STRANGER IN
MY HEART

STRANGER IN MY HEART

Helene Sinclair

Five Star
Unity, Maine

Five Star Romance.
Published in conjunction with the author and the
author's agent, Kidde, Hoyt & Picard Literary Agency.

Cover photograph by Tom Knobloch.

October 1998
Standard Print Hardcover Edition.

Five Star Standard Print Romance Series.

The text of this edition is unabridged.

Set in 11 pt. Plantin by Al Chase.

Printed in the United States on permanent paper.

Library of Congress Cataloging in Publication Data

Sinclair, Helene.
    Stranger in my heart / Helene Sinclair.
      p.   cm.
    ISBN 0-7862-1596-8 (hc : alk. paper)
    I. Title.
PS3569.I5234S77 1998
813'.54—dc21
                                        98-8709

For Doris and Don Lewandowski

*and for a friendship that
has survived both time
and distance*

Chapter 1

"At least give it some thought, Griffin," Nathaniel Kynes urged his grandson. He stirred restlessly in his chair and ran a hand through his silver hair.

The young man standing before the desk viewed his grandfather with angry eyes, his hard expression making him appear somewhat older than his twenty-five years. Dressed in tan breeches and a white cotton shirt, open at the neck, Griffin Kynes stood just over six feet tall. A darkly handsome man, his lean, well-muscled body was deeply suntanned, attesting to the many hours spent beneath the South Carolina sun.

"You're asking me to marry a woman I've never seen?" he demanded. "And a Yankee, at that?" His tone wavered with incredulity.

Nathaniel issued a long, drawn out sigh as he let his gaze travel about the study. It was a pleasant room; his late wife Anne had selected the pale pink marble that graced the mantel over the hearth. She had also purchased the horsehair sofa and dark leather chairs, all with an eye toward his comfort. The rosewood desk, a massive piece with brass ornaments and intricately carved legs, had been imported from Italy more than fifty years ago, when Nathaniel had first built Albemarle.

The morning sun slanted in through tall windows, warming everything it touched — except Nathaniel, who felt the chill of despair penetrate his very bones. He closed the ledger book in front him, then viewed his grandson a moment before speaking again.

"The last crop failed," he murmured in a quiet voice. "And the previous one was barely enough to make ends meet." Nathaniel felt a twinge of conscience as he presented that argument. Griffin was well aware of their financial difficulties and they both knew that the failure of the crop had played only a small part in their present dire circumstances.

"You know the weather was against us," Griffin protested. He placed his hands, palms down, on the polished surface of the desk, his dark eyes intent. "The crop failed, but so did just about everyone else's. This year will be better," he went on, almost pleading. He couldn't quite believe that his grandfather actually wanted him to marry a stranger. "And by spring, we'll be able to send a coffle to Charleston, or even up to New Orleans." He waited hopefully.

Another sigh greeted that. "We can't wait that long. The money's overdue now. Aleceon Edgewood has made it plain that he won't give us anymore time." Nathaniel paused a moment, then, in a low voice, added, "If you don't do this thing, we'll lose Albemarle." He ran his fingertips over the smooth leather of the ledger book as though the volume held all that was dear to him.

"You should never have gotten involved with that old reprobate," Griffin declared heatedly, straightening. "You know what he wants. . . ."

"I do," his grandfather acknowledged sadly. "He wants Albemarle. Unfortunately, he's in a position to get it, one way or the other."

"That man is completely without honor. Not that any Yankee is so endowed," Griffin muttered in reply. He walked toward the fireplace. Putting a hand on the mantel, he stared, brooding, into the black and empty grate. "I should have called him out long ago."

"On what grounds?" his grandfather asked quietly, casting a look in Griffin's direction. "For demanding payment of his debts? Be reasonable, Griff. This could be the way out for all of us. Your sister is now seventeen. In January she'll be presented at Saint Cecelia's. Ah. . . ." He leaned back in his chair in an attitude of dejection. "If only your mother were still alive. I worry about Cammy, I don't mind tellin' you. As for Albemarle, it's been too long without a woman's touch."

"And you expect me to supply the woman." Griffin knew his tone was bitter but he couldn't help himself. The hard look returned as he stared at his grandfather. "A woman I've never even seen!"

A pained expression crossed Nathaniel's creased face. "I'd do this myself, if it were possible," he replied softly, looking away from those accusing eyes.

Contrite now, Griffin crossed the room, coming quickly to his grandfather's side. Feeling ashamed of his outburst, he placed a hand on the thin shoulder, his eyes softening as he viewed the older man. At seventy-one, Nathaniel Kynes was an active man, with a mind that was just as keen and intelligent as it had been fifty years before. His dark brown eyes were speculative and clear, his back ramrod straight, his silver hair adding a touch of distinction rather than age to his overall appearance. Yet, to Griffin's sharp eye, these past twelve months had taken their toll on the man he so dearly loved.

"You mustn't think I blame you," Griffin said at last, tightening the pressure of his hand. "I know that none of this is your fault."

"It's all my fault," Nathaniel observed simply and with a touch of weariness. "I should've gotten out of that game once I began to lose. But I was so certain . . ." He rapped the arm of his chair with a clenched fist and his brows knitted into an anguished scowl. "That last hand — I held four queens . . ." His voice trailed off, but Griffin, having heard it all before, made no comment.

And he had been sure, Nathaniel was thinking with a bitter recollection. So confident had he been, in fact, that he had wagered better than twenty thousand dollars on that one hand of cards — money he didn't have. And so he had put up Albemarle as collateral. Aleceon Edgewood, an experienced and well-known gambler, had been the only other player in the game, which had gone on all night long. When Nathaniel had placed his cards on the table, face up, Aleceon had regarded them for a moment with that small, cold smile of his. Nathaniel had known then, without even looking at the four kings held by his opponent, that he had lost.

That had been over a year ago, a year in which their rice crop had failed, forcing Nathaniel further into debt to buy seed. That money, too, had come from Aleceon Edgewood, who by that time was such a frequent visitor at Albemarle that he had been given his own room on the second floor.

Some months ago, in an effort to pay their debts, Nathaniel had sent a coffle of slaves to market to be sold. But even that resource was being depleted. Last year, there had been better than three hundred slaves to work Albemarle; now there were barely one hundred and sixty.

"All my fault," Nathaniel murmured in fresh anguish. Then, with a sound of resignation, he reached up and patted the hand that still rested on his shoulder. What could he have been thinking of? he chastised himself. Better to let Albemarle go than to ruin his grandson's life. "Never mind, Griff," he said softly. "When Mr. Edgewood arrives later today, I'll tell him that his conditions are unacceptable. We'll just have to make other arrangements —"

"No," Griffin interrupted. But he couldn't prevent the deep sigh that followed. He knew that no bank would lend them the money. Albemarle was already mortgaged to the hilt. "We'll inform Mr. Edgewood that I'll marry his daughter. But only," he added in a terse voice, "if he wipes out every debt, every note in our name."

"Beggin' yore pardon, Masta Nathaniel, suh. . . ."

Both men looked toward the door, viewing the dark-skinned Hausa, who was standing there in respectful submission, waiting for permission to speak.

"What is it, Thomas?" Nathaniel asked, irritated with the interruption.

"It's Jonah, suh. They done caught him." Thomas nodded his head with its graying fringe of woolly hair surrounding his broad forehead. He was almost the same age as his master and was, in fact, the first Negro that Nathaniel had ever purchased.

A nod of satisfaction replaced Nathaniel's irritability. "Put him in the barn. We'll be there directly. Tell Mr. Dobbs I said to shuck that bastard down and string him up."

"The dogs must've worked," Griffin speculated as Thomas closed the door.

Nathaniel nodded at the observation, his expression grave. "Second time that worthless nigger's run. See to it that the patrollers are given fifty dollars, Griff. Then meet me in the barn."

Emerging from the Great House a short time later, Griffin descended the broad front steps, his booted feet echoing his passage, then headed toward the two men who stood by their horses. They were part of a band of patrollers that regularly scouted the area in search of runaways. They were dedicated, but could be, on occasion, ruthless in the pursuit of their quarry. Nearby, four hounds stretched at their leashes, tails wagging and tongues lolling in the late morning sun.

"Mornin', Mr. Kynes," the tallest of the men said. He removed his broad-brimmed hat to reveal an almost bald head.

Griffin smiled affably. "Where'd you find Jonah?"

" 'Bout six miles upriver." The man squinted in the bright sun, appearing earnest as he continued. "I'm afraid the dogs

11

tore him up a bit. Real sorry about that, Mr. Kynes. But we got to him before too much damage was done."

"Don't worry about that." Griffin waved a hand, dismissing the apology. "When Dobbs gets through with that buck, won't be much left of him anyhow. Much obliged to you both."

Reaching into his pocket, Griffin counted out the money, giving the man the customary fifty dollars, which would be split between them. Then, politely, he invited them to stay for dinner.

But the tall man declined for them both. "Still plenty of daylight left," he explained. "We're huntin' a runaway from Four Oaks. Mr. Barrows is plenty upset. He paid twelve hundred dollars for that buck not two months ago."

Griffin inclined his head at the news, reflecting gravely that, lately, hardly a week passed that he didn't receive word from one of the neighboring plantations that one or more of their slaves had tried to escape.

Small incidents perhaps, for almost every runaway was eventually captured; it was, nonetheless, disturbing because it was happening so consistently. Like most people who lived all their lives in the South and around Negroes, Griffin had the thin thread of fear that, like a taut string on a fiddle, would suddenly vibrate into life at the mere thought of a slave revolt. Running was, of course, the first step in that direction. Not that he'd ever seen a revolt. But there were always rumors; rebellion, stealing, disobedience. Isolated, to be sure, but it paid to be on one's guard.

"I'll keep an eye out," he offered at last. He watched a moment as the men mounted their horses, then he headed in the direction of the barn, his eyes surveying the land on which he had been born.

Albemarle was not the largest plantation along the Ashley River, but to Griffin Kynes, it was the most beautiful. Covering better than nine hundred acres and fronting on the river, Albemarle lay some sixteen miles from Charleston.

Griffin could not see the fields from here. They were concealed by a stand of cypress that acted as a buffer, perhaps against those who toiled so ceaselessly on the rich, dark earth. They were Hausa and Kru, Ashanti and Angolan, Dahomean and Fanti. All were referred to as blacks or darkies or niggers, though their skin ranged from ebony to gold.

And they were all slaves.

When his grandfather, then a young man of seventeen and newly arrived from England with his bride, had first built Albemarle, indigo had been the primary crop. That was replaced in 1834 by rice, with some seventy acres devoted to sugar cane, raised mostly for their own use. For some years now, the land had been producing less and less. Last year the crop hadn't even supported expenses.

That had been only the beginning of their troubles. The failure of the crop had been nothing compared to the appearance of Aleceon Edgewood in their lives.

Probably, Griffin reflected as he walked, they would never have met the man if his grandfather hadn't been in New Orleans, indulging in his one weakness: gambling. Not that Griffin blamed his grandfather. Nathaniel had few vices and a man ought to be able to have some enjoyment out of life.

When he reached the stables, Griffin paused, watching a bright-skinned young Negro as he expertly combed and brushed a gray gelding. The animal stood patiently, flanks quivering beneath the gentle, firm strokes.

"How's Thunder doing?" Griffin came closer and ran a hand over the horse's foreleg. The thoroughbred was scheduled to race in January.

"Fine, Masta Griffin," came the prompt reply. "Swellin's jest 'bout gone. He feelin' peppy." With a soft touch, Jude ran

13

his fingertips along a muscle of the horse's leg, injured in a jump only yesterday. For a moment, the hands of the two men came in close proximity. Jude stared, noticing that the color of his own hand was not that much different from the suntanned skin of his young master.

Glancing up at that moment, Griffin caught the intent expression and his eyes narrowed. He didn't like Jude, although he couldn't quite put his finger on the exact cause of his enmity. Probably it was the nigger's eyes, he thought to himself. They were blue. Of all the goddamned tricks of nature, the nigger's eyes were blue. Not a dark blue, either. They were vivid, like the sky on a clear October day. Jude was a quadroon, the oldest son of Minda, the cook. He was also, in Nathaniel's opinion, a showpiece. Physically, Jude, who was almost twenty years old, was a fine specimen. Griffin couldn't argue with that. He was excellent with the horses, he was respectful, obedient . . . yet Griffin sensed — something. He couldn't put a name to the nebulous feeling, but if it were up to him, he'd sell the damned buck tomorrow.

"What're you looking at?" he demanded, his brow deepening into a frown.

Guiltily, and with a small start, Jude tore his gaze away. " to you, masta, suh," he said hastily. "Jest noticin' you got a nasty cut on yore thumb."

Griffin blinked, staring down at his hand which he had accidentally cut with a hunting knife the week before. "Yes . . . well, it's almost healed." He straightened, gave the horse a pat on its rump, and without further words to Jude, turned and strode away.

Leaving the stables, Griffin walked past the carriage house and the smokehouse, approaching the barn, the front part of which was devoted to any chastisement that might be earned by the slaves of Albemarle.

Entering the dim interior, Griffin saw the overseer, Carlie Dobbs, standing beside his grandfather. The thin, wiry man, who was in his early forties, was discussing the punishment to be meted out to the runaway slave, who, having already been stripped, now stood with head bowed and hands shackled, nervously awaiting whatever his masters decided should be his fate. A deep gash on his arm, running from his shoulder to his elbow, was bleeding profusely. Several less severe puncture wounds dotted his muscular body. The dogs, having caught his scent at dawn, had tracked him down with relentless determination. When they finally caught sight of him, they had attacked. Jonah knew perfectly well that if the patrollers hadn't shown up when they did, the dogs would have torn him to shreds.

"Griffin!" Nathaniel called out when he saw the young man. "We've been waitin' for you. Carlie here thinks that seventy-five lashes and a branding would cure this nigger of runnin'. I'm thinkin' that'll ruin him."

"Probably," Griffin agreed, coming closer. "But what's the difference? You're not thinking of keeping him, are you?"

The Negro turned in the direction of his young master, his black face gray with fear. His skin was the color of coal. The dark eyes, set deeply beneath a wide forehead, were filled with an apprehension that bordered on terror. "Please, Masta Griffin, suh. Doan let 'em be seventy-five," he moaned. "Doan run agin me. Learnt my lesson, suh. Learnt it good."

"Shut your black mouth, Jonah," Dobbs growled, frowning at the slave's impertinence. "No one heah's askin' for your say-so." He glared a moment longer, then turned to a massive Negro who was standing nearby, and whose ebony skin gleamed in the light of the brazier he was tending. He was a giant of a man, standing a full six-feet, nine-inches. "Joe!" Dobbs gave a curt motion with his hand. "String this heah nigger up. Mebbe he'll stop his yappin' and let us get on with it."

The overseer watched only a moment as Joe, who was the blacksmith for Albemarle, secured the end of a long rope to the shackles that bound Jonah's wrists, then flung it up over a beam. He pulled on it until Jonah's arms were raised up over his head, then pulled again, until only the slave's toes were in contact with the wooden floor.

"Griff's right, suh," Dobbs said to Nathaniel after a moment. "Won't do no good to keep this one. Spend more time watchin' him than he's worth." With his thumb, he rubbed the bridge of his hawklike nose as he waited for his employer's response.

"Who said anything about keepin' him?" Nathaniel waved an impatient hand. "But he won't fetch a damn cent if he's crippled, you know that."

A slight moan escaped Jonah's full lips, but no one turned in his direction. He hung there, feeling the strain in his arms and back, but knew from experience that the discomfort was nothing compared to what lay ahead of him. The last time he had run, he had been given fifty lashes. It had almost killed him. Seventy-five, he figured, would.

"Won't cripple him," Dobbs argued earnestly with a sharp shake of his head. "Lay him up some. But it'll be months before you get a coffle together. He'll be healed by then." He viewed Jonah's muscular back, already badly scarred. " 'Course, you can always shunt him off on the next trader passin' by," he mused, pursing his thin lips. "He ain't good for nothin' but the cane fields anyway. No sense in even sendin' him to auction."

Nathaniel considered that, then looked toward his grandson. "What do you think, Griff?"

Griffin Kynes shrugged his broad shoulders. "Can't see

16

killing him," he stated after a moment. "Give him fifty. After the branding, rub him down good with capsicum; it'll make him heal faster. Carlie's right about one thing," he turned to face Nathaniel. "Don't bother sending him in the coffle. Next trader comes along can have him at a good price. I don't like having runaways around," he went on firmly. "They're a bad influence."

Nathaniel nodded, pleased with the astuteness of the decision. "All right, let's get on with it. Don't have all day."

Dobbs turned to Joe and jerked his head in the direction of Jonah. "Get to it," he ordered briskly. "And make sure they're well laid on, heah?"

"Yassuh," replied Joe, inclining his great head, his expression placid in the face of his distasteful chore.

With practiced ease and little apparent effort, the huge Negro applied the first of the fifty lashes against the back of the runaway slave. The long rawhide whip sliced through air, then flesh, with a stinging, resonant sound.

At each delivered stroke, Dobbs counted, his voice a monotone that effectively conveyed boredom. Griffin and Nathaniel watched with impassive eyes as the slave screamed, helpless beneath the relentless bite of the lash.

In fact, none of the three white men present displayed, nor felt, compassion at the sight, and would have been greatly surprised if anyone did. Neither Griffin nor his grandfather enjoyed the process of disciplining their slaves; it was simply a necessity, a job that had to be accomplished. Most of the time, it was Carlie Dobbs who wielded the whip. Today was, however, an exception. It was rare for a slave at Albemarle to receive an excess of ten lashes. More than that was considered serious, and Nathaniel and Griffin always made it a point to be present on those occasions.

At last it was over. Joe released the rope and Jonah crumpled to the ground. There was little of his black skin left on his back; it was now a mass of torn and bleeding wounds.

Turning the iron in the brazier, Joe looked at Carlie Dobbs, who nodded. Moving Jonah's head to an angle that suited him, Joe quickly applied the hot iron to the slave's forehead. There was a sharp hissing sound, followed by the sickly-sweet smell of burned flesh. Jonah screamed once, hoarsely, and was still.

"Rub him down with capscium," Dobbs instructed the huge Negro. "Don't want him to bleed to death."

Picking up a rag, Joe dipped it in the pail that contained a solution of salt, water, and red pepper, then applied it liberally to Jonah's back.

"How much do you think we can get for him?" Nathaniel asked as he and Griffin walked back into the yard.

"Not much," Griffin replied, feeling the November sun warm on his back. "Be lucky if we get five hundred for him, marked the way he is."

A dark-skinned girl of about eighteen approached them hesitantly, tears streaming down her satiny cheeks. She was small boned, with an erect carriage that produced a high bosom above well rounded hips.

"Please, Masta Nathaniel, kin I take Jonah to his cabin now?" Her dark eyes viewed the old man, pleading.

Nathaniel shook his head. "Have to lock him up, Zoe," he replied, sounding regretful. "This is the second time your brother's run. . . ."

"But —"

"Go along, Zoe!" Griffin interjected sharply, annoyed by the girl's persistence.

She stood there a moment longer. Then, shoulders slumping beneath her cotton dress, which was the only garment she wore, Zoe walked away, her bare feet kicking up little mounds of ecru dust.

"That wench is too sassy for her own good," Griffin complained, watching the receding figure. "I can't understand why you won't sell her."

"She's a pretty little gal," Nathaniel replied, sounding unconcerned. "I'm hopin' that Jude boy can get her knocked up. She's real black and if she can drop a sucker with her color and Jude's blue eyes, we'll have ourselves a real fancy piece."

Morosely, Griffin reflected that the last thing Albemarle needed was another nigger with blue eyes, but he said nothing, knowing his grandfather's penchant for breeding what he considered "good stock."

They began to walk in the direction of the Great House. Suddenly Nathaniel halted, putting a hand on Griffin's arm. Then he pointed at the carriage coming up the drive. It was a chaise, driven with the top down and hauled by a pair of matched bays. A Negro, dressed only slightly less grand than his master, guided the animals with a quick and sure touch, containing their spiritedness without benefit of whip or harsh words.

Neither Griffin nor Nathaniel gave the Negro driver, whose name was Ben, a second glance. Their attention was riveted on the man who was seated in the chaise and whose bearing suggested that his outing was no more pressing than a Sunday drive.

"It's Aleceon." Nathaniel frowned. "And from the looks of it, it appears like he's plannin' to stay awhile." The frown fell into a scowl at the sight of the baggage strapped to the back of the vehicle. He turned toward Griffin, noting the slightly flushed cheeks that indicated inner anger. "There's still time to change your mind," he began, but the young man shook his head.

"No," Griffin responded firmly. "I'm not turning my home over to that scoundrel." He made a face of disgust.

19

"Wonder what's wrong with her?" he mused in a low voice, keeping his eyes on the approaching carriage.

"Who?"

"His daughter. Must be something wrong with her if he has to twist a man's arm to marry her."

Slowly, Nathaniel shook his head. "Don't know," he conceded. "Never saw her." Privately, he suspected that Griffin's assessment was probably true. A woman who was almost twenty years of age and still unmarried must have a face that would turn a man to stone. Still, once they were married, Griffin didn't have to bother with her much. He had Serena, the high yellow gal that had been his bed wench for over a year now. That one would make any man forget an ugly wife.

The chaise halted before them. Alighting, Aleceon Edgewood stood there a moment regarding Nathaniel and Griffin without speaking, then nodded briefly. He wasn't as tall as Griffin, lacking a good four inches to reach that young man's height, but he was so thin that he gave the appearance of being taller than he actually was. Like the rest of his body, his face was long and angular, with an aquiline nose above a narrow mouth. His dark blond hair was thick, straight, and always neatly combed. His was a fastidious nature, and this was reflected in his clothes and bearing. Aleceon never appeared disheveled, or even rumpled, and there was that about him that could be termed an air of elegance. Even those who disliked him — and they were legion — had to admit that it was so.

Today, as always, Aleceon was dressed in a fashionable manner, his bottle-green frock coat and trousers custom made, his silk vest hand embroidered, his walking stick with its mother-of-pearl handle held at a jaunty angle.

Greeting his visitor in a barely civilized manner, Nathaniel led the way across the sun-dappled front yard into the house, heading for the study. He instructed the hovering Thomas to bring them a full decanter of bourbon. From the nature of their business, he reflected sourly, they'd all need more than one drink.

With a certain degree of familiarity, Aleceon settled himself on the sofa, accepted the preferred glass from Nathaniel, then viewed Griffin's dark and flushed face. "I take it your grandfather has informed you of my proposal?" he remarked.

"A grand name for what you've suggested," Griffin snapped quickly. "Why didn't you just take Albemarle for yourself? Why indulge in all this trickery?" His hands itched with the urge to strike the other man. Fearful of losing control, Griffin plunged them deeply into his pockets.

Calmly, Aleceon sipped at his drink, his manner languid and unhurried. But his blue eyes were alert and piercing as he viewed Griffin in silence for a long moment, apparently giving careful consideration to the question. A gambler for most of his forty-one years, Aleceon had learned the virtue of weighing his words carefully before he spoke.

"Under different circumstances, I might have done just that," he allowed at last, shifting himself into a more comfortable position. He glanced toward Nathaniel, who had seated himself behind his desk, but the older man refused to look at him.

"However," Aleceon continued, again viewing Griffin, who had remained standing, "the truth of the matter is that I know nothing about running a plantation, much less one of this size. Nor am I particularly interested in learning," he added, finishing his drink.

"Doesn't it bother you that what you are doing is . . ." Griffin raised a hand, searching for the right word, "dishonorable? Or is that expression meaningless to you?" His eyes were fierce and bright with anger.

The statement seemed to amuse Aleceon. Getting up, he

casually poured himself another drink. "To a certain extent," he answered quietly, "you are right in your assumption. Honor is a useless impediment, fit only for fools."

Watching as Aleceon once again seated himself, Griffin noted scornfully, "You could not hope to understand."

Resting an elbow on the arm of the sofa, Aleceon twirled the glass in his hands, viewing it thoughtfully. It was clear to him that the young man had a mind of his own, was not in any sense a puppet of his grandfather. Whether he would, or would not, go along with this would be his own decision. Aleceon leaned back against the cushions, pleased with his assumption. He'd been a gambler all his life. This time he was playing for higher stakes than anyone knew. This time it had been Fate who had dealt the cards; a nonwinning hand.

There was a brief silence, then Aleceon said to Griffin, "When you marry my daughter, all outstanding notes will be destroyed. Albemarle will be free and clear. Thereafter, twenty percent of your annual profit will be paid to me."

"All that could be accomplished without a marriage," Griffin noted with a pronounced touch of sarcasm.

Aleceon's nod was slow. He appeared unperturbed by the young man's attitude. "Perhaps," he allowed. "But Morgana can no longer stay in school. And I've no intention of becoming tied down. She's already passed the age when she should be married. Besides . . ." he issued the cold smile that so grated on Griffin's nerves, "as your father-in-law, I'm certain that I will be welcome to make Albemarle my home. I know I don't have to tell you how attached I've become to it."

Griffin's jaw worked visibly and he turned away for a moment. There seemed to be no end to the man's audacity.

Behind his desk, Nathaniel rubbed his face with a gnarled hand, but remained silent, knowing that the decision was Griffin's alone to make.

"And what does your daughter have to say about all this?" Griffin demanded tersely, turning toward Aleceon again. His hands, back in his pockets, tightened into fists. He could feel his pulse accelerate in answer to his mounting anger.

"Morgana?" Aleceon gave a short laugh. "She doesn't even know about our . . . arrangement," he replied. "I thought it better if she were to believe that you were smitten at first sight."

Griffin made a face at that. He gave momentary thought to demanding, at the very least, a physical description of the mysterious Morgana Edgewood. But then he discarded the notion. What the hell did he care what she looked like? It would do him no good if she was beautiful and stupid; nor, conversely, if she was ugly and intelligent. Neither of the choices appealed to him. Certainly she wouldn't be beautiful and intelligent. That would be too much to hope for. Besides, no man pawned off a daughter like that!

"What if your daughter refuses?" Griffin finally asked.

Aleceon calmly studied a well manicured nail for a moment before remarking, "If you play your part well, Griffin, I'm sure she won't. Let's hope that that situation will not arise," he observed ominously, raising his eyes slightly to meet Griffin's hot stare.

"And if I refuse this ridiculous scheme?" Griffin no longer made the effort to conceal his open distaste. Aleceon was on his fourth bourbon and seemed to swallow the stuff as if it were water. He should be drunk, but he wasn't. His grandfather had told him that one of the reasons Aleceon was so successful as a gambler was his ability to remain placid and inscrutable. Griffin was beginning to realize how accurately Nathaniel had judged the man.

Aleceon gestured with a hand that sported an ornate gold ring set with two perfectly matched emeralds. He always wore the ring. He had long discovered that it was a distraction at

23

the card table, giving him a fraction of an advantage, allowing him to observe expressions and nervous habits while his opponent's eyes more often than not strayed to the glittering gems instead of his own face. Nathaniel Kynes had been one of those who had let his attention wander at a crucial time.

It interested Aleceon now that not once since they had begun their conversation had Griffin's eye been caught by the ring. Again, he was pleased.

"If you refuse," Aleceon replied softly, "then Albemarle will be mine — to do with as I see fit." His gaze was level and without humor. "I've already sent for my daughter," he went on. "I expect her to arrive in Charleston by the end of the week."

The cold smile returned to Aleceon's thin lips. The thought often occurred to Griffin that the man would appear only half dressed without it. It seldom, if ever, held any humor; rather, it was condescending and mocking, an attitude that was reinforced by those eyes that were the color of blue smoke.

"I think it might be a good idea if you went to fetch her, Griffin," Aleceon continued quietly, taking the other man's silence for agreement. Then he stood up and put his empty glass on a nearby table. "The long drive back will enable you both to get to know each other. I feel certain that a man of your sophistication will have little trouble in charming an innocent, impressionable young lady."

Aleceon paused, but neither Griffin nor his grandfather made any comment. He waited a moment longer, then, his bearing nonchalant, he left the study, appearing unconcerned or even aware of the hostility his words had generated.

With his departure, Nathaniel and Griffin exchanged looks — the old man's saddened, the young man's rigid with a cold, implacable anger.

Griffin turned away feeling the determination harden

within him. He had plans, plans for himself, for his sister, for Albemarle, which he intended to restore to its former position as one of the most successful plantations in the area.

As for his sister, Cammy must be given the opportunity of making a good marriage. Once she made her debut in January, he intended to persuade her to look upon Clinton Barrows with favor. The eldest son of Farley Barrows, Clinton stood to inherit Four Oaks one day. The two plantations, side by side, united by marriage, sharing resources, was a vision that was very tempting to Griffin.

First, however, Albemarle's debts must be cleared. And right now, there appeared only one way to do that.

Into the silence, Nathaniel at last expulsed a deep breath. "It's no good, Griff," he murmured, shaking his head. "I can't let you do this. . . ."

The young man came closer to the desk, mouth set tight. "You said it before, Grandfather," he pointed out as he poured himself a drink. He lifted the glass to his lips and downed the contents in a long swallow before continuing. "We'll lose Albemarle if I don't." He put the glass beside the decanter. Then, with a last, grim look at his grandfather, Griffin left the study.

Later that evening, although it was not yet nine o'clock, Aleceon retired to his room on the second floor. It was a back bedroom and, as such, did not have access to the piazza, which only the front bedrooms opened onto. But Aleceon liked it because it had windows on two walls. It was therefore bright, and, when nature offered it, had a cross breeze as well. The room was large and square, the four-poster roomy and soft with its down mattress. He wasn't overly fond of the wallpaper, which depicted overblown roses of a dark maroon color that he found depressing. But aside from that flaw, the wardrobe and dresser, as well as the several tables and chairs, were serviceable. And that was all Aleceon wanted or required.

Aleceon had stayed many times at Albemarle over the past two years, and was by now quite familiar with the routine. Because the hands began work in the fields at first light, everyone was awake and functioning at that time, with the result that, soon after darkness fell, the household quieted down for the night.

Closing the door to his room, Aleceon stood there a moment, mouth tight, a hand over his abdomen.

Then, quickly, he withdrew a small bottle from his pocket. Uncapping it, he swallowed the clear liquid. In only moments the laudanum eased the pain in his stomach. It had been growing worse in these past months — it would kill him before too many more passed, that much he knew. Six months to a year, the doctors had told him. That had been four months ago.

His suggestion that Griffin meet Morgana in Charleston had not been a whim. It was based upon the simple fact that he didn't think he had the strength to make the trip there and back, and he wanted to horde what little was left in an effort to see his daughter safely married. Once the notes on Albemarle were destroyed, the plantation should prosper, as it had done in years past. Her life, he reasoned, would be a comfortable one.

He had given Morgana little during her lifetime. Now, with death threatening his own mortality, Aleceon had tried to make arrangements for her security. And the only real security for a woman was, of course, marriage. Griffin Kynes had been far from a casual choice. Aleceon had considered and rejected a score of other young men over the past four months. They had been too old, too young, too poor, too unattractive.

And Aleceon Edgewood had too few months to live to let nature take its course.

Nor did he give any thought to the ensuing relationship

between Morgana and Griffin Kynes. It would work out. Morgana was, after all, her father's daughter. Aleceon almost smiled, but then scowled at the slave who came toward him.

"Get away from me, you black viper," he growled. "Is there no place a man can have a measure of privacy?"

"Yassuh, masta, suh," the Negro replied as he calmly prepared to remove Aleceon's boots. Ben was part Ashanti, his ancestors having come from that western part of Africa known as the Gold Coast, where, it was said, there was a heavy infusion of Arab blood in the people of his tribe. While his skin was a dark and rich reddish-brown, his nose was straight and narrow, his lips well formed and only slightly full, his cheekbones set high in his angular face. His black hair, however, was kinky and lay close to his skull. He topped Aleceon's height by five inches and outweighed him by almost sixty pounds.

Ben had been with Aleceon for over five years and, by now, knew his master as well as anyone. It wasn't so much what Aleceon said, as how he said it, that prompted Ben's responses. Aleceon grumbled and complained constantly, but in a perverse sort of way seemed genuinely fond of his slave.

Ben recognized that, and offered his master a devotion that no other white man had ever received from him. No one else knew about the sickness that daily consumed a part of Aleceon. But Ben knew. The thought at once saddened and terrified him. Even though Aleceon had already informed him that, when the time came, he would be given to Morgana, Ben knew of the coming marriage plans, and he was very well aware that it wouldn't be Morgana, but Griffin Kynes to whom he would belong.

That thought produced nightmares. At least once a year, a coffle of slaves trudged from Albemarle to Charleston, or even up to Savannah, to be sold. Who was to say that he might not be one of them?

"You feelin' bettah, suh?" Ben ventured in his soft voice as he now helped Aleceon to undress.

"Soon I will be," Aleceon murmured, grimacing. The pain was growing stronger day by day, he realized. It took all his energy and willpower to hide it from others. Only with Ben did he relax and give in to it.

"I gits you moah medicine?" Ben offered, taking a step toward the dresser.

Aleceon took a deep breath. The pain was receding to the familiar dull ache which had been his constant companion for the past two weeks. "No," he said tiredly. "I'll sleep now." As he moved toward the bed, Ben leaped forward to turn down the covers.

After his master had settled himself with a deep sigh, Ben sat on his pallet on the floor, his dark eyes never leaving the motionless, thin form. He knew that, within an hour, or two at the outside, Aleceon would need more of the clear, harmless looking liquid that allowed him to function. Occasionally, almost as a mother would do while watching over a sick child, Ben would doze, sitting up, his back against the wall. But at the slightest movement or sound, Ben would be awake, alert to the needs of the man who was not only his master, but who had once saved his life.

Chapter 2

Edith Appleby sat in her office at the Brookshire Academy for Young Women, reading the letter on her desk for the third time since she had received it that morning. It had actually arrived the day before, but yesterday, Monday, she had left her office early, retiring to her private rooms on the second floor to nurse a headache.

In her fifties, the headmistress still bore traces of the patrician handsomeness that nature had bestowed upon her at an early age, giving her a sharp-featured and sometimes forbidding demeanor. Beneath the dark blue dress made of fine lawn, her plump body was tightly corseted. Her hair, although gray, was thick and wavy, drawn back from her small ears into a sweeping pompadour. Hazel eyes, behind steel-rimmed spectacles, had the capacity to warm or chill an observer as the mood struck her.

Turning slightly, she glanced out the window. The day was clear and cold and bright, a respite from two straight days of snow the previous week which had been followed by several more days of sub-zero temperatures and oyster-gray skies that had blanketed upper New York state with a relentless gloom.

Unlike many schools of the day that catered to females, Brookshire was academically oriented. The faculty of twenty-three — all women — were carefully screened by Edith Appleby, who demanded excellence, expertise, and a sincere desire to impart knowledge.

Not all of the young ladies had a thirst for knowledge and more than a few — parents included — thought of Brookshire more in terms of a finishing school, a label Edith Appleby considered ridiculous and demeaning.

Putting her elbows on the desk, she sighed deeply, pressing her fingertips to her temples, massaging the aching throb that was a residue of her recent migraine.

How, she wondered, was she going to tell Morgana?

Unaccountably, she recalled last Christmas Eve, when she and Morgana had sipped eggnog and eaten little almond cakes to celebrate the holidays. They had talked long and seriously, mostly of Morgana's future here at Brookshire. Unlike the rest of the seventy-four girls who comprised the student population, Morgana Edgewood always spent the holidays at school.

Ruefully, and a bit annoyed with herself, Miss Appleby realized that, somewhere along the line, Morgana had become the daughter she never had, and never would have.

Miss Appleby was not married. She had never met a man she could love enough to give up her own independence. Her father had been wealthy, arthritic, and confined to a wheelchair for the seven years that preceded his death. Her mother had died when Edith was only fourteen. From then, until her father's death some ten years later, Edith Appleby had devoted herself to his care and comfort. When he died, he left everything to his only daughter and, thirty years ago, in the spring of 1822, Edith Appleby had founded Brookshire.

In all those years she had never let herself become attached to any of her students, knowing that each in their own turn would, sooner or later, leave her.

With Morgana Edgewood, however, she had broken that rule. Now she would have to pay for that lapse into sentimentality.

Again her eyes drifted to the innocent-appearing piece of paper. It was dated the 16th of November 1852, some four weeks ago, and was from Aleceon Edgewood, Morgana's father.

Just the thought of that man caused a frown, deepening the

already existing creases in her forehead. There had been rumors when he had first brought his daughter here; rumors that his wife, who had died when Morgana was born, had been of a character that was less than admirable, a woman of the streets, it was whispered.

As for Mr. Edgewood himself, it was said that gambling was one of his more respectable occupations.

Since Brookshire was highly selective and, it could be said, one of the most exclusive schools in New York, Edith Appleby quite naturally had had reservations about admitting Morgana Edgewood.

However, it had subsequently come to light that the then thirteen-year-old girl was the niece of Sarah Edgewood Enright, who practically owned the town of Taunset and the mill that bore her name. Of course, Taunset was in Massachusetts and Brookshire was in New York, but even that distance was not so great that Edith Appleby didn't know about the Enrights. Few families were on a par with that most socially acceptable clan.

She had, therefore, with only few misgivings, accepted the girl's application.

Nor had she done the wrong thing, Miss Appleby now thought. Morgana had proved to be not only intelligent and capable, but a definite credit to the school. She was intelligent, well behaved, and conducted herself with a gracefulness that was at once both appealing and charming. She was a bit strong willed at times, but Miss Appleby, having a touch of that trait herself, saw nothing wrong with that endowment.

In fact, so impressed was Edith Appleby with this particular student, that she had — until today — entertained hopes that Morgana would join their teaching staff. It was something the girl herself had requested.

And now . . . Now this.

Laying aside the unwanted message, Edith Appleby at last sent for Morgana Edgewood.

Morgana had already finished her breakfast when she was called to Miss Appleby's office. Having been there many times, the summons didn't even move her to curiosity. It wasn't unusual for the headmistress to request her assistance in grading papers or filing or any other of several chores.

There was, in fact, nothing unusual about this morning. It was like every other weekday morning of the past six years. The bell had rung at six-thirty, announcing the start of another day. She, together with more than seventy other girls ranging in age from thirteen to nineteen, had risen, washed, brushed her teeth, dressed, and had come down to the dining room to eat breakfast. Even that had been the same, oatmeal, orange juice, hot tea laced with rich cream.

Nothing marked today as any different from its predecessors. Nor did Morgana Edgewood desire any change. (Her life contented her, her future was planned.)

When she entered the office, Morgana saw the headmistress standing by the window. The woman did not immediately turn toward her, although Morgana was certain that her presence had been noted.

Patiently, she waited. Buttery yellow sunlight crept in past the plum colored draperies, warming wood, giving a sheen to the leather upholstery and creating sharp points of light across the dark walnut desk. It was all so very familiar to her; she had even helped in the selection of the material for the draperies.

Miss Appleby turned then, regarding Morgana with a somewhat enigmatic expression, seeing a tall, slim girl with eyes so blue they could easily be termed her most arresting feature. She was dressed conservatively, without adornment, in a gray woolen dress with a white collar and cuffs. Her shining blond hair was worn severely, pulled back from her heart-shaped face and knotted in a bun at the nape of her neck.

"Be seated, Morgana," Miss Appleby murmured, still standing by the window.

Puzzled by the intent look and grave tone of voice, Morgana sat down on the straight-backed chair before the desk. She tucked her feet primly beneath her and folded her hands gracefully in her lap as she had been taught to do.

At last Miss Appleby walked to her desk and sat down. Taking off her steel-rimmed spectacles, she placed them carefully before her.

"Morgana," she said quietly, taking a deep breath. "I have received word from your father . . ." She paused, seeing the startled look on the face of the young woman. And why shouldn't she be surprised? the headmistress thought with no little bitterness. Aleceon Edgewood had placed his daughter in this school when she had been all of thirteen years old. That had been more than six years ago. And not once in all that time had he visited or even written her. The bank drafts arrived promptly each month in payment of tuition. Twice a year, additional money arrived for clothing and other necessities. Aside from that, there had been no correspondence at all, not even on the girl's birthdays.

"Is he well?" Morgana asked, thinking of nothing else to say in the face of this unusual occurrence.

Edith Appleby wet her narrow lips. "I assume he is," she answered slowly, toying with a cameo brooch on the collar of her dress. "Quite frankly, he didn't say."

A first nudge of uneasiness coursed through Morgana, caused more by Miss Appleby's attitude than her words. She had seldom seen the woman so disturbed. Could it be, she wondered, that her father had failed to send the money for her tuition? If so, it would be the first time. But the one thing she remembered most about her father was his distressing affinity for losing vast sums at the card table. Still, she thought to herself, keeping a wary eye on Miss Appleby, she could work here if need be. She could tutor. She would even work in the kitchen if she had to. Certainly the headmistress would allow her to do that. She had only six months to go before she would become a fully accredited teacher.

Clasping her hands before her, Miss Appleby's mouth set into firmness before she again spoke. "Your father wants you to return home," she murmured, not looking at Morgana. "Right away. He has made all the arrangements for your trip to," she picked up the letter again, "to Charleston, South Carolina."

Too stunned to speak, Morgana only stared at her. A forewarning chill crept up her spine, leaving tension in its wake. She sat quietly, not moving, trying to absorb the words she had just heard.

Miss Appleby sighed deeply as she stood up. "You'll have to leave today." Although her voice remained soft, she was genuinely irritated by this sudden turn of events. She knew how much Morgana wanted to stay on, to become a teacher. And the loss would be felt by the school, too. Good teachers were difficult to find, and Morgana had the instinct as well as the intellect.

Leave? Morgana was thinking, trying desperately to channel her whirling thoughts. Her father wanted her to come home — but this was her home. She had never even been to Charleston. She had been born in New York and had spent what seemed to her most of her life right here at Brookshire.

Morgana's eyes strayed to the diamond-paned window. Outside, the sun glistened on the Hudson River, less than a mile away. The school was situated on the west bank of the mighty waterway, just outside of Albany. Here and there, nestled in blue shadows, were stubborn patches of snow left over from last week's storm which the winter sun's weak rays had been unable to conquer. Her gaze shifted to the big oak tree, one of many on the well tended grounds. Its branches were bare now, but how many times during the past six years had she sat beneath its leafy boughs, to read, to study, to simply daydream. . . .

"Morgana!" Miss Appleby spoke sharply, alarmed by the pallor she was seeing. "Are you all right?"

Morgana shook off her reverie. "Yes, ma'am," she managed. She straightened in the chair and made a conscious effort to relax tautly held muscles. "You said I had to leave today." She looked up at the woman before her, the woman who was more familiar to her than any member of her own family had ever been. "It's just so . . . sudden." The words emerged choked and seemed to catch in her throat.

Looking a trifle embarrassed, Edith Appleby averted her face. "I know," she whispered. "The letter took several weeks to get here. In fact, it arrived yesterday — but . . . I wasn't here when it came. I read it only an hour ago . . ." Her voice trailed off and was replaced with another sigh.

"Does he say why he wants me to . . . leave here?" Morgana couldn't bring herself to say go home. Those words had no meaning for her.

"No, he made no mention of his reasons." Getting up, Miss Appleby walked to the other side of the desk and stood before Morgana. "Do you want to read it?" she asked, offering the letter.

Morgana shook her head. She didn't even want to touch it. What good would reading it do? she thought unhappily, clasping her hands tightly in her lap. It wouldn't alter the facts, wouldn't allow her to stay.

Standing there, the older woman picked up her glasses from the desk and put them on. "You had better pack," she murmured quietly. "A carriage is coming for you in about an hour. You'll be leaving on the next boat. I'm sorry, dear," she added earnestly, sensing the girl's distress. Coming closer, she bent forward, putting an arm about Morgana in a comforting way. "I know how much it meant to you to stay on here, to become a teacher. But apparently your father has other plans for you."

"I don't want to go to Charleston," Morgana protested, unable to stem the biting edge of resentment that crept into her voice. Why, she wondered angrily, hadn't her father continued to stay out of her life! She had gotten along very well without him all these years and was certain she would continue to do so.

The words produced a frown. Miss Appleby straightened, her expression stern. "You cannot disobey your father, Morgana," she admonished firmly. Visions of her personal selfless devotion to her own father flashed through her mind. The idea of familial disobedience was quite alien to her. "If you were legally of age," she went on, adopting a softer tone, "perhaps you could make your own decision. But since you are not, the subject doesn't bear further discussion."

Morgana made no comment, but her mouth was set obdurately, effectively conveying her disagreement. She knew that, with only a slight encouragement from the headmistress, she would do just that — disobey her father.

Edith Appleby's hand reached out, hovering in the air an instant as if it were going to rest on Morgana's shoulder. Then it moved in a helpless gesture. She bit her lower lip, letting her hand fall to her side. "I do admit, though, that it distresses me that you will be living in the South. A land of barbarians," she murmured, more to herself than to Morgana. Then she brightened and, for the first time, smiled. "But you'll see your father again. I'm sure you're looking forward to that, after all this time." She nodded encouragingly as Morgana stood up.

Morgana managed an appropriate phrase as she left the office, somewhat uncertain of the veracity of Miss Appleby's last statement. It had been so long, she couldn't quite remember what her father looked like; and even if she had, certainly he wouldn't look the same. Doubtless, she thought ruefully, he wouldn't even recognize her.

Slowly, as if she did not want to reach her destination, she walked back to her room. It accommodated four girls, but was spacious enough so as not to be cramped. The beds, two on either side of the room, were narrow but comfortable. Between each bed was a table with a flowered porcelain basin and ewer. The large window, framed with a starched white curtain, overlooked the rear gardens which now, in December, appeared lifeless, the oaks and elms long since having shed their vibrant coverings.

For six years this room had been home to Morgana Edgewood. She felt safe here. Her younger years had been spent moving from place to place as whim overtook her father. There was little warning when these changes occurred, only a brief order to pack. Then they would be gone.

Morgana's eyes swept over the empty room. The others had already gone to class. Desultorily, Morgana wondered what they thought of her absence. Fortunate in her good health, Morgana had never once missed a class in six years. She fought down her resentment, having long ago reached the conclusion that certain things in life were unlikely to change and, therefore, had to be accepted.

She sat down on the edge of her bed, absently running the palm of her hand across the uneven surface of the chenille spread. She stared at the changing pattern of sunlight and shadow that rippled across the polished wood floor. Then her brow furrowed in concentration as she tried to remember her father.

She had an image of a man who was tall and thin, who wore his clothes with an unusual degree of sophistication. His thinness was not so much inherent as it was due to a bout of consumption in his early years. He had never worked a day in his life.

In her very young years, Morgana had had no idea what her father did. This was not unusual, perhaps. Not all young children knew with a certainty what their fathers did for a living. Fathers went out to work and they came home.

The difference, in Morgana's case, was that her father went out to work mostly at night — sometimes all night — while Morgana remained in the care of the current housekeeper. They came and went, nameless women with long forgotten faces who, sometimes after only a few weeks, left in a huff, presumably having discovered that Aleceon Edgewood was not, as he claimed, in the world of finance.

Gradually, as she grew older, Morgana became aware that most of her father's time was spent gambling. There were times when he won handsomely. However, everything he made soon found its way back to the card table, leaving them, at times, in dire straits.

While her father was on his way to a life he coveted, Morgana occupied her time as best she could. She read voraciously, a lot more than any child her age could be expected to do. She also embroidered. It gave her a sense of accomplishment, although most of the things she turned out wound up in her dresser drawer or were lost in moving from place to place.

It was during one of the impoverished times that her cousin, Caroline, had so unexpectedly appeared on their doorstep. That had been when they were living in Boston. Caroline, who was the only daughter of Aleceon's sister, Sarah, had wanted to rid herself of an unwanted child. Morgana's father had made all the arrangements, "assisting" his niece in her hour of need. Then he had tried to blackmail her. When Caroline's mother, Sarah Enright, had learned of all this, she had been justifiably furious with her brother. Both Morgana and her father had been ousted from Somerset Hall, the mansion in which the Enrights lived, and to which Morgana and her father had returned some months after Caroline's visit.

Morgana remembered all of that, but of course had never told anyone about it. Certainly not Miss Appleby, who, she was certain, would have been shocked by it all.

For the short time she had known her Aunt Sarah, Morgana had become very fond of that gracious lady. She thought her aunt returned her feelings; however, she was never entirely certain of that. Once, during these past six years, Morgana had almost written to Sarah Enright. In the end, however, she had torn up the letter. Her aunt had sent them both away; Morgana could only assume that she, like her father, was unwelcome in her aunt's house.

Now, this man . . . this stranger, really . . . wanted her back in his life. And what kind of a life? she wondered with growing apprehension.

Repressing her unease in a determined manner, Morgana got up and crossed the room. Opening the door of her wardrobe, she rummaged through its dim interior. Finally, way in the back, she located her portmanteau. She observed it critically; it wasn't in the best of shape.

Briskly then, without letting her mind dwell upon the coming days, Morgana packed her few belongings.

A short while later, a knock at the door made her turn and she saw Miss Appleby standing on the threshold, a heavy woolen shawl draped about her plump shoulders.

"The carriage is here, Morgana. Are you ready?"

Not trusting herself to speak, Morgana only nodded. Picking up her wool-lined pelisse, she shrugged her arms into it, then buttoned it with hands that were surprisingly steady.

As they walked from the room, Morgana resisted the urge for a backward glance at the haven she was leaving. There was not even time to say a few final words to her friends. And perhaps that was just as well, she reflected glumly. Good-byes were so . . . final. Even now, on her way to God knew what, there was in her mind the small flare of hope that perhaps she would be able to return. The holidays would soon be upon them. Everyone would be going home. This time, for the first time since she had come here, so would she. Maybe, like the others, she too could return.

They didn't speak as they headed downstairs. Morgana was grateful that the headmistress walked with her to the front driveway. It seemed to postpone, if only for a few moments, her departure into the unknown.

But at last they reached the waiting carriage. Morgana viewed it forlornly.

"Your father will meet you at the Charleston pier," Miss Appleby was saying brusquely, handing Morgana the letter. "I'm certain he will know what time the boat docks." She hesitated, then put her arms about the young woman, giving her an affectionate hug. "Please write and let us know how you are."

"I will," Morgana promised, close to tears.

"And take care of yourself," Edith Appleby whispered, her eyes misting. "We will miss you."

The driver had hoisted her bag inside the vehicle and now assisted Morgana in entering.

As it moved away, Morgana waved a gloved hand. Turning, she looked out the rear window until long after the plump form of Edith Appleby had disappeared from view.

Finally, she faced forward, her expression resolute. She glanced only once at the envelope in her hand. Then, without reading it, placed it in her reticule.

Morgana had never wasted time wishing for what might have been, an attitude she considered both unrewarding and unproductive. To a certain point, she was fatalistic, but that peak was reached only after she considered her options and alternatives.

Right now, it appeared that she had no other alternative than to obey her father's injunction. Her plans for her own future would simply have to be shelved for a year or two, she decided. But it would not be forever, she told herself. When she reached twenty-one, she would be her own mistress.

Settling back then, Morgana let her calm gaze drift over the softly rolling hills, determined that this interruption in her life would be of short duration.

Chapter 3

Standing on the deck of the steamboat, its side paddles chugging slowly through the clear blue water, Morgana Edgewood viewed the Charleston Harbor with little interest.

About her, the air was warm and humid, but not unpleasantly so due to a persistent breeze that alleviated both conditions. When she had left New York, it had been cold enough to feel the bite in the frequently gusty winds of December.

Here, it seemed almost like spring. Even flowers were in bloom, creating splashes of color among the pastel shades of the houses. In the distance, she could see sunshine warming slate and tiled roofs, tipping greenery and creating an occasional glitter of light upon a window pane.

The boat neared the shore, angling effortlessly alongside the jutting wooden pier. Seagulls swooped and squawked, flashes of white against blue sky and water as they brazenly approached the many fishing boats that dotted the bay.

Leaning forward on the railing, Morgana scanned the dock for any sign of her father. He was nowhere in sight.

Some twenty minutes later she stood uncertainly, portmanteau by her side, amidst boxes and crates, coils of rope, and milling people, all of whom seemed to have a purpose, a destination in mind.

With a deep sigh of annoyance she loosened the brown woolen shawl draped about her shoulders. The temperature was in the mid-seventies and her heavy clothing clung to her in a most uncomfortable manner. She peered about for any source of shade where she could get out from beneath the blazing sun. But there was only the ticket office and it appeared crowded.

Her annoyance sharpened. There was still no sign of her father. Briefly, she glanced at the small enameled watch pinned to her bodice. It was four-twenty in the afternoon. The boat had been on time; obviously her father wasn't.

"Miss Edgewood?"

The voice startled her. Turning, Morgana regarded the young man who was striding in her direction. "Yes. . . ."

Well, Griffin thought to himself, she's not ugly anyway. He'd had no trouble identifying her. She was the only unaccompanied woman on the pier. His eyes lingered on the heart-shaped face. Her skin was fair and as smooth as cream. She had a small but well defined mouth that, right now, was set primly. Her eyes were very blue, very direct, and were fringed with thick, silky lashes.

He frowned slightly at the sight of her blond hair which she wore pulled back into a severe, most unflattering bun at the nape of her neck. The golden mass was almost hidden beneath a straw bonnet the likes of which he hadn't seen in years. Nor was he impressed by the simple brown muslin dress she was wearing; even though half concealed by her woolen shawl, he could see that it, too, was hopelessly outdated. She was tall, standing a good five-feet, seven-inches — another minus to Griffin's way of thinking. He preferred small, petite women.

When she spoke, her voice was husky, low, not at all like the breathless, somewhat musical voices of the young women he knew.

"Yes?" she said again, a bit impatiently now. She couldn't imagine why the young man was staring at her as if he were taking inventory.

He inclined his head. "My name is Griffin Kynes. Your father couldn't be here to meet you. I've come in his stead."

"Is he ill?" she asked quickly. She looked up at him with some concern.

"No more than usual," he replied, offering no further explanation, not mentioning that Aleceon had long since drunk himself into a stupor.

Bending over, Griffin picked up the shabby portmanteau, then put his hand on her elbow, intending to propel her forward. To his acute surprise, she didn't move. Beneath the slight pressure of his hand, he could feel a rigorous resistance.

Griffin faltered, more than a bit flustered, and just stood there, feeling foolish.

"I don't even know you, sir." She frowned at him, her small mouth returning to primness as she drew away from his touch.

"I just told you who I am!" he responded sharply in a voice thick with exasperation. God, the woman was standing there as if he were about to assault her. She stood very still, eyes viewing him intensely, appearing to be judging his worth. From her expression, Griffin assumed that he didn't measure up too well.

The look, so direct and challenging, unnerved him. "How would I know your name and time of arrival if your father hadn't sent me?" he demanded, mentally cursing Aleceon Edgewood and his strange daughter — whom he was expected to marry!

"My father led me to believe that he would meet me," she insisted, holding her ground. "I have his letter . . ." She began to fumble within her reticule.

Griffin removed his hat and ran an agitated hand through his dark hair. He had wasted the whole blasted day in this foolishness. The drive into the city was three hours coming and three hours going.

He watched her a moment longer, making no effort to repress his irritation. "I don't give a damn about your letter," he exclaimed at last. Ignoring her zealous and indignant protests, Griffin again grasped her arm, this time with greater firmness.

About them, Negroes had ceased their work, travelers had paused in their tracks, and all were staring at the two young people, some with broad grins on their faces.

Griffin could feel his face redden and he clenched his teeth. His eyes fixed straight ahead as he almost dragged Morgana to the waiting carriage.

"Will you be still!" he hissed. "You're making a scene." He threw the portmanteau on the seat. With no warning, he put his hands around her waist, lifted her off her feet and deposited her, none too gently, next to it. Then he got in, seating himself opposite from her.

Her back stiff and straight as she sat down in the vehicle, Morgana glared at him, her eyes shimmering with the iridescence of sapphires. "I am unaccustomed to having strange men approach me," she retorted in clipped tones, quite affronted by his boorish behavior.

He cast a black look in her direction. "I can understand that," he muttered sarcastically, happy to see the flush that crept up her slim neck and stained her cheeks. Turning, he motioned briefly to Jude, who was seated on the driver's bench.

They fell into a strained silence as the carriage moved forward.

Surreptitiously, Morgana moved her head slightly, studying Griffin Kynes. He was, she observed, dressed somewhat informally, unaware that the white shirt, tan breeches and soft leather boots was the apparel he wore most days while on the plantation. He was tall, probably just over six feet. Although he was wearing a wide-brimmed hat, she could see that his hair was black and wavy, his sideburns cropped short. His jaw was square and clean shaven beneath dark eyes that were brooding, intelligent, speculative.

He was a most handsome man — and probably knew it, she decided, feeling an irritation she was hard pressed to explain.

"You indicated that my father was not feeling well," she prompted after a while. She tried not to frown. Something in his attitude set her teeth on edge.

Griffin regarded her coolly a moment before answering. "I did?" He seemed surprised. "There's nothing wrong with your father," he replied brusquely, turning away. "In fact, I suspect he has the heart of an ox," he added in a murmured, disinterested voice. With his thumb he pushed the hat further back on his head and settled himself more comfortably.

Somewhat put off by this callous disregard for her feelings, Morgana's mouth tightened again. She'd always heard that Southerners were supposed to be polite and hospitable. If Griffin Kynes was any indication, she thought ruefully, all the stories were false.

For a time, she studied the passing scenery. The dirt road they were traveling ambled alongside the Ashley River and was lined with live oaks and cypress trees, from which moss hung like tattered gray wisps of lace.

As they passed plantation after plantation, Morgana was struck by the run-down condition of most of the houses. Even the larger ones appeared to be in a state of some disrepair, needing at the very least a new coat of paint. In the fields, she could see the bent backs of the Negroes as they labored beneath the late afternoon sun. Quickly, she averted her eyes and moved restlessly. Like most Northerners, Morgana found the very idea of slavery reprehensible.

It appeared from her father's letter, which she had at last read on the boat, that her final destination was a place called Albemarle. Morgana wondered whether it would be like the houses she could see from the road. She wondered, too, whether it was tended by slaves. It wasn't a very comforting thought.

"I suppose you were unhappy to leave school on such short notice?"

Griffin's voice claimed her attention. Pensively, Morgana regarded him for a moment, feeling a fresh surprise at his obviously unfriendly manner. Although he had addressed her, he wasn't looking at her. His attention seemed focused on the passing landscape. She wondered whether he would even bother to repeat the question if she made no answer.

"I was," she replied at last. She couldn't quite repress her bitter tone, but if he took note of it, he made no comment. "I really don't understand why my father sent for me," she added. She stared at him, hoping for some enlightenment. Who was Griffin Kynes? she wondered. And what was his relationship to her father? Although, she reflected in her usual, practical manner, the fact that she didn't know any of her father's acquaintances was only to be expected under the circumstances.

Griffin observed her with his first show of interest. He hadn't quite believed that she didn't know of her father's plans, but he realized now that she really was unaware of the reason for her being here.

"How long has it been since you've seen Aleceon?" he asked her, feeling some curiosity.

"I've not seen my father since 1846 when he enrolled me in Brookshire."

He raised a brow at that. "Six years?" he murmured, taken aback.

She nodded curtly. "Six years." She gave him a fleeting glance that was glacial in its warning to bestow no pity upon her.

Pity was the last thing on Griffin's mind. He was simply

surprised, for a sense of family was deep within him. He couldn't imagine not seeing Nathaniel or Cammy — much less a child of his own — for that length of time. Settling back, Griffin fell silent again, appearing lost in his own thoughts.

Morgana hesitated, then decided not to pursue the matter further. Instead she inquired, "How much farther do we have to go?"

"A distance," he replied, without turning his eyes in her direction. "But we should reach Albemarle by dark."

Another silence descended. Weary from four days of travel, Morgana began to doze.

At last she became aware that the carriage had left the road and was now proceeding up a long driveway, lined on both sides by massive oaks, the uppermost branches of which entwined, producing a shaded, living arch.

As they neared, Morgana's eyes widened as she took in the sight of the magnificent structure that sat in a clearing, aloofly unaware of the encroaching swamp and wood that surrounded it. Three stories high, it was ringed by a verandah on the lower floor and piazzas on the two upper levels. Tall white columns rose majestically from the ground to the second story. The whole building was suffused with lilac in the gathering twilight.

The carriage halted and Griffin got out, extending a hand in her direction. "Come along," he said peremptorily, leading her up the wide front steps.

The door opened before they reached it. A tall Negro, somewhat on in years but bearing himself with a quiet dignity, smiled at them as they entered the large and spacious foyer.

Glancing up, Morgana noted with some surprise that the ceiling extended all the way to the second floor. From it were suspended two immense crystal chandeliers that splayed prismed candlelight on the parquet flooring. Several hall tables were positioned evenly on either side of the foyer, and all bore

live poinsettia plants, the vivid red of the lush leaves displaying splashes of color so vibrant it seemed to glow.

"Will you be wantin' supper, masta, suh?" Thomas was in-
quiring pleasantly, addressing his question to Griffin, but
viewing Morgana with open curiosity.

"The others have eaten?"

"Yassuh."

"Very well, we'll eat now. Put Miss Edgewood's baggage
in her room." His eyes returned to Morgana. "Both my
grandfather and my sister have apparently retired. I hope you
don't mind if we dine alone." He said the words as if it really
didn't matter to him whether she minded or not. Turning, he
began to walk away.

Irked by his blatant arrogance, Morgana clasped her hands
loosely at her waist and raised her chin defiantly. Surely, she
thought, this man didn't expect her to follow him every time
he issued a command!

"I would like to see my father first," she stated calmly, not
moving from where she stood.

Halting, Griffin turned and gave her a brief glance that held
more than a little exasperation. He had assumed, from the way
Aleceon had spoken, that his daughter was unsophisticated,
innocent, perhaps just a trifle gauche. What he found was a
young woman who handled herself with a cool assurance, was
candid and straightforward to an almost embarrassing degree.
She seemed incapable of dissimulating, even for the sake of
propriety. His mouth twitched with annoyance at his discov-
ery. He was not especially thrilled at the prospect of being
saddled with a wife who displayed such unfeminine traits.

They stared at each other for a moment longer. Griffin was
the first to look away.

"Thomas," he said to the Negro, "see if Master Edgewood
is awake. We'll be in the dining room." He began to walk away

again, not looking back at Morgana.

With little recourse, Morgana removed her shawl and bonnet and placed them carefully on a nearby table. Then she followed Griffin across the spacious hall into a large and airy dining room.

On the south wall, she saw that French doors led out onto the verandah. The west wall was almost entirely taken up by two wide and tall windows framed by dark red velvet draperies. The high backed chairs, table, and sideboard were all made of dark, richly carved teakwood.

The only light came from two brass candelabrums that rested on the long table, which was now in the process of being covered with more food than two people could possibly eat.

As Morgana sat down in a chair held by a young Negro who could be no more than ten years old, she realized that she was very hungry. She hadn't eaten since noon, and that had been no more than a small bowl of stew so highly seasoned as to be virtually impalatable.

But as famished as she was, Morgana took the time to note the snowy white and finely embroidered linen cloth, the gleaming silver, the delicate crystal and the gold bordered china that graced the table. She had only once before in her entire life seen such opulence, and that had been in her aunt's house at Somerset Hall.

They had no sooner settled themselves than Thomas appeared.

"Masta Edgewood is asleep, suh," he offered in his quiet voice, his body bending forward in just the suggestion of a bow. "Shall he be wakened?"

"Oh, no," Morgana replied before Griffin could speak. "Please don't disturb him. I'll see him in the morning." Although she refrained from showing it, she was now truly annoyed with her father. He had known she was arriving today. Even if he couldn't have made it into Charleston, the least he could have done was stay awake and greet her when she had gotten here.

As they began to eat, Griffin allowed himself a small sigh, suspecting that his grandfather had purposefully absented himself, and probably had instructed Cammy to stay in her room as well. Doubtless the old man reasoned that Griffin could use the time alone with his bride-to-be.

Good Lord, Griffin thought to himself, pushing the food around his plate with his fork. How did he ever get himself involved in all this? He wasn't even sure he liked this woman. She certainly didn't know how to talk to a man, to make him feel at ease. All of the young women he knew had been carefully prepared in the social graces of conversation and flirting; they could compliment a man with a sidelong glance or a graceful flutter of their fan.

But this one . . . There was a sense of independence about her that he found disconcerting.

Griffin shook his head, his lean, angular face beset with conflicting emotions. He was sorely tempted to rush upstairs and throttle Aleceon Edgewood, to evict both him and his daughter from Albemarle. Unobtrusively, he darted a black scowl at the young woman seated beside him, but her attention was elsewhere and she didn't notice.

And, viewing her almost perfect profile, Griffin made up his mind.

He didn't like her.

The thought so depressed him that suddenly his whole future loomed, empty and bleak. Lifting some of the food to his mouth, Griffin tasted antagonism, clenching his teeth while it settled in his stomach like an alien intruder bent on disturbing him. He wiped his mouth with his napkin and barely repressed a groan of despair.

The silence lengthened.

51

For a time, Morgana was unsettled by the constant presence of servants. She was unused to being waited upon in what she considered an excessive manner. The boy who had held her chair, and whose name, she learned, was Suky, was now standing behind it, waving a palmetto fan over her. Since the weather was not especially warm now that the sun had set, she reasoned that his purpose was more to keep the flies away than to offer a cooling breeze. A young, light-skinned man, about twenty, hovered constantly at her side, offering bowls and platters at intervals, refilling her cup with coffee as soon as she took a sip. His counterpart was doing the same for Griffin. Both young men were wearing black jackets with matching trousers and white gloves that could be termed no less than immaculate. At intervals, one or the other of them would disappear into the kitchen, which seemed to be just off the dining room, only to appear moments later with still more food.

There was chicken, fried, crispy, tempting; there was a huge platter of shrimp, tiny and succulent and pink; and there were mounds and mounds of rice — Morgana was to learn that it was served with every meal, including breakfast. In addition, there was red gravy, okra, corn, and sweet potatoes. Biscuits with the steam still ricing from fluffy centers together with butter and jam were placed at arm's length, but Morgana never had to reach for them. They were personally offered to her by the attentive servant, who somehow seemed to know whenever she was about to make a move. And finally, there was coffee served with a cream so rich and thick it floated on the surface of the steaming concoction.

To Morgana, it all seemed a terrible waste.

Seeing her expression and apparently guessing at her thoughts, Griffin spoke. "The leftovers go to the house servants," he told her, his tone short. "I assure you, the food will not be wasted."

She bent her head, staring at her plate, embarrassed that he had caught her disapproval. Quickly, she changed the subject. "You don't speak like a Southerner, Mr. Kynes," she observed in her low, well modulated voice. More than one of her classmates at Brookshire had been from the South. All had spoken with a soft, lilting accent that was barely noticeable in his voice.

"I'd prefer that you call me Griffin," he stated, leaning back in his chair as the plates were cleared away. "Adam, bring me a glass of Madeira," he said to one of the servants, then regarded Morgana questioningly, but she shook her head.

"I was born here in this very house," he went on in answer to her observation. "My grandfather came to the Carolinas from England. When I was seven, he hired a tutor for me. When I was fourteen, I was sent back to England, to Oxford, to complete my education."

Morgana raised a brow. "Isn't that unusual?"

"Not at all," he replied, sipping his wine. "There are no adequate schools in the Carolinas." He made a vague gesture. "And even if there were, I suspect that my grandfather would still have sent me back there. Being an Englishman, he regards all schools as inferior to Oxford."

"Your father . . ." Morgana began tentatively.

"My father died fifteen years ago, of smallpox. My mother died some years before that, giving birth to my sister."

"I'm sorry," Morgana whispered.

He regarded her for a moment, then asked, "And what of Brookshire — you did say that was the name of the Academy you attended?"

She nodded. "I consider it a fine school."

"A sort of finishing school?" he suggested with a faint smile.

Morgana heard the slight edge of condescension in his voice as he made that assumption, and couldn't help but smile at

53

the thought of Miss Appleby's reaction to that statement. Few things had infuriated the headmistress more than having her academy classed in such a manner.

"I hardly think it could be termed that," she murmured at last, thinking of all the hours she had spent with her head bent over a book on history or geography, not to mention mathematics and classical literature.

A dark brow arched skeptically. "You were not taught how to dance or play the piano?"

She kept the smile in check, allowing her blue eyes to widen with assumed innocence. "Oh, yes. Yes, as a matter of fact, I was. I can also embroider beautifully."

He looked a bit smug, apparently satisfied that he'd been right in his assumption.

Morgana's eyes were lighted with mischievous amusement as she sipped at her coffee. Looking up just then, she saw a woman standing in the doorway that led to the kitchen, her brown face wreathed in smiles.

"Wantin' to know if ever'thin' be all right, masta, suh." Although she addressed her question to Griffin, her dark eyes were upon Morgana.

Glancing at the woman, Griffin couldn't contain a rueful smile, knowing full well that the cook was merely satisfying her own curiosity. The whole household, of course, knew why Morgana was here.

"As usual, everything was very good," Griffin replied solemnly, nodding his head. He turned toward Morgana. "This is Minda," he explained. "She not only does the cooking, she runs the whole household. She's a bit of a Tartar, I'm afraid." He grinned affectionately at the Negress. "But we all put up with it because, frankly, she's the best cook in these parts."

The compliment produced such a delighted chortle that Morgana had to smile at the boisterous sound. Minda, she saw, was positively statuesque, lacking only about an inch to reach a full six feet. She was a handsome, robust looking woman, big boned, but not fat, and appeared to be about thirty-five years old. Above a red calico dress with a white fichu at the neck, her woolly hair was cropped so short that it gave the appearance of a tight black cap about her well-shaped skull.

Behind Morgana, Suky was grinning impishly at his mother, trying to suppress his ready laughter, which had a tendency to erupt at the most awkward times. Minda caught the look and scowled at her youngest son, effectively silencing any giggle that might emerge.

"Dat boy o' mine actin' uppity, suh?" Minda asked Griffin. She had only recently installed Suky as a houseboy.

"He's doing just fine," Griffin assured her.

"He bettah . . ." Minda threw the boy an ominous look. "Paddle him so's he cain't set down fer a week iffen he doan mind his manners." She again regarded Morgana, now smiling broadly, showing a full set of white and perfect teeth.

"I can't remember when I've had such an enjoyable meal," Morgana said sincerely.

The woman looked long and hard at Morgana. Then, issuing another sound of glee, she turned and left the dining room.

In some perplexity, Morgana glanced at Griffin, who seemed to have noticed nothing unusual. He was placidly staring into space. Perhaps, she thought, it was not unusual for the cook to enter the dining room to view guests.

The room was quiet again. Griffin sipped his wine. Morgana toyed with her spoon.

After some minutes passed, she asked, "What connection does my father have with Albemarle?" The short and bitter laugh that greeted her question generated startled confusion on her part. Griffin Kynes, she decided, was the strangest man she had ever met.

"I suppose you might say that he owns twenty percent of it," Griffin observed acidly. He finished his wine, then got to his feet. "I know that you must be tired. I'll have Thomas show you to your room. Tomorrow, when you are rested, I'll take you on a tour of Albemarle."

She nodded slowly, but was still confused. None of her questions thus far had been answered satisfactorily. It was most annoying.

Getting up, she followed the Negro — whom she assumed was a sort of butler — up the wide, curving staircase and along the landing. Finally he paused, opening a door with a smile and a bow of his graying head.

Entering, Morgana viewed her accommodations with a pleased eye.

It was, actually, two rooms. There was a bedroom of a goodly size, the wooden floor of which was highly veneered and partly covered with a braided rug, and which contained a four-poster, a wardrobe, a dressing table, and a japanned chiffonier. The ceilings were high, fully eighteen feet, she guessed. Separated by an archway was a sitting room, furnished with a wicker chair, a divan, and a writing table. This smaller room led out onto the piazza.

In some surprise, Morgana saw that her portmanteau had already been unpacked, the clothes hung in the wardrobe, her few personal possessions laid out atop the dresser.

A young woman came forward, smiling expectantly. Her skin, although dark, was not black; it was a warm brown with a slightly reddish tint to it. She appeared to be about eighteen years old.

"I'se Bella, miss," she announced, nodding her head and nervously fingering the white apron she wore over her black cotton dress.

Morgana blinked. "I . . . don't really need a maid," she

protested with a small laugh of embarrassment.

The young woman put a hand to her mouth and giggled. "Ain' no maid, miss," she replied, shaking her head. "I'se yore wench. Masta Griffin give me to you."

Morgana's eyes darkened with a sudden surge of anger. How dare that man assume she would accept a slave, she thought indignantly.

"Well," she retorted tartly, "you can return to Master Griffin and tell him that I'm quite capable of caring for myself."

The girl's nervousness increased and she took a step back. "Cain't go, miss," she whispered, almost in tears. "Masta Griffin whip me fer shoah iffen he thinks I doan take care of you prop'ly."

The girl looked so dismayed and upset that Morgana could only stand there in ashamed contrition. "I'm sorry," she murmured, quickly deciding to contain anymore impulsive comments. "I . . . of course you may stay." Morgana fought a feeling of helplessness. Oh, that man! she thought, clenching her small hands into fists. Never in her life had she met someone who annoyed her as much as did Griffin Kynes.

Appearing visibly relieved by the decision, Bella began to bustle happily about the room, turning down the bed and laying out Morgana's nightclothes with exaggerated care.

Shaking her head with resigned acceptance, Morgana walked out onto the piazza. Leaning on the iron railing, she surveyed her surroundings in mounting appreciation.

The moon had already risen, hanging in a purple sky that was lavishly decorated with brilliant stars. The moss looked silvery. Just below her room, a huge magnolia tree shone milky white.

Only a few days ago, Morgana thought to herself as she looked about, she had been in New York, feeling the biting threat of winter; now she was here, in a sort of fairyland, a place touched by the warmth of spring despite the contradiction of the calendar.

And why was she here? Why hadn't her father met her? Why had he sent a stranger to fetch her?

Questions bumped and jogged in her mind — and all had no answer.

Oddly, Morgana was aware of a slight stirring of homesickness. But for what? she asked herself dourly. Brookshire was a school, not a home. Miss Appleby was a headmistress, not the surrogate mother Morgana had occasionally thought her to be.

She sighed, taking a deep breath of the sweet-scented night. Griffin had made mention of a sister, she recalled. Perhaps, with another woman around, she wouldn't feel so lonely.

Then Morgana remembered Griffin's offer to show her around Albemarle tomorrow and she wondered if he felt some obligation toward her to make her feel welcome.

That thought she dismissed as soon as it came to her. Whatever else Griffin Kynes felt, it certainly wasn't the need to make her feel welcome. She couldn't remember the last time she had met such a cold, unfeeling person. He was quite insufferable, really.

And how had it come about, she further speculated, that her father owned twenty percent of Albemarle? From what Griffin had told her, he had been born here. Had Griffin or his grandfather sold a part of their plantation to her father? If so, for what possible reason?

Finally, feeling the night air cool on her arms, Morgana turned and went back inside to the bedroom, somewhat daunted by the futility of her thoughts. Everything would just have to wait until morning. There was nothing she could do tonight, she decided. She suddenly felt very tired and wanted only to sleep.

The young Negro girl came toward her. Reaching out, she calmly began to undo the buttons on Morgana's dress.

Startled, Morgana quickly raised a hand. "What are you doing?" She took a step away, holding her bodice together with both hands.

Bella was confounded by the reaction, surprise and confusion playing across her dark face. For the moment she couldn't even think of a reply.

"Helps you undress?" she said at last, the tentative response sounding more like a question than an answer.

"I do not need anyone to help me undress," Morgana declared emphatically. As if to prove her statement, she walked determinedly toward the four-poster and began to remove her outer clothes. Down to her shift at last, she paused a moment, waiting for Bella to leave the room. When the girl showed no signs of doing so, Morgana uttered a brief sigh of resignation. Doffing the rest of her attire, she quickly put on her nightdress.

When she was at last settled in bed, Bella extinguished the lamps.

With another, deeper sigh, Morgana snuggled down in the softness and fell asleep almost immediately.

Chapter 4

The following morning, Morgana opened her eyes, feeling well rested, but with a sense of it being very early. She stretched, luxuriating in the softness for a moment, then awareness came to her, making her conscious of the unfamiliar surroundings.

Outside in the rosy tinted dawn, dogs were barking, the high spirited sound being punctuated by roosters, who were not to be outdone in the greeting of a new and bright day.

Somewhere a bell was being rung with tedious monotony, and Morgana knew that this was what had awakened her.

Bella, too, got up. In some surprise, Morgana saw that the dark-skinned girl had spent the night on a pallet at the foot of her bed.

"Gits you warm water, miss," the girl announced. She bobbed her head and quickly left the room as if to forestall any protest.

She was back in a few minutes, lugging a pail of warm water which she poured into a porcelain basin. With almost methodical precision, she laid soap and towels within easy reach, then crossed the room to the wardrobe. Opening the panelled door, Bella viewed the collection of plain dresses for a long moment, almost shaking her head in despair. In her considered opinion, not one of the garments was suitable for a lady to wear. Hesitating, she threw Morgana a questioning look.

Having gotten out of bed, Morgana was now washing herself, quite unaware that the black girl was waiting for instructions.

"What you wants to wear dis mornin', miss?" Bella finally

ventured into the silence.

Pausing, Morgana regarded her, frowning slightly, hoping she wouldn't have to go through the same ritual as last night. She sighed with resignation. "The dark blue muslin will be fine, thank you," she murmured.

Bella removed the chosen dress from the wardrobe and contemplated it doubtfully. It didn't look so fine to her. Aside from the somewhat common material from which it was made, it didn't have so much as a bow or a piece of lace to relieve the plainness. Miss Cammy, she thought, would have long since discarded a dress like this one — if she had even thought to buy it in the first place.

A while later, having washed and dressed, Morgana sat at the lovely rosewood dressing table, twisting her shining blond hair into its customary knot. At the sound of a knock on the door, she looked up.

"Come in," she called out, turning.

The door opened. Tentatively, Morgana smiled at the sight of the beautiful young girl who entered. Her hair was black and very fine. Dark brown eyes fringed with black lashes were set in an exquisitely proportioned face. She was dressed in what looked, to Morgana, like a ballgown, with yards and yards of silk and lace surrounding a crinolined skirt.

"Good morning," the girl said, dimpling. "I'm Camellia Kynes — Cammy. You must be Aleceon's daughter."

Morgana acknowledged that as the girl came further into the room. She sat down on the edge of the bed, her dark eyes bright with curiosity.

Her grandfather had, only last night, told Cammy of their financial difficulties — a thing she hadn't known about until now. His reference to mortgages held little meaning for her; she had only the vaguest notion as to what that entailed. But her grandfather had been most emphatic as to her silence on this whole matter. Apparently, Griffin planned to marry this young woman, thereby solving all their problems. That was enough to gain Cammy's acceptance.

Cammy had this while been watching Morgana as she put the finishing touches to her hairdo. "Why are you doing that?" she asked at last, tilting her small head.

Turning slightly in the chair, Morgana regarded her in surprise. "Doing what?"

"Your hair," Cammy responded with a small gesture. "Belle is very good at it."

"Why, I've always done it myself." Morgana's face reflected amusement. She began to wonder if women in this part of the country did anything at all for themselves.

Cammy looked a bit surprised at that, but decided not to pursue the matter. "Will you be staying with us?" she asked.

Morgana nodded. "I guess I will be. Is that all right?"

"Oh, yes," the girl responded with unfeigned enthusiasm. "Sometimes I get bored when we're here. Nobody talks about anything but rice and darkies. When we're in the town house, things are much more interesting."

"I presume that would be in Charleston?" Morgana speculated.

"Yes. We'll all be going there next week," the girl added. Her voice a trifle breathless with her enthusiasm over the coming event, Cammy then proceeded to tell Morgana of her coming debut at Saint Cecelia's in January.

"Perhaps I'll be staying here," Morgana noted doubtfully when she was through.

"Oh, no. No one stays at the plantation during the holidays. Or the summer months, either — it's the fever, you know."

Morgana didn't know. The imagined vision produced a trace of bewilderment. "You mean everyone goes — even the slaves?"

That produced a delighted laugh from the seventeen-year-old girl. "My goodness, no. Only the house servants come with us."

"But don't they catch the fever if they stay here during the summer?"

Cammy shook her head, her glossy black curls swinging freely with the motion. "Swamp fever doesn't affect them," she explained. "For some reason, they never get it. Of course, Mr. Dobbs, our overseer, remains here. The people can't be left unsupervised. They do nothing unless they're told to."

"What about Mr. Dobbs's health?" Morgana picked up her enameled watch from the dresser and pinned it on her bodice.

Cammy shrugged delicately, as if the thought held little interest. "He's careful, I suppose. He doesn't go outside at night." She gave Morgana a charming smile, then went on to ask, "Have you had your breakfast yet?"

"No," Morgana admitted. "Actually, I had hoped to see my father first. Do you know if he is awake?"

Cammy turned to the hovering Bella and waved a hand. "Go and see . . ." She regarded Morgana again, with a suddenly critical eye, noting that the young woman wore neither hoop nor stay beneath her plain blue muslin dress. "Is that what they wear in the North?"

It was said in such a guileless manner that Morgana issued a small laugh, unable to take offense. "Yes. Although I daresay it's a bit outdated," she added with a sigh.

Cammy pursed her rosy lips. "Well, we'll have to get to work then. You'll not be able to wear anything like that when we get to Charleston."

"Why ever not?" Morgana asked in some surprise. She looked down at her dress, which she considered quite serviceable.

"Oh, it won't do. It won't do at all." Cammy was most emphatic. Standing up, she twirled about, her hooped skirt billowing about her in a most appealing way. "Have you ever worn hoops?" she asked, standing quietly again. When Morgana shook her head, Cammy gave a small sigh. "Well then, we'll have to have a few lessons, I suppose."

"To wear a dress?" Morgana laughed delightedly at the ridiculous notion, both captivated and amused by the young girl.

"Oh, yes," Cammy responded seriously. "If you're not careful . . . well, you'll see. My wench, Meg, is very good with a needle. We can alter some of my dresses for you until you get your own." Privately, Cammy was thinking that something would have to be done with Morgana's hair as well as her clothes, but she decided to say nothing about that right now, fearing her remarks might seem rude.

Before Morgana could reply, Bella returned with the information that Aleceon was awake and waiting to see his daughter.

Promising Cammy that they would finish their discussion at another time, Morgana hurried from her room. Following Bella's directions, she knocked on her father's door a short time later.

Entering the room, which she noted was similar to her own except that it faced the rear of the house, she saw him standing by the window. He was dressed in dove gray trousers and a white shirt, over which he wore a black silk vest. A matching cravat was tied neatly around the collar, but he was jacketless.

"Father . . ." Morgana greeted Aleceon quietly, trying to mask her shock at the sight of him.

With her first look at the man she hadn't seen in six years, remembrance flooded Morgana's mind. But how, she wondered uneasily, was it possible for a man to have aged so much in such a relatively short time? He was so thin, she doubted he weighed much more than she did. His pace was drawn, almost haggard, the lines on his forehead and around his nose and mouth deeply etched. His color, too, appeared unhealthy.

Aleceon saw the look she tried so hard to conceal and met it with a wry smile. He'd had an especially bad day yesterday; even the laudanum hadn't helped. It had taken almost a full bottle of brandy to dull the pain and provide the blessed oblivion that offered a few hours respite. Most days he felt reasonably well. Only twice before during his illness had he experienced such a day, but he knew with a terrible certainty that those times would appear more and more in the weeks to come.

"I've had a bout with the fever," he offered by way of explanation. "It's a hazard in this part of the country."

Still uneasy, Morgana gave a small nod. She made no move toward him and stood there, feeling a trifle awkward. Her father was far from a demonstrative person and she knew perfectly well that he would neither kiss nor hug her in greeting. And she knew too that if she made the effort he would merely move away from her.

Aleceon studied her for a long moment, noting with a bit of surprise that she was no longer a child, that she had grown into a lovely young woman. She'd been thirteen when he'd last seen her; somehow, that last image had always remained with him.

"You're looking well," he said quietly, still regarding her.

Morgana found that she really couldn't say the same thing about him. "Are you certain that you are not ill?" she persisted, her brow furrowing in concern. She took a step closer to him.

"I'm not ill," he contradicted irritably in a tone she suddenly remembered so well.

Flustered, she looked about, her eyes resting on the Negro who stood discreetly by the door. He was dark-skinned, with gentle brooding eyes that, right now, were fixed, not on her, but on her father.

Seeing the direction of her glance, Aleceon commented, "His name is Ben. He belongs to me. We've been together for a long time."

She paled and her eyes widened expressively. "You mean you own a slave?" she exclaimed, incredulous.

Glancing toward Ben, Aleceon raised a quizzical brow. "Are you unhappy?" The thought seemed to hold some amusement for him.

The Negro's mouth stretched into a wide grin. "Not since I bin wit you, suh."

Morgana noticed that the smile didn't reach the dark velvety eyes which looked inexplicably saddened. Yet she sensed the man was telling the truth. The realization, however, provided only a small comfort. Somehow she had never envisioned her father as owning slaves, even though she knew he had lived in the South for the past six years.

Turning, Aleceon saw her shocked expression and pursed his lips. "My dear, you're no longer in the North," he pointed out dryly. "Please, for both our sakes, don't bring your abolitionist notions with you down here. I've seen men tarred and feathered for making remarks against the South's peculiar institution."

Morgana bit her lower lip. How was she going to be able to live in this strange place? she wondered. She longed for the comfort of her studies, the sameness of Brookshire, and again vowed that her absence would be only temporary.

"How is old stoneface?" her father asked then. At her blank look, he enlarged, "Miss Appleby."

Morgana appeared surprised, then her fair skin flushed with annoyance. "She's one of the kindest people I know," she protested, upset with her father's disparaging remark.

"If you think that, then I'm glad I took you out of there,"

he commented with a short laugh. "The woman's a gargoyle. . . ."

Morgana's color deepened with outrage. "I will not have you speak of her that way. If it hadn't been for her, I can't imagine how I would have gotten through those first years." Her tone became accusatory. "You never came to see me, or wrote. . . ."

She fell silent at the sight of his suddenly closed look. She hadn't seen her father in six years, she reminded herself sternly. Now was not the time to argue.

"I was busy," he offered bluntly. "As for Miss Appleby's kindness, I assure you, my dear, the woman was well paid for her efforts." He gave her a sharp look. "Your tuition was higher than anyone else's. Did you know that?" he demanded. "Your precious Miss Appleby at first refused to take you; didn't think you were good enough."

At her look of dismay, his expression softened. "Well, it was a long time ago. The woman has served her purpose. But that is all behind you now."

Morgana viewed her father with a level look. "Why have you sent for me?" She sat down on a nearby chair, arranging the folds of her skirt without taking her eyes from his.

Mock surprise drifted across his face. "Don't you think it was about time?" he retorted with a rare display of humor. "Surely you didn't expect to spend the rest of your life in that school."

She lowered her head slightly. "It was so sudden, I thought there might be a reason . . ." Her expression grew intent and she inhaled deeply. "Why didn't you meet me yesterday?"

Walking toward the pier mirror, Aleceon adjusted his cravat more to his liking before commenting, "The drive into Charleston is long and tiring, as you've probably discovered for yourself. And, as I have already told you, I'm recovering from a bout of the fever. It tends to sap a man's strength for months on end."

"I'm sorry," she murmured quietly. "I hadn't realized. . . ."

"Never mind, it's of no matter," he dismissed her apology. Turning, he viewed her in silence a moment. Then, in a deceptively casual voice, he asked, "How do you like Albemarle?"

Her brow furrowed. "I haven't seen much of it yet," she replied. "Mr. Kynes — Griffin — has promised to take me on a tour of it today." She paused a moment, then went on to ask, "Are we to live here?"

He nodded briefly, shrugging his arms into the jacket held by Ben.

"But why?" She made a gesture as she got to her feet. "Who are these people? Why are we living in their house?"

"You're certainly full of questions, aren't you?" He passed a hand under his chin thoughtfully. "Nathaniel Kynes and I are . . . old friends," he explained carefully. "I've lived here, on and off, for the past two years."

"Griffin said you owned twenty percent of this . . . plantation."

He nodded again, buttoning his jacket. "I own the mortgage." He smiled at her surprise. "You are, in fact, a wealthy young woman, Morgana." Extending his hand, he took her arm, leading her toward the door. "Let's get some breakfast. There's no need for you to know the details. Down here, it's considered bad form for a young woman to interest herself in financial matters. Southern belles are far too delicate to be concerned with such things."

"I'm not a Southern belle," Morgana murmured in some annoyance, but her father seemed not to hear her words.

As they entered the dining room a few minutes later, Morgana saw that Griffin and Cammy were already at the table. The girl flashed a bright smile, but Griffin merely offered a brief nod.

The older man seated to Griffin's right she presumed to be their grandfather. He immediately got to his feet. Coming forward, he bowed slightly. Taking her hand, he raised it to his lips while Morgana just stood there in startled surprise.

The man studied her for an uncomfortably long moment, a scrutiny Morgana was at a loss to explain since it seemed more intense than the moment warranted. Then he smiled broadly.

"I'm Nathaniel Kynes," he said. "It's a pleasure to have such a lovely young lady in my home." His head bobbed in approval, and some relief. There didn't appear to be anything wrong with her that he could see. In fact, he thought her quite lovely.

Morgana returned his smile, liking him instantly, and allowed him to lead her to a chair.

Again she marveled at the repast. There were steaming platters of scrambled eggs, fried ham, oysters, and those delectable looking hot biscuits. Dainty bowls of preserves, honey, and butter rested beside grits and red gravy, which Morgana had never before eaten, and which her father urged her to try.

"I hope your trip was a pleasant one," Nathaniel said to her as they began to eat. "It's been some years since I've been in the North," he went on conversationally, not waiting for her answer. "Too much hustle and bustle." He looked toward his grandson, who had resumed eating. "Griffin, it might be a good idea for you to show Miss Morgana about the grounds today."

Griffin nodded, a bit curtly, Morgana thought. "I plan to," he replied brusquely, then regarded Morgana with cool eyes. "Can you ride a horse?"

"No, I'm afraid not," Morgana responded with a small laugh.

"Oh, it isn't difficult at all," Cammy put in. "Let her ride Lady, Griffin," she suggested, turning briefly toward her brother. "She's very gentle, you'll have no problem," she added to an apprehensive Morgana. "I'll lend you one of my riding habits until we can have one made for you."

Tentatively, Morgana nodded, not at all certain she wanted to ride a horse. As far as she was concerned, horses were for hauling carriages and ploughs.

Later that morning, however, having donned the borrowed outfit, Morgana sat sidesaddle, holding on to the pommel for dear life, only half listening to Griffin as he gave her a few brief instructions.

"No need for you to be concerned," he assured her. He mounted his own horse with practiced ease. "Lady is so old she won't go faster than a walk no matter how you prod her on."

Morgana was viewing him with some doubt. She had the disturbing sense of being high off the ground and suffered a moment's vertigo which, thankfully, quickly passed. However, she refused to release her hold on the pommel.

Amusement flickered across Griffin's face as he watched her. She was sitting straight backed and stiffly, as though perched on something precariously fragile.

"Relax," he advised, gripping the reins of his own horse. "You just might enjoy it."

And, much to her surprise, she did. After the first frightening moments when the horse began to move, Morgana's taut muscles began to ease. After another ten minutes passed, she actually began to observe her surroundings.

The game, she noted, was extensive. Mostly small animals and a profusion of birds that was quite awesome. They swooped and wheeled, chattering noisily, creating a panorama of color that was exceeded only by the exotic array of flowers.

After they had ridden about half a mile, Griffin reined in his horse, then pointed ahead. "These are the rice fields. Each field is some fifteen acres in size and divided by those embankments."

She studied the neat, muddy patchwork. "Why are they separated like that?"

"So that one field can be flooded independently of those around it," he replied. "Unlike cotton or sugar, rice takes a great deal of water."

She regarded the scene for many moments, watching as women raked piles of rubble together, then proceeded to burn it.

Seeing her absorbed attention, Griffin went on to explain, "They're destroying what's left of the last crop, as well as any weeds or refuse that might have accumulated. When they're through, the area will be clean and ready to receive the new seed. Come along." He nudged his horse forward.

She followed — or rather, Lady did — as he led the way through the field to another, some distance away. Here, men were ploughing, creating neat furrows that dissected the land with almost geometric precision.

"Do they work at this all day long?" Morgana was beginning to feel the heat of the sun on her back and wondered what is was like in the summer.

Griffin glanced at her. "All day," he affirmed. "Work begins at sunrise."

"When do they eat?"

"Breakfast is brought to them about eight o'clock, the midday meal about noon. Usually, they finish about four in the afternoon. After that, the remainder of the day can be spent in tending to their own patches."

"They have their own land?" Morgana asked. She viewed him in some surprise.

"Sort of," he smiled. "The land, of course, belongs to my grandfather. But we usually assign a quarter-acre to each worker to farm as his own. The produce can be kept for their own use or sold. How well they do depends, of course, on how quickly they complete their task."

"Task?"

Griffin steadied his spirited horse before he replied. "Every hand has a certain amount of work to accomplish in the course of the day. When he's finished, his day is over." He peered about, then pointed. "Look there — see those hands digging ditches?" At her nod, he continued. "They're assigned six hundred feet a day. It's a fair system," he insisted, seeing her dubious expression. "Darkies are lazy; some more than others. If we were to allow a gang to work at their own pace, some would work hard and others would laze away the day, not pulling their own weight. In this way, each one does the same amount of work in his own good time."

They continued to tour the plantation for another hour, Griffin explaining any question she might have, then they began to head back toward the Great House.

"I take it you have reservations about slavery," Griffin commented at one point. He angled his horse closer and now rode at her side.

She detected the coolness in his voice but, nevertheless, she answered truthfully. "I cannot see why you must own them," she murmured. "Wouldn't it be just as easy to hire them, to pay them a wage?"

He seemed to seriously consider that. Actually, Griffin was unaccountably filled with a sense of discomfort, of being on the defensive — and before a woman! He was torn between grim amusement and wariness. The cool assurance she displayed nudged a grudging respect from him. He knew very well that she had been impressed by Albemarle the day before. But she had entered as if she belonged, as if she were used to the scope. There was nothing in her attitude to indicate that she might be out of her element. She had lived six years in a school. No matter how exclusive, he reasoned, it was still a school. Yet she conducted herself with a comportment that struck him as — regal.

Ignoring her comment, Griffin asked, "How much do you think it costs to feed and clothe our people for one year?"

The question took her by surprise. "I . . . have no idea," she confessed, turning to look at him.

"Better than twenty-five dollars a year — for one," Griffin held up a finger. "When our people numbered three hundred, as they did two years back, that came to seventy-five hundred dollars a year to feed and clothe our . . . slaves. On their own, only a fraction of them would work," he went on, "or make anywhere near enough to be able to feed themselves. A good portion of them would probably starve if left to their own devices."

Morgana could think of no immediate answer to that and, for a time, rode in silence.

At last they reached the main compound. "And what is that?" she asked, pointing to the barn. She was sitting on the horse comfortably now, thoroughly enjoying herself.

For the first time Griffin looked uneasy and, for a moment, Morgana thought he wasn't going to reply.

"It's just . . . a barn." He averted his face and offered no further explanation.

Since he had been so accommodating and outgoing with his answers and explanations up to this point, Morgana was slightly baffled by his attitude. However, she was in much too good spirits to dwell upon it, and by the time they reached the Great House, she had quite forgotten the incident.

Again, in the light of day, Morgana admired the large and

imposing structure, noticing that the kitchen, despite her first impression of the night before, was actually a separate wing, connected to the main house by a trellised portico.

Griffin dismounted, handing the reins to the waiting Jude. Then he came toward Morgana to assist her off the horse.

Bending forward, she felt his hands encircle her slim waist. With little effort, he lifted her down.

For a timeless moment, his strong hands remained where they were as he looked down at her with an expression she was hard put to define. His dark eyes seemed to bore right through her. A tingling expectancy came over her, a feeling Morgana had never before experienced. She stood very still, allowing the pleasant sensation to wash over her.

The moment lengthened as they continued to stare at each other. Jude had led the horses in the direction of the stables, but Morgana didn't notice their departure. She was aware of nothing but those dark eyes and couldn't seem to look away from them.

At the jarring noise of a bell, they both turned toward the house to see Minda on the kitchen porch, vigorously pulling on the rope, producing the sound that summoned the family to the midday meal.

After dinner, Cammy insisted that Morgana practice wearing hoops. Amused, Morgana agreed to humor the girl. Nathaniel and Griffin had gone into the fields and her father announced that he was taking his afternoon nap.

Later, standing in her camisole and drawers, viewing what was, to her, a bewildering array of paraphernalia, Morgana was astonished.

Laid out on the bed were stays, hoops, ruffled and beribboned pantaloons, shirtwaists, petticoats . . . Surely, she thought in growing amazement, she wasn't expected to wear all that!

They were in Cammy's bedroom, which was directly across the hall from her own. While the bedroom and sitting room was an exact duplicate of her own insofar as size was concerned, Cammy's room was done entirely in blue and yellow, even to the braided rug which was woven in those two colors. Bella and Meg, a sweet-faced Kru, assisted Morgana as she donned the waiting clothing while Griffin's sister looked on in satisfaction.

When she was at last dressed and tried to move about, Morgana quickly learned what Cammy meant. The hooped skirt, swinging from side to side, almost unbalanced her. And when she sat down, she blushed to think what would have happened if her skirt had risen up to her chin while she had been in public.

Cammy, Bella, and Meg dissolved into helpless laughter as they watched Morgana.

"Jest what you gals up to?"

Minda, hands on her broad hips, her wide feet encased in slippers, glared at them all from the doorway. "Kin heah y'all downstairs," she complained irascibly. "Sounds lak de chicken house when a new rooster comes to call."

"Oh, stop fussing, Minda," Cammy gasped between gales of laughter.

"You gals oughta be actin' lak ladies," Minda insisted, frowning, but her dark eyes glinted with affectionate humor as she took in the scene.

"You must see this," Cammy insisted. Taking a few running steps forward, she grasped the black woman's hand.

"Cain't stop fer foolishness," Minda grumbled. Nevertheless, she allowed herself to be drawn into the room.

"Piffle! It's hours until supper," Cammy pointed out. She kissed the woman's cheek, then turned to Morgana, her eyes shining mischievously. "Show her . . ." She fell into laughter again, joined by Bella and Meg.

Good-naturedly, Morgana again rose, walked unsteadily, and sat herself down with a plop that once again sent the skirt up under her chin.

"Lawd," Minda exclaimed with a great guffaw, clapping her hands. "Ain' dat be a sight fer de gen'mens to see. . . ."

Still chuckling, Minda left the room, shaking her head from side to side. With her departure, the girls again howled in merriment.

"You musn't mind Minda," Cammy said when she caught her breath. "She was my dah and thinks she owns me. I absolutely adore her, but she's always fussing and grumbling like an old bear."

Morgana regarded her curiously, wondering what a "dah" was, but before she could ask, Cammy was off again, walking about the room, her instructions and helpful hints coming fast and furious as she urged Morgana to practice.

"You must take small steps, like this . . ." Cammy minced about in what seemed an exaggerated manner. "And for heaven's sake, don't turn too fast." She twirled gracefully, looking, to Morgana, like a delicate porcelain figure atop a music box. "Slowly . . . slowly. The hoops, you see, have a tendency to sway from side to side; you musn't prod them to and fro . . ."

Obediently, Morgana followed instructions.

It was a gay and spirited afternoon, the four young women, two white and two black, time and again breaking into helpless laughter, clutching at each other for support.

Wiping the tears from her eyes, Morgana reflected happily that the stories and angry rhetoric she had heard were not at all true. From what she had seen so far, slavery was not the terrible thing the abolitionists would have everyone believe. True, the people worked, but mostly at their own pace; they were well fed, clothed, cared for, and, to her untutored eye, quite content with their lot in life.

Supper that evening was animated. The poinsettias Minda had instructed the houseboys to use as decorations added a festive touch to the meal.

The table was replete with baked ham and roast turkey with oyster stuffing, candied yams, sweet potato pie, corn, and peas. For dessert they had pecan pie, rich with rum and molasses.

Even Griffin was in a jovial mood, teasing his sister and lending an attentive ear whenever Morgana spoke, although his gaze was decidedly cool whenever it rested upon Aleceon.

Aleceon pretended not to notice, keeping his voice neutral and his face bland. He could afford to be generous. Nevertheless, he moved and spoke cautiously, well aware that Griffin's hot temper could explode with little warning, thereby ruining all their plans.

Later that night, after supper, Morgana could hear the music and singing wafting up from the slave quarters as the people indulged in their customary Saturday night partying. Not all planters allowed this, she was informed by Cammy, but most in these parts did, feeling it a good outlet after a week's labor in the fields.

And the next day, Sunday, only reinforced Morgana's new-found convictions. There was, of course, no work on this day. The people visited and gossiped, fished in the river, paid calls to friends on neighboring plantations, or simply sat in the sun, dozing.

The next week passed quickly. On Christmas day, when Morgana looked out from her piazza that morning, she was surprised to see all the slaves gathered in the front yard. The women were obviously wearing their best clothes, sporting snowy white fichus brightly colored bandannas. Everyone seemed to be in high spirits, and there was much laughter and joking.

Later that morning, Morgana, with the rest of the household, sat on the verandah while Griffin personally distributed gifts; bolts of vivid cloth to the women, a keg of corn liquor to the men, candy and cookies for the children.

Then he, too, joined the rest of the family on the verandah while Dobbs, with the assistance of Thomas, distributed molasses, flour, and clothing to each family.

Afterward there was singing and dancing as fiddlers and banjo players produced a lively music that set Morgana's foot to tapping.

That evening, after a truly sumptuous meal prepared by Minda, they all went into the front parlor to exchange gifts. Morgana was embarrassed at not having anything to give, but Griffin gallantly assured her that her presence was gift enough for them all.

Cammy was in an especially gay mood, and when she opened her gift from her brother, jumped up to kiss him.

"Oh, Griffin," she cried out in delight. "You remembered."

He gave her an affectionate hug and watched as she held up the exquisite gold lavaliere. "I'm glad you like it, darling," he said, helping her to fasten the chain about her neck.

There was, Morgana saw, watching them, a great similarity between Griffin and his sister; same dark wavy hair, same dark expressive eyes, although Cammy's sparkled with an ebullience that seemed a part of her.

"How does it look?" Cammy asked, turning to face them all.

Everyone agreed that it looked lovely, and again Cammy threw her arms about Griffin. "You are the best brother in the whole world," she exclaimed enthusiastically.

Laughing, Griffin agreed with her. "You little imp." He tweaked her nose. "How could I have forgotten when you made certain you reminded me of it at least once a week since you saw it in the window of Kingsleys?"

She grinned, her eyes reflecting a saucy gleam, and Morgana could sense the deep feeling between Griffin and his lovely young sister.

Finally, over eggnog and rich, dark fruitcake, they all sat quietly, listening to the voices of the Negroes as they sang Christmas carols.

It was, Morgana was to think afterward, the very best Christmas day of her life.

Chapter 5

Late the following morning, they all set out for the town house in Charleston where they were to stay for the remainder of the holiday season, which, Morgana was informed, extended through the whole month of January.

Aleceon had, at the last moment, decided to stay at Albemarle. Morgana had tried to talk him into coming with them, but he had declined, claiming he needed the time to recover fully from his bout of the "fever."

Morgana couldn't argue with the fact that her father looked as though he needed a long rest, but she was uncomfortable with the thought that he would be alone with only Ben in attendance.

"Then I will stay here with you," she had told him, upset with his decision. In spite of herself, she found that she was looking forward to the trip.

For some reason, that made him angry. "Morgana, I do not wish for you to stay," he told her firmly. "Ben is perfectly capable of seeing to my needs. And Nathaniel has given orders for a wench named Zoe to cook in Minda's absence. Believe me," he patted her hand in a reassuring manner. "A few weeks rest and I shall be as good as new."

Finally, with some reluctance, Morgana had acceded to his wishes.

Just before she left, Aleceon pressed a bank draft into her hand with instructions to use it to buy herself a new wardrobe, and at last they were on their way.

Morgana, Griffin, Nathaniel, and Cammy rode in the carriage which was driven by Jude, now resplendent in green livery. Following in the buckboard were most of the house servants, including Minda and Thomas.

The town house was located on Church, a narrow street one block east of Meeting Street. The sidewalk was made of smooth granite block from which a path of pale pink brick led to a walled garden enclosing several magnolia trees so old and so tall they reached to the second floor of the house. Along one wall were dozens of camellias, in full bloom, the flowers appearing almost too perfect against the dark leaves of the bushes.

The house itself was a lovely structure, three stories high and made of baked brick with the inevitable piazzas ringing each floor. All the panelling, including the carved mantels, were made of local cypress. The bedrooms, sitting rooms, parlors, and even the dining room were on the second and third floors, the first level being the servants' quarters and kitchen.

Morgana was absolutely delighted by it all. Having arrived late in the day, Minda hastily prepared a light supper for them all, after which they retired.

At seven the following morning, Morgana awoke to the sound of iron wheels on the granite block of the sidewalk below. Getting up, she crossed the carpeted floor to the window and smiled at the sight of the old vendor pushing his cart, his voice a singsong announcement of the fresh shrimp he had to offer.

Bella had laid out a dress for her to wear — one of Cammy's that Meg had altered. It had a frothy white skirt made of twilled cotton with a wide blue silk sash that encircled the waist. Morgana allowed Bella to help her, for dressing was no longer the simple task she had performed all her life.

That afternoon Griffin took Morgana on a drive through Charleston and now, unlike her arrival the week before, she found herself enchanted with the beautiful city.

A peninsula, Charleston was snuggled between the Ashley and Cooper rivers, the nature of its harbor assuring it as an important place of commerce.

The first thing Morgana noticed as they drove along was that the houses were all set at a peculiar angle, with the side of the house facing the street.

They were, Griffin explained to her, situated in such manner so as to catch the breeze from the sea. Everywhere, decorative and intricately carved wrought iron railings and fences caught and held Morgana's eye. She'd never seen the likes of them before.

As they drove down the broad and cobbled thoroughfare known as Meeting Street, she marveled at the pastel colors of the houses, the steep tiled roofs with their quaint chimneys, and the pathways of exquisite pale pink brick that wended from the street through narrow walks and alleys, terminating in secluded courts and gardens that were breathtaking amidst an array of flowers and trees. She had already discovered that what appeared to be the front door of a house actually led to a covered walkway, which, in turn, took one to the real front entrance.

They drove by White Point Gardens, which Griffin promised to show her at a later date. Finally, stopping the carriage, he took her for a walk along the raised promenade that ambled along the harbor.

The day was clear and sunny and mild. Morgana felt more alive than at any other time in her life.

Looking back on the city, she could see the delicate spire atop of Saint Michael's Church. From this angle, she could see only one of its four clock faces, but could easily hear the sound of the bells pronouncing the passing of each quarter-hour.

"It's truly magnificent," she breathed at last, drinking in the sight. "I had no idea. . . ."

Griffin gazed down at her. He had discarded his usual apparel and was attired in a fawn colored frock coat and matching trousers. A flowered waistcoat over a white ruffled shirt gave an urbane quality to his appearance.

"You're not sorry you came?" he teased.

She flushed, grateful for the cooling breeze upon her face. "No. I'm so very glad . . ." She was aware that her heartbeat quickened beneath his look and was a bit surprised by her own reaction. Morgana was forced to acknowledge to herself that she was finding Griffin Kynes more and more attractive with each passing day she spent in his company. His cold indifference, so noticeable on that first day they met, seemed to have dissipated. "It's all so very lovely," she whispered.

A small smile caught and held the corners of his mouth, softening the angular planes of his face. "It's the only setting in which you belong," he murmured.

And he meant it. Dressed now in more fashionable clothes, her hair curled into soft ringlets, Griffin saw that she had a quiet beauty, quite breathtaking in its own way. She was smiling at him, and he couldn't help but stare at the transformation wrought by the ordinary expression. She had beautiful teeth, strong and white and even, and the most adorable dimple on the side of her mouth. Bemused, he noticed that it was only on the right side.

With his remark, Morgana had darted a small glance at him to see if he was serious. Was it possible, she wondered, to learn to care for a man in so short a time? She had no way of knowing, no basis for comparison.

Morgana continued to regard Griffin, who was still smiling at her. He was so very handsome, she thought, studying his rough-hewn features. He emanated virility and strength with each movement he made.

She did care, Morgana suddenly realized. The thought made her a trifle uneasy. Surely a man like this would never look twice at her, she reasoned.

"I'd like to thank you for being so kind and for showing me your splendid city," she said after awhile, when they had resumed walking.

"Oh, there's much more to Charleston than what you've just seen," he responded with a small laugh that, nevertheless, had a ring of pride in it. Just ahead of them, he noticed a group of young boys skimming stones into the water, their boisterous actions accompanied by shouts of hilarity. Griffin placed his hand on Morgana's elbow, steering her to the other side of the promenade. When they were safely past the boys, he released her. "Next month will be especially busy," he went on, glancing down at her as they strolled along. "Have you ever been to the races?"

She shook her head, not wanting to tell him that she'd been nowhere at all. She was acutely aware of his brief touch. Her arm still tingled with the contact.

"I think you'll enjoy that," he mused. "We have a horse entered. My grandfather has high hopes of winning. And, of course, Saint Cecelia's will be having its annual ball. Cammy is to be presented, as you probably already know."

"Yes," Morgana murmured, liking the sound of his voice. "She's been talking about little else. It all sounds very exciting."

"It is," he agreed. "And when we return in the summer, things will be just as exciting. There will be outdoor musicals at Orange Gardens, plays at the Dock Street Theater, concerts, parties, teas. . . ."

She laughed at his enthusiasm, tilting her head to look up at him. "How do you find the time for it all?"

"Oh, we manage." He thought her laughter was like a golden waterfall. The sound of it pleased him. "Whatever else my fair city offers, I assure you, boredom is not among the choices."

And Griffin was right. The next six weeks were a whirlwind in Morgana's mind.

Accompanied by Cammy, with Bella and Meg in attendance, Morgana shopped in all the quaint stores on King Street, spending several afternoons on the pleasurable pastime. She had never seen so many splendid dresses and accessories. With Cammy's help, she selected an entire new wardrobe, but hardly made a dent in the money her father had given her for the purpose.

The dress Morgana decided upon for the Saint Cecelia's ball was an off-the-shoulder creation made of pale blue satin. A full ten yards of material were needed for just the skirt. Cammy, of course, was restricted to white, and chose a brocade material that was to be sewn with tiny seed pearls about the neckline. Both of them would wear the traditional long gloves that rose above the elbow.

The night of the ball was to linger forever in Morgana's memory. Six hundred people attended the fashionable event. The Society had its own orchestra, the finest musicians available both locally and in Europe.

When they arrived, the orchestra had already begun to play a waltz and the music filtered down to the gallery, which was on the first floor.

Cammy led Morgana to the ladies' cloak room where they shed their outer wraps and viewed themselves in the looking glass for a final critical inspection before going upstairs to the ballroom.

When they returned to the gallery, Nathaniel brought their dance cards to them and, following Cammy's lead, Morgana looped it over her wrist. Then, curious, she read it. Except for Nathaniel and Griffin, it was filled with names she didn't even know. Griffin's name appeared only three times, for the third, ninth, and sixteenth dances.

Peering over her shoulder, Cammy giggled, then pointed to number sixteen. "It's the special dance," she whispered confidingly. In a graceful movement she raised her lace fan to shield her lips. "Reserved for wives and . . . sweethearts."

Morgana blushed furiously and made a valiant attempt to regain her composure as they entered the ballroom. At the sight that greeted her eye, she caught her breath in delight. The huge room was a marvel. There were countless white and scented candles in the chandeliers and wall sconces. White fluted columns shone almost gold in the reflected, flickering light. Large pots of camellias had been placed around the raised platform where the musicians sat. The flowers were, of course, in full bloom. The whole room was infused with their sweet fragrance. On either side of the platform were long tables draped in white satin and holding silver bowls that were filled with sparkling punch and fresh orange slices. And there were endless platters of canapes and hors d'oeuvres.

The ambience was truly glittering. Ladies moved lissomely, gowned in their best finery and most treasured gems. The gentlemen, attired in their black dress suits, all managed to look tall and elegant, even if they were not.

With the others, Morgana watched as Nathaniel led Cammy in the Grand March, his pride visible for all to see.

Morgana found herself waiting for the third dance with an eagerness she couldn't deny. When it finally arrived, the orchestra chose to play "The Blue Danube," and as Morgana stepped into Griffin's arms for the beautiful waltz, she knew it wasn't the dance she had been waiting for, but the opportunity to be held within the embrace of those strong arms.

Effortlessly, he guided her about the large dance floor, twirling and gliding in perfect movements to the three-quarter time.

Griffin was a marvelous dancer, and Morgana felt as though she were floating. She felt almost giddy beneath his warm smile of approval as he discovered that she, too, was an accomplished dancer.

They hardly spoke, but never took their eyes from one another. The rest of the assemblage seemed to drift into the background and Morgana was left with the impression that there was no else in the room except Griffin and herself. She wished with all her heart that the dance would never end, but, of course, it did. Griffin then led her to one of the long tables. While they both sipped from glasses of champagne handed to them by one of the attentive black waiters, he smiled down at her.

"I've never danced with a partner as graceful as you are," he murmured. His dark eyes flashed with sincere admiration.

"Nor I," she responded, conscious that her ears were tingling from the flush of delight that coursed through her at his compliment.

They were still smiling at each other when Nathaniel's voice intruded.

"Come now, Griffin," the old man admonished, clapping his grandson on the shoulder. "I'll not allow you to monopolize the time of the most beautiful woman in the room." He directed a surprisingly youthful grin at Morgana. "Age has its prerogatives, my dear." He gave a courtly bow and held out his arm. "I believe that I'm the fortunate recipient of this next dance."

Laughing, flushed with happiness, Morgana put down her glass of champagne and allowed Nathaniel to lead her out onto the dance floor. While Nathaniel was not as accomplished a dancer as Griffin, he was enthusiastic to a degree that left her breathless.

The evening seemed to race by, and Morgana was astonished when the sixteenth dance arrived. Again she gave herself up to the delicious sensation aroused by Griffin's arms around her.

"Is it true," she asked him at one point, "that the sixteenth dance is a . . . special one?"

He glanced down at her for a long moment, then tightened the pressure of his hand upon hers. "Yes, it's true."

He said no more, but Morgana felt as though she finished the dance on a cloud.

During the days that followed, Griffin remained attentive. Though the only time he touched her was when they danced, his eyes sought hers more and more. Morgana was thrilled and excited by the message they seemed to hold.

So enthralled was Morgana with Griffin that she was only slightly aware that Cammy's ebullience seemed to fade in those next days, a situation Morgana was at a loss to explain. The young girl seemed most popular. The day after her debut saw the town house literally filled with flowers from admirers, most of which came from a pleasant faced young man named Clinton Barrows, who, Morgana distinctly remembered, had been penned on Cammy's card for the sixteenth dance. He arrived nearly every day, bouquet in one hand, calling card in the other. But Cammy remained distant and, at times, almost angry with the constant attention.

No doubt, Morgana reflected to herself as they at last made their way back to Albemarle, Cammy most likely had her bonnet set for the one young blade who had not shown an interest in her.

But Cammy's problem — if indeed she had one — went

completely unnoticed by Morgana, for on the day after their return to the plantation, an event took place that forever changed her life.

It was early afternoon. Griffin insisted that she ride with him so that he could show her the canefields, which lay a distance away.

The planting of the sugar cane was in full progress. The roots — or ratoons as they were called — were being laid end to end in long narrow furrows cut into the dark earth.

"By July," Griffin explained to her, "the cane will be better than five feet high. It requires little care from that point until the grinding season. That should be in October. During that time, everyone works an eighteen-hour day."

"Is it so difficult to harvest?" Morgana asked. She viewed the scene with interest.

"It isn't the harvesting, but the grinding that requires constant attention," he replied, then pointed to a wooden building a short distance away. "That's the sugarhouse. When the cane is ground, the resulting juice is put into large black iron sugar kettles. It boils continually, night and day, until it granulates."

Morgana returned her gaze to the workers. "There are quite a few children in the fields," she noted. Her brow deepened into a frown of disapproval. She recalled that in the rice fields, too, there had been children among the workers.

Griffin hesitated a moment, then murmured, "I understand that the mills and factories of the North employ very young children. . . ."

Morgana's expression tightened. "I've heard that argument before, Griffin," she pointed out, fixing him with a level look.

Morgana's voice held that hint of challenge and Griffin almost smiled. He was becoming used to it. As he looked at her it occurred to him that, when she was around, his eyes kept straying to her face. She had a proud bearing and a stubborn set to her chin. He didn't know why, but she was beginning to fascinate him. Time and again she caught him off guard, but for some reason he was beginning to find it stimulating.

"It's not all that difficult to argue with the truth," he noted, still staring at her. Was his mind playing tricks on him? he wondered. His attention had, in a sense, been forced to focus upon this young woman. Was that the reason he found her stunningly attractive? But no, he had to admit to himself. Dammit, she *was* attractive, unlike anyone he'd ever known.

"I don't see how you can compare one with the other," Morgana protested.

Griffin's response was offered in a mild voice. "Just how young are they when they are allowed to go to work in the factories?"

Her glance was a trifle annoyed. "As young as five," she admitted tersely, "but —"

"And how many hours a day do they work?" he interrupted quietly, watching her closely.

She raised her chin. "I . . . would guess the normal factory hours."

"That would be twelve to fourteen hours a day?" At her curt nod, Griffin smiled in satisfaction. "No child younger than twelve works here — at anything. And when they are sent into the fields, their task consumes only three to four hours, depending on how fast they work."

She floundered and his smile broadened. "Don't waste your sympathy on the little black rascals," Griffin said, laughing now. Gripping the reins, he moved his horse forward. "They're just quarter-hands. Their task is only twenty-five percent of what a prime hand is assigned."

As they left the fields, Griffin set a leisurely pace, angling down toward the Ashley, keeping the horses at a walk. It was a beautiful, nearly perfect day. A warm sun blazed down from a cerulean sky, unimpeded by clouds. The trees seemed greener, the moss more delicate, the very shadows appeared to have been painted with warm umber.

The river moved serenely, the tide just at the turning point when the water would flow back to the sea. Sunlight ribboned the surface, glinting and shifting, throwing darts of gold about.

A covey of birds took wing, disturbed by their approach, then soared and dipped in noisy confusion until again settling down some distance away.

At last Griffin halted and helped her from her horse. Morgana gave the animal an affectionate pat on her silky nose. She was becoming most fond of Lady.

This part of the river cut inland, creating a small sandy cove, completely surrounded by moss-laden cypress.

"It's like a little island," she exclaimed delightedly, looking about her.

"This is where I went swimming when I was a child," Griffin informed her. "And still do, on occasion. My dah used to bring me here when the weather was warm enough."

She looked up at him, recognizing the word she had heard Cammy use once before. "Dah?"

He pursed his lips. "I suppose you might say nursemaid, or nanny," he mused. "But they are, in fact, more than that. A second mother, perhaps." Griffin tethered both horses to a branch of a tree.

"And Minda is, or was, Cammy's dah?" Morgana inquired. He nodded and she went on to ask, "Was she yours as well?"

"No." He came back to her side. "My dah was a woman named Coralee. She was Thomas's wife." His voice grew low. "She died while I was in England."

She heard the sadness in his voice, and noted quietly, "You must have loved her a great deal."

He nodded again. "She was a fine woman." He raised both brows in an appealing expression that made Morgana's heart lurch. "And she never thought twice about paddling me when I needed it."

She grinned at him. "I suspect you must have needed it about once a day."

"Too close to the truth," he admitted carefully, then joined her delighted laughter.

They were standing close. As Griffin looked down at her, his laughter faded and his dark eyes grew serious.

"I'm so glad you came to us," he murmured, noticing how delicately her features were molded, sculpted into clean lines from cheek to chin. There was little, if any, soft and rounded prettiness to her face — a prettiness he suddenly considered mundane.

She was viewing him with an expression as serious as his own. "I am, too," she whispered.

He put his hand on her cheek, then, bending forward, kissed her, moving his tongue between her soft lips. His hand slipped downward and cupped her firm breast.

Morgana's arms went around his neck and she pressed closer to him, wishing the moment would never end. As he drew her down upon the soft sand, she went willingly, clinging to him.

Moving his mouth to her throat, Griffin could feel her pulse quicken. Slowly, he began to undo the lace ribbon at the top of her bodice. She murmured a small sound of uncertainty. Griffin paused for just a moment, then placed his lips back on hers, his hands now unfastening buttons.

Morgana felt her bodice being loosened. Although she made a token effort toward resistance, she knew, in advance, that it was futile. The feel of his lips on her ear was arousing a sensual quickening deep inside her. It had a mesmerizing effect on her.

His mouth now moved along her white neck to the soft hollow between her bared breasts. Against his lips he could feel the rapid beating of her heart and he felt his own body throb with an answering desire.

With unhurried movements, Griffin undressed her, stopping now and again when he sensed a resistance on her part, at those times kissing her long and deeply. His hands caressed her with feathery movements that made her tremble beneath his touch.

When she was at last unclothed, he removed his own garments and lay down at her side.

Although she had never in her life seen a man naked, Morgana found, much to her surprise, that she was without embarrassment. Instead, her eyes were delighted by the play of muscle, lean flanks, soft black body hair. He was so perfectly formed that he appeared to her a work of art, a living sculpture created by a master.

Griffin's hands were exploring every contour of her body; a satiny smooth shoulder, the clean line of her collarbone, a sweetly rounded arm.

"You're so very beautiful," he murmured, letting his eyes travel the perfection of her form. His hands were now upon her back, patiently massaging tightly held muscles that gradually relaxed beneath his practiced touch. His fingertips then traced the gentle curve of her spine, dropping to the small of her back and finding the delicious swell of her buttocks. All the while, he was kissing her face and nibbling on her sensitive ear until her whole body quivered and she could only gasp between her quickening breaths.

His hands moved to the warmth between her thighs, again hesitating, not wishing to hurry or frighten her, for he didn't need to be told that no man had ever before touched her. His fingertips found her most secret place and she moaned, gripping him tighter in an almost reflexive movement.

Gently, Griffin pushed her backward and covered her body with his own.

Entering her warmth, he met resistance, and for a moment lay still, giving her time to overcome her fear while his hands and lips continued to caress her.

When he sensed she was ready, he gave a strong thrust and broke the barrier of her womanhood. Her sharp gasp of pain was followed by a wave of pleasure that caused her to shudder with its intensity. Griffin moved slowly, controlling himself until he was certain that her level of desire matched his own.

Morgana clung to his rocking body, urging him to continue until at last her body shook with an ecstacy that tore the breath from her throat.

Afterward, he stayed within her, holding her close to him, murmuring her name, his lips on her ear, his warm breath continuing the waves of golden joy that spread throughout her.

Morgana felt the lassitude of contentment course through her, leaving a pleasant languor in its wake. She felt she could remain in Griffin's embrace forever. She was fascinated by the dark curls on his chest and kept running her fingers through the softness, delighting in the feel of it against her breast.

"I love you, Griffin," she heard herself declare fervently, mildly surprised by her own forwardness. But she had spoken the truth, she realized, gazing up at his now very dear face. She loved this man and had no intention of denying the wondrous feeling, whatever the consequence. Griffin had made her feel beautiful, desirable; it was a heady wine that she knew she must taste again and again.

Once more he kissed her, this time gently, with a lingering tenderness. For a long time they lay there, holding each other, touching, kissing, until the fires of passion blossomed anew. This time Morgana experienced only joy, and her responses were as ardent and heated as his own.

At last Griffin raised himself up on an elbow and looked down at her. With slow movements, he caressed the smoothness of her cheek, letting his fingers move down her throat to the curve of her rounded breast, still dampened with the heat of desire.

"Marry me, Morgana," he whispered, searching her face for the answer he hoped would be there.

Morgana's answer was immediate. She neither thought of, nor regretted releasing her hold on the dream of becoming a teacher. That life was now in the past. Her future was all that mattered. Her arms went around his neck.

"Oh, yes," she breathed, viewing him with love-filled eyes.

"Right away," he insisted. He drew her closer to him, burying his lips in her fragrant hair. "I couldn't bear to have you around and not make love to you each day."

"I'll marry you whenever you say, Griffin," she replied quietly. "Today, if you want . . ." The thought of being with Griffin each day caused her to again shudder in joy and she tightened her grip, letting her hands play across the muscles of his back.

That evening, just before supper when they were all gathered in the front parlor, Griffin made the announcement that he and Morgana were to be married.

Aleceon seemed greatly pleased. Morgana was relieved — if somewhat surprised — by her father's attitude. For some reason she had thought he might object; not because Griffin wasn't suitable, but because of the suddenness of it all. She had, after all, known Griffin Kynes for only two months.

Instead, Aleceon was in a rare, jocular mood, joining Nathaniel as they both congratulated the couple several times in succession.

Finally, Aleceon raised his glass of wine for a toast. "Many,

many years of life and happiness to you both," he pronounced. Gazing at his daughter's happy and flushed face, Aleceon felt a momentary twinge of conscience, regretting his underhanded machinations in bringing about this union. He wondered if perhaps it would have worked out without his interference.

But no, he decided, placing the glass on a table. It was too risky to leave something so important in the hands of fate. No one knew better than he how fickle luck could be. Still and all, he was greatly relieved that it hadn't been necessary to order Morgana to take this step.

Comforted by his assumptions, Aleceon then gallantly offered his arm to his daughter as they all made their way into the dining room.

Seating himself at the table, Griffin's eyes glinted dangerously, although his expression remained amiable enough. He felt he could almost see the wheels spinning in Aleceon's mind, could almost sense the other man's greed and satisfaction. He had never in his life hated anyone as much as he hated Aleceon Edgewood at this moment.

So strong was his feeling of antipathy that Griffin turned a cool eye in Morgana's direction, and for a fleeting moment imagined he saw the image of Aleceon superimposed upon her smiling face.

Chapter 6

The wedding of Griffin Kynes and Morgana Edgewood took place at Albemarle a week later. The minister, a portly, dour man named Henry Olive, had been summoned from Charleston to officiate.

Farley Barrows, his wife Amelia, and their three sons came from Four Oaks to attend the ceremony, but were the only outsiders in attendance.

Morgana immediately liked Farley, a bluff and hearty man in his late sixties. He had a ready smile and a charming, if somewhat garrulous way about him. Amelia, five years younger than her husband, was a thin, nervous woman who managed to frown even when she was smiling. Their eldest son, Clinton, was a gangling young man who once again showered attention upon Cammy, and looked crestfallen at her lack of response to his overtures.

During the preceding week, both Bella and Meg had labored long hours, transforming a bolt of ivory satin into a wedding gown. Acting on Morgana's preferences, they carefully copied the gown from a picture in *Godoy's Lady's Book*. It was long-sleeved, the cuffs coming to a sharp point on the back of the hand. Beneath a boat neckline the bodice also came to a point, hugging the waist neatly before flaring into deep folds that reached the ankle in the front and flowed into a three-foot train in the back. The headdress was really a coronet of pearls from which a delicate white lace veil fell back and across the shoulders.

Minda, too, had made her contribution, toiling in the kitchen from first light, producing a three-tiered wedding cake which she herself carried with much pride into the dining room.

All through supper that evening, Morgana's eyes went from Griffin to her gold wedding ring, seeing how it caught and reflected the candlelight when she moved her hand. It was a lovely ring. The band itself was of yellow gold. The center was fashioned into a rose blossom made of white gold and sported two tiny diamond dewdrops. The ring had belonged to Anne Kynes and was given by Nathaniel to Griffin. Morgana had at first — somewhat halfheartedly — protested that it should really be given to Cammy. But Griffin had assured her that Cammy was in possession of their mother's jewelry, which included the wedding ring that had belonged to her.

That night, in her own room, Bella having helped her to undress, Morgana lay in the large four-poster, excited anticipation coloring her cheeks with a pink glow. She had never in her life been as happy as she was at this moment. Nathaniel had promised to refurbish Griffin's room from top to bottom as a wedding present for them both. Until it was completed, they would stay here, in her room.

At last the door opened. Griffin, with a curt nod at Bella who quickly exited, looked at Morgana and his expression softened at the sight of her. In the light from the single burning lamp on the bedside table, she appeared very young. Her blond hair, unbound, tumbled about her shoulders and had the sheen of silk.

Coming forward, he sat on the edge of the bed. "Shall I extinguish the lamp?" he asked. Reaching out, he touched the softness of her hair, rubbing the strands with his fingertips.

Morgana nodded, gazing at him with adoration.

He held her gaze a moment longer, then turned down the lamp until the yellow glow faded and was gone.

In the dimness she was aware that he was undressing. Only moments later he was beside her. His hands were gentle yet insistent as he undid the buttons of her nightgown. Morgana made no resistance as he lifted it up over her head and flung it aside.

Pale silvery moonlight illuminated their bodies as Griffin bent forward, placing his lips upon hers. For many moments he kissed her, his hand caressing the smoothness of her breast, slipping to her waist and then to her inner thigh.

Now, as before, he raised her desire to a fever pitch until at last, with a small cry, Morgana's arms entwined about him as she pulled him closer to her. Her hands strayed about his body, delighting in the feel of him. She felt no shyness, no reservation as she eagerly grasped the most private part of him, guiding him into her willing warmth, once again losing herself in the exquisite sensation of being one with the man she loved.

Afterward, Morgana nuzzled against him, resting her head on his broad chest. Only moments later, her deep and even breathing bespoke sleep.

Griffin, however, lay there, hands clasped behind his head, staring up into the darkness, trying to fathom his feelings. From the time he had been fifteen and had taken his first wench, right here at Albemarle, he'd made love to many women. Most were black and didn't really count. But more than a few of them were white, for Griffin, when he chose to be, could be very persuasive.

But with Morgana it had been different. Why? he wondered. She hadn't been the first virgin he had bedded. The others had been, for the most part, unsatisfying. He preferred a woman with experience, not someone he had to coddle along. Yet both times with this woman he had reached a degree of satisfaction he'd thought impossible.

Why? he wondered again, puzzled with his own reaction. Did he love her? If so, when had it happened?

And he shouldn't love her. Her father was responsible for all their ills. . . .

The drifting, ethereal moonlight that crept in through the window found his expression set into almost angry lines. Aleceon had gotten his way — now he'd better pay off, Griffin thought to himself.

One other person lay awake far into the night.

Getting up from the corn husk mattress she shared with Jude, Zoe glanced down at him, assuring herself that he was fast asleep.

Silently, she let herself out of the cabin, then went around to the rear. It took only a moment to locate the heavy-handled hoe she had hidden in the tall grass earlier in the day.

Tonight was, she thought, perfect. Everyone had stayed up later than usual because of the wedding and so should sleep soundly. Masta Nathaniel had graciously given them all extra rations of corn liquor to celebrate the happy event. Prudently, Zoe had touched none of it.

Gripping the hoe tightly, Zoe walked as quietly as she was able, her bare feet gliding noiselessly over the dirt road. She made her way slowly, hesitating now and then, casting a wary eye in all directions, until at last she arrived at Jonah's cabin. It had been eight weeks since her brother had been so severely beaten. He was now almost fully recovered.

Zoe knew that he would soon be sold, and not through any auction where he just might have a chance, but to a slave trader. Masta Nathaniel had made that perfectly clear. She was well aware that those rednecks bought only what nobody else wanted. Their coffles almost invariably wound up in the canefields of Mississippi or Louisiana. For Jonah, as well as for any other slave who might meet that fate, there was nothing to look forward to except death under those circumstances.

Although she was frightened, Zoe knew that she was Jonah's only hope. He would be awake and ready because, today, when she had brought his food to him, she had whispered that tonight she would come to him. She could tell him no more. As always, Carlie Dobbs hovered nearby, waiting to lock the door again after she left.

At last she stood before the small log cabin, regarding the iron padlock on the door. Studying it, she frowned. There was no way of breaking it, she knew. But there was a chance that she could break the surrounding wood into which it was nailed.

Placing the sharp tip of the hoe between the lock and the wood, Zoe tried to pry it apart. At first, nothing happened, so she exerted more pressure. Twice the hoe slipped, and as metal grated on metal she paused, holding her breath. Somewhere a dog barked in the distance, but otherwise all was still.

Again, Zoe stuck the hoe behind the piece of metal from which the padlock was suspended, grunting softly as she strained, pushing against the wooden handle as hard as she was able. She felt it give slightly and renewed her effort. Finally, she heard the sound of wood splintering, and at last the contrivance loosened. With a bit more prying and pulling, the lock fell away.

She pushed the door inward and whispered her brother's name. Then she felt his arms go around her, hugging her tightly.

"Zoe, gal," Jonah murmured in a low voice. "Ain' nobody smart as you." He peered outside, then turned to her again. "Dis time, ain' nobody catchin' me. . . ."

She grabbed at his arm, feeling the rough cotton of his sleeve beneath her palm. "You stay offen de road," she urged strongly, frightened for his welfare. "Pat'rollers be goin' up an' down lak always. Iffen dey catches you agin. . . ." She gave a soft sob.

"Kills 'em first," he vowed fiercely, keeping his voice soft.

"An' listen fer de dogs," she pressed, tightening her grip on his arm.

"Doan worry none 'bout me," he muttered quickly, brushing aside her concern with a wave of his hand. "Gonna walk in de water much as I kin. Dogs cain't track in de river." In the dimness, his eyes glittered with determination. "Bin hearin' 'bout de underground peoples who he'ps us'ns. Gonna find 'em iffen I kin."

Jonah glanced into the yard, assuring himself that no one was around. He hesitated a moment, wanting to take his sister with him, but knowing she would only delay his passage.

He put his hands on her shoulders. "Won't forget you, Zoe," he promised. Bending forward, Jonah gave her a quick kiss. Cautiously, he stepped outside, almost immediately becoming as one with the black night.

Zoe watched him only a moment. Then, as quietly as she came, she made her way back to her own cabin.

The next morning, although Morgana awakened early, Griffin was already gone from her bed.

Dressing quickly, she hurried downstairs, hoping that he was still at breakfast. Excitement coursed through her each time she thought of her husband and she knew of a certainty that she would feel this way for the rest of her life. The thought birthed a smile of pure joy.

At the foot of the stairs, Morgana paused, hearing voices coming from the study, one of which she recognized as Griffin's. His voice contained an enormous amount of anger. She moved closer, the smile fading from her lips. The door was opened and she could hear the words very clearly.

"It is done!" Griffin was saying in a harsh voice she'd never heard him use. "The marriage has been effected and consummated. Just as planned. I've held up my side of the bargain,

Aleceon. And I fully expect you to hold up yours. Every note, every debt against Albemarle is to be destroyed."

Standing in the hall, Morgana could feel the blood leave her face. Swaying slightly, she gripped the balustrade with hands that felt suddenly icy. She didn't comprehend it all at once, although something deep inside her realized the awfulness of what she had just heard. The words floated for a time inside her head: *the marriage has been effected and consummated. Just as planned.* . . . They hung there as if awaiting her awareness, as though her own body was making a valiant attempt to protect her mind.

Her father's answering response was a mere murmur, or perhaps, over the drumming in her ears, Morgana just couldn't hear it.

"Damn you!" Griffin shouted now. His fist came down on top of the desk with resounding force. "Your word is not good enough. I want to see it done. Now!"

A moment later, both men, followed by Nathaniel, emerged from the study. At the sight of her, they all fell silent. Morgana looked only at Griffin. Seeing her, he halted abruptly. His face was a curious mixture of surprise and dismay, overlaid with a faint residue of anger. He blinked, drawing his breath sharply, and extended a hand in her direction.

But before anyone could speak, Morgana spun around and raced back upstairs to her room. Closing the door, she bolted it from the inside. Trembling, she rested her cheek against the carved surface. It felt cool on her hot skin.

A few moments later, when she heard the knock followed by Griffin's soft entreaty, Morgana put her hands over her ears to block out the sound. The pain she felt was so acute it struck at her very soul, threatening to destroy her.

Bella stood close by, watching her, her dark eyes solemn, silently commiserating with Morgana. At the sight of her stricken mistress, she put a hand to her lips, issuing a soft moan.

When Morgana began to sob, Bella stepped forward, putting her arms around her. "Doan you cry, Miz Morgana," she pleaded, close to tears herself. "Breaks dis gal's heart to see you takin' on so. . . ."

Raising her head, Morgana regarded the black girl's saddened face. "Did you know?" she whispered brokenly.

Slowly, Bella nodded, looking more unhappy than ever. "Ever'body know dat Masta Griffin gonna marry up wit you. Doan know why, 'ceptin' your daddy say it got to be dat way."

Upon hearing that, Morgana's tears ceased. The cold feeling returned. She moved away from the comforting arms and walked out onto the piazza. It seemed to her that her heart had suddenly turned to stone.

Looking down, she saw Griffin mount his horse, then ride off in the direction of the fields.

So much for love, she thought grimly, at that moment hating the man who was now her husband. For the first and only time in her life, she had fallen in love with a man only to see her dreams crushed beneath the harsh light of reality. Griffin had married her to save his precious Albemarle. He had lied to her, used her in the most contemptible way a man could use a woman.

Incongruously, there flashed before her mind's eye the picture of herself and Griffin on the warm sand, sheltered by the cypress and moss. She could feel her face flush, remembering her warm responses to his ardent caresses.

She had professed her love so eagerly. And now, thinking with a clear rage, Morgana realized that Griffin had never done so. Oh, his words had been sweet enough, but they had been empty.

"I love you . . ." She said the words aloud, testing them,

for they were still new to her. But they were as ashes upon her tongue and she gritted her teeth.

How could she have been such a fool? she thought, feeling the anger rise and spread throughout her. She refused to excuse herself on the basis of not having had any experience with men. Time and again over the past several years she had listened to her friends, sympathizing with their heartbroken accounts of a love that had turned sour, of a man who had vowed loyalty only to betray that vow.

Probably, she reflected, Griffin now thought her devastated, broken by the revelation, for there was no doubt in her mind that he knew how much she loved him.

No! she corrected herself with sternness. Once, she had loved him; yesterday — a lifetime ago.

But she would survive. Absently, she twisted the wedding ring on her hand. Looking down at it, Morgana was of a mind to tear it from her finger and fling it across the room. Instead, she clasped her hands tightly, feeling the edge of the metal cut into her flesh. She was filled with the sense of having been manipulated, and she was furious.

Two could play at that game, she decided, staring at Griffin's receding figure with eyes that resembled mountain snow in the twilight. Then she smiled coldly, and only those who knew Aleceon Edgewood well would have noticed the eerie resemblance of that expression upon the face of his daughter.

As for her father . . . Morgana's eyes narrowed. He had obviously played a part in all this. Yet, for what possible reason?

That, at least, could be explained.

Turning abruptly, Morgana left her room. Moments later, she knocked on the door to her father's room. There was a brief pause before it was opened by Ben.

Entering, she saw her father seated at the writing table. Although she was certain that he knew she was there, he didn't turn, just continued with whatever he was writing. He had removed his jacket, but still wore his vest over a white ruffled shirt.

Morgana's gaze drifted to the fireplace, noting the smoldering ashes that were all that was left of recently burning papers. The sight of it caused the pulse at the base of her throat to throb with quickening emotion.

"Why?" she asked without preamble, her eyes returning to her father.

Looking up then, Aleceon raised a brow, the corners of his mouth tightening with what she took to be annoyance.

"Why!" she demanded when he made no immediate response.

"You are being childish, Morgana," Aleceon said with slow deliberation. He indicated for her to take a seat. With exaggerated care, he folded the paper on which he had been writing and laid it aside before again speaking. "I thought your years at Brookshire would have at least taught you how to behave in a ladylike manner," he commented.

Her eyes flashed as she seated herself on the chair before the writing table. "We are talking about deception, Father, not ladylike manners." She viewed him stonily, her back rigid. "You are obviously the instigator in this little farce. I'd like to know why."

"You are nineteen, almost twenty years of age," he noted quietly, ignoring her agitated state. "I thought it was about time you were married."

"I find it difficult to believe that you had my welfare in mind," she shot back with heavy sarcasm. "For six years you didn't even know whether I was alive or not, and I doubt you cared. Now, suddenly, you make plans for the rest of my life without bothering to consult me." She leaned forward, intent and angry. "Did it ever occur to you that I might have had plans of my own?"

Her blue eyes were gleaming with a formidable anger, for the moment unsettling Aleceon, who suddenly recognized in his daughter a strength of will that far exceeded his own. The idea, however, did not distress him; rather, he was grateful for its existence.

"Did it!" she demanded again, feeling a hot impatience with his digression.

"Please, my dear," Aleceon murmured then, appearing pained. He passed a hand across his forehead. "Don't raise your voice." He sighed. "I can understand that you've suffered a bit of a blow to your vanity, had your feathers ruffled, so to speak —"

"Dammit! I will not be spoken to as if I were a child. Not even by you!"

Aleceon blinked, quite astonished at the outburst. Then he adopted a placating tone. "You're right, of course. I confess that I sometimes forget that you are now a woman."

She was not mollified. "I will not be put off," she said through clenched teeth. She strove to keep her temper in check. "Why was it a condition that Griffin Kynes marry me before you returned his notes of indebtedness?"

Aleceon took a deep breath and a look passed between him and Ben that, in her agitated state, Morgana didn't notice.

For just a moment, Aleceon wavered, tempted to tell her the truth. The moment passed. He didn't want her pity, didn't want anyone's pity. Dying, he suddenly realized, was a very personal thing, a very private experience. Aleceon felt he could accomplish it with more dignity if no one knew about it until the very end.

How unfortunate, though, that she had discovered Griffin's part in all this, he thought, dismayed that his carefully laid plans had gone awry. Yet she was married. And, unless he missed his guess, loved her husband. Further, unless he misinterpreted the look in Griffin's eyes, that man was not without feeling for Morgana.

Time, then. Aleceon didn't have it, but the two young people had many years of that precious commodity.

Morgana was still glaring at him and Aleceon made his decision.

"Very well," he said at last, getting to his feet. "You were put in school six years ago because . . . well, because you were troublesome. I'm sure you'll agree that a man cannot go about his business saddled with a child. Doubtless you can understand that, at least," he stated, running a hand through his dark blond hair. "And what was I to do now?" he demanded. "Certainly you couldn't have stayed in that school much longer. You must have damned near been the oldest one there."

"I was," she agreed curtly. Her attitude plainly indicated that he should continue. One part of Morgana felt restless, tingling with the desire to move, to smash, to scream her fury to the skies. But she forced herself to remain still, ignoring the self-indulgent inclination, which she knew would serve no useful purpose.

"Well, then," Aleceon went on, wetting his lips. "Was I to bring you home and have you underfoot again? Simply put, I arranged what I considered a more than suitable union for you. Griffin Kynes is an attractive man," he argued. "You must admit that."

"He is." The comment was expressed coldly.

"And he is, or will be one day, rich," he added, appearing to wait for her approval. When she made no response, he continued, a thin, shimmering strand of sarcasm threading his words. "And it certainly appeared to me, from your enthusiastic response to his proposal, that you loved the man."

"What do you know of love?" she challenged quickly. "I

doubt you have ever loved anything or anyone in your entire life!"

He refused to be goaded. "We are not discussing my emotions, Morgana," he pointed out in a lazy voice.

Morgana stared at her father. Her feeling of betrayal was strong, hurtful. She had always overlooked her father's single-minded, self-centered absorption with his own well-being. She had found excuses for his strangeness, his aloofness, and accepted him as he was. But this — this was too much to accept, too much to forgive.

"And," Aleceon mused, almost as an afterthought, "I must admit to wanting Albemarle." His fingertip traced an indefinable pattern on the writing table as he seemed to collect his thoughts. "I can't run it, but I want to live here. The life of a gentleman planter appeals to me."

"So you used me as a pawn." Morgana's tone was bitter. She shifted her weight in the chair and made a conscious effort to relax her tautly held muscles. All the truths she had known about her father and had never wanted to admit to herself now rushed forward, crowding her mind with contempt. To Aleceon Edgewood, nothing was sacred — not even his own daughter; least of all his daughter.

Aleceon was now moving about the room in a disquieted manner, casting an occasional glance at her rigid demeanor. "You are a little fool!" The words erupted in a curious sound of exasperation that was at odds with his almost pleading look. He paused before her, hands in his pockets, expression now stern. "Can't you see what I've done for you? Instead of complaining, get down on your knees and count your blessings."

Morgana got to her feet, her eyes steady and unforgiving. "I have," she replied tersely. "They add up to . . . nothing."

With that, she turned and left the room without looking at him again, closing the door firmly behind her.

For long moments after she had gone, Aleceon just stood there, his face expressionless. Yet his eyes revealed a pain that had nothing to do with his condition.

"Why didn't you tell missy de truf?" Ben ventured after awhile. He had listened to the conversation between father and daughter with mounting dismay.

Turning, Aleceon glared at his slave "And what is the truth, you black viper?" he demanded in a tight voice.

Ben hesitated, then whispered, "Dat you dyin' an' wants to make missy's life safe. . . ."

Ignoring that, Aleceon walked toward the table. Picking up the decanter, he poured himself a stiff brandy.

"Kin do dat fer you, suh." Ben came quickly forward.

"It isn't necessary for you to jump every time I make a move!" Aleceon declared irritably, motioning him away. "I'm not one of those Southern fops who can't even pour himself a drink."

Ben halted and sighed deeply. "Knows you ain'," he agreed quietly. He watched his master for a moment, then took a breath of determination. "But you should have tol' her," he insisted.

"No!" Aleceon's smoky blue eyes were fierce. "And don't you, either. Besides," he added with a flash of insight, "it's not my intentions that she's concerned with; it's Griffin's. And my reasons will not alter his. There is nothing I can say that will make her see the obvious. She will not believe that her husband loves her. And," he mused quietly, giving it thought, "perhaps Griffin himself is unaware of it." He fell silent a moment, then fixed the Negro with a hard look. "You are to say nothing of this. If you so much as say a word, I'll string you up by your heels. Understand?"

Resigned, Ben raised his hands. "My lips sealed with wax, suh. You knows dat."

Aleceon grunted as he returned to the window, then gave a deep, drawn out sigh. "I've never loved a woman," he mused idly. "Never found one that rated a second look."

"Have to be a special lady fer you to notice her, suh," Ben agreed sagely with a nod of his woolly head.

Aleceon seemed not to have heard him. He stood there quietly, almost motionless. "I married her mother because I needed her," he went on in a barely audible voice. "Kitty was a good girl. She was a whore, you know." Lifting the glass to his lips, he drank his brandy.

Ben nodded cautiously, a bit surprised at the revelation, but knowing that Aleceon was, in a sense, talking to himself.

"She was only sixteen," Aleceon went on. "But she was street wise. She died when Morgana was born."

"Must've bin a fine lady," Ben murmured in the face of that somewhat disjointed disclosure. "Miz Morgana shoah is."

Aleceon turned to view Ben. "She is, isn't she?" he demanded, as if he had just discovered that fact. When Ben fervently agreed, he turned away again to contemplate the scenery outside. "Still, I didn't love Kitty. Never found a woman I could love," he said again, with another deep sigh. "But Morgana . . . I loved her from the time she was a little girl. Always wanted the best for her. But . . ." he trailed off and morosely regarded his empty glass. He held it out and Ben moved quickly to refill it.

"Morgana was a strange little thing," Aleceon went on after taking a swallow of the fiery liquid. "Quiet, you know. Not going on at the mouth like most women. That's the thing I can't stand about them. Always preaching. Like to drive a man crazy with their sermonizing. My sister was like that. A real pain in the ass."

Ben made no comment to that. He avoided even agreeing with an uncomplimentary comment about white women.

Aleceon fell silent then, sinking into one of his frequent dark moods of melancholy with which, by now, Ben was thoroughly familiar.

Anxiously, Ben kept an eye on the thin, gaunt back of the man who, inexplicably, had saved his life five years before. For as long as he lived, the memory would remain with him, as would his devotion for this man.

Ben had been born on a cotton plantation in Mississippi, some thirty-seven years ago. His master, a thoroughly frightening individual by the name of Warren Fiske, had beaten Ben's mother to death for malingering. Ben had been only seven at the time. At nineteen, he had married a wench named Tildy. The marriage, however, lasted less than a year. Tildy had been taken to auction and sold.

When Ben reached thirty years of age, Fiske had sold him to a passing slave trader, along with several other Negroes he considered past their prime. Eventually, Ben had wound up on a nameless plantation some ten miles out of New Orleans, where the only crop raised was sugar cane.

Toiling in the cotton fields, he soon learned, was child's play compared to the canefields, where a slave's life expectancy could be numbered in a mere five years. The work was unrelenting, from dawn to dusk, and sickness was not an excuse for absenteeism. The drivers were a surly lot, always in poor temper, always ready with the whip.

For Ben, and for the rest of the field hands, exhaustion was a constant companion, not only because of the long hours but because their diet was sadly deficient in protein. Meat was a luxury granted once a year on Christmas day, in spite of the law requiring that it be served once a week. The fact that it was a sugar plantation notwithstanding, blackstrap was doled out only every four months, the quantity so slight as to insure its disappearance after only one week. Vegetables were plentiful enough in the summer and spring, but their availability declined during fall and winter. The staples were grits and pone, enough to ward off hunger, but not enough to sustain a man for labor in the fields for eighteen hours a day. During grinding season they even worked on Sundays. Six hours was all the rest time allowed.

Ben knew, after only two years during which his health declined rapidly, that he would die if he didn't get away.

And so, for the first time in his life, he had run.

The patrollers caught him only three days later. His new master, one Samuel Carver, decided to make an example out of Ben. After giving his recalcitrant slave one hundred lashes, Carver had given orders for Ben to be staked out on a clearing in front of Slave Row as a reminder to the rest of his people of what would happen if they ever decided to run.

And there, tied down and waiting to die beneath the relentless Louisiana sun, left without food or water, was where Aleceon had found him.

Aleceon had been on his way to New Orleans and had stopped at Carver's for the night. There being no inns or any other type of public houses in the vicinity, it was customary for travelers to seek lodgings at any plantation they came across.

Thus it was that Aleceon Edgewood came to Carver's at the most crucial time in Ben's life.

Ben had been staked out for one whole day and night when he opened his eyes that morning to see the thin, aristocratic form of Aleceon Edgewood, who was viewing him somberly and listening to Carver's explanation of why his slave was being punished in such manner.

"He looks half dead now," Aleceon commented when Carver was through.

"Will be, before another day or two goes by," Carver announced in satisfaction, hooking his thumbs in his belt. He was a big and gruff-voiced man who prided himself on being able to turn out more hogsheads of sugar per acre than any of his neighbors. He went to great lengths to keep that dubious record intact.

Aleceon turned his smoky blue eyes upon his host. "How much do you want for him?" he asked casually, leaning on his walking stick.

Carver viewed him in open surprise. "He ain't for sale," he protested in his gravel-toned voice. "Gonna make an example out of this heah bastid."

"I'd say you've already done that," Aleceon murmured dryly with a brief glance at Ben's wracked body. "I'll give you three hundred dollars for him."

Pausing, Carver scratched his head. "Why in hell you wanta buy a worthless nigger like this one? He's a runner. 'Sides, like you said, he's half dead."

Aleceon shrugged and moved his ringed hand in a vague gesture. "I need a body servant," he explained. "And right now I can't afford a prime one."

Carver guffawed and hitched up his breeches. "This one ain't been trained to do nothing but work in the fields," he pointed out in a somewhat condescending voice, recognizing his visitor as a novice. "Why, he ain't even been housebroken. Wouldn't know the first thing about being a body servant." He rested a hand on Aleceon's shoulder. "Look heah, I've got some fine young bucks. Be glad to have you inspect them, if you want."

Aleceon shook his head firmly. "No. I want this one. And I'll give you three hundred dollars for him."

Ben had listened to the conversation in growing amazement, with the wild hope that Carver would agree. He wasn't exactly certain what a body servant was, but he knew it would be a damn sight better than dying.

114

The bickering continued for several more minutes. Eventually, unable to resist the tempting offer of hard cash for a half dead slave, Carver had agreed.

After being untied, Ben was then carried to his cabin, being too weak to walk. One of the wenches washed and dressed the wounds on his back. After being fed and drinking his fill of water, Ben began to think that he just might live, after all.

Later that day, Aleceon came to his cabin.

Ben had made the effort to get up off his pallet, but Aleceon motioned for him to remain where he was.

"How are you feeling?" Aleceon asked, looking down at him.

"Fine, suh," Ben replied, not quite truthfully. He was awed by this man who dressed in clothes the likes of which he had never before seen, and who spoke with a curious accent that made Ben, at times, uncertain of his meaning. "Wantin' to thank you, masta, suh, fer buyin' dis no good nigger. . . ."

"You were all I could afford," Aleceon said softly with a half smile hovering about his thin lips. Then he grew serious. "Do you think you'll be able to travel in a week's time?"

"Yassuh," Ben replied swiftly, raising himself up on an elbow to indicate his willingness. "Goes wit you now, iffen you want."

Aleceon smiled again at the obvious enthusiasm. "No. I'm not taking any chances with my three hundred dollar investment. I've left instructions that you are to be well fed and well cared for until I come back for you next week." He turned to go. Then, glancing back, he added sternly, "And, you black viper, you'd best serve me well."

Aleceon had returned, just as he'd promised, the following week. With him, he brought a mule for Ben to ride. Then the two of them had returned to New Orleans and Ben had begun to live a life he never knew existed.

Aleceon outfitted his new body servant in clothes of a quality only slightly less grand than his own. For the first time in his life Ben wore shoes — something that took a bit of getting used to. When money was won, Ben shared in the profits, for Aleceon was generous when he was lucky. When funds were in short supply, they both made do as best they could.

If it was possible for a slave to grow to idolize his master, Ben learned to do so over the next five years, to such an extent that he would have gladly given his own life to save that of the man who had rescued him from the pain and drudgery of the canefields.

Still watching the wasted form of Aleceon as he stared moodily out of the window, Ben sighed deeply, thinking of all this. The man who had saved his life was dying and Ben was helpless in the face of it.

Downstairs, at that very moment, Carlie Dobbs was pacing the verandah, glancing from time to time at Griffin, who was seated in a wicker chair.

"Goddamn that black bastid," Dobbs raged angrily, waving his arms in acute agitation. "This time I'll beat his ass till it falls off his worthless hide!"

To that, Griffin said a fervent amen. The overseer had just told him of Jonah's latest escape. After hastily writing a pass for Joe, Griffin had sent the huge Negro into Charleston to put a notice in the newspapers.

"Niggers are gettin' out of hand," Carlie muttered, still agitated. "Yestiddy, I heard Four Oaks lost another one. Disappeared overnight. Last week, Farraday had two of 'em take off into the swamp. The goddamn Underground Railroad is makin' a mess of trouble."

For a moment, Griffin made no response, having been only half listening to the overseer's rantings. Once again, as had happened all day long, his thoughts had returned to what had happened between him and Morgana that morning. He couldn't seem to get his mind off of it. Certainly he had never intended for her to find out, to be hurt. She wouldn't talk to him, had locked herself in her room all day. But she would have to come out sooner or later, he reasoned, determined to make the effort to at least try and explain the situation to her.

Aware that Dobbs had fallen silent and was regarding him curiously, Griffin brought himself back to the moment at hand. "The Underground's the least of our problems." Leaning forward in his chair, he took the glass of whiskey from the tray offered by Thomas. "There's two of those damn Yankee Abolitionists preaching in Charleston. I hear they're drawing bigger crowds each day."

"I heard 'em," Carlie said, then spat over the railing. "Spewin' their filthy venom to anyone who'll listen. We ought to tar and feather the bastids, like they did with those in Natchez." He regarded Griffin earnestly. "Run 'em right out of town on a rail, like they did. It stirs up the niggers when they heah that kind of stuff. Gets 'em riled, and to thinkin' they're as good as anybody else. Christ, Griff, can you imagine what would happen if they were freed? Randy bucks runnin' loose, rapin' and killin'? We ought to put those preaching Abolitionists in a roomful of niggers and lock the door," he pronounced with a sharp nod of his head. "They'd change their tune in a hurry."

Griffin finished his drink. "That'll never happen, Carlie," he said calmly. "Them being free, I mean. The South would never stand for it."

Carlie paused to finish his own drink, then picked up his hat which was balanced precariously on the railing. "I hope you're right, Griff," he said quietly. " 'Cause if you ain't, we're all in a passel of trouble."

Supper was over before Griffin had a chance to approach Morgana. She had spoken to no one during the meal, not even Cammy, and when she was through, she had immediately gotten up and left the room.

Quickly, Griffin went after her, seeing her about to ascend the stairs.

"Morgana, wait. You're acting foolish." He grabbed her arm, effectively halting her progress. "Look, I know how it sounded . . . I know what you think, but —"

"Do you?" The mocking words glittered icily. His attitude of patient condescension only infuriated her further. To her, he didn't look at all contrite or even sorry for what he had done. She glanced down at the hand on her arm, then up at him.

His jaw worked visibly as he withdrew his hand. He tried again. "It's not the way it seems at all."

"You didn't marry me to free Albemarle from debt?" Her voice was soft and deadly as she regarded his handsome face with exaggerated interest.

Griffin ran a hand through his hair. "Yes, but —"

"It isn't necessary to explain further, Griffin," she interrupted in the same tone of voice. "I'm not interested in your reasons or excuses!"

She spun around and grasped her skirt with both hands. Hoisting it an inch or two, she ran up the stairs without a backward glance, not wanting to give him the satisfaction of seeing her eyes bright with tears.

It took all her willpower to prevent herself from turning, from throwing herself into his arms.

Reaching her room, she entered, locked the door, and flung herself onto the bed. Burying her head in the pillow, she wept, allowing herself the tears she vowed he would never see.

Chapter 7

The next morning, after carefully avoiding Griffin at breakfast, Morgana wandered about the house in an aimless fashion, too restless to sit still. After a few tentative, sympathetic overtures, Cammy had otherwise occupied herself, sensing Morgana's need to work out her problems alone.

Toward the rear of the downstairs hallway, Morgana came across closed doors which she had not before noticed.

Hesitating only a moment, she opened them, blinking in surprise at the sight of the lovely drawing room with its molded panelling and cream colored walls. On the far side, pocket doors connected this room with the front parlor. These, too, were closed.

Entering, she saw that the furniture was of a delicate construction with fluted back- and armrests, all richly upholstered in a pale rose damask that was repeated in the draperies that covered rose-point lace curtains.

As lovely as it was, the room had about it an air of being unused. Everything was situated too perfectly. The lace doilies on the head- and armrests of the chairs and settee were not even a fraction of an inch off center. A crystal vase on top of a small table with drop leaves was positioned dead center, and empty of flowers. A candle stand sported a brass candelabra, its white candles never having been lit. In a corner, between two bow windows, was a baby grand piano with a fringed shawl draped over the top of it. Italian marble graced the fireplace, over which hung a portrait of a lovely young woman gowned in an elaborately ruffled yellow silk dress. She was holding a bouquet of white star jessamine in her arms.

Moving closer, Morgana stared, struck by the beautiful face

that gazed serenely down, a slight, almost secret smile about the lips.

"Her name was Anne. . . ."

Startled, Morgana spun around to see Nathaniel. She hadn't heard him enter the room. He, too, was looking at the portrait.

"That was Griffin's grandmother," Nathaniel said softly.

"She . . . she was very beautiful."

He nodded solemnly at the observation, eyes still on the portrait.

Morgana felt suddenly uncomfortable. "I hope it's all right that I came in here. . . ."

"Oh, yes," Nathaniel quickly assured her. "This is your home now. The only reason this room has been closed off is because . . . well, since Anne died, we don't do much entertaining here at Albemarle. There have been times in years past when the house was filled with laughter and music. But with just me and Griff, and Cammy still a child . . ." He sighed.

"Anne was your wife," Morgana noted, still feeling as if she had intruded. The room was like a shrine.

"Yes." His eyes again returned to the portrait. "You would have liked her, I think. She was a bit straightforward; that sometimes bothered people. But she was honest in a way few people seem to achieve."

"I'm sure I would have liked her," Morgana whispered, not knowing what else to say. She clasped her hands together, wanting to leave, wanting to be alone with her thoughts, but she couldn't find it within herself to simply turn and leave the room. She sensed that Nathaniel had something to say to her, but she was uncertain as to whether or not she wanted to hear it.

Nathaniel walked over to the piano, rubbing his fingers across the polished surface. "This was hers. She used to play every day. The music is still there, in the bench, just as she left it." He looked at Morgana with grave eyes. "Do you play?"

"Yes. A bit," Morgana replied, still feeling uncomfortable. "I was taught at school."

He nodded again. "Then feel free to use it anytime you want. It . . . would be nice to have music in the house again."

A small silence descended. Nathaniel looked suddenly embarrassed. He turned away, staring out of the window. His hands moved restlessly, as if he didn't quite know what to do with them.

"You mustn't think harshly of Griffin," he murmured after a moment, not looking at her.

Morgana's mouth compressed. "I . . . don't think of him at all," she replied tartly. And that was a lie, she told herself. She couldn't seem to stop thinking about him.

Nathaniel turned then, his face reflecting the sort of tired sadness that only a person of his years could express. "You shouldn't blame Griffin," he entreated. His voice fell to an anguished whisper. "If anyone's to blame, it's me. Griffin did what he had to do. . . ."

Morgana raised her chin. Her eyes flashed as anger returned in full force. "He knew he was going to marry me even before I came here. Didn't he?"

Nathaniel's sigh was long and deep. "Yes," he admitted quietly. "But I think, after he met you, he wanted to."

She gave a short laugh at that. "Please, Nathaniel. I would appreciate it if you didn't play me for more of a fool than I have already been."

Unhappily, he looked down at the floor, then at her. "Is that what you think?"

"Oh, I don't know what to think," she cried out. She put a palm to her cheek. It felt warm and flushed. But then, at the sight of his stricken face, she relented. "I'm sorry. I should never have spoken like that to you."

"You and Griffin are married now," Nathaniel reminded her. "For better or worse."

She made a bitter sound which he chose to ignore.

"What you do now will set the pattern of your marriage for the rest of your life," he went on in an earnest manner. He came closer and raised a hand as if to place it on her shoulder, but then apparently thought better of it and allowed it to fall to his side. "Morgana, it would be best for all concerned if you would forget what happened, if you would put it from your mind."

"Forget?" She was astonished by his words. "Forget that my husband married me only because he had to?" She could feel the hot tears scald her eyes. Rather than display them, Morgana ran from the room.

When they sat down to eat that evening, Morgana refused to meet Griffin's eye. The conversation at the supper table was strained and awkward, with only Cammy and Nathaniel making an attempt to fill the increasing silence with bright, meaningless chatter. Aleceon had prudently absented himself, taking his meal in his room.

Morgana tried to keep a cool composure, unwilling to let them see how betrayed she felt. By "them" she meant Griffin and her father. Somehow she couldn't find it in her heart to censure either Cammy or Nathaniel, though most certainly they both had known what was going on. Cammy, she felt certain, had not really been a part of it; most likely she only found out after the arrangements had been made. Nathaniel, on the other hand, had certainly had an active hand in the plot. Still, Morgana couldn't fault him, for he had looked so unhappy, so genuinely contrite this morning, she almost felt sorry for him.

That left Griffin and her father. And even Aleceon, as angry and as exasperated as she was with him, Morgana couldn't hold entirely to blame. She had always known how he was, how he acted first in his own interests.

But Griffin . . . The end result was that all the pain she felt was caused solely by him.

That night, when Griffin knocked on her bedroom door, his voice a soft entreaty, Morgana refused to allow Bella to open it. She sat alone in the darkness with only her thoughts for company. A yawning sense of futility loomed before her as she thought of the days, the months, the years that lay ahead of her, living a life that was not of her making, living with a man she loved, but knowing she could never permit herself to give in to the feeling.

For the next three nights Morgana heard, and did not respond to, the soft knock on her door.

On the fourth night there was silence.

Morgana knew that she was alienating herself from her husband and father, to whom she barely spoke. But she was helpless in her anger and hurt to do otherwise.

Gradually, over the next two weeks, an uneasy truce was reached during the day and a certain semblance of normalcy returned to Albemarle.

Coming out of her room one morning, Morgana paused as Griffin's door suddenly opened and a young girl dressed in a plain white cotton shift that fell to her ankles emerged. Her skin was the color of honey. The girl halted abruptly at the sight of Morgana, her eyes wide, much as a startled doe when danger threatens. Even in her rising anger, Morgana had to admit that the girl was one of the most beautiful creatures she had ever laid eyes upon.

Their gazes locked for a moment, then the girl's slid away. She began to move quietly down the hall, her head lowered.

Stepping back into her room, Morgana viewed Bella with

eyes like blue stone. She described the girl, then asked, "Who is she?"

Bella stared at the braided carpet on the floor as if she would find the answer there, and again, sharply, Morgana repeated the question.

"Dat's Serena, missus," came the whispered reply.

"Serena?"

"Yassum." Bella was still studying the carpet with an engrossed look.

Morgana's delicate nostrils flared. "And who is Serena?" she inquired in measured tones. She stared at the black girl, but Bella refused to meet her eye.

"Jest a wench, missus. . . ."

"I've not seen her before . . ." Morgana raised a questioning brow and her eyes seemed to turn a darker shade of blue.

Bella shrugged with increasing uneasiness. "Serena works in de kitchen. Sometimes," she qualified.

"How long has she been here?" Morgana's outer calm concealed the raging turbulence within her.

"Masta Griffin done bought her las' year, when he went to Savannah."

"He purchased a girl like that for a kitchen wench?" Morgana's tone conveyed utter disbelief. "Then what was she doing coming out of his room at this time of the morning?"

Bella bit her full lip in thought. "Doan know, missus," she decided at last with a guileless look that did nothing to deceive her mistress.

"She's Master Griffin's wench, isn't she!" Morgana demanded, taking a step closer.

Again Bella's eyes sought the carpet. "S'pose so," she admitted with another shrug. Then, glancing at Morgana's darkening countenance, hastened to add, "Doan mean nothin'

124

though. All de gen'mens has dey wenches." She regarded Morgana earnestly.

Although she had no reason to doubt Bella, Morgana was genuinely outraged. She had never heard of such a thing. Her mouth tightened. All "gen'mens" might do it, she thought, furious, but she'd be damned if she'd have such goings-on in her own home!

Turning swiftly, Morgana left the room. Walking across the carpeted hall with a determined step, she opened Griffin's door without knocking.

He was lying on the rumpled bed, only a sheet covering him from the waist down. At her abrupt entrance, he raised a brow, but made no other move.

"I will not have it!" Morgana blurted out, trying to control the urge to strike that handsome face.

A lazy smile greeted that. "Somehow, I was hoping to hear softer words from your lips than that." He threw back the sheet and she could see that he was naked. Annoyed, she felt her face flush. He patted the rumpled bed. "Come here," he said softly. "We'll talk about whatever is bothering your Northern sensibilities."

Morgana glared at him, feeling the heat on her face, but her eyes remained steady. "That . . . girl. I saw her when she came out of your room."

The black brows rose higher. "What girl?" he asked innocently.

"Damn you, Griffin!" she said through clenched teeth. "I'm in no mood for your foolishness."

He watched her for a moment, then, getting up, he crossed the room and stood before her. With some effort, Morgana kept her gaze at eye level. It seemed to amuse him, and again he smiled.

"The situation can be easily remedied," he remarked softly, the infuriating grin still in place. Reaching out, he gently traced her jaw with a fingertip. "If you will allow me back into your bed, it won't be necessary to bring anyone to mine."

Her cheeks turned scarlet, but she was uncertain as to whether it was embarrassment or rage that was coursing through her. The light touch on her face sent a flame throughout her whole body.

He took another step toward her and Morgana stiffened. "Don't come any closer," she warned, acutely irritated by the wavering tone of her voice.

Once more, amusement slanted from his dark eyes as he looked down at her, hands on his lean hips. "There's a rosy glow to your cheeks that's very becoming," he noted with a wicked glint in his eye, appearing to enjoy her discomfort. "Am I the cause, or have you been dipping your fingertips into the paint pot?"

She was infuriated. The glow deepened, heightening the blue of her eyes. "Don't change the subject!" she snapped. "I don't care what your . . . traditions are," she cried out, trying to calm her racing pulse. He was so close she could feel the heat from his body. It burned through her and her anger rose to new heights. She was furious with herself as well as with him, and she began to tremble. "I cannot believe that decent men live this way. I will not have it!" she said again, eyes blazing at him.

This time, he grinned broadly. "I never said I was decent," he protested mildly. "In fact, there are those who say I'm a regular scoundrel."

Before she could move, he grabbed her, holding her tightly against him. Even through her clothing, she could feel the hardness of him and she fought vainly against the weakness that came over her. She was certain that if he released her she would collapse because her legs seemed unable to support her weight.

He continued to stare down at her, his eyes mocking her.

With a gasping cry, Morgana tore herself from his embrace and rushed from the room. Her eyes stung with tears of impotent rage and she blinked them away quickly.

Outside, she breathed deeply, waiting for her heart to cease its pounding.

Did she still love that man after all that had happened? she wondered. She was deeply annoyed with herself and with her uncontrollable reactions to his nearness.

Yes. The thought gnawed at her, but she refused to give in to it. She had, once before, innocently offered her love and devotion. She would not make that foolish mistake again, she vowed fervently.

At last she calmed a bit. With a nervous glance back at the house, she began to walk in the direction of the group of cabins known as Slave Row. She had little purpose in mind, she just didn't want to face Griffin over the breakfast table, didn't want to see his hateful, mocking face, didn't want those taunting eyes upon her.

Approaching the slave quarters, she paused a moment, enjoying the sight of a group of black children playing in the dirt road. Their laughter was shrill and enthusiastic as they cavorted about. They were very young — toddlers really — and naked as the day they had been born.

At the sight of her, they all fell silent, eyes round. Not wishing to disrupt their game, Morgana flashed a smile of encouragement at them, then hurried on.

The cabins were small, she noticed, only one room, and made of logs. A somewhat larger cabin, consisting of two rooms, she found out later, belonged to Minda.

But the largest structure of them all was a combination hospital and nursery, and was presided over by an ancient Negress called Auntie Flora.

Despite her height, which could have been no more than five feet, and her age, which had to be in the upward reaches of seventy, Auntie Flora was an imposing sight. She stood with a proud stance, her dark eyes more direct and level than any slave Morgana had so far seen. There was an immense dignity about the woman, and if she was in any way intimidated by her status, it wasn't apparent.

The only occupant as Morgana entered was a young woman with skin the color of light chocolate. The room was sparsely furnished, containing only a table, a chair, and several husk mattresses which were positioned on the floor. There was only one small window, but the walls were whitewashed, giving one the appearance of a certain degree of airiness.

Auntie Flora nodded calmly at Morgana. She didn't appear surprised by the unexpected visit. "Dis heah's Tansy, missus," she explained, motioning toward the woman on the husk mattress. "She done had herse'f a baby gal, jest las' night."

"And where is the baby?" Morgana asked, looking about the otherwise empty room.

"Doan keep suckahs heah, missus. Dey's kept in de nurs'ry." She pointed to a closed door.

Morgana was surprised at that. "But why? Why aren't the babies with their mothers? Who feeds them?"

"Got wet nurses fer de chillens. Takes good care of 'em, we do. Doan you worry yore pretty se'f 'bout dat." She folded her fleshless arms across an almost flat bosom.

Sensing evasion, Morgana frowned. "Why aren't the babies kept with their mother?" she asked again in a low voice.

There was no way for Auntie Flora to refuse to answer, although Morgana was, as yet, unaware of that simple fact; but the old woman's lined face looked saddened as she replied.

"Some o' de wenches," she explained carefully, "gits it in

dey haids dat dere suckahs bettah off daid den slaves. An' so . . . dey kills de poor babies. Not ever'one feels lak dat," she added hastily in the face of Morgana's horrified expression. "On'y some do. But . . ." she shrugged her bony shoulders, "best fer baby an' de momma, dey be sep'rated fer awhile. Den, after de suckah a few weeks old an' de momma gits to know 'em, cain't kill 'em no more."

For a moment, Morgana was silent, feeling a sudden, over-whelming sense of depression. Then she regarded the young woman on the mattress. "Would you kill your baby?" she asked quietly.

The dark eyes brimmed with tears. "No, missus. Wouldn't do sech a thing. . . ."

Morgana smiled, then viewed Auntie Flora again. "Bring this woman's child to her." At the sight of the doubtful expression that crossed the black face, she added softly, "Please, do as I say."

Reluctantly, Auntie Flora nodded. Morgana turned away. Getting down on her knees, she put her hand on the young woman's forehead. Feeling the cool skin, she inclined her head in satisfaction.

"Has a doctor seen her?" she asked, looking over her shoulder at the old woman.

Raising both hands, Auntie Flora chortled, delighted with what she thought was a deliberate effort toward a joke. "Lawd, missus," she exclaimed. "Ain' no doctor 'round heah. 'Cept, o' cose, fer Dr. Foxworth. But he be de white folkses doctor. Doan treat us niggers."

Morgana's brow creased in consternation. "Then who took care of this woman when she was having her baby?"

Auntie Flora's black eyes grew round. "Why, dis heah ole nigger woman do it. Yassum," she nodded her head in a vigor-ous manner at Morgana's surprised look. "Dese wenches doan need no coddlin' when dey's givin' birf. Havin' babies easy fer 'em."

"But what if there are complications?" Morgana said quickly, upset with what she was hearing. "What if the baby is in a wrong position?"

Auntie Flora grinned broadly, displaying an almost toothless smile as she held up her gnarled hands for Morgana to see. "Kin turn 'em 'round," she stated, appearing unconcerned. "Done it lots o' times."

Morgana could only regard the old woman in amazed wonder. "And what if anyone is sick?" she ventured, half prepared for the answer.

"Treats 'em, I do," Auntie Flora offered with a shake of her gray and woolly head.

"Where did you learn to do all this?" asked an astonished Morgana.

The old woman cackled again. "Learnt in Africa. I'se an African nigger, you know, missus." She said that with a certain pride.

Morgana got to her feet, her expression reflecting confusion. "An African . . ." she made a vague gesture. "I thought you all were African."

"Lawd, missus, dat ain' so," Auntie Flora disclaimed, again exposing her gums in a grin. "Most o' dese niggers borned right heah, in dis country. Doan know no more 'bout Africa den a sparrow do. I'se an African." She pointed a black finger at her sagging breast, again displaying pride.

"And you learned how to care for sick people there?"

"Yassum. Nacherly, has to make do wit de herbs an' barks we got heah. Works fine. Most de times," she added fatalistically, then walked slowly toward the other room.

Morgana waited until Tansy's baby was brought to her. She gave a nod of satisfaction as the young woman eagerly reached for her child. Then, smiling to herself, she left the "hospital" and the wonder called Auntie Flora.

The children were still playing in the road, having been joined by a large yellow dog. At the sight of Morgana, the animal came closer, tail wagging, ears flattened as he panted a welcome.

She paused long enough to rumple the soft fur before continuing on her way.

As she walked up the narrow street that separated the rows of cabins, Morgana saw Carlie Dobbs roughly hauling a Negro into the barn. Curious, she headed in their direction.

She heard the sound of the whip before she got there, and broke into a run.

Entering the barn a few moments later, she gasped at the sight of Dobbs ruthlessly lashing the man whose hands were tied around a wooden pillar.

Appalled, she shouted, "Stop it! Stop it!" She ran forward, "What are you doing to him? You'll kill him. . . ."

Dobbs halted, arm in midair, staring at her with open surprise. "You shouldn't be heah, Miz Morgana," he protested. "This ain't no place for a white lady. Please go back into the house."

"I want you to untie that man — immediately!" she insisted, her face reddening with indignant anger.

Striving to hide his exasperation, Dobbs muttered, "No need to concern yourself with this sort of thing."

"Untie him!"

"Can't do that," Dobbs protested, shaking his head from side to side. The overseer had recovered from his surprise at seeing her and was now regarding her with a sullen expression, only barely checking the annoyance from showing on his face. He didn't like Morgana; didn't like Northerners period. He especially disliked Northern women. They seemed to approach the question of slavery with an evangelistic ferver that raised his hackles.

She was still staring at him, angry and flushed, and Dobbs took a deep breath. "Look, I caught him stealing some tools so he could sell 'em to buy whiskey," he tried to explain. "That's an offense that calls for ten lashes. Now please, get out of here and let me get on with it."

Dobbs again raised his arm and the Negro cringed, turning his face away. Morgana quickly stepped forward, grabbing the overseer's shirt with such determination that the pocket tore beneath her grasp.

"Stop it, I say . . ." Her voice rose to a shout as she began to struggle with the man, trying to pull the whip from his hand.

"What the hell's going on here?"

Morgana turned to see Griffin and Nathaniel standing in the doorway. Both men looked angry.

"Griffin!" Morgana came toward him. "Mr. Dobbs was viciously beating this man," she exclaimed in an excited voice, pointing toward the bound Negro. "You must do something!"

Griffin looked at Dobbs, who, in an almost weary tone, explained the situation.

When the overseer was through, Griffin gave a curt nod. "Get on with it," he ordered.

Morgana's eyes widened. "Aren't you even going to question this man?" she demanded, again pointing to the slave. "Perhaps he has an explanation."

"I'm not interested in his explanations," Griffin pronounced tersely. "If Carlie says he's guilty, then he is!"

As Morgana again began to protest, Griffin took hold of her arm in a rough gesture and almost dragged her outside into the yard.

"You are, without a doubt, the most aggravating woman I've ever known," he growled. His mouth set into a grim line. "I don't want you to interfere with Dobbs again!" he ordered sternly.

In a sudden motion, she wrenched her hand away from him, her eyes blazing. "You're despicable," she shouted at him. Then she winced as she heard the whip striking flesh and the loud wail that accompanied it. "How can you do such a thing?" she demanded, close to tears.

"We do what needs to be done," he stated coldly, unmoved. "And I will thank you not to make a nuisance of yourself."

Furious, Morgana raised her hand, intending to strike him, but he easily caught her arm, holding it in a painful grip as he turned to Nathaniel.

"Take her into the house," he said to his grandfather. "And try to persuade her to stay out from underfoot." He released Morgana, who was sputtering in rage, then strode away without looking back.

Tentatively, in an almost apologetic way, Nathaniel touched Morgana's arm. "Come along, girl. Let's go into the house now," he entreated.

She resisted a moment, then, with a deep, audible sigh, followed the old man. She was still trembling with the force of her anger and outrage.

Inside the house, Nathaniel led her into his study and closed the door. Shaking his head, he remarked, "Lots you don't understand, Morgana. Sit down," he motioned. "Sit down and stop prancin' about like a restless filly."

"Now," he went on after she had reluctantly seated herself. "You got to understand how it is, and why folks hereabouts tend to keep a tight rein on their people." He sat down in a nearby chair.

"I think what I saw was a bit more than that," she began indignantly.

Nathaniel ignored her observation. Leaning back in his

chair, he squinted, looking up toward the ceiling as if it would be there where he'd find the threads of his remembrance.

"It was in the summer of '22, I recall," he began slowly. "I was a young man in my thirties then. Alicia, well, she wasn't but eighteen at the time. And my wife, Anne — she was alive then, too."

He paused, a wistful smile hovering about his lips while Morgana fidgeted impatiently. She wondered if that poor man in the barn had been seriously injured and mentally cursed Carlie Dobbs for his savage brutality.

But Nathaniel wasn't to be hurried. "We were all in Charleston for the summer — fever, you know," he waited for her nod, then continued. "There was this nigger by the name of Denmark Vesey. He was a free man, or so he claimed. Well, this Vesey got it into his kinky head to lead the slaves in a revolt. Must've been planning it for months," he mused, rubbing his chin.

Morgana took a breath and shifted herself to a more comfortable position. "I hardly think that man outside was planning a revolt," she noted caustically.

"Their stealing and sabotaging are a form of it," he objected mildly, refusing to be goaded.

She looked at him in surprise. "Sabotage?"

"Oh, yes. They break tools, hide things. Left alone, they'd damage the crop if they could. They're just like children, you know."

"Since when would you treat a child like that!" she exclaimed sharply, pointing toward the window in the general direction of the barn.

"You're missing the point . . ." He fell silent a moment, trying to repress his exasperation.

"Have you?" she demanded. She leaned forward in the chair, eyes bright.

Nathaniel drew his brows together. "Have I what?"

"Ever done that to a child? Have you ever tied up a child and beat him?"

"Of course not!" Nathaniel seemed genuinely shocked by her words. He waited a moment and when she didn't speak, continued with his story. "Anyway, this Vesey managed to get close to a thousand blacks involved — from Charleston and the plantations along the Ashley and Cooper rivers. They planned to burn down Charleston, then kill as many white people as they were able to."

In spite of herself, Morgana found she was regarding him intently. "What happened?"

"Well, seems like George Farraday's cook got wind of it — he owns a plantation along the Cooper — and she told George about it only days before it was to happen."

Morgana leaned back in the chair again. "So they never actually attacked Charleston?" she observed.

"Oh, they tried, all right. Critters were armed with pikes and knives, probably made over the previous months by the blacksmiths. But by the time they got ready — the militia was ready, too. Only caught about thirty-five of them, though," he related, sounding regretful. "The rest skedaddled on home."

"And I suppose they were all killed?" Morgana noted with a sigh. "The ones that got caught, I mean."

"You bet they were," Nathaniel affirmed with a short and harsh laugh. "Hanged the lot of them. But how many of us would they have slaughtered if they hadn't been stopped?" he demanded, fixing her with a hard look.

"Well, I agree that that sort of situation could be truly frightening. Still, it was a black who saved you, wasn't it?" she pointed out logically.

"That time," he agreed with a curt nod of his head. "But the folks in Virginia weren't so lucky some years later. Ever hear of Nat Turner?"

Morgana admitted that she had not.

"No black called an alarm that time. Him and about seventy other niggers went on a bloody rampage in the summer of '31. Traveled from plantation to plantation, killin' and lootin' as they went. Before they were stopped, the bastards murdered better than fifty people. Children, too — little babies. And I won't offend you by tellin' you what they did to the women before they killed them."

Nathaniel's face was grim now, uncompromising, and he noted Morgana's paleness with satisfaction.

"So, you see, girl, we can't give no quarter. Where the slaves are concerned, we've got to keep the upper hand. And it's why we put up with the patrollers," he added as an afterthought. "There's those as calls them white trash. And I'm not one to argue the point. Fact of the matter is, most of them are. But we need them. And I'm not one to chide a man on how he makes his living. Listen," he leaned forward, his eyes imploring her understanding. "Neither me nor Griff likes it when we got to discipline our people. Some do, you know." He wagged a finger for emphasis. "Ashamed to admit that, but it's so."

Morgana fell silent. She had learned things today — and not all of them were pleasant. Slavery was not a benevolent institution, despite her first impressions. It had a dark and evil side that loomed larger and larger with each new experience she encountered.

As she looked out of the window at the peaceful scene beyond, it struck her that there were six white people here at Albemarle — and more than a hundred and fifty blacks. If the slaves here ever decided to revolt . . . She gave a shudder at just the thought.

★ ★ ★ ★ ★

That night at the supper table, the conversation was, once again, strained. Griffin made no effort at all to ease the situation, but more than once Morgana was aware of those taunting eyes, which she refused to meet.

As soon as she was able, she left the table and went outside. The sun was low, the western sky streaked with brilliant apricot slashes.

Griffin had watched her leave. As soon as she did, he wiped his mouth with his napkin and got up. It was time he had it out with her, he thought to himself. This foolishness had gone on long enough.

With determined steps he left the house, seeing Morgana a distance away, walking in the direction of the river.

She turned just then, the waning sun setting her hair ablaze with golden light, washing the flawless skin with a rosy color. She looked so beautiful that Griffin paused in his tracks. Staring, he caught his breath at the sight of her. How was it, he thought to himself, amazed, that he could have been so blind at the beginning?

His mouth felt dry and he swallowed. He wanted to approach her, to take her in his arms, to ravish her, consume her . . . but his limbs wouldn't respond. He felt suddenly clumsy, awkward, like a schoolboy.

The realization prompted a dark surge of anger.

Who was this woman to so provoke him? his mind demanded. Who was this damn Yankee female, with her airs and principles . . . She was his wife, by God. His wife! And as such, he was entitled to his rights, and his privileges.

He strode in her direction, full of purpose, his jaw set with new determination.

Having noted his approach, Morgana faced him, eyes cool as a sea breeze, her body relaxed, demeanor calm.

Griffin paused before her, looking down at her face as if he had never before seen it. Then he grabbed her shoulders none too gently and pulled her toward him. His mouth sought hers, forcing her soft lips to part. His tongue tasted the sweetness of her mouth and he could feel himself becoming aroused almost beyond control.

For a moment, Morgana remained passive within his embrace. Then she began to struggle, placing her small hands against his chest, trying to push him from her.

He tore his mouth away, breathing heavily. "Goddamn you," he muttered. "You're my wife. You belong to me!"

Delicate nostrils flared and whitened, and blue eyes flashed a storm warning. "I belong to no one," she spat, twisting away from him. It was a determined move, leaving no room for argument or entreaty and, sensing that, Griffin's hands fell to his side. "I'm not one of your nigger wenches," she said. The words were low and contemptuous. "You can command Serena," she declared, her eyes still blazing. "But you can't command me." She took a step back from him, hands clenched at her sides.

Griffin's face bore an expression of uncertainty that, for the moment, intrigued her. Then she turned away, unwilling to allow herself to show any interest.

"Morgana," he pleaded, as she began to walk away.

Pausing, she turned, regarding him in wintry silence before she spoke. "You got what you wanted, Griffin," she said quietly. "Albemarle is yours. But I'm not, and never will be."

Griffin heard the coldness in her voice, saw the scorn in her eyes, and in a quick motion, he turned away. He was a proud man; proud of who he was, how he lived, and, yes, proud of his Southland. He wouldn't beg for his wife's favors, or acquiesce to her foolish outbursts. He would, he decided as he walked back to the house, be accepted on his own terms or not at all.

Morgana remained where she was for a few minutes longer, then she made her way slowly back to the house.

On the way to her room, Cammy beckoned to her. After a brief hesitation, Morgana went to her.

"Come in," Cammy insisted, grasping her hand. She drew Morgana toward the bed and sat on it, pulling her down beside her. "I heard about what happened today. . . ."

For the moment, Morgana just stared at her. So many things had happened, she was uncertain which one Cammy was referring to.

"It doesn't happen often," Cammy went on, her expression entreating Morgana's understanding. "That business with Ramus . . . He's the slave you saw being punished," she went on to explain, confronted by Morgana's questioning look. "It's just that, well . . . sometimes the people get out of hand —" She broke off at Morgana's deep sigh.

"Your grandfather explained that to me," Morgana murmured wearily.

Cammy continued to regard her, then suddenly flung her arms about Morgana, hugging her. "Oh, I do want you to be happy here," she cried. "Things will work out with Griffin, too. I know it!" She said the words as though willing it to happen.

Morgana just smiled sadly and patted the slim arm, thinking of nothing to say.

"Oh, Morgana," Cammy exclaimed, close to tears. "Please give us a chance. I know it's all strange to you . . . and that business with the mortgage," she sighed, not noticing the bitterness return to Morgana's face. "I don't really understand it all," she mused, now plucking absently at the covers with her fingers. "But I do know one thing," she again viewed Morgana, this time intently. "My brother didn't marry you because he had to."

"Oh, Cammy," Morgana protested tiredly, shaking her head at the girl's so obvious attempt to smooth things over.

Cammy gripped her hand tightly, leaning forward. "I know my brother, Morgana. I know him well. The expression on his face in those days just before you were married . . ." She shook her head once, emphatically. "I've not seen that look before. . . ."

Morgana tilted her head, the sad smile returning. She was grateful — and even a bit amused — at Cammy's attempt to make her feel better. But it was useless. Words wouldn't change what had happened, wouldn't heal her bruised heart.

Griffin's sister was regarding her with such a pleading look that Morgana kissed the petal soft cheek before she got to her feet. "Thank you, Cammy," she said softly.

"Would you like to stay with me tonight?" the girl offered quickly. "Perhaps you shouldn't be alone so much. . . ."

Gently, Morgana shook her head. "I really am tired." She headed for the door. "Good night, dear."

Lying on her bed a while later, unable to sleep, Morgana could hear the sound of someone singing. The voice, rich and mellifluous, was coming from the slave quarters. It was a sad song, almost a lament, and it suited her present state of mind perfectly.

When she thought of the events of the day, Morgana realized that the anger had left her, or perhaps she was simply too weary to give credence to it. In its place was a profound sadness, a sadness for what might have been, for what almost had been hers.

She put a fingertip to her lips. Only a short time ago, Griffin's mouth had been upon those very lips. He would never know how close she had come to yielding. Agitated, she sat up

140

in bed, motioning for Bella to remain where she was. The dark-skinned girl had immediately risen when she heard Morgana stir.

Perhaps she *was* being foolish, Morgana thought. Getting up, she walked back and forth across her room, knowing that, only a few steps away, Griffin was lying in his bed. She could go to him, lie beside him, let him quell the terrible heat he had aroused within her and which she was unable to quench. Only he could do that.

With a soft sob, Morgana headed for the door, her body trembling with its need.

Opening the door quietly, she froze. She was just in time to see Serena enter Griffin's room.

The anger returned, stronger. The cold and deadly feeling effectively doused her passion, and she clenched the knob of the door so tightly the metal bruised her palm.

Closing the door, she leaned her back against it. Her eyes narrowed with her fury, part of which was directed at herself. Once again she had almost played the fool.

"But damn you, Griffin Kynes," she whispered fiercely into the dimness, "I shall not make that mistake again."

Chapter 8

The following morning, Griffin and Nathaniel decided to ride to the neighboring plantation of Four Oaks, not only to visit Farley Barrows, who was an old friend, but to learn whether the planter had recovered his runaway slave.

From her piazza, which faced directly over the front yard, Cammy watched as her brother and grandfather rode away.

There was a subdued excitement about her as she stood there, dressed in the morning gown of blue sprigged muslin that she had worn at breakfast. Her eyes were shining and her lips were parted slightly to accommodate the quickening breaths she took.

Catching Meg's curious glance at her, Cammy brought herself under control, striving for a casualness she didn't feel.

"Get my riding clothes," she ordered preemptorily. Turning, she went back into her bedroom. "Stop dawdling!" she exclaimed, irritated with the slave's hesitancy.

With Meg's assistance, Cammy hurriedly donned the light gray habit which was trimmed with a dark blue velvet collar and velvet-covered buttons. Disdaining the matching hat, she picked up a book from her writing table, then almost ran downstairs and out into the sunwashed day. Slowing her steps to reflect a more sedate pace, she secreted the book inside her jacket.

Arriving at the stables a few minutes later, Cammy's dark eyes swept over Jude as he groomed a horse, noting the play of muscles beneath his cotton shirt as his arms moved about. It should have been a familiar sight to her because she had seen him every single day for her whole life. But the sight of Jude was anything but ordinary to her of late.

Seeing her, Jude now straightened, his manner unexpectedly cautious.

"You be wantin' to ride today, Miss Cammy?" he asked her, laying the brush on a small wooden stool. The horse turned its head, nudging Jude's arm in a silent plea for a continuation of his attention. Absently, he moved his hand to the animal's nose, rubbing the softness, never taking his eyes from Cammy.

She frowned at his words, but nodded, following him as he walked inside to one of the stalls, adjusting her eyes to the cool dimness. There were twelve stalls, six on either side of the wooden structure which had a dirt floor. Bales of hay were stacked at the rear, and harnesses, saddles and trappings were hung on the walls and from the beamed ceiling.

Jude led a sleek, reddish-brown mare forward, then hoisted a heavy saddle over the shiny back as if it were weightless. After he secured the straps, he cupped his hands for his young mistress.

Coming toward him, Cammy raised a small booted foot. Then, faking a stumble, she leaned her young body up against his.

Jude stood very still. Her hips pressed against him sent a flood of heat through his loins. Her white arms went about his neck and she gazed up at him, a smile curving her soft lips.

"You ought'n be doin' dat, Miss Cammy," he said in a strangled voice, keeping his hands at his sides.

"I hate it when you talk like that," she said in a low voice, but moved away from him.

"You knows I cain't talk no other way," he protested mildly.

"Stop it, I say!" She took a step back, hands on her rounded hips, her small breasts thrust forward.

He made no comment, only shook his head once, lowering his eyes. He knew that Cammy objected to his manner of speech, but knew also that to speak otherwise was to invite dire repercussions.

Jude had been born on Albemarle. His mother, Minda, was the cook. The only thing he knew about his father was the fact that he was white. When Nathaniel Kynes had first purchased Minda, she had been barely sixteen years old. She had been raped by a man who had been no more than a casual visitor at Albemarle. The result of that night had been Jude; and since Minda was a mulatto, and his father a white man, Jude was a quadroon, a high yellow. He also, thanks to Cammy, spoke better than most white people did, an accomplishment he took great care in concealing.

Watching him, Cammy bit her lip. "Come with me to the grove," she whispered.

Looking up, his blue eyes widened. "Cain't," he exclaimed, upset with her sudden brazenness. Cammy was usually very discreet about their meetings. "Not today. Got me too much to do around heah."

Glancing about to make certain that no one was within earshot, Cammy reached inside the jacket of her riding habit and drew forth the book.

"See here," she said to Jude, her tone now eager. "It's the new one by Mr. Dickens. Adam brought it back with yesterday's post. We'll read it together, just like we did with the others."

Fear momentarily paralyzed Jude, but he couldn't disguise the hunger in his eyes as he looked at the book.

Cammy returned the volume to its hiding place, then mounted her horse without assistance. She looked down at him. "Wait about five minutes, then follow me. I'll be waiting for you." She let her eyes travel insolently from his face to the bulge in his breeches, grinning impudently. Then, grasping the reins, she nudged the horse forward.

Jude managed a nod, swallowing through a throat that felt numb. He went outside, standing there for a long moment, watching until she was out of sight.

He didn't need to be told that following his young mistress was an offense that could lead to his death. Yet it was a threat that he'd been living with for years, ever since they had been children.

Only now, since last week, the danger had become acute. He didn't quite know how it had happened, but they had made love.

Peering about him and seeing that no one was in the immediate vicinity, Jude at last walked away from the stables.

When he arrived at the cypress grove some ten minutes later, Cammy was seated on the soft grass by the river, the book in her lap.

Her face lit up when she saw him. "Come, sit beside me." She waited until he settled himself, then handed him the book. "Read it aloud," she said to him as he opened it.

For a time, Jude read, Cammy correcting him when he mispronounced a word. These occasions were few, however, for she had begun his lessons some five years before, when she was twelve and he was fourteen.

Listening to him, Cammy recalled that first day they had come here. They had slipped past Minda and run to the grove like two wild and uninhibited young animals.

Jude had gone to the river's edge. With a string and a pin, and using a small rock as an anchor, he began to fish.

Cammy kicked off her shoes, sat down, and dunked her feet in the water, wriggling her toes in the delicious feel of it.

"Gonna scare de fish," Jude had complained, giving her an irritated glance. "Ain' gonna catch nothin' iffen you keeps doin' dat."

She had looked at him, for the first time conscious of his

speech. "Why do you talk like that?" she had asked him, genuinely curious with all the newly awakened awareness of her twelve years. Until that very moment she had honestly given it no thought. The sound of Jude's voice — as well as the other Negroes that surrounded her all her life — was like the sound of birds: accepted, never questioned.

Turning, he had stared at her, surprised. "Talks lak ever'body else," he had defended himself.

She thought about it, then shook her head. "No. No, you don't. You talk like a darkie."

He gave a short laugh. "What you think dis heah boy is?" Having felt a tug at the end of the string, Jude was momentarily diverted.

Not so Cammy, in whose mind sprouted the beginnings of an idea.

"If you could read, then you would know how to say the words correctly," she told him.

The notion did not immediately appeal to Jude. "Doan want to read," he stated firmly, still concentrating on the movement of the string in the water.

"Why not?" she persisted, pouting at his lack of enthusiasm.

Another of those glances came her way. " 'Cause, what good it gonna do me? Got no books anyways. 'Sides," he added in a practical vein, "gits whipped iffen masta catches me wit a book."

"Grandfather would never whip you." Cammy dismissed the very thought of such a happening.

But even at twelve she knew the rules. She knew it was against the law for a slave to read, but she didn't know why. All of a sudden it seemed like a stupid law, not worth thinking about.

Her tutor still came twice a week to give her lessons, as he had been doing for the past three years and would continue to do for the next two. Nathaniel was of the opinion that women need learn only reading, writing, penmanship, and be given a basic instruction in ciphering; perhaps a bit of music if they were so inclined. Cammy wasn't.

"I know how to read," she informed him in a tone that suggested she was imparting a secret.

"So what," he shot back, unimpressed.

"I could teach you. . . ."

"Cain't do no learnin'."

"Why not!" She became irked, then adopted an impervious manner. "Tomorrow, when we come here, I'll bring a book. . . ."

The fish Jude had been struggling with finally broke loose. Completely exasperated, he dropped the string with a muttered imprecation. Then, looking at her, he got a wicked gleam in his blue eyes. Reaching out, he grabbed her ankle with one hand, her arm with the other, and dumped her into the water, laughing at her spurious squeal of fright. Cammy could swim as well as he could.

But the very next day, despite his misgivings, Jude was introduced to the mystery of letters, letters that formed words, words that formed stories, stories that led him to places he had never even dreamed about.

After that, whenever they could avoid Minda's watchful eye, they had escaped to the grove, spending hour after hour with their heads bent over the marvelous volumes.

Jude was mesmerized, entranced. Nor had his excitement diminished even to this day.

Now, having finished the first chapter of *David Copperfield*, Jude closed the book.

The young girl, having been utterly captivated by the sound of his rich, golden voice, smiled at him. "You don't need any more lessons," she observed quietly.

"I know," he murmured, rubbing his thumb along the leather binding. "Wish I could finish the story."

"You can," she said quickly. "Take the book with you. Read it at night, in your cabin. . . ."

Slowly, he shook his head. "It's too dangerous. Not only for me, but for you as well. You know how Zoe is. That wench of mine can't keep her mouth shut about anything."

At the mention of Zoe, Cammy's eyes darkened. She hated the thought of that wench being in Jude's cabin even though she knew that Jude had no say in the matter. She was about to urge Jude to take the book anyway, but then sighed deeply, for she knew that Jude was right. She had broken a very serious law when she had taught him to read and write. But she had loved him since they were children. And so strong was her feeling that she saw nothing wrong with it, although she knew very well what would happen if her brother or her grandfather ever discovered their relationship. But that, Cammy vowed, would never happen. Not until it was too late for them to do anything about it. Griffin, she knew, had a crazy notion that she would consent to marry Clinton Barrows. But that would never come about. She had room in her heart for only one man, and that man was Jude.

Jude had started to get to his feet. Quickly, she put a hand on his arm.

"You don't have to leave yet," she protested, eyes pleading with him. "Griffin and grandfather have gone to Four Oaks. They won't be back until suppertime."

Glancing up, Jude noted the changing position of the late morning sun. There would be questions asked if his task for the day remained uncompleted. Despite her plea, he again made the attempt to get to his feet.

"Stay, Jude," she urged. "We must talk. . . ."

Sinking down again, he allowed himself a small sigh.

"There's nothing for us to talk about, Cammy," he murmured. "We've been through all this before. . . ."

She leaned forward, placing her hands along each side of his face. "You know how much I love you," she said in a quiet and serious voice. "Someday, I'll find a way out for us. I promise." She moved further into his embrace, her arms tightening about him.

He was a bit saddened by her naivete. She had been saying a variation of those words for years now. But there was no way out. For him, perhaps, if he could escape to the North, but for "them," no. Even most of the Northern states had laws against miscegenation. He was light-skinned, but not enough to pass for white. No one would ever believe he was other than what he was. Sometimes, when he was dressed in livery, walking or riding through Charleston, Jude would look at the young white men about him and wonder what it was like to grow to manhood in freedom. Did they know what they had, those men on the threshold of life? Doubtless they did not, for the simple reason that they took their freedom for granted.

And, thinking of those young and white and privileged young men, Jude hated — and envied — every one of them.

"Jude," Cammy whispered, aware of his drifting attention. Her lips brushed his cheek. "What are you thinking about?"

His arm went around her, his hand caressing the small of her back. "Us," he answered. knowing that that was the answer she expected.

She murmured in contentment as he drew her closer to him, but Jude's thoughts were still turned inward. For years now, he knew that Cammy had entertained the thought that, one day, they could leave here and live happily ever after. Jude knew that was no more than a fantasy. And yet . . . if he were ever to get away, he knew it could be only with her help. Cammy was foolish and naive, but he needed her.

Nor could he delay much longer, Jude thought, only half responding as Cammy nuzzled his neck. So far, he'd been able to keep Zoe from discovering his secret, but he shuddered to think what might happen if she ever found out. Zoe loved him, although he had no feelings for her. She was no more than a convenience as far as he was concerned. But she was jealous and spiteful and he didn't even want to guess as to what her reaction would be if she found out what was going on.

His mother knew that he and Cammy occasionally met. They'd been doing it for years. Minda disapproved violently, of course, but she, like the few others who knew, thought that Cammy was only teaching him to read and write.

And, until about two weeks ago, that's just what was happening. Now, though, their relationship had moved to a different plane. A much more dangerous one.

Cammy's lips were very close to his. Moving his head forward slightly, Jude kissed her.

With a small moan, her arms tightened about him. She clung to him fiercely as the tip of his tongue sent darts of fire through her young body.

With hands that were clumsy in their haste, Cammy undid her bodice. Drawing his head to her breast, she gasped as his mouth encircled her nipple. She lay there for awhile, too weak to even move. Her breath came in whimpers as she clutched at his muscular shoulders, trying to bring him even closer to her.

She could stand it no longer. Reaching down, Cammy hoisted her skirt and shimmied out of her pantalettes, begrudging the time it took for Jude to shuck his breeches. His breath was now as quick as her own.

In a simultaneous movement they came together. Jude closed his eyes as he thrust into the willing and eager young flesh beneath his own.

About them, the droning insects and chattering birds were the only witnesses to the frenzied coupling of the two young lovers and Cammy's cry of pleasure caused only a brief cessation of nature's song before it again continued with its serenade.

When Jude returned to the stables sometime later he saw, in dismay, that his mother was heading in his direction. He barely stifled a groan, hoping he wasn't in for another lecture.

"Where you bin at?" she demanded, sounding angry. It had been Meg who had alerted her to the fact that Miss Cammy had left the house with a book tucked into her riding habit.

"Wasn't nowhere," he mumbled, not looking at her, taking care to slip back into the accepted pattern of speech.

Minda raised her hand and Jude ducked the blow aimed at his head. Over the years he had become most proficient at doing that; Minda's hand was as quick as her tongue.

"What I tell you 'bout stayin' away from Miss Cammy?"

"Wasn't nowhere near her," he protested. Despite the lie, he met her eyes squarely.

Minda's angry expression held a moment longer, then crumbled into sharp anxiety. She knew he was lying.

"Jude," she pleaded, resisting the urge to clasp the young man to her breast. "You courtin' the devil, actin' lak you do. Ain' gonna make you happy, readin' dem books . . ." She folded her hands in an almost prayerful manner. "Please, Jude. Listen to yore Momma. Knows what's best fer you, I do. An' tellin' you, you got a powerful lot o' trouble waitin' for you. . . ."

In an attitude of disgust, Jude reached for a rag hanging on a nail just inside the door. From a shelf above it, he grasped a bottle filled with oil, then poured some of it onto the rag.

"Someday, we be free," he muttered fiercely, applying the rag to a leather harness. "Den we gots to know how to do all de things de white folks do."

Minda looked saddened at his words and her eyes brimmed with unshed tears. "Ain' never gonna be free, son," she murmured in a grieving tone. "You jest foolin' yorese'f, thinkin' lak dat. White mens bin talkin' 'bout freein' us'ns fer a long time." She shook her head solemnly. "Ain' gonna happen. Dey jest talkin', dat's all. Bin hearin' 'bout it since I wuz a li'l chile."

"Cain't believe dat!" Jude exclaimed quickly, sharply. His brow knitted into a scowl. "Iffen I do, ain' no reason to live no more."

"Jude. . . ."

"Means it, Momma!"

Minda took a deep breath. "Mebbe you right, son," she said placatingly, not for one minute believing her own words. "Dey free us'ns one day. But, till de Lawd Jesus see fit to give us'ns dat great day of jubilation, you gots to watch yore step and doan cause no trouble."

Dourly, Jude reflected to himself that the Lord Jesus had little, if anything, to do with their freedom. But he kept such thoughts to himself, knowing his mother's deeply held religious convictions. Besides, his mother was the only person in the world for whom he had feelings that could be said to approximate love. There were times, though, when he viewed her with something akin to resentment. Had she been lighter in color, had she possessed features that were not so obviously Negroid, then he might have been able to pass for white. It would have made things so much simpler, for Jude, at nineteen, had no intention of remaining a slave for the rest of his life. He had nothing but contempt for those, like Joe, who accepted their lot in life with a placid stoicism that angered and baffled him.

Standing there, Minda watched for a moment in silence as Jude worked the oil into the leather until it was smooth and pliable in his hands.

"Anyways," she stated quietly, "it doan be readin' what's on my mind. An' knows it, you do. Wuz diff'rent when you wuz both chillens. Ain't fittin' now dat Miss Cammy be a young lady. . . ."

Jude paused, glaring at her. "What you wantin' me to do?" he snapped. "When Miss Cammy tells me sumpin, gots to do what she says." There was no immediate response and he added, "Ain' it so?"

Slowly, she nodded, wishing with all her heart that Miss Cammy would find herself a nice young gentleman and get married. Only then would her Jude be safe.

Minda's sadness increased and the sorrow pressed down upon her until she thought she could no longer bear its weight. She recognized her son's discontent. Hadn't she seen it in the eyes of the other men? Not all, to be sure. Not all men who were born slaves had the stamina or the will to fight their circumstances, even if only in their mind.

"Mebbe iffen you spend moah time wit Zoe," Minda suggested at last, "you gits dis foolishness out'n yore haid."

Jude threw the rag to the ground in a vicious motion. "Doan want dat black wench nowhere near me," he declared strongly. "She smell worse den de horses do."

Minda gave a great sigh, not for the first time wishing that her son had been born black. Then her mouth set determinedly and she again viewed Jude with sternness, hands on her hips. "Next time missy axin you to go wit her, you say no. Heah? Even if you gots to sass, you say no!" She bent her head forward, staring intently, her mouth tight.

Jude was about to retort sharply, but a look at his mother's severe countenance quickly changed his mind. He turned away from Minda's piercing eyes — those ebony pools of awareness. At times he had the feeling that his mother's eyes could peer into his soul. He shook off the disturbing feeling. His mother knew what he wanted her to know, he reminded himself sternly. She knew nothing of his plans, his capabilities. She knew only that he could read and write his name. Certainly she didn't know that he could speak as well as any white man — and better than some.

Minda was still glaring, waiting for a response.

"Awright, awright," he mumbled ungraciously. Bending over, he picked up a pail. "Gots to feed de horses," he announced. With a long stride, he walked into the stables without looking back at her.

Minda continued to stand there for many minutes, wondering if she had accomplished anything at all. Then, shaking her head in despair, she headed slowly back toward her kitchen.

Chapter 9

In April the pace of activity at Albemarle quickened. Vegetable crops were planted, fields were drained and ploughed, and in the Great House, under Minda's stern eye, spring cleaning was undertaken with a vengeance.

And, after three mornings of recurring nausea, Morgana's suspicions were confirmed: she was to have a child.

On this afternoon, she sat on the verandah in a rocking chair, a forgotten piece of embroidery in her lap. The weather was gray and dismal, holding the threat of rain and cooling the air. No breeze stirred the delicate moss as it hung motionless from the trees.

Griffin and Nathaniel had gone into the fields, and only moments ago Cammy had gone off, riding her horse as she did almost every day at this time.

Most of the hands went about their daily task. The afternoon was peaceful and quiet.

Morgana rocked slowly, her mind on the life that was, at this very minute, growing inside her. After an initial stab of dismay, she found herself more and more thrilled at the prospect of becoming a mother.

She would have to tell them soon, she thought, although the crinolined skirts were a marvelous concealment. She suspected that a woman could practically go her full term without her condition becoming noticeable.

For some reason she wanted to tell her father first, but Aleceon hadn't left his room in the past three days. A bad cold, Ben had solemnly reported to anyone who might be interested, and, except for Morgana, no one seemed to be.

She wasn't entirely certain in her own mind as to why she

should even bother to tell her father anything at all. Their relationship was still strained. Oddly, she saw very little of him, even though they were both living in the same house. Aleceon spent most of his days in his room, appearing only for meals, and sometimes not even then. Although heaven only knew what he occupied his time with, she thought, sighing.

She wondered what Griffin would think when she told him about the baby, unaware that once Bella knew, the whole household became aware of the impending event.

Morgana was so wrapped up in her approaching motherhood that she never noticed Nathaniel's solicitation or Griffin's anxious glances in her direction.

Rocking to and fro, soothed by the monotonous motion, Morgana had closed her eyes and was, therefore, startled when she heard Ben's voice.

" 'Pologizes fer disturbin' you, Miz Morgana," he said to her, his stance awkward as he bowed slightly. "But axin' you to please come to yore daddy's room. He be wantin' to talk wit you."

She felt a prick of annoyance. "Why can't he come down here?" she countered with a suggestion of petulance, not wishing to move from her comfortable spot.

"Cain't, missus," Ben murmured. Sniffing, he wiped his nose with the back of his hand.

Looking at him more closely, Morgana became alarmed at the sight of his stricken face. He appeared about to cry. She ceased rocking and sat straighter. "What's wrong, Ben? Is my father feeling worse?"

"Yore daddy bin sick fer a long time, Miz Morgana," he explained in a voice that was low and grieving. "Doctor be tellin' him months ago he doan be havin' much time left. Wouldn't let me tell nobody. An' dese last three days he bin in

156

sech mis'ry, couldn't git hisself up. An' now . . . well, he callin' for you."

Morgana was left astonished and trembling at the report. Her father, dying? The thought was too awesome, too frightening to comprehend all at once.

Somewhat shakily, she got to her feet, heedless of the embroidery that fell from her lap. She stared at Ben for a long moment, then turned and headed for the stairs, almost running up the steps, with Ben behind her.

Outside Aleceon's door, she paused a moment, trying to catch her breath and allow her heart to return to its normal beat.

Then, without knocking, she entered her father's room.

He was in bed. Now that she could see his arms bared, his thin frame appeared shockingly wasted.

Feeling a trembling unease, she walked toward the bed, sitting on the chair that was already placed there and from which Ben had moved only rarely in the past three days, ever since Aleceon had begun to spit up blood.

"Father . . ." Morgana was appalled at the sight of him. He looked positively cadaverous, his face waxy, except for his lips, which were a ghastly white.

At the sound of her soft voice, Aleceon opened his eyes, attempted to smile, and gave it up.

"Don't feel sorry for me, Morgana," he murmured in a halting voice that was, nevertheless, a command. "I've lived my life in my own way, and I'd just as soon die without any fuss . . ." He waved a hand with a trace of his usual impatience as she started to speak and she bit her lip. "There's not much time, so you must listen to me. . . ."

"Oh, Father," Morgana cried out, unable to keep quiet any longer. "Why didn't you tell me? We can take you to New York, to Boston . . . They have the best doctors . . ." She fell silent as he raised a hand.

"I've been to the doctors, several of them," he protested weakly. "I've known for months now that there was nothing they could do."

"But there must be something!" she insisted, trying to stem her frightened tears. She had never really been close to her father, but now, suddenly, she was feeling a wrenching loss for what might have been.

"Nothing to be done . . ." An uncharacteristic sadness came upon him as he looked at the only human being he had ever loved. "I'm sorry for all those years we were separated," he whispered. "I thought the school would be good for you. . . ."

"It was," she said quickly. She clasped her hands tightly in her lap. "I was happy there. You must believe that."

A wry ghost of a smile played at the corners of his mouth. "I'm glad you were not unhappy there. I suspect life with me would have provided you with an education you'd be better off without . . ." He broke off, coughing, his frail chest heaving with the exertion.

Immediately, Ben stepped forward with a glass of clear liquid. Placing one massive arm about the wracked body of his master, he held him as one would a child. Then, when Aleceon calmed a bit, Ben brought the glass to the white lips.

"Drinks yore medicine, suh," he coaxed, nodding in satisfaction as Aleceon did so.

"Black viper thinks I'm his baby," Aleceon grumbled as he sank back on the pillows, but Morgana could sense the very real affection between the two men, as well as their dependence upon each other.

Then Aleceon turned to his daughter once more, his smoky blue eyes luminous with fever in his ashen face. "When I brought you here . . ." he sighed, and the sound tore at her heart, ". . . I thought I was finally doing the right thing for you." His look was pleading. "I never meant for you to find out. . . ."

"Please . . ." Morgana reached out a hand, grasping the hot, dry flesh, and was struck by the fact that it had been years since she had touched her father. She couldn't even remember him ever kissing her, or hugging her. The urge came upon her, strong, and bending over, she placed her lips upon his cheek. "Don't talk of this anymore," she begged.

"There will never be another time," he noted simply. How really fine she was, he thought to himself, carefully keeping his face bland. If he had nothing else in his life to be proud of, he could feel pride in Morgana.

Then, with more urgency, he continued. "Do you remember when we left Somerset Hall?" At her tearful nod, he went on. "Sarah wanted you to stay. I . . . wouldn't allow it." He gave a sound of disgust that was obviously directed at himself. "I would rather have seen my daughter grow up with strangers than with those who loved her," he added with deep bitterness. He closed his eyes and turned his head on the pillow, averting his face. "When you were a very young girl, you used to ask me about your mother. . . ."

She smiled, a slight, sad expression. "But you never wanted to talk about her," she noted softly.

He was silent for a long moment. Turning toward her, he seemed to search her face for something that would have meaning only to him. "You were, I thought, too young to understand," he said finally.

Her face clouded. She compressed her lips and viewed her folded hands in her lap. "Then, it's true?" she whispered. When there was no response, she looked at him, her eyes just as searching as his. "There were rumors . . ." She appeared embarrassed. "I . . . heard things. . . ."

"You always were too intelligent and too perceptive for your own good," he observed wryly, and sighed. "Your mother was a good woman," he said at last. "Whatever else she was — and circumstances forced her into a life she would not have otherwise chosen — she was a decent and caring person. I . . ." he hesitated, "I wasn't good enough for her. She deserved better. She was so young . . ." His voice trailed off. "So very young. Only seventeen when she had you. In those months before you were born, she was so excited, so looking forward to having a child. . . ."

"Did you love her?" Morgana asked from curiosity. She couldn't really imagine her father loving anyone.

In that, she was almost right. But, looking at his daughter, Aleceon found himself compelled to give only one answer. "Yes," he replied. "I loved your mother very much."

The words seemed to comfort Morgana and he was content. She would never know the feeling of pride, of overwhelming love he had experienced when first he looked upon his newborn daughter. Kitty was already dead by then. Aleceon had given her no further thought. He had married her on the spur of the moment, out of necessity. He had been, at most, fond of Kitty. She was a pretty thing, with auburn hair and a pleasing body that had accommodated many men. Over the years, Aleceon had often wondered how the two of them had produced a child like Morgana. Nature must have been very selective, he thought to himself. He had never expressed his feeling of love and pride to his daughter, for those words did not come easy to him; indeed, he rarely gave it conscious thought. It was just a feeling, lying deep within him. And even now, he couldn't find the words with which to tell her.

"It seems we are ruled by the past," he murmured, sounding dreadfully weak to Morgana. She leaned forward to catch his words. "No matter how we try to ignore it, it's always there, waiting."

His breathing sounded labored, and Morgana felt a terrifying need to do something, anything. But she just sat there, knowing in her heart that there was nothing she could do, knowing that there was nothing anyone could do now.

After awhile, Aleceon looked at her again. "If you ever need a place to go — go to your aunt. . . ."

"I will, Father. Please, don't worry about me." She gave a shaky laugh. "I'm a married woman now. And," she added, a bit shyly, "I'm not entirely certain and I've not told anyone yet, but I think I'm to have a child. . . ."

A slow, wistful smile drifted across his face. "That makes me very happy," he whispered. "I hope it eases things between you and Griffin. He's not a bad sort . . . It's just that he's a proud man, and sometimes . . . well, sometimes that gets in the way of a man's judgment." He took a deep and rasping breath. Then pain made itself felt. It was fierce, gnawing at his insides, drawing his life's breath from his body, leaving behind what felt like a pile of burning embers in his stomach. He grimaced at the now familiar intrusion, waiting until the spasm passed before he again spoke.

"Ben . . ." He motioned to the Negro and the man came immediately forward. "Show my daughter," he paused, groaning. "Show her where it is. . . ."

The black man got down on his hands and knees. Reaching under the bed, he drew forth a metal box. He placed it at Morgana's feet.

"What is it?" Morgana viewed the receptacle with curious eyes.

"Money. Gold. Keep it with you in case you ever need it."

She stared at him in some perplexity for a moment.

"Don't let Griffin know you have it," Aleceon urged, bending forward slightly. He rested a hand on her arm. "Don't let anyone know. Someday, if you should ever need it, then use it.

161

There is more than five thousand dollars in there . . ." He fell silent at the sound of her gasp, then smiled wryly. "I'll not tell you how I came upon it. It's best that you not know." He sank back again, incredibly weary from the effort of speaking at length.

"I'll do as you say, Father," Morgana tried to comfort him. She still couldn't believe that this was happening.

After several moments passed, Aleceon found the strength to continue. "Keep it in a safe place. Here . . ." Reaching up, he removed a thin gold chain from about his neck, from which was suspended a small key. He handed it to her. "This, too, should be kept in a safe place, It's the key that will unlock the box. One more thing . . ." Aleceon glanced at the hovering Negro. Ben's dark eyes had not once moved from Aleceon's face. "This black viper is more trouble than he's worth," he said, his voice sounding raspy and dry. "But I give him to you. Over there," he pointed to the desk with a trembling finger. "You'll find his papers in the top drawer. I've already made them out in your name." He fixed Ben with a stern look. "Promise me that you will serve your mistress well and guard her life with your own."

Ben sank to his knees, tears streaming down his black cheeks. "Serves her lak I serves you, suh," he whispered in a choked voice.

Extending a hand, Aleceon patted the woolly head. "I ask for no more than that, my friend," he murmured.

Morgana frowned, not wishing to deny her father anything in his hour of extremity, but she couldn't keep silent. "I cannot own a slave," she said quietly.

Regarding her solemn, fine-featured face, Aleceon gave a short laugh at her words. "Through your marriage, you own close to two hundred of them," he reminded her. "However, if you feel that strongly, then free him. But," he admonished,

162

raising a hand, "if you free him, make certain that he is cared for. Don't let your high ideals be responsible for further injury. Once free, how will he live? Who will provide for him?"

Confusion sank upon Morgana, who had never before thought of that. She regarded Ben thoughtfully for a long moment. "Do you want your freedom?" she asked him, leaning forward.

Ben hesitated. "Would rather be yore slave, missus. But," he added, almost as an afterthought, "doan want to be sold to nobody else."

"I would never do that," Morgana promised quickly. The thought, however, still troubled her. Then her face brightened. "I'll file the papers for your manumission," she told him. "Then, you'll be free to stay or go, whenever you decide. . . ."

She glanced at Aleceon for his approval, and the smile froze upon her face. Without even touching him, she knew, knew that the appearance of sleep was a deception, a false comfort.

For a long moment she held her breath, staring, waiting for her father to speak, to move, to smile, but, of course, he did nothing.

She shivered, feeling suddenly alone, although it was ironic that after all these years such a sensation would fall upon her. Had there ever been a time when she hadn't been alone?

A small drop of blood glimmered like a malevolent ruby at the corner of Aleceon's mouth. Removing her handkerchief from her sleeve, Morgana wiped it away, her hand as steady and as gentle as if it were living flesh she touched.

As she heard the sound of a heartbreaking sob, her hand automatically reached out to Ben, resting on his broad shoulder. The Negro was still kneeling, his cheeks glistening wetly as he released his sorrow.

How strange, Morgana thought, aware of her own dry eyes,

how strange that she was doing the comforting instead of receiving it.

Sitting there, Morgana searched her mind for memories of closeness to her father, memories to hang onto, memories to take out and savor in the years to come.

But no such time existed. Her father had never raised a hand to her in either anger or love.

Glancing out of the window, she was surprised to see the fine misty rain that had finally broken through the clouds and now fell gently and silently upon the land.

Had she ever loved her father? she wondered dully, again viewing the motionless form on the bed. It was a question she honestly couldn't answer.

Aleceon was buried the following day in the small cemetery at Albemarle. It was a pleasant spot about a half mile from the Great House, set in a clearing that was neatly enclosed by a decorative, wrought iron fence. There were only three headstones, all crafted from white marble: one for Roger Kynes, Griffin's father; one for Alicia Saunders Kynes, Griffin's mother; and one for Anne Mary Kynes, Nathaniel's wife.

It was Nathaniel who, with the aid of his worn family Bible, conducted the simple ceremony. Both he and Griffin were dressed in black frock coats over black trousers.

The air was fresh, the sun warm and bright as it sparkled on rain-washed trees and bushes. The pleasantness of the spring day irked Morgana. Everything was alive and growing, almost mocking the solemn occasion. It was, she thought, a day of death, not a day to be even thinking of such things as life and growth.

Morgana, dressed in the plain brown dress in which she had first arrived at Albemarle, remained placid through the short service, a feeling of unreality crowding in upon her. She couldn't quite accept the fact that her father was dead, that he lay in the hastily constructed wooden box that was almost completely concealed by a profusion of spring flowers.

To the side, standing in respectful silence, heads lowered, were the two slaves who had dug the grave and who now waited to fill it with earth once again. Morgana glanced briefly at Ben, hearing his quiet sobs. Beside him stood a man who was very black and whom Morgana didn't immediately recognize. He was burly and muscular with a somewhat sullen expression that dissolved into a meaningless smile as he noticed Morgana's eyes upon him.

Atlas, she thought absently, that was the slave's name. Then she returned her attention to Nathaniel's resonant voice as he continued with the simple service.

When it was over, Cammy moved closer. She had, for once, forsaken her hoops and stays and was clad in a dark blue cotton dress with a broad white collar. A bit timidly, she touched Morgana's arm.

"I'm sorry about your father," she said quietly. "It must have been an awful shock for you. I . . ." she faltered, feeling helpless. "That is to say, none of us realized how ill he was. He never said anything. . . ."

Morgana patted the slim arm. "I know," she replied simply. "He never said anything to me, either."

They began to walk back to the house, Nathaniel and Griffin following a short distance behind. Ben and Atlas remained at the small cemetery to shovel the dirt back into the open grave.

"Were you close to your father?" Cammy asked as they made their way along the narrow path. She was well aware of the recent estrangement, but was curious as to their previous relationship.

Morgana hesitated a long moment, thinking on it. "No,"

she said at last. "Not really." Turning her head, she regarded Cammy, who sighed.

"I don't remember my father at all," the girl said as they walked slowly. "He died when I was two. I guess . . ." she made a gesture. "I guess both Griffin and I tend to think of grandfather in that way." She inclined her head, glancing at Morgana. "Your mother?"

Morgana shook her head. "Like yours, my mother died when I was born."

Cammy hooked an arm through hers in a silent gesture of companionship. "But you have a family now," she murmured with a shy smile. "You are the sister I never had."

When she went upstairs that night after supper, Morgana found that Ben had moved her father's trunk and the metal box into her room.

The box she shoved under her bed. The trunk she just left in a corner, not having the heart to go through his things just yet.

Another, smaller box lay upon her bed and, curious, Morgana opened it. A pair of dueling pistols rested on the blue velvet that lined the case. She stared a moment, then, not knowing what else to do with it, put it away in a dresser drawer. She wasn't afraid of guns. Long ago, her father had shown her how to load and fire a pistol. It was part of the strange education she had received while living with a man of Aleceon's character.

"Miz Morgana?"

Bella's soft voice reached her, and Morgana turned.

"Dat Ben sayin' he wants to talk wit you." She made an exasperated face. "Tol' him he got no business botherin' you at dis time, but —"

"It's all right, Bella," Morgana interrupted softly. "Tell him to come in."

Muttering to herself, Bella did as she was instructed. Ben was waiting in the hall, and when he entered stood just inside the doorway, looking awkward and out of place. He kept his head lowered, staring at the floor until Morgana spoke to him.

"Thank you for bringing my father's belongings in here." She regarded him questioningly, wondering what it was he wanted.

"Got to tell you sumpin, Miz Morgana." Ben spoke in a voice that was no more than a whisper. "Masta Aleceon tol' me never to tell you, but —" His voice broke and he wiped his nose with the back of his hand.

"Tell me what, Ben?" she prompted, taking a step closer to him.

It took a moment for the Negro to gain control of himself and Morgana could see how deeply affected he was by her father's death.

He swallowed, shifting his weight from foot to foot. "Yore daddy not tellin' you de truf when he say why he brung you heah. . . ."

She inclined her head, surprised by his words. "And what is the truth?" she asked quietly, watching him closely.

He hesitated only a moment, then raised his head to look at her with saddened eyes. "He be knowin' fer months dat he wuz gonna die. Wantin' to see you safe before dat happen." He shook his head sorrowfully. "Wasn't true what he said 'bout you bein' underfoot. Before we come heah, yore daddy wuz visitin' lots of Great Houses, lookin' fer de right husband fer you to marry up wit. Wasn't tryin' to do you no harm, Miz Morgana," he said earnestly. "Wuz on'y tryin' to do good fer you."

At the recital, Morgana sighed and averted her face. "Why couldn't he have told me that?" she murmured. Although, she was thinking, it would have hardly made any difference insofar

167

as Griffin was concerned.

" 'Cause den he would have to tell you he wuz dyin', an' he didn't want you to know dat. Wuz a proud man, yore daddy." Ben's dark eyes brimmed with tears. "An' he be tellin' me dat he loved you more den anybody in de world. Thinkin' on'y of you when he done what he did. . . ."

Morgana bit her lip, feeling her own eyes smart, and for a time was silent. Though she had no reason to doubt Ben, she couldn't quite believe that her father really loved her. Yet he would have no other reason for doing what he did, she realized.

"Thank you, Ben," she whispered at last. Then, in a brisker voice, asked, "Where are you staying?"

"Masta Nathaniel give me a cabin. Sayin' I kin help Joe in de smithy."

She frowned slightly. "Do you want to work there?"

Ben shrugged. "Doan mind," he answered blithely. "Laks it fine, I do," he decided after a moment.

"Very well. But I meant what I said," she told him. "As soon as I can, I will file your papers. And Ben," she added as he turned to go. "If you have any problems with Mr. Dobbs, I want you to come and tell me immediately. Do you understand?"

"Yassum."

After Ben left, Morgana walked out onto the piazza. The sun had set, but it was not yet dark. It was calm and still. The very air seemed painted in hues of lilac and gold. Morgana leaned on the railing, feeling very tired and dispirited. Restlessness coursed through her. She knew that if she lay down on her bed, she would be unable to sleep.

Perhaps a walk, she thought. Heading back inside, she reached in her wardrobe for a light shawl. Leaving her room, she went downstairs and out into the evening.

She walked along the driveway down to the carriage gate,

even in her melancholy state admiring the brilliant panorama of color that streaked the western sky. Foliage and moss were outlined in black in the deepening twilight, hanging limp and still, as if at rest. Only a few yards away the river hummed softly on its journey to the sea. An early evening mist hovered over the water, thick and with a pearly translucency along the banks.

Morgana realized that, sometime during these past months, she had grown to love this land, this countryside that was so vastly different from any she had ever known in her lifetime.

The thought saddened her. She was uncertain as to what her future would be once her child was born.

Could she stay here? Could she stay with a man who didn't want or love her? There was no doubt in her mind that Griffin would honor the contract of marriage. But that was the crux of the problem: it was just a contract. Morgana was uncertain that she could live her life on those terms.

Tightening her shawl, she began to walk slowly back to the house. Ahead, she saw Griffin emerge from the stables. She called to him, waiting until he turned, a surprised look upon his face. Immediately, he headed toward her.

"What are you doing out at this time of night?" he asked, surprise turning to concern.

She shrugged, not answering that. Instead, she said, "I would like to thank you and your grandfather for allowing my father to stay here . . . and for the ceremony. . . ."

"It isn't necessary," he said quickly. "Your father was . . . a fine man." The words stuck in his throat. But then, suddenly, he realized that Aleceon must have known he was dying, must have known that he would never live to see a profit from Albemarle.

Morgana's expression closed somewhat as she sensed his insincerity. Whatever else Aleceon Edgewood was, he had been

169

her father; whatever he had done — and if his convoluted manner of thinking had produced her present dilemma — she couldn't deny that his last acts and thoughts had been for her benefit.

"I'm perfectly aware that my father made it a condition that you marry me . . ." Morgana had mixed feelings about Ben's disclosures. The fact that she now understood her father's motives for bringing her here did not alter the fact that Griffin had acted with a somewhat less altruistic reason in mind. While she could class her father's deceit as benevolent, she found she could not excuse Griffin on that or any other basis.

"Morgana . . ." Griffin took a step closer, then halted as she raised her hand.

"Please don't," she said wearily. She took a deep breath. "If it were possible, I would leave now and release you from . . . all of it." He began to speak, but she wouldn't allow him to do so. She was in no mood for any spurious explanation he might feel it necessary to utter. "However, I am unable to leave at this time. You see," she faltered, moistening her lips, "I am to have a child."

He smiled, not wanting to tell her that he already knew. "That's wonderful," he exclaimed, taking another step forward. Her expression again halted him. Her blue eyes were viewing him with cool speculation.

"I thought you would be pleased," she murmured dryly. "I can imagine how much it means for you to have an heir . . . for Albemarle." She knew her words were sarcastic, but she couldn't help herself. No matter how her mind revolved about all that had happened, what she was left with, finally, was a feeling of betrayal. Her emotions felt like a pile of smoldering ashes waiting to spark into life at the least provocation.

Griffin fell silent a moment, his eyes searching her face. "You once said you loved me," he whispered tentatively. He

170

longed to reach for her, but he knew if he did that she would turn him away. His pride couldn't stand that rebuff yet one more time. He knew, too, that if he told her that he loved her, she would smile that small cold smile that reminded him so much of Aleceon and would disbelieve his words.

Her brows arched. "Love is only an illusion," noted the Morgana who had lived, survived and adjusted for her whole life, mostly on her own.

A deep sigh greeted that. "We didn't know each other long enough for it to become a reality," Griffin pointed out mildly.

Morgana allowed the silence to lengthen before she again spoke. "Nor will we," she retorted coldly. Her eyes were level and unforgiving.

Then, for a moment too fast for her to see, there appeared on his face an expression of anguish that darkened his eyes and tightened his jaw. But before it was fully formed, it was gone, buried beneath a coldness that matched her own. Even though it was there, Griffin fought back his desire for this woman, this woman who had come into his life unbidden and who now had such a hold on him that he couldn't explain it even to himself.

Morgana watched him turn and walk away. Her expression retained its rigid scorn until he was almost out of sight. Then she bit her lip hard, trying to stem the rush of loneliness that engulfed her. Tears sprang to her eyes, but only the moon looked down at her bitter sadness and only the night creatures heard her sob of longing and despair.

She could not deny that Griffin had her love, although Morgana conceded that with some reluctance. She would have torn it from her heart had she been able. But her trust . . . that was not beyond her. It had once been given willingly. It would now have to be earned many times over.

Although she was certain that she would find no rest this

night, Morgana walked slowly back to the house, trying vainly to free her mind of any thought of Griffin, struggling within herself to keep fresh anguish from returning. She felt emotionally battered and yearned only for the blissful oblivion of sleep.

Late the following morning, a man rode up the driveway, his horse at a walk. Behind him in a forlorn procession were six Negroes, all male, their wrists spanceled and their ankles bearing leg irons with just enough chain between each to allow them to take a small step.

Hearing the dogs bark, Morgana walked out onto the piazza. Looking down, she viewed the scene below with curious eyes. Motioning to Bella, she asked, "Who is that man?"

The dark-skinned girl gave only a cursory glance into the yard. "Dat's Masta Will Parkins, missus. He be a slave trader." She folded her arms beneath her breast, her expression contemptuous. "He be stoppin' by 'bout once each year. Buys on'y no-good niggers what nobody else wants."

In the yard, Nathaniel and Griffin were approaching the slave trader. As Morgana watched, she saw her husband shake his head in denial.

Then, calling to Joe, who was working at his anvil, his black skin glistening with the sweat of his labor, Griffin apparently gave instructions for the small coffle of slaves to be put in the barn, for they all now trailed along after the huge Negro.

There was more discussion, and laughter from Nathaniel as he summoned Jude, who had been waiting nearby in anticipation of caring for the trader's horse. Having dismounted, the man was peering intently at Jude, all the while talking earnestly to Nathaniel, who shook his head in an emphatic way.

At the sight, Bella issued a short laugh. "He do dat ever' time he come heah," she explained to Morgana. "Always wantin' to buy dat Jude. Sayin' he kin git a fancy price fer dat buck."

Regarding the chained and silent Negroes who were now filing into the barn, Morgana frowned. "Well, I certainly hope he won't sell Jude to that man," she mused. The sight of the chained Negroes shuffling along, heads lowered, was not a pleasant one to see. Her frown deepened.

"Oh, naw, Miz Morgana," Bella replied. She waved a hand, dismissing even the thought. "Masta Nathaniel right proud of Jude. Shows him off ever' chance he gits."

The two women watched for a while longer, then the men headed for the verandah and were lost from view.

That evening when she came downstairs, Morgana was a bit surprised to find Will Parkins at the supper table. He wasn't a tall man, standing no more than five-feet, six-inches, but he was so massive in the chest and arms that he gave the appearance of being much bigger than he was. His features were rough and coarse, his speech and manners not much better.

At first happy to see a new face at the table, Morgana found herself disliking the man before she had even finished her soup.

By the time the first course was cleared away, Parkins had sunk in her esteem to a position just below that of Carlie Dobbs. At least, she thought in growing annoyance, Dobbs didn't eat with them. He ate in his own cabin.

So far, Parkins had entertained them with tales of lynchings, public floggings, and several mutilations he considered particularly interesting.

Morgana's appetite was fast leaving her. However, as she looked about the table, she noticed that Griffin and Nathaniel were both regarding the man with a certain degree of interest; Cammy merely looked bored, as if she'd heard it all before. As for the houseboys, they moved about quietly, faces devoid of any expression whatsoever.

"Good meal, suh," Parkins said at last. He patted his stomach and nodded in Nathaniel's direction.

"Pleasure to have you share it with us, Mr. Parkins," Nathaniel responded hospitably. "Feel free to stay with us as long as you like."

Morgana winced at that, but relaxed when she heard Parkins decline.

"Have to be movin' on," he advised. "But it grieves me that you don't have any of your stock for sale. From what I saw this afternoon, you've got quite a few prime hands. And as for that buck with the blue eyes . . ." He shook his head. "Could offer a good price, if you'll reconsider . . ." He regarded Griffin expectantly.

Seated beside Parkins, Cammy stiffened noticeably, clasping her hands tightly in her lap.

"We're not selling now," Griffin advised the man firmly, unaware of his sister's reaction. "In fact, we're getting ready to buy a few."

"That so?" Parkins fumbled about in his shirt pocket for a moment. "You might be interested in this, then." Leaning forward across the table, he handed Griffin the piece of paper which was an advertised notice of a slave auction to be held in Savannah. "Heard they got some prime ones sent down from Virginia."

Griffin read a minute, then looked up. "Thank you, Mr. Parkins. I'll look into it." He handed the piece of paper to Nathaniel and then leaned back in his chair, regarding the trader. "Too bad you didn't stop by a few weeks back. We had a buck that was a runner. Would have gladly sold him to you for a good price."

"Where is he now?" Parkins asked with a show of interest. He finished the last of his coffee with an audible smacking of his lips.

Slowly, Griffin shook his head. "Can't say. He managed to escape again."

Putting down his cup, Parkins looked surprised at that. "Didn't you hide him?"

"Gave him fifty good ones," Nathaniel put in. "We had him locked up in his cabin, but he managed to get out anyway."

"Sounds like a bad sort," Parkins contemplated, sucking at his teeth. "Best to keep runners spanceled," he advised sagely.

Nathaniel nodded ruefully. "The truth, suh. The truth."

"Although, personally, I prefer to hamstring 'em," the trader mused thoughtfully after a moment. "Cuts down on their value, but they can still work in the fields."

Unable to contain herself, Morgana eyed the man angrily, her face flushing. "Are you discussing men or animals?" she demanded, fixing him with an icy stare.

Parkins viewed her, then blinked in surprise. "We're discussin' niggers, ma'am," he murmured, disconcerted by her tone.

"You must excuse my wife," Griffin interrupted smoothly. He cast a warning look in Morgana's direction. "She's a Northerner and doesn't quite understand the intricacies of our peculiar institution."

In an angry gesture, Morgana threw her napkin on her plate. She was furious with Griffin's patronizing tone.

Parkins raised a hand in a conciliatory manner. "No offense taken, suh," he said hastily. "Shouldn't be discussin' these things in front of the ladies anyhow." He pushed his chair back and got up, avoiding Morgana's eye. "If y'all will excuse me, I'll check on my stock and then retire. . . ."

Nathaniel stood up. If he was disturbed by Morgana's outburst he gave no visible indication as he addressed the trader. "I'll have Thomas show you to your room when you're ready."

The two men walked toward the front hall. With an almost apologetic glance at Morgana, Cammy followed.

"I will thank you to show a bit more courtesy to our guest,"

Griffin said stiffly when they were alone.

Defiantly, Morgana glared at him as she got to her feet. "As you have pointed out, Griffin, I am not a Southerner. I feel no obligation to extend courtesy in the face of rude or offensive behavior."

"I saw no sign of either," Griffin shot back quickly, his brow furrowing. Standing up, he regarded her with a sternness that increased Morgana's anger. "I can appreciate your sensitivity at this time," he remarked with a brief glance at her stomach. "And I will agree that Parkins is a crude sort. But whatever else he is, he *is* a guest in my home. As such, he will be made to feel welcome. And he shall be treated with courtesy for the length of time he remains here!"

Griffin's voice had risen, and Morgana's outrage grew in direct proportion to his tone.

"In view of the fact that I feel myself unable to obey your command . . . Master Griffin," she said tartly, "I shall remain in my room until that man leaves."

Her skirts swirling from her indignation, Morgana walked from the room, head high, leaving Griffin to stand there alone, a scowl upon his face.

Chapter 10

By the 10th of May they all returned to Charleston, with the exception of Griffin, who went to Savannah to attend the auction that had advertised the sale of prime slaves.

This time, though, Morgana's social activities were severely curtailed due to her condition. There was one thing, however, that she did do. With Nathaniel's assistance — and a few expressed misgivings on his part which she refused to heed — she filed the papers that would manumit Ben.

And Nathaniel, bearing in mind that her child was due in October, insisted that they return in September so that his first grandchild would be born at Albemarle. By then, Griffin had joined them in Charleston, and together they all returned to the plantation.

A week after the family had returned from Charleston, Zoe was standing in the open doorway of her cabin, watching for Jude.

Directly across the dirt road known as Slave Row was the cabin shared by Joe, his wife Pearl, and the couple's three children, all of whom were too young yet to work in the fields. The three children, two girls and a boy, were a distance away at the far end of the road, playing with their friends.

The September day was uncomfortably warm, the air damp and heavy, the breeze so slight that it didn't even disturb the flies and mosquitoes; they droned incessantly, an irritating, never ending nuisance to those who had to live within their proximity.

Usually this late in the day, the breeze would quicken, providing some relief as it swept across the river, at times bringing the salty tang of the sea with it, depending on the tide. When it flowed inward it brought with it the salt water from the Atlantic. When it flowed outward, the water turned fresh. It was only at these times that the fields would be flooded with the life giving substance.

The tide had just turned and most of the hands were still in the fields. The yard was quiet and empty of inhabitants save for the children and dogs, and they, too, seemed disinclined to cavort in the heavy atmosphere.

Standing there, Zoe wiped her damp brow with her hand as she waited.

As soon as she saw Jude emerge from the carriage house, she took the food out of the bucket, spooning it onto a tin plate which she placed on the solitary wooden table. Aside from two chairs and a small, three-legged stool, the only other furnishing in the small cabin was a corn husk mattress positioned in a corner of the single room. There were no windows, but there was a small hearth for cooking and, on those occasions when it was required, for heat.

Most slaves did their own cooking in the evening, usually pone or grits, possibly pork or fish, and whatever vegetables were available in garden patches, but Zoe was able to bring theirs from the kitchen. Sometimes, when Jude went fishing — and caught some — they'd eat that, but mostly it was what Minda saved for them from the day before. Today it was cold beef, red gravy and biscuits left over from yesterday's meal at the Great House.

Zoe had been with Jude for almost a year now. They weren't married and wouldn't be until there was a child. It had been Nathaniel who had installed Zoe in Jude's cabin, a situation that had made her deliriously happy — at first. However, it soon became painfully apparent that Jude didn't want her at all. She could leave and return to her own cabin, previously shared with her brother Jonah, anytime she wanted to. The trouble was, she loved Jude too much to even consider taking that step.

But if Jude didn't love her, he seemed not to love anyone else, either. He was a loner, something rare among her people. The only one he seemed to bother with was Miss Cammy. But of course he couldn't possibly be in love with her, Zoe reflected dourly. Still, they met occasionally. Everyone seemed to know about it except for Masta Nathaniel and Masta Griffin — and certainly no black was going to tell them.

Jude thought that she didn't know, but Zoe heard things: Minda whispering worriedly to Thomas, one day; a few of the house servants discussing it, another day. They all fell silent when she approached, but Zoe had heard enough to piece some of it together.

She was consumed by curiosity over the nature of these meetings. It didn't happen often, but today it had happened again, for the first time since he had returned from Charleston a week ago. Not being a house servant, Zoe was never included in these trips.

And today, Zoe was bound and determined to find out what was going on.

Jude entered, his handsome face set in a scowl. He was wearing his usual attire of a linsey-woolsey shirt and breeches that were string tied at the waist. Like Zoe and everyone else save the house servants, he wore no undergarments. In town, of course, he wore his livery. But as soon as he returned to the plantation, he gave that splendid outfit to Minda, who personally washed and ironed it, then put it away for the next time.

Zoe watched Jude as he now sat down. He viewed his meal, but made no move toward it. His silence wasn't all that unusual; he spoke to her only when he had to.

"Jude, man," she said at last in a low, cajoling voice. "Eat yore supper. You bin frettin' fer days now, ever since you come home." Her dark face turned anxious as she wondered if perhaps he was ill. Usually his appetite was good and he ate whatever she put in front of him. But lately he seemed too preoccupied to even eat his food.

"Jude. . . ."

With a grunt of annoyance and a quick irritated glance at her, Jude began to eat.

For a while, she stared at him. Lawd, but he was a powerful handsome buck, she thought, her own expression wavering between anger and dismay. If only he would let her, she would love him with everything she had to give to that emotion. As it was, it was bottled up inside her with no means of escape, and, like a festering wound, was causing her more and more distress.

"Gits you grits wit sweet'nin', iffen you wants," Zoe offered after a bit. She took a step toward the table.

He didn't bother to look up. "Doan want none."

With a sigh, Zoe moved back to the doorway. She leaned on the frame in a careless attitude. "Looked fer you dis mornin'," she murmured, absently viewing her bare feet. "Noticin' you wuz gone off somewheres. . . ."

Jude tensed, but kept on eating. "Ain' no business of yourn what I do," he muttered. He wished she wouldn't talk so much. He would rather be alone with his own thoughts. How was a man to think with a prattling woman around him all the time? He hunched over the tin plate, shoveling food into his mouth without really tasting it.

"Thinkin' mebbe it is my business," she contradicted. She stared outside at a lone chicken scratching in a tuft of grass. "Seen Miss Cammy when she go off, ridin' her horse." She turned slightly and gave him a sidelong glance. "An' seen you goin' in de same direction on'y a few minutes after dat. . . ."

Startled, Jude looked up at her, glaring. "You ever say a word 'bout dat, I'll shet yore black mouf forever."

She was a bit disconcerted by his fiercely angry look, and a bit surprised by the force of it. But she was also determined. After a moment she worked up enough courage to ask, "What you doin' when you meets Missy?"

"None of yore goddamn business," he snapped, returning his attention to his plate. He picked up a biscuit, rolled it around in the red gravy, and ate it in two bites.

Zoe's broad nostrils flared indignantly at his tone. "Wants to know," she insisted. She folded her arms across her high bosom and viewed him with level eyes.

In a violent motion, Jude threw the wooden spoon on the table where it landed with a clatter. Then, getting up, he began to pace the small cabin, casting angry looks in her direction.

"What you thinks we doin', heh?" he jibed. "What you thinks?" His chin jutted out and his breath came heavy, expanding his broad chest until it strained against cotton.

Her gaze slipped away. "Doan know," she mumbled. "But wants you to tell me."

"Well, wants to know, do you?" he muttered savagely. His blue eyes glinted like an approaching storm. He knew Zoe well enough to know that, like a dog with a bone, she wouldn't cease her questioning until he answered her. She would hound him for days, even weeks, until she got what she wanted. And under no circumstances must she learn the truth, at least that part of it that was so dangerous to him.

"Awright," he said at last in a tone that suggested compliance. He took a deep breath. "Tells you. Missy teachin' me to read." He nodded at her suitably shocked expression.

A fearful look came into Zoe's dark eyes. "You crazy?" she hissed. "Wants to git yorese'f kilt? You gots to stop it now! Doan learn no more. . . ."

His laughter was harsh as he viewed her stricken face. "I already know how to read and write," he informed her softly, dropping the idiom that had become so hateful to him.

She stared blankly at the sound of his voice, unable to believe her ears. Even the timbre of it had changed. Had she closed her eyes she would have thought that it was a white man talking.

"Did you hear me, Zoe?" he asked in the same soft tone. He brought his face close to hers, enjoying her unsettled state. "You wanted to know what we were doing; now, I think you know."

"Sweet Baby Jesus," Zoe gasped as fear knotted in her throat. "You stop talkin' lak dat! Stop it dis minute, 'fore someone hears you . . ." She stood there, breathing deeply, peering about the small cabin as if it were suddenly peopled by unseen demons. A slave could be sold, shipped to the canefields, if it was even suspected that he could read, much less write. A slave who could write could easily pen himself a pass. She'd heard stories of slaves who had had their hands chopped off for possessing such a skill.

At last she regarded Jude, her own fury mounting. What he was doing could get them all in serious trouble. White men were not selective when their anger was aroused.

"An' what you think you gonna do wit dat learnin'?" she demanded, her brow furrowing in consternation. Her breath came so fast that her words were rushed. "Cain't use it nohow. Masta thinks you bein' uppity, he take de skin offen yore back."

Raising his chin, Jude's blue eyes narrowed. He knew he shouldn't tell her anymore, but the temptation was irresistible.

"With Miss Cammy's help, I'm going North," he stated at last, his voice barely a whisper. He glanced through the open doorway to assure himself that no one was around. Then he viewed Zoe again. "It won't be long before all slaves are freed.

When that time comes," he pointed a thumb at his chest, "I'll be ready."

"Freed?" She gave a short, bitter laugh, expressing heavy skepticism. Jude moved to the other side of the table. Zoe walked away from the doorway, coming closer to him. One corner of her mouth curled downward as she looked at him. "You daft in de haid, honey man. Ain' no white folks gonna free us'ns. Think dey's gonna do de plantin' and de ploughin' all by deyselves?" She put her hands on her hips and viewed him with open scorn.

He grimaced at her ignorance. "They'll pay us to work, you little fool," he growled. "But I don't aim to work in any field. . . ."

He appeared so confident, Zoe faltered, feeling uncertain. "You really thinks it gonna happen? Thinks we gonna be free?" The thought scared her a bit, for Zoe, at eighteen, had known no other life than the one she lived at Albemarle. She had never even been to Charleston. Her mother, Linny, had been pregnant with Zoe when Masta Nathaniel had bought her. Linny had died when Zoe was thirteen years old. Jonah had been two years older than that. Since then, Zoe had been doing just what she did now: the washing and ironing for the people who lived in the Great House and helping Minda in the kitchen in the afternoons. The work she wouldn't miss at all. But where would she go if freedom actually came? Who would supply her food, her clothes? She didn't even have a husband. . . .

"It will happen," Jude was affirming strongly, inclining his head in a solemn manner. "It's not only books I read, I read the newspapers, too." He couldn't prevent the pride that crept into his voice with the statement.

Zoe considered that for a long moment, the possibility at last beginning to excite her. Her mind ran wild with the possibilities. She could go anywhere, do anything she pleased. There would be no one to stop her, to give her orders, to threaten her with a beating if she refused.

Eager now, Zoe reached out and clutched at Jude's sleeve. "Den, takes me wit you," she begged, her eyes imploring. "When you goes, takes me wit you. . . ."

Impatiently, he brushed aside her hand. "You?" The word was threaded with a shimmering strand of mockery that caused Zoe's lip to tremble. He laughed at the thought, shaking his head from side to side.

Zoe clasped her hands tightly, her dark eyes never leaving him. "Won't be no trouble." Her voice wavered with anticipation. "Promises you. Do ever'thin' you tells me . . ." She broke off when the laughter continued. The sound of it struck at her heart like a heavy fist.

"Don't plan on spending the rest of my life with the likes of you," Jude pronounced firmly when he had his amusement under control. "Besides," he added, turning away from her, "you'd only get in my way. I'm not going to saddle myself with an ignorant black wench like you." He didn't dare tell her that Cammy was planning to run with him. As her coachman, no one would question him when they rode away from here.

Zoe fell silent, more hurt and bitter than at any other time in her life. She watched with quiet resentment as Jude shucked his shirt and breeches and lay down on the husk mattress.

She should be there, at his side, but knew it would be futile. The heat would spring up, flooding her belly with desire. But Jude, as she knew from experience, would probably turn away, muttering disdainfully. He did that more often than not.

Having completely forgotten Zoe, Jude lay, hands behind his head, staring up at the ceiling, impatient for his plans to become a reality. He could, of course, write his own pass anytime he wanted to, had even practiced forging Master

Griffin's bold scrawl, always being careful to burn the papers afterward. But, having given it great and deep thought, Jude was also too smart to try it. He knew very well that he would have only one chance at freedom, only one; therefore, his escape would have to be foolproof.

If he did forge a pass, it would get him as far as Charleston. Then what? Having been born and raised on Albemarle, Jude had never been further than Charleston. He did know the quickest means of travel North was by boat. Only a fool like Jonah would attempt it overland. Jude had no doubt that sooner or later Jonah would be caught again, despite the fact that he had remained at large for almost seven months now. Probably the fool was hiding in the swamp, he thought contemptuously.

However, to get on a boat, Jude reflected, still staring up at the ceiling, one needed money as well as a pass. He had saved some, but he didn't want to spend it until he had to.

No, the only foolproof way was with Cammy. Once North, he would of course have to send her back home. He wouldn't put it past Griffin to come after his sister with murder in his heart. Jude would never feel safe if he had to continually look over his shoulder, waiting for Cammy's brother to suddenly appear. On his own, he could mix and blend in with the free colored community until such time as freedom became a fact.

But Cammy wouldn't suffer too long, he reasoned. It was to be expected that her brother and grandfather would raise holy hell for a while. Then they'd marry her off to some respectable white man and the matter would be ended.

And so Jude daydreamed, his thoughts turned inward, seeing with his mind's eye the stories he had read, the pictures he had seen. Oh, it would be a good life, he thought in satisfaction, a broad lazy smile finding its way to his full lips. And, best of all, he would be free.

★ ★ ★ ★ ★

The next morning, Zoe emerged from the washhouse, lugging a basketful of freshly washed laundry, muttering to herself as she went to hang it up.

All day long, it seemed to her, she washed and ironed, then had to help Minda in the kitchen.

"An' you would think," she said out loud, though there was no one around to hear, "dat after you wuz done, Zoe gal, you could at least count on yore man to pleasure wit you. But naw, dat buck got his mind someplace else . . . an' ever'body knowin' jest where."

She dropped the basket on the ground. Straightening, she stood with her hands on her rounded hips, a sour look on her black face.

"An' jest what he doin' when he follows missy to de grove?" She gave a sharp, unpleasant laugh. "Readin', he sez," she continued with her solitary monologue. "So when he gits Nawth, he kin be somebody . . ." She gave a snort of disgust.

Picking up a ruffled white shirt that belonged to Nathaniel, she shook it out, snapping it, then secured it to the wash line with wooden clothespins.

For a time she continued with her task, her mind filled with thoughts of Jude and how she could persuade him to take her along when he made his escape.

Even thinking on it, Zoe doubted that she could change his mind. But that wouldn't prevent her from trying, she decided firmly. Whatever peril was involved, she would willingly share it with him.

Perhaps, she thought, pinning a petticoat to the line, she could threaten Jude into changing his mind. Tell him that she would reveal all she knew about his plans unless he took her along with him.

The basket was now empty. Peering in the direction of the

186

stables, Zoe's black eyes narrowed. Jude was nowhere about. Most days at this time she could see him grooming horses, repairing straps and harnesses or otherwise making himself useful.

But today he was nowhere around.

Glancing about in the late morning quiet, Zoe moved furtively in the direction of the wooded area that surrounded the main compound. Last night, Jude had told her that he was getting ready to run. Did he already do it? she wondered. Or was he with Miss Cammy again?

She would, Zoe suddenly decided, see for herself just what kind of lessons missy was giving her Jude.

Sometime later, Zoe stood, concealed by moss and the heavy, drooping branches of a great gnarled cypress. And what she saw filled her with an anger so great, she could hardly contain herself.

They were naked, the rich golden color of her man's skin in sharp contrast with the white and flawless skin of her young mistress.

The look on the face of Jude as he found a sudden release from his passion was one that Zoe had never seen. On those rare occasions when Jude condescended to couple with her, it was a quick and brutal thing he did, as if he couldn't wait to get it over and done.

No wonder she hadn't conceived in all these months, Zoe thought, enraged. That Jude was dumping his seed before he ever got to her.

Cammy still had her white arms about Jude, kissing him, teasing him, her laughter trilling through the grove like that of a contented bird. Jude laughed, too, as she tickled him and playfully bit on his ear. Grabbing her, Jude held her tight against him, murmuring words Zoe couldn't hear. And then there was silence as the lovers kissed, deeply and passionately.

Zoe compressed her lips tightly, afraid that the angry thoughts in her mind would come rushing out through her mouth. With effort, she swallowed, then turned away, unwilling to witness the couple's heated embraces. As quietly as she had come, Zoe now made her way back to the yard.

Unaware of anything amiss, Cammy finally sat up, smoothing her hair with her hands. She stared down at Jude, stretched out languorously on the blanket. With her finger, she traced the muscles on his shoulder, trailing down the smooth, golden skin to his flat abdomen. The feel of his bare flesh caused her to shudder in delight.

"Cammy . . ." he murmured warningly, not opening his eyes.

She gave a soft laugh, then lay down beside him, putting her head on his warm chest.

After a bit, she glanced up at his still closed eyes. "Jude . . ." she whispered, then bit her lip. "There's something I've got to tell you. . . ."

He grunted but made no move. He was half asleep.

"I'm going to have a baby. . . ."

Beneath her body, Cammy felt him go rigid. In a slow movement, he opened his eyes, then raised himself up on an elbow, almost tumbling her off of him.

She was frightened at the look of him, never having seen such a truculent expression upon his face. "It will be all right," she tried to assure him. "We'll just have to leave sooner than we planned, that's all."

His blue eyes stared steadily, almost hatefully, into her own. His hands balled into fists. For a long moment, fear and anger battled within him. Fear proved stronger. He turned from her. Drawing up his knees, he folded his arms across them and put his head down in an attitude of utter dejection.

Cammy placed a small hand on his arm. "Listen to me,

Jude," she entreated earnestly. "I know exactly what we're going to do. I'm going to tell Morgana."

He raised his head, staring at her in dumb astonishment. "You can't tell nobody!" he protested hoarsely. "You want to see me get killed? Oh, Jesus," he muttered, turning away again. The fear spread throughout him, leaving him breathless with the force of it.

"Will you please listen?" she begged. "Morgana will help us. I know she will. And besides, she comes from the North. She can tell us the best place to go. . . ."

Jude listened dully to her plans, too overwhelmed to do anything else. For having been taught to read, he could be sold. For this . . . When they were through with him, death would be a welcome blessing. His mind presented increasingly grotesque possibilities to him. His body actually cringed at the thought of the indignities that would be visited upon it. How many strokes of the lash did it take to kill a man? he wondered, growing more frantic. He shuddered, feeling icy cold beneath the warm sun.

Finally he turned, aware that Cammy was shaking his arm.

"Are you listening to me?" At his brief nod, she said, "And once we get there, we can be married . . ." She paused at the look he gave her and her lips trembled. "Don't you want to marry me?"

He gave an impatient gesture, summoning his remaining strength to bring himself under control. "Yes, of course," he lied. "But how do you plan to keep the baby a secret until we leave?"

She looked down at her almost flat stomach. "Nothing shows," she observed. "We have at least a month to plan —"

"A month!" He couldn't wait that long, he thought distractedly. He was filled with the urge to run, right now!

She nodded, eager again. "Morgana won't be able to come

with us until she has her own baby. You and I can't possibly go into Charleston alone," she explained patiently, although she knew he was perfectly aware of that simple fact. "But Morgana and I can go on the pretext of doing some shopping. You will, of course, drive us."

He gave her a doubtful look, the fear still crouched in his belly, waiting to spring up in his throat. "What makes you think she'll do all this?"

"I know she will," Cammy insisted firmly. "You don't know her like I do."

"Have you talked to her yet?" he asked skeptically, relaxing only slightly.

"Not yet," she admitted. "But I will, today," she added quickly, seeing his expression close again. She put her arms around him. "Please trust me, Jude," she whispered, her mouth against his neck.

Jude's only answer was another deep sigh. He had, he reflected dispiritedly, no other choice.

Back in her cabin, Zoe's anger spewed forth and boiled over like a pot of unwatched milk. She prowled the small cabin like a caged cat seeking escape. Occasionally, she paused by the open door, peering across the yard to the stables. Jude had still not returned.

Within her frail body, hate took shape and grew, spreading throughout her like water poured on sand.

"Goin' Nawth, is he?" She clenched her teeth as she stared outside into the sun-dappled yard.

She knew now why Jude had been so confident. Probably, she thought in rising agitation, even if Jude was caught trying to run, Miss Cammy would see to it that the whip wouldn't scar that handsome body.

Not like her brother, Jonah. Poor Jonah was too ignorant,

too dumb to get away. He had run twice and been caught both times; though, this time, luck seemed to be with him. But he didn't have a white lady to help him. Miss Cammy wouldn't look twice at a buck like Jonah. Her brother didn't have blue eyes and his skin was black as night. Jonah was a nigger, but Jude. . . .

Well, goddamn them all, Zoe thought in the heat of her rage. Jude was just as much a nigger as Jonah. Maybe it was time for honey man to learn that. . . .

Chapter 11

It was hot. The late September air was heavy and humid and uncomfortable, as it had been all week long since their return. In the distance thunder rumbled against a sullen sky. Creatures in the woods and swamps paused a moment, hearing in the ominous sound a prelude to the approaching storm.

After the cooling breeze that had been present in Charleston, Morgana found Albemarle stifling. Both Griffin and Nathaniel had urged her to stay indoors, at least until the danger of fever had passed. But as she sat in her room, fanning herself in an effort to find some relief from the heat, Morgana couldn't resist going out onto the piazza, having instructed Bella to move the divan out there.

Supper was over, and here in the privacy of her own room, Morgana had discarded hoops and stays, wearing no more than a cotton nightgown over which she wore a thin wrap of the same material.

Sitting herself down, Morgana viewed the darkening sky, studying the silvery mist that crept up from the river, hovering almost caressingly about the trunks of the cypress and oaks. She fervently wished for October, and her baby, to arrive.

Feeling disgruntled, Morgana sighed deeply. Lately, waiting seemed to fill her life.

Bella brought her lemonade, offering yet another admonishment against sitting in the night air. Garbed in her usual black dress and white apron, Bella wore a red bandana about her head, tied in such an intricate manner that it suggested a fashionable turban.

"Shouldn't be heah, Miz Morgana," she grumbled. "Best you go inside." Putting the glass down on a small table, she

192

stood with hands on her hips, viewing her mistress as though she were a naughty child.

"It's so very warm," Morgana protested tiredly, waving a hand. "At least there's a bit of a breeze out here."

Bella clucked her disapproval. "It's de breeze what comes from de river dat brings de fever," she advised solemnly, nodding her turbaned head for emphasis. "An' when de fever gits a'holt of you, doan let go. Keeps comin' back. Makes a body right sickly, it do."

With a certain wariness, Bella turned and eyed the bronzed sky with a flicker of apprehension. She always breathed a sigh of relief when September, and the chance of hurricanes, passed. The first year she had come to the Carolinas, September had birthed just such a fearsome spectacle and she hoped to never again see the likes of it.

Watching her, Morgana smiled with true affection. Bella was, she thought, a godsend. The girl constantly hovered, alert to Morgana's needs, whether it was a cool drink of water or a change of perspiration-dampened clothing. Morgana had long since put herself in Bella's capable hands, and had actually grown very fond of her.

"I promise I'll go inside in just a few minutes," she said at last in an effort to placate her.

"Iffen you doan, Masta Griffin paddles me for shoah," Bella murmured darkly with an audible sigh.

Morgana regarded the black girl with a suddenly intent look. "Have you ever been . . . paddled?" She felt angry at just the thought.

"Not since I come heah," Bella replied offhandedly. She went inside, emerging a moment later with a palmetto fan in her hand.

Morgana was looking at her in surprise. "I thought you were born here. . . ."

"Oh, no, missus. I wuz borned in Virginny." She made a vague gesture with the fan. "Doan rightly know where dat is, but it's a long ways from heah. Took days an' days fer us'ns to walk to New Orleans. Dat's where de auction wuz," she elaborated.

"How long ago was that?"

Bella screwed up her face in thought, mentally counting the plantings, then, finally, held up three fingers. "Dat long ago."

"You were about fifteen when you were sold?" Morgana speculated.

" 'Spects so," Bella agreed blithely. She laid the fan on the table within Morgana's reach.

"Is that where my husband bought you?'

Straightening, Bella shook her head. "Wasn't Masta Griffin. Was Masta Dabney Pritchard what bought me." At Morgana's look of confusion, she went on to explain, "Masta Dabney lost dis gal while he wuz playin' cards. An' it wuz Masta Nathaniel who won me."

Leaning back, Morgana gave a sigh, but made no comment. She wondered how long it was going to take for her to get used to this sort of thing.

At the sound of a knock on the door, Bella went inside again. Morgana sipped a bit of the tangy lemonade, then looked up to see Cammy.

"I . . . just wanted to talk to you," she said, sounding a bit breathless.

"Of course," Morgana responded quickly. She patted the divan. "Come, sit beside me. I'm grateful for your company." She noticed that Cammy was still wearing the gown she had worn at the supper table, a ruffled and beribboned pale blue merino creation over a wide, crinolined skirt. Just the sight of it made Morgana feel warm. Reaching out, she picked up the palmetto fan from the table beside her.

Cammy hesitated a moment, then turned to Bella. "Leave us alone." She waited until the slave left, then sat herself down. She was silent for a time, twisting her handkerchief with nervous movements.

At last Cammy turned toward Morgana. "How are you feeling?" she asked. She was perched on the edge of the divan as if she were about to take flight.

"Except for being a bit uncomfortable with the heat, I'm fine." Morgana gave a rueful smile. "I certainly hope that you're not going to tell me to go back into that hot room," she murmured, fanning herself. "Belle's been hounding me since I came out here."

Cammy smiled at her, a stiff parody of that expression, too bright, too affected to be meaningful. "You like Bella?" she asked.

A bit surprised by the question, Morgana laughed. "Of course I do. At first I was unsettled by having someone around me all the time," she admitted. "But now I confess that I'd be lost without her."

Turning away, Cammy was quiet for a long moment and when she did speak, Morgana was again, jolted by surprise.

"Do you think that slavery will ever be abolished?" the girl asked in a deceptively casual voice.

"Why, I don't know," Morgana answered slowly, considering it. "I certainly hope it will be, one day." She took another sip of the lemonade.

"You don't regard the darkies as inferior?"

"Certainly not," Morgana stated, turning to look at her. "They are uneducated, but that's hardly their fault, is it? There is a big difference between being ignorant and being uninformed."

"It's against the law to teach Negroes to read or write," the girl mused. She regarded Morgana with some curiosity. "Do you believe that, if they were educated — informed — they would be just like we are?"

Morgana shrugged. She put the fan back on the table, feeling too weary to even use it. "I don't see why not." She gave a short laugh. "Of course, I wouldn't want to argue the point with your grandfather," she murmured wryly, inclining her head. "He seems to feel they are like children."

Cammy looked down at her lap and managed to keep her voice steady. "I used to think that way, too," she whispered. "Does everyone in the North feel as you do?" she asked after a bit, not looking at Morgana.

"I can't speak for everyone," Morgana responded quietly, wondering at the seriousness of the girl's tone. She had the oddest sensation that Cammy was talking about one subject and thinking of another. The feeling was disconcerting, but transitory. The heat was stifling even her reactions. "But, yes. I think that most Northerners agree that slavery is a terrible thing. Some, in fact, are quite outspoken in their beliefs."

"Then, if a Negro were to live there, no one would bother him, is that right?"

Morgana frowned in perplexity. "Cammy, what are you getting at?"

The girl wet her lips, hesitated, then mopped her face with the crumpled handkerchief. "I need your help," she murmured, turning her dark eyes on Morgana. "You're the only one . . ." Her mouth set into a tense line. This morning, when she had thought it all out, it had seemed so simple. Now, faced with the moment of truth, Cammy found herself searching for the right words.

Studying her young sister-in-law, Morgana felt a prodding of unease. The girl was pale and her eyes seemed darker and larger than usual. Her face was grave, troubled, displaying none of the usual mischievous energy that Morgana was used to see-

196

ing. The handkerchief in her hands had been reduced to an undefinable wad. "I'll do whatever I can," she said quickly, alarmed. "But first you'd better tell me what this is all about."

"I . . . I'm in love with someone, and . . ." Cammy bit her lower lip, shifting her position restlessly on the divan.

The smile returned to Morgana's lips and she relaxed once more. So that's what all this was about, she thought in relief. "That's wonderful," she began, then her brow creased in thought. Since no young man had called here at Albemarle, obviously Cammy's young man was in Charleston, or perhaps at a neighboring plantation. "Is it Mr. Barrows?" she prompted, thinking of the young man who had called most often while they were in the town house.

Cammy stared blankly a moment, then shook her head. "No. No, it isn't Clinton. . . ."

"Someone that your grandfather doesn't approve of?" Morgana probed tentatively when the girl showed no sign of continuing.

Cammy swallowed. "It's . . . Jude." Her voice was so low, her words were barely audible.

It was Morgana's turn to stare blankly. "Jude?" For the moment she didn't even recognize the name, trying as she was to place it with one of the fresh young faces she had seen in Charleston.

"Jude." Cammy was staring in a determined manner.

Morgana blinked. "I don't —" she began, then fell silent. Her blue eyes suddenly widened with comprehension. "You mean . . . *our* Jude?" At Cammy's brief nod, Morgana felt a rush of dismay so strong that it produced a feeling of nausea in her throat. She took a deep breath in order to fight down the unpleasant sensation, then closed her eyes in an effort to assimilate her thoughts. For the immediate present she was too stunned to speak.

197

Cammy continued to watch her closely, almost holding her breath in anticipation of Morgana's reaction.

"But you can't marry him," Morgana breathed at last. She gripped Cammy's small hand. "Neither your grandfather nor Griffin would ever allow it." Whatever could the girl be thinking of? she wondered distractedly.

"I know," Cammy quickly agreed with a brief nod of her head. She appeared almost relieved now that the first hurdle had been accomplished. "That's why we must leave here."

"Where could you possibly go?" Morgana was astounded by the girl's calm statement.

"North. I've never been there. Neither, of course, has Jude, so you must tell us where to go. But first, we must return to Charleston. I can't go by myself, with only Jude driving. Grandfather would never allow it. But if you came with us. . . ."

Bewilderment settled upon Morgana as she tried to follow the rush of words. She tried to make sense out of what she was hearing, but her mind couldn't absorb it all. Cammy seemed to have entirely forgotten that she was unable to travel.

"We'll have to wait until after your baby is born," Cammy said quickly, sensing her thoughts. "We had planned to wait until next year, but —"

"You cannot run away with Jude," Morgana interrupted firmly. She straightened. "You mustn't even think of such a thing! Your grandfather . . ." She made a gesture, feeling helpless in the face of just the thought of Nathaniel's reaction to this situation. Cammy herself had noted that her grandfather would not allow her to drive into the city with only Jude in attendance. Whatever possessed the girl to think that Nathaniel would accept this!

"But I love him," Cammy cried out. At the sight of Morgana's freshly stricken face, the girl exclaimed, "You don't understand. Jude and I — we grew up together. I've known him all my life. He's the kindest, most gentle person in the whole world."

"I'm trying to understand," Morgana offered patiently. She took another deep breath. "But —"

"Oh," Cammy made a sharp, disparaging gesture with her hand, "how could you understand? You're a Northerner, a Yankee . . ." Her eyes brightened with a sudden anger and she regarded Morgana sharply. "Or is it just that when your convictions are tested, you find yourself lacking. . . ."

Stung, Morgana frowned in consternation. "That's not it at all," she protested strongly. "You're being unfair! We are not discussing abolition. Even in the North, feeling would run high against a marriage of this sort —"

"I don't care," Cammy interjected heatedly, her back rigid. "I don't care what people think."

Upset, Morgana's finger went to her lips in an effort to caution Cammy, whose voice had risen. Getting up, she went to the iron railing and peered into the yard. It was quiet, with only the usual sound of the dogs barking and an occasional laugh that wafted up from Slave Row.

It was completely dark now, the black sky unrelieved by stars, which were hidden by the clouds. The air hung still and unmoving, the slight breeze having retreated in the calm before the storm.

Satisfied that there was no one in the immediate vicinity, Morgana walked back to the divan. "You don't mean that," she objected softly as she sat down again.

Cammy's eyes were bright. "I do. I do mean it! And besides," her voice fell to a whisper, "if I stay here, Griffin will make me marry Clinton Barrows." Absently, she plucked at the tatted edging of the handkerchief, unraveling it. "At least he will try," she added grimly, her mouth tightening. "And I will not do that. I cannot abide him."

"Is that why Clinton came to call so often while we were in Charleston?"

Cammy made an exasperated face and put what was left of the handkerchief on the small table. "Exactly. They seem to think I'll change my mind eventually. I've told Griffin that I would not consider Clinton Barrows under any circumstance." She sighed. "My brother patted my hand and told me I'll see things differently in a year or so."

"He seems like a nice young man," Morgana ventured tentatively.

Cammy was silent a moment, studying the changing pattern of light on the piazza floor created by the flickering oil lamp in the bedroom and the deepening shadows outside. Then, turning her head, she regarded Morgana with a level look. "I cannot marry Clinton because . . ." Her resolve deserted her and she reached out to take Morgana's hand, holding it tightly. "You've seen Jude. He's not like the others. Nor," she went on, "is he ignorant, as he pretends to be. I've taught him. From the time we were children, I've taught him. He can read and write. And," she continued with a trace of bitterness, "he speaks as well as you or me. He's just afraid to, you see." She was watching Morgana closely, her lips trembling, her brimming eyes pleading for understanding.

Morgana sensed the unbridled, unspoken emotion. Cammy, she had long since learned, was never casual about anything, and if ordinary things goaded her toward excitement, what would love do?

In a quick motion, Morgana clasped the girl in her arms, giving her a hug. "Oh, my dear Cammy. If it were up to me, you and Jude could marry this instant. Please, don't think I'm censuring you."

Cammy's expression turned eager. "Then you'll help us?"

"What can I possibly do?" Morgana responded sadly, leaning back against the soft cushions again. Her finely drawn features displayed unutterable sympathy. "Even if you ran away, you know that Griffin would follow you and bring you back here."

"He won't if we are already married."

"I doubt that even that would stop him," Morgana replied with a shake of her head. She knew perfectly well how much Griffin thought of his sister. She had, this while, been thinking of Nathaniel's reaction, but now she realized that Griffin would be just as angry, if not more, were he to learn of all this.

The girl drew away, her face hardening. "He'll have to." She got to her feet, hands clasped at her waist, and looked down at Morgana. "I'm to have Jude's baby."

A muted, rolling sound of thunder punctuated her statement. White-faced, Morgana just stared at her.

"Oh, dear God," she murmured, putting a hand to her pale cheek. She glanced at Cammy's waist, but the crinolined skirt gave her no indication. "How long. . . ."

"Not for more than four months yet. That's why it is so important that we leave as soon as possible."

"Does anyone know? Have you told Jude?"

Cammy nodded slowly. "Just this morning. No one else knows. I think I've been able to keep Meg from discovering it, but I'm not entirely certain. I have an idea she suspects. However," she added hastily, "Meg would never tell, even if she did know."

Cammy continued to watch her, waiting for a response, but when Morgana didn't speak, a cold feeling of abandonment crept over her. She rubbed her bare arms, feeling suddenly chilled. She hadn't realized until this minute just how much she had been counting on Morgana's help.

"There must be another alternative," Morgana said after a brief pause. "To your running away, I mean."

"There is no other way," Cammy stated flatly, then sighed. "I've known for a long time that one day I would have to make this decision."

Morgana leaned forward, still unconvinced. "Is there any chance, any chance at all, that your grandfather could be persuaded to free Jude —" She broke off at Cammy's mirthless laugh. "But surely, under the circumstances, he would at least consider it. The baby might change his mind."

The girl shook her head firmly. "If he or my brother ever found out before we could get away . . . ." She averted her face as if to escape the sound of her own words. "They'd kill Jude." Her voice ended on a strangled sob.

Startled, Morgana's eyes widened. However, despite the girl's conviction, she couldn't believe that that was a possibility. They might sell Jude, she thought, and that would be bad enough, but they would never kill him. The idea was out of her realm of imagination.

"Cammy," she said after a bit, "are you sure, very sure, that this is what you want? Once you take this step, there will be no turning back."

"Morgana, I love Jude," Cammy whispered softly, almost sadly. "I know it's difficult for you to understand, but I've known him all my life. To me he isn't a slave, or black. He's just . . . Jude."

Looking away, Morgana felt despair crowd in upon her. She wished she could refute Cammy, point out the illogic of the whole situation. And, if it weren't for the coming child, she might have made the attempt in spite of Cammy's plaintive words.

"Morgana, will you help us?"

Overwhelmed by the heat and by Cammy's distressing tale, Morgana just sat there. Absently, she glanced at the sky, noting the approaching storm with distant eyes. She didn't know what to do or what to say. She had a sudden longing to rush from the room, to creep into Griffin's strong arms and rest there, sheltered. What matter if he didn't love her? she thought wildly, brushing the dampened tendrils of her hair from her forehead. She loved him — wasn't that enough?

But it *did* matter, she told herself sternly, upset with her inclination. She wasn't about to throw herself into Griffin's arms whatever the provocation. She had done that once and she had learned a bitter lesson for her rashness.

Coming forward, Cammy touched her arm, shaking her out of her reverie, demanding, with her eyes, Morgana's strength and fortitude.

The moment of weakness passed and Morgana sat up straighter as she gathered her inner resources about her, forcing herself to think clearly.

A thought began to form in her mind, and as Morgana considered it, she felt certain that it would work. Both Griffin and Nathaniel would be angry; that was only to be expected. But she sensed that Cammy was prepared to go through with her plan of running away with or without her help. On their own, she reasoned, they would probably be caught before they even left Charleston.

"I have an aunt in Massachusetts," she said at last, turning to look at Cammy again. "Perhaps you and Jude can go there. The two of you can be married and stay there until the baby comes, and until you both decide where to live, and what to do."

"Would your aunt allow us to stay?" Cammy asked excitedly, bending toward her.

Morgana pursed her lips. It was a question she could not, of course, answer with any degree of accuracy. "I'll write to her tomorrow," she decided with a firm nod of her head. "I've been meaning to do it ever since my father died. When we receive her answer, we'll know what to do." She glanced down at her swollen stomach; her child wasn't due for another three weeks. "I'm not entirely sure I'll be able to go with you. But if it's at all possible, I'll take you there myself."

The more Morgana thought about it, the more feasible it sounded. Besides, she thought, it would be good for her to get away from here for a while. Decisions would have to be made and she needed time and a haven to think clearly.

Cammy's dark eyes flared with hope. "Oh, if only it could be so . . ." She pressed a trembling hand to her lips.

"Of course it will," Morgana tried to assure her. She sighed deeply. "I can't say I approve of what you have done . . ." Her voice trailed off. My God! Morgana thought to herself, suddenly ashamed of her words. Who was she to talk? She had given herself to the man she loved before they were married. What right did she have to condemn anyone else?

First one, then another fat drop of rain began to pelt her shoulders, and Morgana finally got to her feet. Cammy, she thought, had been right about one thing: Morgana felt that Cammy was the sister she never had. The thought was, in some ways, at once disturbing and demanding. Still and all, she felt a very real responsibility for this girl's welfare. Morgana knew she couldn't let Cammy down, whatever the cost to herself or her marriage. That last caused her mouth to twist in irony. What marriage? she wondered. When a man marries a woman under a threat it is no true marriage, it is a desecration of vows.

Putting an arm about Cammy, Morgana spoke briskly as they walked back into the bedroom. "Now, don't you worry. Everything will turn out all right."

Morgana felt certain of her words. But Morgana hadn't lived in the South long enough to realize just how improbable her statement was.

That night, Morgana lay on her rumpled bed, tossing and turning for more than an hour. The rain had cooled the air a bit, but had increased the humidity, adding to her discomfort.

At one point Bella got up from her pallet. Reaching for the palmetto fan, she began to wave it over Morgana. Morgana motioned the slave away.

"Just because I'm restless is no reason for you to spend a sleepless night," she protested, insisting that Bella return to her pallet.

After that, Morgana made the attempt to lie still, her thoughts on Cammy. Running away and getting married was one thing. But what, she wondered worriedly, would the two young people do afterward? Could Jude earn a living? Could he support a wife and child? Morgana took some comfort in the fact that she could give them some of the money her father had left her. But what would they do when it was gone? Perhaps by then, she thought, Nathaniel would relent and allow them to return home.

Hearing the sound of a door open and close in the hall, Morgana raised her head, listening. She figured it was well after midnight; time and more for the whole household to have settled down.

She put her head back on the pillow and compressed her lips tightly, certain that it was Griffin's door that had issued the noise. And there was only one reason for someone to be entering his room at this time of night. It must have been Serena.

Even though it was quiet now, Morgana buried her head deeper into the pillow, imagining it was possible for her to hear the sounds of lovemaking from across the hall.

Morgana's moan of despair was muffled in the downy softness. How did Griffin make love to that . . . wench? Was it an expression of love or sex? Was it a hurried act to relieve his need or did he enjoy it? Did he spend endless minutes caressing her? Morgana couldn't erase the imagined pictures from her mind no matter how she tried. Visions tormented her, goading her still further toward wakefulness; Griffin's strong muscular arms about the satiny smooth, honey colored skin; his mouth pressed upon rose-tinted lips. . . .

"Oh, God," she murmured, suppressing a sob of longing.

At the foot of the bed, Bella's head again appeared as she sat up, peering anxiously through the dimness at her mistress. She waited a full minute, but Morgana remained quiet. Presently, Bella lay down again, falling asleep almost immediately.

But Morgana lay there, wide awake, listening to the pattering of the rain that continued almost until it was light. Not until she heard Griffin's door open and close again did she fall into a restless, troubled sleep. She dreamed of Griffin, dreamed that she continually reached for him only to have him laughingly elude her outstretched arms.

At last the morning dawned, clear and fresh and sparkling. Morgana awoke feeling as tired as if she had not slept at all.

Bella regarded her with a worried frown, noting the dark smudges of weariness beneath Morgana's eyes. "You jest stay in bed, Miz Morgana," she urged. "Brings yore breakfast up heah."

Before Morgana could protest, Bella was gone. She sank back against the pillows, and before Bella had returned, fell into a light and dreamless sleep.

She awoke some time later feeling much better and ate heartily of the bacon and eggs Bella put before her.

After having eaten and dressed, Morgana took a stroll in the direction of the stables, relieved to find Jude alone at his chores.

When he saw her, his blue eyes turned suddenly wary. Even so, Morgana had to admit, now that she studied him with care, he was a very handsome young man. He possessed features that were almost Caucasian — his lips perhaps a trifle full, his nostrils only slightly flared. His black hair, while tightly curled, wasn't kinky. If it wasn't for his coppery gold skin . . . Yes, she decided in that instant, she could understand Cammy's attraction, if not her love.

"Miz Morgana," he murmured respectfully as she neared. "Kin I do sumpin fer you?"

She smiled slightly, although there was little humor in the expression. "I was told that you could speak English as well as I can," she commented dryly.

His eyes grew round and fearful and he took a step back from her.

"I mean you no harm," she exclaimed quickly, seeing his reaction. "I . . . just wanted to be certain." She looked about to assure herself that no one was around. "Cammy told me everything last night," she said, dropping her voice to the merest whisper.

Jude studied the ground for a moment, then met her eye. "And what are you going to do?"

"Help you both, if I can," she responded quietly. Even though prepared, Morgana felt a slight shock at the difference in his voice.

With her words, Jude seemed to relax, although his attitude remained cautious.

"Do you love Cammy as much as she loves you?" Morgana asked then.

Gravely, he nodded his head. And the beginnings of new hope surged through him. Jude had no misgivings about using white people when the opportunity presented itself. "I'm so glad you understand," he murmured, striving for sincerity and hiding his jubilation. With both Cammy and Morgana helping him, freedom was assured. The thought was intoxicating.

"Do you have money?" Morgana asked him.

"Some," he admitted. "About three hundred dollars."

She raised a surprised brow.

"I don't spend my money on foolishness," he supplied quickly, sounding a bit pontifical. "Whatever I make, I save."

She nodded once, satisfied. "It will not, of course, be enough. But I have some money of my own. I'll be glad to give it to you and Cammy."

He looked grateful. "Will we be going North?" Jude asked. At her nod of affirmation, he was sorely tempted to enlist her aid in leaving immediately. Wisely, he checked himself. "Cammy said you would know what to do," he whispered. "I thank God for your help. . . ."

When Morgana left Jude, she was completely certain that she was doing the right thing. It was so obvious, she thought, that the two young people were in love. There was no one else who would help them, she realized. In spite of the ensuing repercussions — and Morgana did not fool herself into thinking that there would be none — she knew that she would have to be the one.

Returning to her room, Morgana sat down at her writing table and carefully penned a letter to her Aunt Sarah. Then she gave it to Adam, the slave who made the trip into Charleston twice a week to pick up mail and newspapers. She could make no further plans until she received a reply. Morgana hoped it would arrive quickly, for all their sakes.

Chapter 12

With few exceptions, notably coffee and tea, salt and flour, shrimp and beef, most of the food consumed at Albemarle was grown right on the premises. The land abounded with game, the river with fish, the soil generous with its constant supply of vegetables, rice, sweet potatoes, and sugar cane.

It was not so unusual, therefore, that the kitchen was large and well stocked. When Nathaniel had first built Albemarle, he had taken great care in the selection of a suitable site. The pantry, which was an addition to the kitchen itself, had been constructed directly over an underground spring, with the result that, even in the hottest weather, the room, having two-foot-thick walls, remained cool.

There was even a wood burning stove, but Minda preferred the brick hearth with its roomy bake oven on one side for creating most of her culinary achievements. The kitchen was her domain. Since the death of Anne Kynes, Minda had ruled supreme. She'd had a few misgivings when she first learned that Masta Griffin was planning to take a wife, but Miz Morgana, like Miss Cammy, was content to leave things under Minda's capable jurisdiction.

Mostly she worked alone, but in the late afternoon Zoe came in to help with supper. Occasionally, Serena would appear. But, Minda often thought grumpily, that yellow gal was no more than a hothouse flower. Couldn't boil water if her life depended on it. In truth, the only reason Serena even came into the kitchen was to give her the semblance of a task. The girl really had only one function to perform, and being a scullery maid wasn't it. She was here for the sole purpose of giving pleasure to her master whenever he chose to summon her to his room. He never did that directly, of course, he always left word with Thomas when he desired her company.

On this bright and sunny Saturday afternoon, Serena was nowhere in sight. Minda was happy for that state of affairs because the girl had a tendency to chatter in an endless fashion while accomplishing absolutely nothing.

Absorbed in her chore, Minda's large brown hands were kneading dough with a fierce determination. Now and then she glanced toward the young black woman seated at the well scrubbed kitchen table, peeling potatoes in a lackadaisical manner.

"Doan got all day, Zoe," Minda muttered with a show of irritation that wrinkled her normally smooth brow. "You shoah bin draggin' yore butt aroun' lately." Straightening, she wiped her hands on her apron and scowled. "You knocked up or sumpin?"

Zoe's glance at Minda was sullen. "Ain' knocked up," she mumbled, the irascible expression on her face destroying what prettiness she possessed.

"Well, you lookin' peaked enuf to be," Minda commented sarcastically as she put the dough into the pan. Walking to the open back door, she stuck her head outside. "Suky!" she called out with lusty enthusiasm. "Suky! Git yore black ass to movin'."

The young boy was supposed to be cutting and stacking firewood, but the day was too warm, so he had been merely sitting beneath a tree, dozing. At his mother's call, he reluctantly got to his feet and ambled slowly in her direction.

As he passed her, Minda's brown hand shot out and delivered a sharp slap to the kinky head of her youngest son.

"Ashes up to de ceiling an' you sittin' lak you wuz roy'lty or sumpin," she scolded the boy, who only grinned at her.

With a semblance of diligence, the lad began to rake the hearth clear of ashes.

Minda watched him a moment, then moved back to the table, her slippers flapping on the wooden floor with each step she took. With a heavy sigh, she sat down, fanning herself with her apron. "Lawd, it gits hotter each year," she commented to no one in particular. Then she peered sharply at Zoe, who had ceased working altogether and was just staring out of the window. "You shoah you ain' knocked up?" she demanded, her eyes narrowing.

Her attention captured, Zoe made a face, but didn't bother to answer the question again. "Be a miracle iffen I wuz," she declared in an acid voice. "That worthless nigger son of yourn ain' good fer nothin'. Thinks he be too fine fer me."

"What you talkin' about, gal?" Minda demanded sharply, eyes flashing beneath her broad forehead. Her regal bosom heaved with indignation. She was outraged that anyone would speak disparagingly of her eldest son. "Jude's de finest buck you'll ever see. Thank de Lawd Jesus you got him. Cain't do no better."

"Dat so? Humph." Zoe's slim shoulders jerked with her agitation. "Ain' no man a'tall, dat one." She opened her mouth to say more, then thought better of it. Besides, she knew what she was going to do and Minda wasn't going to stop her. She picked up the knife again and savagely attacked the potatoes.

Minda watched her suspiciously for a moment, but, as always, the preparation of food claimed her first attention. Supper was due in just over an hour and Minda wasn't about to ruin it because this black gal was acting strangely.

Getting to her feet, she crossed the room to the oven, carefully removing a ham that was glistening with molasses and cloves. She regarded it with a critical eye for a moment, then, satisfied, put it on the table.

211

Zoe was crazy anyway, Minda decided as she sliced the moist pink meat. It was no wonder her Jude didn't pay her no mind. It was too bad that Masta Nathaniel had insisted that Jude take Zoe for a wench, she thought to herself. He was too good for the likes of her.

Suky had completed his simple chore and Minda now gave him a sugar cookie, prodding him out the door again with firm instructions to refill the wood bin before supper. Then, walking to the cupboard, she reached for the tin can that held the brown sugar. Strewing a generous portion of the sweet stuff into the pan drippings, she commenced to stir it vigorously with a wooden spoon.

Minda was troubled about her oldest son, but that wasn't anything new. Jude had been different from the day he had been born. She faced that fact with a certain amount of pride, but was wise enough to realize that a slave who was different could arouse more than admiration from his masters. And as fond as Masta Nathaniel was of her boy, Minda knew with a certainty that he wouldn't take kindly to what had been going on right under his nose for years now.

When Jude and Cammy had been children, Minda hadn't minded so much. It wasn't that unusual for children — black and white — to play together, especially when the family was in residence on the plantation. The fact of the matter was that there were no other children, except black, to play with, and so everyone viewed the association with a tolerant eye.

But while, from Minda's viewpoint, Miss Cammy was still little more than her baby, Jude had long since left his childhood behind. The situation was now fraught with danger — for Jude.

The only reason they had been able to get away with it for so long, Minda reflected, adding a bit of flour to the gravy, was that there had been no white mistress to take charge of Albemarle. Men had their own concerns, and the fields and crops were what occupied most of their waking hours. Minda had tried, even in the beginning, to discourage the association of Jude and Cammy. Unfortunately, trying to outwit her had become almost a game to the two children. Nor had Minda ever dared to ask Masta Nathaniel to intervene. By that time, young Masta Griffin had been packed off to England and there was, in effect, no one to gainsay the wishes of Miss Cammy.

She had tried to talk some sense into Jude, pleading with him to cease his dangerous pastime. He wouldn't listen. But then, Minda was forced to admit, he couldn't very well refuse his young mistress, either. Although what her son would do with his book learning escaped her. It was all, really, a waste of time.

As Minda moved about her kitchen, her mind on her own worrisome thoughts, Zoe surreptitiously watched the front yard, knowing full well when Griffin returned from his afternoon rounds. When she was certain that Minda was otherwise occupied, Zoe slipped outside, and by the time Griffin reached the front steps, she was waiting for him.

"Masta, suh," she said to him in her most deferential tone of voice. "Kin I talk wit you?"

Griffin looked down at the slight figure, taking a moment to place the name with the face. He registered surprise. "Zoe! What the hell are you doing here? Aren't you supposed to be in the kitchen?"

"Yassah." Zoe seemed a bit breathless, and, in point of fact, she had never before addressed her master on a personal basis. She was more than a bit frightened, but her anger at Jude had climbed to monumental proportions, making her careless of any consequences that might befall her.

Griffin displayed exasperation. He was hot and tired, and wanted a cool drink before he ate. "Dammit, gal. Speak your piece or get back into the kitchen where you belong."

Zoe swallowed nervously, shifting her weight from foot to foot. "Please, suh. Gots to talk wit you. It's 'portent dat you knows. . . ."

"Know what?" He glared, then his expression suddenly softened. "You knocked up, is that it?" His grandfather, he thought, would be pleased. It had been almost a year now. They were both beginning to think that Zoe might be barren, or that Jude had no sap in him. "You'll get a silver dollar if it's a boy," he assured her, smiling. He patted her shoulder.

Lawd Jesus, Zoe thought in growing exasperation. Why did everyone just look at her and pronounce her knocked up? "Ain' dat, suh," she said at last. Taking a deep breath, she continued in a resolute manner. "Wants to talk wit you in private . . ." She pressed her full lips together, giving the appearance of obstinacy.

The frown returned.

"It's 'bout my Jude, suh," she went on before he could protest. "He . . ." She paused and glanced about them. There was no one within earshot that she could see, but she knew very well that didn't mean a damn thing. If someone saw her talking to Masta Griffin, they'd make every effort to learn what was going on.

"What about Jude?" Griffin plucked a handkerchief from his pocket and, removing his hat, wiped the back of his neck. Damn all niggers, he was thinking. A man needed the patience of a saint when dealing with them.

"Masta, suh," Zoe entreated in a stronger voice, close to tears of frustration. "Shouldn't be talkin' 'bout it heah, in de open."

Griffin issued a long, drawn out sigh. "Christ," he muttered. "Come inside. At least I can have a drink."

Obediently, Zoe followed him, her eyes avid as she took in the spacious and opulent surroundings. It wasn't often that she got past the kitchen. Once, when there had been guests, she had made it into the dining room. But when she had clumsily spilled a tureen of soup, Minda had banished her forever from anything but the most menial of chores.

At last Griffin paused, looking into the study. Seeing that it was empty, he beckoned to her. "In here. And, by God, Zoe, it had better be important or I'll see to it personally that you can't sit down for a week."

With a deep sigh, Griffin settled wearily in a chair and flung his hat on the desk. Seeing Thomas standing in the doorway, he ordered him to fetch a bourbon and branch water.

After the door had closed, Griffin viewed Zoe again. Impatience furrowed his brow. "Now, get on with it. You've wasted enough of my time."

The girl plucked at her cotton shift with nervous fingers. "Masta Griffin, suh. Jude's got hisself a . . . another gal . . ." She faltered, biting her lip.

Muttering an oath, Griffin passed a hand across his eyes. He hated to involve himself in his people's squabbles. "Well, just what the hell do you want me to do about it?" he demanded at last. "You said it was important!" He glared at her. "Damn your black hide, you need your ass warmed by the paddle."

Zoe's large dark eyes glistened with frustrated tears. If only he'd let her tell him in her own way. She was about to speak again, but at the sound of a discreet tap on the door and Griffin's booming voice as he shouted at Thomas to enter, she fell silent.

The butler deftly removed the glass from the small silver tray he was carrying and set it in front of Griffin. It was a tribute to his many years of service that Thomas did not look in Zoe's direction. But his heart thumped painfully as he left the room, closing the door again, because he, as did just about every house servant at Albemarle, knew all about Jude and Cammy, knew that she had been teaching him to read and write. That was not a secret that could be kept. If Zoe was about to tell Masta Griffin that, then Jude was in serious danger of being sold. That, he knew, would break Minda's heart.

In the hall, Thomas hovered close enough to hear voices in the study. Taking a handkerchief from his breast pocket, he carefully began to dust an already dust free table.

Inside, Griffin took a long, appreciative sip of his drink, then regarded the black woman, indicating for her to continue.

"It's de woman, suh," Zoe said, desperate now. "She's . . . she's a white lady." Her voice fell to the merest whisper and her trembling began, increasing until her frail body began to shake as if she had the fever.

Griffin just stared at her. His face paled and flushed as his emotions rose and ebbed with the force of his outrage. For one small moment in time, he credited Zoe with lying. The thought was, however, short-lived. No matter how riled, she would never dare lie about anything like that.

His anger settled into a cold knot in the pit of his stomach. "You've just killed Jude," he noted in a quiet, flat voice. "You know that?"

"Yassuh." Zoe looked down at the floor, scuffing her bare toe in the softness of the carpet.

"You hate him that much?"

She swallowed again, visibly, wiping her mouth with the back of her hand.

"Answer me!"

"Yassuh, masta, suh."

"Then why am I to believe that you're telling me the truth?"

She looked up at him. "Doan lie, suh," she protested, shaking her head. "Saw it wit my own eyes." Her voice ended on a dry sob. "Dey wuz in de grove, de two of 'em . . ." She couldn't keep her hands still, and now clasped them behind her back. Although she knew that Griffin was staring at her, she couldn't bring herself to look at him and kept her head lowered.

Griffin's eyes had narrowed dangerously. "And what, exactly, were they doing in the grove?" His voice was deceptively soft.

"Dey wuz . . ." She looked up now, feeling helpless. He continued to stare at her, waiting for her answer. His hand, still clutching his drink, had tightened to the point where the glass was in jeopardy of being broken.

"Answer me." The voice was still soft.

"Dey wuz . . . pleasurin' wit each other. . . ."

For a moment, Griffin thought of that day when he and Morgana had first made love. Had they been spied upon, too?

"You little bitch," Griffin growled in a menacing voice. Getting to his feet, he approached her until he was standing right in front of her. Then he slapped her, hard. She flinched, reeled, but stood her ground.

"Whips me iffen you likes, suh, but it doan change de truf," she insisted stubbornly, again staring at the floor.

Griffin felt he could have killed her then. With great effort, he stayed his hand. He turned away from the black woman, trying to collect his turbulent thoughts.

Jude hadn't left Albemarle since last May, when they had all gone to Charleston. Zoe, of course, had remained here, as she always did. That was four months ago. Obviously, Zoe wouldn't be coming to him now unless it was someone right here, in the house. And there were only two white women. Cammy, he dismissed immediately, without even giving it conscious thought. That left. . . .

"Morgana." He wasn't even aware that he had spoken the name aloud. This was her way of getting even with him, he thought, enraged. A chilling thought struck — she was pregnant. By Christ, he'd kill her.

Zoe was watching him, by now almost paralyzed with fear. Even her trembling had ceased. "Naw, suh," she managed with great effort. "Ain' Miz Morgana. Ain' yore wife. She's a fine lady, Miz Morgana is. . . ."

Griffin spun around to look at her, his face really dreadful to see. For the moment Zoe closed her eyes to blot out the sight.

Griffin grabbed her by the shoulders and shook her so violently that the breath left her lungs and she gasped.

"Do you know what it feels like to have a hundred lashes?" he demanded in a loud voice. "Do you? You little black bitch!" His voice rose to a shout. "If it wasn't my wife, then who?"

"Miss Cammy," Zoe whispered, really terrified now. Masta Griffin looked like a madman, his eyes wild and staring, his nose pinched and white. His mouth was compressed so tightly that the nerves in his jaw pounded in protest against the enforced restriction.

Griffin stopped shaking her and stared for a moment suspended in eternity. Then his fist shot out, landing on her jaw. Zoe fell, feeling the blood filling her mouth where her teeth had loosened. In a black rage, control gone, Griffin kicked at her helpless form.

"Griffin!"

Nathaniel's voice cut through his rage and Griffin turned to stare at his grandfather.

"What the devil's going on here? Can't a man get a quiet drink before supper?" Nathaniel viewed Zoe's crumpled form and frowned. "What's that black wench doing in the house? She causin' trouble?"

The comment was so ludicrous that Griffin almost laughed aloud. He opened his mouth to speak, but could find no words to express the appalling charge made by Zoe against his sister.

He just stood there, hands clenched at his sides, gripped with a feeling of mute helplessness.

"Griff, boy. You feeling sick? What's the matter with you?" Nathaniel glared at Zoe. "Get up, gal. I want to know what's going on, and I want to know it now!"

"Jus' tol' Masta Griffin de truf, suh," Zoe mumbled, getting to her feet. Her jaw was beginning to swell and she touched it tentatively, wincing as she did so.

"What's this wench talkin' about, Griff?" Nathaniel looked toward his grandson, but Griffin had sat down at the desk, his head in his hands, and he made no reply.

Nathaniel again viewed Zoe, his expression commanding an answer.

The black woman hesitated as long as she dared. Then, in a halting voice, she repeated her tale.

Nathaniel looked like he was about to be ill. "Get out," he yelled in a strangled voice when she was through. "And if you so much as breathe a word of this, I'll have your tongue cut out. Then I'll feed the rest of your black carcass to the hogs!"

Zoe stumbled from the room, not looking at either man. She wasn't sorry for what she had done. Jude deserved whatever was coming to him. In spite of Masta Griffin's words, Jude wouldn't be killed; she knew that. He was the pride and joy of Masta Nathaniel, who showed him off every chance he got. But Jude would get a whippin' the likes of which he'd never had before. And serves him right, Zoe thought in grim satisfaction. As for Miss Cammy — nothing would happen to her, Zoe reasoned. She was a white lady.

When the door closed, Nathaniel turned to view Griffin, who hadn't moved since the last time he'd looked at him. "You think that wench was tellin' the truth?" he murmured. He came closer to the desk.

Griffin's answer was a deep, despairing sigh. He had no

doubt that Zoe was telling the truth. There was, in fact, no reason for Zoe to lie. If Griffin had been informed that his sister had committed murder, he could have more easily accepted that deed than the one that had taken place.

"Goddamn women," Nathaniel muttered angrily. He slapped the desk with the palm of his hand. "Black or white, they don't have the sense God gave a turnip." He walked around the desk and put a hand on Griffin's broad shoulder. "We'll have to send her away, Griff," he said quietly. "Cammy can't stay here now. If that black wench knows, then they all know." He gave a sharp sound of disgust. "Their blasted grapevine will have the news all over the state." When he received no response, Nathaniel frowned. "Griffin! Snap out of it, boy. You know as well as I this is not the first time something like this has happened. The thing's over and done with. We've got to think about your sister now. . . ."

There was a soft knock at the door and Nathaniel cast angry eyes in that direction. "What is it?" he called out irritably. His anger turned to surprise as he saw Morgana enter the room.

The "grapevine" Nathaniel had spoken about was already in action: Thomas to Minda and to Meg — who had been in the kitchen, sipping a companionable cup of coffee with the cook. Minda had collapsed, moaning in fright. Meg had raced upstairs to her mistress, who had fled to Morgana in hysterical tears.

"We're busy right now," Nathaniel began awkwardly, attempting a smile.

"I know why Zoe was here," Morgana informed him quietly, closing the door again. Her face was grave and solemn as she viewed the old man. She had already dressed for supper when Cammy had burst into her room, and was clad in a pale green silk dress over a wide crinolined skirt that almost concealed her advanced pregnancy.

"Jesus," Nathaniel muttered with her comment. He ran a trembling hand through his silver hair. "I sometimes wonder who owns who," he sighed, sinking heavily into a nearby chair. "Where the hell is my granddaughter?" He viewed Morgana, who bit her lower lip.

"She's upstairs. She's . . . very upset."

"Upset!" Nathaniel was visibly incredulous. "She wreaks havoc on us all — and she's upset!" He got up again, too agitated to remain still for any length of time. "Well, she won't be much longer," he declared with firmness. "We're going to send her away. England, maybe." Pausing, he glanced at Griffin, who still appeared to be in a state of shock. He hadn't even looked up when Morgana came into the room.

"I . . . don't think that would be wise," Morgana said in the same quiet tone. Mentally, she tried to prepare herself for the furious anger she knew her words would generate. "At least, not now."

Griffin looked up then, his dark eyes hot and anguished. "Oh, she'll go," he said suddenly, harshly, before Morgana could respond. He gave his wife a hard look. "You tell that — my sister, to have her bags packed and be ready to leave in the morning." He finally stood up and his face was implacable as he continued. "And between now and then," he advised in a tight voice, "I don't want to set eyes on her!"

"Now, Griff . . ." Nathaniel began placatingly. The young man turned a fierce gaze in his direction.

"I don't want to see her!" Griffin shot back. "She has thrown away whatever future she may have had." And, he thought in silent despair, a part of his own dream as well. No white man would marry Cammy now, certainly not Clinton Barrows. The young man's father would never permit it. Clinton himself would probably balk at such a union, Griffin thought, further distressed.

Morgana was about to angrily remind him of Serena, but then thought better of it. Instead, she took a deep breath. "Cammy will be unable to travel for at least four months."

The words hung there as the two men turned to look at her. Their expressions were blank, uncomprehending at first.

"You mean . . ." Nathaniel couldn't quite speak the words. His color had turned ashen and his lips trembled visibly.

Morgana's nod was solemn. "She is to have a child."

"Oh, my God," Nathaniel groaned, sitting down again. His shoulders slumped and he suddenly looked every one of his seventy-one years. "Hate to lose that Jude," he mumbled to no one in particular. He covered his eyes with a hand and seemed to sink further into the chair.

"That nigger won't live out the day," Griffin stated grimly. He headed for the door with long strides, brushing past Morgana as if he didn't even see her.

Morgana's eyes widened. "Wait! No . . ." But Griffin was gone and so she turned to Nathaniel. A heavy feeling of apprehension settled in the pit of her stomach and she fought off a dizzying sense of nausea. With some effort she gained control of herself once more. Going to Nathaniel's side, she knelt before him, taking his cold hand in her own warm one. "What is Griffin going to do?" she asked fearfully.

Lowering his other hand to the armrest, Nathaniel's eyes were glazed as he viewed his grandson's wife. He appeared a bit surprised that she was still there.

"Nathaniel!" Morgana squeezed his hand in an effort to gain his attention. "What is Griffin going to do?"

"Do?" the old man repeated inanely. "No buck can live after rapin' a white woman." He turned away and sighed.

In a sharp movement, Morgana shook her head. "No, no. It wasn't like that at all," she protested. She tightened her grip on his hand. "They're in love. . . ."

Nathaniel blinked, his pale skin reddening with her words. "Don't you be talkin' like that, young woman!"

"But it's true," she insisted, desperate for him to understand. "They've loved each other for years." He made no answer, so she continued. "When Cammy leaves, you must allow Jude to go with her," she urged strongly. "They can go North, or even, as you said, to England. . . ."

In a curt gesture, Nathaniel withdrew his hand and glared at her. "You think I'd give my granddaughter to a black buck?" he exclaimed, incredulous at the thought. "I'd see her dead first."

"You are a hypocrite, Nathaniel!" she shouted at him, getting to her feet. Tears of anger threatened, but Morgana kept herself under control.

Startled, he turned to look at her.

"What about Serena?" she demanded, her mouth tightening. "What about your grandson and that . . . black wench! I've never heard you speak out against that." She waited for his answer, but Nathaniel merely looked embarrassed and made no response. Softening her voice, Morgana said, "Cammy is not the first woman to have a child out of wedlock. . . ."

Nathaniel was now regarding her with pity, as though she were a child who simply did not understand. "I wish it were as simple as that," he murmured at last, looking away.

"There is nothing difficult about it," she declared firmly. "At least Cammy acted out of love."

Nathaniel moved restlessly in his chair, refusing to meet Morgana's level, accusing eyes. Then, in a quieter voice, he said, "Love has nothing to do with it, Morgana. It has to do with the children." He looked at her again. "If Serena ever has a child," he explained carefully, "it will be black — and a slave." He paused for a moment, then added, "In the eyes of the law and society, the child — my granddaughter will have —

will also be black. And a slave."

Appalled, Morgana could only stare at him. "Why can't you let them go away?" she cried, desperate now. "What you are about to do will destroy Cammy. Let them alone," she begged. "Let them be married, if that's what they both want —" She broke off at his suddenly fierce look.

Nathaniel got to his feet, his face an even darker shade of red than before. At his temple, a pulse throbbed with his agitation. "No granddaughter of mine is going to go before a judge and swear she's got colored blood!" At the sight of Morgana's surprised face, he nodded curtly. "That's how it's done, girl. She'd have to claim *she's* a nigger."

Nathaniel turned then, and with slow steps left the study without a backward glance.

Chapter 13

For a long moment after Nathaniel left the study, Morgana just stood there, feeling drained. She had expected both Griffin and Nathaniel to be angry and upset with what had taken place. But she had not expected the cold fury Griffin had displayed nor the dark despair evidenced by Nathaniel.

Quickly then, heedless of her condition, Morgana ran into the hall. She glanced once at the stairs, torn between wanting to go to Cammy and wanting to try to prevent Griffin from killing Jude.

The immediacy of one was more important than the other, she decided, heading for the front door.

On the verandah, she halted abruptly, puzzled by the activity she was seeing. Only a few feet from where she was standing, Nathaniel stood quietly, his face expressionless as he viewed the preparations taking place. The sun was low now, the front yard ribboned with gold and lilac.

It seemed to Morgana that every slave on the plantation was suddenly gathered in the yard. Even the children were there, eyes wide with fear as they viewed the unusual happenings. Of Jude, though, there was no sign. Perhaps, she thought with a surge of relief, he had managed to escape.

But a glance at her husband dashed that hope. Griffin was watching everything, his demeanor, to all outward appearances, calm, if grim. He stood with his feet planted wide, holding his riding crop with both hands. He issued no instructions, yet the slaves were working in silence beneath his black scrutiny, apparently knowing what to do.

Wood and brush had been gathered and laid out in a sort of rectangle, about seven feet long and about two feet wide. It was just now being ignited. It burned smoky at first, but then, as the wood caught and held, the low blaze burned clear.

Dear God, Morgana thought, her heart beating wildly. Were they going to burn him? She put a hand to her throat at the thought. But, she tried to console herself, it wasn't a very large fire. . . .

Then, at each end of the rectangle of fire, Morgana saw a slave place a stout oaken pillar, the top of which had been carved into a U-shape.

A high thin wail broke the unnatural stillness as Minda suddenly rushed forward, skirts billowing with her haste. Her eyes were round, filled with a terror that made her motions stiff and clumsy. She ran past Griffin, who never even turned his head, and fell at Nathaniel's feet.

"Doan let him kill Jude," she cried out piteously. She clutched at his boots with hands that were shaking. "Please, Masta Nathaniel, doan kill my boy . . ." Tears streamed down her black cheeks and her great bosom heaved with the force of her anguish.

Nathaniel looked down at her. For the first time since this business had started, Morgana thought she detected a look of pity on his face. But it was gone in an instant.

"Get back to the kitchen, Minda," Nathaniel said, not unkindly. Then, hands behind his back, he raised his head and stared over her, refusing her any more of his attention.

For a while, Minda didn't move. She crouched, sobbing as if her heart would break. At last, Suky approached his mother, his step hesitant, his large dark eyes looking fearfully at Nathaniel, who paid him no mind.

Grabbing Minda's sleeve, the ten-year-old boy urged her to move, terrified that whatever punishment had fallen to his brother would somehow be visited upon his mother as well.

For a time, Minda resisted, or perhaps she was just too weak in her grief to move. But at last, in a quick movement that seemed almost desperate, she clasped her young son to her breast. Getting up, she lifted the boy off his feet, holding him so tightly that his small body squirmed in discomfort.

Then, still sobbing, Minda stumbled away in the direction of the kitchen.

The group of Negroes parted now and Morgana finally saw Jude. He was held fast by two slaves on either side of him, his face fierce, eyes bright, although with anger or fear, she wasn't able to tell.

Behind the trio came Joe, who was dragging the trunk of a tree in his wake. It was freshly cut, about seven feet long, and in some confusion, Morgana watched as a few of the slaves began to douse the wood with water.

Finally, under the direction of a grim-faced Carlie Dobbs, who had brought up the strange procession, Jude was stripped of his clothing and lashed to the tree trunk, stomach down.

After the leather thongs were tightened, the huge log was then raised to the oaken pillar, each end resting snugly within the U-shaped tops.

As the full horror of what she was seeing washed over her, Morgana gave a shrill cry and started forward, only to be caught by Nathaniel, who gripped her arms with surprising strength.

"Get back into the house," he ordered in an angry voice, unaware that she had been standing there.

"You can't!" Morgana cried out. Her voice sounded thin and unrecognizable even to her own ears. "It will take hours for him to die . . ." Her breath was coming in short, rapid pants, as if she couldn't get enough air into her lungs. Her pulse throbbed and drummed in her ears and a cold dread weakened her limbs.

"He'll be roasted like the piece of worthless meat he is," Nathaniel said to her in a gruff tone. "Now, go back inside.

You can't stop anything." Regarding her, his face softened a bit at the sight of her wide and horrified eyes. "Go to Cammy," he whispered, bending forward slightly.

Cammy! Oh, dear God, Morgana thought, breaking away. Her bedroom was directly over the front yard. As she raced up the stairs, Morgana reflected bitterly that that was probably the reason why Griffin had chosen the site.

Pausing before Cammy's door, Morgana took a moment to catch her breath, both hands on her swollen stomach. She listened, but heard nothing. And so she entered.

Relief flooded over Morgana when she saw Cammy on the bed. Clad only in a camisole and pantalettes, she was lying on her back, staring up at the ceiling. Morgana had expected to find the girl in hysterics, but she appeared almost calm. Too calm, perhaps.

"Cammy," Morgana murmured softly, coming forward. She felt overwhelmed with pity.

"Do you know why they saturate the tree trunk with water?" Cammy asked tonelessly, not turning toward her.

Startled by the question, Morgana sank down on the bed. She stroked the girl's hair. "Don't think about it. Please. . . ."

Cammy turned slightly to look at her. "It's so the wood doesn't catch fire and burn." She spoke the words as if teaching a young child a lesson.

"Oh, please, Cammy," Morgana cried out, fighting her tears. She took the girl's hand in her own. It felt like ice and she began to chafe it. "Let us get out of here," she begged, fearing the girl was in shock. "Let's go for a walk. Or we can get the carriage — I'll tell Ben to drive us into Charleston. . . ."

But made no move. She just lay there as though she hadn't heard a word Morgana said. Her face was so pale she looked like a fragile porcelain doll.

"No," she murmured at last. "I can't leave until it's over.

Jude will know that I'm here. He'll know that I'm with him to the end. Then I'll go." A note of raw bitterness crept into her voice and her small hands balled into fists. "I'll stay until my baby is born. Then I'll go and never come back. I hate them. I hate them both, Griffin and my grandfather. I hate them!"

Morgana was about to take the girl in her arms in an attempt to comfort her when the first anguished scream rent the September air. It was a horrifying sound, the long drawn-out howl of an animal in mortal distress.

Cammy froze, her slight body stiffening. She didn't even appear to be breathing. Only the pulse at her throat indicated life. Another scream followed as Jude cried out in agony.

Although Morgana tried to stop her, Cammy insisted on going out onto the piazza. The girl stumbled on legs that appeared wooden and unresponsive. Weakly, she leaned on the railing, her dark eyes riveted on the terrible scene being acted out below.

Coming to her side, Morgana looked down, unable to suppress her revulsion. Except for Jude's hysterical screams, there was a great and awful silence in the yard. Morgana saw Zoe standing to the side. Confronted with the fruits of her treachery, the woman's face was gray and tormented.

Bella and Meg were there, too, holding onto each other in their fear. Even Serena was in the crowd, her delicate hands covering her face, shielding her eyes. Morgana began to understand why all the slaves were gathered. Obviously, they had all been commanded to attend.

A movement caught her eye. Unable to believe what she was witnessing, Morgana saw two of the slaves turn the tree trunk slightly.

My God, Morgana thought in horror, catching her breath, they're roasting him like a pig! Revulsion left her, swamped in a wave of anger that grew to awesome proportions.

She glanced down at Cammy, who had sunk to the floor in a crumpled heap, her hands gripping the iron bars of the railing. Her lovely face was ghastly in its paleness. She looked so small, so vulnerable, that Morgana's heart twisted in compassion.

Enough!

The thought presented itself, and Morgana acted. She knew she couldn't prevent Jude's death — but she damn well could prevent this senseless torture, she thought, enraged.

She gave little thought to what she did next. She acted on emotion alone, and that emotion was a pure, white-hot anger.

Leaving Cammy's room, Morgana went to her own, trying without much success to shut out the piercing, blood-curdling screams that rose and ebbed with chilling repetition. Flinging open dresser drawers with a furious carelessness, Morgana located her father's dueling pistols, making certain that they were loaded.

Then she went downstairs quickly, her hand at her side, one of the guns concealed in the folds of her skirt.

As she emerged outside, no one turned to look at her. It was completely dark now, the glow of the embers lighting in a grotesque manner the horror that was Jude. Nathaniel had moved from the verandah and now stood quietly at Griffin's side. All eyes were on the writhing, groaning form of Jude as he struggled futilely against the thongs that bound him so securely in place. He had passed the point of being able to scream.

Morgana saw that the wood and brush had burned down to glowing, red-hot coals, not as high, but hotter than actual flames. There was no hesitation in her, no questioning as to right or wrong.

Morgana came as close as she dared, close enough to feel

the shimmering curtain of heat that wavered in the still air, distorting images as one peered through it. Then, raising the gun, she pointed it directly at Jude's head.

When the shot rang out, there was no immediate reaction. Eyes blinked, viewed the spreading stain of blood that flowed from Jude's forehead, then, in an almost concerted movement, turned in her direction.

But no one moved.

Morgana's hand, still holding the gun, dropped to her side. Then she released her hold, allowing it to fall to the ground. She turned her furious gaze upon her husband — and met an anger that matched her own.

Slowly, Griffin began to walk toward her, his face a rigid mask of fury, the riding crop clenched in his hand as though it were a weapon.

Morgana stood where she was, facing them all, her expression daring them, challenging them to take exception to what she had done. And, although she didn't notice it, every black face was regarding her with a gratitude that bordered upon veneration, including Zoe's. Even Nathaniel's expression had fallen into a strange look of relief. Only Dobbs and Griffin appeared angry at what had taken place.

At last Griffin stopped before her. She raised her head slightly, so as to meet his smoldering eyes with her own cool gaze.

"You —" he choked, unable to get the words past his tightened throat. Twin spots of color appeared in his cheeks, testimony of the rage he was barely able to contain.

Morgana continued to look up at her husband, one part of her mind wondering if he were going to strike her, but feeling no fear at the prospect.

For an endless moment, the silence lengthened. Griffin was still staring at her. He seemed incapable of speech.

Suddenly, Morgana's eyes widened as she felt a sharp and searing pain. Unable to help herself, she gasped with the force of it. It began in her lower back, then quickly, with a vicious stab, it worked its way forward to her abdomen. She wrapped both arms around her stomach and gasped again, bending forward until her head almost touched Griffin's chest.

In a reflex motion, his hand shot out to steady her. Morgana moaned as the pain came again, stronger. Stupidly, Griffin just stood there.

With quick steps, Nathaniel came to Griffin's side. He took one look at Morgana, then exclaimed, "It's the baby! Get her upstairs, Griff. I'll send for Doc Foxworth."

Hesitating only a moment, Griffin dropped the riding crop. Reaching for Morgana, he carried her into the house and up the stairs to her room, where he laid her carefully on the bed.

He motioned to Bella, who had followed him and now stood uncertainly in the doorway. "Do something!" he cried out anxiously, aware that his hands were shaking.

Quickly, Bella moved forward and began to undress Morgana, pausing when her mistress groaned and turned on her side.

Feeling utterly helpless, Griffin backed from the room and closed the door.

When the contraction passed, Bella removed the rest of Morgana's clothing. Then, moving efficiently, she tore a sheet in half, tying one strip on either side of the bedpost. Knotting the ends firmly, she placed one in each of Morgana's hands.

"Now, you pull on dat," she crooned, wiping Morgana's glistening brow with the tip of her apron. "Pull hard — and you jest holler all you wants. . . ."

Bella kept up the meaningless, comforting chatter, praying for the doctor to arrive soon.

But it wasn't the doctor who delivered Morgana of her

daughter some four hours later — it was Auntie Flora, hurriedly summoned when it became apparent that the physician wasn't going to make it in time.

Morgana's recovery was slow. Although her labor had been brief, it had been violent, and when the doctor arrived almost an hour after the baby had been born, he found Morgana in a severely weakened condition, bleeding heavily and only half conscious.

After examining her, he packed her with linen gauze, showing Bella how to change it at intervals when it became saturated. Then he gave her a sleeping draught. For the next two days, the doctor stayed at Albemarle, until he could safely pronounce Morgana out of danger.

Tansy was summoned to the Great House to serve as a temporary wet nurse until Morgana was strong enough to take over that function for herself.

At times during those two days, Morgana thought she saw Griffin's anxious face hovering over her. But by the time she came fully to her senses, she was uncertain as to where the line between imagery and reality began and ended.

It was on the third day when Cammy came to visit her.

The girl appeared wan and drawn as she approached the bed. Clad only in a nightgown and cotton wrap, her hair was twisted into one long, thick braid. Morgana wondered if she'd had any sleep at all during the previous two nights. From the look of the dark and purple smudges beneath Cammy's eyes, she sincerely doubted it.

For a moment the two young women stared at each other. Then, with a wrenching sob, Cammy threw herself forward, embracing Morgana.

"Can you forgive me?" Morgana whispered to her sister-in-law.

Cammy raised her head and with tear-filled eyes, attempted a smile. "Forgive you?" She gripped Morgana's hand tightly. "I get down on my knees and thank you. You were the only one with courage enough to do what had to be done . . ." The sobs came again. For a time, Morgana held the girl until she calmed.

At last Cammy sat up, wiping her cheeks with the back of her hand. She gave a deep, shuddering breath.

"Cammy," Morgana said quietly. "You have your whole life ahead of you." She placed a hand on the girl's arm. "From this day forward, you must live for yourself and for your child. . . ."

Cammy gave a small, sad smile, accompanied by a slow nod. "I thank God for the baby," she said simply. "That, at least, cannot be taken from me." She held Morgana's eye a moment longer, then turned, looking toward Bella. "And where is my new niece?" she asked with an attempt at brightness.

Bella summoned Tansy from the sitting room. The girl came forward, holding the child in her arms.

Her face softening, Cammy reached for the infant. "Oh, she's so beautiful . . ." She glanced toward Morgana, who was unable to contain the smile of pride that curved her lips. "Have you decided what to name her?"

Morgana nodded. "Anne."

Cammy offered a small smile that never reached her eyes. "That will please my grandfather," she murmured. She bent her head, putting a cheek against the softness of the infant.

Watching her, Morgana was greatly relieved. Cammy would be all right, she told herself, refusing to believe otherwise. She was strong and she was young. In time, perhaps, she would forget. . . .

Later that day, Griffin entered her room. Tansy, who was breast feeding the baby, smiled up at him.

"Shoah is a fine li'l chile, Masta Griffin," she said enthusiastically as he looked down at his daughter. The baby was contentedly suckling, a tiny white hand against a full brown breast.

Tansy was quite happy with her new position, even if it was only temporary. She was eating better than she ever had. For the first time in her whole life, she was eating the same fare that was served to her masters. Of course, she had to feed Anne first, before she fed her own daughter, but so far this was not creating undue problems. At present, she was producing enough nourishment for both infants.

Griffin nodded, but didn't bother to answer her. Finally, he turned and walked slowly toward the bed, regarding Morgana as she rested against the softness of two downy pillows. Her shimmering blond hair was unbound and tumbled about her shoulders in appealing disarray. Her blue eyes were level as she looked at him.

"Are you feeling better today?" he asked in an almost formal manner.

"Yes," she replied, aware that her own response sounded just as stilted. "Although I will be glad to be up and out of this bed," she added, still watching him.

"The doctor said you must rest for at least ten days," he reminded her sternly.

She sighed, then gave a brief nod of acquiescence. "Griffin," she murmured, sitting up a bit straighter. "I know you are angry over what has happened, but —"

"This is not the time to discuss it," he said shortly, interrupting her.

"I don't see why not," she flared hotly, annoyed by his pompous attitude. "We can't ignore it . . ." She fell silent at the look of his angered eyes and compressed mouth. Then she leaned back against the pillows again, feeling exhausted by just the small effort she had expended. Perhaps he was right, she thought wearily, seeing him turn and leave the room. In any event, she didn't seem to have the strength to speak at length, much less argue at this time.

She had no intention of justifying her actions, anyway. Morgana couldn't prevent the unwanted picture of Jude's last agonizing moments that taunted her memory. She shuddered, wincing in pain as her muscles reacted against the sudden intrusion. Still, it was there; the coppery skin disfigured by horrible blisters, the black hair singed and smoldering. . . .

No! she thought with renewed determination. She had done the right thing, the only thing under the circumstances. Griffin wouldn't hesitate to kill a horse that was suffering in pain, yet he had committed that terrible act against another human being. Even now it amazed her.

Nor did he seem to feel that he had acted wrongly. In a very odd way, that was the only thing that kept her from judging Griffin too harshly. He actually thought that he had been performing a necessary function. Going over in her mind what Nathaniel had said to her, Morgana realized that he, too, felt the same way.

Morgana shifted her weight in bed, restless, wishing that she could relax, wishing that she could sleep. She felt empty and alone. Finally, with a cry of despair that she couldn't repress, she beckoned for Tansy to bring her baby to her.

The brown-skinned woman got up, came forward, and gently placed Anne in her arms. The child was now sleeping peacefully, a small fist against her pink lips.

Comforted by the warm little body against her own, Morgana at last slept. Tansy took the baby from her then. Bella tucked the light blankets closer around Morgana.

For a moment, both black women stood there looking down

at the sleeping form of their mistress. At last Bella shook her head slowly.

"Dem two peoples got deyselves a powerful anger 'tween 'em," she mused quietly. "Hopin' Miz Morgana doan git it in her haid to take her chile an' leave heah. Wouldn't want to be 'round Masta Griffin, nohow."

Tansy nodded solemnly at the observation. Like everyone else, she was still shaken by what had taken place earlier in the week. "Seems lak white folks got deyselves moah trouble what dey kin handle," she agreed, rocking Anne in her arms. "Wonder what Masta Griffin gonna do when Miss Cammy has her baby. . . ."

Bella rolled her eyes and raised both her hands. "Lawd, doan even want to be thinkin' o' dat," she declared. "Had us enuf trouble to las' dis heah gal fer a lifetime."

The two women moved to the sitting room. Tansy placed Anne in the cradle, then sat down.

"Thinkin' Miss Cammy really wantin' to marry up wit dat boy?" Tansy asked musingly after a while.

Bella shrugged. "Doan know. She wuz learnin' Jude his letters, dat's fer shoah. Ever'body knowed dat. But it doan do him no good now."

Tansy leaned forward, lowering her voice. "Dat Meg tellin' me dat Miss Cammy real upset by all whats happened. She jest cry all de time, Meg sez. Waitin' till her chile be borned, den she goin' away."

Bella shifted in her chair, giving her friend a sharp look. "Where at she goin'?"

"Doan rightly know. Prob'ly Nawth."

Bella snorted as she leaned back again. "How dat li'l gal gonna git herself Nawth? Cain't git herse'f to Charleston, lessen somebody he'ps her."

Tansy made a vague gesture, not responding, and for a time

the two women sat quietly.

"Seems lak it all dat Zoe's fault," Tansy muttered resentfully after some minutes went by.

"Humph. Dat gal hidin' in her cabin, she is. Doan dare go in de kitchen. Minda gonna carve her hide up, right pretty lak." It didn't strike Bella as odd that Minda blamed not her masters for the death of her son, but Zoe. "Wouldn't su'prise me none iffen dat gal gits herse'f sol'," Bella concluded with a firm and righteous nod of her head.

"An' serves her right," Tansy declared quickly. Then her light brown face fell into a thoughtful expression. "Gots to admit, though, dat Jude boy wuz a powerful handsome buck." Catching Bella's somewhat disapproving look, she hastened to add, "Nacherly, he not as handsome as my Adam. Jest means dat he wuz a pretty boy. Mebbe kin un'erstan' why Zoe done it."

Bella made a wry face and crossed her arms under her breast. "Yore Adam heahs you talkin' lak dat, gonna be de las' time you talkin' 'bout anythin'," she advised darkly.

Tansy looked sheepish, then broke into a wide grin.

Putting their hands across their faces to stifle the noise, both young women began to giggle.

Despite her early appearance, Anne was a sturdy child with rosy cheeks and a mop of fine, wispy black hair that covered her small, well shaped head.

When, after two weeks, it became apparent that Morgana wasn't producing enough milk for the child, Nathaniel hurried off to Charleston in search of a suitable wet nurse, returning a few days later with a sixteen-year-old girl named Celia, whose child had recently died. Morgana was immediately taken with the girl, who was a light-skinned Kru with a ready smile and amiable manner.

The sitting room was hastily converted into a nursery and, for a time, Bella was a bit put out by what she considered an invasion of her territory. But it soon became apparent that Celia, when she put her mind to it, could charm the birds out the trees, and it wasn't long before she and Bella were fast friends.

Another week went by before Morgana was well enough to get out of bed. Each day, Griffin visited his wife and his daughter, but Morgana had the distinct impression that he came more from a sense of duty than anything else. He seemed, to Morgana, to be a changed man. He was quiet, withdrawn, uncommunicative.

Griffin studiously avoided speaking to his sister, a situation that didn't seem to bother Cammy at all, for, as she told Morgana, she didn't have anything to say to her brother.

While Griffin refused to speak to Cammy, he was barely civil to Morgana, and not once did he refer to or even agree to discuss the incident with Jude.

Nathaniel urged patience. But Morgana was discovering that she was far from a patient woman. More than once she considered leaving Albemarle. However, her daughter and Cammy were powerful inducements for staying. In any event, the baby was too young to travel, and, of course, she couldn't possibly go without Celia, who was not, strictly speaking, her property, but belonged to Nathaniel.

As for Cammy, she would need all the help and support Morgana could give her when her time came. Nathaniel seemed to have softened in his attitude toward his granddaughter, although he showed no inclination of directly crossing Griffin, and any words of kindness or understanding came when his grandson was absent.

At the beginning of November, Cammy took to her room and refused to leave it, ignoring Morgana's pleas to get out of the house for at least an hour each day.

"You need your exercise," Morgana urged, distressed by the lethargy she was seeing. "You cannot lie about all day long like this. . . ."

But Cammy refused to listen. She seemed to have sunk back into the depression she had experienced just after Jude's death.

One day, during the latter part of November, Meg came to Morgana's room in tears.

"Missy won't eat," Meg cried unhappily, wringing her hands as if it were somehow her fault. "Dat Minda makin' all kinds o' vittals she thinkin' will tempt Miss Cammy. But dat chile jest doan even look at it. Jest lays dere an' cries lak her heart bin broke. Den she sleeps. When she wakes, it start all over agin. . . ."

Morgana listened to the report, tight-lipped. When Meg concluded, she walked into the nursery, looking down at her daughter for a long moment. Then, lifting Anne from her cradle, Morgana went to Cammy's room, her face set with severe determination.

Cammy was in bed. Although it was past four in the afternoon, she hadn't bothered to dress and still wore her nightgown.

Morgana hesitated a moment. Then, her mouth set firmly she walked across the floor. Bending over, she deposited Anne in Cammy's arms.

Startled, the girl automatically held the infant. Anne was awake, her eyes bright and darting. She squirmed, making baby noises and, reaching out, rested a tiny hand on Cammy's chin.

Standing at the foot of the bed, Morgana viewed her sister-in-law with uncharacteristic sternness, hands on her hips, brows drawn down in open disapproval.

"This is what you carry inside of you," she said shortly. "A

240

child. Your child. You can deprive yourself, Cammy, but can you deny your baby?" Her voice lowered a bit, became almost pleading. "I can hand Anne to Celia," she noted quietly. "But right now, your child has no one but you. . . ."

The baby continued with her gurgles of happiness, then began to kick her legs, her small feet pushing at Cammy's abdomen.

If the image of Jude's last moments had plagued Morgana, they were etched indelibly in Cammy's mind. It was permanently seared into her memory, just as if it had been branded there with a hot iron the way Dobbs marked runaways. She had only to close her eyes to see it. So strong, so intense was her remembrance of those awful minutes that even the recollection of their pleasant times together could not compensate, could not erase that horror.

For a long time Cammy looked down at the child in her arms, her expression unreadable.

Then the tears began to slip down her cheeks, silently, unstoppable, until finally Cammy gave a great sob, burying her head against the child. Frightened by the change, the baby now began to cry with lusty indignation. Quickly, Morgana motioned to Meg, instructing her to take the child back to Celia.

Sitting down on the edge of the bed, Morgana held Cammy while the girl sobbed as if her heart would break. Morgana made no attempt to calm her; she allowed the solace of weeping to run its course.

But the ploy had worked. Cammy finally roused herself. While she still stayed in her room most of the day, she not only ate, she walked about the grounds with Morgana for about an hour each morning

At the beginning of December, Morgana finally received an answering letter from her Aunt Sarah, who apologized profusely for the delay, explaining that she had just returned from Europe. The letter was lengthy and expressed the feeling that Morgana was welcome anytime she chose to return to Somerset Hall. The invitation, Sarah was careful to explain, included anyone that Morgana might wish to bring with her. After reading it, Morgana put the letter in a drawer of her writing table and did not mention its arrival to Cammy.

It was the day before Christmas when Cammy at last went into labor.

Morgana had come to Cammy's room to fetch her for their morning walk. But Cammy, in her nightgown, was clinging to the wooden post of the bed, her face contorted with pain.

"De baby's comin'," Meg announced somewhat unnecessarily. She was rubbing Cammy's back.

Morgana moved closer and Cammy managed a smile. "It's true," she whispered. She appeared almost relieved.

"I'll send for the doctor." Morgana began to walk toward the door.

"No!" Cammy reached out a hand. "No doctor. Meg has already sent for Auntie Flora."

Morgana paused, uncertain.

"Please," Cammy pleaded. "I want Auntie Flora . . . and you." Another spasm gripped her and for the moment she was unable to speak.

Morgana remained uncertain a moment longer, but then, remembering Auntie Flora's gentle touch upon her own body, nodded. And, though she hated to admit it to herself, she thought there was a chance that Griffin and Nathaniel would probably refuse to send for the doctor. They both still had the ridiculous notion of keeping this whole thing a secret.

With a brisk step, Morgana returned to Cammy's side and helped Meg get her back into bed. She didn't bother to send word to Nathaniel or Griffin, knowing that they would realize what was happening soon enough.

Nine hours later, Morgana bent over Cammy's straining body, her eyes frantic with worry. Meg was diligently sponging her mistress's sweating brow.

Turning, Morgana regarded Auntie Flora, who didn't appear the least concerned. "Is she all right?"

The ancient Negress cracked her toothless grin. "Missy havin' a baby, missus. She ain' sick."

"But she's so narrow." Morgana gave another worried glance at the girl on the bed, wondering if there was still time to send for the doctor.

Just then, Cammy gave a great shriek and Auntie Flora bent over her. "It's comin' now. Kin see its haid." Her gnarled hands reached for the emerging infant, and only moments later she held the child up for view. "It's a boy!" she pronounced triumphantly, severing the cord with a knife.

Cammy's smile was as triumphant as the old woman's tone as she reached for her son. She clasped the baby close to her breast and wept happy tears.

Cammy named the child Jamie. He had black curly hair, much like Cammy's own. And his eyes were blue. His skin was almost white, with only the barest hint of a golden hue to mark his heritage.

"A mustee," Nathaniel breathed as he viewed his grandson for the first time the next morning. Shaking his head, he left the room.

Griffin refused to look upon the child.

Chapter 14

The December night was quite cool but calm. Only the drone of insects and the flickering fireflies disturbed the quiet, somehow intensifying the silence instead of alleviating it.

At the edge of the clearing, Jonah stood quietly, his black eyes straining through the darkness as he surveyed the Great House that sat on a rise about a hundred feet away from him.

Clad in a light jacket which he had stolen, Jonah still wore the same cotton shirt and breeches that he'd had when he left Albemarle. On his feet he wore a pair of brogans. The roughly made shoes, usually worn by slaves only in the winter months, had also been stolen.

Beside him stood another runaway named Zack. A head shorter and nowhere near as muscular as Jonah, Zack had been a field hand at White Manors, the very plantation they were now viewing.

Behind them, the wooded area led into the swamp where, together with eight other runaways, they had built crude shelters for themselves amongst the cypress and gum trees.

Jonah had come across Zack while stumbling through the swamp some three days after his escape from Albemarle. Zack, who was thirty-four years old, had been at large for seven weeks, leaving the relative safety of the swamp only to steal food and, when he could manage it, tools. He had watched Jonah's progress for more than an hour before he had felt safe enough to approach, assuring himself that the newcomer was not being followed by the patrollers.

At that time Zack had no more than a lean-to, a few boards hastily lashed together to keep the rain from falling upon him while he slept. With Jonah's help, a cabin had been constructed.

Others, subsequently, had joined them.

As the days passed, hope had risen. For the most part, the patrollers avoided the swamp, fearing the quicksand that lie in wait for the unwary. Too, the place was alive with cottonmouth moccasins, coral snakes, and even alligators. Under the circumstances, the dogs were virtually useless and would themselves be placed at great risk. Only the desperate or the determined, ventured into the swamp. Jonah and his cohorts were both.

Jonah's previous inclination of finding the Underground and heading North had been temporarily put aside. At first, there had been only Zack and himself. But before too long a time had gone by, they had been joined by other runaways. Soon their number would increase until there were enough of them for a full-scale revolt.

They had weapons of a sort; knives, hoes, scythes. But they had no guns. However, Tampa, the brooding Fanti who had run from Four Oaks, assured them that he knew where Farley Barrows kept his guns. When the time came and their number assured success, that would be their first stop.

Albemarle, Jonah insisted, would be their second. Not only did he want to rescue his sister, Zoe, he had scores to settle. His scarred body was a constant reminder, lest he forget his goal.

Now Jonah took a step forward. It was after ten o'clock and the Great House was dark and silent.

"Mebbe we could git into de kitchen," he speculated, thinking of the tempting array of knives that was no doubt just lying about.

"Naw," Zack shook his head sharply. They had come here with the express purpose of raiding the toolshed and he didn't want to press their luck. "Too dangerous with jest us'ns. Masta Whitney got hisself five sons, all growed. An' dey mean bastids. Seen one of dem beat a wench till she up an' died 'cause she wouldn't come to his room lessen she wuz dragged."

"Doan call him masta," Jonah insisted, bringing his face closer to Zack. "Doan call no white man dat no moah. We our own mastas now."

Zack shrugged, but made no comment. While the thought of an insurrection gave him a great deal of satisfaction, he was unable to drum up the zeal that infected Jonah, a zeal that had made the man, in effect, their leader.

"Ain' dere no white lady?" Jonah asked him, glancing at the house again.

"Yeah. But Miz Whitney bin poorly fer years. Stays in her room most times. Doan rightly know what's goin' on."

"When we git ready, mebbe we come heah first," Jonah suggested. "Could kill 'em all iffen we wants."

Zack considered that tempting possibility for a long moment. His mental process was sluggish, but then, until recently, he hadn't had to think for himself. But he remembered all the whippings he had endured since he had arrived at White Manors as a boy of twelve, remembered all the hours, the endlessly hot and bitter hours, he had toiled in the fields. There would be great satisfaction, he thought, in seeing his white masters die. However, without guns, they wouldn't stand a chance. Zack's father had been one of those slaves who had joined the insurrection led by Denmark Vesey more than thirty years ago. And there were valuable lessons to be learned from the abortive attempt at freedom.

No, they needed guns. One pistol, one rifle was worth more than a hundred knives and hoes.

"Naw," Zack said finally. "Dat Tampa's right. Wouldn't do no good to come heah. Four Oaks is where de guns is at. Collects 'em, dey do. An' Farley Barrows got on'y three sons, one of 'em jest a baby, an' another no more den a saplin'. Naw," he repeated with a firm shake of his head. "Best we stay wit de plan."

"Doan day got guns heah?" Jonah asked after a moment, reluctant to give up on the possibility.

Zack grunted an affirmation. "But dey ain' in one place. Each one got his own and keeps it in dey room." Seeing the hesitation on his companion's face, Zack grabbed his arm. "Tells you, Jonah, it be too dangerous. Let's go! We git de tools, den we go back."

Jonah resisted a moment. In the velvety darkness of night his eyes seemed to glow, reflecting an inner light that was ignited by visions only he could see. And that vision was total insurrection, every plantation burned to the ground, every slave — man, woman, and child — set free.

And it was a possibility. Overall, the blacks outnumbered the whites by more than four to one. In some areas it was, of course, many times higher than that.

Jonah had no doubt that most of his people would heed the call to freedom. There would be those, he knew, who would resist out of fear or some misguided feeling of loyalty. Those would have to be killed. But it was, he thought, a small price to pay for what would eventually be accomplished.

"Come on, Jonah," Zack urged in a stronger voice, sensing the other's continued hesitation. "Doan want us'ns to git caught, do you?"

Shaken from his introspection, Jonah viewed his friend a moment, then nodded slowly. He followed the other man as they both hugged the shadows on the edge of the clearing, making their way toward the toolshed.

Jonah moved with care. He wasn't about to be caught. This time, he thought with grim fortitude, this time he would fight to the death.

And before they were through, Jonah vowed, clenching his massive fists, he would see Carlie Dobbs and Griffin Kynes in hell.

Chapter 15

It was the first week of the new year, and Morgana hoped that 1854 would be a more pleasant one than its predecessor. It had been mutually and tacitly agreed that, this year, they would all forgo the trek into Charleston. Cammy had recovered quickly from her confinement and the joy of having her son had greatly restored her spirits. She seemed, for the time being, to have achieved a certain degree of contentment. Unlike Morgana, Cammy was able to nurse her own baby and refused to allow anyone to take over that most enjoyable task.

The morning dawned clear, if a bit cool, and Morgana awoke to the sound of Anne's fretful cry. Before she could get up and don a robe, Celia had already taken the child to her breast.

Although it was still early, not yet seven-thirty, Morgana decided to get up, in view of the fact that she was now wide awake.

Bella seemed subdued and quiet as she assisted Morgana in dressing, but Morgana made no comment on the somewhat unusual state of affairs, reasoning that if Bella had a problem, she would come to her in her own good time.

Having washed and dressed, Morgana walked into the sitting room and kissed her daughter, who was now back in the cradle. Hearing the rumble and creaking of a wagon, she walked out onto the piazza. In the distance, a group of about ten slaves, all in the back of the buckboard, were being driven through the gates and along the road to Charleston. Morgana's brow wrinkled in perplexity as she watched the little scene with curious eyes.

"Dey's bein' sold," Bella murmured, coming to stand at

Morgana's side as the buckboard rumbled away.

Morgana glanced at the black woman. "Why?"

"Do it ever' year," Bella responded, then cleared her throat. "Miz Morgana . . ." Agitation took hold of her and she bit her lip, which had begun to tremble.

Morgana now turned to study her more closely. "What is it, Bella? What's wrong?" she asked in consternation, noticing that the young woman seemed nervous and upset.

"Oh, Miz Morgana," Bella cried out, wringing her hands and close to tears. "Masta Griffin whips me fer shoah . . . Sez de first one who breathes a word gits skinned alive. . . ."

Morgana frowned at the recital. "Bella! What on earth are you talking about?" She put her hands on the slim shoulders. "If there is something I should know," she said quietly, "then you must tell me."

Bella regarded her mistress with wide, fearful eyes. "You won't tell Masta Griffin I tol' you?" she pleaded, sounding truly distraught.

"Of course not. Nor," Morgana added, mouth tight, "will I allow him to whip you."

The assurance was enough for Bella. Like most of the slaves at Albemarle, Bella had learned to trust Morgana. Still, her words came in spurts, between small sobs. "It's de baby, Miz Morgana. Oh, Lawd Jesus, what Miss Cammy gonna do when she finds out?" Bella put her hands to her face and wept in earnest.

"What are you talking about?" Morgana exclaimed sharply. Reaching out, she took hold of the girl's wrists, pulling them away from her black face. "Tell me! What about Jamie? Is he sick?"

"No, missus. He ain' sick." Bella glanced outside. The coffle was out of sight. "He's wit Tansy," she whispered. "Masta Griffin gonna sell 'em both. Gave Tansy Miss Cammy's baby.

Gonna sell 'em as a pair . . . Sellin' Zoe, too, but Miss Cammy's baby too light to be passed off as her'n, so he give it to Tansy." Bella's voice ended on a wail.

The blood left Morgana's face. "Oh, my God . . ." She turned and hurried from the room, almost colliding with Celia in her haste.

She screamed Griffin's name as she ran down the stairs, only to be informed by Thomas that her husband had accompanied the coffle to Charleston.

Dismayed, she ran outside, skirts swirling around her ankles. There, on the verandah, she spied Nathaniel. Though it was barely eight o'clock in the morning, he was seated in the rocking chair, sipping a drink. He didn't seem surprised to see her, but he avoided her eye as she stormed in his direction.

"How could you have let this happen?" she demanded angrily, sounding breathless. She was dumbfounded that Griffin would have done this in the first place, and further shocked that Nathaniel had made no move to stop it.

Nathaniel took a long sip of his toddy before replying. It was his third and it helped blunt his thoughts. "Damned grapevine," he complained irascibly. "Can't understand how the hell they do it."

"Nathaniel!" Morgana spoke sharply, resisting the urge to shake the old man. "You must send someone after that child. I will not allow this to happen."

"Can't stop it now," Nathaniel said. Although his voice was quiet enough, his chest rose and fell more quickly than if he had in truth been calm. He downed his drink. "Thomas!" he shouted, waving his glass. "Damned buck's never around when you want him." He hunched lower in the rocker.

"Nathaniel —" Morgana broke off as Thomas brought another toddy. The Negro cast her a look full of despair as he retreated.

"Can't do nothin'," Nathaniel mumbled. Turning slightly, he gave her a brief glance. His eyes appeared sunken, shadowed with pain. "Boy's a nigger, just like the rest of them." He turned away again.

"That child's no more black than you or I," Morgana all but shouted, then fell silent as she heard the scream. It was loud, piercing, as if the person who had uttered it was in mortal anguish.

With one more glance at Nathaniel, who seemed not to have heard the commotion, Morgana ran back into the house.

She was about to go upstairs when she saw Cammy coming down. The girl's hair was disheveled. Her cotton robe was untied, revealing the white flannel nightgown she wore underneath it. She was standing a few steps down from the landing, leaning on the banister, a crazed look upon her face. In her right hand, a pair of scissors gleamed dully. Behind her, Meg hovered anxiously, hands outstretched, but not daring to touch her mistress.

"Cammy . . ." Morgana tried to keep her voice quiet and steady. She started up the stairs. The girl looked down at her as if a stranger were approaching.

"I'll kill him!" she cried out in a low and ragged voice. "I'll kill my brother for this!" She raised the scissors in a threatening gesture.

Morgana paused. She took a deep breath, forcing herself to be calm. Her heart was beating painfully fast, causing a throbbing in her ears. Slowly, she climbed, one step at a time, never taking her eyes from Cammy's distraught face.

"We'll get him back," Morgana murmured in the same quiet tone. She extended a hand. "I promise you, we'll get your baby back. . . ."

Drawing away slightly, Cammy regarded her with bright, suspicious eyes. "He sold my baby. He took him away and sold him!" She repeated it over and over, as though she herself couldn't believe it.

Coming closer, Morgana put her arms about the slim figure, and turning her around, led her back to her bedroom. Cammy went docilely enough, but wouldn't allow Morgana to take the scissors, which she clung to in a fierce, determined manner. Her face was a curious mixture of dazed, hysterical anger.

After the door closed, Morgana sat Cammy gently down on the bed. "Listen to me," she murmured in slow, measured tones. She bent forward to better see Cammy's face. "I will bring your baby home. Cammy," she shook the girl, trying to gain her full attention. "I will bring him back to you. But to do that, I must leave you and go into Charleston." She peered closer. "Will you promise me you will do nothing foolish while I am gone?"

Cammy finally looked directly at Morgana, the words at last penetrating her fogged state of mind. "How?"

Morgana gave a small breath of relief. It was the first thing Cammy had said in a coherent manner. "You leave that to me." She cupped Cammy's chin with her hand. "Do you understand everything I've said?"

Slowly, Cammy nodded, and this time made no protest when Morgana took the scissors from her grasp and handed them to Meg.

Straightening, Morgana regarded the frightened slave. "I want you to stay with your mistress," she instructed the wide-eyed Meg. "Don't leave her for a moment. Do you hear me?"

"Yassum," Meg replied readily. She took a step closer to Cammy as if to indicate her willingness to comply. "Stay's by her side, ever' minute. Promises you."

Morgana nodded, satisfied. Then she regarded Cammy again. She was sitting on the bed, her shoulders slumped, hands loose and limp in her lap. "I'll return as soon as I'm able.

252

Although," she stressed, "I doubt that I'll get back today."

As Morgana turned to go, Cammy's murmured voice halted her. "He won't listen. You can talk as much as you want, but Griffin won't listen. He's going to sell my baby . . ." Her voice broke as she began to sob. Meg came closer and put her arms around her mistress, appearing as if she, too, was ready to burst into tears.

Morgana's lips curved into a humorless, cold smile. "I have no intention of trying to change Griffin's mind," she stated. She continued toward the door where she paused, looking back at Cammy. "I'll be leaving in a little while. When I return, Jamie will be with me."

As she closed the door, Morgana closed her eyes and offered a brief, fervent prayer that her words were true. Feeling an acute sense of urgency, she summoned Bella and Ben to her room.

A while later, Morgana rummaged through her father's trunk, finally locating a leather poke among the contents. Then, with Ben's assistance, she dragged the locked metal box from beneath her bed. Kneeling on the floor, she unlocked it, then began to stuff the gold into the poke.

Glancing up at Ben, she asked, "How much does it cost to buy a slave?"

"Depends, Miz Morgana," he answered, scratching his woolly head. "A prime buck kin bring eighteen hun'erd." He looked sheepish then. "Masta Aleceon bought this worthless nigger fer only three."

Morgana frowned at him. "I don't ever want to hear you say that again, Ben," she admonished sternly. "You're not worthless."

"Yassum."

"But a baby, Ben," she went on. "How much does a baby cost?"

Ben shook his head. "Dey doan sell suckahs by deyselves, Miz Morgana," he said slowly. "Always wit a wench."

"Well, how much then?" she demanded, growing impatient.

He shrugged. "Kin go for, mebbe eight, nine hun'erd. Depends on de wench."

Morgana chewed her lower lip in contemplation, still on her knees. "Well, there's about two thousand dollars in the poke. That ought to be enough." She got to her feet, brushing her skirt with her hands. "Ben, you go and get the carriage ready."

Bella stood by, regarding her mistress doubtfully. "You plannin' on goin' to de auction, Miz Morgana?"

"Yes," she answered shortly, giving the woman a brief nod. "And I'll outbid any man there if it takes every cent I've got," she added grimly. Going to the wardrobe, she took out a shawl.

Bella's doubt increased and her expression turned skeptical. "Never seen a white lady theah before, Miz Morgana," she mused slowly. "Thinkin' dey's holdin' sep'rate auctions for 'em."

Morgana halted abruptly, staring at her. "You mean they don't allow women at these . . . auctions?"

"Never seen one, Miz Morgana," Bella responded. "But I on'y bin sol' once. Jest not shoah."

Morgana hadn't considered that obstacle. She stood, pensive, her mind working with its usual agility. Then her eye lit upon the open trunk and she gave a slow smile.

"Well, we won't take any chances," she murmured softly. Removing her shawl, she threw it carelessly on the bed. "Come, help me." She walked over to the trunk and began to pick up first one, then another article of clothing. Thank God her father had been so thin and gaunt, she thought, as she began to undress.

Bella watched her actions with wide, incredulous eyes.

Morgana pulled on a pair of fawn colored trousers, at first over her pantalettes. Looking at herself in the mirror, she frowned at the bulge of material. Without hesitation, she stripped down to her skin. Again the trousers went on, this time fitting smoothly, just a bit loose in the waist, and about an inch too long.

"Hurry, Bella," she said, waving a hand. "Get your needle. Just tack the cuffs. I'll pin the waist. No one will see it beneath the jacket anyway."

She stood with as much patience as she could muster while Bella accomplished the few stitches on either side of the cuffs. Grabbing one of her petticoats, Morgana hastily tore it lengthwise, then put one of the pieces across her breasts. Turning, she said to Bella, "Tie it." She looked down. "A bit tighter."

A white ruffled shirt went on next, and completely confused by the intricacies of the cravat, Morgana submitted to the ministrations of Bella, who deftly accomplished the task. She could not, she realized, wear the boots. They were too big. Her own would have to do, but the trousers would hide the tops.

Bella helped Morgana into the frock coat that matched the trousers. It fit surprisingly well. The shoulders were a bit large, but not noticeably so.

Viewing her, Bella shook her head and pursed her full lips. "Ain' nobody gonna think yore a man wit dat hair," she noted wryly, gesturing at the golden mass.

Morgana looked into the pier mirror and gave a short laugh. "I daresay you're right. Is there a hat in there?" she pointed to the trunk.

"Yassum," Bella replied after a brief search. "An' a walkin' stick, too."

Quickly, Morgana piled her hair atop her head, pinning it securely. Then she put on the hat. "There. Is that better?"

Carefully, Bella studied her mistress from head to toe. "You wait jest a minute, Miz Morgana," she said.

Before Morgana could protest, Bella hurried from the room, returning a short while later with a piece of coal. With light, deft strokes, she began to darken Morgana's eyebrows, thickening them slightly, then did the same with the bit of hair that was visible just in front of her ears.

Viewing herself once more, Morgana smiled delightedly. "Hand me the walking stick, Bella. I'm going to Charleston."

It was late in the day when Morgana finally reached the city, grateful that Ben knew the way to where the auction would be held. But then, why shouldn't he know? she reflected angrily. She doubted there was a slave in the South who didn't know where the auctions were held in their area.

The carriage halted on the cobbled street before what looked like a common warehouse. Morgana got out and approached the front entrance, which was securely locked. Then, in dismay, she read the posted notice on the door. The auction was not to be held until ten o'clock the following morning.

"But where are the slaves now, Ben?" she asked worriedly, looking about. There was no one around; the whole area seemed deserted.

Ben pointed to a one-story building across the street from where they were standing. Several citrus trees and a huge wisteria vine did little to conceal the structure's dilapidated condition. "Dey's in de jail, Miz Morgana," he answered, turning to look at her. "Dat's where dey spen' de night. Calls it a barracoon, but it's jest a jail."

Morgana started to move across the street, then stopped in her tracks. She realized the only way to purchase a slave right out of the barracoon, without attending the auction, would be to deal directly with the owner. In this case, Griffin. That was a chance she couldn't possibly take. With a sigh, she viewed Ben, who nodded, having sensed her intentions.

"Best you waits fer de auction, Miz Morgana," he advised solemnly. "Be a crowd of peoples aroun' den. Safer dat way."

Morgana nodded, then gave him a sharp look. "Ben, you must call me Master Morgan. Please, try to remember."

"Yes, Miz — ah, Masta Morgan."

"Good. Until this is over, you call me that even when we're alone," she instructed firmly. "Understand?"

"Yassuh, Masta Morgan, suh." He grinned broadly at her nod of approval.

"Now. Where can I stay until morning?"

Ben pondered. "Dere's a place on Meetin' Street where de ladies stay, an' it's mos' respectable. Nobody bother you dere."

She made a face at the suggestion. "I can't walk into a place like that, dressed like this," she reminded him.

That produced a sheepish grin from Ben. "Yassum — Masta, suh. Gen'mens stay at de Charleston Hotel."

"All right." She began to get back into the carriage, then paused, glancing at him. "Can you stay there?"

He nodded in affirmation. "Got a place in back by de kitchen," he assured her, closing the carriage door as she settled herself.

"Fine. Then that's where we'll go."

Awhile later, Morgana entered the crowded lobby of the fashionable hotel, Ben following a few steps behind her. She was nervous and her eyes darted about, scanning the red velvet chairs that were positioned amongst the potted plants. What if she met Griffin? The thought caused her stomach to tighten as she approached the front desk.

"I'd like a room for the night," she said to the clerk. She tried to lower her naturally husky voice and carefully avoided eye contact.

However, the clerk, a thin, pasty-faced individual in his early thirties, gave her no more than a cursory glance. He was always busy at auction time because of the swelling numbers of out-of-town clientele that the function generated.

"Three dollars," he mumbled brusquely, pushing a key in her direction. Looking toward Ben, he added, "Your nigger stayin'?"

She nodded.

"Want him fed?"

"Of course!"

"Another six bits," he informed her, barely stifling a yawn.

She paid the money, then turned away, feeling weak. A group of men were discussing the auction in loud and raucous tones. She walked quickly past them to where Ben was standing by the front door. "You know where to go?" she asked him, coming closer.

He nodded. "Doan worry 'bout me, suh."

"I worry for us both," she replied with a small laugh. "Come for me in the morning, right after breakfast." She glanced at the key she held in her hand. "Number twenty-four."

"Be there. . . suh." Ben gave a slight bow.

She turned then and walked hurriedly across the carpeted lobby. She looked neither right nor left and prayed that she wouldn't come across her husband. She was hungry, but didn't dare go into the dining room. That, she thought, would be tempting fate too far.

Walking up two flights, Morgana located number twenty-four. Closing the door behind her, she leaned against it, a deep sigh following soon thereafter.

It was not a large room, but the bed appeared comfortable enough. After a moment, she took off her hat, placing it on the mahogany dresser. The jacket she put over the single chair. Then she removed her boots. She would never be able to retie the cravat, she thought tiredly, and lay down on the bed with the rest of her clothes on.

Although it was not yet dark, she felt weary, both in mind and in body. Wistfully, she thought of Griffin — not the Griffin of today, but the one she first knew and loved. Sometimes her yearning almost got the better of her; her treacherous body remembered, even if her mind sought forgetfulness.

What she was about to do would again anger him, she realized, taking a deep breath of resignation. She closed her eyes, unwilling to face that, knowing in her own heart that she was doing the right thing.

She turned over on her stomach and plumped the pillow with several vicious jabs before resting her head on its dubious softness.

Oh, Griffin, her mind silently cried out, even with all that's happened I still love you so. . . .

Morgana knew that she had given herself countless excuses for not leaving Griffin. In the beginning she told herself she could not leave because she had no money. After her father died, she told herself she could not go because of the coming child. Yet, deep inside herself, Morgana was aware of the gentle deceptions her heart offered as excuses for her staying at Albemarle.

During the week before she and Griffin had been married, Morgana had had many daydreams of what their life together would be like. They had been such pretty dreams, she thought sadly, and now they lay like broken toys, mangled in the grip of an ill-tempered child. Nothing had turned out the way she had imagined it would. Nothing.

What kind of a charade had her life become? Morgana thought miserably.

Although she was very tired, Morgana laid there for hours, her mind filled with thoughts of Griffin. It was well after midnight before she finally fell into a restless sleep.

When she awoke, bright sunlight was streaming in through the window. She sat up quickly and peered about the strange room, taking a brief moment to orient herself.

What time was it? she wondered frantically, struggling into her boots. Hastily, she donned the jacket and hat. The mirror over the dresser was cracked, but she was reassured by what she saw. She looked the same as she had yesterday.

Opening the door, she blinked as she saw Ben. He was seated on the floor. When he saw her, he smiled as he got to his feet.

"What time is it?" she asked him worriedly.

"Jest a bit after eight, suh. Plenty o' time. You eat yore breakfast . . ."

She shook her head as she closed the door. "If Griffin is there. . . ."

"Ain' dere," Ben assured her. "Seen him, I did. 'Bout thirty minutes ago. He long since gone. You eat yore breakfast," he repeated with a patient nod of his head.

"Have you eaten?" she asked as they walked down the hall.

"Yassum . . . suh. Doan you worry none 'bout Ben." He chuckled, following her down the stairs. "Got me some grits wit molasses, I did. Dat gal whats in de kitchen, she knows a fine buck when she sees one."

"All right," Morgana was unable to repress a smile. "I'll get something to eat. But I won't be long," she stressed. "Be in the carriage when I get there."

"Be there, suh," Ben promised solemnly.

In spite of Ben's assurance that Griffin was not around, Morgana entered the dining room a few minutes later with no little trepidation. She crossed the carpeted floor and found a small table in the corner. As she seated herself, she let her gaze travel the room. There were only a sprinkling of women, most of the occupants were men. Griffin wasn't among them.

A waiter appeared, a spurious smile appearing carved into his black face.

Morgana glanced briefly at the bill of fare and ordered scrambled eggs, bacon, and coffee. Then she waited, feeling a gnawing sense of impatience. She hoped fervently that she would be able to accomplish what she had set out to do. She had never in her life attended an auction — much less one where they sold people. She hadn't the faintest idea of what to expect.

When the waiter finally put the plate in front of her, Morgana bolted her food down in a most unladylike manner. As she wiped her mouth with a linen napkin, she couldn't help but wonder what Miss Appleby would think of her performance . . . Then the frivolous thought fled her mind as she rushed outside.

Ben was there, waiting. But despite her early confidence, Morgana began to tremble with what lie ahead.

Chapter 16

Unlike yesterday, the street was now filled with horses, carriages, liveried servants, well dressed — and some not so well dressed — men. The air was cool on this January morning, but the sun was warm, the breeze so slight it barely nudged the leaves.

When they arrived, Morgana sat in the carriage for a full two minutes studying the crowd.

A group of Negro drivers and servants congregated near the hitching rail, to which were tied a dozen or so horses. For them, she could see, this was not an auction, it was a social event. News was being exchanged, gossip from the Great Houses, which of their friends had been, or were to be, sold, who had been punished and why.

Listening to their muted voices and laughter, Morgana's eye finally lit upon Atlas, and she frowned. The burly Angolan had been installed as groom and stableboy in place of Jude. He was standing somewhat apart from the others, engaged in conversation with one of the liveried drivers. So far he had not noticed her arrival.

Motioning to Ben, Morgana called his attention to the slave. She didn't think he would recognize her, but he would certainly recognize Ben.

"He doan see us'ns yet," Ben noted quietly. He glanced across the cobbled street, squinting slightly in the sun. "Drives de carriage behind de jail, an' waits for you dere," he suggested.

Taking a deep breath, Morgana nodded in agreement, trusting Ben. Then, not seeing Griffin anywhere in sight, she finally got out of the carriage and headed for the entrance. Nobody gave her a second glance.

The building in which the auction was to be held was a one-story wooden structure, some sixty by a hundred feet in size, the only notable structural achievement being the white-pillared portico in front. Inside it was furnished with true spartan frugality. Against one wall was a wooden platform about two feet high with steps on one side. Along the same wall stood the slaves that were to be sold this day.

Except for a rickety table where a clerk sat, prepared to make out the bills of sale and collect the money, the room held no other furnishings.

Most of the men were standing in small groups, conversing, laughing, gossiping. The front doors had been left open, as had the two windows on either side of the room, but already the air was dense with cigar smoke. Gauzy sunlight streamed in through one of the windows, producing slanting, wavering rays as it cut through smoke and dust. When Morgana entered, her gaze swept the crowd in search of Griffin. He was standing with two other men, deep in conversation. Quickly, she moved to the other side of the room, putting as much distance between them as she could.

Selecting her position, Morgana stood quietly, leaning only lightly on the walking stick, trying her best to adopt the stance of some of the men she was viewing. She was nervous, but not unbearably so; rather, her attitude was one of caution. She was more concerned about the baby than she was about herself.

She wondered how Cammy was faring and prayed that the girl would do nothing rash while left alone. Although, in truth, Morgana couldn't blame Cammy. It didn't take much on her part to realize what her own reaction would be if she were in the same predicament.

The room was becoming crowded now. Morgana was certain that even if Griffin glanced in her direction he wouldn't see her. There were so many bodies between them she had to peer around heads to catch a glimpse of him.

Relaxing a bit, she studied the slaves, easily recognizing Zoe. The young woman was standing in an attitude of utter dejection, her eyes lowered. Next to her stood Tansy, who was holding Jamie in her arms. There were only seven women and they all stood together. They were obviously wearing their best clothes, black calico dresses with white fichus. All had bright red bandannas tied about their heads.

The rest of the slaves were men, about twenty-five in all. They were clad only in cotton breeches. All the men wore iron spangels on their wrists.

Morgana found the sight terribly depressing. Shifting her position a bit, she tried to avoid looking at the forlorn group of men and women who, through no more than a happenstance of nature, had to live in such a harsh environment.

The auctioneer, a short, balding man with a potbelly and quick, birdlike movements, now mounted the platform. He gave a brief announcement, informing the gathering that the sale would begin in about twenty minutes. "And if any of you gentlemen wish to examine any of the wenches in private, we've a shed just outside for your accommodation," he concluded, rubbing his hands together in an anticipatory manner.

There was a slight flurry of movement as a few of the men now stepped forward to avail themselves of this service. Zoe and one other Negress were led outside. In some relief, Morgana noted that Tansy had remained where she was standing, possibly because of the encumbrance of the baby in her arms.

"Now, that's a likely lookin' buck, wouldn't you say?"

Startled, Morgana turned to the man who had come up beside her, then quickly averted her face.

"See the one I mean?" he persisted, pointing to a tall and muscular Negro. "Ashanti, I'm thinkin' . . . Make good fighters." He turned to Morgana. "Pearson's my name, suh." He nodded his head in a friendly greeting. He was a heavyset man with a paunch that caused the buttons on his yellow silk vest to strain with each breath he took. His graying sideburns were sparse and crept down his cheek in a tentative manner, disappearing at his jawline. Age had plucked the hair from the top of his head, leaving a shiny pate that gave him the appearance of a benevolent friar.

Morgana gave him only a brief glance. "Morgan, sir," she offered at last, still not looking directly at him. "George Morgan."

He moved closer. "Do you live in Charleston, Morgan?"

"No. I'm from . . . New Orleans."

"Ah," he beamed, rocking on his heels. "Fine city. Visited there about two years ago. Had the time of my life. Not many cities to compare with that one."

Morgana wet her lips, wishing the man would go, but he showed no inclination of doing so.

"You lookin' for a buck or a wench?" he went on after a minute's silence.

"A . . . wench."

"Aha. Thought so, suh. Fine lookin' young fella like yourself." He nudged her with his elbow, jerking his head in the direction of Tansy. "Notice that little high yeller? Pretty a piece as I've ever seen. Well tittied out, too." He sighed wistfully, not noticing how the "young man" beside him blushed hotly. "Wife'd never let me bring that one home," he mused, hooking his thumbs in his vest pocket. "Here to buy a fightin' buck, myself. Wife doesn't approve of that, either," he added sourly. "But I told her a man's got to have some enjoyment out of life." He turned again to Morgana, who had managed to get herself under control. "You a married man, Morgan?"

"No."

Pearson nodded his head in an almost approving manner.

Reaching into his coat pocket, he brought forth a cigar, bit off the end, and stuck it in his mouth, unlit.

"Must be plenty of fine wenches for sale in New Orleans," he speculated casually after a minute, his words coming a bit garbled as he chewed on the cigar. When there was no immediate response, he regarded Morgana questioningly.

"I suppose there are," she offered shortly. She was growing irked by his insistent prattle, but she dared not take the chance of moving away.

"Had me a quadroon once," Pearson went on, much to Morgana's annoyance. "She was sixteen. Fanciest little wench you'd ever want to see. Bought her right here, in Charleston. Gave me two bright-skinned suckers. Had to sell the lot of 'em when I got married, though. That was about seven years back." He expulsed his breath in a deep sigh. "Sure wish I had them to sell now. Price of niggers keeps going up and up. Why, today, I could've asked twice the price and got it easy."

Morgana's hand tightened on the walking stick. She had an almost uncontrollable urge to hit the pompous oaf over the head with it. Bright-skinned suckers, indeed, she thought with rising fury. The man had actually sold his own children, yet his only regret seemed to be that he could have gotten more money had he waited. It was on the tip of her tongue to ask if one of the children had been a girl. Had he sold his own daughter, sold her so that she could be purchased for the same intentions as had her mother? Morgana decided she didn't really want to know the answer.

"Excuse me, sir," she said finally, aware that her voice was tight and angry. "I think they're about to begin."

Morgana moved quickly, afraid that her temper would get the better of her, but was cautious enough to keep an eye on Griffin's whereabouts. She moved closer to the platform so she would not have to shout when the time came to bid. Griffin,

266

she noticed, had not moved and, fortunately, had his back to her.

Zoe and the other young black woman had been returned to the group and once again the auctioneer mounted the wooden platform.

The first slave to be sold was the huge Negro that Pearson had pointed out as a likely fighter. The man was so black his skin had little, if any, highlights; from head to toe he was unrelieved ebony. He was tall, an inch, perhaps two, over six feet and had broad, muscular shoulders. Dressed only in cotton breeches, he stood quietly, almost proudly, despite the incongruity of the iron manacles on his wrists. He displayed no fear as a few of the men crowded close while the auctioneer began to extol the prime condition of his merchandise.

Pearson was among the men. Reaching up, he motioned for the Negro to bend down and open his mouth. Poking his pudgy fingers into the dark cavity, he diligently inspected the man's teeth. Apparently satisfied, he ran his hands over the muscular body, prodding at the man's genitals, squeezing the thighs, punching at his abdomen with quick jabbing thrusts. One or two of the other men were doing the same thing as the auctioneer continued with his enthusiastic spiel.

The bidding, begun at eight hundred dollars, was intense and energetic, and ended with Pearson's bid of nineteen hundred and fifty dollars. Looking immensely pleased with himself, Pearson then stepped up to the table to claim his bill of sale.

The whole process made Morgana ill. For a moment, she turned away. It took all her control to stand quietly and watch, to avoid calling attention to herself by berating the egotistical men about her who were displaying such a careless superiority.

As unobtrusively as possible, she continued to keep an eye on Griffin. Thankfully, he wasn't milling about. He was still with the same two men she had seen him with when she had entered.

Listening to the proceedings, Morgana couldn't help but wonder what would become of the slaves that were being sold. At least one, she knew, was destined to become a fighter. But the rest — where would they end up? Would they be ill treated? She shook herself away from her wandering thoughts, forcing herself to concentrate on the moment at hand.

An hour passed. Tansy, the baby still in her arms, at last mounted the platform, her eyes cast down. Zoe had already been sold. For once, Morgana had watched the process with dispassionate eyes, uncaring of the fate in store for the young Negress.

"Look lively, gal!" The auctioneer gave Tansy a poke in the ribs with his finger. While his tone was jocular enough, his little black eyes narrowed menacingly.

Tansy straightened, a bright smile plastered upon her face. Even from where she was standing, Morgana could see the girl trembling.

The auctioneer laughed heartily, then addressed the group in an almost conspiratorial manner, his voice at the level of a stage whisper.

"This little yeller can warm my bed anytime," he informed them all with a broad grin.

Frowning, Morgana began to understand why white women were not welcome in a gathering of this sort.

Amidst the good-natured laughter that followed the auctioneer's remark, Morgana glanced once at Griffin. However, his back was still toward her and she couldn't see his expression. He didn't appear to be laughing, although the two men he was standing with were displaying high amusement. The auctioneer continued, and Morgana returned her attention to the platform.

"Now this heah's Tansy," the man pronounced, raising his voice slightly to indicate that he was getting down to serious business. "She's unmarked and docile. Only eighteen years old, but already a fine breeding wench, as you can see." He made a brief gesture toward the child in her arms. "She'd make a fine wet nurse for any of you gentlemen as has such a need in your family. She's primarily a field hand, but young enough to be housebroken." He glanced down at his notes to refresh himself. "Tansy comes from Albemarle and is the property of Mr. Griffin Kynes, who wishes to sell her at this time." He looked out upon the crowd expectantly.

One of the men bid three hundred dollars. Morgana quickly upped it to four.

"Four-fifty," came the return bid.

Taking a deep breath, Morgana raised a hand. "Six hundred."

There was a brief pause, then, "And fifty!"

"Eight hundred," Morgana called out, still taking care to distort her voice as much as possible.

After that, there was silence.

Gazing about the smoke-filled room and seeing no other indications, the auctioneer shouted, "Sold!" Then he quickly proceeded to the next slave.

Morgana moved through the crowd, making her way to the table. She paid the money and collected a bill of sale, keeping her back always in the direction of Griffin, who, at any rate, hadn't shown undue attention to the person who had bought Tansy and her supposed child.

Beckoning the brown-skinned girl to follow her, Morgana then walked out into the bright afternoon sunshine. Crossing the street with hurried steps, she went to the rear of the jail, where Ben was waiting beside the carriage.

Morgana entered and motioned for Tansy to get in. The girl halted abruptly, recognizing both the carriage and Ben, then stared stupidly at Morgana.

"Get in!" Morgana instructed sharply, anxious to be on their way.

When Tansy finally did, the carriage moved forward at a smart pace. Tansy couldn't take her eyes off Morgana, still not recognizing her, until, at last, Morgana spoke in her normal voice.

"It's Miss Morgana, Tansy," she murmured quietly.

There was no immediate reaction. Then the girl's eyes grew round. "Lawd Jesus, missus," she breathed. "What you doin' heah, dressed lak dat?" Her eyes grew even wider as they surveyed Morgana from head to toe, unable to believe what she was seeing.

Bending forward, Morgana checked to see that the baby was all right before she answered. Satisfied that he was sleeping peacefully, she said, "Tansy, how would you like to go North, to be free?"

Turning somber, the girl just stared at her, dark eyes turning wary. She knew perfectly well what she was supposed to say anytime anyone asked her that question. For a slave to admit to wanting freedom was to invite consequences too awful to even think about.

"Wants to be yore slave, missus," Tansy replied dutifully after a moment's consideration. She gave a short nod of her head for emphasis, then shifted the baby to a more comfortable position in her lap.

The answer confounded Morgana, who was, for the moment, at a loss for words. She heard Ben chuckle. Then the Negro glanced over his shoulder at Tansy.

"Best you speaks de truf, gal," he noted quietly. "Miz Morgana meanin' what she says."

Again the girl regarded Morgana, still uncertain, still unable to believe her mistress was serious. It wasn't that she didn't trust Miz Morgana; she did. But she knew very well that white

270

folks were to be trusted only so far. Tansy glanced at Ben, whose attention was again centered on the road. Miz Morgana, she knew, *had* freed Ben, although, for reasons of his own, he continued to serve her.

Morgana was regarding Tansy quizzically, not understanding the hesitation. "Do you want to go North?" she repeated in a stronger voice.

The girl looked away for a moment, then back at Morgana, still a bit uncertain. "How do I git dere?" she responded at last.

Morgana patted the slim brown hand. "You just leave that to me."

"Kin I take my baby?" Tansy spoke hesitantly, not wishing to jeopardize her sudden good fortune.

Leaning back on the seat, Morgana looked dismayed at the suggestion. Good Lord, she had forgotten all about Tansy's baby. She bit her lip. Then, determined, she nodded. "Yes. Yes, we will take your baby with us."

They fell silent then. Occasionally, Morgana turned around and glanced out of the small rear window in the carriage, hoping and praying that she wouldn't see the buckboard on the road behind them. She consoled herself by reasoning that Griffin would surely stay until the end of the auction. When she had left, there were still seven slaves to be sold. Taking a deep breath, she tried to relax.

When they arrived at Albemarle some hours later, Nathaniel was standing on the verandah. Incredulous, he watched as Morgana stepped out of the carriage, followed by Tansy and the baby. Having gone into the fields shortly after he spoke to Morgana the previous morning, he hadn't even known she was gone. Cammy hadn't left her room and Nathaniel had supposed that Morgana was with her.

"What the hell," was all he could think to say as Morgana

removed the hat, allowing her golden hair to tumble about her shoulders.

As she walked toward him, Morgana felt a pressing need for haste. She was, at best, an hour or two ahead of Griffin, and knew she couldn't leave until after the household settled down for the night. The next few hours would be critical.

Just then, Cammy came rushing from the house, still in her nightgown, her wrap billowing and flapping about her slim body as she raced down the broad front steps. Laughing and crying at the same time, she reached for her son, burying her face in the child's soft and warm neck.

Morgana allowed them a brief moment, then she stepped close to Cammy. "We are leaving in a few hours," she said quietly. "Do you want to come with us?"

"Oh, yes. Yes!" Cammy cried out, still clutching her son to her breast.

Morgana placed a hand on her sister-in-law's arm. "Tansy and the baby will have to stay in Ben's cabin until we're ready to leave," she said. "You stay in your room until then. Pack only what you can put in one bag. And remember, Cammy, it will be cold where we're going."

Unable to speak, Cammy only nodded, reluctantly handing the child back to Tansy.

Morgana turned. "Ben, you put the carriage and horses in the barn. But be ready to leave when I come for you."

"Yassum," Ben nodded smartly. He climbed back up on the driver's seat and prodded the horses forward.

Then Morgana turned to Nathaniel, who stood with his mouth open, still unable to believe what he was seeing. Taking him gently by the arm, she led him inside to the parlor.

Closing the pocket doors, Morgana faced Nathaniel, almost amused by the look of dumb astonishment on his face.

Still staring at her, Nathaniel sat down heavily, as if his legs would no longer support him. "How the hell did you do that?" he asked, waving a hand in the general direction of the front yard.

Morgana couldn't repress the small smile that found its way to her lips. "I admit that I never thought I would be buying slaves," she commented dryly, with a slight shake of her head. "But it appears that I have just bought two of them."

"But . . . but how?" he sputtered. He wanted to comment on her attire, but he couldn't seem to find the words, so he just stared at her.

Quickly, and in as few words as possible, Morgana told him.

"But the money," Nathaniel persisted, raising both brows. "Where did you get the money?"

That, too, she told him. When she was through, Nathaniel regarded her in silence for a long moment, then slapped his knee. "By God," he exclaimed, giving a great guffaw of a laugh. "By God!" He repeated that several times, laughing until the tears came. "You're some kind of a woman, Morgana," he said when he caught his breath. Fumbling in his pocket, he brought forth a handkerchief and wiped his eyes.

Then he quieted and grew serious. "But what're you going to do now? When Griff finds out about all this . . ." He shook his head, his lined face reflecting deep concern. He knew how hotheaded his grandson could be when provoked.

"I hope he won't find out until we have already left. And that's up to you, Nathaniel," Morgana added quietly, watching him closely. At this moment the fate of them all rested with this man. Morgana prayed she had not misjudged him.

"Leave?" Nathaniel raised his head, eyes widening. "Where are you going?"

"I'm taking Cammy and the baby, as well as Tansy and Ben to my aunt in Massachusetts. They'll be safe there. But

Griffin mustn't know until we're gone." She took a step closer, her voice falling to a whisper. "Please, Nathaniel, say you'll help us."

He looked at her for an agonizing moment. Then, almost sadly, he nodded.

She came to his side and kissed his weather-beaten cheek with true affection. "Thank you," she murmured, squeezing his arm.

As she reached the door, his voice halted her. "Are you coming back, Morgana?"

She turned to look at his anxious face.

"Please come back," he entreated. "We need you."

Chapter 17

An hour later, Morgana stood on the piazza just outside her bedroom. Hidden in the shadows, she watched for Griffin's return, tightening the woolen shawl about her shoulders. The sun had set and the air had turned chilly. Although she had discarded the jacket and cravat, she had not taken the time to change the rest of her clothes and still wore the outfit she had worn to the auction.

She was a bit tense with the enforced wait, even though she knew it was necessary. She couldn't chance leaving now and meeting Griffin on the road. Her nerves were taut and she prayed that Nathaniel would keep his promise and remain silent. He had already gone to his room and she took heart from that.

Now all she had to do was hope that no one else would tell Griffin. She didn't think anyone would; still, she knew very well that she wouldn't relax entirely until they were actually on the boat and away from here.

Morgana refused to allow herself to dwell upon the future. Right now she had committed herself to getting Cammy and her baby to safety. After that, she could work on her own problems.

At Morgana's side, Bella was fearful and agitated. While she greatly admired what her mistress had done, Bella wished she could be anywhere else but here when Masta Griffin found out about all this. The fact that Masta Nathaniel seemed to have tacitly agreed with what was going on offered only small comfort. Her young master was a man with a fearful temper and it was best to stay out of his way when he was riled.

Time and again Bella's eyes anxiously sought her mistress.

She was trembling and longed to sit down, but she knew that she couldn't do that unless Morgana did. So she stood, clasping and unclasping her black hands, murmuring audible prayers until, at last, with rising impatience, Morgana ordered her to be quiet.

Turning, Morgana glanced into the sitting room. Anne was in the cradle, sound asleep. Celia was standing beside it, twisting her apron with nervous hands. Occasionally she reached out to rock the cradle and peer at the sleeping child.

Morgana's heart wrenched at the thought of being separated from her daughter, even for a short period of time. But the journey would be difficult enough with two babies in tow, and she herself couldn't nurse Anne. Tansy could, but if and when Morgana returned, Tansy wouldn't be with her. She shook her head. No. Anne would have to stay. Resolutely, Morgana returned her attention to the yard, hoping that Griffin would get back soon. What, she wondered distractedly, would they do if Griffin decided to spend the night in Charleston?

Twilight had deepened into a purple haze by the time the buckboard, driven by Atlas, creaked up the driveway.

With little expression, Morgana watched as her husband got down from the bench seat and strode wearily into the house. She wondered if he had regrets about what he had done, or tried to do. Somehow, she doubted it. As with Jude, Griffin probably reasoned that he was doing the right thing for all concerned.

It seemed to her that an eternity went by before she finally heard Griffin make his way up the stairs.

Standing behind her closed door, ear pressed against the solid wood, Morgana thought he paused outside her room, but couldn't be certain. Nevertheless, her heart pounded until, finally, she heard his door close.

Glancing at Bella and Celia, she put a finger to her lips,

cautioning them against making any kind of a sound. Then, carefully, she opened her own door and peered into the empty hall, listening. The whole household had settled into a hushed quiet.

She waited then, a full hour before she felt safe enough to leave. During that time she dressed herself in the brown woolen dress she had arrived in. It was the warmest she owned. Over the matching pelisse she draped a woolen shawl. Then, with a last look at her daughter — one that caused her heart to ache within her breast — Morgana left her room.

The hall was dark and silent. Not even one candle burned in the wall sconces. She stood quietly a moment, letting her eyes adjust to the dimness. Then she walked slowly, hand on the wall, until she reached Cammy's room.

A light tap on Cammy's door brought an immediate response. Without words, dressed in a wine colored pelisse and carrying a heavy cloak she had never even worn, the girl fell into step. Both of them had, earlier, had Ben pick up their baggage and take it out to the carriage.

Noiselessly, they both made their way down the stairs and out to the barn without incident, although by now there was only one person on the plantation who didn't know what was going on.

Tansy was already waiting for them, having left her cabin when she saw the light extinguished in Griffin's bedroom. Both infants were, thankfully, asleep.

From the barn to the road, Ben walked beside the horses, holding the bit of one of them in his hands, allowing the animals to move only at a very slow walk.

On the road at last, he climbed up onto the driver's seat, then prodded the horses forward at a rapid pace.

Three hours later they were back in Charleston.

By now it was after one o'clock in the morning. They all,

with the exception of Tansy and the two babies, had no sleep.

Morgana directed Ben to drive to the pier. The ticket office was, of course, closed, a posted sign in the window informing them that it would reopen at six A.M.

Wearily, she suggested that they all sleep as they could in the carriage. It was pointless, she thought, to go to a hotel at this ungodly hour.

Outside it was dark, and the moon had already risen from its resting place. The whiteness was pale and thin, dusting the bay with a silvery glow that melted into blue shadows along the shoreline.

Eventually, Cammy slept. Ben, stretched out on the driver's seat, dozed intermittently.

But for Morgana sleep was a luxury she couldn't afford. She became uncomfortably aware that five people were depending upon her, at least three of them for their very lives. It was a responsibility that weighed heavily.

She wondered what Griffin would do when he found out about what she had done. With a little luck — and Nathaniel's help — there was a possibility that he could go a day, or even more, before he discovered Cammy's absence. But what about her own absence? That he would most likely discover before the day was gone.

Morgana wished that she'd had time to write to her aunt and let her know they were coming. In a way, she supposed that Sarah was expecting them, for she had written about Cammy and Jude. But Sarah didn't know when they would arrive; now there was no way for Morgana to let her know.

She sighed, watching the first faint rays of the pearly dawn lighten the sky.

Quite a few boats were anchored in the harbor, not an unusual state of affairs. Vessels from such faraway places as London, Glasgow, and the West Indies put in here to load indigo, turpentine, and tar, as well as rice, corn, and other produce.

Small fishing boats were now coming in, some of them from James Island, their catch heading for the market which opened at five-thirty in the morning.

There were at least two steamboats that she could see. Morgana said a quick prayer that at least one of them would be heading North — and that there would be space available for all of them.

As soon as the sun tipped the horizon, the activity began as Negroes set to loading and unloading the various cargoes. Seagulls spread great white wings, swooping between tall masted ships in hopes of gleaning their morning meal.

The ticket office opened, finally, at six-fifteen. Morgana was first in line. Happily, one of the steamboats was headed for New York. From there, they could transfer to a packet going to Boston.

The boat, however, was not scheduled to leave until ten o'clock.

Morgana had Ben take them all to the Charleston Hotel where they had breakfast. From the hotel, Ben drove the women and children back to the pier. He then drove to the livery stables, leaving the horses and carriage there, requesting the owner to send word to Albemarle in a day or two and have someone come and fetch the rig.

Then he walked back to the pier.

Shortly after ten o'clock, the *Delta Fox* began to move, its side paddles slicing neatly through blue water as it headed out toward the Atlantic.

Tansy, as supposed "dah" for Jamie, had been allowed to share the stateroom occupied by Cammy and Morgana. Ben, however, had had to be booked into a lower cabin, in an area set aside for Negroes.

Standing on the deck beside Morgana, Cammy viewed the receding shoreline, unable to repress a small sigh of relief. After a while, she turned to Morgana, a worried frown creasing her brow. "You didn't have time to let your aunt know we were coming, did you?"

"It will be all right," Morgana assured her with a firm nod of her head. "I don't want you to concern yourself with that. She was most emphatic in her letter. I know we'll all be welcome at Somerset Hall." She put a hand on Cammy's arm. "Come, let's go down to our cabin and see how Tansy and the children are doing."

The cold was absolutely chilling when they arrived in Boston four days later. Prodded by a howling wind, it seemed to penetrate the heaviest clothing.

After Ben had collected their luggage, Morgana secured a hired cab and instructed the driver to take them to Taunset, seven miles distant.

Cammy was silent for most of the trip. At first, she had just been glad to leave Albemarle, to get away from her brother, to get her child to safety. But in these past few days the enormity of her predicament left her quite shaken. She had, in effect, cut herself off from her family, had no money, no means with which to support herself and Jamie. She hoped that Morgana was correct in her assumption that they would all be welcome at Somerset Hall. If so, then she and Jamie would have a safe haven — at least for the immediate future.

And Cammy refused to think beyond that.

Her aunt looked just as Morgana remembered her. Time had been very gentle with Sarah Enright. At forty-seven, her chestnut brown hair was still rich in color and texture, even if dusted with silver at her temples. Her gray eyes were still clear and brilliant — and right now wide with surprised pleasure.

"Morgana!" she exclaimed, embracing her niece. "How good it is to see you." She drew back, her dark green satin gown rustling softly with her movement. "I was sorry to hear about your father . . ." Her lovely eyes shadowed. "As you know, my brother and I were not close in these past years. But," she smiled sadly, "I confess to having loved him, despite his faults. His death came as a shock to me."

"He spoke of you . . . at the end," Morgana murmured as her aunt led them into the rear parlor. "I think he regretted many things. . . ."

Sarah patted Morgana's arm in a consoling way. "You and I will have a long talk, dear," she whispered. Then she motioned to the three people waiting in the large, well-furnished room. "Do you remember your cousin Benjamin?" Sarah looked at Morgana.

"Yes, of course I do." Morgana smiled at the man who came forward, kissing her cheek. At twenty-nine, Benjamin Enright had an appealing face and an engaging smile beneath a shock of red-gold hair. His blue eyes welcomed her, as did his quick hug of affection.

"The last time I saw you," he said, studying Morgana's face, "you were just a little waif with big and somber eyes."

Morgana laughed delightedly at the description of herself as a child. "You haven't changed much, Benjamin," she commented, viewing him.

He grinned, gesturing to the young woman standing by his side. "My wife, Hannah."

Morgana clasped the outstretched hand, smiling at the delicate, fine-boned young woman with the silver-blond hair and vivid green eyes.

"And, of course, Nicholas," Sarah interjected, nodding at her younger son. "He is now a lawyer," she added with an un-

281

abashed touch of pride.

Younger by some four years than his brother Benjamin, Nicholas Enright had dark hair and dark eyes set in a good-looking, even featured face. The brothers didn't resemble each other very much, Morgana noted. Even their taste in clothes seemed to be at odds, Nicholas tending toward a conservatism that was expressed by a dark gray frock coat and a somber black cravat. Benjamin, on the other hand, was wearing a buff colored jacket and his vest was a bright red with tiny yellow flowers embroidered on the fabric.

Despite his courteous welcome and cousinly kiss, Nicholas Enright's attention seemed to have focused upon Cammy, and he only briefly nodded at Morgana's acknowledgment.

"Come along," Sarah said, placing a hand on Morgana's shoulder. "I know you'll all want to freshen up before supper."

Morgana was led to the room she considered her own, it having been the one she had stayed in when she lived at Somerset Hall more than seven years ago.

For a time she walked about, touching the furniture, an ache growing in her throat with her memories. She remembered everything about this room. Her fingertips felt for the nick in the rosewood dresser top. It was still there. The large four-poster looked just as it had when last she slept in it, even to the brightly colored patchwork quilt that covered it.

This room had been a sanctuary to her — but it had lasted such a few short weeks before she had once again been uprooted. Now, she thought to herself, it was once again a sanctuary.

Later, having rested and changed their clothes, Morgana and Cammy met the others in the dining room. Tansy and Ben were in the large kitchen having their supper with the household staff.

As the conversation flowed smoothly, Morgana happened to

glance at her cousin Nicholas. She raised her napkin to her lips in an effort to conceal her smile. The young man was gazing at Cammy with such unconcealed admiration and interest that his face positively glowed. He couldn't seem to look away and appeared oblivious to everyone else at the table.

Cammy, of course, couldn't help but notice. Her cheeks flushed prettily as she tried to ignore the intense scrutiny.

When they were settled in the parlor again, the talk turned to more serious matters.

Sarah informed her niece that, despite the threat of secession by several Southern states, it wantonly a matter of time before abolition became a fact.

"But surely the North cannot feel so strongly that it would actually take the chance of having the Southern states secede?" Morgana protested at one point.

Sarah, who had changed into a mauve silk gown for supper, shrugged. "Right now, the Abolitionists are in the minority," she conceded, then made a vague gesture with a ringed hand. "But there are very powerful people dedicated to the cause." She looked at Morgana. "Mr. Garrison, as you well know, is tireless in his efforts to abolish slavery."

A maid entered the parlor just then, carrying a large silver tray with a pot of coffee and a plate of butter cookies studded with nuts and raisins. With practiced ease, she placed it on the low, glass-topped table between the two settees that faced each other.

"The South will never abolish slavery," Morgana murmured with a shake of her head. Glancing at Cammy, she saw the girl's nod of agreement.

"They'll have to, if it becomes law," Hannah interjected solemnly. The young woman was standing by the fireplace and now moved toward the settee. "As for secession — I sincerely doubt that they would go that far." She began to pour the steaming coffee into the delicate porcelain cups.

"But they would!" Morgana insisted, recalling everything she had seen and heard this past year. "I've lived there, I know they would. And it wouldn't surprise me in the least if South Carolina was the first state to secede," she added grimly, reaching for the cream pitcher.

Sarah extended a hand toward her niece. "Morgana, you must not return to the South. Stay here with us," she begged.

"I can't," Morgana replied with a deep sigh. She stirred the coffee once, then rested the spoon on the saucer. "My daughter —"

"Bring her back here," Sarah interrupted, leaning forward. "Nicholas will be glad to escort you."

"I will indeed," Nicholas offered promptly, with a nod of his head. "Sooner or later, this situation will become acute. I'm certain of it." He shook his head as he picked up his cup. "And I fear the time is not all that far distant."

Cammy regarded the young man frankly, and a bit depreciatingly. "There has been talk of abolition for years," she pointed out, still viewing Nicholas, who blushed with her attention. "I've been hearing arguments on that subject since I've been a little girl."

Seated beside Hannah, Benjamin cleared his throat, his face somber. "Have either of you heard of the new party that's been organized?" Both Cammy and Morgana indicated they had not, so he continued. "A Major Alvan Bovay out in Ripon, Wisconsin has formed a new political group — they're calling themselves Republicans."

Morgana gave a mirthless laugh at the news. "There have always been new parties, Benjamin," she stated, reaching for a cookie. "The American Party has been trying to unseat the Democrats and the Whigs for years."

Benjamin nodded at the observation. "I agree, the

Know-Nothings are a small threat. But, in increasing numbers, they are joining the Republicans. And now that Horace Greeley is beginning to show an interest, the movement seems to be gaining momentum. They're going to hold their first formal convention in July and plan to name candidates at that time."

Morgana frowned at the report as she wiped her hands on the provided napkin. "But why do you think the Republicans are different from any other fledgling party?" she asked her cousin.

"Because their main platform will be to abolish slavery," Benjamin replied. "In all states. I seriously doubt that they can win the next election. They're not yet that strong. But if they manage to select a man who is in any way forceful and charismatic, then I believe they have a good chance at the presidency."

"And you think that such a man would actually pass a law, abolishing slavery in the South?" Morgana asked, finding it difficult to believe.

Benjamin's nod was serious. "Yes, I do."

Morgana paled. "They'll never stand for it!"

He nodded again, slowly, his lips pursed. "I'm afraid you're right. And if there is a move toward secession, the government would have no alternative but to take up arms. Of course, if it were only South Carolina, the fighting would be brief. However, if the rest of the South joins with them . . ." He turned away, viewing the darting flames in the tiled hearth before again facing Morgana. "I don't even want to think of what might happen."

When Morgana retired later that night she felt an unease that threaded its way through her mind, stopping just short of outright fear.

She'd heard nothing of all this at Albemarle. There, day followed placid day, the river rose and ebbed with the tide, crops were planted and harvested. . . .

But no one spoke of abolition as anything other than a hypothetical occurrence — one they all agreed the North would not be so foolish as to instigate.

Fretful, she tossed and turned for some hours before she finally fell asleep. Her last thoughts were of Griffin. By now, he must know what she had done. She didn't need to guess that his reaction would be anger. She knew that. What she did wonder was if her absence mattered to him. She had thought that, once away from Albemarle — and her husband — she would be able to see things with a more circumspect eye; so far, that had not happened.

But of one thing she was certain. What she had done would not help matters in her relations with Griffin anymore than had the incident with Jude.

Chapter 18

A week after their arrival, Cammy, having borrowed a heavy, fur-lined cloak and matching muff from Hannah, took a walk around the vast grounds that comprised Somerset Hall, enjoying the sting of cold upon her cheeks.

She was fascinated by the snow, the New England countryside, and the invigorating weather. About a mile from where she was standing, the Taunton River appeared just as gray as the day itself. Somerset Hall was situated on a gently rolling hill about two miles from the milltown of Taunset, but a silvery mist precluded her from seeing anything more than vague outlines in the distance.

Light snow had been falling since early morning and the January day had a dim yet luminous look about it. Flakes were fluttering about like so many feathers, taking their time before they reached the ground.

Tansy refused to set foot outside, claiming the cold gave her aches and pains in places she never knew she had. Cammy didn't insist upon her company, rather enjoying the quiet solitude.

For the first time in many weeks she felt safe. She grieved for Jude, but it was now a quiet sorrow, not the overwhelming despair she had experienced at the beginning. She had Jamie, who was a part of Jude. Cammy made a silent vow that her son would grow up to know his father and to cherish his memory. Just as she would.

She had gone only a short distance when the sound of boots crunching in the snow made her turn around. In some surprise, Cammy saw Nicholas Enright heading in her direction. He was wearing a greatcoat and a hat of some soft material, the bright red woolen scarf around his neck offering the only vivid slash of color in his otherwise somber attire.

Approaching, he smiled a bit hesitantly, as if fearing he might not be welcome. "Miss Kynes, may I walk along with you?" he asked.

She nodded. "Of course, Mr. Enright."

"I hope I'm not intruding . . ." He fell in step, matching her slow pace.

"On the contrary, I would be pleased for the company."

For a time they walked in silence, Nicholas occasionally looking down at her, until at last Cammy paused at the end of the driveway. She gave Nicholas a shy glance, disconcerted by the intense way he was looking at her.

"I'm sorry," he murmured, embarrassed as he caught her questioning look. "I didn't mean to stare at you. It's just that . . ." He gave a soft laugh, his warm breath hanging in the frigid air for a fleeting second. "I've never seen anyone quite as beautiful as you are."

She flushed a rosy tint and lowered her eyes. "That's very kind of you, Mr. Enright," she murmured graciously.

"Oh, I meant it," he hastened to say. Nicholas couldn't look away from her. A few of her dark and shiny curls peeped out from under her bonnet, tantalizing him with their softness. The blue cloak — which he recognized as belonging to Hannah — set off the incredible perfection of her ivory tinted skin. And her eyes . . . Nicholas was certain that he could easily get lost in their fascinating depths.

At last he cleared his throat. "Ah . . . I was wondering if you would care to attend a lyceum with me this Saturday night — if you like that sort of thing." He watched her expectantly, unaware that he was holding his breath.

Cammy grew somber, not quite meeting his eyes. She felt a sudden heaviness around her heart. The young man seemed so sweet, so innocent to her. She felt bowed down by the weight of experience. "I . . ." She bit her lip, then regarded him with level eyes. "You do . . . know about me, don't you?" she whispered. She raised a hand and brushed a few snowflakes from her cheeks, but she kept her head up to look at him.

"Yes," Nicholas replied quietly. He admitted to himself that his initial reaction had been one of shock when he first heard Cammy's story. He and his brother Benjamin had been in the room when Morgana told his mother of all that had happened. Following soon on the heels of his first shock had come a rush of pity; the girl was so young, so vulnerable, he thought. It didn't seem right that she should have suffered so much. Then pity, too, dissipated, for each time he looked at Cammy, he became more and more mesmerized.

"It doesn't matter to me," he said in a rush, when she remained silent. "What's in the past is over and done with."

She contemplated that for a moment before observing, "There are not too many gentlemen who would feel that way."

Nicholas took a breath. "You must have . . . loved him very much." The words seemed to cause him pain. He turned away, studying the white scenery. When she didn't answer him, he turned to her again, his eyes searching her face. "If you don't want to talk about it, I understand," he said quickly.

Cammy shook her head. "No, it's all right." She met his eye. "I did," she said. "I loved him very much."

Nicholas nodded gravely at her words. "Then he must have been a fine man," he stated sincerely.

Cammy's eyes moistened and she blinked rapidly against the hot sting. "He could have been — if things were otherwise."

Nicholas seemed about to reach for her, but then thought better of it. "I think you did the right thing," he said to her in a low voice. "To bring your son here, I mean. He's a fine boy."

Her breath was a soft shudder as they turned and began to walk back to the house. On either side of the driveway, tall poplars dropped beneath their burden of snow. Cammy thought they looked like silent white sentinels.

"You like children, Mr. Enright?" Cammy asked after a while, when her emotions were again under control.

"I certainly do." He glanced down at her. "I hope that someday I will have a houseful. . . ."

His enthusiasm brought a smile to her lips. "Then I'm surprised you have not yet married."

Nicholas grew serious again. "I have not yet married for the simple reason that I've not found a woman with whom I wish to share my life. Until now," he added in a barely audible murmur. He didn't look at her as he said that. He seemed to be profoundly interested in the tips of his boots.

Wonderingly, Cammy glanced up at him, but made no comment.

Just before they reached the front steps, Nicholas paused, regarding her with dark, searching eyes. "I know it's too soon to speak of these things," he began. "I'm certain you need time to forget your loss . . . But, if you would consider it, I'd very much like to get to know you better."

Her smile was tremulous, warm. "I'd like that, too, Mr. Enright."

His grin made him appear suddenly boyish. Extending his hand, he put it on her elbow. "Let me help you, Miss Kynes. The steps can be slick. . . ."

Another week passed. One day, as soon as she opened her eyes in the morning, Morgana knew she would have to return to Albemarle.

She had been wrestling with her thoughts and options for days; remaining here, returning with Nicholas and bringing her daughter back North — or just returning and staying.

This morning, almost as if her subconscious mind had made the decision for her during sleep, Morgana awoke knowing the answer. Whatever problems existed between her and Griffin, they had Anne to consider now. Morgana hadn't wanted to admit just how much she missed her daughter, but when she looked upon Jamie her arms ached with a longing that cut right through her.

She would return — but she would not ask for Griffin's forgiveness for what she had done.

As expected, Sarah immediately tried to dissuade her. "From what you've told me about the man you married, I cannot understand your decision to return to him," she exclaimed, truly dismayed. "I thought you would be glad to get away. After all he's done, I shouldn't think you'd ever want to see him again."

"There have been times when I felt that way," Morgana admitted with a nod. "And yet," she smiled softly, "I think I knew from that very first day I saw Griffin that there would never be anyone else for me. And as for Anne . . ." Her sigh caught in her throat, ending in a sob. "Oh, I miss her so. . . ."

"Of course you do." Sarah gave Morgana a quick hug. Then she sighed with resignation. "I feel I have found you only to lose you again," she murmured softly.

Morgana gripped her aunt's hand. "You are so very dear to me," she whispered. "I can never thank you for all you've done. . . ."

Sarah bit her lip. "You will come back to visit?"

Morgana smiled through her tears. "I promise I will."

After her discussion with her aunt, Morgana sought out Ben. She found the Negro in the back yard, splitting firewood — a task he had taken upon himself for want of anything better to do.

As she approached, Ben gave a final chop, leaving the ax

buried in the log. Then he straightened, smiling at her.

"I'm going back home, Ben," she said quietly.

He nodded as if he'd known that all along. Sitting down on a log, he wiped his brow on the sleeve of his jacket. Despite the cold, the work had produced a thin film of perspiration on his black face.

She watched him a moment, then suddenly asked, "Ben, how old are you?" Sitting down beside him, she arranged her heavy woolen skirt about her ankles.

"Doan rightly know, Miz Morgana," he answered. "Thirty-seven, I reckon; mebbe thirty-eight."

"Have you ever been married?"

The question didn't seem to cause him any surprise. "Had me a wife once, but she got sold. Never seen her agin." He sighed heavily, although from his words or his recent exertion, she couldn't tell.

Morgana shifted her weight a couple of times until she felt comfortable on the hard wood. "Does that mean you're still married?" she asked him.

He shook his head. "Naw, Miz Morgana. Ain' married no more. When de preacher sayin' de words of marriage, he say, 'until death — or distance — do you part.' " He spoke the phrase slowly and clearly, as if he had memorized it.

Morgana struggled with the anger which, of late, seemed her constant companion. "You mean a marriage is dissolved whenever the husband or wife is . . . sold?"

"Yassum," Ben acknowledged with a nod of his head. " 'Spects my Tildy got herself another husband by now," he speculated.

"Do these . . . separations happen often?" she inquired, a bit astonished at how little she knew about how these people lived, even having been in their proximity for more than a year now.

Ben shrugged. "Iffen you got a good masta, it doan happen so much. But my ole Masta Fiske . . ." He shook his head slowly from side to side. "He be one fearful man. Kilt my momma, he did. Whipped my Tildy, sayin' she sassed him. Den he sol' her."

Morgana turned away and bit her lip, not wanting to hear anymore. For a time they sat in silence.

"What do you think of Tansy?" Morgana asked after a few minutes had gone by.

"She be a right pretty gal," he answered after a moment's thought. "She spirited."

Morgana turned to look at him. "Would you be willing to marry her?"

Ben seemed to consider that. "Marries her iffen you want me to, Miz Morgana," he said at last. "But goin' back wit you when you goes home," he added firmly.

"You mustn't do that!" Morgana exclaimed quickly. "Here, you're free. But even with your papers, once you go back there, you'll be in danger of becoming a slave again." She was astounded and dismayed that he would even consider such a thing.

"Knows dat, I do, Miz Morgana," Ben replied solemnly, inclining his head. He tightened the scarf around his neck, pulling it up to cover his ears against the cold.

"Don't you like it here?" she persisted, bending toward him.

"Lak it fine," Ben assured her. "Pretty, wit de snow an' all. An' dese people bin good to me. Yassum, laks it fine," he repeated, his full lips curving into a smile.

She sighed, feeling exasperated. "They why won't you stay here?"

Ben regarded her for a long moment, his expression turning serious. "Promised yore daddy I watch over you," he said in a low voice. "Cain't go back on my word to dat man."

Morgana smiled slightly, touched by the simple statement. "You were very fond of my father, weren't you?" she asked softly. Reaching down, she picked up a handful of snow, absently fashioning it into a round ball.

"Yassum," Ben responded with quiet conviction. "Saved my life, he did. Was wit him fer five years, an' it wuz de happies' time in my life. Traveled lots, us. An' I wuz dressed fine all de time." His dark eyes sparkled with his memories. "An' ever' time Masta Aleceon won at de cards, he give Ben some of de money to spend." He chuckled, slapping his knee. "Dem gals in New Orleans would do dey fanciest struttin' ever' time dey seen Ben comin' along."

She was silent a moment, then sighed deeply as she lobbed the snowball at a tree. It landed with a soft splat, shattering into a spray of white.

"Very well," she said at last, brushing her hands against one another. "It isn't for me to ask you to marry anyone. And since you are now a free man, I can no longer tell you what to do." She got to her feet. "If it's your decision to return with me, I won't try to change your mind."

Later that day, Cammy burst into tears when Morgana told her of her decision. But Cammy's welfare no longer troubled Morgana. She knew that Sarah would let her stay indefinitely, and it didn't take much perception on her part to see that Nicholas and Cammy were growing more and more attracted to one another with every day that passed.

"But you can't," the girl cried out, persisting even in the face of Morgana's firm decision. "Please, Morgana. Send for Anne. Stay here . . ."

"Cammy, I must go back," Morgana retaliated, not fully explaining even to herself why she felt it necessary to return to Albemarle.

In spite of everything that had happened, Morgana knew

that she loved Griffin Kynes as much today as when she had married him, more than a year ago. There was that to be said, and no more. It was not something she could change at will, however much she may have wanted to. Somehow, some way, she would have to pick up the threads of her life and begin anew.

And her life was with Griffin.

Two days later, with expressed misgivings on the part of her family and copious tears from Cammy, who clung to her, weeping, Morgana and Ben left Somerset Hall.

Chapter 19

The February evening was damp and cold. Outside, the rain fell steadily, without let up, as it had been for the past two days now.

Standing by the window in the study, hands in the pockets of his tan breeches, Griffin contemplated the silver rivulets of water that coursed down the diamond-shaped panes of glass, eventually forming small gullies that threaded through the front yard.

The rain, he thought to himself worriedly, was starting much too early. The ground was already so saturated that the new water wasn't running off easily. The fields were becoming flooded under the onslaught. If the weather didn't clear, and soon, the crop would be irreparably damaged.

"Masta, suh . . . Yore supper's ready," Thomas reminded him in his soft voice as he entered the study for the second time in the past fifteen minutes. When there was no immediate response, he added, "Masta Nathaniel already sittin' down." He waited hopefully.

Without looking at Thomas, Griffin nodded then. With one more look at the gray and wet weather, he headed for the dining room.

In the hall, Griffin paused abruptly, seeing Serena about to ascend the stairs. She was dressed in the red silk gown with its black lace overskirt that he had purchased for her on an impulse when last he had been to New Orleans. It was her one piece of finery, and she wore it every chance she got. Her long black curly hair was piled atop her small head and secured with an onyx comb, another gift he had given her.

Viewing him with her dark and beautiful eyes, the girl whispered a question. "Waits for you in yore room, suh?"

Serena's expression was a silent plea, for she was very much in love with her strong and virile master. Like everyone else on that night four weeks ago, Serena had known that Morgana was about to leave Albemarle. She had hugged the knowledge to herself in secret joy, feeling that now she would have Griffin all to herself.

From the very day he had purchased her in Savannah more than two years ago when she had been sixteen, Serena had loved Griffin Kynes. She had been a virgin then, terrified of what her fate was to be.

Fortunately — or perhaps unfortunately for her — Serena's fate had been to fall in love with her master. She had no aspirations of rising above her station. She asked for nothing other than to be his slave.

Even though Griffin, in these past weeks since his wife had left him, had, for some reason, been unable to make love to her, Serena couldn't find it in her heart to censure him. Just being allowed to lay at his side was bliss enough for her.

Now, one delicate hand on the balustrade, Serena continued to wait for his answer, her eyes bright with anticipation.

But Griffin frowned at her, an expression Serena had seen often of late. His voice emerged unintentionally gruff. "No. Go back to your cabin."

Her eyes filled with tears as she turned. Although the sight would have, at one time, caused him to relent, Griffin said no more as the girl withdrew. With slow steps, he continued on to the dining room.

As he sat down at the table a few moments later, Griffin thought to himself that he wasn't very hungry. He viewed the chicken, fried just the way he liked it, the platter of tiny shrimp, the bowls of rice, the tempting golden mound of biscuits, and, sighing, picked up his glass of Madeira.

To Griffin's right, Nathaniel sat, eating with his usual appetite.

Although it was not yet seven o'clock, the lowering and sullen weather had already brought with it the darkness of night. Both of the silver candelabrums sported lighted candles and the two brass lamps on the sideboard were turned high, casting a flickering yellow glow that prodded at shadows in the corners.

The room was quiet with just the two of them there. It seemed empty despite the presence of the four houseboys who moved about on slippered feet. One of them offered the platter of chicken to Griffin, but he shook his head, moving his hand in a curt dismissal.

"You're not eatin', boy," Nathaniel observed, wiping his mouth with his napkin. He gestured to Adam and the light-skinned Hausa immediately spooned more rice and shrimp onto the empty plate.

"I'm not hungry," Griffin replied, sipping his wine. "Too much pie for dinner."

The old man snorted. "You didn't eat enough to fill a bird," he contradicted. He picked up his fork again and plunged it into the rice.

Griffin just shrugged and motioned for his glass to be refilled.

"Got to drain the west fields tomorrow," Nathaniel noted after a while, scraping the last of the shrimp from his plate.

"I know."

Eventually, Nathaniel put down the fork and leaned back in his chair. He viewed his grandson for a long moment with a worried eye. "You got to talk about it sometime, Griff," he murmured at last.

Griffin's eyes were steely as he darted a quick look at the older man. "Talk about what?"

Brows drawn down, Nathaniel pushed his chair back and got to his feet. "Come on, boy. I could use a brandy and so could you."

Griffin issued a deep sigh of resignation, but got up and followed his grandfather into the study.

The night was cool and a small fire had been laid in the grate. Nathaniel sat down in one of the two wing chairs before the comfortable blaze, rubbing his hands together in satisfaction while Griffin poured their drinks.

"Feels good," Nathaniel murmured in contentment. "Cold seems to reach my bones more than it used to. Think mebbe I'm gettin' old."

Griffin smiled slightly as he handed Nathaniel a glass. Then he sat down. "You're not so old."

"Almost seventy-two now; that's not young." Nathaniel took a deep sip of the brandy and felt the warmth settle in his stomach. Then he put the glass on the table beside his chair. He sat back, fixing Griffin with a level and knowing look. "Got to talk about it, Griffin," he said again, this time more firmly. "It's been weeks now and you're actin' like nothing happened. Can't keep it bottled inside you. Bad for the digestion," he pronounced sagely. "No wonder you can't eat." He leaned forward, clasping his work-worn hands between his knees. "What're you going to do about Morgana?"

Griffin's expression closed as annoyance tugged at him. He didn't even want to think about her, much less talk about her.

"What're you going to do about your wife?" Nathaniel persisted in measured tones, undeterred by his grandson's attitude.

"What the hell do you want me to do?" Griffin exploded in exasperation. He ran a hand through his dark hair. "She's gone. And good riddance," he muttered, draining his glass.

Nathaniel's mouth hardened into a thin line of censure.

"You don't mean that, boy," he murmured, shaking his head in an almost sorrowful manner. "You got the look of a man who's lost something mighty precious to him. Man wants to get rid of his wife, he looks relieved when she goes; he don't look like you."

"After what she's done, I don't want her back!"

Griffin's fierce look was meant to silence Nathaniel who simply ignored it. He was determined to have his say. He was not one for interfering between man and wife, for some things are better left to the principals involved. But this situation was different than most, Nathaniel reasoned. He himself had had a hand in it, and so had a right to speak.

"What did she do?" he asked finally. At Griffin's glowering look, he repeated, "I mean it, Griff. What did she do? Think about it." He waved a hand. "Saved the life of your sister's child? Put a buck out of his misery? Hell, that woman's got more gumption than any ten put together."

Having had his say, Nathaniel rested back again and, for a time, neither of them spoke.

Outside, the rain quickened, driven by a wind that bent branches and whistled along the eaves of the house.

Nathaniel stared into space, thinking of his wife, Anne. With her at his side, he had discovered the meaning of life. She had joined him on his trip to America, sharing his determination for a new life in a new country. All that any man could desire had been in Anne. In Morgana, he recognized the same type of woman. Difficult — but impossible to live without. They made it all worthwhile, gave meaning to a man's life and accomplishments.

Nathaniel had never even considered taking another wife after Anne's death. She had been too perfect a mate to ever be replaced. She had struggled and toiled by his side when they had come to this new land. And she had died before fully reaping the rewards from both their efforts. When their son Roger had fallen ill with smallpox fifteen years ago, Anne had nursed him day and night in her own tireless and courageous way. On the very day Roger had died, Anne had come down with the dreaded disease, and before the week was gone she, too, had succumbed.

Turning his head slightly, Nathaniel viewed his brooding grandson. Griffin, from the day he had been born twenty-six years ago, had found a special place in Nathaniel's heart. Although he had never told a living soul, Nathaniel had always been somewhat disappointed in his own son. Roger had been a soft spoken man with an intellect more suited to a poet than a planter. He'd been a dreamer all his life, and the only thing of worth his son had ever accomplished — in Nathaniel's eyes — was his marriage to Alicia Saunders, a beautiful and gentle-bred Charleston girl whose family now lived on James Island. William Saunders, a retired lawyer, had been violently opposed to the marriage of his only daughter to Roger Kynes, whom he considered unworthy of the lovely and gracious Alicia. In that, Nathaniel had to admit, the old barrister had been right.

But Griffin . . . From the beginning, he had been the recipient of his grandfather's love and pride. Nor, Nathaniel reflected ruefully, had Griffin ever disappointed him. Until now.

"Reminds me of your grandmother," Nathaniel mused at last, putting his thoughts into words as if his mind had never left the subject. "Your mama, now, she was a sweet little thing." He cast a quick look at the young man, who continued to remain silent. Griffin was sunk deep in the chair, legs stretched out before him. "You remember your mama, boy?"

Griffin muttered a brief affirmation. He got up, poured himself another drink, and sat down again. He continued to stare moodily into the little blaze in the grate.

"She was a fine lady," Nathaniel continued with a slow nod. "That's what she was — a lady. But your grandmama . . ." A soft smile crept across his lined face. "Ah . . . She was a woman." He peered sharply at Griffin's averted face. "You know the difference, boy?" he demanded.

Griffin groaned inwardly. The old man just wasn't going to give up, he thought. But his only answer was another deep sigh.

"You got yourself a woman." Nathaniel gave a small chuckle and took another sip of his brandy. "Takes a man to handle one of them," he declared knowledgeably. He gave his grandson a sly, sidelong glance. "Want to know how she did it?" He spoke in a deceptively soft and casual voice.

Griffin at last looked directly at his grandfather. "Did what?" he asked, although he knew very well to what Nathaniel was referring. He *had* wondered how Morgana had managed to buy Tansy and the baby, then spirit them away. All Nathaniel had told him was that she bought them, then took them North. Upon hearing that, he had flown into a black rage, refusing to even speak of her again.

Nathaniel gave another chuckle, pleased with the response he had received. "You should have seen her," he murmured, his eyes lighting with remembrance. "Never seen a woman dressed like a man before . . ." He rubbed his chin, unobtrusively watching the younger man.

Griffin's brow creased in perplexity. He wondered whether his grandfather had had too much brandy.

Seeing the look, Nathaniel nodded his head, his expression positively gleeful. "That's how she did it!" he exclaimed, sitting up straighter, aware that he now had Griffin's full attention. "Dressed herself in her daddy's clothes — walkin' stick and all. Then she took herself off to Charleston, went to the auction and, cool as you please, outbid every man there." He laughed in sincere delight, then finished his brandy in one long swallow.

Dumbfounded, Griffin just stared at him.

"Yessir!" Nathaniel gave a vigorous movement of his silver head. "Brought 'em all back here. They were here when you came home," he confided. "Then, after you went to bed, she had Ben drive them to Charleston where they took the next boat North."

Sitting there, Griffin tried to conjure up the sight of Morgana dressed as a man. But his imagination failed him, projecting an image so ludicrous that, in spite of himself, the corners of his mouth softened in the beginnings of a smile.

Noting that, Nathaniel's eyes gleamed in satisfaction. "Now — what're you going to do about that woman of yours?"

Griffin made no immediate answer. He was thinking about that day when Morgana shot Jude. Approaching her, he had been about to strike her with his riding crop. The defiant look in her eyes had stayed his hand, made him incapable of carrying out his intention. And, knowing her as he now did, he realized that even if he had struck her, she wouldn't have flinched; she probably would have struck back.

He felt his chest expand with unconscious pride as he thought that, even though his mouth was twisted with a grim sadness. He sighed, turning morose again.

"There's nothing I can do," he said at last.

"You love her?" Nathaniel peered intently, his dark eyes bright with speculation. He knew the answer, had for months, but he wondered if Griffin knew.

Griffin hesitated, then nodded slowly.

"Well then, seems like you oughta tell her that."

"It wouldn't do any good," Griffin replied quietly. "Besides," he averted his face, "I . . . tried to tell her once, but she wouldn't listen."

Nathaniel's sound of disgust was sharp and he shifted his

weight in the chair, displaying agitation. "No woman alive who wouldn't listen to a thing like that," he muttered. Then, frowning, he jabbed a finger in Griffin's direction. "You ought to go after her, tell her. . . ."

Griffin turned to look at the old man. "Where, exactly, would I go?" he asked impatiently and just a bit sarcastically.

Nathaniel's frail shoulders slumped as he sank back in his chair. "Don't rightly remember," he admitted sadly, then thought on it for a long moment. Finally, he snapped his fingers. "Massachusetts! That's it. To an aunt in Massachusetts."

At that, Griffin gave a short, humorless laugh. "That's a pretty big place," he noted wryly, again picking up his glass.

A silence descended as the two men each fell into their own thoughts. The baby began to cry, the sound of her fretful wails carrying easily downstairs and through the open door of the study. Abruptly it ceased as, upstairs, Celia took the child to her breast. Then it was quiet again, with only the sound of the rain to punctuate the passing minutes.

"Seems to me that a woman like that wouldn't leave her baby for too long a time," Nathaniel mused at last. His gaze rested upon Griffin, who had again sunk into a dour contemplation of the darting flames. "Wouldn't surprise me a'tall," he went on quietly, "if she were to come back soon, if for no other reason than to see her baby. . . ."

Having offered that assumption, Nathaniel leaned his head back, absently contemplating the shelves that marched up the wall on either side of the tiled fireplace. They were filled with an assortment of volumes that Nathaniel had collected over the years and which he had always intended to read when he found the time. But time, for Nathaniel Kynes, always seemed to be at a premium, and so most of the books languished, unread.

But he would get to them one day, he thought, closing his eyes.

The warmth of the fire and the brandy combined to prod Nathaniel toward sleep. After only a few more minutes passed, his head began to nod until, finally, his chin came to rest on his chest and he slept.

Griffin continued to sit there, staring at nothing, his thoughts alive with Morgana.

The anger really hadn't left him, but it was becoming unfocused. Was it directed at himself? Morgana? Cammy? He wasn't sure. He wasn't sure about anything anymore. At the time he had punished Jude and sold Jamie, he had felt very strong in his convictions. The fact that Morgana had thwarted him both times provoked a righteous rage within him that continued to simmer long after the events had taken place.

But in these past two weeks, he had become aware of a new emotion, one he had never before felt: loneliness. And loneliness, Griffin reflected morosely, was not something a person got used to. Suddenly, nothing seemed very important anymore. The very house seemed to echo with emptiness. As much as possible, he had avoided thinking about Morgana. But at odd times of the day, her image would invade his mind, provoking a bleak despair that almost made him physically ill.

As for the nights . . . During the four weeks that Morgana had been gone, he had summoned Serena to his bed on more than one occasion. To his utter dismay, even her young and warm body couldn't rouse him from his lethargy.

Against his will, he found himself remembering things, how the solitary dimple in her smooth cheek deepened when she was amused, the flash of her eyes when she was angered, the rare golden laugh that haunted him with its never-to-be-forgotten sound, and the soft and white body, so pliant, so willing beneath his touch. . . .

"Oh, God," he moaned, unable to bear the memories that stalked through his mind. He had never realized it was possible to love so deeply. And the realization had, for him, come too late. At night, in the darkness of his room, even with Serena at his side, he kept hearing Morgana's voice. "I love you, Griffin," she had said. "I love you." Griffin felt the despair churn within him. Would he ever hear those words again? Ever hear them from the only person who mattered?

Leaning his head back, Griffin closed his eyes. Weariness etched his face, somehow more profound because it was of the mind, not the body.

He was more than a little drunk, and the lack of food wasn't helping matters. But then, in these past weeks, that had been the only way in which he was able to summon the comfort of sleep. And oblivion.

Just before he drifted into the void of blackness that beckoned so invitingly, Griffin wondered whether his grandfather had been right.

Perhaps Morgana would come back — if for no other reason than their daughter.

Chapter 20

This time when the boat docked at Charleston, Morgana felt as if she were coming home. The soft and gentle breeze, tangy with salt spray, kissed her cheeks in welcome. Almost avidly, her eyes took in the now familiar sight of slate and tiled roofs, the beautifully decorative ironwork, the majestic spire of Saint Michael's Church. She breathed deeply of the sweet and pungent March air that was filled with the scent of flowers and citrus.

After collecting their baggage, she sent Ben to rent a carriage. A while later, they were on the road to Albemarle. She felt deliciously giddy at the prospect of again seeing Griffin, even though her feeling was tempered with cautious restraint.

Since the boat hadn't docked until after five in the afternoon, she knew they wouldn't get to their destination until well after dark.

And what would her reception be? Morgana wondered, a bit nervously. Nathaniel would be glad to see her, she knew. But what about Griffin? Would he welcome her — or would he send her away again?

Although she was tired, Morgana couldn't relax enough to sleep. She was, therefore, wide awake about two hours later when she felt the carriage come to an abrupt halt.

"Where you goin', Nigger!"

The menacing voice boomed from the darkness, shattering the quiet evening.

Startled by the gruff and sinister voice, Morgana looked outside to see the patrollers approaching. There were more than twenty of them. Some were carrying torches, the wavering golden glare cutting sharply through the black shadows along the dirt road. All of them held guns.

"What do you want?" Morgana demanded, upset by the delay. "Who are you?"

The leader peered suspiciously, then relaxed, but only slightly. Angling his horse forward, he came closer.

"Sorry, ma'am," he apologized. He removed his broad-brimmed hat in an almost deferential manner. He was of medium height, his body thick and compact without an ounce of spare flesh upon it. A high-bridged nose dominated an otherwise unprepossessing face. "Name's Drover. Jake Drover. Excuse me, ma'am, but you shouldn't be out tonight. . . ."

"What are you talking about?" Morgana frowned at the man. She knew patrollers were necessary, but she didn't like them. They were a rough and mean sort, their numbers drawn from the so-called poor white trash. "Get those men out of the way," she ordered, waving a hand at the others. "They're blocking the road."

His expression didn't change, nor did his attitude of tense watchfulness. Although his rifle wasn't pointed at her and was being held with an outward display of casualness, Morgana noticed uneasily that it was aimed directly at Ben.

"You shouldn't be out tonight, ma'am," he repeated firmly. "There's trouble. . . ."

"Let us pass!" Morgana was growing exasperated with the man's stubbornness. "We're on our way to Albemarle."

The man cast a hard look at Ben, who was nervously trying to maintain his composure.

"You trust this heah buck?" he demanded of Morgana.

"Of course I do!" she retorted angrily. "You have no right to stop us this way. . . ."

"Didn't mean no disrespect to you ma'am," he hastened to say, but the hard expression remained. "There's a gang of niggers on the prowl, led by a renegade buck named Jonah. We caught one of the black devils about an hour ago. But the rest of 'em headed into the swamp. Killed one of my men and set fire to Barrow's house over at Four Oaks." He looked closely at Morgana, who had paled at the report. "That's only about six miles from Albemarle, ma'am," he reminded her in a quiet voice.

Sobered, Morgana nodded slowly. "Well, we can't go back," she decided. She was silent a moment, then viewed the waiting patroller. "You said they headed into the swamp?"

"Yes, ma'am. But no tellin' how long they're going to stay there. They're crazy . . . and they're likkered up, too. You better ride along with us."

"Where are you going?"

Drover pointed back in the direction from which she had come. "One of my men lives about an hour's ride from here. We're going to get his dogs, then come back again. Can't do no tracking in the dark without the dogs."

Morgana chewed her lower lip thoughtfully. "That's almost clear back to Charleston," she pointed out. She shook her head firmly. "No, Mr. Drover. We'll continue on. Besides, we'd only hold you up."

The man saw the truth in that. He gave a slow nod and put his hat back on his head. "All right," he agreed, but with reluctance. "I'll send two of my men to ride along with you. Although," he added, "I doubt it'll be too much protection for you. When the renegades left Four Oaks, they stole some guns. They're not only crazy, they're armed."

After assigning two men as an escort, the patroller rode off into the night, the rest following closely.

Ben removed the whip from the whip socket to the side of the driver's seat and flicked it over the rump of the horses, spurring them forward, this time at a quicker pace as they hurried toward Albemarle.

There was no thought of rest now as Morgana anxiously looked out into the dark night. There wasn't even a moon to alleviate the relentless blackness. One of the patrollers had insisted that Ben extinguish the small lamps bobbing atop the carriage, and now there wasn't even that bit of light to guide them. Ben was apparently trusting to the horses' instincts to stay on the road. Morgana could only hope that his confidence was not misplaced.

The two patrollers were only a small comfort, she realized uneasily. If they were suddenly attacked by a gang of renegade slaves, the two men could easily be overcome. Then what? The stories Nathaniel had told her came rushing to her mind and she shuddered at the prospect of what might happen.

Supposing they had already attacked Albemarle? She bit her lip and moaned, thinking of her child. Babies, Nathaniel had said. They had killed helpless babies. . . .

Why did they seem to be going so slow! And why hadn't she thought to send word she was coming?

"How far away are we?" she called out to Ben, her anxiety growing.

"Jest a couple of miles, Miz Morgana," Ben answered over his shoulder, not bothering to turn around. He, too, sounded worried. "Be there soon."

But it seemed to take forever.

She smelled the smoke before she saw the flames.

Little by little, the blackness became invaded by an ominous glow. Four Oaks, Morgana thought, recalling that the patroller had told her that the house had been set ablaze.

Before they had gone another half mile, however, Morgana realized that the flames she could see shooting up into the moonless sky came, not from the neighboring plantation, but from Albemarle. . . .

Vague and frightening fancies tormented her in those har-

310

rowing minutes; Griffin slain, her child murdered.

Oh, God! She put her trembling hands to her face. Better she were to die as well, rather than live with such a horror waiting to be envisioned each day of her remaining life.

When they at last drove through the gates, Morgana could see that it was not the house, but the barn, that was on fire.

Now she could hear screams, shouts, the sound of gunfire. The terror pressed down upon her. People were running back and forth, all of them black. She wondered frantically if the slaves of Albemarle had joined the revolt. If so, they were all doomed.

The carriage was careening forward. Ben was standing up, gripping the reins in his hands, shouting for everyone to get out of the way.

A figure leaped out of the darkness and tried to jump up on the carriage seat, but a well placed shot from one of the patrollers caught the man in the chest. With a wild yell, he fell backward.

At last they reached the Great House. Before Ben could get to her, Morgana had opened the carriage door and was racing up the steps.

Griffin, Nathaniel, and Carlie Dobbs were on the verandah, rifles at ready, and were soon joined by the two patrollers.

There was no time for amenities or greetings as Morgana, followed by Ben, ran into the house and up the curved staircase.

Entering her room, Morgana gave a sob of wild relief. Both Celia and Bella were huddled in a corner, shielding the baby with their bodies, their faces terror-stricken in that moment before they recognized Morgana and Ben.

At the sight of her, they both began to wail, clutching at her as if for protection.

Quickly, Morgana tried to calm them down. She then went for the mate to the pistol she had once before used. Checking to see that it was loaded, she regarded the two cringing women.

"Lock the door when I leave," she instructed in what she hoped was a calm voice. "Let no one in until I return."

"Has to git over my daid body to git to dis heah chile," Celia cried out in a high, thin voice. She clasped Anne tightly to her breast.

Morgana attempted a smile, but managed only a weak grimace. Then she and Ben went into the hall. She waited until she heard the sound of the bolt. Nodding at Ben, they both went downstairs.

The five men were standing close to the front door, attitudes wary and cautious as they watched the rampaging Negroes. So far, they hadn't approached the house.

Catching sight of her, Griffin snapped, "Get back into the house!"

"I can help," Morgana informed him quietly, producing the gun. "I . . . know how to use it," she reminded him.

She couldn't define the look he gave her, but it was brief, then he returned his gaze to the yard.

"Some of those bastids got guns," Carlie noted grimly, peering at the renegades with narrowed eyes.

"Got 'em at Four Oaks," one of the patrollers commented. "Mister Barrows got a whole collection of 'em, but most don't work. And even if they did, wouldn't be enough ammunition, 'cept maybe for two or three of 'em."

"Is Farley all right?" Nathaniel asked quickly. He gave the man a searching glance as he inquired after his old friend.

"Don't know, suh," the man replied. "Was when we left."

"Where are the patrollers now?" Griffin asked angrily, then listened to the man's words with a disgusted expression. "They should have stayed here, dammit!"

"Thought they headed into the swamp," the patroller tried to explain in a voice that hovered on the edge of a whine.

"Well, they're not in the swamp now," Griffin muttered through clenched teeth, gripping the rifle in his hands.

The renegades had this while been whooping and hollering in glee at the sight of the burning barn. Their laughter sounded maniacal. Finally, with a thundering retort, the structure collapsed to the ground in a shower of brilliant sparks.

Morgana moved closer to Nathaniel. "Are our people involved in this?" she asked quietly. She was amazed at her own calmness.

Nathaniel shrugged his thin shoulders. "Hard to tell, girl," he murmured. "Certainly, not all of them are. . . ."

"Why don't we bring those who aren't up here with us?" she suggested.

Turning slightly, he gave her a wry smile. "How're you gonna tell the difference?" he wanted to know. "Besides, we can't give them any guns, it's against the law." His expression softened and he touched her arm, giving it a slight squeeze.

Morgana felt the sincere welcome. Tears burned her eyes, but she couldn't give in to them. So far, Griffin had shown her no indication of his feelings about her return. He looked worried, tense, but she knew that had nothing to do with her.

"That nigger's makin' me nervous," one of the patrollers complained, looking at Ben, who was standing at Morgana's side.

"He stays here," Morgana stated firmly. She stared at the man until he turned away with a muttered oath. Griffin glanced at her again, but made no comment. His expression was inscrutable and it unnerved her. She couldn't tell what his reaction was to her return. He looked noticeably thinner to her and she felt a small stab of alarm, wondering if perhaps he had been ill.

Then Morgana heard Nathaniel draw in his breath sharply. She turned toward him.

"They're comin'," he said in a strained voice. He raised his rifle. "They've had their fun. Now they're comin' after us. . . ."

Looking into the yard, Morgana saw that he was right. They had grouped, crouching low in the waning embers of the fire. But as yet they made no move forward.

"They're waiting for the fire to die out," Griffin observed tersely. "It'll be really dark then. We'd better get into the house."

Carefully, they all backed in through the front door, Ben positioning himself in front of Morgana.

Turning, Griffin raised his rifle in a threatening gesture, aiming it at Thomas, who had suddenly appeared.

The terrified Negro quickly raised his hands. "Doan shoot, masta, suh," he cried out fearfully. "Comin' to help you. . . ."

"Get the hell out of here," Griffin ordered harshly, not lowering the rifle nor taking his eyes from the trembling man.

"Where I gonna go?" Thomas wailed, looking miserable.

"Let him alone, Griff," Nathaniel said. His brows dipped into a severe frown. "If Thomas is gonna attack, he'll have to fight me first."

A shot rang out and they all started as the ball crashed into the outside wall.

With a shriek of animal fear, Thomas bounded up the stairs, heading for the attic.

Griffin, Nathaniel, and the two patrollers aimed their rifles at the front door, which Griffin had locked. Carlie Dobbs, his attitude tense, moved a few steps forward, standing with his back against the wall.

Morgana, pistol in hand, was a bit disconcerted to find her target was the back of Ben, who was still standing in front of her.

There was a sound of a sharp retort as something slammed with great force against the front door. Again and again it sounded, and they all knew that the door would soon be broken down.

314

Griffin looked toward his grandfather. "The study. It has a door that locks, and a window if we need it. Let's not barricade ourselves in a room we can't get out of."

In a sudden movement, Morgana turned and began to run up the stairs.

"Where are you going?" Griffin shouted after her.

"To get Anne!"

Morgana was only halfway to the landing when the front door caved in under the constant battering onslaught.

For a timeless moment, they all froze as Jonah, the other blacks crowded close behind him, stepped into the hall.

In that instant, Morgana saw that most of the blacks were carrying knives and only three had guns: Jonah, a Negro she didn't recognize — and Atlas, the burly Angolan who had replaced Jude and who had apparently joined the renegades.

Then, everyone began to shoot at the same time.

The next agonizing moments were an incoherent jumble in Morgana's mind. Ben raced up the stairs. A shot caught him in the back just as he reached her and he fell heavily against her, knocking her down.

One of the patrollers fell, blood streaming from his forehead. The force of a ball in his chest slammed Carlie Dobbs against the wall. Only two of the renegades were cut down.

After the first volley of shots, the blacks came rushing forward with a yell, overpowering Griffin, Nathaniel, and the remaining patroller.

"Now I gonna whip his white ass to death," Jonah shouted triumphantly. He was holding Griffin in a vicelike grip.

Atlas was making his way up the stairs, crouching like an animal, a hideous grin on his black face.

For the first time, Morgana looked upon a Negro and thought him less than human. Indeed, the black face of Atlas, his eyes wild and savage, thick lips drawn back in a parody of a smile, appeared more beast than man to her.

Terrified, Morgana tried to push Ben off of her, struggling with the weight of him across her lower body. She had dropped the gun when she had fallen, and now frantically groped around, not daring to take her eyes from Atlas.

At last her hand closed around metal. But before she could aim it, the Negro dived at her, knocking the pistol from her grip.

Lying almost on top of Morgana, Atlas leered down at her, bringing his black face so close she could smell his whiskey-laden breath. That, combined with his musky body scent, made her gag. She put both hands on his chest and pushed with all her strength.

Her effort produced no more than a laugh from the muscular slave. Bending down, he put his mouth on hers.

The terror rose up in her throat. Morgana could feel the steps cut into her back and lower spine as she struggled. She was aware of his hand fumbling with her skirt as he tried to push it up, but the weight of his own body was impeding his progress.

"Bring dat wench down heah!" Jonah called out. "Wants her to see what a hun'erd lashes look lak on a white back!" When Atlas gave no indication of hearing the command, Jonah raised his voice to a shout. "Goddamn you, nigger! Iffen I come up dere, gonna crack yore kinky haid open!"

Atlas turned then, casting a sullen look in Jonah's direction. Then he got up. His hand went around Morgana's wrist in a grip so tight it made her wince in pain. With a yank, he pulled her up, then began to walk downstairs. "We has our fun later," he muttered to her, dragging her along.

In the yard, there wasn't a soul about. Atlas was the only Albemarle slave who had joined the rebellion. The rest were all in their cabins, doors shut tightly. They would not join, but they would not help, either.

The smokehouse and the carriage house had been set afire and the combined blaze threw shafts of golden light about that danced crazily in the black shadows of night. The air was acrid with the smell of smoke and burning wood. In the stables, the horses were hysterical, their neighing cries shrill with terror as they smelled the smoke.

Morgana resisted the urge to look up toward her room, praying that Bella and Celia had had sense enough to get out of the bedroom. Using the back stairs, they could get out through the rear door. The renegades had not yet fired the house, but she knew they soon would.

Right now, however, they had other things on their mind.

Three of the oak trees that lined the driveway now sported a man lashed to the trunks. Griffin, Nathaniel, and the patroller had all been stripped to the waist. Each one of them was now tied to a tree.

Griffin turned slightly, trying to catch a glimpse of Morgana, his expression reflecting anguished concern for her safety. He struggled against his bonds, sweat beading his face with his effort, but was secured as strongly as was Morgana, held in the grip of Atlas.

Nathaniel was still and, as much as was possible under the circumstances, stood with dignity, his mouth grim.

The patroller, however, was cursing loudly in a furious rage, struggling against the ropes that bound him.

Grinning, his face appearing evil in the shifting firelight, Jonah stepped slowly toward him, a rawhide whip coiled in his right hand. His eyes were gleaming with triumphant satisfaction. All his plans were coming to fruition. He had tasted freedom and found it sweet. Revenge, he thought, would taste even sweeter. He still felt the rage that had flooded him when Atlas had told him that Zoe had been sold. It was yet one more score to settle.

"Thinkin' you makin' too much noise, *masta, suh,*" Jonah said to the patroller in a voice that was laced heavily with sarcasm.

The patroller's answer was a string of invectives so vitriolic and expressive that Morgana had never even heard most of the words he used.

Jonah only kept on smiling. Even after the first stroke drew a screeching yell from the man, he kept the smile in place.

The rest of the renegades howled in delight, urging Jonah onward and begging for a chance to use the whip.

"When I gits tired, y'all kin have yore turn," Jonah assured them magnanimously. He again raised his arm.

With each blow of the whip, Morgana could feel her insides cringe, her mind imagining that it was Griffin's back receiving the punishment.

Frantically, she looked about the yard. There were over one hundred people little more than a stone's throw away — where the hell were they?

Glancing down at her, Atlas grinned, then pulled her in front of him, her back against his chest. His arms went about her waist. He was holding her so tightly against him that she could feel his arousal even through her voluminous skirt.

"Ain' nobody gonna save you, missy," he whispered, his mouth against the back of her neck. "Dese people knows enuf to stay in dere cabins. Dey come out, we kills 'em. Knows it, dey do."

Morgana bent her head in an effort to get away from his searching mouth, but he raised a sinewy arm to her throat, forcing her head back again.

"You watch," he ordered softly. "Gonna see how it is to be a slave." He nuzzled her neck. "Den I gonna teach you how it is to be a wench. Likes it, you will. Promises you."

Morgana took a deep breath, then swallowed in an effort to

318

keep from screaming. She refused to allow herself to sink into the hysteria that was threatening to overwhelm her.

Her eyes darted about, viewing the renegades. They were all, she saw, very drunk, and getting more so. Having raided Nathaniel's stock of whiskey, the Negroes were now passing the bottles around, each man drinking long and deeply before handing it to another.

Watching them, she was astounded at how she had been fooled by their attitude of subservience, of gentle good humor, of apparently genuine regard for their masters. It had all been a hoax. These were no more than savages who lay in wait for the first opportunity to torture and murder.

In the midst of these sharp and bitter conclusions, there came the thought of Ben, and Morgana felt ashamed. That man lay dead on the stairs because of her. He could have easily joined the renegades. He could have easily stayed in Massachusetts. Instead, he had chosen to give his life to save her own.

The patroller had ceased his cursing, crying out now only in agony as Jonah, appearing tireless, continued with the savage beating.

Then, over the screams of the patroller, the howling of the renegades, and the whispering, menacing voice of Atlas, Morgana heard the faint sound of yapping dogs.

She ceased her struggles and stood very still, for the moment not even breathing. The sound was coming closer. But so far, no one seemed to have noticed. She reasoned that she could hear it because she and Atlas were standing a distance away from the mob of men, who were now so drunk and noisy it would take a cannon shot to capture their attention.

But Morgana realized that, even if the majority of them hadn't yet heard, Atlas soon would. He was drunk, but not sodden. Somehow, she would have to keep him engrossed with her for a few minutes longer. If the blacks heard the oncoming patrollers, they would probably kill Griffin and Nathaniel before they ran — and probably take her with them!

She began to struggle again, this time with purpose. Each time she moved, she rubbed her buttocks up against him until Atlas was breathing so heavily only the sound of his own gasps reached his ears.

At last he spun her around to face him and Morgana allowed him to do so, all the while keeping the pretext of fighting him. She began to scream now, placing her mouth close to one of his ears, putting a hand against his head, palm over his other ear.

Atlas was now wild with desire. With clumsy hands he began to tear at her clothes.

Morgana could feel herself tiring. She knew she couldn't fight him off much longer. Her body felt like a mass of aches and bruises.

With a grunt and a sudden movement, Atlas sank to the ground, dragging her down, cursing at the impediment of her skirts.

A shot rang out, but Atlas paid no mind. Beneath her, Morgana could feel the drumming sound of horses' hooves vibrating through the ground.

She began to fight in earnest, clawing at Atlas's face, her nails leaving trails of angry red scratches in the black skin.

Men were shouting, shots were being fired, dogs were growling fiercely as their canine teeth sunk into black flesh, and still Morgana fought, her breath now coming in whimpering, gasping sobs.

Tiring of the little game, Atlas put his hands about her neck, squeezing, his eyes inflamed with lust or murder, she couldn't tell. For the moment her vision blurred. Even the hateful face lost its outline and blended in with the shadows behind him. Her throat muscles strained, grew rigid. As if in the distance, Morgana thought she heard her name being called with a terrible urgency.

Suddenly she saw Griffin, his face rigid with fury as he came up behind Atlas. Jumping on the man's back, he put his arm about Atlas's throat, bracing his knee against the slave's spine. Increasing the pressure of his grip, Griffin forced Atlas's head backward, straining until the muscles in his temple throbbed with the effort.

Morgana had managed to squirm out from under Atlas and now sat on the ground, too weak in her relief to even get to her feet.

Griffin then placed the palm of his free hand on Atlas's forehead, pushing the Negro's head even further back. He again increased pressure until, at last, with a sickening crunch, he broke the man's neck.

Griffin held him a moment longer, then released him. Atlas's lifeless body crumpled, his head at an awkward angle.

Morgana began to sob, unaware that she was doing so. Coming toward her, Griffin picked her up in his strong arms and carried her into the house.

He walked up the stairs, stepping around Ben. Morgana continued to sob, clinging to him, her tears falling in droplets upon his bare chest. Reaching her door, Griffin kicked at it with his foot.

"Open it, dammit!" he shouted.

Recognizing his voice, Bella hastened to obey, her eyes round with fear.

Walking toward the bed, Griffin gently laid Morgana upon its soft surface. Straightening, he glanced at Celia, who was holding the sleeping Anne. Then he addressed Bella.

"See to your mistress. Don't leave her alone." He looked down at Morgana, who had calmed somewhat and was lying there, an arm across her eyes. She appeared utterly exhausted. Then he left the room.

On the steps again, Griffin stooped down and turned Ben over so that he was face up. Bending forward, he placed his head on the black man's chest. There was a faint, thready heartbeat.

Calling for Thomas, who had finally come out of hiding, Griffin gave instructions for Ben to be carried to Auntie Flora's cabin.

"Then fetch the doctor," he added, continuing on downstairs.

The patroller in the hall was dead. So was Carlie Dobbs. Briefly, Griffin viewed the two dead Negroes. Then, with a grim expression, he headed outside. He saw Nathaniel conversing with the newly arrived patrollers and he headed in their direction.

Of the twenty renegades, eight had been killed outright, including the two in the front hall. Another four were seriously wounded. The remaining eight, including Jonah, were standing in quiet dejection, hands tied behind their backs. They were guarded by several patrollers and the dogs, who occasionally strained at their leashes in an effort to get to their quarry.

The patroller who had been beaten was now lying on the grass, being tended to by several of his friends. He was cursing once more with vivid enthusiasm.

Nathaniel, having taken the time to put his shirt on again, turned as Griffin neared. "I've told Joe to round up some of the hands and clear away the bodies. They'll bury them in the swamp." Griffin nodded and Nathaniel went on to ask, "Is Carlie dead?"

Griffin nodded again. "And so is one of your men," he added with a look at Jake Drover.

"We'll take him with us," the man responded. "Now, where

can we string up these niggers?" He motioned in the direction of the renegades. "Jonah's your buck, ain't he? Want to handle him yourself?"

"No," Griffin responded quickly, before Nathaniel could reply. Right now, he felt as if he'd had enough killing to last him a lifetime. "Get them all out of here, including Jonah. Do what you have to, but do it elsewhere."

Jake Drover shrugged, nodded, then went to join his men.

"How is Morgana?" Nathaniel asked. His lined face reflected concern as he buttoned his shirt.

"She's resting. I've already sent for the doctor."

The words were no sooner spoken than Griffin looked up to see Daniel Foxworth's buggy rumbling up the driveway.

"I was over at Four Oaks," the doctor explained as he climbed down. He was a tall man, but on the lean side, which gave him an appearance of lanky uncoordination. His black moustache was full, looking somewhat oversized for his face. "I saw the flames and figured you might need help," he went on, reaching back inside the buggy for his satchel. "Is everybody okay here?"

Griffin regarded the man in gratitude, then quickly explained the situation. "I want you to take a look at my wife first," he said as they headed for the house. "After that, there's a buck that's needing attention. I put him in Auntie Flora's cabin."

The doctor chuckled and gave a short shake of his head. "He's in good hands then," he observed blithely. "Sometimes I think that old wench of yours is a witch."

Normally, Foxworth did not treat slaves. His reasons, however, were strictly pragmatic and not from any sense of prejudice. The doctors who tended slaves — and for the most part they were a motley crew, drunk more often than not — were immediately classed as "nigger doctors." The only time a white person would submit to their ministrations was in a time of emergency.

The reverse was also true. In times of emergency it was quite acceptable for a doctor of Foxworth's standing to treat Negroes.

The doctor went upstairs and Griffin poured himself a drink while he waited in the study. Looking out of the window, he saw the patrollers ride away, the renegades in tow. Those that couldn't walk were strapped on the horses like oversized saddlebags. Griffin knew that each and every one of them would be hung.

The bodies had been removed and Nathaniel had organized a bucket brigade to douse the remaining fires. The carriage house and the smokehouse were gutted. The barn was burned to the ground.

Only now did the full import of what had taken place make itself known to Griffin. They could have all been killed. When he thought of Morgana in the grip of that black buck and what could have happened to her, his hands began to shake.

Griffin had finished his drink when the doctor came downstairs again.

"She's all right," Foxworth reported. "A few cuts and bruises, but nothing serious. I admire the way she's got herself under control," he added, rubbing the back of his neck in a gesture of weariness. "Most women would be in hysterics after what she's been through. Had to dope up Amelia Barrows. Couldn't quiet her down at all."

Griffin viewed the doctor with a serious expression. "Any casualties over at Four Oaks?"

Foxworth shrugged. "Nobody killed, if that's what you mean. Farley took the missus and his sons and got the hell out of there when he saw them coming. But the bastards did plenty of damage before they left. Well," he said, heading for the door,

"I'll see to your buck now."

"He's not mine," Griffin explained as he walked with the doctor into the hall. "Used to be Morgana's, but she freed him."

Pausing, the doctor turned, staring at Griffin in some surprise. Most people in these parts refused to even consider such a step, regardless of the circumstances. Certainly no slave of Albemarle had ever been freed.

"Do the best you can for him," Griffin went on. He appeared almost embarrassed. Few were as outspoken as he when it came to manumission. "He saved my wife's life."

When the doctor left, Griffin went upstairs slowly. Outside Morgana's room, he paused a long moment before entering, motioning for Bella and Celia to leave.

Morgana wasn't in bed. She was seated on the chair by her dressing table. Dark bruises on her throat and upper arm were the only outward indication of what she'd been through. She had changed her clothes and brushed her hair. It lay soft and shining about her shoulders. Like everything else about her, Griffin thought it incredibly beautiful.

She was watching him, but she wasn't smiling as he came closer. Her expression was one of quiet contemplation.

Viewing her, Griffin felt such a rush of love for this woman, that, for the moment, he couldn't even speak. There was pride and there was strength, he could see it in her bearing and in her face. Both he recognized as a mirror image of his own pride and strength. A man needed those in a woman, he thought to himself. Needed them almost as much as gentleness and softness.

But above all, he needed love. To feel it or give it — Griffin somehow thought the former the necessity. To give love was rewarding; to feel it was to feel life itself.

For a few tense minutes, neither of them said anything. But

the very air seemed charged with emotion, with the sort of tingling expectancy that one senses before a summer storm.

Although thoughts and words crowded his mind, what Griffin finally said, was, "So you came back. . . ."

"Yes," she whispered. Her eyes were level as she continued to watch him.

He gave her a sharp look. "Was it because of Anne?" His breath seemed to still within him as he waited for her reply.

She hesitated, viewed her folded hands in her lap, then raised her face to him again. "Not entirely."

A small silence descended. Once or twice, Griffin opened his mouth to speak, then closed it again. Morgana continued to sit calmly, making no effort to break the awkward quiet.

Griffin began to move about the room, hands in his pockets. "When I discovered what you did," he said after a while, his voice barely audible, "I wanted to thrash you to within an inch of your life. . . ."

"And now?" she asked softly, tilting her head slightly.

Pausing, he turned toward her. "Oh, Morgana," he murmured with a small, sad smile. For a moment he seemed incapable of speech. Moving across the room, he sat down in a chair across from her, elbows on his knees, face in his hands. "At first, I was so angry, I couldn't even think straight. And then . . . I'm glad you got them away," he whispered, his voice muffled. "That child . . ." He looked up at her, expression anguished. "I never meant him harm. I was just so wild with the thought of Cammy. . . ."

"Your sister and her child are safe," she assured him quickly, smiling. "In fact, I believe that she and my cousin have discovered a mutual attraction for each other. I hope it works out for them. He seems genuinely fond of the baby, too."

Griffin continued to regard her for a long moment, wanting to know more about his sister's welfare. But he couldn't quite bring himself to ask. Not yet. Perhaps in time. Right now the thought of Cammy was like an open wound.

Finally, Griffin got up and came toward her. Kneeling at her feet, he took her soft hands in his own. "We got off to such a bad start . . ." His voice caught and he wet his lips. "But . . . I love you, Morgana," he whispered. "You must believe me. Whatever else I am or have done, I love you very much. . . ."

Her eyes shone with tears as she looked down at him. "That's the first time you've ever said that to me. . . ."

Reaching up, Griffin put his hands on each side of her face and looked deeply into her eyes. "Can you learn to love me again?"

Her eyes sought and found his, and it was as if they looked into each other's soul.

"I have never stopped loving you," she replied simply.

His breath seemed to catch in his throat and it was a moment before he could continue. "And can you forgive me? For everything?"

She nodded, not trusting herself to speak.

"That day when we first made love . . ." Griffin's voice was halting, as if he were searching for the words. "I want you to know that, for me, it had never been like that before. . . ."

"Oh, my darling," she murmured with a gentle laugh. "That was the easy part." She squeezed his hand. "For us, it will always be the easy part." Her smile was warm as she gazed into his eyes. "It's the loving with your heart and with yourself that takes time and understanding. . . ."

"And can we?" he asked with urgency, his dark eyes never leaving hers. "Can we learn the difficult part?"

"I think we already have, my darling," she replied softly. "I know that nothing will ever destroy the love I have for you."

His heart seemed to swell within him as he heard the words

he thought he'd never hear again. They were like cool spring water to his parched and arid senses. Getting to his feet, Griffin raised her up, embracing her. "Promise me," he said huskily, holding her tightly against his bare chest. "Promise that you'll never leave me again. While you were gone, there was nothing — nothing at all. Everything became meaningless . . ." His voice broke. "I'd thought you'd gone forever. . . ."

"I'll never leave you again, Griffin," she replied, feeling the joy blossom within her. She felt his love like a tangible thing, enveloping her with its warmth and security.

He hugged her tightly, feeling a contentment he had long been without.

Then, hearing his named called, Griffin went out onto the piazza, Morgana at his side. He looked down into the yard as Dr. Foxworth waved at him.

"The buck's going to be all right," the doctor shouted, a hand cupping his mouth. "Be sore for a few weeks, but he's going to make it."

Griffin nodded, smiling, and returned the wave of the departing physician.

"Thank God," Morgana murmured, her eyes glistening.

"Ben will have a home here for as long as he wants it," Griffin assured her. "In fact, I'll deed him a few acres of land to work as his own. . . ."

She couldn't prevent the few tears that coursed down her cheeks with his words.

His brows drew together. "That's something I don't ever want to see again," he murmured, tracing the silvery rivulets on her face with his fingertips. "There'll be no more tears for you, not ever . . ." Gently, he prodded the corners of her soft mouth until the dimple appeared to tantalize him. Bending forward, he put his lips on the adorable indentation, and in response, Morgana smiled tremulously. "That's better," he said, still holding her close, his chin against her hair.

For a long moment they stood within each other's arms, bodies pressed together, feeling the warmth that flowed through them with the contact.

Drawing back slightly, Griffin looked down at Morgana, searching her eyes for the answering response to his growing desire.

Without speaking, he picked her up and carried her to the bed, helping her to undress. When he had removed his own clothing, he lay down beside her and drew her into his arms. Beneath his lips, her skin felt like satin and tasted the way he imagined a rose petal would taste.

They came together naturally, without restraint, each delighting in the texture of the other, in the sensations aroused.

They made love sweetly, tenderly, and, at last, with the remembered passion each had to give to the other.

Afterward, as they lay quietly, arms entwined, Morgana looked at Griffin, wanting to tell him all she had learned, of the dark clouds brewing both in the North and South — but she knew he'd never leave his beloved Albemarle. She knew, too, as she rested her head on his chest, that whatever the future held for them, they would face it together.

shiji
wenxue
60jia

世纪文学 **60** 家

阿城著

阿城精选集

北京燕山出版社

"世纪文学60家"书系总策划:

白烨、陈骏涛、倪培耕、贺绍俊、张红梅

"世纪文学60家"评选专家名单:

(以姓氏笔画为序)

丁　帆　南京大学中文系教授

王中忱　清华大学中文系教授

王晓明　华东师范大学中文系教授

王富仁　汕头大学中文系教授

白　烨　中国社会科学院文学研究所研究员

孙　郁　鲁迅博物馆研究员

吴思敬　首都师范大学文学院教授

陈思和　复旦大学中文系教授

陈晓明　北京大学中文系教授

陈骏涛　中国社会科学院文学研究所研究员

陈子善　华东师范大学中文系教授

孟繁华　沈阳师范大学教授

於可训　武汉大学文学院教授

杨匡汉　中国社会科学院文学研究所研究员

杨　义　中国社会科学院文学研究所研究员

张　炯　中国社会科学院文学研究所研究员

张　健　北京师范大学文学院教授

张中良　中国社会科学院文学研究所研究员

赵　园　中国社会科学院文学研究所研究员

洪子诚　北京大学中文系教授

贺绍俊　沈阳师范大学教授

谢　冕　北京大学中文系教授

程光炜　中国人民大学中文系教授

雷　达　中国作家协会创研部研究员

黎湘萍　中国社会科学院文学研究所研究员

出版前言

20世纪的社会生活风云激荡,沧桑巨变,20世纪的华文文学也波澜壮阔,气象万千。上承19世纪,下启21世纪的20世纪华文文学,在与社会生活的密切连接和与时代情绪的遥相呼应中,积极地开拓进取和不断地自我革新,以其大起大伏、大开大阖的自身演进,书写了中华民族五千年华彩乐章中光辉灿烂的一页。这是一个古老民族焕发出青春活力的精神写照,更是一笔浓墨重彩、彪炳史册的文化财富。20世纪的华文文学必将成为中华民族文化传统中的重要构成为后世所传承,20世纪的那些杰出的华文文学作品必将作为经典为后人所记取。

抱着共同的目的和相同的旨趣,以"世界文学文库"树立了良好品牌形象的北京燕山出版社,得到以中国社会科学院文学研究所为核心的文学研究权威机构的支持和帮助,由著名文学批评家和出版家白烨、倪培耕、著名学者和文学批评家陈骏涛、贺绍俊总策划,开始了这项以"世纪文学60家"命名的策划、评选活动。

"世纪文学60家"书系的创编与推出,旨在以名家联袂名作的方式,检阅和展示20世纪中国文学所取得的丰硕成果与长足进步,进一步促进先进文化的积累与经典作品的传播,满足新一代文学爱好者的阅读需求。为使"世纪文学60家"书系的评选、出版活动,既体现文学专家的学术见识,又吸纳文学读者的有益意见,我们采取了专家评选与读者投票相结合的方式,秉承客观、公平、公开的原则,力图综合各个方面的意愿与要求,反映20

世纪华文文学发展的实际情形，体现文学研究专家的普遍共识和读者对 20 世纪华文文学作品的阅读取向。

　　基于上述评选宗旨和评选原则，经专家推荐，我们依据 20 世纪华文作家在中国现当代文学史上的地位与影响，经过反复推敲和斟酌，确定了 100 位作家及其代表作作为候选名单。其后，又约请 25 位中国现当代文学专家组成"世纪文学 60 家"评选委员会，在 100 位候选人名单的基础上进行书面记名投票，以得票多少为顺序，产生了"世纪文学 60 家"的专家评选结果。为了吸纳广大读者对 20 世纪华文作家及作品的相关看法和阅读意向，我们得到了在国内最具人气的"新浪网·读书频道"的鼎力支持和全力合作，展开了为期两个月的"华文'世纪文学 60 家'全民网络大评选"活动。2005 年 12 月 16 日，读者评选结果在"新浪网·读书频道"正式公布。

　　为了使"世纪文学 60 家"的评选与编选，能够比较客观地反映专家和读者两方面的意见，经过反复协商，最终以各占 50% 的权重，得出了"世纪文学 60 家"书系入选名单。

　　"世纪文学 60 家"书系入选作家，均以"精选集"的方式收入其代表性的作品。在作品之外，我们还约请有关专家撰写了研究性序言，编制了作家的创作要目，其意都在于为读者了解作家作品及其创作上的特点和其在文学史上的地位，提供必要的导读和更多的资讯。

　　"世纪文学 60 家"书系的出版，旨在囊括 20 世纪华文创作的精华，展示具有经典意义的作家作品，打造一份适于典藏的精品书目。她凝聚了数十位专家的心血，寄托着数以万计的热爱中国现当代文学读者的殷切希望。我们期望此书系能够经受住时间的考验和历史的淘洗，像那些支持这项事业的朋友们所祝愿的那样："世纪文学 60 家"将作为各大图书馆的馆藏经典，高等学校文科学生和文学爱好者的必读书目为世人所瞩目。

目　录

散文编

(本书目由贺绍俊选定)

冷峻客观的小说

[法]诺埃尔·迪特莱

这个介入的题目是受了阿城本人1991年3月寄给我的一封信①的启发,他对我是这样说的:

> 早先,笔记小说(essai ou note)在中国十分发达。在某些阶段,它的地位几乎与散文平起平坐。后来,自1949年以来,甚至自1919年"五四运动"以来,散文经历了前所未有的飞跃。可以这么说,半个世纪以来,尤其自1949年以来,散文经历了它的"黄金时代",以鲁迅为代表。这一阶段,文化人差不多个个写过杂文(zawen)。同时,短篇小说同样得到了极大的发展。这种飞跃的原因之一得力于西方小说的翻译——小说在中国的地位很低,所

---

① 信原文见本序言附录。此处阿城信的引文保持了从法文转译,发表在《当代作家评论》(1994.6)时的原貌。——编者注

以，人们称之为小说（"menus propos"或"discours mineurs"，据安德烈·莱维的译法）。长篇小说（long menus propos）这一术语里有一个矛盾。所以在中国出现了与传统章回小说不同的小说。然而，我认为，中国并不存在任何为西方术语接受的小说。我想，这是因为，中国文学传统基于诗，而散文，文学传统则基于《史记》，司马迁的《史记》、笔记、话本、章回小说（《史记》是具有文学特点的各种描写的开端，已不再是历史传统）。所以，目前，小说（甚至长篇小说）的写作是可能的，但不是"长"小说。然而，笔记这一文类消失了。这是我想写笔记小说的理由之一。1984年，我开始一段一段地写我的《遍地风流》，差不多在1985年，杭州的李庆西确认了"新杂文"（就像人们讨论"新小说"一样）。接着又有一些人写了笔记小说。在写笔记小说的当代作家中，我偏爱汪曾祺。说实话，汪曾祺是忠实于笔记小说的唯一作家。

这种文类大概同时具有诗、散文、随笔和小说的特征。可以通过它把我们的许多遗产传之后世，同时可以在描写中超前进行各种各样的实验，例如句子的节奏、句调、结构、视角等等。我喜欢西方音乐，我记得，正是一边听着贝多芬的最后弦乐四重奏的某些乐章时，我突然领悟到我的一些随笔应该如何写。

这封来信是一份宣言。阿城在信中向西方证实,他不采纳传奇故事式的形式,他清楚地将此形式区别于传统的中国小说:章回小说(roman aepisode)。这一尝试与阿城的美学追求相吻合,被两位评论家苏丁和仲呈祥所指明。他们指出阿城在当代文学思潮中如何附属于中国传统,有如中国水墨画,与张辛欣、刘心武、张贤亮那样的作家紧密依附西方传统成为对照,确切地说,他们的作品令人想起西方的油画。

阿城本人在1986年1月出版的香港《九十年代》杂志上,就他的创作手法发表了一篇长篇访谈录,他在访谈录中表达了自己的看法。他指出,他不可能在一种激动状态下写作,他追求某种思想状态的展示,这种状态他不能确定,但对他来说是必不可少的。因此,至少在表面上,他远不是一个钟情于写作,一百次重复这样那样的句子的作家。阿城举了《棋王》中的主人公王一生和九名对手的著名棋局。他在绝对安静中一句接一句写了这一段,未感到丝毫激动。"激动的是读者,而不是我。"

形　式

阿城的作品总共包括三个中篇小说:《棋王》(1984),《树王》(1985),《孩子王》(1985);六个短篇小说:《迷路》,《傻子》,《周转》,《卧铺》,《会餐》,《树桩》(1985)。最后还有以《遍地风流》(1986)为题的,由很短的文章组成的系列。阿城从没有写过长篇小说。另外,他每两月一次在每一期《九十年代》杂志上发表一篇很短的文章,他已发表了三十三篇这种类型的文章。按照发表时间先后，可以发现，阿城在他的短文中，舍弃了浪漫传奇式的形式，使之成为新形式，他确认为随笔或笔记小说。

假如查一查艾田蒲提出的标准，长篇小说从五万字算起，一万字以上就不再是短篇小说。在一万字到五万字之间的短长篇和长中篇，与中国人所称的中篇小说相当。在"三王"中，《棋王》二万六千字，《树王》二万四千五百字，《孩子王》二万八千字。因此，阿城的所有作品，可称为短篇或杂著一类。

作品的构思

一部长篇小说的写作需要一种总体的构思：一个提纲的确定，人物之间的关系，人物之间的行为变化。阿城的举动独辟蹊径。事实上，他处在中国传统小说起源的直线上——口头。在当作家以前，阿城一直画画，随后受到喜欢听他讲故事的朋友的催促，他本人说，想到作者的权利会使他冬天买到白菜，于是决定写作。他那说书人的才能来源于当知青的阅历：他向农民和他的伙伴们讲书中的故事，让他们得到消遣，那些书他在父母的书斋中读过，他的母亲让他卖给书商以便养家糊口！于是阿城从口头转到了笔头，就像中国文人通过文字转述街道里巷故事，并记录在"话本"中一样。这就解释了为什么作品和故事的构思在他的第一篇小说《棋王》中极为简明扼要：一个青年家中困难重重，首先寻求他的生活保障，然后寻求活下去的新理由：弈棋。从那以后，按阿城自己所说,其余的事接踵而来。他限于按事件发生先后讲述事件。《棋王》的创作是下乡这一偶然事件的成果。阿城获得了某种人生经验,他的朋友们促使他回北京后重新誊抄,他根本没有期待引起轰动,因为他说,"我写过的东西与眼下人们可以读到的东西截然不同"。而正是这种新颖给阿城带来了成功。

阿城一旦成名,他会试着写一些包含更复杂的情节和人物,结构更完整的长篇小说吗?他创作构思本身不允许他这样做。他清晰明确地指出,他需要一种特殊状态下的感觉才能写作(比如听贝多芬的四重奏),即使平静会胜过激动。继《棋王》之后发表的两篇小说是文学杂志总编约稿的结果。阿城离群索居,写作《树王》。然而,作品的总构思是相同的:叙述者按照年代先后讲述故事,他到云南的一个农场时,事件在他那个村里发生。游离于《树王》之外的补充方面是他那神奇和奥秘的观点与实行党的指示的知青的理性态度。在《孩子王》中,作品的构思也同样简洁。一个知青被指定为云南边远学校的小学教师,他试图让他教的孩子们获得汉语的一些初步概念,而不是通过官方课本和报刊口号的"木头语"(langue de bois)。他的方法使他的上级不悦,于是他被辞退了。

阿城说,他本来想写"八王"故事,集中起来以《八王》为总题目。因此他觉得,在某一时期他似乎试图"规划"他的写作。同时他又说,他不能肯定能否处在好的状态中写他的小说,并说也许永远写不出来。他动身去美国大概极大地改变了他看待事物的方式。实际上，他从未写（至少据我所知）所缺的"五王"。在"三王"之后，阿城集中写三个很短的小说，然后写笔记小说。在小说中，他不再描写大量很有限的人物和动人的境遇。人物以其自己的方式经受得住空虚和生活的困难，但是他们沉浸在大自然的广袤无垠中，大自然的生机在结束部分中重新掌握自己的权利：一缕月光，一道薄雾，睡意袭来，太阳升起，等等。

正是在题为《遍地风流》的那些文字中，阿城最充分地施展了自己的才能。非常精炼的语言本身接近非常文学性的古汉语（比如不用代词，读者会看到）。他描写叙述者与他描写的自然和谐一致，这一事实把他带到对生活的深刻思考之中。在《雪山》中，叙述者在做任何一件事前必定观望群山。这种绝对需要为他的作品提供了一些玄奥的方面。

众所周知，在流寓美国后，阿城专心致志地写发表于《九十年代》杂志上的短文。他有时重操已描写过的主题：知青们的生活，乡下的饥饿，可是他的探寻领域大大地扩展了。事实上，他的写作构成一幅由连贯的细小笔触描画的中国社会的巨大图景。人的小心眼，抑或是人的正直，都被调侃地描写出来。初读这些作品的读者常常不能理解作者想表达什么，一些文章看起来没有头尾。但是只要更深入地阅读下去，就会揭示出对所描述情境的极其细腻深邃的分析。

写作技巧

第一人称的使用。

在他的小说《棋王》、《树王》、《孩子王》、《卧铺》、《傻子》和《迷路》中,阿城用第一人称说话。读者碰到一个自称"我"的叙述者,面对着他生活的外部世界。"我"在各种情况下遇到一个或几个奇特人物:棋呆子,迷棋的青年;"树王",一个与大自然相依为命,以致当有人砍掉他试图救下的"树王"时死去的奇特人物;王福,一个想背词典,试图过更好生活的青年学生。在《孩子王》中,自称"我"的人物处于小说的中心,因为他自己就是"孩子王",即小学教师。在《卧铺》中,"我"在他的车厢里遇到几个富有情趣的人物;在《迷路》中,和他作伴的是一个所谓的"傻子",但多亏了他的医学知识,挽救了局面,最后,在《傻子》中,他在他的朋友老李身上发现了一个"傻孩子"的存在,他一直不怀疑其存在。在别的作品(《树桩》或《周转》)中,"我"不出现。这是第三人称叙述。在题为《遍地风流》的作品里,"我"以一种极其漫不经心的、有时含蓄的方式出现。例如,在《溜索》一篇中,第一人称的"我"字从未出现(在翻译中,必须使其准确)。这是一种强调手法,使得自叙者和所描写的风景与情境融为一体。

第一人称的运用使阿城的最初几篇作品具有一种文献价值,生活阅历深深地吸引了读者。可是这并不是简单的报道。它们表明了一个人(叙述者)面对生活及其兴衰的态度。阿城笔下人物的冷峻、严肃和伦理道义被自称"我"的叙述者所注意观察,使中国广大读者激动不已。

我还想就阿城的写作描写一点细节。在《孩子王》中,教师试图造一个汉字。他在注视正在做作文的学生时，开始想到他当教师之前放的那些吃草的牛，他想起这些牲畜喜欢喝尿到了何种地步。这时候，他重新开始在黑板上写字，而且由于疏忽和观念联合，他在黑板上画了一幅由汉字"牛"和"水"构成的表意文字。孩子们提醒他，他慌忙擦掉。从这里可以看到作者逃脱语言枷锁的一种不自觉的意图，很快放弃的意图……这种"经验"可能比较接近中国造型艺术家的经验。他们发明一些汉字来写几本难懂的书，随后编一些由连他们也不懂的字构成的词典。

风　格

在《孩子王》中，阿城清楚地解释了他在写作方面的观点。他让教师对学生解释如何写一篇作文：

> 那写些什么呢？听好，我每次出一个题目，这样吧，也不出题目了。怎么办呢？你们自己写，就写一件事，随便写什么，字不在多，但一定要把这件事老老实实、清清楚楚地写出来。别给我写些花样，什么"红旗飘扬，战鼓震天"，你们见过几面红旗？你们谁听过打仗的鼓。分场的那一只破鼓，哪里会震天？把这些都给我去掉，没用！

他的意思显而易见：应以正确的方式、朴实的方式写作。王蒙在一篇想必是"大力推荐"阿城的荣誉的文章中是这样评价的:"美不胜收——口语化而不流俗,古典美而不迂腐,民族化而不过'土'"。

正是手法的简练使阿城的读者最为感动。作者用一种近乎古汉语的语言替代了一种很口语化的语言。最动人的例证是《棋王》的段落。捡烂纸的老头儿用文言教棋呆子赢棋的道教方法。同时棋王的对话甚至尊重人物的外地风尚,在一种口语中写成。

《周转》的作品文本也是阿城文学语言运用的一个好的说明。开头两段是很凝炼的句子,四字一句,两次出现,后面紧接一句更长的句子,使人想到袁宏道《游记》(note de voyage)的风格。

阿城的散文诗最有力的作品之一《雪山》,是以富有韵律的、凝炼的风格写成的。由于很短,七百字略多,给人留下一种与读日本俳句相同的印象:一闪而过,却留下难忘的记忆。这篇作品不含任何人称代词。故事在天黑和太阳升起之间发生,让雪山显现,凝望雪山是绝对必须的。阿城在小说中描写了与大自然接触这一意识的唤醒过程。

阿城在《九十年代》杂志上发表了用新手法写的作品,这些作品舍弃了其诗意的力量。这是一些严厉、尖刻、充满冷嘲热讽的作品。作者的简洁风格行之有效。譬如阿城用一版篇幅描画一群知识分子的肖像:一些人被送到田野里,在那里负责除粪(《大风》);一个把光阴花在观察周围的一切事物上的人,他在"文化大革命"中曾险些丧生;一个有洁癖者;一个舍命也不放弃"真"的僧人等等。在

《九十年代》上发表的最后几篇作品中，有一篇《成长》似乎是一种展示：一个在楼里劳动的老"知青"被派往毛泽东纪念堂建筑工地。阿城描写了这个人物，在最完整的共产主义正统观念中成长，而他一边凝望天安门广场和毛的画像，一边眼里充满眼泪，从纪念堂高处往下撒尿。阿城用一版篇幅，就共产主义这盘棋和曾经满怀信念的年轻人的失望，与张贤亮的一部长篇小说说了同样的话。

小说到短文，经由散文诗，构成阿城作品有机统一的，是各种手法的和谐。没有冗长的描写，只用几个很快的笔触来描绘一种局面。人常常有处于一个传统之前的印象，人消失在其风景中。在这方面，阿城接近汪曾祺或韩少功。在《棋王》中，譬如，有一处描写特别代表阿城的风格：

> 这时已近傍晚。太阳垂在两山之间，江面上金子一样滚动，岸边石头也如热铁般红起来。有鸟儿在水面上掠来掠去。叫声传得很远。对岸有人在拖长声音吼山歌，却不见影子，只觉声音慢慢小了。大家都凝了神看。许久，王一生长叹一声，却不说什么。

阿城致力于细节的描写，而这些细节特别意味深长，对《棋王》的主人公"吃相"的描写非常有名。因此，人们谈论过"饥饿文学"。甚至题为《会餐》的极短的小说中，知青们筹划安排的一盘蛇肉会餐，同样十分动人心魄。无论被剥夺了一切的知青,还是内蒙古旗的头头,在中国农村深处安排会餐,其实质,就是"吃"这样一种事实,而阿城对这类氛围的描写十分出色。

结　　论

假如一部小说是由一个有结构的现实生活本身构成,或者,小说家至少意识到好像是经过安排的一种文学形式,那么,人们就会比较清楚地理解为什么阿城对这种文学形式根本不感兴趣。事实上,具有一定结构的现实生活与小说形式毫不相干。正在这一点上,他不同于同时代的作家。他用知青七十年代在乡下的生活作为一种背景而不是主题。现实只不过像他的人物行进的框架使他感兴趣。相反,短篇形式(小说,还有散文)允许他把注意力集中于现实的一个细节,一个片段上。阿城以一个一生描绘虾或小鸡的中国画家试图抓住重建的现实的方式,描写了风景、人物、奇特或普通的情境,他乐此不疲,以便描绘一幅巨大的画图。

阿城给当代中国文学带来的巨大独创性,是他保持古典文学的表现财富的能力(大概多亏他来自"口述"的缘由)。阅读、领会十九世纪和二十世纪世界文学的经典巨著,运用小说和杂文那样的文学形式是他的选择。最后,他决定实验发展最适合他的文学形式:杂文或笔记小说。这种志愿之举说明他在创作了他最初的、应付一种需要的作品之后,对写作本身进行思考。概括起来,我要说,"三王"应付了一种必须,接下来的小说表明,集中在《遍地风流》题下的作品是向诗性散文的转变,在美国写的文本是作者理论思考的成就。

最后,应该认识到,阿城的创作远远没有结束。他最近的作品虽然在美国写成,却表现了在中国生活的各种人。人们拭目以待,看阿城现在居住的国家是否能成为一道引发灵感的源泉,看笔记小说是否仍然是他的表达形式。

(刘 阳 编译)当代作家评论199406

附录:

阿城致诺埃尔·迪特莱的信

Noel Dutrait 先生:

(前略)

　　我不知道你在翻译中有什么问题没有？笔记小说在中国原来是很发达的,有些时期甚至与散文的地位难分上下。但是一九四九年以后,或者说,一九一九年的五四以后,杂文空前的兴盛,可以说,半个世纪以来,尤其是四九年以前,杂文有过它的黄金时期,代表人物是鲁迅。当时的文化人,差不多都写过杂文。同时短篇小说也很发达,原因之一是对西方短篇小说的翻译,西方的长篇小说(小说在中国的地位低,所以才叫小说。另外「长篇小说」在词的组合上是一个矛盾)的翻译,使中国迅速出现不同于传统章回小说的长篇小说,但我认为中国至今还没有一部西方意义的长篇小说。我想这是因为中国的传统是诗、散文,文学传统是《史记》(《史记》发文学性描写的开端,已经有悖史的传统了)、笔记、话本、章回。于是现在的短篇可以写好,扩展至中篇也好,长篇不好,但笔记消失了,这也是我为什么要写笔记小说的原因之一。我在一九八四年开始一组一组地发表《遍地风流》,大约是一九八五年,杭州的李庆西把我的这类小说称为"新笔记小说",之后这几年又有许多人在写笔记小说。当代作家里我最喜欢汪曾祺的笔记小说，实际清况是，汪曾祺是五四以来笔记小说的唯一坚持者。

笔记小说可以具有诗、散文、笔记和小说的特点，有大量的遗产可以继承，同时又可以进行各种叙述试验，例如节奏，语音，句法，视角等等。（后略）

好，就此打住。祝你顺利。

阿城

一九九一年三月

Noel Dutrait 先生：

（前略）

《遍地风流》是我七十年代随手写下的一些文字，有关一些情绪，一些场景，一些人物和事物的印象。这些文字，通常很短，失散的也很多。从乡下回到北京后，曾投给文学杂志，被退回来，大概是无法归类，小说？散文？笔记？《棋王》发表后，各种杂志要稿很多，又很急，并且要求字数也多，于是两三篇合为一组拿去发表，即你看到的〈之一〉、〈之三〉等等。当时给出去很多，后来都想不清楚谁拿走了，还记得给过湖北一个工厂的厂办刊物一组，但要我现在说出这个工厂和刊物的名字，实在是想不起来了。我没见过这个刊物，我想它大概是没有出版登记号的，只限于工厂内，印给工人看。另外我能记得的就是发表在《上海文学》的〈之三〉，是《人民文学》的退稿。

不必按〈之一〉、〈之二〉排列，把它们打散，按你自己的意思排列。

《遍地风流》中"遍地"的意思是"到处"，everywhere，也就是我七十年代在中国流浪所至之处。"风流"不好解，"风"原是交配、交媾的意思，后来转变为"风俗"的意思。"风流"中的"风"，是"风度"，我此处结合了风俗、风度两层意思，每个短篇中亦是在捕捉风俗和风度，包括自然景物的风度。"风流"在中国当代语言中多指男女之事，我用它的古义。宋朝苏轼的《念奴娇·赤壁怀古》的名句"大江东去，浪淘尽千古风流人物，"用的是"杰出"的意思，但他在前面描写了杰出人物的风度，我是只取"我看到的或喜欢的风度"，不管杰出不杰出，因为"杰出"的标准未必人人都同意。

我不知道和"风流"对应的英文是什么，但我猜法文会有这种意思的字。

Prosper Merimee 写过 CARMAN，我想他是写出了一种风度。风度是指不自觉的时候，自觉了，就是摹仿出来的，也就不是风度了。总之，《遍地风流》用直白的话说，就是"这块土地上的各种风度"。但是，你？可以以你对这些短篇的看法起一个法国式的题目。

至于你想写的研究文章，我手上没有评论文章，所以在朋友中找了找，复印给你。另外，寄给你的《节日》，发表在去年的《女性人》（第三期）杂志上，我记得大概是八五年或八六年写的。你如果有兴趣，可以纳入短篇小说集里。

先写这些，祝你一切都好！

阿城

一九九一年八月十八日

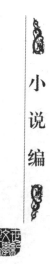

小说编

棋　　王

一

　　车站是乱得不能再乱，成千上万的人都在说话。谁也不去注意那条临时挂起来的大红布标语。这标语大约挂了不少次，字纸都折得有些坏。喇叭里放着一首又一首的语录歌儿，唱得大家心更慌。

　　我的几个朋友，都已被我送走插队，现在轮到我了，竟没有人来送。父母生前颇有些污点，运动一开始即被打翻死去。家具上都有机关的铝牌编号，于是统统收走，倒也名正言顺。我虽孤身一人，却算不得独子，不在留城政策之内。我野狼似的转悠一年多，终于还是决定要走。此去的地方按月有二十几元工资，我便很向往，争了要去，居然就批了。因为所去之地与别国相邻，斗争之中除了阶级，尚有国际，出身孬一些，组织上不太放心。我争得这个信任和权利，欢喜是不用说的，更重要的是，每月二十几元，一个人如何用得完？只是没人来送，就有些不耐烦，于是先钻进车厢，想找个地方坐下,任凭站台上千万人话别。

车厢里靠站台一面的窗子已经挤满各校的知青,都探出身去说笑哭泣。另一面的窗子朝南,冬日的阳光斜射进来,冷清清地照在北边儿众多的屁股上。两边儿行李架上塞满了东西。我走动着找我的座位号,却发现还有一个精瘦的学生孤坐着,手笼在袖管儿里,隔窗望着车站南边儿的空车皮。

我的座位恰与他在一个格儿里,是斜对面儿,于是就坐下了,也把手笼在袖里。那个学生瞄了我一下,眼里突然放出光来,问:"下棋吗?"倒吓了我一跳,急忙摆手说:"不会!"他不相信地看着我说:"这些细长的手指头,就是个捏棋子儿的,你肯定会。来一盘吧,我带着家伙呢。"说着就抬身从窗钩上取下书包,往里掏着。我说:"我只会马走日,象走田。你没人送吗?"他已把棋盘拿出来,放在茶几上。塑料棋盘却搁不下,他想了想,就横摆了,说:"不碍事,一样下。来来来,你先走。"我笑起来,说:"你没人送吗? 这么乱,下什么棋?"他一边码好最后一个棋子,一边说:"我他妈要谁送? 去的是有饭吃的地方,闹得这么哭哭啼啼的。来,你先走。"我奇怪了,可还是拈起炮,往当头上一移。我的棋还没移到,他的马却"啪"的一声跳好,比我还快。我就故意将炮移过当头的地方停下。他很快地看了一眼我的下巴,说:"你还说不会? 这炮二平六的开局,我在郑州遇见一个名手,就是这么走,险些输给他。炮二平五当头炮,是老开局,可有气势,而且是最稳的。嗯? 你走。"我倒不知怎么走了,手在棋盘上游移着。他不动声色地看着整个棋盘,又把手袖笼起来。

就在这时，车厢乱了起来。好多人拥进来，隔着玻璃往外招手。我就站起身，也隔着玻璃往北看月台上。站上的人都拥到车厢前，都在叫，乱成一片。车身忽地一动，人群"嗡"地一下，哭声四起。我的背被谁捅了一下，回头一看，他一手护着棋盘，说："没你这么下棋的，走哇！"我实在没心思下棋，而且心里有些酸，就硬硬地说："我不下了。这是什么时候！"他很惊愕地看着我，忽然像明白了，身子软下去，不再说话。

　　车开了一会儿，车厢开始平静下来。有水送过来，大家就掏出缸子要水。我旁边的人打了水，说："谁的棋？收了放缸子。"他很可怜的样子，问："下棋吗？"要放缸子的人说："反正没意思，来一盘吧。"他就很高兴，连忙码好棋子。对手说："这横着算怎么回事儿？没法儿看。"他搓着手说："凑合了，平常看棋的时候，棋盘不等于是横着的？你先走。"对手很老练地拿起棋子儿，嘴里叫着："当头炮。"他跟着跳上马。对手马上把他的卒吃了，他也立刻用马吃了对方的炮。我看这种简单的开局没有大意思，又实在对象棋不感兴趣，就转了头。

　　这时一个同学走过来，像在找什么人，一眼望到我，就说："来来来，四缺一，就差你了。"我知道他们是在打牌，就摇摇头。同学走到我们这一格，正待伸手拉我，忽然大叫："棋呆子，你怎么在这儿？你妹妹刚才把你找苦了，我说没见啊。没想到你在我们学校这节车厢里，气儿都不吭一声儿。你瞧你瞧，又下上了。"

棋呆子红了脸，没好气儿地说："你管天管地，还管我下棋？走，该你走了。"就又催促我身边的对手。我这时听出点音儿来，就问同学："他就是王一生？"同学睁了眼，说："你不认识他？唉呀，你白活了。你不知道棋呆子？"我说："我知道棋呆子就是王一生，可不知道王一生就是他。"说着，就仔细看着这个精瘦的学生。王一生勉强笑一笑，只看着棋盘。

王一生简直大名鼎鼎。我们学校与旁边几个中学常常有学生之间的象棋厮杀，后来拼出几个高手。几个高手之间常摆擂台，渐渐地，几乎每次冠军就都是王一生了。我因为不喜欢象棋，也就不去关心什么象棋冠军，但王一生的大名，却常被班上几个棋篓子供在嘴上，我也就对其事迹略闻一二，知道王一生外号棋呆子，棋下得很神不用说，而且在他们学校那一年级里数理成绩总是前数名。我想棋下得好而有个数学脑子，这很合情理，可我又不信人们说的那些王一生的呆事，觉得不过是大家寻逸闻鄙事以快言论罢了。后来运动起来，忽然有一天大家传说棋呆子在串连时犯了事儿，被人押回学校了。我对棋呆子能出去串连表示怀疑，因为以前大家对他的描述说明他不可能解决串连时的吃喝问题。可大家说呆子确实去串连了，因为老下棋，被人瞄中，就同他各处走，常常送他一点儿钱，他也不问，只是收下。后来才知道，每到一处，呆子必然挤地头看下棋。看上一盘，必然把输家挤开，与赢家杀一盘。初时大家看他其貌不扬，不与他下。他执意要杀，于是就杀。几步下来，对方出了小汗，嘴却不软。呆子也不说话，只是出手极快，像是连想都不想。待到对方终于闭了嘴,连一圈儿观棋的人也要慢慢思索棋路而不再支招儿的时候,与呆子同行的人就开始摸包儿。大家正看得紧张,哪里想到钱包已经易主?待三盘下来,众人都摸头。这时呆子倒成了棋主,连问可有谁还要杀?有那不服的,就坐下来杀,最后仍是无一盘得利。后来常常是众人齐做一方,七嘴八舌与呆子对手。呆子也不忙,反倒促众人快走,因为师傅多了,常为一步棋如何走自家争吵起来。就这样,在一处呆子可以连杀上一天,后来有那观棋的人发觉钱包丢了,闹嚷起来。慢慢有几个有心计的人暗中观察,看见有人掏包,也不响,之后见那晚上来邀呆子走,就发一声喊,将扒手与呆子一齐绑了,由造反队审。呆子糊糊涂涂,只说别人常给他钱,大约是可怜他,也不知钱如何来,自己只是喜欢下棋。审主看他呆相,就命人押了回来,一时各校传为逸事。后来听说呆子认为外省马路棋手高手不多,不能长进,就托人找城里名手邀战。有个同学就带他去见自己的父亲,据说是国内名手。名手见了呆子,也不多说,只摆一副据传是宋时留下的残局,要呆子走。呆子看了半晌,一五一十道来,替古人赢了。名手很惊奇,要收呆子为徒。不料呆子却问:"这残局你可走通了?"名手没反应过来,就说:"还未通。"呆子说:"那我为什么要做你的徒弟?"名手只好请呆子开路,事后对自己的儿子说:"你这个同学桀骜不驯,棋品连着人品,照这样下去,棋品必劣。"又举了一些最新指示,说若能好好学习,棋锋必健。后来呆子认识了一个捡烂纸的老头儿,被老头儿连杀三天而仅赢一盘。呆子就执意要替老头儿去撕大字报纸，不要老头儿劳动。不料有一天撕了某造反团刚贴的"檄文"，被人拿获，又被这造反团栽诬于对立派，说对方"施阴谋，弄诡计"，必讨之，而且是可忍，孰不可忍！对立派又阴使人偷出呆子，用了呆子的名义，对先前的造反团反戈一击。一时呆子的大名"王一生"贴得满街都是，许多外省来取经的革命战士许久才明白王一生原来是个棋呆子，就有人请了去外省会一些江湖名手。交手之后，各有胜负，不过呆子的棋据说是越下越精了。只可惜全国忙于革命，否则呆子不知会有什么造就。

这时，我旁边的人也明白对手是王一生，连说不下了。王一生便很沮丧。我说："你妹妹来送你，你也不知道和家里人说说话儿，倒拉着我下棋！"王一生看着我说："你哪儿知道我们这些人是怎么回事儿！你们这些人好日子过惯了，世上不明白的事儿多着呢！你家父母大约是舍不得你走了？"我怔了怔，看着手说："哪儿来父母，都死球了。"我的同学就添油加醋地叙了我一番，我有些不耐烦，说："我家死人，你倒有了故事了。"王一生想了想，对我说："那你这两年靠什么活着？"我说："混一天算一天。"王一生就看定了我问："怎么混？"我不答。待了一会儿，王一生叹一声，说："混可不易。一天不吃饭，棋路都乱。不管怎么说，你父母在时，你家日子还好过。"我不服气，说："你父母在，当然要说风凉话。"我的同学见话不投机，就岔开说："呆子，这里没有你的对手，走，和我们打牌去吧。"呆子笑一笑，说："牌算什么，瞌睡着也能赢你们。"我旁边儿的人说："据说你下棋可以不吃饭？"我说：

"人一迷上什么,吃饭倒是不重要的事。大约能干出什么事儿的人,总免不了有这种傻事。"王一生想一想,又摇摇头,说:"我可不是这样。"说完就去看窗外。

一路下去,慢慢我发觉我和王一生之间,既开始有互相的信任和基于经验的同情,又有各自的疑问。他总是问我与他认识之前是怎么生活的,尤其是父母死后的两年是怎么混的。我大略地告诉了他,可他又特别在一些细节上详细地打听,主要是关于吃。例如讲到有一次我一天没有吃到东西,他就问:"一点儿也没吃到吗?"我说:"一点儿也没有。"他又问:"那你后来吃到东西是在什么时候?"我说:"后来碰到一个同学,他要用书包装很多东西,就把书包翻倒过来腾干净,里面有一个干馒头,掉在桌上就碎了。我一边儿和他说话,一边儿就把这些碎馒头吃下去。不过,说老实话,干烧饼比干馒头解饱得多,而且顶时候儿。"他同意我关于干烧饼的见解,可马上又问:"我是说,你吃到这个干馒头的时候是几点?过了当天夜里十二点吗?"我说:"噢,不。是晚上十点吧。"他又问:"那第二天你吃了什么?"讲老实话,我不太愿意复述这些事情,尤其是细节。我说:"当天晚上我睡在那个同学家。第二天早上,同学买了两个油饼,我吃了一个。上午我随他去跑一些事,中午他请我在街上吃。晚上嘛,我不好意思再在他那儿吃,可另一个同学来了,知道我没什么着落,硬拉了我去他家,当然吃得还可以。怎么样?还有什么不清楚?"他笑了,说:"你才不是你刚才说的什么'一天没吃东西',你十二点以前吃了一个馒头,没有超过二十四小时。更何况第二天你的伙食水平不低，平均下来，你两天的热量还是可以的。"我说："你恐怕还是有些呆！要知道，人吃饭，不但是肚子的需要，而且是一种精神需要。不知道下一顿在什么地方，人就特别想到吃，而且，饿得快。"他说："你家道尚好的时候，有这种精神压力吗？有，也只不过是想好上再好，那是馋。馋是你们这些人的特点。"我承认他说得有些道理，禁不住问他："你总在说你们、你们，可你算什么人？"他迅速看着其他地方，只是不看我，说："我当然不同了。我主要是对吃要求得比较实在。唉，不说这些了，你真的不喜欢下棋？何以解忧？唯有象棋。"我瞧着他说："你有什么忧？"他仍然不看我，"没有什么忧，没有。'忧'这玩意儿，是他妈文人的佐料儿。我们这种人，没有什么忧，顶多有些不痛快。何以解不痛快？唯有象棋。"

　　我看他对吃很感兴趣，就注意他吃的时候。列车上给我们这几节知青车厢送饭时，他若心思不在下棋上，就稍稍有些不安。听见前面大家拿吃时铝盒的碰撞声，他常常闭上眼，嘴巴紧紧收着，倒好像有些恶心。拿到饭后，马上就开始吃，吃得很快，喉节一缩一缩的，脸上绷满了筋。常常突然停下来，很小心地将嘴边或下巴上的饭粒儿和汤水油花儿用整个儿食指抹进嘴里。若饭粒儿落在衣服上，就马上一按，拈进嘴里。若一个没按住，饭粒儿由衣服上掉下地，他也立刻双脚不再移动，转了上身找。这时候他若碰上我的目光，就放慢速度。吃完以后，他把两只筷子舔了，拿水把饭盒冲满，先将上面一层油花吸净，然后就带着安全抵岸的神色小口小口地呷。有一次，他在下棋，左手轻轻地叩茶几。一粒干缩了的饭粒儿也轻轻跳着。他一下注意到了，就迅速将那个干饭粒儿放进嘴里，腮上立刻显出筋络。我知道这种干饭粒儿很容易嵌到槽牙里，巴在那儿，舌头是赶它不出的。果然，待了一会儿，他就伸手到嘴里去抠，终于嚼完和着一大股口水，"咕"地一声儿咽下去，喉节慢慢移下来，眼睛里有了泪花。他对吃是虔诚的，而且很精细。有时你会可怜那些饭被他吃得一个渣儿都不剩，真有点儿惨无人道。我在火车上一直看他下棋，发现他同样是精细的，但就有气度得多。他常常在我们还根本看不出已是败局时就开始重码棋子，说："再来一盘吧。"有的人不服输，非要下完，总觉得被他那样暗示死刑存些侥幸，他也奉陪，用四五步棋逼死对方，说："非要听'将'，有瘾?"

我每看到他吃饭，就回想起杰克·伦敦的《热爱生命》，终于在一次饭后他小口呷汤时讲了这个故事，我因为有过饥饿的经验，所以特别渲染了故事中的饥饿感觉。他不再喝汤，只是把饭盒端在嘴边儿，一边不动地听我讲。我讲完了，他呆了许久，凝视着饭盒里的水，轻轻吸了一口，才很严肃地看着我说："这个人是对的。他当然要把饼干藏在褥子底下。照你讲，他是对失去食物发生精神上的恐惧，是精神病? 不，他有道理，太有道理了。写书的人怎么可以这么理解这个人呢? 杰……杰什么? 嗯，杰克·伦敦，这个小子他妈真是饱汉子不知饿汉子饥。"我马上指出杰克·伦敦是一个如何如何的人。他说："是呀，不管怎么样，像你说的，杰克·伦敦后来出了名，肯定不愁吃的，他当然会叼着根烟，写些嘲笑饥饿的故事。"我说："杰克·伦敦丝毫也没有嘲笑饥饿，他是……"他不耐烦地打断我说："怎么不是嘲笑？把一个特别清楚饥饿是怎么回事儿的人写成发了神经，我不喜欢。"我只好苦笑，不再说什么。可是一没人和他下棋了，他就又问我："嗯？再讲个吃的故事？其实杰克·伦敦那个故事挺好。"我有些不高兴地说："那根本不是个吃的故事，那是一个讲生命的故事。你不愧为棋呆子。"大约是我脸上有种表情，他于是不知怎么办才好。我心里有一种东西升上来，我还是喜欢他的，就说："好吧，巴尔扎克的《邦斯舅舅》听过吗？"他摇摇头。我就又好好儿描述一下邦斯这个老饕。不料他听完，马上就说："这个故事不好，这是一个馋的故事，不是吃的故事。邦斯这个老头儿若只是吃而不馋，不会死。我不喜欢这个故事。"他马上意识到这最后一句话，就急忙说："倒也不是不喜欢。不过洋人总和咱们不一样，隔着一层。我给你讲个故事吧。"我马上感了兴趣：棋呆子居然也有故事！他把身体靠得舒服一些，说："从前哪，"笑了笑，又说："老是他妈从前，可这个故事是我们院儿的五奶奶讲的。嗯——老辈子的时候，有这么一家子，吃喝不愁。粮食一囤一囤的，顿顿想吃多少吃多少，嘿，可美气了。后来呢，娶了个儿媳妇。那真能干，就没说把饭做糊过，不干不稀，特解饱。可这媳妇，每做一顿饭，必抓出一把米藏好……"听到这儿，我忍不住插嘴："老掉牙的故事了，还不是后来遇到荒年，大家没饭吃，媳妇把每日攒下的米拿出来，不但自家有了，还分给穷人？"他很惊奇地坐直了，看着我说："你知道这个故事？可那米没有分给别人，五奶奶没有说分给别人。"我笑了，说："这是教育小孩儿要节约的故事，你还拿来有滋有味儿地讲，你真是呆子，还不是一个吃的故事。"他摇摇头，说："这太是吃的故事了，首先得有饭，才能吃，这家子有一囤一囤的粮食，可光穷吃不行，得记着断顿儿的时候，每顿都要欠一点儿。老话儿说'半饥半饱日子长'嘛。"我想笑但没笑出来，似乎明白了一些什么。为了打消这种异样的感触，就说："呆子，我跟你下棋吧。"他一下高兴起来，紧一紧手脸，啪啪啪就把棋码好，说："对，说什么吃的故事，还是下棋。下棋最好，何以解不痛快？唯有下象棋。啊？哈哈哈，你先走。"我又是当头炮，他随后把马跳好。我随便动了一个子儿，他很快地把兵移前一格儿。我并不真心下棋，心想他念到中学，大约是读过不少书的，就问："你读过曹操的《短歌行》？"他说："什么《短歌行》？"我说："那你怎么知道'何以解忧，唯有杜康'？"他愣了，问："杜康是什么？"我说："杜康是一个造酒的人，后来也就代表酒，你把杜康换成象棋，倒也风趣。"他摆了一下头，说："啊，不是。这句话是一个老头儿说的，我每回和他下棋，他总说这句。"我想起了传闻中的捡烂纸的老头儿，就问："是捡烂纸的老头儿吗？"他看了我一眼，说："不是。不过，捡烂纸儿棋下得好，我在他那儿学到不少东西。"我很感"这老头儿是个什么人？怎么下得一手好棋还轻地笑了一下，说："下棋不当饭。老头儿纸。可不知他以前是什么人。有一回，怎么找不到了，以为当垃圾倒出去了，就到垃圾站去翻，正翻着，这个老头推着筐过来了，指着我说：'你个大小伙子，怎么抢我的买卖？'我说不是，是找丢了的东西，他问什么东西，我没搭理他。可他问个不停，'钱？存折儿？结婚帖子？'我只好说是棋谱，正说着，就找着了。他说叫他看看。他在路灯底下挺快就看完了，说'这棋没根哪'。我说这是以前市里的象棋比赛。可他说，'哪儿的比赛也没用，你瞧这，这叫棋路？狗脑子。'我心想怕是遇上异人了，就问他当怎么走，老头儿哗哗说了一通谱儿，我一听，真的不凡，就提出要跟他下一盘。老头让我先。我们俩就在垃圾站下盲棋，我是连输五盘。老头儿棋路猛，听头几步，没什么，可着子真阴真狠，打闪一般，网得开，收得又紧又快。后来我们见天儿在垃圾站下盲棋，每天回去我就琢磨他的棋路，以后居然跟他平过一盘，还赢过一盘，其实赢的那盘我们一共才走了十几步。老头儿用铅丝扒子敲了半天地面，叹一声，'你赢了。'我高兴了，直说要到他那儿去看看。老头儿白了我一眼，说，'撑的?!'告诉我明天晚上再在这儿等他。第二天我去了，见他推着筐远远来了。到了跟前，从筐里取出一个小布包，递到我手上，说这也是谱儿，让我拿回去，看瞧得懂不。又说哪天有走不动的棋，让我到这儿来说给他听听，兴许他就走动了。我赶紧回到家里，打开一看，还真他妈不懂。这是本异书，也不知是哪朝哪代的，手抄，边边角角儿，补了又补。上面写的东西，不像是说象棋，好像是说另外的什么事儿。我第二天去找老头儿，说我看不懂，他哈哈一笑，说他先给我说一段儿,提个醒儿。他一开说,把我吓了一跳。原来开宗明义,是讲男女的事儿,我说这是'四旧'。老头儿叹了,说什么是旧?我这每天捡烂纸是不是在捡旧?可我回去把它们分门别类,卖了钱,养活自己,不是新?又说咱们中国道家讲阴阳,这开篇是借男女讲阴阳之气。阴阳之气相游相交,初不可太盛,太盛则折。折就是'折断'的'折'。"我点点头。"'太盛则折,太弱则泻。'老头儿说我的毛病是太盛。又说,若对手盛,则以柔化之。可要在化的同时,造成克势。柔不是弱,是容,是收,是含。含而化之,让对手入你的势。这势要你造,需无为而无不为。无为即是道,也就是棋运之大不可变,你想变,就不是象棋,输不用说了,连棋边儿都沾不上。棋运不可悖,但每局的势要自己造。棋运和势既有,那可就无所不为了。玄是真玄,可细琢磨,是那么个理儿。我说,这么讲是真提气,可这下棋,千变万化,怎么才能准赢呢? 老头儿说这就是造势的学问了。造势妙在契机。谁也不走子儿,这棋没法儿下。可只要对方一动,势就可入,就可导。高手你入他很难,这就要损。损他一个子儿,损自己一个子儿,先导开,或找眼钉下,止住他的入势,铺排下自己的入势。这时你万不可死损,势式要相机而变。势式有相因之气,势套势,小势导开,大势含而化之,根连根,别人就奈何不得。老头儿说我只有套,势不太明。套可以算出百步之远,但无势,不成气候。又说我脑子好,有琢磨劲儿,后来输我的那一盘,就是大势已破,再下,就是玩了。老头儿说他日子不多了,无儿无女,遇见我,就传给我吧。我说你老人家棋道这么好,怎么还干这种营生呢？老头儿叹了一口气，说这棋是祖上传下来的，但有训——'为棋不为生'，为棋是养性，生会坏性，所以生不可太盛。又说他从小没学过什么谋生本事，现在想来，倒是训坏了他。"我似乎听明白了一些棋道，可很奇怪。就问："棋道与生道难道有什么不同么？"王一生说："我也是这么说，而且魔症起来，问他天下大势。老头儿说，棋就是这么几个子儿，棋盘就这么大，无非是道同势不同，可这子儿你全能看在眼底。天下的事，不知道的太多。这每天的大字报，张张都新鲜，虽看出点道儿，可不能究底。子儿不全摆上，这棋就没法儿下。"

　　我就又问那本棋谱。王一生很沮丧地说："我每天带在身上，反复地看。后来你知道，我撕大字报被造反团捉住，书就被他们搜了去，说是'四旧'，给毁了，而且是当着我的面儿毁的。好在书已在我的脑子里，不怕他们。"我就又和王一生感叹了许久。

　　火车终于到了。所有的知识青年都又被用卡车运到农场。在总场，各分场的人上来领我们。我找到王一生，说："呆子，要分手了，别忘了交情，有事儿没事儿，互相走动。"他说当然。

<h2 style="text-align:center">二</h2>

　　这个农场在大山林里，活计就是砍树，烧山，挖坑，再栽树。不栽树的时候，就种点儿粮食。交通不便，运输不够，常常就买不到煤油点灯。晚上黑灯瞎火，大家凑在一起臭聊，

天南地北。又因为常割资本主义尾巴,生活就清苦得很,常常一个月每人只有五钱油,吃饭钟一敲,大家就疾跑如飞。大锅菜是先煮后搁油,油又少,只在汤上浮几个大花儿。落在后边,常常就只能吃清水南瓜或清水茄子。米倒是不缺,国家供应商品粮,每人每月四十二斤。可没油水,挖山又不是轻活,肚子就越吃越大。我倒是没什么,毕竟强似讨吃。每月又有二十几元工薪,家里没有人惦记着,又没有找女朋友,就买了烟学抽,不料越抽越凶。

山上活儿紧时,常常累翻,就想:呆子不知怎么干?那么精瘦的一个人。晚上大家闲聊,多是精神会餐。我又想,呆子的吃相可能更恶了。我父亲在时,炒得一手好菜,母亲都比不上他。星期天常邀了同事,专事品尝,我自然精于此道,因此聊起来,常常是主角,说得大家个个儿腮胀,常常发一声喊,将我按倒在地上,说像我这样儿的人实在是祸害,不如宰了炒吃。下雨时节,大家都慌忙上山去挖笋,又到沟里捉田鸡,无奈没有油,常常吃得胃酸。山上总要放火,野兽们都惊走了,极难打到。即使打到,野物们走惯了,没膘,熬不得油。尺把长的老鼠也捉来吃,因鼠是吃粮的,大家说鼠肉就是人肉,也算吃人吧。我又常想,呆子难道不馋?好上加好,固然是馋,其实饿时更馋。不馋,吃的本能不能发挥,也不得寄托。又想,呆子不知还下不下棋。我们分场与他们分场隔着近百里,来去一趟不容易,也就见不着。

转眼到了夏季,有一天,我正在山上干活儿,远远望见山下小路上有一个人。大家觉得影儿生,就议论是什么人。有人说是小毛的男的吧。小毛是队里一个女知青,新近在外场找了一个朋友,可谁也没见过。大家就议论这个人可能是来找小毛,于是满山喊小毛,说她的汉子来了。小毛丢了锄,跌跌撞撞跑过来,伸了脖子看。还没待小毛看好,我却认出来人是王一生——棋呆子。于是大叫,别人倒吓了一跳,都问:"找你的?"我很得意。我们这个队有四个省市的知青,与我同来的不多,自然他们不认识王一生。我这时正代理一个管三四个人的小组长,于是对大家说:"散了,不干了。大家也别回去,帮我看看山上可有什么吃的弄点儿。到钟点儿再下山,拿到我那儿去烧。你们打了饭,都过来一起吃。"大家于是就钻进乱草里去寻了。

我跳着跑下山,王一生已经站住,一脸高兴的样子,远远地问:"你怎么知道是我?"我到了他跟前说:"远远就看你呆头呆脑,还真是你。你怎么老也不来看我?"他跟我并排走着,说:"你也老不来看我呀!"我见他背上的汗浸出衣衫,头发已是一绺一绺的,一脸的灰土,只有眼睛和牙齿放光,嘴上也是一层土,干得起皱,就说:"你怎么摸来的?"他说:"搭一段儿车,走一段儿路,出来半个月了。"我吓了一跳,问:"不到百里,怎么走这么多天?"他说:"回去细说。"

说话间已经到了沟底队里,场上几只猪跑来跑去,个个儿瘦得赛狗。还不到下班时间,冷冷清清的,只有队上伙房隐隐传来丁丁当当的声音。

到了我的宿舍,就直进去。这里并不锁门,都没有多余的东西可拿,不必防谁。我放了盆,叫他等着,就提桶打热水来给他洗。到了伙房，与炊事员讲，我这个月的五钱油全数领出来，以后就领生菜，不再打熟菜。炊事员问："来客了？"我说："可不!"炊事员就打开锁了的柜子，舀一小匙油找了个碗盛给我，又拿了三只长茄子，说："明天还来打菜吧，从后天算起，方便。"我从锅里舀了热水，提回宿舍。

王一生把衣裳脱了，只剩一条裤衩，呼噜呼噜地洗。洗完后，将脏衣服按在水里泡着，然后一件一件搓，洗好涮好，拧干晾在门口绳上。我说："你还挺麻利的。"他说："从小自己干，惯了。几件衣服，也不费事。"说着就在床上坐下，弯过手臂，去挠后背，肋骨一根根动着。我拿出烟来请他抽。他很老练地敲出一支，舔了一头儿，倒过来叼着。我先给他点了，自己也点上。他支起肩深吸进去，慢慢地吐出来，浑身荡一下，笑了，说："真不错。"我说："怎么样？也抽上了？日子过得不错呀。"他看看草顶，又看看在门口转来转去的猪，低下头，轻轻拍着净是绿筋的瘦腿，半晌才说："不错，真的不错。还说什么呢？粮？钱？还要什么呢？不错，真不错。你怎么样？"他透过烟雾问我。我也感叹了，说："钱是不少，粮也多，没错儿，可没油哇。大锅菜吃得胃酸。主要是没什么玩儿的，没书，没电，没电影儿。去哪儿也不容易，老在这个沟儿里转，闷得无聊。"他看看我，摇一下头，说："你们这些人哪! 没法儿说，想的净是锦上添花。我挺知足，还要什么呢？你呀，你就是叫书害了。你在车上给我讲的两个故事，我琢磨了，后来挺喜欢的。你不错，读了不少书。可是，归到底，解决什么呢？是呀，一个人拼命想活着，最后都神经了，后来好了，活下来了，可接着怎么活呢？像邦斯那样？有吃，有喝，好收藏个什么，可有个馋的毛病，人家不请吃就活得不痛快。人要知足，顿顿饱就是福。"他不说了，看着自己的脚趾动来动去，又用后脚跟去擦另一只脚的背，吐出一口烟，用手在腿上掸了掸。

我很后悔用油来表示我对生活的不满意，还用书和电影儿这种可有可无的东西表示我对生活的不满足，因为这些在他看来，实在是超出基准线之上的东西，他不会为这些烦闷。我突然觉得很泄气，有些同意他的说法。是呀，还要什么呢？我不是也感到挺好了吗？不用吃了上顿惦记着下顿，床不管怎么烂，也还是自己的，不用蹿来蹿去找刷夜的地方。可我常常烦闷的是什么呢？为什么就那么想看看随便什么一本书呢？电影儿这种东西，灯一亮就全醒过来了，图个什么呢？可我隐隐有一种欲望在心里，说不清楚，但我大致觉出是关于活着的什么东西。

我问他："你还下棋吗？"他就像走棋那么快地说："当然，还用说？"我说："是呀，你觉得一切都好，干嘛还要下棋呢？下棋不多余吗？"他把烟卷儿停在半空，摸了一下脸，说："我迷象棋。一下棋，就什么都忘了。呆在棋里舒服。就是没有棋盘、棋子儿，我在心里就能下，碍谁的事儿啦？"我说："假如有一天不让你下棋，也不许你想走棋的事儿，你觉得怎么样？"他挺奇怪地看着我说："不可能，那怎么可能？我能在心里下呀！还能把我脑子挖了？你净说些不可能的事儿。"我叹了一口气，说："下棋这事儿看来是不错。看了一本儿书，你不能老在脑子里过篇儿，老想看看新的。可棋不一样了，自己能变着花样儿玩。"他笑着对我说："怎么样，学棋吧？咱们现在吃喝不愁了，顶多是照你说的，不够好，又活不出个大意思来。书你哪儿找去？下棋吧，有忧下棋解。"我想了想，说："我实在对棋不感兴趣。我们队倒有个人，据说下得不错。"他把烟屁股使劲儿扔出门外，眼睛又放出光来："真的？有下棋的？嘿，我真还来对了。他在哪儿？"我说："还没下班呢。看你急的，你不是来看我的吗？"他双手抱着脖子仰在我的被子上，看着自己松松的肚皮，说："我这半年，就找不到下棋。后来想，天下异人多得很，这野林子里我就不信找不到个下棋下得好的。现在我请了事假，一路找人下棋，就找到你这儿来了。"我说："你不挣钱了？怎么活着呢？"他说："你不知道，我妹妹在城里分了工矿，挣钱啦，我也就不用给家寄那么多钱了。我就想，趁这工夫儿，会会棋手。怎么样？你一会儿把你说的那人找来下一盘？"我说当然，心里一动，就又问他："你家里到底是怎么个情况呢？"他叹了一口气，望着屋顶，很久才说："穷。困难啊！我们家三口儿人，母亲死了，只有父亲、妹妹和我。我父亲嘛，挣得少，按平均生活费的说法儿，我们一人才不到十块。我母亲死后，父亲就喝酒，而且越喝越多，手里有俩钱儿就喝，就骂人。邻居劝，他不是不听，就是一把鼻涕一把泪，弄得人家也挺难过。我有一回跟我父亲说，'你不喝就不行？有什么好处呢？'他说，'你不知道酒是什么玩意儿，它是老爷们儿的觉啊！咱们这日子挺不易，你妈去了，你们又小。我烦哪，我没文化，这把年纪，一辈子这点子钱算是到头儿了。你妈死的时候,嘱咐了,怎么着也要供你念完初中再挣钱。你们让我喝口酒,啊？对老人有什么过不去的,下辈子算吧。'"他看了看我,又说:"不瞒你说,我母亲解放前是窑子里的。后来大概是有人看上了,做了人家的小,也算从良。有烟吗?"我扔过一根烟给他,他点上了,把烟头儿吹得红红的,两眼不错眼珠儿地盯着,许久才说:"后来,我妈又跟人跑了。据说买她的那家欺负她,当老妈子不说,还打。后来跟的这个是什么人,我不知道,我只知道我是我妈跟这个人生的,刚一解放,我妈跟的那个人就不见了。当时我妈怀着我,吃穿无着,就跟了我现在这个父亲。我这个后爹是卖力气的,可临到解放的时候儿,身子骨儿不行了,又没文化,钱就挣得少。和我妈过了以后,原指着相帮着好一点儿,可没想到添了我妹妹后,我妈一天不如一天。那时候我才上小学,脑筋好,老师都喜欢我。可学校春游、看电影我都不去,给家里省一点儿是一点儿。我妈怕委屈了我,拖累着个身子,到处找活。有一回,我和我母亲给印刷厂叠书页子,是一本讲象棋的书。叠好了,我妈还没送去,我就一篇一篇对着看。不承想,就看出点儿意思来。于是有空儿就到街上看人家下棋。看了有些日子,就手痒痒,没敢跟家里要钱,自己用硬纸剪了一副棋,拿到学校去下。下着下着就熟了。于是又到街上和别人下。原先我看人家下得挺好,可我这一跟他们真下,还就赢了。一家伙就下了一晚上,饭也没吃。我妈找了来,把我打回去。唉,我妈身子弱,都打不疼我。到了家,她竟给我跪下了,说,'小祖宗,我就指望你了！你若不好好儿念书，妈就死在这儿。'我一听这话吓坏了，忙说，'妈，我没不好好儿念书。您起来，我不下棋了。'我把我妈扶起来坐着。那天晚上，我跟我妈叠页子，叠着叠着，就走了神儿，想着一路棋。我妈叹一口气说，'你也是，看不上电影儿，也不去公园，就玩儿这么个棋。唉，下吧。可妈的话你得记着，不许玩儿疯了。功课要是落下了，我不饶你。我和你爹都不识字儿，可我们会问老师。老师若说你功课跟不上，你再说什么也不行。'我答应了。我怎么会把功课落下呢？学校的算术，我跟玩儿似的。这以后，我放了学，先做功课，完了就下棋，吃完饭，就帮我妈干活儿，一直到睡觉。因为叠页子不用动脑筋，所以就在脑子里走棋，有的时候，魔症了，会突然一拍书页，喊棋步，把家里人都吓一跳。"我说："怨不得你棋下得这么好，小时候棋就都在你脑子里呢！"他苦笑笑说："是呀，后来老师就让我去少年宫象棋组，说好好儿学，将来能拿大冠军呢！可我妈说，'咱们不去什么象棋组，要学，就学有用的本事。下棋下得好，还当饭吃了？有那点儿工夫，在学校多学点儿东西比什么不好？你跟你们老师说，不去象棋组，要是你们老师还有没教你的本事，你就跟老师说，你教了我，将来有大用呢。啊？专学下棋？这以前都是有钱人干的！妈以前见过这种人，那都有身份，他们不指着下棋吃饭。妈以前待过的地方，也有女的会下棋，可要的钱也多。唉，你不知道，你不懂。下下玩儿可以，别专学，啊？'我跟老师说了，老师想了想，没说什么。后来老师买了一副棋送我，我拿给妈看，妈说，'唉，这是善心人哪！可你记住，先说吃,再说下棋。等你挣了钱,养活家了,爱怎么下就怎么下,随你。'"我感叹了,说:"这下儿好了,你挣钱了,你就能撒着欢儿地下了,你妈也就放心了。"王一生把脚搬上床,盘了坐,两只手互相捏着腕子,看着地下说:"我妈看不见我挣钱了。家里供我念到初一,我妈就死了。死之前,特别跟我说,'这一条街都说你棋下得好,妈信,可妈在棋上疼不了你。你在棋上怎么出息,到底不是饭碗。妈不能看你念完初中,跟你爹说了,怎么着困难,也要念完。高中,妈打听了,那是为上大学,咱们家用不着上大学,你爹也不行了,你妹妹还小,等你初中念完了就挣钱,家里就靠你了。妈要走了,一辈子也没给你留下什么,只捡人家的牙刷把,给你磨了一副棋。'说着,就叫我从枕头底下拿出一个小布包来,打开一看,都是一小点儿大的子儿,磨得是光了又光,赛象牙,可上头没字儿。妈说,'我不识字,怕刻不对。你拿了去,自己刻吧,也算妈疼你好下棋。'我们家多困难,我没哭过,哭管什么呢?可看着这副没字儿的棋,我绷不住了。"

我鼻子有些酸,就低了眼,叹道:"唉,当母亲的。"王一生不再说话,只是抽烟。

山上的人下来了,打到两条蛇。大家见了王一生,都很客气,问是几分场的,那边儿伙食怎么样。王一生答了,就过去摸一摸晾着的衣裤,还没有干。我让他先穿我的,他说吃饭要出汗,先光着吧。大家见他很随和,也就随便聊起来。我自然将王一生的棋道吹了一番,以示来者不凡。大家就都说让队里的高手"脚卵"来与王一生下。一个人跑去喊,不一刻,脚卵来了。脚卵是南方大城市的知识青年,个子非常高,又非常瘦。动作起来颇有些文气,衣服总要穿得整整齐齐,有时候走在山间小路上,看到这样一个高个儿纤尘不染,衣冠楚楚,真令人生疑。脚卵弯腰进来,很远就伸出手来要握,王一生糊涂了一下,马上明白了,也伸出手去,脸却红了。握过手,脚卵把双手捏在一起端在肚子前面,说:"我叫倪斌,人儿倪,文武斌。因为腿长,大家叫我脚卵。卵是很粗俗的话,请不要介意,这里的人文化水平是很低的。贵姓?"王一生比倪斌矮下去两个头,就仰着头说:"我姓王,叫王一生。"倪斌说:"王一生? 蛮好,蛮好,名字蛮好的。一生是哪两个字?"王一生一直仰着脖子,说:"一二三的一,生活的生。"倪斌说:"蛮好,蛮好。"就把长臂曲着往外一摆,说:"请坐。听说你钻研象棋? 蛮好,蛮好,象棋是很高级的文化。我父亲是下得很好的,有些名气,喏,他们都知道的。我会走一点点,很爱好,不过在这里没有对手。你请坐。"王一生坐回床上,很尴尬地笑着,不知说什么好。倪斌并不坐下,只把手虚放在胸前,微微向前侧了一下身子,说:"对不起,我刚刚下班,还没有梳洗,你候一下好了,我马上就来。噢,问一下,乃父也是棋道里的人么?"王一生很快地摇头,刚要说什么,但只是喘了一口气。倪斌说:"蛮好,蛮好。好,一会儿我再来。"我说:"脚卵洗了澡,来吃蛇肉。"倪斌一边退出去,一边说:"不必了,不必了。好的,好的。"大家笑起来,向外嚷:"你到底来是不来? 什么'不必了,好的'!"倪斌在门外说:"蛇肉当然是要吃的,一会儿下棋是要动脑筋的。"

大家笑着脚卵，关了门，三四个人精着屁股，上上下下地洗，互相开着身体的玩笑。王一生不知在想什么，坐在床里边，让开擦身的人。我一边将蛇头撕下来，一边对王一生说："别理脚卵，他就是这神神道道的一个人。"有一个人对我说："你的这个朋友要是真有两下子，今天有一场好杀。脚卵的父亲在我们市里，真是很有名气哩。"另外的人说："爹是爹，儿是儿，棋还遗传了?"王一生说："家传的棋，有厉害的。几代沉下的棋路，不可小看。一会儿起来看吧。"说着就紧一紧手脸。我把蛇挂起来，将皮剥下，不洗，放在案板上，用竹刀把肉划开，并不切断，盘在一个大碗内，放进一个大锅里，锅底蓄上水，叫："洗完了没有？我可开门了!"大家慌忙穿上短裤。我到外边地上摆三块土坯，中间架起柴引着，就将锅放在土坯上，把猪吆喝远了，说："谁来看着？别叫猪拱了。开锅后十分钟端下来。"就进屋收拾茄子。

　　有人把脸盆洗干净，到伙房打了四五斤饭和一小盆清水茄子，捎回来一棵葱和两瓣野蒜、一小块姜，我说还缺盐，就又有人跑去拿来一块，捣碎在纸上放着。

　　脚卵远远地来了，手里抓着一个黑木盒子。我问："脚卵，可有酱油膏?"脚卵迟疑了一下，返身回去。我又大叫："有醋精拿点儿来!"

　　蛇肉到了时间，端进屋里，掀开锅，一大团蒸气冒出来，大家并不缩头，慢慢看清了，都叫一声好。两大条蛇肉亮晶晶地盘在碗里，粉粉地冒鲜气。我嗖地一下将碗端出来，吹吹手指，说："开始准备胃液吧!"王一生也挤过来看，问："整着怎么吃?"我说:"蛇肉碰不得铁,碰铁就腥,所以不切,用筷子撕着蘸料吃。"我又将切好的茄块儿放进锅里蒸。

脚卵来了,用纸包了一小块儿酱油膏,又用一张小纸包了几颗白色的小粒儿,我问是什么,脚卵说:"这是草酸,去污用的,不过可以代替醋。我没有醋精,酱油膏也没有了,就这一点点。"我说:"凑合了。"脚卵把盒子放在床上,打开,原来是一副棋,乌木做的棋子,暗暗的发亮。字用刀刻出来,笔划很细,却是篆字,用金丝银丝嵌了,古色古香。棋盘是一幅绢,中间亦是篆字:楚河汉界。大家凑过去看,脚卵就很得意,说:"这是古董,明朝的,很值钱。我来的时候,我父亲给我的。以前和你们下棋,用不到这么好的棋。今天王一生来嘛,我们好好下。"王一生大约从来没有见过这么精彩的棋具,很小心地摸,又紧一紧手脸。

我将酱油膏和草酸冲好水,把葱末、姜末和蒜末投进去,叫声:"吃起来!"大家就乒乒乓乓地盛饭,伸筷撕那蛇肉蘸料,刚入嘴嚼,纷纷嚷鲜。

我问王一生是不是有些像蟹肉,王一生一边儿嚼着,一边儿说:"我没吃过螃蟹,不知道。"脚卵伸过头去问:"你没吃过螃蟹?怎么会呢?"王一生也不答话,只顾吃。脚卵就放下碗筷,说:"年年中秋节,我父亲就约一些名人到家里来,吃螃蟹,下棋,品酒,做诗。都是些很高雅的人,诗做得很好的,还要互相写在扇子上。这些扇子过多少年也是很值钱的。"大家并不理会他,只顾吃。脚卵眼看蛇肉渐少,也急忙捏起筷子来,不再说什么。

不一刻，蛇肉吃完，只剩两副蛇骨在碗里。我又把蒸熟的茄块儿端上来，放少许蒜和盐拌了。再将锅里热水倒掉，续上新水，把蛇骨放进去熬汤。大家喘一口气，接着伸筷，不一刻，茄子也吃净。我便把汤端上来，蛇骨已经煮散，在锅底刷拉刷拉地响。这里屋外常有一二处小丛的野茴香，我就拔来几棵，揪在汤里，立刻屋里异香扑鼻。大家这时饭已吃净，纷纷舀了汤在碗里，热热的小口呷，不似刚才紧张，话也多起来了。

脚卵抹一抹头发，说："蛮好，蛮好的。"就拿出一支烟，先让了王一生，又自己叼了一支，烟包正待放回衣袋里，想了想，便放在小饭桌上，摆一摆手说："今天吃的，都是山珍，海味是吃不到了。我家里常吃海味的，非常讲究。据我父亲讲，我爷爷在时，专雇一个老太婆，整天就是从燕窝里拔脏东西。燕窝这种东西，是海鸟叼来小鱼小虾，用口水粘起来的。所以里面各种脏东西多得很，要很细心地一点一点清理，一天也就能搞清一个，再用小火慢慢地蒸。每天吃一点，对身体非常好。"王一生听呆了，问："一个人每天就专门是管做燕窝的？好家伙！自己买来鱼虾，熬在一起，不等于燕窝吗？"脚卵微微一笑，说："要不怎么燕窝贵呢？第一，这燕窝长在海中峭壁上，要舍命去挖。第二，这海鸟的口水是很珍贵的东西，是温补的。因此，舍命，费工时，又是补品；能吃燕窝，也是说明家里有钱和有身份。"大家就说这燕窝一定非常好吃。脚卵又微微一笑，说："我吃过的，很腥。"大家就感叹了，说费这么多钱，吃一口腥，太划不来。

天黑下来,早升在半空的月亮渐渐亮了。我点起油灯,立刻四壁都是人影子。脚卵就说:"王一生,我们下一盘?"王一生大概还没有从燕窝里醒过来,听见脚卵问,只微微点一点头。脚卵出去了。王一生奇怪了,问:"嗯?"大家笑而不答。一会儿,脚卵又来了,穿得笔挺,身后随来许多人,进屋都看着王一生。脚卵慢慢摆好棋,问:"你先走?"王一生说:"你吧。"大家就上上下下围了看。

走出十多步,王一生有些不安,但也只是暗暗捻一下手指。走过三十几步,王一生很快地:"重摆吧。"大家奇怪,看看王一生,又看看脚卵,不知是谁赢了。脚卵微微一笑,说:"一赢不算胜。"就伸手抽一棵烟点上。王一生没有表情,默默地把棋重新码好。两人又走。又走到十多步,脚卵半天不动,直到把一根烟吸完,又走了几步,脚卵慢慢地说:"再来一盘。"大家又奇怪是谁赢了,纷纷问。王一生很快地将棋码成一个方堆,看着脚卵问:"走盲棋?"脚卵沉吟了一下,点点头。两人就口述棋步。好几个人摸摸头,摸摸脖子,说下得好没意思,不知道谁是赢家,就有几个人离开走出去,把油灯带得一明一暗。

我觉出有点儿冷,就问王一生:"你不穿点我衣裳?"王一生没有理我。我感到没有意思,就坐在床里,看大家也是一会儿看看脚卵,一会儿看看王一生,像是瞧从来没见过的两个怪物。油灯下,王一生抱了双膝,锁骨后陷下两个深窝,盯着油灯,时不时拍一下身上的蚊虫。脚卵两条长腿抵在胸口,一只大手将整个儿脸遮了,另一只大手飞快地将指头捏来弄去。说了许久，脚卵放下手，很快地笑一笑，说："我乱了，记不得。"就又摆了棋再下。不久，脚卵抬起头，看着王一生说："天下是你的。"抽出一支烟给王一生，又说："你的棋是跟谁学的？"王一生也看着脚卵，说："跟天下人。"脚卵说："蛮好，蛮好，你的棋蛮好。"大家看出是谁赢了，都高兴得松动起来，盯着王一生看。

　　脚卵把手搓来搓去，说："我们这里没有会下棋的人，我的棋路生了。今天碰到你，蛮高兴的，我们做个朋友。"王一生说："将来有机会，一定见见你父亲。"脚卵很高兴，说："那好，好极了，有机会一定去见见他。我不过是玩玩棋。"停了一会儿，又说："你参加地区的比赛，没有问题。"王一生问："什么比赛？"脚卵说："咱们地区，要组织一个运动会，其中有棋类。地区管文教的书记我认得，他早年在我们市里，与我父亲认识。我到农场来，我父亲给他带过信，请他照顾。我找过他，他说我不如打篮球。我怎么会打篮球呢？那是很野蛮的运动，要伤身体的。这次运动会，他来信告诉我，让我争取参加农场的棋类队到地区比赛，赢了，调动自然好说。你棋下到这个地步，参加农场队，不成问题。你回你们场，去报名就可以了。将来总场选拔，肯定会有你。"王一生很高兴，起来把衣裳穿上，显得更瘦，大家又聊了很久。

　　将近午夜，大家都散去，只剩下宿舍里同住的四个人与王一生、脚卵。脚卵站起来，说："我去拿些东西来吃。"大家都很兴奋，等着他。一会儿，脚卵弯腰进来，把东西放在床上，摆出六颗巧克力，半袋麦乳精，纸包的一斤精白挂面。巧克力大家都一口咽了，来回舔着嘴唇。麦乳精冲成稀稀的六碗，喝得满屋喉咙响。王一生笑嘻嘻地说："世界上还有这种东西？苦甜苦甜的。"我又把火生起来，开了锅，把面下了，说："可惜没有调料。"脚卵说："我还有酱油膏。"我说："你不是只有一小块儿了吗？"脚卵不好意思地说："咳，今天不容易，王一生来了，我再贡献一些。"就又拿了来。

大家吃了，纷纷点起烟，打着哈欠，说没想到脚卵还有如许存货，藏得倒严实，脚卵急忙申辩这是剩下的全部了。大家吵着要去翻，王一生说："不要闹，人家的是人家的，从来农场存到现在，说明人会过日子。倪斌，你说，这比赛什么时候开始呢？"脚卵说："起码还有半年。"王一生不再说话。我说："好了，休息吧。王一生，你和我睡在我的床上。脚卵，明天再聊。"大家就起身收拾床铺，放蚊帐。我和王一生送脚卵到门口，看他高高的个子在青白的月光下远远去了。王一生叹一口气，说："倪斌是个好人。"

王一生又待了一天，第三天早上，执意要走。脚卵穿了破衣服，掮着锄来送。两人握了手，倪斌说："后会有期。"大家远远在山坡上招手。我送王一生出了山沟，王一生拦住，说："回去吧。"我嘱咐他，到了别的分场，有什么困难，托人来告诉我，若回来路过，再来玩儿。王一生整了整书包带儿，就急急地顺公路走了，脚下扬起细土，衣裳晃来晃去，裤管儿前后荡着，像是没有屁股。

三

这以后，大家没事儿，常提起王一生，津津有味儿地回忆王一生光膀子大战脚卵。我说了王一生如何如何不容易，脚卵说："我父亲说过的，'寒门出高士'。据我父亲讲，我们祖上是元朝的倪云林。倪祖很爱干净，开始的时候，家里有钱，当然是讲究的。后来兵荒马乱，家道败了，倪祖就卖了家产，到处走，常在荒村野店投宿，很遇到一些高士。后来与一个会下棋的村野之人相识，学得一手好棋。现在大家只晓得倪云林是元四家里的一个，诗书画绝佳，却不晓得倪云林还会下棋。倪祖后来信佛参禅，将棋炼进禅宗，自成一路。这棋只我们这一宗传下来。王一生赢了我，不晓得他是什么路，总归是高手了。"大家都不知道倪云林是什么人，只听脚卵神吹，将信将疑，可也认定脚卵的棋有些来路，王一生既赢了脚卵，当然更了不起。这里的知青在城里都是平民出身，多是寒苦的，自然更看重王一生。

将近半年，王一生不再露面。只是这里那里传来消息，说有个叫王一生的，外号棋呆子，在某处与某某下棋，赢了某某。大家也很高兴，即使有输的消息，都一致否认，说王一生怎么会输呢？我给王一生所在的分场队里写了信，也不见回音，大家就催我去一趟。我因为这样那样的事，加上农场知青常常斗殴，又输进火药枪互相射击，路途险恶，终于没有去。

一天脚卵在山上对我说，他已经报名参加棋类比赛了，过两天就去总场，问王一生可有消息？我说没有。大家就说王一生肯定会到总场比赛，相约一起请假去总场看看。

过了两天，队里的活儿稀松，大家就纷纷找了各种借口请假到总场,盼着能见着王一生。我也请了假出来。

总场就在地区所在地,大家走了两天才到。这个地区虽是省以下的行政单位,却只有交叉的两条街,沿街有一些商店,货架上不是空的,即是"展品概不出售"。可是大家仍然很兴奋,觉得到了繁华地界,就沿街一个馆子一个馆子地吃,都先只叫净肉,一盘一盘地吞下去,拍拍肚子出来,觉得日光晃眼,竟有些肉醉,就找了一处草地,躺下来抽烟,又纷纷昏睡过去。

醒来后,大家又回到街上细细吃了一些面食,然后到总场去。

一行人高高兴兴到了总场,找到文体干事,问可有一个叫王一生的来报到。干事翻了半天花名册,说没有。大家不信,拿过花名册来七手八脚地找,真的没有,就问干事是不是搞漏掉了。干事说花名册是按各分场报上来的名字编的,都已分好号码,编好组,只等明天开赛。大家你望望我,我望望你,搞不清是怎么回事。我说:"找脚卵去。"脚卵在运动员们住下的草棚里,见了他,大家就问。脚卵说:"我也奇怪呢。这里乱糟糟的,我的号是棋类,可把我分到球类组来住,让我今晚就参加总场联队训练,说了半天也不行,还说主要靠我进球得分。"大家笑起来,说:"管他赛什么,你们的伙食差不了。可王一生没来太可惜了。"

直到比赛开始,也没有见王一生的影子。问了他们分场来的人,都说很久没见王一生了。大家有些慌,又没办法,只好去看脚卵赛篮球。脚卵痛苦不堪,规矩一点儿不懂,球也抓不住,投出去总是三不沾,抢得猛一些,他就抽身出来,瞪着大眼看别人争。文体干事急得抓耳挠腮,大家又笑得前仰后合。每场下来,脚卵总是嚷野蛮,埋怨脏。

赛了两天,决出总场各类运动代表队,到地区参加地区决赛。大家看看王一生还没有影子,就都相约要回去了。脚卵要留在地区文教书记家再待一两天,就送我们走一段。快到街口,忽然有人一指:"那不是王一生?"大家顺着方向一看,真是他。王一生在街另一面急急地走来,没有看见我们。我们一齐大叫,他猛地站住,看见我们,就横过街向我们跑来。到了跟前,大家纷纷问他怎么不来参加比赛?王一生很着急的样子,说:"这半年我总请事假出来下棋,等我知道报名赶回去,分场说我表现不好,不准我出来参加比赛,连名都没报上。我刚找了由头儿,跑上来看看赛得怎么样。怎么样?赛得怎么样?"大家一迭声儿说早赛完了,现在是参加与各县代表的比赛,夺地区冠军。王一生愣了半晌,说:"也好,夺地区冠军必是各县高手,看看也不赖。"我说:"你还没吃东西吧?走,街上随便吃点儿什么去。"脚卵与王一生握过手,也惋惜不已。大家就又拥到一家小馆儿,买了一些饭菜,边吃边叹息。王一生说:"我是要看看地区的象棋大赛。你们怎么样?要回去了吗?"大家都说出来的时间太长,要回去。我说:"我再陪你一两天吧。脚卵也在这里。"于是又有两三个人也说留下来再耍一耍。

脚卵就领留下的人去文教书记家,说是看看王一生还有没有参加比赛的可能。走不多久,就到了。只见一扇小铁门紧闭着，进去就有人问找谁，见了脚卵，不再说什么，只让等一下。一会儿叫进了，大家一起走进一幢大房子，只见窗台上摆了一溜儿花草，伺候得很滋润。大大的一面墙上只一幅毛主席诗词的挂轴儿，绫子黄黄的很浅。屋内只摆几把藤椅，茶几上放着几张大报与油印的简报。不一会儿，书记出来，胖胖的，很快地与每个人握手，又叫人把简报收走，就请大家坐下来。大家没见过管着几个县的人的家，头都转来转去地看。书记呆了一下，就问："都是倪斌的同学吗？"大家纷纷回过头看书记，不知该谁回答。脚卵欠一欠身，说："都是我们队上的。这一位就是王一生。"说着用手掌向王一生一倾。书记看着王一生说："噢，你就是王一生？好。这两天，倪斌常提到你。怎么样，选到地区来赛了吗？"王一生正想答话，倪斌马上就说："王一生这次有些事耽误了，没有报上名。现在事情办完了，看看还能不能参加地区比赛。您看呢？"书记用胖手在扶手上轻轻拍了两下，又轻轻用中指很慢地擦着鼻沟儿，说："啊，是这样。不好办。你没有取得县一级的资格，不好办。听说你很有天才，可是没有取得资格去参加比赛，下面要说话的，啊？"王一生低了头，说："我也不是要参加比赛，只是来看看。"书记说："那是可以的，那欢迎。倪斌，你去桌上，左边的那个桌子，上面有一份打印的比赛日程。你拿来看看，象棋类是怎么安排的。"倪斌早一步跨进里屋，马上把材料拿出来，看了一下，说："要赛三天呢！"就递给书记。书记也不看，把它放在茶几上，掸一掸手，说："是啊，几个县嘛。啊？还有什么问题吗？"大家都站起来，说走了。书记与离他近的人很快地握了手，说："倪斌，你晚上来，嗯？"倪斌欠欠身说好的，就和大家一起出来。大家到了街上，舒了一口气，说笑起来。

大家漫无目的地在街上走，讲起来还要在这里待三天，恐怕身上的钱支持不住。王一生说他可以找到睡觉的地方，人多一点恐怕还是有办法，这样就能不去住店，省下不少钱。倪斌不好意思地说他可以住在书记家。于是大家一起随王一生去找住的地方。

原来王一生已经来过几次地区，认识了一个文化馆画画儿的，于是便带了我们投奔这位画家。到了文化馆，一进去，就听见远远有唱的，有拉的，有吹的，便猜是宣传队在演练，只见三四个女的，穿着蓝线衣裤，胸撅得不能再高，一扭一扭地走过来，近了，并不让路，直脖直脸地过去。我们赶紧闪在一边儿，都有点儿脸红。倪斌低低地说："这几位是地区的名角。在小地方，有她们这样的功夫，蛮不容易的。"大家就又回过头去看名角。

画家住在一个小角落里，门口鸡鸭转来转去，沿墙摆了一溜儿各类杂物，草就在杂物中间长出来。门又被许多晒着的衣裤布单遮住。王一生领我们从衣裤中弯腰过去，叫那画家。马上就乒乒乓乓出来一个人，见了王一生，说："来了？都进来吧。"画家只是一间小屋，里面一张小木床，到处是书、杂志、颜色和纸笔。墙上钉满了画的画儿。大家顺序进去，画家就把东西挪来挪去腾地方，大家挤着坐下，不敢再动。画家又迈过大家出去，一会儿提来一个暖瓶，给大家倒水。

大家传着各式的缸子、碗，都有了，捧着喝。画家也坐下来，问王一生："参加运动会了吗？"王一生叹着将事情讲了一遍。画家说："只好这样了，要待几天呢？"王一生就说："正是为这事来找你。这些都是我的朋友。你看能不能找个地方，大家挤一挤睡？"画家沉吟半晌，说："你每次来，在我这里挤还凑合。这么多人，嗯——让我看看。"他忽然眼里放出光来，说："文化馆有个礼堂，舞台倒是很大。今天晚上为运动会的人演出，演出之后，你们就在舞台上睡，怎么样？今天我还可以带你们进去看演出。电工与我很熟的，跟他说一声，进去睡没问题。只不过脏一些。"大家都纷纷说再好不过了。脚卵放下心的样子，小心地站起来，说："那好，诸位，我先走一步。"大家要站起来送，却谁也站不起来。脚卵按住大家，连说不必了，一脚就迈出屋外。画家说："好大的个子！是打球的吧？"大家笑起来，讲了脚卵的笑话。画家听了，说："是啊，你们也都够脏的。走，去洗洗澡，我也去。"大家就一个一个顺序出去，还是碰得丁当乱响。

原来这地区所在地，有一条江远远流过。大家走了许久，方才到了。江面不甚宽阔，水却很急，近岸的地方，有一些小洼儿。四处无人，大家脱了衣裤，都很认真地洗，将画家带来的一块肥皂用完。又把衣裤泡了，在石头上抽打，拧干后铺在石头上晒，除了游水的，其余便纷纷趴在岸上晒。画家早就洗完，坐在一边儿，掏出个本子在画。我发觉了，过去站在他身后看。原来他在画我们几个人的裸体速写。经他这一画，我倒发现我们这些每日在山上苦的人，却矫健异常，不禁赞叹起来。大家又围过来看,屁股白白的晃来晃去。画家说:"干活儿的人,肌肉线条极有特点,又很分明,虽然各部分发展可能不太平衡,可真的人体,常常是这样,变化万端,我以前在学院画人体,女人体居多,太往标准处靠,男人体也常静在那里,感觉不出肌肉滚动,越画越死。今天真是个难得的机会。"有人说羞处不好看,画家就在纸上用笔把说的人的羞处涂成一个疙瘩,大家就都笑起来。衣裤干了,纷纷穿上。

这时已近傍晚,太阳垂在两山之间,江面上便金子一般滚动,岸边石头也如热铁般红起来。有鸟儿在水面上掠来掠去,叫声传得很远。对岸有人在拖长声音吼山歌,却不见影子,只觉声音慢慢小了。大家都凝了神看。许久,王一生长叹一声,却不说什么。

大家又都往回走,在街上拉了画家一起吃些东西,画家倒好酒量。天黑了,画家领我们到礼堂后台入口,与一个人点头说了,招呼大家悄悄进去,缩在边幕上看。时间到了,幕并不开,说是书记还未来。演员们都化了妆,在后台走来走去,抻一抻手脚,互相取笑着。忽然外面响动起来,我拨了幕布一看,只见书记缓缓进来,在前排坐下,周围空着,后面黑压压一礼堂人。于是开演,演出甚为激烈,尘土四起。演员们在台上泪光闪闪,退下来一过边幕,就喜笑颜开,连说怎么怎么错了。王一生倒很入戏,脸上时阴时晴,嘴一直张着,全没有在棋盘前的镇静。戏一结束,王一生一个人在边幕拍起手来,我连忙止住他,向台下望去,书记不知什么时候已经走了，前两排仍然空着。

　　大家出来，摸黑拐到画家家里，脚卵已在屋里，见我们来了，就与画家出来和大家在外面站着，画家说："王一生，你可以参加比赛了。"王一生问："怎么回事儿？"脚卵说，晚上他在书记家里，书记跟他叙起家常，说十几年前常去他家，见过不少字画儿，不知运动起来，损失了没有？脚卵说还有一些，书记就不说话了。过了一会儿书记又说，脚卵的调动大约不成问题，到地区文教部门找个位置，跟下面打个招呼，办起来也快，让脚卵写信回家讲一讲。于是又谈起字画古董，说大家现在都不知道这些东西的价值，书记自己倒是常在心里想着。脚卵就说，他写信给家里，看能不能送书记一两幅，既然书记帮了这么大忙，感谢是应该的。又说，自己在队里有一副明朝的乌木棋，极是考究，书记若是还看得上，下次带上来。书记很高兴，连说带上来看看。又说你的朋友王一生，他倒可以和下面的人说一说，一个地区的比赛，不必那么严格，举贤不避私嘛。就挂了电话，电话里回答说，没有问题，请书记放心，叫王一生明天就参加比赛。

　　大家听了，都很高兴，称赞脚卵路道粗。王一生却没说话。脚卵走后，画家带了大家找到电工，开了礼堂后门，悄悄进去。电工说天凉了，问要不要把幕布放下来垫盖着？大家都说好，就七手八脚爬上去摘下幕布铺在台上。一个人走到台边，对着空空的座位一敬礼，尖着嗓子学报幕员，说："下一个节目——睡觉。现在开始。"大家悄悄地笑，纷纷钻进幕布躺下了。

躺下许久，我发觉王一生还没有睡着，就说："睡吧，明天要参加比赛呢！"王一生在黑暗里说："我不赛了，没意思。倪斌是好心，可我不想赛了。"我说："咳，管它！你能赛棋，脚卵能调上来，一副棋算什么？"王一生说："那是他父亲的棋呀！东西好坏不说，是个信物。我妈留给我的那副无字棋，我一直性命一样存着，现在生活好了，妈的话，我也忘不了。倪斌怎么就可以送人呢？"我说："脚卵家里有钱，一副棋算什么呢？他家里知道儿子活得好一些了，棋是舍得的。"王一生说："我反正是不赛了，被人做了交易，倒像是我占了便宜。我下得赢下不赢是我自己的事，这样赛，被人戳脊梁骨。"不知是谁也没睡着，大约都听见了，咕噜一声："呆子。"

四

第二天一早儿，大家满身是土地起来，找水擦了擦，又约画家到街上去吃。画家执意不肯，正说着，脚卵来了，很高兴的样子。王一生对他说："我不参加这个比赛。"大家呆了，脚卵问："蛮好的，怎么不赛了呢？省里还下来人视察呢！"王一生说："不赛就不赛了。"我说了说，脚卵叹道："书记是个文化人，蛮喜欢这些的。棋虽然是家里传下的，可我实在受不了农场这个罪，我只想有个干净的地方住一住，不要每天脏兮兮的。棋不能当饭吃的，用它通一些关节，还是值的。家里也不很景气，不会怪我。"画家把双臂抱在胸前，抬起一只手摸了摸脸，看着天说："倪斌，不能怪你。你没有什么了不得的要求。我这两年，也常常犯糊涂，生活太具体了。幸亏我还会画画儿。何以解忧？唯有——唉。"王一生很惊奇地看着画家，慢慢转了脸对脚卵说："倪斌，谢谢你。这次比赛决出高手，我登门去与他们下。我不参加这次比赛了。"脚卵忽然很兴奋，攥起大手一顿，说："这样，这样！我呢，去跟书记说一下，组织一个友谊赛。你要是赢了这次的冠军，无疑是真正的冠军。输了呢，也不太失身份。"王一生呆了呆："千万不要跟什么书记说，我自己找他们下。要下，就与前三名都下。"

大家也不好再说什么，就去看各种比赛，倒也热闹，王一生只钻在棋类场地外面，看各局的明棋。第三天，决出前三名。之后是发奖，又是演出，会场乱哄哄的，也听不清谁得的是什么奖。

脚卵让我们在会场等着，过了不久，就领来两个人，都是制服打扮。脚卵作了介绍，原来是象棋比赛的第二、三名。脚卵说："这就是王一生，棋蛮厉害的，想与你们两位高手下一下，大家也是一个互相学习的机会。"两个人看了看王一生，问："那怎么不参加比赛呢？我们在这里待了许多天，要回去了。"王一生说："我不耽误你们，与你们两人同时下。"两人互相看了看，忽然悟到，说："盲棋？"王一生点一点头，两人立刻变了态度，笑着说："我们没下过盲棋。"王一生说："不要紧，你们看着明棋下。来，咱们找个地方儿。"话不知怎么就传了出去，立刻嚷动了，全场上各县的人都说有一个农场的小子没有赛着，不服气，要同时与亚、季军比试。百十个人把我们围了起来，挤来挤去地看，大家觉得有了责任，便站在王一生身边儿。王一生倒低了头,对两个人说:"走吧,走吧,太扎眼。"有一个人挤了进来,说:"哪个要下棋?就是你吗?我们大爷这次是冠军,听说你不服气,我来请你。"王一生慢慢地说:"不必。你大爷要是肯下,我和你们三人同下。"众人都轰动了,拥着往棋场走去。到了街上,百十人走成一片。行人见了,纷纷问怎么回事,可是知青打架?待明白了,就都跟着走。走过半条街,竟有上千人跟着跑来跑去。商店里的店员和顾客也都站出来张望。长途车路过这里开不过,乘客们纷纷探出头来,只见一街人头攒动,尘土飞起多高,轰轰的,乱纸踏得嚓嚓响。一个傻子呆呆地在街中心,咿咿呀呀地唱,有人发了善心,把他拖开,傻子就依了墙根儿唱。四五条狗蹿来蹿去,觉得是它们在引路打狼,汪汪叫着。

到了棋场,竟有数千人围住,土扬在半空,许久落不下来。棋场的标语标志早已摘除,出来一个人,见这么多人,脸都白了。脚卵上去与他交涉,他很快地看着众人,连连点头儿,半天才明白是借场子用,急忙打开门,连说"可以可以",见众人都要进去,就急了。我们几个,马上到门口守住,放进脚卵、王一生和两个得了荣誉的人。这时有一个人走出来,对我们说:"高手既然和三个人下,多我一个也不怕,我也算一个。"众人又嚷动了,又有人报名。我不知怎么办好,只得进去告诉王一生。王一生咬一咬嘴说:"你们两个怎么样?"那两个人赶紧站起来,连说可以。我出去统计了,连冠军在内,对手共是十人。脚卵说:"十不吉利的,九个人好了。"于是就九个人。冠军总不见来,有人来报,既是下盲棋,冠军只在家里，命人传棋。王一生想了想，说好吧。九个人就关在场里，墙外一副明棋不够用，于是有人拿来八张整开白纸，很快地画了格儿。又有人用硬纸剪了百十个方棋子儿，用红黑颜色写了，背后粘上细绳，挂在棋格儿的钉子上，风一吹，轻轻地晃成一片，街上人们也喊成一片。

人是越来越多。后来的人拼命往前挤，挤不进去，就抓住人打听，以为是杀人的告示。妇女们也抱着孩子们，远远围成一片。又有许多人支了自行车，站在后架上伸脖子看，人群一挤，连着倒，喊成一团。半大的孩子们钻来钻去，被大人们用腿拱出去。数千人闹闹嚷嚷，街上像半空响着闷雷。

王一生坐在场当中一个靠背椅上，把手放在两条腿上，眼睛虚望着，一头一脸都是土，像是被传讯的歹人。我不禁笑起来，过去给他拍一拍土。他按住我的手，我觉出他有些抖。王一生低低地说："事情闹大了。你们几个朋友看好，一有动静，一起跑。"我说："不会。只要你赢了，什么都好办。争口气，怎么样？有把握吗？九个人哪！头三名都在这里！"王一生沉吟了一下，说："怕江湖的不怕朝廷的，参加过比赛的人的棋路我都看了，就不知道其他六个人会不会冒出冤家。书包你拿着，不管怎么样，书包不能丢。书包里有……"王一生看了看我，"我妈的无字棋。"他的瘦脸上又干又脏，鼻沟儿也黑了，头发立着，喉咙一动一动的，两眼黑得吓人。我知道他拼了，心里有些酸，只说："保重！"就离了他。他一个人空空地在场中央，谁也不看，静静的像一块铁。

棋开始了。上千人不再出声儿。只有自愿服务的人一会儿紧一会儿慢地用话传出棋步,外边儿自愿服务的人就变动着棋子儿。风吹得八张大纸哗哗地响,棋子儿荡来荡去。太阳斜斜地照在一切上,烧得耀眼。前几十排的人都坐下了,仰起来看,后面的人也挤得紧紧的,一个个土眉土眼,头发长长短短吹得飘,再没人动一下,似乎都要把命放在棋里搏。

我心里忽然有一种很古的东西涌上来,喉咙紧紧地往上走。读过的书,有的近了,有的远了,模糊了。平时十分佩服的项羽、刘邦都在目瞪口呆,倒是尸横遍野的那些黑脸士兵,从地下爬起来,哑了喉咙,慢慢移动。一个樵夫,提了斧在野唱。忽然又仿佛见了呆子的母亲,用一双弱手一张一张地折书页。

我不由伸手到王一生的书包里去掏摸,捏到一个小布包儿,拽出来一看,是个旧蓝斜纹布的小口袋,上面用线绣了一只蝙蝠。布的四边儿都用线做了圈口,针脚很是细密。取出一个棋子,确实很小,在太阳底下竟是半透明的,像是一只眼睛,正柔和地瞧着。我把它攥在手里。

太阳终于落下去,立刻爽快了。人们仍在看着,但议论起来。里边儿传出一句王一生的棋步,外边儿的就嚷动一下。专有几个人骑车为在家的冠军传送着棋步,大家就不太客气,笑话起来。

我又进去,看见脚卵很高兴的样子,心里就松开一些,问:"怎么样?我不懂棋。"脚卵抹一抹头发,说:"蛮好,蛮好。这种阵势,我从来也没见过,你想想看,九个人与他一个人下，九局连环！车轮大战！我要写信给我的父亲，把这次的棋谱都寄给他。"这时有两个人从各自的棋盘前站起来，朝着王一生一鞠躬，说："甘拜下风。"就捏着手出去了。王一生点点头儿，看了他们的位置一眼。

王一生的姿势没有变，仍旧是双手扶膝，眼平视着，像是望着极远极远的远处，又像是盯着极近极近的近处，瘦瘦的肩挑着宽大的衣服，土没拍干净，东一块儿，西一块儿。喉节许久才动一下。我第一次承认象棋也是运动，而且是马拉松，是多一倍的马拉松！我在学校时，参加过长跑，开始后的五百米，确实极累，但过了一个限度，就像不是在用脑子跑，而像一架无人驾驶的飞机，又像是一架到了高度的滑翔机，只管滑翔下去。可这象棋，始终是处在一种机敏的运动之中，兜捕对手，逼向死角，不能疏忽。我忽然担心起王一生的身体来。这几天，大家因为钱紧，不敢怎么吃，晚上睡得又晚，谁也没想到会有这么一个场面。看着王一生稳稳地坐在那里，我又替他赌一口气：死顶吧！我们在山上扛木料，两个人一根，不管路不是路，沟不是沟，也得咬牙，死活不能放手。谁若是顶不住软了，自己伤了不说，另一个也得被木头震得吐血。可这回是王一生一个人过沟过坎儿，我们帮不上忙。我找了点儿凉水来，悄悄走近他，在他眼前一挡，他抖了一下，眼睛刀子似的看了我一下，一会儿才认出是我，就干干地笑了一下。我指指水碗，他接过去，正要喝，一个局号报了棋步。他把碗高高地平端着，水纹丝儿不动。他看着碗边儿，回报了棋步，就把碗缓缓凑到嘴边儿。这时下一个局号又报了棋步,他把嘴定在碗边儿,半晌,回报了棋步,才咽一口水下去,"咕"的一声儿,声音大得可怕,眼里有了泪花。他把碗递过来,眼睛望望我,有一种说不出的东西在里面游动,嘴角儿缓缓流下一滴水,把下巴和脖子上的土冲开一道沟儿。我又把碗递过去,他竖起手掌止住我,回到他的世界里去了。

我出来,天已黑了。有山民打着松枝火把,有人用手电照着,黄乎乎的,一团明亮。大约是地区的各种单位下班了,人更多了,狗也在人前蹲着,看人挂动棋子,眼神凄凄的,像是在担忧。几个同来的队上知青,各被人围了打听。不一会儿,"王一生"、"棋呆子"、"是个知青"、"棋是道家的棋",就在人们嘴上传。我有些发噱,本想到人群里说说,但又止住了,随人们传吧,我开始高兴起来。这时墙上只有三局在下了。

忽然人群发一声喊。我回头一看,原来只剩了一盘,恰是与冠军的那一盘,盘上只有不多几个子儿。王一生的黑子儿远远近近地峙在对方棋营格里,后方老帅稳稳地待着,尚有一"士"伴着,好像帝王与近侍在聊天儿,等着前方将士得胜回朝;又似乎隐隐看见有人在伺候酒宴,点起尺把长的红蜡烛,有人在悄悄地调整管弦,单等有人跪奏捷报,鼓乐齐鸣。我的肚子拖长了音儿在响,脚下觉得软了,就拣个地方坐下,仰头看最后的围猎,生怕有什么差池。

红子儿半天不动,大家不耐烦了,纷纷看骑车的人来没来,嗡嗡地响成一片。忽然人群乱起来,纷纷闪开。只见一老者,精光头皮,由旁人搀着,慢慢走出来,嘴嚼动着,上上下下看着八张定局残子。众人纷纷传着，这就是本届地区冠军，是这个山区的一个世家后人，这次"出山"玩玩儿棋，不想就夺了头把交椅，评了这次比赛的大势，直叹棋道不兴。老者看完了棋，轻轻抻一抻衣衫，跺一跺土，昂了头，由人搀进棋场。众人都一拥而起。我急忙抢进了大门，跟在后面。只见老者进了大门，立定，往前看去。

王一生孤身一人坐在大屋子中央，瞪眼看着我们，双手支在膝上，铁铸一个细树桩，似无所见，似无所闻。高高的一盏电灯，暗暗地照在他脸上，眼睛深陷进去，黑黑的似俯视大千世界，茫茫宇宙。那生命像聚在一头乱发中，久久不散，又慢慢弥漫开来，灼得人脸热。

众人都呆了，都不说话。外面传了半天，眼前却是一个瘦小黑鬼，静静地坐着，众人都不禁吸了一口凉气。

半晌，老者咳嗽一下，底气很足，十分洪亮，在屋里荡来荡去。王一生忽然目光短了，发觉了众人，轻轻地挣了一下，却动不了。老者推开搀的人，向前迈了几步，立定，双手合在腹前摩挲了一下，朗声叫道："后生，老朽身有不便，不能亲赴沙场。使人传棋，实出无奈。你小小年纪，就有这般棋道，我看了，汇道禅于一炉，神机妙算，先声有势，后发制人，遣龙治水，气贯阴阳，古今儒将，不过如此。老朽有幸与你接手，感触不少，中华棋道，毕竟不颓，愿与你做个忘年之交。老朽这盘棋下到这里，权做赏玩，不知你可愿意平手言和，给老朽一点面子？"

王一生再挣了一下，仍起不来。我和脚卵急忙过去，托住他的腋下,提他起来。他的腿仍然是坐着的样子,直不了,半空悬着。我感到手里好像只有几斤的分量,就示意脚卵把王一生放下,用手去揉他的双腿。大家都拥过来,老者摇头叹息着。脚卵用大手在王一生身上、脸上、脖子上缓缓地用力揉。半响,王一生的身子软下来,靠在我们手上,喉咙嘶嘶地响着,慢慢把嘴张开,又合上,再张开,"啊啊"着。很久,才呜呜地说:"和了吧。"

老者很感动的样子,说:"今晚你是不是就在我那儿歇了?养息两天,我们谈谈棋?"王一生摇摇头,轻轻地说:"不了,我还有朋友。大家一起出来的,还是大家在一起吧。我们到、到文化馆去,那里有个朋友。"画家就在人群里喊:"走吧,到我那里去,我已经买好了吃的,你们几个一起去。真不容易啊。"大家慢慢拥了我们出来,火把一圈儿照着。山民和地区的人层层围了,争睹棋王风采,又都点头儿叹息。

我挽了王一生慢慢走,光亮一直随着。进了文化馆,到了画家的屋子,虽然有人帮着劝散,窗上还是挤满了人,慌得画家急忙把一些画儿藏了。

人渐渐散了,王一生还有些木。我忽然觉出左手还攥着那个棋子,就张了手给王一生看。王一生呆呆地盯着,似乎不认得,可喉咙里就有了响声,猛然"哇"地一声儿吐出一些黏液,呜呜地说:"妈,儿今天……妈——"大家都有些酸,扫了地下,打来水,劝了。王一生哭过,滞气调理过来,有了精神,就一起吃饭。画家竟喝得大醉,也不管大家,一个人倒在木床上睡去。电工领了我们,脚卵也跟着,一齐到礼堂台上去睡。

夜黑黑的,伸手不见五指。王一生已经睡死。我却还似乎耳边人声嚷动,眼前火把通明,山民们铁了脸,掮着柴火在林中走,咿咿呀呀地唱。我笑起来,想:不做俗人,哪儿会知道这般乐趣? 家破人亡,平了头每日荷锄,却自有真人生在里面,识到了,即是幸,即是福。衣食是本,自有人类,就是每日在忙这个。可囿在其中,终于还不太像人。倦意渐渐上来,就拥了幕布,沉沉睡去。

树　王

一

运知青的拖拉机进了山沟，终于在一小片平地中停下来。知青们正赞叹着一路野景，这时知道是目的地，都十分兴奋，纷纷跳下车来。

平地一边有数间草房，草房前高高矮矮、老老少少站了一溜儿人，张了嘴向我们望，不大动。孩子们如鱼般远远游动着。带队来的支书便不耐烦，喊道："都来欢迎欢迎嘛！"于是走出一个矮汉子，把笑容硬在脸上，慌慌地和我们握手。女知青们伸出手去，那汉子不握，自己的手互相擦一下，只与男知青们握。我见与他握过手的人脸上都有些异样，心里正不明白，就轮到我了。我一边伸出手去，说着"你好"，一边看这个矮汉子。不料手好似被门缝狠狠挤了一下，正要失声，矮汉子已去和另外的人握手了。男知青们要强，被这样握过以后，都不做声，只抽空甩一下手。

支书过来，说："肖疙瘩，莫握手了，去帮学生们下行李。"

矮汉子便不与人握手,走到拖斗一边,接上面递下的行李。

知青中,李立是好读书的人。行李中便有一只大木箱,里面都是他的书。这只木箱,要四个人才移得动。大家因都是上过学的,所以便对这只木箱有敬意,极小心地抬,嘴里互相嘱咐着:"小心!小心!"移至车厢边,下边只站着一个肖疙瘩,大家于是叫:"再来三个人!"还未等另外三个人过来,那书箱却像自己走到肖疙瘩肩上,肖疙瘩一只手扶着,上身略歪,脚连着走开了。大家都呆了,提着一颗心。待肖疙瘩走到草房前要下肩时,大家又一齐叫起来:"小心!"肖疙瘩似无所闻,另一只手扶上去,肩略一颠,腿屈下,双手把书箱稳稳放在地下。

大家正说不出话,肖疙瘩已走回车厢边,拍一拍车板,望着歇手的知青们,略略有些疑惑。知青们回过神,慌忙推一排行李到车厢边。肖疙瘩一手扯一件,板着胸,脚连着提走。在省城往汽车上和在总场往拖拉机上倒换行李时,大家都累得不行,半天才完。在队上却不知不觉,一会儿就完了。

大家卸完行李,进到草房里,房中一长条竹床,用十多丈长的大竹破开铺好,床头有一排竹笆,隔壁又是一间,分给女知青住。床原来是通过去的,合起来可各睡二十多人。大家惊叹竹子之大,纷纷占了位置,铺上褥子,又各自将自己的箱子摆好。李立叫了三个人帮他把书箱放好。放好了,李立呆呆地看着书箱,说:"这个家伙!他有多大的力气呢?"大家也都围过来,像是看一个怪物。这书箱漆着赭色,上面又用黄漆喷了一轮有光的太阳,"广阔天地,大有作为"几个字围了半圈。有人问:"李立,是什么珍贵的书?"李立就浑身上下摸钥匙。

天已暗下来,大家等着开箱,并没有觉得。这时支书捏了一只小油灯进来,说:"都收拾好了? 这里比不得大城市,没有电,先用这个吧。"大家这才悟过来没有电灯,连忙感谢着支书,小心地将油灯放在一摞箱子上。李立找到钥匙,弯下腰去开锁。大家围着,支书也凑近来,问:"打失东西了?"有人就介绍李立有一箱书,都是极好的。支书于是也弯下腰去看。箱盖掀开,昏暗中书籍漫出沿口,大家纷纷拿了对着亮看。原来都是政治读物,四卷雄文自不必说,尚有半尺厚的《列宁选集》,繁体字,青灰漆布面,翻开,字是竖排。又有很厚的《干部必读》、《资本论》、《马恩选集》、全套单行本《九评》,还有各种装潢的《毛主席语录》与林副主席语录。大家都惊叹李立如何收得这样齐整,简直可以开一个图书馆。李立慢慢地说:"这都是我父母的。我来这里,母亲的一套给我,父亲的一套他们还要用。老一辈仍然有一个需要学习的问题。但希望是在我们身上,未来要靠我们脚踏实地去干。"大家都感叹了。支书看得眼呆,却听不太明白,问:"看这么多书,还要学习文什么?"李立沉沉地说:"当然。"支书拣起一本书说:"这本是什么? 我拿去看看。"大家忍住笑,说这就是《毛泽东选集》。支书说既是毛选,他已有两套,想拿一本新的。李立于是拿了一本什么给他。

收拾停当,又洗涮,之后消停下来,等队上饭熟。门口不免围了一群孩子,于是大家掏摸出糖果散掉。孩子们尖叫着纷纷跑回家,不一会儿又嘴里鼓鼓地吮着继续围来门口,眼里少了惊奇,多了快乐,也敢近前偎在人身边。支书领着队长及各种干部进进出出地互相介绍,问长问短,糖果自然又散掉一些。大人们仔细地剥开糖纸,不吃,都给了孩子们。孩子们于是掏出嘴里化了大半的糖粒,互相比较着颜色。

正闹着,饭来了,提在房前场上。月亮已从山上升出,淡着半边,照在场上,很亮。大家在月光下盛了饭,围着菜盆吃。不料先吃的人纷纷叫起来。我也夹了一筷子菜放进嘴里,立刻像舌头上着了一鞭,胀得痛,慌忙吐在碗里对着月光看,不得要领。周围的大人与孩子们都很高兴,问:"城里不吃辣子么?"女知青们问:"以后都这么辣吗?"支书说:"狗日的!"于是讨了一副筷,夹菜吃进嘴里,嚼嚼,看看月亮,说:"不辣嘛。"女知青们半哭着说:"还不辣?"大家于是只吃饭,菜满满地剩着。吃完了,来人将菜端走。孩子们都跳着脚说:"明早有得肉吃了!"知青们这才觉出菜里原来有荤腥。

吃完了饭,有表的知青说还不到八点,屋里又只有小油灯,不如在场里坐坐。李立就提议来个营火晚会。支书说柴火有的是,于是喊肖疙瘩。肖疙瘩远远跑来,知道了,就去拖一个极大的树干来,用一个斧劈。李立要过斧来说自己劈。第一斧偏了,削下一块皮,飞出多远。李立吐了唾沫在手心,捏紧了斧柄抡起来。"嗨"的一声劈下去。那斧正砍中一个杈口,却怎么也拔不出来。大家都拥上来要显显身手。斧却像生就的,树干晃得乱动,就是不下来。正忙着,肖疙瘩过来,一脚踏住树干,一手落在斧柄上,斧就乖乖地斜松下来。

肖疙瘩将斧拿在手里,并不抡高,像切豆腐一样,不一会儿,树干就分成几条。大家看时,木质原来是扭着的。有知青指出这是庖丁解牛,另有人就说解这木牛,劲小的庖丁怕不行。肖疙瘩又用手去掰分开的柴,山沟里劈劈啪啪地就像放爆竹。有掰不动的,肖疙瘩就捏住一头在地上摔断。一个丈长的弯树,不一刻就架成一堆。李立去屋里寻纸来引。肖疙瘩却摸出火柴,蹲下,划着,伸到柴堆里去点。初时只有一寸的火苗,后来就像有风,蹿成一尺。待李立寻来纸,柴已燃得劈啪作响。大家都很高兴,一个人便去拨火。不料一动,柴就塌下来,火眼看要灭,女知青们一迭声地埋怨。肖疙瘩仍不说话,用一根长柴伸进去轻轻一挑,火又蹿起来。

我说:"老肖,来,一起坐。"肖疙瘩有些不好意思,说:"你们耍。"那声音形容不出,因为他不再说话,只慢慢走开,我竟觉得他没有说过那三个字。

支书说:"肖疙瘩,莫要忘记明天多四十个人吃饭。"肖疙瘩不说话,不远不近地蹲到场边一个土坡上,火照不到他,只月光勾出他小小的一圈。

火越来越大。有火星不断歪曲着升上去,热气灼得人脸紧,又将对面的脸晃得陌生。大家望着,都有些异样。李立站起来,说:"战斗的生活就要开始了,唱起歌来迎接它吧。"我突然觉得,走了这么久的路来到这里,绝不是在学校时的下乡劳动,但来临的生活是什么也不知道。大火令我生出无限的幻想与神秘,我不禁站起来想在月光下走开,看看这个生产队的范围。

大家以为我站起来是要唱歌，都望着我。我忽然明白了，窘迫中想了一个理由："厕所在哪儿?"大家哄笑起来。支书指了一个地方，我就真的走过去，经过肖疙瘩身边。

肖疙瘩望望我，说："屙尿?"我点点头，肖疙瘩就站起来在我前面走。望着他小小的身影，真搞不清怎么会是他劈了一大堆柴并且升起一大堆火。正想着，就到了生产队尽头。肖疙瘩指一指一栋小草房，说："左首。"我哪里有尿? 就站住脚向山上望去。

生产队就在大山缝脚下，从站的地方望上去，森森的林子似乎要压下来，月光下只觉得如同鬼魅。我问："这是原始森林吗?"肖疙瘩望望我，说："不屙尿?"我说："看看。这森林很古老吗?"肖疙瘩忽然很警觉的样子，听了一下，说："麂子。"我这时才觉到远远有短促的叫声，于是有些紧张，就问："有老虎吗?"肖疙瘩用手在肚子上勾一勾，说："虎? 不有的。有熊，有豹，有野猪，有野牛。"我说："有蛇吗?"肖疙瘩不再听那叫声，蹲下了，说："蛇? 多得很。有野鸡，有竹鼠，有马鹿，有麝猫。多得很。"我说："啊，这么多动物，打来吃嘛。"肖疙瘩又站起来，回头望望远处场上的火光，竟叹了一口气，说："快不有了，快不有了。"我奇怪了，问："为什么呢?"肖疙瘩不看我，搓一搓手，问："他们唱哪样?"我这时听出远处火堆那里传来女知青的重唱。几句过后，就对肖疙瘩说："这是唱我们划船，就是在水上划小船。"肖疙瘩说："捉鱼么?"我笑了，说："不捉鱼，玩儿。"肖疙瘩忽然在月光下看定了我，问："你们是接到命令到这里砍树么?"我思索了一下，说："不。

是接受贫下中农再教育,建设祖国,保卫祖国,改变一穷二白。"肖疙瘩说:"那为哪样要砍树呢?"我们在来的时候大约知道了要干的活计,我于是说:"把没用的树砍掉,种上有用的树。树好砍吗?"肖疙瘩低了头,说:"树又不会躲哪个。"向前走了几步,哗哗撒了一泡尿,问我:"不屙尿?"我摇摇头,随他走回去。营火晚会进行到很晚,露气降下来,柴也只剩下红炭,大家才去睡觉。夜里有人翻身,竹床便浪一样滚,大家时时醒来,断断续续闹了一夜。

二

第二天一早,我们爬起来,洗脸,刷牙,又纷纷拿了碗,用匙儿和筷子敲着,准备吃饭。这时司务长来了,一人发给一张饭卡,上面油印了一个月口粮的各种两数,告诉我们吃多少,炊事员就划掉多少。大家都知道这张纸是珍贵的了,就很小心地收在兜里。司务长又介绍最好将饭卡粘在一张硬纸上,不易损坏。大家于是又纷纷找硬纸,找胶水,贴好,之后到伙房去打饭吃。菜仍旧辣,于是仍旧只吃饭。队上的人都高高兴兴地将菜打回去。有人派孩子来打,于是孩子们一边拨拉着菜里的肉吃,一边走。

饭吃好了,队长来发锄,发刀。大家把工具在手上舞弄着,恨不能马上到山上干起来。队长笑着说:"今天先不干活,先上山看看。"大家于是跟了队长向山上走去。

原来这山并不是随便从什么地方就可以上去的。队长领着大家在山根沿一条小道横走着,远远见到一片菜地,一地零零落落的洋白菜，灰绿的叶子支张着，叶上有大小不等的窟窿。大家正评论着这菜长得如此难看，就见肖疙瘩从菜地里出来，捏一把刀。队长说："老肖。"肖疙瘩问："上山么？"队长说："带学生们上山看看。"肖疙瘩对大家看看，就蹲下去用刀砍洋白菜的叶子。几刀过后，外面的叶子落净，手上只剩一个球大的疙瘩，很嫩的样子。肖疙瘩又将落在地上的叶子拾在一起，放进一只筐里。有个知青很老练的气度，说："这是喂猪的。"队长说："喂猪？这是好东西。拿来渍酸菜，下得饭。"大家不安了，都说脏。肖疙瘩不说话，仍旧在弄他的。队长说："老肖，到山上转转？"肖疙瘩仍不说话，仍在弄他的。队长也不再说，领了我们走。

山上原来极难走。树、草、藤都掺在一起，要时时用刀砍断拦路的东西，蹚了深草走。女知青们怕有蛇，极小心地贼一样走。男知青们要显顽勇，劈劈啪啪地什么都砍一下，初时兴奋不觉得，渐渐就闷热起来。又觉得飞虫极多，手挥来挥去地赶，像染了神经病。队长说："莫乱砍，虫子就不多。"大家于是又都不砍，喘着气钻来钻去地走。走了约一个多钟头，队长站下来，大家喘着气四下一望，原来已经到了山顶。沟里队上的草房微小如豆，又认出其中的伙房，有烟气扭动着浮上去，渐渐淡没。远处的山只剩了颜色，蓝蓝的颤巍着伸展，一层浅着一层。大家呆呆地喘气，纷纷张着嘴，却说不出话。我忽然觉得这山像人脑的沟回，只不知其中思想着什么。又想，一个国家若都是山，那实际的面积比只有平原要多很多。常说夜郎自大，那夜郎踞在川贵山地，自大，恐怕有几何上的道理。

队长说："你们来了，人手多。农场今年要开万亩山地，都种上有用的树。"说着用手一指对面的一座山。大家这时才看出那山上只有深草，树已没有。细细辨认，才觉出有无数细树，层层排排地种了一山，只那山顶上，有一株独独的大树。李立问："这些山，"用手一划，"都种上有用的树吗？"队长说是。李立反叉了腰，深深地吸一口气，说："伟大。改造中国，伟大。"大家都同意着。队长又说："咱们站的这座山，把树放倒，烧一把火，挖上梯田带，再挖穴，种上有用的树。农场的活嘛，就是干这个。"有一个人指了对面山上那棵大树，问："为什么那棵树不砍倒？"队长看了看，说："砍不得。"大家纷纷问为什么。队长拍落脸上的一只什么虫，说："这树成了精了。哪个砍哪个要糟。"大家又问怎么糟？队长说："死。"大家笑起来，都说怎么会。队长说："咋个不会？我们在这里多少年了，凡是这种树精，连树王都不砍，别人就更不敢砍了。"大家又都笑说怎么会有成精的树？又有树王？李立说："迷信。植物的生长，新陈代谢，自然规律。太大了，太老了，人就迷信为精。队长，从来没有人试着砍过吗？"队长说："砍那座山的时候，我砍过。可砍了几刀，就浑身不自在，树王说，不能砍，就不敢再砍了。"大家问："谁是树王？"队长忽然迟疑了，说："啊，树王，树王么——啊，树——"用手挠一挠头，又说："走吧，下山去。大家知道了，以后就干了。"大家不走，逼着问树王是谁，队长很后悔的样子，一边走，一边说："唉，莫提，莫提。"大家想那人大约是反革命之类的人，在城里这类人也是不太好提的。李立说："肯定是搞迷信活动。农场的工人觉悟就这么低？他说不能砍就不砍了？"队长不再说话，默默地一直下到山底。

到了队上，大家不免又看那棵树，都很纳闷。听说下午是整理内务，几个人吃了午饭就相约爬上去看一看。

中午的太阳极辣。山上的草叶都有些垂卷，远远近近似乎有爆裂的声音。吃了午饭，大家看准了一条路，只管爬上去。

正弯腰抬腿地昏走，忽然见一个小娃赤着脚，黑黑的肩脊，闪着汗亮，抢了一柄小锄在挖什么。大家站住脚，喘着气问："挖什么？"小娃把锄拄在手下，说："山药。"李立用手比了一个圆形，问："土豆儿？"小娃眼睛一细，笑着说："山药就是山药。"有一个人问："能吃吗？"小娃说："吃得。粉得很。"大家就围过去看。只见斜坡已被小娃刨开一道窄沟，未见有什么东西。小娃见我们疑惑，就打开地上一件团着的衣服，只见有扁长的柱形数块，黄黄的，断口极白。小娃说："你们吃。"大家都掐了一点在嘴里，很滑，没有什么味儿，于是互相说意思不大。小娃笑了，说要蒸熟才更好吃。我们歇过来了，就问："到山顶上怎么走？"小娃说："一直走。"李立说："小朋友，带我们去。"小娃说："我还要挖。"想了想，又说："好走得很嘛，走。"说着就将包山药的衣服提着，捎了锄沿路走上去。

小娃走得飞快，引得我们好苦，全无东瞧西看的兴致，似乎只是为了走路。不一刻，汗淌到眼睛里，杀得很。汗又将衣衫捉到背上，裤子也吸在腿上。正坚持不住，只听得小娃在上面喊："可是要到这里？"大家拼命紧上几步，方知到了。

大家四下一看，不免一惊。早上远远望见的那棵独独的树，原来竟是百米高的一擎天伞。枝枝杈杈蔓延开去，遮住一亩大小的地方。大家呆呆地慢慢移上前去，用手摸一摸树干。树皮一点不老，指甲便划得出嫩绿，手摸上去又温温的似乎一跳一跳，令人疑心这树有脉。李立围树走了一圈，忽然狂喊一声："树王就是它，不是人！"大家张了嘴，又抬头望树上。树叶密密层层，风吹来，先是一边晃动，慢慢才动到另一边。叶间闪出一些空隙，天在其中蓝得发黑。又有阳光渗下无数斑点，似万只眼睛在眨。

我生平从未见过这样大的树，一时竟脑子空空如洗，慢慢就羞悔枉生一张嘴，说不得唱不得，倘若发音，必如野兽一般。

许久，大家才很异样地互相看看，都只咽下一口什么，慢慢走动起来。

那小娃一直掮着锄四下望着，这时忽然伸开细细的胳膊，回头看了我们一下，眼里闪出光来。大家正不明白，只见他慢慢将锄捏在手里，脊背收成窄窄的一条，一下将锄死命地丢出去。那锄在空中翻滚了几下，远远落在草里，草里就蹿出黄黄的一条，平平地飘走。大家一齐"呀"地喊起来，原来是一只小鹿。

小鹿跑到山顶尽头，倏地停住，将头回转来，一只耳朵微微摆一摆。身子如印在那里，一动不动。大家回过神来，又发一声喊,刚要抬脚,那小鹿却将短尾一平,碎着蹄脚移动几步,又一探头颈,黄光一闪,如梦般不见了。

小娃笑着去草里寻锄。大家说:"你怎么会打得着鹿?"小娃说:"这是麂子嘛,不是马鹿。"我想起昨晚的叫声,原来就是这种东西发出来的,就说:"这家伙叫起来很怪。"大家不信,问我怎么会知道。我说:"昨天晚上我就听见了,肖疙瘩说是麂子叫。"小娃很严肃地说:"我爹说是麂子叫,就是麂子叫。这山里还有一种叫声:咕、嘎。这是蛤蚧,肉好吃得很。"大家明白这原来是肖疙瘩的小孩。我不由得问:"你叫什么?"小娃将身体摆了一下,把一只手背过去,很坏的样子眯起一只眼睛,说:"肖六爪。"大家正不明白是哪几个字,我却明白了:"六指。把手拿来看看。"肖六爪迟疑了一下,又很无所谓的样子把手伸出来,手背朝上,大家一看,果然在小指旁边还长出一只指头,肖六爪将那个小指头立起来独独地转了一圈,又捏起拳头,只剩下第六个指头,伸到鼻子里掏,再拽出来,飞快地弹一下。一个人不由得闪了一下,大家都笑起来。肖六爪很骄傲的样子,说:"我这个指头好得很,不是残废,打起草排来比别人快。"大家不明白什么打草排,肖六爪很老练的样子,说:"将来你们也要打,草房顶要换呢。"

我拍拍六爪的头,说:"你爸爸力气很大。"六爪把两条细腿叉开,浑身扭一下,说:"我爹当过兵,侦察兵,去过外国。我爹说:外国跟这里一样,也是山,山上也是树。"我心里估摸了一下,问:"去朝鲜?"六爪愣了一下,摇摇头,用手一指,说:"那边。"大家都早知道这里不远就是国境,不免张望起来。

可除了山，还是山，看不出名堂。

大家慢慢往回走，又回头望望树王。树王静静地立在山顶，像是自言自语，又像是逗着百十个孩子，叶子哗哗地响。李立忽然站住了，说："这棵树要占多少地啊！它把阳光都遮住了，种的树还会长吗？"大家都悟过来这个道理，但不明白他为什么说这个。一个人说："树王嘛。"李立不再说什么，随大家一齐下山。

三

第三天，大家便开始上山干活。活计自然是砍树。千百年没人动过这原始森林，于是整个森林长成一团。树都互相躲让着，又都互相争夺着，从上到下，无有闲处。藤子从这棵树爬到那棵树，就像爱串门子的妇女，形象却如老妪。草极盛，年年枯萎后，积一层厚壳，新草又破壳而出。一脚踏下去，"噗"的一声，有时深了，有时浅了。树极难砍。明明断了，斜溜下去，却不倒，不是叫藤扯着，就是被近旁的树架住。一架大山，百多号人，整整砍了一个多月，还没弄出个眉目来。这期间，农场不断有命令下来，传达着精神，要求不怕苦、不怕死，多干快干。各分场，各生产队又不断有挑应战。成绩天天上报，再天天公布出来，慢慢就比出几位英雄好汉，令大家敬仰。这其中只有一个知青，即是李立。

李立原并不十分强壮，却有一股狠劲儿，是别人比不得的。开始大家都不太会干，一个钟头后就常常擦汗，擦的时间渐渐长久，于是不免东张西望，并发现许多比砍树更有趣的事情。例如有云飘过，大家就一动不动地看阴影在山上移动；又有野雉拖一条长尾快快地飞走，大家就在心中比较着它与家鸡的味道；更有蛇被发现，大家围着打；还常常寻到一些异果，初时谁也不敢吃，于是必有人担起神农的责任，众目睽睽之下，镇静地慢慢嚼，大家在紧张中咽下口水。但所有这些均与李立无关。李立只是舍命地砍，仅在树倒时望望天。有人见李立如此认真，便不好意思，就好好去干，将兴趣藏起。

我慢慢终于会砍山上的一切。以我的知识，以为砍树必斧无疑，初时对用刀尚不以为然，后来才明白，假若山上只有树，斧当然极方便。但斧如何砍得草？队上发的刀，约有六七斤重，用来砍树，用力便砍得进；用来砍藤，一刀即断；用来砍草，只消平抡了一排涮过去。在城里时，父亲好厨，他常指点我：若做得好菜，一要刀，二要火。他又常常亲自磨刀，之后立起刃来微微动着看，刃上无亮线即是锋利了。这样的刀可切极薄的肉与极细的菜丝。有父亲的同事来做饕客，热心的就来帮厨，总是被割去指甲还不知道，待白菜渗红，才感叹着离开。后来磨刀的事自然落在我身上，竟使我磨刀成癖。又学了书上，将头发放在刃上吹，总也不断，才知道增加吹的力量，也是一种功夫。队上发刀的头一天，我便用了三个钟头将刀磨得锋快。人有利器，易起杀心。上到山上，逢物便砍，自觉英雄无比。只是一到砍树，刃常常损缺。

在山上砍到一个多月，便有些油起来，活自然会干，更会的是休息。休息时常常远望，总能望到树王，于是不免与大家一起议论若满山是树时，树王如何放倒。方案百出，却不料终于也要砍到这样一棵大树。

这棵大树也像树王立在山顶，初时不显，待慢慢由山下砍上来而只剩山顶时，它便显出大来。但我发现，老职工们开始转移到山的另一面干活去了，不再在这里砍。知青们慢慢也都发觉，议论起来，认为是工时的原因。

这里每天砍山，下工前便由文书用皮尺丈量每人砍了多少面积，所报的成绩，便是这个内容。按理来说，树越大，所占的面积越大，但树大到一定程度，砍倒所费的工时便与面积不成比例。有经验的人，就借了各种原因，避开大树，去砍树冠大而树干细的树。眼看终于要砍这棵大树了，许多人就只去扫清外围。

这天，大家又上到山上，先纷纷坐下喘气休息，正闲聊间，李立站起来，捏了刀在手里，慢慢走近那棵大树，大家都不说话，只见李立围树走了一圈，把手拳在嘴前，看定了一个地方，举起刀，又抬头望望，重新选了一个地方，一刀砍下去。大家明白了，松了一口气，纷纷站起来，也走到大树近旁，看李立砍。

若要砍粗的树倒，便要破一个三角进去。树越粗，三角越大。李立要砍的这棵大树，上刀与下刀的距离，便有一公尺半的样子。有知青算了，若要树倒，总要砍出一立方的木头，而且大约要四天。大家兴致来了，都说合力来砍，不去计较工时，又公推由我负责磨刀，我自然答应下来，于是扛了四把砍刀，返身下山，回到队上。

狠狠地磨了三把刀，已近中午。正在磨第四把，忽然觉得有影子罩住我。抬头看时，是肖疙瘩双手抱了肩膀立在一边。见我停下，他弯下身去拾起一把磨好的刀，将右手拇指在锋上慢慢移一下，又端枪一样将刀平着瞄一瞄，点一点头，蹲下来，看看石头，问："你会磨刀？"我自然得意，也将手中的刀举起微微一晃，说："凑合。"肖疙瘩不说话，拿起一把磨好的刀，看到近旁有一截树桩，走过去，双手将刀略略一举，嗖地一下砍进去，又将右肩缩紧，刀便拔出来。肖疙瘩举起刀看一看刃，又只用右手一抡，刀便又砍进树桩，他松了手，招呼我说："你拔下来看刃。"我有些不解，但还是过去用双手将刀拔出。看刃时，吃了一惊，原来刃口小有损缺。肖疙瘩将手掌伸直，说："直直地砍进去，直直地拔出来，刃便不会缺。这刀的钢火脆，你用力歪了，刃便会缺，于是要再磨。这等于是不会磨刀。"我有些不舒服，便说："肖疙瘩，你什么时候剃胡子？"肖疙瘩不由摸摸下巴，说："早呢。"我说："这四把刀任你拿一把，若刮胡子痛了，我这左手由你切了去。右手嘛，我还要写字。"肖疙瘩用眼睛笑笑，撩一些水在石头上面，拿一把刀来磨，只十几下，便用手将刀上的水抹去，又提刀走到树桩前面，招呼我说："你在这里砍上一刀。"说着用手在刚才砍的地方下面半尺左右处一比。我走过去，接过刀，用力砍一下，不料刀刚一停，半尺长的一块木片便飞起来，在空中翻了一个斤斗，白晃晃地落在地上。自砍树以来，我从来没有两刀便能砍下这么大一块木头，高兴了，又两刀砍下一大块来。肖疙瘩摩一摩手，说："你望一下刃。"我将刀举到眼前,刃无损缺,却发现刃的一侧被磨了不宽的一个面。我有些省悟,便点点头。肖疙瘩又将双手伸直合在一起,说:"薄薄的刃,当然快,不消说。"他再将手掌底沿连在一起,将上面分开,做成角形,说:"角子砍进去,向两边挤。树片能下来,便是挤下来的。即便刀有些晃,角子刃不会损。你要剃头吗?刃也还是快。"我笑了,说:"痛就砍你右手。"肖疙瘩仍用眼睛笑一笑,说:"好狠。"

我高兴了,说:"我这刀切菜最好了。"肖疙瘩说:"山上有菜吗?"我说:"反正不管怎么说,在快这一点上,你承认不承认我磨得好?"肖疙瘩想一想,不说话,伸手从腰后抽出一柄不长的刀来递给我。我拿过来,发现木刀把上还连着一条细皮绳,另一端系在身后。我问:"刀连着绳干什么?"肖疙瘩说:"你看看刃我再告诉你。"我将刀端起来一看,这刀原来是双面刃的,一面的刃很薄,一面的刃却像他刚才磨的样子。整个刀被磨得如电镀一般,刃面平平展展,我的脸映在上面,几乎不走样。我心下明白,刃面磨到这般宽而且平,我的功力还赶不上。再细看时,刃面上又有隐隐的一道细纹,我说:"你包了钢了?"肖疙瘩点点头,说:"用弹簧钢包的,韧得很。"我将拇指在刃上轻轻一移,有些发涩,知道刃已吃住皮,不禁赞叹说:"老肖,这把刀卖给我了!"于是抬头认真地看着肖疙瘩。肖疙瘩又笑了,我忽然发现有些异样。原来肖疙瘩的上唇很紧,平时看不出来,一笑,上唇不动,只两片脸肉扯开,慢慢将嘴唇抻得很薄。我说:"老肖,你的嘴动过手术吗?"肖疙瘩还未笑完,就几乎嘴唇不动地说:"我这嘴磕破过,动了手术,就紧了。"我说:"怎么磕得这么厉害?"肖疙瘩不笑了,声音清楚了许多,说:"爬崖头。"我想起他当过兵,就问:"侦察?"他望望我,说:"哪个说?"我说:"六爪。"他有些慌:"小狗日的!他还说些哪样?"我说:"怎么了? 就说当侦察兵呀。"他想了想,看了看手,伸给我一只,说:"苦得很,你摸摸,苦得很,大比武,苦得很。"我摸一摸肖疙瘩的手。这手极硬,若在黑暗中触到,认为是手的可能性极小。而且这手的指头短而粗。肖疙瘩将手背翻过来,指甲极小,背上的肉也如一层石壳。肖疙瘩再将手拳起来,指关节便挤得颜色有些发浅。我推一推这拳头,心中一颤,不敢做声。

肖疙瘩忽然将两条胳膊伸直压在腿旁,全身挺直,一动不动,下巴收紧,几乎贴住脖子。又将腿直直地迈开向前走了两步,一碰脚跟,立定,把下巴伸出去,声音很怪而且短促,吼道:"是! 出列!"两只眼睛,只有方向而无目标,吼完又将下巴贴回脖子。我木木地看着他,又见他全身一软,额头的光也收回去,眼睛细了,怪怪地笑着,却非常好看,说:"怎么样? 正规训练!"我也兴奋了,说:"训练什么?"肖疙瘩将右手打在左掌上:"哪! 擒拿,攀登,击拳,射击,用匕首。"我想象不出肖疙瘩会将脚跳来跳去地打拳,就说:"你拳打得好?"肖疙瘩看一下我,不说话,用左掌紧紧地推右拳,忽然蹲下去,同时将右拳平举过肩。待完全蹲下去时的一刹那,右拳也砸在磨刀的石头上,并不叫,站起来,指一下石头。我一看,不由得下巴松了,原来这石头断裂成两半。我拉过肖疙瘩的右手,沉甸甸的在手上察看,却不能发现痕迹。肖疙瘩抽回手,比出食指与中指，说："要连打二十块。"我说："到底是解放军。"肖疙瘩用手揉一下鼻子，说："走，到我家去，另拿一块好石头你磨刀。"

我于是随肖疙瘩到他的草房去。到了，进去，房里很暗，肖疙瘩跪在地上探身到床底，捱出一块方石，又探身向床底寻了一会儿，忽然大叫："六爪！"门口的小草棚里响动了一下，我回身一看，六爪已经赤脚蹿了进来，问："整哪样？"肖疙瘩跪在地上，问："那块青石呢？找来给叔叔磨刀。"六爪看一看我，眯起一只眼睛，用手招招，示意我凑近。我弯下腰，将脸移近他。他将手括在嘴上，悄悄地问："有糖么？"我直起身，说："没有了，明天去买来给你。"六爪说："青石是明天才用么？"我料不到他会有这个心计，正要笑，肖疙瘩已经站起来，扬起右手，吼道："小狗日的！找打么？"六爪急忙跑到门口，吸一下鼻子，哼着说："你有本事，打叔叔！青石我马上拿来，叔叔明天能买来糖？去县里要走一天，回来又是一天，好耍的地方叔叔能只待一天？起码四天！"肖疙瘩又吼道："我叫你吃嘴巴子！"六爪嗖地一下不见了。

我心里很过意不去，便说："老肖，别凶孩子，我找找看谁那里还有。"肖疙瘩眼睛柔和了，叹一口气，捱一下床单，说："坐。孩子也苦。我哪里有钱给他买糖？再说人大了，山上能吃的东西多得很，自己找去吧。"肖疙瘩平日不甚言语，但生产队小，各家情况，不需多日便可明了。肖疙瘩家有三口人，六爪之外，尚有肖疙瘩的老婆，每月挣二十九元。两人每月合有七十元，三人吃喝，却不知为什么过得紧紧巴巴。我坐在床上，见床单边沿薄而且透朽，细看图案，原来是将边沿缝拼作中间，中间换作边沿，仍在使用。一床薄被，隐隐发黄绿的面子，是军队的格式；两只枕头，形状古怪，非要用心，才会悟出是由两只袖子扎成。屋内无桌，一个自制木箱垫了土坯，摆在墙角，除此之外，家具便只有床了。看来看去，就明白一家的财产大约都在箱中，可箱上并无锁，又令人生疑其中没有什么。我说："老肖，你来农场几年了？"肖疙瘩进进出出地忙倒水，正要将一缸热茶递给我，听见问，仰头想想，短粗的手指略动动，说："哪！九年了。"我接过缸子，吹一吹浮着的茶，水很烫，薄薄地吸一口，说："这里这么多树，为什么不做些家具呢？"肖疙瘩摩一摩手，转一转眼睛，吸了一口气，却没有说话，又将气吐出来。

这时六爪将青石搬来。肖疙瘩将青石与方石摆在一起，又叫六爪打一些水来，从四把刀中拿出一把，先在方石上磨十几下，看一下，又在青石上缓缓地用力磨。几下之后，将手指放在刃上试试，在地上放好，正要再磨一把，忽然问："磨四把整哪样？"我将山上的事讲了一遍，肖疙瘩不再磨刀，蹲在地下，叹了一口气。我以为肖疙瘩累了，便放下缸子，蹲下去将剩下的两把刀磨好，说声："我上山去。"于是辞了肖疙瘩，走出门外。六爪在门口用那只异指挖鼻孔，轻轻叫一声："叔叔。"我明白他的意思，抚一下他的头，他便很高兴，钻到门口的小草棚里去了。

上到山上，远远见那棵大树已被砍出一大块浅处，我吆喝说："快刀来了！"大家跑过来拿了刀走近大树。我捏一把

069

刀说:"看我砍。"便上一刀、下一刀地砍。我尽量摆出老练的样子,不做拼力状,木片一块块飞起来,大家都喝彩。我得意了,停住刀,将刀伸给大家看,大家不明白有什么奥秘,我说:"你们看刃。刃不缺损。你们再看,注意刃的角度。上一刀砍好,这下一刀在砍进的同时,产生两个力,这条斜边的力将木片挤离树干。这是科学。"李立将刀拿过去仔细看了,说:"有道理。我来试试。"李立一气砍下去,大家呆呆地看。四把刀轮流换人砍,进度飞快。

　　到下午时,大树居然被砍进一半。李立高兴地说:"我们今天把这棵树拿下来,创造一个纪录!"大家都很兴奋。我自报奋勇,将两把刀带下山去再磨。

　　下到山底时,远远望见肖疙瘩在菜地里,便对他喊说:"老肖!那棵树今天就能倒了呢!"肖疙瘩静静地等我走到跟前,没有说话。我正要再说,忽然觉出肖疙瘩似在审视我的样子,于是将我的兴奋按下去,说:"你不信吗? 全亏了你的方法呢!"肖疙瘩目光散掉,仍不说话,蹲下去弄菜。我走回队里,磨刀时,远远见肖疙瘩挑一挑菜走过去。

四

　　快下工时,太阳将落入远山,天仍旧亮,月亮却已从另一边升起,极大而且昏黄。队上的其他人沿路慢慢走下山去,李立说:"你们先回吧。我把这棵树砍倒再回去。"大家眼看大树要倒,都说倒了再回,于是仍旧轮流砍。大树干上的缺口已经很大而且深了,在黄昏中似乎比天色还亮。我想不会再要好久就会完工，于是觉出有尿，便离开大家找一个方便去处。山上已然十分静寂，而且渐生凉气，迎着昏黄的月亮走出十多步远，隐在草里，正在掏，忽然心中一紧，定睛望去，草丛的另一边分明有一个矮矮立着的人。月亮恰恰压在那人的肩上，于是那人便被衬得很暗。我镇定下来，一边问是哪个，一边走过去。

原来是肖疙瘩。

我这才觉出，肖疙瘩一直在菜地班，没有到山上来过，心中不免有突兀之感。我说："老肖，收工了。"肖疙瘩转过头静静地看着我，并不说什么。我背过他，正在撒尿，远远听一阵呐喊，知道树要倒了，便急忙跳出草丛跑去看。

大家早都闪在一边。那大树似蜷起一只脚，却还立着，不倒，也无声息。天已暗下来，一树的枝叶黑成一片，呆呆地静着，傻了一般。我正纳闷，就听得啪啪两声，看时，树仍静着。又是三声，又是一声，树还静着，只是枝叶有些抖。李立向大树走了两步，大家都叫起来，李立便停住了。半晌，大树毫无动静，只那巨大的缺口像眼白一样，似乎是一只眼睛在暗中凝视着什么。李立动了一下，又是近前，猛然一片断裂声，有如一座山在咳嗽。树顶慢慢移动，我却觉得天在斜，不觉将腿叉开。树顶越移越快，叶子与细枝开始飘起来，树咳嗽得喘不上气来。天忽然亮了。

大家的心正随着沉下去，不料一切又都悄无声息。树明明倒了，却没有巨大的声响。大家似在做梦，奇怪极了，正纷纷要近前去，便听得背后短短的一声吼："嗨！"

大家都回过身来，只见肖疙瘩静静地立着，闹不清是不是他刚才吼了一声。肖疙瘩见大家停住，便抬起脚迈草过来，不看大家，径直向大树走去。大家都跟上去，肖疙瘩又猛地转回身，竖起一只手，大家明白有危险，又都停下来。

　　肖疙瘩向大树走去，愈近大树，愈小心，没有声息。李立开始慢慢向前走，大家有些好奇而且胆怯，也慢慢向前走。

　　原来大树很低地斜在那里。细看时，才知道大树被无数的藤缠着，藤又被周围的树扯住。藤从四面八方绷住大树，抻得有如弓弦，隐隐有铮铮的响声。猛然间，天空中一声脆响，一根藤断了，扬起多高，慢慢落下来。大树晃动一下，惊得大家回身便走，远远停住，再回身看时，大树又不动了，只肖疙瘩一人在离树很近的地方立着。大家再也不敢近前，更不敢出声，恐怕喊动了那棵大树，天塌地陷，伤着肖疙瘩。

　　肖疙瘩静静地立着，许久，无声无息地在树旁绕，终于在一处停下来，慢慢从腰后抽出一把刀。我明白那便是有皮绳的那柄双面刃的刀。肖疙瘩微微曲下右腿，上身随之也向右倾，身体猛然一直，寒光一闪，那柄刀直飞上去，愈近高处，似乎慢了下来，还未等大家看清楚，一根藤早飞将起来，又斜斜地飘落，刚听到"啪"的一声响，一座山便晃动起来。大家急忙退开去，远远听得一片的断裂声，藤一根根飞扬起来，大树终于着地，顷刻间又弹跳起来，再着地，再跳一下，再跳一下，慢慢在暗影里滚动，终于停下来，一个世界不再有声响。

　　大家都呆了，说不出话，看肖疙瘩时，却找不着。正惊慌着，只见肖疙瘩从距原处一丈远的地方慢慢立起来。大家发一声喊,一拥而上,却又被肖疙瘩转身短短一吼止住了。肖疙瘩慢慢扯动皮绳,将刀从枝叶中收回来,前前后后查看着,时时手起,刀落时必有枝藤绷断,大树又微微动了几下,彻底平安下来。

我忽然觉得风冷,回过神来,才觉出一身凉汗,见大家也都有些缩头缩脑,开始有话,只是低低地说。肖疙瘩将刀藏回身上,望一望,说:"下山吧。"便走开了。大家跟在肖疙瘩身后,兴奋起来,各有感叹,将危险渲染起来,又互相取笑着,慢慢下山。天更暗了,月亮不再黄,青白地照过来,一山的断树奇奇怪怪。

肖疙瘩没有话,下到山下,仍没有话。到了队上,远远见肖疙瘩家的门开着,屋内油灯的光衬出门口一个孩子,想必是六爪。肖疙瘩慢慢走回去,门口的孩子一晃不见了。

五

大家回到屋里,纷纷换衣洗漱,话题不离大树。我记起六爪要的糖,便问谁还有糖。大家都说没有,又笑我怎么馋起来了。我不理会,隔了竹笆问隔壁的女生,却只听见水响,无人答话。这边的人于是又笑我脸皮太厚。我说:"肖疙瘩的六爪要一块糖,我答应了,谁有谁就拿一块,少他妈废话!"大家一下都不做声,慢慢又纷纷说没有了。我很后悔在大家聚到一起时讨糖。一个多月下来,大家已经尝到苦头,多辣的菜大家也敢吃,还嚷不够,又嫌没油,渍酸菜早已被女知青们做零食收着。从城里带来的零食很快变成金子,存有的人悄悄藏好。常常有人半夜偷偷塞一块糖在舌底下,五分钟蒙起头咽一下口水。老鼠是极机灵的生物,自然会去舔人。半夜若有谁惊叫起来并且大骂老鼠,大家便在肚里笑,很关心地劝骂的人含一只辣椒在嘴里以防骚扰。我在城里的境况不好,没有带来什么奢侈食品,只好将馋咽进肚里,狠狠地吃伙房的饭,倒也觉得负担小些。现在听到大家笑我馋与脸皮厚,自觉无趣,暗暗决定请假去县里给六爪买糖。

洗涮完毕,大家都去伙房打饭来吃。吃完毕,大家纷纷坐下来,就着一盏油灯东拉西扯,几个女生也过来闲扯。有人讲起以前的电影,强调着其中高尚的爱情关系,于是又有几个女生过来坐下听。我正在心中算计怎么请假,忽然觉得有人拉我一下,左右一看,李立向我点了一下头,自己走出去。我不知是什么事,爬起来跟出去。李立在月光下走到离草房远些,站住,望着月亮等我。我走近了,李立不看我,说:"你真是为六爪要糖吗?"我觉得脖子粗了一下,慢慢将肚子里的气吐出,脸上开始懒起来,便不开口,返身就走。李立在后面叫:"你回来。"我说:"外面有什么意思?"李立跟上来,拉住我的手,我便觉得手中多了硬硬的两块。

我看看李立。李立不安了一下,说:"也不是我的。"李立平日修身极严,常在思索,偶尔会紧张地独自喘息,之后咽一下,眼睛的焦点越过大家,慢慢地吐一些感想。例如"伟大就是坚定","坚定就是纯洁","事业的伟大培养着伟大的人格"。大家这时都不太好意思看着他,又觉得应该严肃,便沉默着。女知青们尤其敬佩李立,又不知怎么得到他的注意,有几个便不免用天真代替严肃,似乎越活岁数越小。我已到了对女性感兴趣的年龄,有时去讨好她们,她们却常将李立比在我上,暗示知识女性对我缺乏高尚的兴趣,令我十分沮丧。于是我也常常练着沉思,确实有些收益,只是觉得累,马脚又多。我想这糖大约是哪个女知青对他的心意,便不说什么,转身向远处肖疙瘩的草房走去。

月光照得一地惨白,到处清清楚楚,可我却连着让石头绊着。近到草房,发现门口的小草棚里有灯光,便靠近门向里望望,却见着六爪伏在一张小方桌上看什么,头与油灯凑得很近,身后生出一大片影子。影子里模模糊糊坐着两个人。六爪听到动静,睁眼向门口看来,一下认出是我,很高兴地叫:"叔叔!"我迈进门,看清影子里一个人是队长,一个人是肖疙瘩的老婆。队长见是我,便站起来说:"你们在,我走了。"肖疙瘩的老婆低低地说:"你在嘛,忙哪样?"我说:"我来看看。"队长不看我,嘴里含含糊糊地说了些什么,又慢慢扶着膝头坐下来。我忽然觉得气氛有些尴尬,好像走错了地方,想想手里的糖,就蹲下去对六爪说:"六爪,看什么?"六爪有些不好意思,弯出小小的舌头舐住下唇,把一本书推过来,肖疙瘩的老婆见我蹲下,忙把她屁股下的小凳递过来,说:"你坐,你坐。"我推让了一下,又去辨认六爪的书。肖疙瘩的老婆一边让着我,一边慌忙在各处寻座头,油灯摇晃起来。终于大家都坐下了,我也看出六爪的书是一本连环画,前后翻翻,没头没尾。六爪说:"你给我讲。"我便仔细地读图画下面的字,翻了几页,明白是《水浒》中宋江杀惜一段。六爪很着急地点着画问:"这一个男的一个女的在搞哪样? 我认得,这个男的杀了这个女的,可为哪样?"这样的书在城里是"四旧",早已绝迹,不料却在这野林中冒出一本,且被昏暗的灯照着,有如极远的回忆。我忽然觉得革命的几年中原来是极累的,这样一个古老的杀人故事竟如缓缓的歌谣,令人从头到脚松懈下来。正说不出话,六爪忽然眯起一只眼,把小手放在我的手背上,笑着说:"叔叔,你可是让我猜你手里是哪样东西?"我一下明白我的手一直拳着,也笑着说:"你比老鼠还灵,不用猜。"说着就把手翻过来张开。六爪把肩耸起来,两只手慢慢举起来抓,忽然又把手垂下去,握住自己的脚腕,回头看一看他的母亲。队长和肖疙瘩的老婆一齐看着我手中的糖,都有些笑意,但都不说话。我说:"六爪,这是给你的。"肖疙瘩的老婆急忙对我说:"呀! 你自己吃!"六爪看看我,垂下头。我把糖啪地拍在桌上,灯火跳了一跳,说:"六爪,拿去。"六爪又看看他的母亲。肖疙瘩的老婆低低地说:"拿着吧。慢慢吃。"六爪稳稳地伸出手,把糖拿起,凑近灯火翻看,闻一闻,把一颗糖攥在左手心,小心地剥另一颗糖,右手上那只异指翘着,微微有些颤。六爪将糖放进嘴里,闭紧了,呆呆地望着灯火,忽然扭脸看我,眼睛亮极了。

　　我问六爪:"我们刚来时你吃到几颗?"六爪一下将糖吐在纸上,说:"我爹不让我去讨别人的东西。"肖疙瘩的老婆笑着说:"他爹的脾气犟,不得好死。"队长呆呆地看着六爪,叹一口气,站起来,说:"老肖回来,叫他找我。"我问:"老肖上哪儿啦?"六爪很高兴地说:"我爹去打野物。打了野物,托人去县上卖了，便有钱。"说完小心地将糖用原来的纸包好，一起攥在左手里。肖疙瘩的老婆一边留着队长，一边送队长出去。队长在门口停下来，忽然问："老肖没有跟你们说什么吧？"我见队长看着我，但不明白问的什么意思，不自觉地摇摇头，队长便走了。

六爪很高兴地与我说东说西，我心里惦记着队长的意思，失了心思，也辞了六爪与他的母亲出来。

月光仍旧很亮，我不由站在场上，四下望望。目力所及的山上，树都已翻倒，如同尸体，再没有初来时的神秘。不知从什么地方空空隐隐地传来几声麂子叫，心里就想，也不知肖疙瘩听到没有，又想象着山上已经乱七八糟，肖疙瘩失了熟悉的路径，大约有些尴尬。慢慢觉得凉气钻到裤裆里，便回去睡觉。

六

山上的树木终于都被砍倒。每日早晨的太阳便觉得格外刺眼。队里的活计稀松下来，我于是请假去县里买糖块，顺便要一要。天还未亮，便起身赶十里山路去分场搭车。终于挤上一辆拖拉机，整整走了五个小时，方才到县里。一路上随处可见斩翻树木的山，如随手乱剃的光头，全不似初来时的景象。一车的人都在议论过不了半月，便可放火烧山，历年烧山都是小打小闹，今年一定好看。到了县上，自然先将糖买下，忍不住吃了几粒，不料竟似吃了盐一般，口渴起来，便转来转去地找水来喝。又细细地将县上几家饭馆吃遍,再买票看了一场电影,内容是将样板京戏放大到银幕上,板眼是极熟的,著名唱段总有人在座位上随唱,忽然又觉得糖实在好吃,免不了黑暗中又一粒一粒地吃起来,后来觉出好笑与珍贵,便留起来不再吃。这样荡了两天,才搭拖拉机回到山里。

沿着山路渐渐走近生产队,远远望见一些人在用锄锄什么。走近了,原来是几个知青在锄防火带,见我回来了,劈头就问:"买了什么好吃的东西?"我很高兴地说:"糖。"大家纷纷伸手讨吃。我说:"我是给六爪买的。"一个人便说:"肖疙瘩出事了。"我吃了一惊,问:"怎么? 出了什么事?"大家索性搁了锄,极有兴趣地说起来。

原来肖疙瘩本是贵州的一个山民,年轻时从家乡入伍。部队上见他顽勇,又吃得苦,善攀登,便叫他干侦察。六二年部队练兵大比武,肖疙瘩成绩好,于是被提为一个侦察班长。恰在此时,境外邻国不堪一股残匪骚扰,便请求这边部队协助剿除。残匪有着背景,武器装备精良,要剿除不免需打几场狠仗,肖疙瘩的班极为精悍,于是被委为尖刀,先期插入残匪地区。肖疙瘩领着七八个人,昼夜急行,迂回穿插,摸到残匪司令部。这司令部建在一个奇绝的崖上,自然是重兵把守。可攀崖头是肖疙瘩的拿手好戏,于是领了战士,五十米直用手指头抠上去。残匪司令部当然料不到,枪响不到一声,已被拿下。肖疙瘩命手下人用残匪电台直呼自己部队,指挥部便有令让他将电台送回,其他的仗不要他打。肖疙瘩于是带了一个四川兵将电台扛回来。电台不是轻家伙,一路走得自然极累而且焦渴。偏偏一路山高无水，专找水源，又怕耽误命令。可巧就遇到一片桔林。四川兵是吃惯桔子的，便请求吃一两个。肖疙瘩初不肯答应，说是违反纪律。又想想部下实在不容易，就说："吃一个吧，放钱在树下。"待吃完才发现自己的钱邻国是不能用的，又无什么可以抵替，想想仅只一个桔子，就马虎了，赶路回来。战役大获全胜，部队集合。肖疙瘩一班人的作用是明摆着的，于是记集体一等功。征尘未及清扫，就脏兮兮地立在头排接受首长检阅。首长坐车一阵风地来了，趋前向战士们问好，战士们撼天动地地回答。首长爱兵如子，不免握手抚肩，为肖疙瘩的一班人舒展衣角。首长为那个四川兵做这些时，碰到他口袋里鼓鼓的一块，便很和蔼的笑问是什么。四川兵脸一下白掉，肖疙瘩叫四川兵回答首长询问。四川兵慢慢将那个东西掏出来。原来是个桔子！肖疙瘩当即血就上头了，不容分说，跨上一步，抬腿就是一脚。侦察兵的腿脚是好动的？四川兵当即腿骨折断，倒在地下。首长还未闹清怎么一回事，见肖疙瘩野蛮，勃然大怒，立即以军阀作风撤销肖疙瘩的一等功，待问明情由，又将一班的集体功撤销，整肃全军。肖疙瘩气得七窍生烟，想想委屈，却又全不在理，便申请复员。部队军纪极严，不留他，但满足了肖疙瘩不回原籍的请求。肖疙瘩背了一个处分，觉得无颜见山林父老，便到农场来，终日在大山里钻，倒也熟悉。只是渐渐不能明白为什么要将好端端的森林断倒烧掉，用有用的树换有用的树，半斤八两的账算不清，自然有些怀疑怨言。"文化大革命"一起，肖疙瘩竟被以坏人揪出来作为造反的功绩,罚种菜,不许干扰垦殖事业。日前我们砍的那棵大树,肖疙瘩下山后对支书说,不能让学生自己砍,否则要出危险。支书便说小将们愿意自己闯,而且很有成绩,上面也在表扬,不需肖疙瘩来显示关怀,又记起自己负有监督改造的责任,就汇报上面,把肖疙瘩的言语当作新动向。

我叹了,说:"肖疙瘩也是,在支书面前说失职,支书当然面子上下不来。"另一个人说:"李立也是抽疯,说是要砍对面山上那棵树王,破除迷信。"大家都说李立多事,我也不以为然。说话间到了下班时间,大家便一路说着,问了我在县上如何耍,一路走回队上。

回到队上,未及洗涮,我就捏了糖去找六爪。六爪见了糖,欢喜得疯了,蹿来蹿去地喊母亲找东西来装,并且拿来两张糖纸给我看。我见糖纸各破有一个洞,不明白什么意思,六爪便很气愤地说:"老鼠!老鼠!"骂完老鼠,又仔细地将糖纸展平夹进连环画里,说是糖纸上面有金的光,再破也是好的,将来自己做了工人有一把刀后,把这糖纸粘在刀把上,会是全农场最好的刀。肖疙瘩的老婆找来一只竹筒,六爪认为绝对不行,老鼠的牙连木箱都会咬破,竹子算什么?我忽然瞥见屋内有一只空瓶,便说老鼠咬不动玻璃。六爪一边称赞着,一边将糖一粒一粒地装进瓶里。瓶里装满了,桌上尚余三粒。六爪慢慢地推了一粒在我面前,忽然又很快地调换了一块绿的给我,说我那块是红的。又慢慢推了一粒在他母亲面前,说是让母亲吃。肖疙瘩的老婆将糖推给六爪,六爪想了想,又将糖推在小桌中央,说是留给父亲吃。我也将我的一块推到小桌中央。六爪看看,说:"爹吃两块么?"我说:"你有一瓶呢!"六爪省悟过来,将自己的一块也推到小桌中央。我看着六爪细细地将桌上微小的糖屑用异指粘进嘴里,说:"你爸呢?"六爪并不停止动作,说:"菜地。"我辞了母子二人出来,肖疙瘩的老婆连连问着价钱,我坚决不要她拿钱出来,肖疙瘩的老婆为难地说:"六爪的爹知道了要骂,你拿些干笋去吧。"我又坚决不收,肖疙瘩的老婆便忧忧地看着我离开。

我打了饭回宿舍吃,大家又都问县里的见闻。仅过了两个多月,大家便有些土头土脑,以为山沟之外,都是饮食天堂,纷纷说等烧了山,一齐出去耍一下。李立并不加入谈话,第一个吃完,用水洗了碗筷,放好,双手支在床上坐着,打断大家对我说:"你再磨几把刀吧。"我看看李立。李立换个姿势,将肘支在膝头,看着手说:"我和支书说了,今天下午去砍树王。"有人说:"下午还要锄防火带呢。"李立说:"也不要多少人。刀磨快了,我想,叫上肖疙瘩,他还是把好手。"我慢慢嚼着,说:"磨刀没有什么。可是,为什么非要砍树王呢?"李立说:"它在的位置不科学。"我说:"科学不科学,挺好的树,不可惜?"有人说:"每天干的就是这个,可惜就别干了。"我想了想,说:"也许队上的人不愿砍,要砍,早就砍了。"李立不以为然,站起来说:"重要的问题是教育农民。旧的东西,是要具体去破的。树王砍不砍,说到底,没什么。可是,树王一倒,一种观念就被破除了,迷信还在其次,重要的是,人在如何建设的问题上将会思想为之一新,得到净化。"说完便不再说话,气氛有些严肃,大家便说些别的岔开。

我自然对磨刀有特殊的兴趣,于是快快将刀磨好。下午一出工,我和几个人便随李立上另一面的山上去砍树王。我去叫肖疙瘩,他的老婆说:丢下饭碗便走了,晓不得在哪里。六爪在床上睡觉,怀里还抱着那只装糖的瓶子。我们几个在队里场上走过,发现队里许多老职工立在自己家的草房前,静静地看着我们。李立叫了支书,支书并不拿刀,叫了队长,队长也不拿刀,大家一齐上山。

七

太阳依旧辣,山上飘着热气,草发着生生熟熟的味道。走到半山,支书站下,向山下队里大喊:"都去上工!都去上工!"大家一看,原来人们都站到太阳底下向我们望,听到支书喊,便开始走动。

走不到好久,便望到树王了。树王的叶子在烈日下有些垂,但仍微微动着,将空隙间的阳光隔得闪闪烁烁。有鸟从远处缓缓飞来,近了,箭一样射进树冠里去,找不到踪影。不一会儿,又忽地飞出一群,前后上下地绕树盘旋,叫声似乎被阳光罩住,干干的极短促。一亩大小的阴影使平地生风,自成世界,暑气远远地避开,不敢靠近。队长忽然迟疑着站住,支书也犹疑着,我们便超过支书和队长向大树走去。待有些走近了,才发现巨大的树根间,坐着一个小小的人。那人将头缓缓扬起,我心中一动:是肖疙瘩。

肖疙瘩并不站起来,将双肘盘在膝上,眼睛直直地望着我们,一个脸都是紧的。李立望望树,很随便地对肖疙瘩说:

"老肖,上来了?"又望望树,说:"老肖,你说这树,从什么地方砍呢?"肖疙瘩于是只直直地望着李立,不说话,嘴紧紧地闭成一条线。李立招呼我们说:"来吧。"便绕开肖疙瘩,走到树王的另一侧,用眼睛上下打量了一下,扬起手中的刀。

肖疙瘩忽然说话了,那声音模糊而陌生:"学生,那里不是砍的地方。"李立转过头来看着肖疙瘩,将刀放下,有些惊奇地问:"那你说是哪儿呢?"肖疙瘩仍坐着不动,只把左手微微抬起,拍一拍右臂:"这里。"李立不明白,探过头去看,肖疙瘩张开两只胳膊,稳稳地立起来,站好,又用右手指住胸口:"这里也行。"大家一下省悟过来。

李立的脸一下白了,我也觉得心忽然跳起来,大家都呆住,觉得还是太阳底下暖和。

李立张了张嘴,没有说出什么。静了一静,咽一下,说:"老肖,不要开玩笑。"肖疙瘩将右手放下:"我晓不得开玩笑。"李立说:"那你说到底砍哪儿?"肖疙瘩又将右手指着胸口:"学生,我说过了,这里。"

李立有些恼了,想一想,又很平和地说:"这棵树砍不得吗?"肖疙瘩手不放下,静静地说:"这里砍得。"李立真的恼了,冲冲地说:"这棵树就是要砍倒!它占了这么多地方。这些地方,完全可以用来种有用的树!"肖疙瘩问:"这棵树没有用吗?"李立说:"当然没有用。它能干什么呢?烧柴?做桌椅?盖房子?没有多大的经济价值。"肖疙瘩说:"我看有用。我是粗人,说不来有什么用。可它长成这么大,不容易。它要是个娃儿,养它的人不能砍它。"李立烦躁地晃晃头,说:

"谁也没来种这棵树。这种野树太多了。没有这种野树，我们早完成垦殖大业了。一张白纸，好画最新最美的图画。这种野树，是障碍，要砍掉，这是革命，根本不是养什么小孩!"

肖疙瘩浑身抖了一下，垂下眼睛，说:"你们有那么多树可砍，我管不了。"李立说:"你是管不了!"肖疙瘩仍垂着眼睛:"可这棵树要留下来，一个世界都砍光了，也要留下一棵，有个证明。"李立问:"证明什么?"肖疙瘩说:"证明老天爷干过的事。"李立哈哈笑了:"人定胜天。老天爷开过田吗? 没有，人开出来了，养活自己。老天爷炼过铁吗? 没有，人炼出来了，造成工具，改造自然，当然包括你的老天爷。"

肖疙瘩不说话，仍立在树根当中，李立微笑着，招呼我们。我们都松了一口气，提了刀，走近大树。李立抬起刀，说:"老肖，帮我们把这棵树王砍倒吧。"肖疙瘩一愣，看着李立，似乎有些疑惑，随即平静下来。

李立举起刀，全身拧过去，刀从肩上扬起，寒光一闪，却梦一般，没有砍下的声响。大家眨一下眼，才发现肖疙瘩一双手早钳住李立的刀，刀离树王只有半尺。李立挣了一下。我心下明白，刀休想再移动半分。

李立狂吼一声:"你要干什么?"浑身扭动起来，刀却生在肖疙瘩手上。肖疙瘩将嘴闭住，一个脸胀得青亮青亮的，筋在腮上颤动。大家"呀"的一声，纷纷退后，静下来。

寂静中忽然有支书的说话声:"肖疙瘩! 你疯了!"大家回头一看，支书远远地过来，队长仍站在原地，下巴垂下来，眼睛凄凄的。支书走近了，指一指刀:"松开!"李立松开刀，退后了半步。肖疙瘩仍捏着刀，不说话，不动，立着。支书说："肖疙瘩，你够了！你要我开你的会吗？你是什么人，你不清楚？你找死呀！"说着伸出手："把刀给我？"肖疙瘩不看支书，脸一会儿大了，一会小了，额头渗出寒光，那光沿鼻梁漫开，眉头急急一颤，眼角抖起来，慢慢有一滴亮。

支书走开，又回过身，缓缓地说："老肖哇，你不是糊涂人。你那点子错误，说出天，在我手下，我给你包着。你种你的菜，树你管得了吗？农场的事，国家的事，你管得了吗？我一个屁眼大的官，管不了。你还在我屁眼里，你发什么疯？学生们造反，皇帝都拉下马了，人家砍了头说是有个碗大的疤。你砍了头，可有碗大的疤？就是有，你那个疤值几个钱？糊涂！老肖，这砍树的手艺，全场你最拿手，我知道，要不你怎么落个'树王'的称呼呢？你受罪，我也清楚。可我是支书，就要谋这个差事。你这不是给我下不来台吗？学生们要革命，要共产主义，你拦？"

肖疙瘩缓缓地松下来，脸上有一道亮亮的痕，喉咙提上去，久久不下来。我们都呆了，眼睛干干地定着，想不起眨。原来护着树根的这个矮小汉子，才是树王！心头如粗石狠狠擦了一下，颤颤的，脑后硬起来。

真树王呆呆地立着，一动不动，手慢慢松开，刀哐当一声落在树根上。余音沿树升上去，正要没有，忽然如哭声一般，十数只鸟箭一样，发一阵喊，飞离大树，鸟儿斜斜地沿山势滑飞下去，静静地又升起来，翅膀纷纷抖动，散乱成一团黑点，越来越小，越来越小。

李立呆呆地看看大家，精神失了许多。大家也你看看我，我看看你。支书不说话，过去把刀拾起来，交给李立。李立呆呆地看看刀，一动不动。

肖疙瘩慢慢与树根断开，垂着手，到了离大树一丈远的地方立下，大家却不明白他是怎么走过去的。

支书说："砍吧，总归是要砍，学生们有道理，不破不立，砍。"回头招呼着："队长，你过来。"队长仍远远站着，说："你们砍，学生们砍。"却不过来。

李立抬起头，谁也不看，极平静地举起刀，砍下去。

八

大树整整砍了四天，肖疙瘩也整整在旁边守了四天，一句话不说，定定地看刀在树上起落。肖疙瘩的老婆做了饭，叫六爪送到山上去，肖疙瘩扒了几口，不再吃，叫六爪回去拿些衣服来。六爪失了往日的顽皮，慌慌地回到队上。天一黑下来，六爪便和他的母亲坐在草房前向山上望着。月亮一天比一天晚出来，一天比一天残。队上的人常常在什么地方站下来，呆呆地听着传来的微微的砍伐声，之后慢慢地走，互相碰着了，马上低下头分开。

我心中乱得很，搞不太清砍与不砍的是非，只是不去山上参加砍伐，也不与李立说话。知青中自有几个人积极得很，每次下山来，高声地说笑，极无所谓的样子，李立的眼睛只与他们交流着，变得动不动就笑，其余的人便沉默着，眼睛移开砍树的几个人。

第四天收工时,砍树的几个人下山来,高声在场上叫:"倒喽!倒喽!"我心中忽然一松,觉出四天的紧张。李立进到屋里,找出笔墨,写一些字,再将写好字的纸贴在他的书箱上边。我仰在床上。远远望去,见到五个大字:我们是希望。其余的人都看到了,都不说话,该干什么干什么。

我晚上到肖疙瘩的草房去。肖疙瘩呆呆地坐在矮凳上,见我来了,慢慢地移眼看我,那眼极干涩,失了精神,模模糊糊。我心中一酸,说:"老肖。"只四天,肖疙瘩头发便长出许多,根根立着,竟是灰白杂色;一脸的皱纹,愈近额头与耳朵便愈密集;上唇缩着,下唇松了;脖子上的皮松顺下去,似乎泄走一身力气。肖疙瘩慢慢垂下眼睛,不说话。我在床边坐下,说:"老肖。"转脸看见门口立着六爪与他的母亲,便招呼六爪过来,六爪看着他的父亲,慢慢走到我身边,轻轻靠着,一直看着自己的父亲。

肖疙瘩静静地坐着,慢慢地动了一下,缓缓转身打开箱子,在杂物中取出一个破本,很专心地看。我远远望去,隐约是一些数字。六爪的母亲见肖疙瘩取出本子,便低头离开门口到小草棚去。我坐了一会儿,见肖疙瘩如无魂的一个人,只有悄悄回来。

九

防火带终于锄好,队长宣布要烧山了,嘱咐大家严密注意着,不要自己的草房生出意外。

太阳将要落山,大家都出来站在草房前。队长和几个老职工点了火把,沿山脚跑动着,隔一丈点一下。不一刻,山脚就连成一条火线,劈劈啪啪的声音传过来。忽然风起了,我扭头一望,太阳沉下山峰,只留亮亮的天际。风一起,山脚的火便振奋起来,急急地向山上跑。山下的火越大,山头便愈黑。树都静静躺着,让人替它们着急。

火越来越大,开始有巨大的爆裂声,热气腾升上去,山颤动起来。烟开始逃离火,火星追着烟,上去十多丈,散散乱乱。队长几个人围山跑了一圈回来,喘着气站下看火。火更大了,轰轰的,地皮抖起来,草房上的草刷刷地响。突然一声巨响,随着嘶嘶的哨音,火扭做一团,又猛地散开。大家看时,火中一棵大树腾空而起,飞到半空,带起万千火星,折一个斤斗,又落下来,溅起无数火把,大一些的落下来,小一些的仍旧上升,百十丈处,翻腾良久,缓缓飘下。火已烧到接近山顶,七八里长的山顶一线,映得如同白昼。我忽然心中一动,回头向肖疙瘩的草房望去,远远见到肖疙瘩一家人蹲在房前。我想了想,就向肖疙瘩的草房走去。场上此时也映得如同白昼,红红的令人疑心烫脚。我慢慢走到肖疙瘩一家人前,他们谁也不看我,都静静地望山上。我站下来,仰头望望天空。天空已成红紫,火星如流星般穿梭着。

忽然六爪尖声叫起来:"呀!麂子!麂子!"我急忙向火中用眼搜寻,便见如同白昼的山顶,极小的一只麂子箭一般冲来冲去,时时腾跃起来,半空中划一道弧,刚一落地,又扭身箭一样地跑。队上的人这时都发现了这只麂子,发一片喊声,与热气一道升上去散开。火将山顶渐渐围满,麂子终于不动,慢慢跪了前腿,头垂下去。大家屏住气,最后看一眼那麂子,不料那生灵突然将身耸起,头昂得与脖子成一竖直线,又慢慢将前腿抬起,后腿支在地上,还没待大家明白,便箭一样向大火冲去,蹚起一串火星,又高高地一跃,侧身掉进火里,不再出现。大火霎时封了山顶,两边的火撞在一起,腾起几百丈高,须仰视才见。那火的顶端,舔着通红的天底。我这才明白,我从未真正见过火,也未见过毁灭,更不知新生。

山上是彻底地沸腾了。数万棵大树在火焰中离开大地,升向天空。正以为它们要飞去,却又缓缓飘下来,在空中互相撞击着,断裂开,于是再升起来,升得更高,再飘下来,再升上去,升上去,升上去。热气四面逼来,我的头发忽地一下立起,手却不敢扶它们,生怕它们脆而且碎掉,散到空中去。山如烫伤一般,发出各种怪叫,一个宇宙都惊慌起来。

忽然,震耳的轰鸣中,我分明听见有人的话语:"冷。冷啊。回去吧。"看时,六爪的母亲慢慢扶着肖疙瘩,肖疙瘩一只手扶着六爪,三个人缓缓向自己的草房里去了。我急忙也过去搀扶肖疙瘩,手摸上去,肖疙瘩的肋下急急地抖着,硬硬软软,似千斤重,忽又轻不及两,令人恍惚。

肖疙瘩在搀扶下,进到屋里,慢慢躺在床上,外面大火的红光透过竹笆的缝隙,抖动着在肖疙瘩的身上爬来爬去。我将肖疙瘩的手放上床,打得碎石头的手掌散着指头,粉一样无力,烫烫的如一段热炭。

十

这之后,肖疙瘩便一病不起。我每日去看他,日见其枯缩。原来十分强悍而沉默的一个汉子,现在沉默依旧,强悍却渐渐消失。我连连劝他不要因为一棵树而想不开。他慢慢地点头,一双失了焦点的眼睛对着草顶,不知究竟在想什么。六爪不再顽皮,终日帮母亲做事,闲了,便默默地翻看残破了的宋江杀惜的书,来来回回地看,极其认真;或者默默地站在父亲身边,呆呆地看着父亲。肖疙瘩只有在儿子面前,才渗出一些笑容,但无话,只静静地躺着。

队上的人都有些异样,只李立几个人仍旧说笑,渐渐有些发颠。队长也常常去看肖疙瘩,却默默无言,之后慢慢离去。队上的老职工常常派了女人与孩子送些食物,也时时自己去,说几句话,再默默离去。大火烧失了大家的精神,大家又似乎觉得要有个结果,才得寄托。

半月后,一天,我因病未去出工,身子渐渐有些发冷,便拿了一截木头坐在草房外面晒太阳。十点钟的太阳就开始烫人,晒了一会儿,觉得还是回去的好。正转身要进门里,就听见六爪的声音:"叔叔,我爹叫你去。"回头一看,六爪用异指勾弄着衣角站在场中。我随了六爪到他家。一进门,见肖疙瘩斜起上身靠在床上,不觉心中一喜,说:"呀!老肖,好多了吗?"肖疙瘩扬起手指,示意我坐在床边。我坐下了,看着肖疙瘩,肖疙瘩仍旧枯缩,极慢地说,没有喉音:"我求你一件事,你必要答应我。"我赶紧点头。肖疙瘩停一停,又说:"我有一个战友,现在四川,在部队上残废了,回家生活苦得很,这自然是我对不住他。我每月寄十五元给他,月月不敢怠慢。现在我不行了——"我心下明白,急忙说:"老肖,你不要着急,我有钱,先寄给他——"肖疙瘩不动,半天才有力气再说:"不是要你寄钱。我的女人与娃儿不识字,我不行了,要写一封书信给他,说我最后还是对不起他,请他原谅我先走了——"我呆了,心紧紧一缩,说不出话。肖疙瘩叫六爪过来,让他从箱里取出一个信封,黄皮纸,中间一个红框格。上面有着四川的地址。我仔细收好,点点头,说:"老肖,你放心,我误不了事。"转头一看,却噤声不得。

肖疙瘩头歪向一边,静静地斜垂着,上唇平平的,下唇掉下来,露出几点牙齿。我慌了,去扶,手是冰凉的。我刚要去叫六爪的母亲,想想不行,便将身挡住肖疙瘩,叫六爪去喊他的母亲。

六爪和他的母亲很快便来了。肖疙瘩的老婆并不十分惊慌,长长叹一口气,与我将肖疙瘩摆平。死去的肖疙瘩显得极沉,险些使我跌一下。之后,这女人便在床边静静地立着。六爪并不哭,紧随母亲立着,并且摸一摸父亲的手。我一时竟疑惑起来,搞不清这母子俩是不是明白肖疙瘩已经死去,何无忧伤?何无悲泣?

六爪立了一会儿,跌跌地转身去小草棚里拿来那本残书,翻开,拣出两张残破的糖纸,之后轻轻地将糖纸放在父亲的手中,一边一张。阳光透过草顶的些微细隙,射到床上,圆圆的一粒一粒。其中极亮的一粒,稳稳地横移着,极慢地检阅着肖疙瘩的脸。那圆点移到哪里,哪里的肉便如活起来,幽幽地闪光,之后又慢慢熄灭下去。

支书来了,在肖疙瘩身旁立了很久,呆呆的不说话,之后痴痴的出去。队上人都来望了。李立几个人也都来看了,再也无笑声,默默地离去,肖疙瘩的老婆与队上说要土葬,讲这是肖疙瘩生前嘱咐给她的。

队长便派工用厚厚的木板制了一副棺材。葬的地方肖疙瘩也说过,就在离那棵巨树一丈远的地方。大家抬了棺材,上山,在树桩根边挖了坑,埋了。那棵巨树仍仰翻在那里,断口刀痕累累,枝叶已经枯掉,却不脱落,仍有鸟儿飞来立在横倒的树身上栖息。六爪在父亲的坟前将装糖的瓶子立放着,糖粒还有一半,被玻璃隔成绿色。

当天便有大雨。晚上息了一下,又大起来,竟下了一个星期才住。烧过的山上的木炭被雨水冲下来,黑黑的积得极厚。一条山沟里,终日弥漫着酸酸的味道,熏得眼睛流泪。雨住了,大家上山出工。一座山秃秃的,尚有未烧完的大树残枝,黑黑的立着,如同宇宙有箭飞来,深深射入山的裸体,只留黑羽箭尾在外面。大家都有些悚然,倚了锄呆呆地望,一星期的大雨,这里那里竟冒出一丛丛的草,短短的立着,黄黄绿绿。忽然有人叫起来:"看对面山上!"大家一齐望过去,都呆住了。

远远可见肖疙瘩的坟胀开了,白白的棺木高高地托在坟土上,阳光映成一小片亮。大家一齐跑下山,又爬上对面的山,慢慢走近。队长哑了喉咙,说:"山不容人啊!"几个胆大的过去将棺材抬放到地上。大家一看,原来放棺材的土里,狠狠长出许多乱乱的短枝。计算起来,恐怕是倒掉的巨树根系庞大,失了养料的送去处,大雨一浇,根便胀发了新芽,这里土松,新芽自然长得快。那玻璃瓶子里糖没有了,灌满了雨水,内中淹死了一团一团的蚂蚁。

队长与肖疙瘩的寡妇商议火化。女人终于同意。于是便在山顶上架起一人高的柴火,将棺材放在上面,从下面点着,火慢慢烧上去,碰了棺材,便生有黑烟。那日无风,黑烟一直升上去,到百多米处,忽然打一个团,顿了一下,又直直地升上去,渐渐淡没。

肖疙瘩的骨殖仍埋在原来的葬处。这地方渐渐就长出一片草,生白花。有懂得的人说:这草是药,极是医得刀伤。大家在山上干活时,常常歇下来望,便能看到那棵巨大的树桩,有如人跌破后留下的疤;也能看到那片白花,有如肢体被砍伤,露出白白的骨。

孩子王

一

一九七六年，我在生产队已经干了七年。砍坝，烧荒，挖穴，挑苗，锄带，翻地，种谷，喂猪，脱坯，割草，都已会做，只是身体弱，样样不能做到人先。自己心下却还坦然，觉得毕竟是自食其力。

一月里一天，队里支书唤我到他屋里。我不知是什么事，进了门，就蹲在门槛上，等支书开口。支书远远扔过一支烟来，我没有看见，就掉在地上，发觉了，急忙捡起来，抬头笑笑。支书又扔过火来，我自己点上，吸了一口，说："'金沙江'？"支书点点头，呼噜呼噜地吸他自己的水烟筒。

待吸完了水烟，支书把竹筒斜靠在壁上，掸着一双粗手，又擤擤鼻子，说："队里的生活可还苦得？"我望望支书，点点头。支书又说："你是个人才。"我吓了一跳，以为支书在调理我，心里推磨一样想了一圈儿，并没有做错什么事，就笑着说："支书开我的玩笑。有什么我能干的活，只管派吧，我用得上心。"支书说："我可派不了你的工了。分场调你去学校教书，明天报到。到了学校，要好好干，不能辜负了。我家老三你认得，书念得吃力，你在学校，扯他一把，闹了就打，不怕的，告诉我，我也打。"说着就递过一张纸来，上面都明明白白写着，下面有一个大红油戳，证明不是假的。

我很高兴，离了支书屋里，回宿舍打点铺盖。同屋的老黑，正盘腿在床上挑脚底的刺，见我叠被卷褥子，并不理会，等到看我用绳捆行李，才伸脖子问："搞哪样名堂？"我稳住气，轻描淡写了一番。老黑一下蹦到地上，一边往上提着裤子，一边嚷："我日你先人！怎么会让你去教书？"我说："我怎么知道？上边来了通知，写得明白。难道咱们队还有哪个和我重名重姓？"老黑趿拉上两只鞋，拍着屁股出去了。

一会儿，男男女女来了一大帮，都笑嘻嘻地看着我，说你个龟儿时来运转，苦出头了，美美地教娃娃认字，风吹日晒总在屋顶下。又说我是蔫土匪，逼我说使了什么好处打通关节，调到学校去吃粮。我很坦然，说大家尽可以去学校打听，我若使了半点好处，我是——我刚想用上队里的公骂，想想毕竟是要教书了，嘴不好再野，就含糊一下。

大家都说，谁要去查你，只是去了不要忘了大家，将来开会、看电影路过学校，也有个落脚之地。我说当然。

老黑说："锄头、砍刀留给我吧，你用不着了。"我很舍不得，嘴里说："谁说用不着了？听说学校每星期也要劳动呢。"老黑说："那种劳动，糊弄鸡巴。"我说："锄你先拿着，刀不能给。若是学校还要用锄，我就来讨。"老黑很不以为然，又说：

"明天报到，你今天打什么行李？想快离了我们？再睡一夜明天我送你去。"我也好笑，觉得有点儿太那个，就拆了行李，慢慢收拾。大家仍围了说笑，感叹着我中学上了四年，毕竟不一样。

当晚，几个平时要好的知青，各弄了一些菜，提一瓶酒，闹闹嚷嚷地喝，一时我成了人人挂在嘴边的人物，好像我要去驻联合国，要上月球。要吃香的喝辣的了。

喝了几口苞谷酒，心里觉得有些恋恋的，就说："我虽去教书，可将来大家有什么求我，我不会忘了朋友。再说将来大家结婚有了小娃，少不了要在我手上识字，我也不会辜负了大家的娃娃。"大家都说当然。虽然都是知青，识了字的来抢锄，可将来娃娃们还是要识字，不能瞎着眼接着抢锄。

在队里做饭的来娣，也进屋来摸着坐下，眼睛有情有意地望着我，说："还真舍不得呢！"大家就笑她，说她见别人吃学校的粮了，就来叙感情，怕是想调学校去做饭了。来娣就叉开两条肥腿，双手支在腰上，头一摆，喝道："别以为老娘只会烧火，我会唱歌呢。我识得简谱，怎么就不可以去学校教音乐？'老杆儿'，"我因为瘦，所以落得这么个绰号，"你到了学校，替我问问。我的本事你晓得的，只要是有谱的歌，半个钟头就叫它一个学校唱起来！"说着自己倒了一杯酒，朝我举了一下，说："你若替老娘办了，我再敬你十杯！"说完一仰脖，自己先喝了。老黑说："咦？别人的酒，好这么喝的？"来娣脸也不红，把酒杯一顿，斜了老黑一眼："什么狗尿，这么稀罕！几个小伙子，半天才抿下一个脖子的酒，怕是没有女的跟你们做老婆。"大家笑起来，纷纷再倒酒。

　　夜里，老黑打了一盆水，放在我床边，说："洗吧。"我瞧瞧他，说："嗬！出了什么怪星星，倒要你来给我打水？"老黑笑笑，躺在床上，扔过一支烟，自己也点着一支，说："唉，你是先生了嘛。"我说："什么先生不先生，天知道怎么会叫我去教书！字怕是都忘了怎么写，去了不要闹笑话。"老黑说："字怎么会忘！这就像学凫水，骑单车，只要会了，就忘不掉。"我望着草顶，自言自语地说："墨是黑下一个土。的是名词、形容词连名词，地是形容词连动词，得是——得是怎么用呢？"老黑说："别穷叨叨啦，知道世上还有什么名词形容词就不错，就能教，我连这些还不知道呢。我才算上了小学就来这儿了，上学也是念语录，唉，不会有出息啦！"看时间不早，我们就都睡下。我想了许久，心里有些紧张，想不通为什么要我去教书，又觉得有些得意，毕竟有人看得起，只是不知是谁。

　　第二天一早，漫天的大雾，山沟里潮冷潮冷的。我穿上一双新尼龙丝袜，脚上茧子厚，扯着袜子哑拉哑拉响，又套上一双新解放鞋，换了一身干净裤褂，特意将白衬领扯高一些，搓一搓手脸，准备上路。我刚要提行李，老黑早将行李卷一下甩到肩上，又提了装脸盆杂物的网兜。我实在过意不去，就把砍刀抢在手里，一起走出来。

　　场上大家正准备上山干活，一个个破衣烂衫，脏得像活猴，我就有些不好意思，想低了头快走。大家见了，都嚷："你个憨包，还拿砍刀干什么？快扔了，还不学个教书的样子？"我反而更攥紧了刀，迸出一股力，只一挥，就把路边一株小臂粗的矮树棵子斜劈了。大家都喝彩,说:"学生闹了,就这么打。"我举刀告别,和老黑上路。

队上离学校只十里山路,一个钟头便到了。望见学校,心里有些跳,刀就隐在袖管里,叫住人打听教务处在哪儿。

有人指点了,我们走过去,从没遮拦的窗框上向里张望。里面有人发觉了,就出来问:"你是来报到的吗?"我点点头,他便招我进去。

我和老黑进去,那人便很热情地招呼座位和热水。屋里还有两位女同志,想来是老师,各坐在木桌上一本一本地改什么,这时都抬了头望我,上上下下地打量。我和老黑坐下不由得也打量一下这间办公室,只见也是草房,与队上没什么两样,只是有数张桌子。招呼我们的人就笑眯眯地说,带很重的广东腔:"还好吧? 我们昨天发了通知,你来得好快。我们正好缺老师上课,前几天一个老师调走了,要有人补他的课。我们查了查,整个分场知青里只剩下你真正上过高中,所以调你来。还好吧?"我这才明白了原由,就说:"高中我才上过一年就来了,算不得上过。这书,我也没教过,不知教得了教不了。您怎么称呼呢?"那人笑一笑,说:"我叫陈林呢,就叫我老陈好了。教书嘛,也不是哪个生来就会,在干中学嘛。"我说:"怕误人子弟呢。"老陈说:"不好这么说。来,喝水,喝水。"我忘了袖里还有一把刀,伸手去接水碗,刀就溜出来掉在地上,哐当一声。窗户上就有孩子在笑。原来上课时间未到,许多学生来看新老师。我红了脸,拾起刀,靠在桌子边上,抬起头,发现老陈的桌上有一本小小的新华字典。

老陈见了，说："好。学校里也要劳动，你带了就好。"老黑说："学校还劳什么动？"老陈说："咦？学校也要换茅草顶，也要种菜，也要带学生上山干活呢！"我说："怎么样？老黑，下回来，把锄带来给我。"老黑摸摸脸，不吭声。

老陈与我们说了一会儿话，望望窗外立起身来说："好吧，我们去安排一下住处？"我和老黑连忙也立起身，三个人走出来。大约是快开始上课了，教室前的空地上学生们都在抓紧时间打闹，飞快地跑着，尖声尖气地叫。我脱离学校生活将近十年，这般景象早已淡忘，忽然又置身其中，不觉笑起来，叹了一口气。老黑愣着眼，说："哼，不是个松事！"老陈似无所见似无所闻，只在前面走，两个学生追打到他跟前，他出乎意料地灵巧，一闪身就过了，跑在前面的那个学生反倒一跤跌翻在地，后面的学生骑上去，两个人扭在一起，叫叫嚷嚷，裤子脱下一截。

教室草房后面，有一长排草房，房前立了五棵木桩，上面长长地连了一条铁线，挂着被褥，各色破布和一些很鲜艳的衣衫。老陈在一个门前招手，我和老黑走过去。老陈说："这间就是你的了，床也有，桌椅也有。收拾收拾，住起来还好。"我钻进去，黑黑的先是什么也看不清，慢慢就辨出一块五六平方米的间隔来。只见竹笆壁上糊了一层报纸，有的地方已经脱翻下来，一张矮桌靠近竹笆壁，有屉格而无抽屉，底还在，可放书物。桌前的壁上贴了一些画片，一张年历已被撕坏，李铁梅的身段竖着没了半边，另半边擎着一只红灯。一地乱纸，一只矮凳仰在上面。一张极粗笨的木床在另一边壁前,床是只有横档而无床板。我抬头望望屋顶,整个草房都是串通的,只是在这一个大草顶下,用竹笆隔了许多小间,隔壁的白帐顶露出来,已有不少蛛网横斜着,这格局和景象与生产队上并无二致。我问老陈:"不漏吗?"老陈正笑眯眯地四下环顾,用脚翻捡地上的纸片,听见问,就仰了脖看着草顶上说:"不漏,去年才换的呢。就是漏,用棍子伸上去拨一拨草,就不漏了。"

老黑把行李放在桌上,走过去踢一踢床,恨恨地说:"真他妈一毛不拔,走了还把竹笆带走。老陈,学校可有竹笆?有拿来几块铺上。"老陈很惊奇的样子,说:"你们没带竹笆来吗?学校没有呢。这床架是公家的,竹笆都是私人打的,人家调走,当然要带走。这桌,这椅,是公家的,人家没带走嘛。"老黑瞧瞧我,摸一摸头。我说:"看来还得回队上把我床上的竹笆拿来。"老黑说:"好吧,连锄一起拿来,我还以为你会享了福呢。"我笑笑,说:"都是在山沟里,福能享到哪儿去呢?"老陈说:"你既带了刀,到这后边山上砍一根竹子,剖开就能用。"我说:"新竹子潮,不好睡,还是拿队上我的吧。"

前面学校的钟响了,老陈说:"你们收拾一下,我去看看。"就钻出门,甩着胳膊去了。我和老黑将乱纸扫出屋外,点一把火烧掉,又将壁上的纸整整齐,屋里于是显得干净顺眼。我让老黑在凳上歇,他不肯,坐到桌上让我坐凳。我心里畅快了,递给老黑一支烟,自己叼了一支,都点着了,长长吐出一口,慢慢坐在凳上,不想一跤翻在地上。坐起来一看,凳的四只脚剩了三只,另一只撇在一边。老黑笑得浑身乱颤,我看桌子也晃来晃去,连忙爬起,叫老黑下来,都坐到床档上。

二

上午收拾停当,下午便开始教书了。老陈叫我去,交给我一个很脏的课本和一盒粉笔,还有红、蓝墨水,一支蘸水钢笔,一个备课本。老陈说:"课本不要搞丢,丢了,不好再找。"我见课本实在脏得可以,已被折得很软,捏在手里沉甸甸的有些凉,翻开,当中用铅笔钢笔批注了许多,杂以粉笔灰,便有些嫌恶,说:"这是谁的课本? 没有病吧?"办公室里几个女教师笑起来,说:"当然有病。"我看看她们,见她们面前的书本都干干净净,就自己捏住书脊抖。老陈也笑起来,说:"哪里有病? 走了的李老师有些马虎,不太注意就是了。可他课本没有搞丢,就不容易了。你看,这是课表。"说着递给我一张纸。我看看,心里一颤,说:"怎么? 教初三? 我高中才念了一年,如何能教初三?"老陈笑眯眯地说:"怎么不能教? 教就是了,不难的。"我坚决推辞,说了无数理由,其中主要是学历太浅。老陈摸摸桌子,说:"那谁教呢? 我教? 我才完小毕业,更不行了。试一试吧? 干起来再说。"我又说初三是毕业班,升高中是很吃功夫的。老陈说:"不怕。这里又没有什么高中,学完就是了,试一试吧。"我心里打着鼓,便不说话。老陈松了一口气,站起来,说:"等一下上课,我带你去班里。"我还要辩,见几位老师都异样地看着我,其中一个女老师说:"怕哪样? 我们也都是不行的,不也教下来了么?"我还要说,上课钟响了,老陈一边往外走,一边招我随去。我只好拿了一应教具,慌慌地跟老陈出去。

老陈走到一间草房门前,站下,说:"进去吧。"我见房里很黑,只有门口可见几个学生在望着我,便觉得如同上刑,又忽然想起来,问:"教到第几课了?"老陈想一想,说:"刚开学,大约是第一课吧。"这时房里隐隐有些闹,老陈便进去,大声说:"今天,由新老师给你们——不要闹,听见没有?闹是没有好下场的!今天,由新老师给你们上课,大家要注意听!"说着就走出来。我体会该我进去了,便一咬牙,一脚迈进去。

刚一进门,猛然听到一声吆喝:"起立!"桌椅乒乒乓乓响,教室里立起一大片人。我吃了一惊,就站住了。又是一声吆喝,桌椅乒乒乓乓又响,一大片人又纷纷坐下。一个学生喊:"老师没叫坐下,咋个坐下了?"桌椅乒乒乓乓再响起来,一大片人再站起来。我急忙说:"坐下了。坐下了。"学生们笑起来,乒乒乓乓坐下去。

我走到黑板前的桌子后面,放下教具,慢慢抬起头,看学生们。

山野里很难有这种景象,这样多的蓬头垢面的娃子如分吃什么般聚坐在一起。桌椅是极简陋的,无漆,却又脏得露不出本色。椅是极长的矮凳,整棵树劈成,被屁股们蹭得如同敷蜡。数十只眼睛亮亮地瞪着。前排的娃子极小,似乎不是上初三的年龄;后排的却已长出胡须,且有喉节。

我定下心,清一清喉咙,说:"嗯。开始上课。你们已经学到第几课了呢?"话一出口,心里虚了一下,觉得不是老师问的话。学生们却不理会，纷纷叫着："第一课！第一课！该第二课了。"我拿起沉甸甸的课本，翻到第二课，说："大家打开第四页。"却听不到学生们翻书的声音，抬头看时，学生们都望着我，不动。我说："翻到第四页。"学生们仍无反应。我有些不满，便指了最近的一个学生问："书呢？拿出来，翻到第四页。"这个学生仰了头问我："什么书？没得书。"学生们乱乱地吵起来，说没有书。我扫看着，果然都没有书，于是生气了，啪地将课本扔在讲台上，说："没有书？上学来，不带书，上的哪样学？谁是班长？"于是立起一个瘦瘦的小姑娘，头发黄黄的，有些害怕地说："没有书。每次上课，都是李老师把课文抄在黑板上，教多少，抄多少，我们抄在本本上。"我呆了，想一想，说："学校不发书吗？"班长说："没有。"我一下乱了，说："哈！做官没有印，读书不发书。读书的事情，是闹着玩儿的？我上学的时候，开学第一件事，便是领书本，新新的，包上皮，每天背来，上什么课，拿出什么书。好，我去和学校说，这是什么事！"说着就走出草房，背后一下乱起来，我返身回去，说："不要闹！"就又折身去找老陈。

老陈正在仔细地看作业，见我进来，说："还要什么？"我沉一沉气："我倒没忘什么，可学校忘了给学生发书了。"老陈笑起来，说："呀，忘了，忘了说给你。书是没有的。咱们地方小，订了书，到县里去领，常常就没有了，说是印不出来，不够分。别的年级来了几本，学生们伙着用，大部分还是要抄的。这里和大城市不一样呢。"我奇怪了，说："国家为什么印不出书来？纸多得很嘛！生产队上一发批判学习材料就是多少，怎么会课本印不够?"老陈正色道:"不要乱说,大批判放松不得,是国家大事。课本印不够,总是国家有困难,我们抄一抄,克服一下,嗯?"我自知失言,嘟囔几下,走回去上课。

进了教室,学生们一下静下来,都望着我。我拿起课本,说:"抄吧。"学生们纷纷拿出各式各样的本子,翻好,各种姿势坐着,握着笔,等着。

我翻到第二课,捏了粉笔,转身在黑板上写下题目,又一句一句地写课文。学生们也都专心地抄。远处山上有人在吆喝牛,声音隐隐传来,我忽然分了心,想那牛大约是吃了什么不该吃的东西,被人赶开。我在队上放过不少时间的牛。牛是极犟的东西,而且有气度,任打任骂,慢慢眨着眼吃它想吃的东西。我总想,大约哲学家便是这种样子,否则学问如何做得成功?但"哲学家"们也有慌张的时候,那必是我撒尿了。牛馋咸,尿咸,于是牛们攒头攒脑地聚来接尿吃,极是快活。我甚至常憋了尿,专门到山上时喂给牛们,那是一滴也不会浪费的。凡是给牛喂过尿的,牛便死心塌地地听你吆喝,敬如父母。我也常常是领了一群朋党,快快乐乐以尿做领袖。

忽然有学生说:"老师,牛下面一个水是什么字?"我醒悟过来,赶忙擦了,继续写下去。

一个黑板写完,学生们仍在抄,我便放了课本,看学生们抄,不觉将手抄在背后,快活起来,想:学生比牛好管多了。

一段课文抄完,自然想要讲解,我清清喉咙,正待要讲,忽然隔壁教室歌声大作,震天价响,又是时下推荐的一首歌,绝似吵架斗嘴。这歌唱得屋顶上的草也抖起来。我隔了竹笆缝望过去，那边正有一个女教师在鼓动着，学生们大约也是闷了，正好发泄，喊得地动山摇。

我没有办法，只好转过身望着学生们。学生们并不惊奇，开始交头接耳，有些兴奋，隔壁的歌声一停，我又待要讲，下课钟就敲起来。我摇摇头，说："下课吧。"班长大喊："起立!"学生们乒乒乓乓站起来，夺门跑出去。

我在学生后面走出来，见那女教师也出来，便问她："你的音乐课吗?"她望望我，说："不是呀。"我说："那怎么唱起来了? 闹得我没法讲课。"她说："要下课了嘛。唱一唱，学生们高兴，也没有一两分钟。你也可以唱的。"

教室前的空地上如我初来的景象，大大小小的学生们奔来跑去，尘土四起。不一刻，钟又敲了，学生们纷纷回来，坐好。班长自然又大喊起立，学生们站起来。我叹了一口气，说："书都没有，老起什么立? 算了，坐下接着抄课文吧。"

学生们继续抄，我在教室里走来走去。因凳都是联着的，不好迈到后排去，又只好在黑板前晃，又不免时时挡住学生的眼睛，便移到门口立着，渐渐觉得无聊。

教室前的场子没了学生，显出空旷。阳光落在地面，有些晃眼。一只极小的猪跑过去，忽然停下来，很认真地在想，又思索着慢慢走。我便集了全部兴趣，替它数步。小猪忽然又跑起来，数目便全乱了。正懊恼间，忽然又发现远处一只母鸡在随便啄食，一只公鸡绕来绕去，母鸡却全不理会，佯作无知。公鸡终于靠近，抖着身体，面红耳赤。母鸡轻轻跑几步,极清高地易地啄食,公鸡撇一下毛,昂首阔步,得体地东张西望儿下,慢慢迁回前去。我很高兴,便注意公鸡的得手情况。忽然有学生说:"老师,抄好了。"我回过头,见有几个学生望着我。我问:"都抄好了?"没有抄好的学生们大叫:"没有!没有!"我一边说"快点儿",一边又去望鸡,却见公鸡母鸡都在撇着羽毛,事已完毕。心里后悔了一下,便将心收拢回来,笑着自己,查点尚未抄完的学生。

学生们终于抄好,纷纷抬头望我。我知道该我了,便沉吟了一下,说:"大家抄也抄完了,可明白说的是什么?"学生们仍望着我,无人回答。我又说:"这课文很明白,是讲了一个村子的故事。你们看不懂这个故事?"学生们仍不说话。我不由说得响一些:"咦?真怪了!你们识了这么多年字,应该能看懂故事了嘛。这篇课文,再明白不过。"随手指了一个学生,"你,说说看。"这个学生是个男娃,犹犹豫豫站起来,望望我,又望望黑板,又望望别的学生,笑一笑,说:"认不得。"就坐下了。我说:"站着。怎么会不知道?这么明白的故事,你又不是傻瓜。"那学生又站起来,有些不自在,忽然说:"我要认得了,要你教什么?"学生们一下都笑起来,看着我。我有些恼,说:"一个地主搞破坏,被贫下中农揪出来,于是这个村子的生产便搞上去了。这还不明白?这还要教?怪!"我指一指班长:"你说说看。"班长站起来,回忆着慢慢说:"一个地主搞破坏,被贫下中农揪出来,于是那——这个村子的生产便搞上去了。"我说:"你倒学得快。"话刚一说完,后排一个学生突然大声说:"你这个老师真不咋样!没见过你这么教书的。该教什么就教什么嘛,先教生字,再教划分段落,再教段落大意,再教主题思想,再教写作方法。该背的背,该留作业的留作业。我都会教。你肯定在队上干活就不咋样,跑到这里来混饭吃。"我望着这个学生,只见他极大的一颗头,比得脖子有些细,昏暗中眼白转来转去地闪,不紧不慢地说,用手抹一抹嘴,竟叹了一口气。学生们都望着我,不说话。我一时竟想不出什么,呆了呆,说:"大家都叫什么名字,报一报。"学生们仍不说话,我便指了前排最左边的学生:"你。报一报。"学生们便一个一个地报过来。

我看准了,说:"王福,你说你都会教,那你来教一下我看。"王福站起来,瞪眼看着我,说:"你可是要整我?"我说:"不要整你。我才来学校,上课前才拿到书,就这么一本。讲老实话,字,我倒是认得不少;书,没教过,不知道该教你们什么。你说说看,李老师是怎么教的?"王福松懈下来,说:"我不过是气话,怎么就真会教?"我说:"你来前面,在黑板上说说。第一,哪些字不认识? 你们以前识了多少字,我不知道。"王福想了想,便离开座位,迈到前边来。

王福穿一件极短的上衣,胳膊露出半截。裤也极短,揪皱着,一双赤脚极大。他用手拈起一支粉笔,手极大。我说:"你把你不识的字在底下划一横。"王福看了一会儿,慢慢在几个字底下划上短线,划完了,又看看,说:"没得了。"便抬脚迈回到后排坐下。我说:"好,我先来告诉你们这几个字。"正要讲,忽然有一个学生叫:"我还有字认不得呢!"这一叫,又有几个学生也纷纷叫有认不得的字。我说:"好嘛。都上来

107

划。"于是学生们一窝蜂地上来拿粉笔。我说:"一个一个来。"学生们就拥在黑板前,七手八脚划了一大片字。我粗粗一看,一黑板的课文,竟有三分之二学生认不得的字。我笑了,说:"你们是怎么念到初三的呢? 怪不得你们不知道这篇课文讲的是什么。这里有一半的字都应该在小学就认识了。"王福在后面说:"我划的三个字,是以前没有教过的。我可以给你找出证明来。"我看一看黑板,说:"这样吧,凡是划上的字,我都来告诉你们,我们慢慢再来整理真正的生字。"学生们都说好。

一字一字教好,又有一间教室歌声大作,我知道要下课了,便说:"我们也来唱一支歌。你们会什么呢?"学生们七嘴八舌地提,我定了一首,班长起了音,几十条喉咙便也震天动地地吼起来。我收拾着一应教具,觉得这两节课尚有收获,结结实实地教了几个字,有如一天用锄翻了几分山地,计工员来量了,认认真真地记在账上。歌声一停,钟就响了,我看看班长,说:"散吧。"班长说:"作业呢? 要留作业呢!"我想一想,说:"作业就是把今天的生字记好,明天我来问。就这样。"班长于是大喊起立,学生们乒乒乓乓地立起来,在我之前蹿出去。

我将要出门,见王福从我身边过去,便叫住他,说:"王福,你来。"王福微微有些呆,看看门外,过来立住。我说:"你说你能证明哪些是真正的生字,怎么证明呢?"王福见我问的是这个,便高兴地说:"每年抄的课文,凡是所有的生字,我都另写在纸上。我认识多少字,我有数,我可以拿来给你看。"

说罢迈到他自己的位子,拿出一只布包,四角打开,取出一个本子,又将包包好,放回去,迈到前边来,将本子递给我。我翻开一看,是一本奖给学习毛著积极分子的本子,上写奖给"王七桶"。我心里"呀"了一声,这王七桶我是认识的。

王七桶绰号王稀屎。稀屎是称呼得极怪的,因为王七桶长得虽然不高,却极结实,两百斤的米包,扛走如飞,绝不似稀屎。我初与他结识是去县里拉粮食。山里吃粮,需坐拖拉机走上百多里到县里粮库拉回。这粮库极大,米是山一样堆在大屋里,用簸箕一下下收到麻袋里,再一袋袋扛出去装上车斗。那一次是两个生产队的粮派一个拖拉机出山去拉。早上六点,我们队和三队拉粮的人便聚来车队,一个带拖斗的"东方红"拉了去县里。一上车,我们队的司务长便笑着对三队的一个人说:"稀屎来了?"被称作稀屎的人不说话,只缩在车角闷坐着。我因被派了这次工,也来车上坐着,恰与他是对面,见他衣衫破旧,耳上的泥结成一层壳,且面相凶恶,手脚奇大,不免有些防他。两个队的人互相让了烟,都没有人让他。我想了想,便将手上的烟指给他,说:"抽?"他转过眼睛,一脸的凶肉忽然都顺了,点一点头,将双手在裤上使劲擦一擦,筒箩一样伸过来接。三队的司务长见了,说:"稀屎,抽烟治不了哑巴。"大家都笑起来。我疑惑了,看着他。他脸红起来,摸出火柴自己点上,吸一大口,吐出来,将头低下,一支细白的烟卷像插在树节上。车开到半路遇到泥泞,他总是爬下去。一车的人如不知觉一般仍坐在车上。他一人在下死劲扛车帮,车头轰几下,爬上来,继续往前开,他便跑几步,用手勾住后车板,自己翻上来,颠簸着坐下。别人仍若无其事地说笑着,似乎他只是一个机器部件。出了故障,自然便有这个部件的用途。我因不常出山,没坐过几回车,所以车第二次陷在泥里时,便随他下车去推。车爬上去时,与他追了几步。他自己翻上去了,我没有经验,连车都没有扒上。他坐下后,见我还在后面跑,就弓起身子怪叫着,车上人于是发现我,喊叫起来,司机停下车。他一直弓着身子,直到我爬上车斗,方才坐下,笑一笑。三队的司务长说:"你真笨,车都扒不上么?"我喘息未定,急急地说:"你不笨,要不怎么不下车呢?"三队的司务长说:"稀屎一个人就够了嘛!"车到县里,停在粮库门前。三队来拉粮的人除了司务长在交接手续,别的人都去街上逛,只余他一人在。我们队的人进到库房里,七手八脚地装粮食。装到差不多,停下一看,那边只他一人在装,却也装得差不多了。我们队的人一袋一袋地上车,三队却仍只有他一人上车。百多斤的麻袋,他一人扛走如飞。待差不多时,三队的人买了各样东西回来,将剩下的一两袋扔上车斗,车便开到街上。我们队的人跳下去逛街,三队的人也跳下再去逛街,仍是余他一人守车。我跳下来,仰了头问他:"你不买些东西?"他摇一摇头,坐在麻袋上,竟是快乐的。我一边走,一边问三队的司务长:"哑巴叫什么?"司务长说:"王七桶。"我问:"为什么叫稀屎呢?"司务长说:"稀屎就是稀屎。"我说:"稀屎可比你们队的干屎顶用。"司务长笑了,说:"所以我才每次拉粮只带他出来。"我奇怪了,问:"那几个人不是来拉粮的?"司务长看看我,说:"他们是出来办自己的事的。"我说:"你也太狠了,只带一个人出来拉一个队的粮,回去只补助一个人的钱。"司务长笑笑,说:"省心。"我在街上逛了一回,多买了一包烟。回到车边,见王七桶仍坐在车上,就将烟扔给他,说:"你去吃饭,我吃了来的。"王七桶指一指嘴,用另一只手拦一下,再用指嘴的手向下一指,表示吃过了。我想大约他是带了吃的,便爬上车,在麻袋上躺下来。忽然有人捅一捅我,我侧头一看,见王七桶将我给他的烟放在我旁边,烟包撕开了,他自己手上捏着一支。我说:"你抽。"他举一举手上的烟。我坐起来,说:"这烟给你。"将烟扔给他。他拿了烟包,又弓身放回到我旁边。我自己抽出一支,点上,慢慢将烟吐出来,看着他。逛街的人都回来了,三队的司务长对王七桶说:"你要的字典还是没有。"王七桶"啊、啊"着,眼睛异样了一下,筐箩一样的手松下来,似乎觉出一天劳作的累来。司机开了车,一路回到山里,先到我们队上将粮卸了,又拉了王七桶一队的粮与人开走。我扛完麻袋回到场上,将将与远去的王七桶举手打个招呼。

我于是知道王福是王七桶的儿子,就说:"你爹我知道,很能干。"王福脸有些红,不说话。我翻开这个本子,见一个本子密密麻麻写满了独个的字,便很有兴趣地翻看完,问王福:"好。有多少字呢?"王福问:"算上今天的吗?"我呆了一下,点点头。王福说:"算上今天的一共三千四百五十一个字。"我吃了一惊,说:"这么精确?"王福说:"不信你数。"我知道我不会去数,但还是翻开本子又看,说:"一二三四五六七八九十,这十个数目字你算十个字吗?"王福说:"当然,不算十个字,算什么呢? 算一个字?"我笑了,说:"那么三千四百五十一便是三千四百五十一个字了?"王福没有听出玩笑,认真地说:"十字后面是百、千、万、亿、兆。这兆字现在还没有学到,但我认得。凡我认得而课文中没有教的字,我都收在另一个本上。这样的字有四百三十七个。"我说:"你倒是学得很认真。我现在还不知道我学了多少字呢。"王福说:"老师当然学得多。"这时钟响了,我便将本子还给王福,出去回到办公室。

老陈见我回来了,笑眯眯地问:"怎么样? 还好吧? 刚开始的时候有些那个,一下就会习惯的。"我在分给我的桌子后面坐下来,将课本放在桌子上,想了想,对老陈说:"这课的教法是不是有规定? 恐怕还是不能乱教。课本既然是全国统一的,那怎么教也应该有个标准,才好让人明白是教对了。比如说吧,一篇文章,应划几个段落? 段落大意是什么? 主题思想又是什么? 写作方法是怎么个方法? 我说是这样了,别的学校又教是那样。这语文不比数学。一加一等于二,世界上哪儿都是统一的。语文课应该有个规定才踏实。"老陈说:"是呀,有一种备课教材书,上面都写得有,也是各省编的。但是这种书我们更买不到了。"我笑了起来,说:"谁有,你指个路子,我去抄嘛。"老陈望望外面,说:"难。"我说:"老陈,那我可就随便教了,符不符合规格,我不管。"老陈叹了一口气,说:"教吧。规定十八岁人才可以参加工作,才得工资,这些孩子就是不学,也没有事干,在这里学一学,总是好的。"我轻松起来,便伏在桌上一课一课地先看一遍。

课于是好教起来，虽然不免常常犯疑。但我认定识字为本，依了王福的本子为根据，一个字一个字地落实。语文课自然有作文项目，初时学生的作文如同天书，常常要猜字到半夜。作文又常常仅有几十字，中间多是时尚的语句，读来令人瞌睡，想想又不是看小说，倒也心平气和。只是渐渐怀疑学生们写这些东西于将来有什么用。

这样教了几天，白天很热闹，晚上又极冷清，便有些想队里，终于趁了一个星期天，回队里去耍。老黑见我回来，很是高兴，拍拍床铺叫我坐下，又出去喊来往日要好的，自然免不了议论一下吃什么，立刻有人去准备。来娣听说了，也聚来屋里，上上下下看一看我，就在铺的另一边靠我坐下。床往下一沉，老黑跳起来说："我这个床睡不得三个人！"来娣倒反整个坐上去，说："那你就不要来睡，碍着我和老师叙话。"大家笑起来，老黑便蹲到地下。来娣撩撩头发，很亲热地说："呀，到底是在屋里教书，看白了呢！"我打开来娣伸过来的胖手，说："不要乱动。"来娣一下叫起来："咦？真是尊贵了，我们劳动人民碰不得了。告诉你，你就是教一百年书，我还不是知道你身上长着什么？哼，才几天，就夹起来装斯文！"我笑着说："我斯文什么？学生比我斯文呢。王七桶，就是三队的王稀屎，知道吧？他有个儿子叫王福，就在我的班上，识得三千八百八十八个字。第一节课我就出了洋相，还是他教我怎么教书的呢。"大家都不相信，我便把那天的课讲了一遍。大家听了，都说："真的，咱们识得几个字呢？谁数过？"我说："我倒有一个法子。我上学时，语文老师见班上有同学学习

113

不耐烦，就说：'别的本事我不知道你们有多大，就单说识字吧。一本新华字典，你们随便翻开一页。这一页上你们若没有一个不会读、书、解的字，我就服。以后有这本事的人上课闹，我管我不姓我的姓。'大家不信，当场拿来新华字典一翻，真是这样。瞧着挺熟的字，读不出来；以为会读的字，一看拼音，原来自己读错了；不认识，不会解释的字就更多了。大家全服了。后来一打听，我们这位老师每年都拿这个法子治学生，没一回不灵的。"大家听了，都将信将疑，纷纷要找本新华字典来试一试，但想来想去没有人有字典，我说我也没有字典，大约还是没有卖的。来娣一直不说话，这时才慢慢地说："没有字典，当什么孩子王？拉倒吧！老娘倒是有一本。"我急忙说："拿来给我。"来娣脸上放一下光，将身仰倒，肘撑在床上，把胖腿架起来，说："那是要有条件的。"大家微笑着问她有什么条件。来娣慢慢团身坐起来，用脚够上鞋，站到地上，抻一抻衣服，拢一拢头，向门口走去，将腰以下扭起来，说："哎，支部书记嘛，咱们不要当；党委书记嘛，咱们也不要当，也就是当个音乐老师。怎么样？一本字典还抵不上个老师？真老师还没有字典呢！"大家都看着我，笑着。我挠一挠头，说："字典有什么稀奇，可以去买，再说了，老陈还不是有？我可以去借。"来娣在门口停下来，很泄气地转回身来，想一想，说："真的，老杆儿，学校的音乐课怎么样？尽教些什么歌？"我笑了，把被歌声吓了一跳的事讲述了一遍。来娣把双手叉在腰上，头一摆，说："那也叫歌？真见了鬼。我告诉你，那种歌叫'说'歌，根本不是唱歌。老杆儿，你回去跟学校说,就说咱们队有个来娣,歌子多得来没处放,可以请她去随便教几支。"我说:"我又不是领导,怎么能批准你去?"来娣想了想,说:"这样吧,你写个词,我来作个曲。你把我作的歌教给你们班上的学生唱,肯定和别的班的歌子不一样,领导问起来,你就说是来娣作的。领导信了我的本事,笃定会叫我去教音乐课。"大家都笑来娣异想天开。我望望来娣。来娣问:"怎么样?"我说:"可以,可以。"老黑站起来说:"什么可以?作曲你以为是闹着玩儿的?那要大学毕业,专门学。那叫艺术,懂吗?艺术!看还狂得没边儿了!"来娣涨红了脸,望着我。我说:"我才念了几年书,现在竟去教初三。世界上的事儿难说,什么人能干什么事真说不准。"来娣哼了一声说:"作曲有什么难?我自己就常哼哼,其实写下来,就是曲子,我看比现在的那些歌都好听。"说完又过来一屁股坐在床上,一拍我的肩膀:"怎么样,老杆儿?就这么着。"

出去搜寻东西的人都回来了,有干笋,有茄子、南瓜,还有野猪肉干巴,酒自然也有。老黑劈些柴来,来娣支起锅灶,乒乒乓乓地整治,半个钟头后竟做出十样荤菜。大家围在地下一圈,讲些各种传闻及队里的事,笑一回,骂一回,慢慢吃酒吃菜。我说:"还是队里快活。学校里学生一散,冷清得很,好寂寞。"来娣说:"我看学校里不是很有几个女老师吗?"我说:"不知哪里来的些斯文人,晚上活着都没有声响。"大家笑了起来,问:"要什么声响?"我也笑了,说:"总归是斯文,教起书来有板有眼,我其实哪里会教?"老黑喝了一小口酒,说:"照你一说,我看确是识字为本。识了字,就好办。"有人说:

"上到初三的学生,字比咱们识得多。可我看咱们用不上,他们将来也未必有用。"来娣说:"这种地方,识了字,能写信,能读报,写得批判稿就行,何必按部就班念好多年?"老黑说:"怕是写不明白,看不懂呢。我前几天听半导体,里面讲什么是文盲。我告诉你们,识了字,还是文盲,非得读懂了文章,明白那里面的许多意思,才不是文盲。"大家都愣了,疑惑起来,说:"这才怪了! 扫盲班就是识字班嘛。识了字,就不是文盲了嘛。我们还不都是知识青年?"我想一想,说:"不识字,大约是文字盲,读不懂,大约是文化盲。老黑听的这个,有道理,但好像大家都不这么分着讲。"老黑说:"当然了,那广播是英国的中文台,讲得好清楚。"大家笑起来,来娣把手指逼到老黑的眼前,叫:"老黑,你听敌台,我去领导那里揭发你!"老黑也叫起来:"哈,你告嘛! 支书还不是听? 国家的事,百姓还不知道,人家马上就说了。林秃子死在温都尔汗,支书当天就在耳机子里听到了,瘟头瘟脑地好几天,不肯相信。中央宣布了,他还很得意,说什么早就知道了。其实大家也早知道了,只是不敢说,来娣,你的那些乱七八糟的歌哪里来的? 还不是你每天从敌台学来的! 什么甲壳虫,什么埃巴,什么雷侬,乱七八糟,你多得很!"来娣夹了一口菜,嚼着说:"中央台不清楚嘛,谁叫咱们在天边地角呢。告诉你,老黑,中央台就是有杂音,我也每天还是听。"老黑说:"中央台说了上句,我就能对出下句,那都是套路,我摸得很熟,不消听。"我笑起来,说:"大约全国人民都很熟。我那个班上的学生,写作文,社论上的话来得个熟,不用教。你出个庆祝国庆的作文题,他能把去年的十一社论抄来,你还觉得一点儿不过时。"大家都点头说不错,老黑说:"大概我也能教书。"我说:"肯定。"

　　饭菜吃完,都微微有些冒汗。来娣用脸盆将碗筷收拾了拿去洗,桌上的残余扫了丢出门外,鸡、猪、狗聚来挤吃。大家都站到门外,望望四面大山,舌头在嘴里搅来搅去,将余渣咽净。我看看忙碌的猪狗,嘴脸都还是原来的样子,不觉笑了,说:"山中方七日,学校已千年。我还以为过了多少日子呢。"正说着,支书远远过来,望见我,将手背在屁股上,笑着问:"回来了?书教得还好?"我说:"挺好。"支书近到眼前,接了老黑递的烟,点着,蹲下,将烟吐给一只狗。那狗打了一个喷嚏,摇摇尾巴走开。支书说:"老话说:家有隔夜粮,不当孩子王。学生们可闹?"我说:"闹不到哪里去。"支书说:"听说你教的是初三,不得了!那小学毕业,在以前就是秀才;初中,就是举人;高中,大约就是状元了。举人不得了,在老辈子,就是不做官,也是地方上的声望,巴结得很。你教举人,不得了。"我笑了,说:"你的儿子将来也要念到举人。"支书脸上放出光来,说:"唉,哪里有举人的水平。老辈子的举人要考呢。现在的学生也不考,随便就念,到了岁数,回到队上干活,识字就得。我那儿子,写封信给内地老家,三天就回信了,我叫儿子念给我,结结巴巴地他也不懂,我也不懂。"来娣正端了碗筷回来,听见了,说:"又在说你那封信,也不怕臊人。"支书笑眯眯地不说话,只抽烟。来娣对了我们说:"支书请到我,说叫我看看写的是什么。我看来看去不对头,就问支书：'你是谁的爷公?'支书说：'我还做不到爷公。'我说：'这是写给爷公的。'弄来弄去，原来是他儿子写的那封信退回来了，还假模假式地当收信念。收信地址嘛，写在了下面，寄信的地址嘛，写在了上面。狗爬一样的字，认都认不清；读来读去，把舌头都咬了。"大家都哄笑起来，支书也笑起来，很快活的样子，说："唉，说不得，说不得。"

我在队里转来转去，要了一天，将晚饭吃了，便要回去。老黑说："今夜在我这儿睡，明天一早去。"我说："还是回去吧。回去准备准备，一早上课，从从容容的好。"老黑说也好，便送我上路。我反留住他，说常回来耍，自己一个人慢慢回去。老黑便只送到队外，摇摇手回去了。

天色正是将晚，却有红红的一条云在天上傍近山尖。林子中一条土路有些模糊，心想这几天正是无月，十里路赶回去，黑了怕有些踌躇，便加快脚步疾走。才走不到好远，猛然路旁闪出一个人来。我一惊，问："哪个?"那人先笑了，说："这么快走，赶头刀吗?"原来是来娣，我放下心，便慢慢走着，说："好晚了，你怎么上山了?"来娣说："咦? 你站下。我问你，你走了，怎么也不跟老娘告别一下?"我笑了，说："老嘴老脸的，告别什么。我常回来。"来娣停了一下，忽然异声异气地说："老杆儿，你说的那个事情可是真的?"我疑惑了，问："什么事?"来娣说："说你斯文，你倒觍着脸做贵人，怎么一天还没过就忘事?"我望一望天，眼睛移来移去地想，终于想不出。来娣忽然羞涩起来，嗯了一会儿。我从未见来娣如此忸怩过，心头猛然一撞，脸上热起来，脖子有些粗，硬将头低下

118

去。来娣叹了一口气，说："唉，你真忘了？你不是说作个曲子吗？"我头上的脉管一下缩回去，骂了自己一下，说："怎么是我忘了？那是你说的嘛。"来娣说："别管是谁说的，你觉得怎样？"我本没有将这事过心，见来娣认真，就想一想，说："可以吧。不就是编个歌吗？你编，我叫我们班上唱。"我又忽然兴奋起来，舔一舔嘴，说："真的，我们搞一个歌，唱起来跟别的歌都不一样，嘿！好！"来娣也很兴奋，说："走，老娘陪你走一段，我们商量商量看。"我说："你别总在老子面前称老娘。老子比你大着呢。"来娣笑了："好嘛，老子写词，老娘编曲。"我说："词恐怕我写不来。"来娣说："刚说的，你怎么就要退了？不行，你写词，就这么定了。"我想一想，说："那现在也写不出来。"来娣说："哪个叫你现在写？我半路上等你，就是为这个，老黑几个老以为我只会烧火做饭，老娘要悄悄做出一件事，叫他们服气。"我看看天几乎完全黑下来，便说："行，就这么定了，你等我的词。我得走了。"说完便快快向前走去。走不多远，突然又听来娣在后面喊："老杆儿，你看我糊涂的，把正事都忘了！"我停下来转身望去，来娣的身影急急地移近，只觉一件硬东西杵到我的腹上。我用手抓住，方方的一块，被来娣的热手托着。来娣说："喏，这是字典，你拿去用。"我呆了呆，正要推辞，又感激地说："好。可你不用吗？"来娣在暗虚中说："你用。"我再也想不出什么话，只好说："我走了，你回吧。"说罢转身便走，走不多远，站下听听，回身喊道："来娣，回吧！"黑暗中静了一会，有脚步慢慢地响起来。

三

当晚想了很久的歌子,却总是一些陈词在盘旋,终于觉得脱不了滥调,便索性睡去。又想一想来娣,觉得太胖,量一量自己的手脚,有些惭愧,于是慢慢数数儿,渐渐睡着。

一早起来,雾中提来凉水洗涮了,有些兴奋,但不知可干些什么,就坐下来吸烟,一下瞥见来娣给的字典,随手拿来翻了,慢慢觉得比小说还读得,上课钟响了,方才省转来,急急忙忙地去上课。

学生们也刚坐好。礼毕之后,我在黑板前走了几步,对学生们说:"大家听好,我要彻底清理一下大家的功课。你们学了九年语文……"学生们叫起来:"哪里来九年?八年!"我疑问了,学生们算给我小学只有五年,我才知道教育改革省去小学一年,就说:"好,就是八年。可你们现在的汉语本领,也就是小学五年级,也许还不如。这样下去,再上八年,也是白搭,不如老老实实地返回来学,还有些用处。比如说字,王福那里有统计,是三千多字,有这三千多字,按说足够用了。可你们的文章,错字不说,别字不说,写都写不清楚。若写给别人看,就要写清楚,否则还不如放个臭屁有效果。"学生们乱笑起来,我正色道:"笑什么呢?你们自己害了自己。其实认真一些就可以了。我现在要求,字,第一要清楚,写不好看没关系,但一定要清楚,一笔一画。第二——嗯,没有第二,就是第一,字要清楚。听清楚了没有?"学生们可着嗓子吼:"听清楚了!"我笑了,说:"有志不在声高。咱们规定下,今后不清楚的字,一律算错字,重写五十遍。"学生们"欧"地哄起来。我说:"我知道。可你们想想,这是为你们好。念了八年书,出去都写不成个字,臊不臊?你们这几年没有考试,糊里糊涂。大道理我不讲,你们都清楚。我是说,你们起码要对得起你们自己,讲别的没用,既学了这么长时间,总要抓到一两样,才算有本钱。好,第二件事,就是作文不能再抄社论,不管抄什么,反正是不能再抄了。不抄,那写些什么呢?听好,我每次出一个题目,这样吧,也不出题目了。怎么办呢?你们自己写,就写一件事,随便写什么,字不在多,但一定要把这件事老老实实、清清楚楚地写出来。别给我写些花样,什么'红旗飘扬,战鼓震天',你们见过几面红旗?你们谁听过打仗的鼓?分场那一只破鼓,哪里会震天?把这些都给我去掉,没用!清清楚楚地写一件事,比如,写上学,那你就写:早上几点起来,干些什么,怎么走到学校来,路上见到些什么——"学生们又有人叫起来:"以前的老师说那是流水账!"我说:"流水账就流水账,能把流水账写清楚就不错。别看你们上了九年,你们试试瞧。好,咱们现在就做起来。大家拿出纸笔来,写一篇流水账。就写——就写上学吧。"

学生们乱哄哄地说起来,纷纷在书包里掏。我一气说了许多,竟有些冒汗,却畅快许多,好像出了一口闷气,学生们拿出纸笔,开始写起来。不到一分钟,就有人大叫:"老师,咋个写呀?"我说:"就按我说的写。"学生说:"写不出来。"我说:"慢慢写,不着急。"学生说:"我想不起我怎么上学嘛。"我靠在门边,扫看着各种姿势的学生,说:"会想起来的。自

121

己干的事情,自己清楚。"

教室里静了许久,隔壁有女老师在教课,声音尖尖地传过来,很是激昂,有板有眼。我忽然觉得,愈是简单的事,也许真的愈不容易做,于是走动着,慢慢看学生们写。

王福忽然抬起头来,我望望他,他又不好意思地低下头,将手里的笔放下。我问:"王福,你写好了?"王福点点头。我迈到后面,取过王福的纸,见学生们都抬起头看王福,就说:"都写好了?"学生们又都急忙低下头去写。我慢慢看那纸上,一字一句写道:

> 我家没有表,我起来了,我穿起衣服,我洗脸,我去
> 伙房打饭,我吃了饭,洗了碗,我拿了书包,我没有表,
> 我走了多久,山有雾,我到学校,我坐下,上课。

我不觉笑起来,说:"好。"迈到前边,将纸放在桌上。学生们都扬起头看我。我问:"还有谁写完了?"又有一个学生交了过来,我见上面写道:

> 上学,走,到学校教室,我上学走。

我又说:"好。"学生们兴奋起来,互相看看,各自写下去。

学生们已渐渐交齐,说起话来,有些闹。终于钟敲起来。我说了下课,学生们却并不出去,拥到前边来问。我说:"出去玩,上课再说。"学生们仍不散去,互相议论着。王福静静

地坐在位子上,时时看我一眼,眼睛里问着究竟。

钟又敲了,学生们纷纷回到座位上,看着我。我拿起王福的作文,说:"王福写得好。第一,没有错字,清楚。第二,有内容。我念念。"念完了,学生们笑起来。我说:"不要笑。'我'是多了。讲了一个'我',人家明白了,就不必再有'我'。事情还是写了一些,而且看到有雾,别的同学就谁也没有写到雾。大体也明白,只是逗号太多,一逗到底。不过这是以后纠正的事。"我又拿了第二篇,念了,学生们又笑起来。我说:"可笑吧?念了八年书,写一件事情,写得像兔子尾巴。不过这篇起码写了一个'走'字。我明白,他不是跑来的,也不是飞来的,更不是叫人背来的,而是走来的。就这样,慢慢就会写得多而且清楚,总比抄些东西好。"

王福很高兴,眼白闪起来,抹一抹嘴。我一篇一篇念下去,大家笑个不停。终于又是下课,学生们一拥出去,我也慢慢出来。隔壁的女老师也出来了,见到我,问:"你念些什么怪东西,笑了一节课?"我说:"笑笑好,省得将来耽误事。"

四

课文于是不再教,终日只是认字,选各种事情来写。半月之后,学生们慢慢有些叫苦,焦躁起来。我不免有些犹豫,但眼看学生们渐渐能写清楚,虽然呆板,却是过了自家眼手的,便决心再折磨一阵。

转眼已过去半个月,学校酝酿着一次大行动,计划砍些竹木,将草房顶的朽料换下来。初三班是最高年级,自然担负着进山砍料运料的任务。我在班上说了此事,各队来的学生都嚷到自己队上去砍,决定不下。我问了老陈,老陈说还有几天才动,到时再说吧。

　　终于到了要行动的前一天。将近下课,我说:"明天大家带来砍刀,咱们班负责二百三十根料,今天就分好组,选出组长,争取一上午砍好,下午运出来。"学生们问:"究竟到哪个队去砍呢?"我说:"就到我们队,我熟悉,不必花工夫乱找,去了就能砍。只是路有些远,男同学要帮着女同学。"女学生们叫起来:"哪个要他们帮!经常做的活路,不比他们差。"忽然有学生问:"回来可是要作文?"我笑了,说:"不要先想什么作文,干活就痛痛快快干,想些乱七八糟的东西,小心出危险。"学生说:"肯定要作文,以前李老师都是出这种题目,一有活动,就是记什么什么活动,还不如先说题目,我们今天就写好。"我说:"你看你看,活动还没有,你就能写出来,肯定是抄。"王福突然望着我,隐隐有些笑意,说:"定了题目,我今天就能写,而且绝对不是抄。信不信?"我说:"王福,你若能写你父母结婚别人来吃喜酒的事情,那你就能今天写明天怎么砍料。"大家笑起来,看着王福。王福把一只大手举起来,说:"好,我打下赌!"我说:"打什么赌?"王福看定了我,脸涨得很红,说:"真的打赌?"我见王福有些异样,心里恍惚了一下,忽然想到这是再明白不过的事,就说:"当然。而且全班为证。"学生们都兴奋起来,看着王福和我。我说:"王福,你赌什么?"王福眼里放出光来,刚要说,忽然低下头去。我说:"我出赌吧。我若输了,我的东西,随便你要。"学生们"欧"

地哄起来,纷纷说要我的钢笔,要我的字典。王福听到字典,大叫一声:"老师,要字典。"我的字典早已成为班上的圣物,学生中有家境好一些的,已经出山去县里购买,县里竟没有,于是这本字典愈加神圣。我每次上课,必将它放在我的讲桌上,成为镇物。王福常常借去翻看,会突然问我一些字,我当然不能全答出,王福就轻轻叹一口气,说:"这是老师的老师。"我见王福赌我的字典,并不惧怕,说:"完全可以。"我将字典递给班长。学生们高兴地看着班长,又看着我。我说:"收好了,不要给我弄脏。"王福把双手在胸前抹一抹,慢慢地说:"但有一个条件。"我说:"什么条件都行。"王福又看定我,说:"料要到我们三队去砍。"我说:"当然可以。哪个队都可以,到三队也可以,不要以为明天到三队去砍,今天你就可以事先写出来。明天的劳动,大家作证,过程有与你写的不符合的,就算你输。不说别的,明天的天气你就不知道。"王福并不泄气,说:"好,明天我在队里等大家。"

我在傍晚将刀磨好,天色尚明,就坐在门前看隔壁的女老师洗头发,想一想说:"明天劳动,今天洗什么头发,白搭工夫。"女老师说:"脏了就洗,有什么不可以?对了,明天你带学生到几队去?"我说:"到三队。"女老师说:"三队料多?"我说:"那倒不一定,但我和学生打了赌。"女老师说:"你净搞些歪门邪道,和学生们打什么赌?告诉你,你每天瞎教学生,听说总场教育科都知道了,说是要整顿呢!不骗你,你可小心。"我笑了,说:"我怎么是瞎教?我一个一个教字,一点儿不瞎,教就教有用的。"女老师将水泼出去,惊起远处的鸡,又用手撩开垂在脸前的湿发,歪着眼睛看我,说:"统一教材你不教,查问起来,看你怎么交待?"我说:"教材倒真是统一,我都分不清语文课和政治课的区别。学生们学了语文,将来回到队上,是要当支书吗?"女老师说:"德育嘛。"我说:"是嘛,我看汉语改德语好了。"女老师扑哧一笑,说:"反正你小心。"

晚上闲了无聊,忽然记起与来娣约好编歌的事,便找一张纸来在上面划写。改来改去,忽然一个"辜负"的"辜"字竟想不起古字下面是什么,明明觉得很熟,却无论如何想不起来,于是出去找老陈借字典来查。黑暗中摸到老陈的门外,问:"老陈在吗?"老陈在里面答道:"在呢在呢,进来进来。"我推门进去,见老陈正在一张矮桌前改作业本,看清是我,就说:"坐吧,怎么样? 还好吧?"我说:"我不打扰,只是查一个字,借一下字典,就在这里用。"老陈问:"你不是有了一本字典吗?"我说:"咳,今天和王福打赌,我跟他赌字典,字典先放在公证人那里了。"老陈笑一笑,说:"你总脱不了队上的习气,跟学生打什么赌? 虽说不讲什么师道尊严,可还要降得住学生。你若输了,学生可就管不住了。"我说:"我绝不会输。"老陈问:"为什么呢?"我说:"王福说他能今天写出一篇明天劳动的作文,你说他能赢吗? 我扳了他们这么多日子老老实实写作文的毛病,他倒更来虚的了。王福是极用功的学生,可再用功也编不出来明天的具体事儿,你等着看我赢吧。"老陈呆了许久,轻轻敲一敲桌子,不看我,说:"你还是要注意一下。学校里没什么,反正就是教学生嘛。可不知总场怎么知道你不教课本的事。我倒觉得抓一抓基础还是好的,可你还是不要太离谱,啊?"我说:"学生们也没机会念高中,更说不上上大学了。回到队里,干什么事情都能写清楚,也不枉学校一场。情况明摆着的,学什么不学什么,有用就行。要不然,真应了那句话,越多越没用。"老陈叹了一口气,不说什么。

我查了字典,笑话着自己的记性,辞了老陈回去。月亮晚晚地出来,黄黄的半隐在山头,明而不亮,我望了望,忽然疑惑起来:王福是个极认真的学生,今天为什么这么坚决呢?于是隐隐有一种预感,好像有什么不妙。又想一想,怎么会呢?回去躺在床上时,终于还是认为我肯定不会输,反而觉得赢得太容易了。

第二天一早,我起来吃了早饭,提了刀,集合了其他队来的学生,向三队走去。在山路上走,露水很大。学生们都赤着脚,沾了水,于是拍出响声,好像是一队鼓掌而行的队伍。大家都很高兴,说王福真傻,一致要做证明,不让他把老师的字典骗了去。

走了近一个钟头,到了三队。大约队上的人已经出工,见不到什么人,冷冷清清。我远远看到进山沟的口上立着一个紧短衣裤的孩子,想必是王福无疑。那孩子望见我们,慢慢地弯下腰,抬起一根长竹,放在肩上,一晃一晃地过来。我看清确是王福,正要喊,却见王福将肩一斜,长竹落在地下,我这才发现路旁草里已有几十根长竹,都杯口粗细。大家走近了,问:"王福,给家里扛料吗?"王福笑嘻嘻地看着我,说:"我赢了。"我说:"还没开始呢,怎么你就赢了?"王福擦了一把脸上的水,头发湿湿地贴在头皮上,衣裤无一处干,也都湿湿地贴在身上,颜色很深。王福说:"走,我带你们进沟,大家做个见证。"大家互相望望,奇怪起来。我一下紧张了,四面望望,迟疑着与学生们一路进去。

山中湿气蔓延开,渐渐升高成为云雾。太阳白白地现出一个圆圈,在雾中走着。林中的露水在叶上聚合,滴落下来,星星点点,多了,如在下雨。

忽然,只见一面山坡上散乱地倒着百多棵长竹,一个人在用刀清理枝杈,手起刀落。声音在山谷中钝钝地响来响去。大家走近了,慢慢站住。那人停下刀,回转身,极凶恶的一张脸,目光扫过来。

我立刻认出了,那人是王七桶。王七桶极慢地露出笑容,抹一抹脸,一脸的肉顺起来。我走上前去,说:"老王,搞什么名堂?"王七桶怪声笑着,向我点头,又指指坡上的长竹,打了一圈的手势,伸一伸拇指。王福走到前面,笑眯眯地说:"我和我爹,昨天晚上八点开始上山砍料,砍够了二百三十棵,抬出去几十棵,就去写作文,半夜以前写好,现在在家里放着,有知青作证。"王福看一看班长,说:"你做公证吧。字典,"王福忽然羞涩起来,声音低下去,有些颤,"我赢了。"

我呆了,看看王福,看看王七桶。王七桶停了怪笑,仍旧去砍枝杈。学生们看着百多根长竹,又看看我。我说:"好。王福。"却心里明白过来,不知怎么对王福表示。

王福看着班长。班长望望我,慢慢从挎包里取出一个纸包,走过去,递到王福手上。王福看看我,我叹了一口气,说:

"王福,这字典是我送你的,不是你赢的。"王福急了,说:"我把作文拿来。"我说:"不消了。我们说好是你昨天写今天的劳动,你虽然作文是昨天写的,但劳动也是昨天的。记录一件事,永远在事后,这个道理是扳不动的。你是极认真的孩子,并且为班上做了这么多事,我就把字典送给你吧。"学生们都不说话,王福慢慢把纸包打开,字典露出来,方方的一块。忽然王福极快地将纸包包好,一下塞到班长手里,抬眼望我,说:"我输了。我不要。我要——我要把字典抄下来。每天抄,五万字,一天抄一百,五百天。我们抄书,抄了八年呢。"

我想了很久,说:"抄吧。"

五

自此,每日放了学,王福便在屋中抄字典。我每每点一支烟在旁边望他抄。有时怀疑起来,是不是我害了学生?书究竟可以这样教吗?学也究竟可以这样学吗?初时将教书看得严重,现在又将学习搞得如此呆板,我于教书,到底要负怎样的责任?但看看王福抄得日渐其多,便想,还是要教认真,要教诚实,心下于是安静下来,只是替王福苦。

忽一日,分场来了放映队。电影在山里极其稀罕,常要年把才得瞻仰一次。放映队来,自然便是山里的节日。一整天学生们都在说这件事,下午放学,路远的学生便不回去,也不找饭吃,早早去分场占地位。我估摸队上老黑他们会来学校歇脚,便从教室扛了两条长凳回自己屋里,好请他们来了坐。待回到屋里,却发现王福早坐在我的桌前又在抄每日的字典,便说:"王福,你不去占地位吗?电影听说很好呢!"王福不抬头,说:"不怕的,就抄完了,电影还早。"我说:"也好。你抄着,我整饭来吃,就在我这里吃。抄完,吃好,去看电影。"王福仍不抬头,只说着"我不吃",仍旧抄下去。

老黑他们果然来了,在前面空场便大叫,我急忙过去,见大家都换了新的衣衫,裤线是笔挺的。来娣更是鲜艳,衣裤裁得极俏,将男人没有的部位绷紧。我笑着说:"来娣,队上的伙食也叫你偷吃得够了,有了钱,不要再吃,买些布来做件富余的衣衫。看你这一身,穷紧得戳眼。"来娣用手扶一扶头发,说:"少跟老娘来这一套。男人眼穷,你怎么也学得贼公鸡一样?今天你们看吧,各队都得穿出好衣衫,暗中比试呢。你们要还是老娘的儿,都替老娘凑凑威风。"老黑将头朝后仰起,又将腰大大一弓,头几乎冲到地下,狠狠地"呸"了一下。来娣笑着,说:"老杆儿,看看你每天上课的地方。"我领了大家,进到初三班的教室。大家四下看了,都说像狗窝,又一个个挤到桌子后面坐好。老黑说:"老杆儿,来,给咱们上一课。"我说:"谁喊起立呢?"来娣说:"我来。"我就迈出门外,重新进来,来娣大喝一声"起立",老黑几个就挤着站起来,将桌子顶倒。大家一齐笑起来,扶好桌子坐下。我清一清嗓子,说:"好,上课。今天的这课,极重要,大家要用心听。我先把课文读一遍。"来娣扶一扶头发,看看其他的人,眼睛放出光来,定定地望着我。我一边在黑板前慢慢走动,一边竖起一个手指,说:"听好。从前,有座山,山里有座庙,庙里有个和尚,讲故事。讲的什么呢? 从前,有座山,山里有座庙,庙里有个和尚讲——"老黑他们明白过来,极严肃地一齐吼道:"故事。讲的什么呢? 从前有座山,山里有座庙,庙里有个和尚讲故事。讲的什么呢? 从前有座山,山里有座庙……"大家一齐吼着这个循环故事,极有节奏,并且声音越来越大,有如在山上扛极重的木料,大家随口编些号子调整步伐,又故意喊得一条山沟嗡嗡响。

闹过了,我看看天色将晚,就说:"你们快去占位子。我吃了饭就来。"大家说好,纷纷向分场走去。来娣说:"老黑,你替我占好位子,我去老杆儿宿舍看看。"大家笑起来,说:"你不是什么都知道么? 还看什么?"来娣说:"我去帮老杆儿做做饭嘛。"大家仍在笑,说:"好,要得,做饭是第一步。"便一路唱着走了。

我与来娣转到后面,指了我的门口,来娣走进去,在里面叫道:"咦? 你在罚学生么?"我跟进去,见王福还在抄,灯也未点,便一面点起油灯,一面说:"王福,别抄了。吃饭。"来娣看着王福,说:"这就是王福吗? 好用功,怪不得老杆儿夸你。留了许多功课吗?"王福不好意思地说:"不是。我在抄老师的字典。"来娣低头看了,高兴地说:"妈的,这是我的字典嘛!"我一面将米在舀出的水里洗,一面将王福抄字典的缘故讲给来娣。来娣听了,将字典拿起,啪地一下摔在另一只手上,伸给王福,说:"拿去。我送给你。"王福不说话,看看我,慢慢退开,又蹲下帮我做事。我说:"字典是她送给我的。我送给你,你不要,现在真正的主人来送给你,你就收下。"王福轻轻地说:"我抄。抄记得牢。我爹说既然没有帮我赢到,将来找机会到省里去拉粮食,看省里可买得到。"来娣说:"你爹?王稀——"我将眼睛用力向来娣盯过去,来娣一下将一个脸涨起来,看我一眼,挤过来说:"去去去,我来搞。你们慢得要死。"于是乒乒乓乓地操持,不再说话。

吃过饭,王福将书用布包了,夹在腋下,说是他爹一定来了,要赶快去,便跑走了。我收拾收拾,说:"去看吧。"来娣坐下来,说:"空场上演电影,哪里也能看,不着急。"我想一想,就慢慢坐到床上。

油灯昏昏地亮着,我渐渐觉出尴尬,就找话来说。来娣慢慢翻着字典,时时看我一下,眼睛却比油灯还亮。我忽然想起,急忙高兴地说:"歌词快写好了呢!"来娣一下转过来,说:"我还以为你忘了呢!拿来看看。"我起身翻出来写完的歌词,递给来娣,点起一支烟,望着她。来娣快快地看着歌词,笑着说:"这词实在不斯文,我真把你看高了!"我吐出一口烟,看它们在油灯前扭来扭去,说:"要什么斯文?实话实说,唱起来好听。只怕编曲子的本领是你吹的。"来娣点点头,忽然说:"副歌呢?"我说:"还要副歌?"来娣看着我:"当然。你现在就写,两句就行。前面的曲子我已经有了。"我望望她。来娣很得意地从椅子上站起来,在屋里旋了半圈,又看看我,喝道:"还不快写!"

我兴奋了,在油灯下又看了一遍歌词,略想一想,写下几句,也站起来,喝道:"看你的了!"来娣侧身过去,低头看看,一屁股坐在椅上,将腿叉开到桌子两旁,用笔嚓嚓地写。

远处分场隐隐传来电影的开场音乐声,时高时低。山里放电影颇有些不便,需数人轮番脚踩一个链式发电机。踩的人有时累了,电就不稳,喇叭里声音于是便怪声怪气,将著名唱段歪曲。又使银幕上令人景仰的英雄动作忽而坚决,忽而犹豫,但一个山沟的人照样看得有趣。有时踩电的人故意变换频率,搞些即兴的创作,使老片子为大家生出无限快乐。

　　正想着,来娣已经写完,跳起来叫我看。我试着哼起来,刚有些上口,来娣一把推开我,说:"不要贼公鸡似的在嗓子里嘶嘶,这样——"便锐声高唱起来。

　　那歌声确实有些特别,带些来娣家乡的音型,切分有些妙,又略呈摇曳,孩子们唱起来,绝对是一首特别的歌。

　　来娣正起劲地唱第二遍,门却忽然打开了。老黑一帮人钻进来,哈哈笑着:"来娣,你又搞些什么糖衣炮弹?唱得四邻不安,还能把老杆儿拉下水么?"我说:"怎么不看了?"老黑说:"八百年来一回,又是那个片子,还不如到你这里来吹牛。来娣,你太亏了。五队的娟子,今天占了风头。有人从界那边街子上给她搞来一条喇叭裤,说是世界上穿的。屁股绷得像开花馒头,真开了眼。不过也好,你免受刺激。"来娣不似往常,却高兴地说:"屁股算什么?老娘的曲子出来了。我教你们,你们都来唱。"

　　大家热热闹闹地学,不多时,熟悉了,来娣起了一个头,齐声吼起来:

一二三四五

初三班真苦
识字过三千
毕业能读书

五四三二一
初三班争气
脑袋在肩上
文章靠自己

又有副歌，转了一个五度。老黑唱得有些左，来娣狠狠盯他一眼，老黑便不再唱，红了脸，只用手击腿。

歌毕，大家有些兴奋，都说这歌解乏，来娣说："可惜词差了一些。"我叹了，说写词实在不是一件容易的事，凑合能写清楚就不错。平时教学生容易严格，正如总场下达生产任务，轮到自己，不由得才同情学生，慢慢思量应该教得快活些才好。

六

第二天一早上课，恰恰轮到作文。学生们都笑嘻嘻地说肯定是写昨天的电影。我说："昨天的电影？报上评论了好多年了，何消你们来写？我们写了不少的事，写了不少我们看到的事。今天嘛，写一篇你们熟悉的人。人是活动的东西，不好写。大家先试试，在咱们以前的基础上多一点东西。多什么呢？看你们自己，我们以后就来讲这个多。"班长说：

"我写我们队的做饭的。"我说:"可以。"又有学生说写我。我笑了,说:"你们熟悉我吗?咱们才在一起一个多月,你们怕是不知道我睡觉打不打呼噜。"学生们笑起来,我又说:"随便你们,我也可以做个活靶子嘛。"

学生们都埋了头写。我忽然想起歌子的事,就慢慢走动着说:"今天放学以后,大家稍留一留,我有一支好歌教你们唱。"学生们停了笔,很感兴趣。我让学生们好好写作文,下午再说。

太阳已经升起很高,空场亮堂堂的。我很高兴,就站在门里慢慢望。远远见老陈陪了一个面生的人穿过空场,又站下,老陈指指我的方向,那人便也望望我这里,之后与老陈进到办公室。我想大约是老陈的朋友来访他,他陪朋友观看学校的教舍。场上又有猪鸡在散步,时时遗下一些污迹,又互相在不同对方的粪便里觅食。我不由暗暗庆幸自己今生是人。若是畜类,被人类这样观看,真是惭愧。

又是王福先交上来。我拿在手中慢慢地看,不由吃了一惊。上面写道:

我的父亲

我的父亲是世界中力气最大的人。他在队里扛麻袋,别人都比不过他。我的父亲又是世界中吃饭最多的人。家里的饭,都是母亲让他吃饱。这很对,因为父亲要做工,每月拿钱来养活一家人。但是父亲说:"我没有王福力气大,因为王福在识字。"

父亲是一个不能讲话的人，但我懂他的意思。队上有人欺负他，我明白。所以我要好好学文化，替他说话。父亲很辛苦，今天他病了，后来慢慢爬起来，还要去干活，不愿失去一天的钱。我要上学，现在还替不了他。早上出的白太阳，父亲在山上走，走进白太阳里去。我想，父亲有力气啦。

我呆了很久，将王福的这张纸放在桌上，向王福望去。王福低着头在写什么，大约是别科的功课，有些黄的头发，当中一个旋对着我。我慢慢看外面，地面热得有些颤动。我忽然觉得眼睛干涩，便挤一挤眼睛，想，我能教那多的东西么？

终于是下课。我收好了作文，正要转去宿舍，又想一想，还是走到办公室去。进了办公室，见老陈与那面生的人坐成对面。老陈招呼我说："你来。"我走近去，老陈便指了那人说："这是总场教育科的吴干事。他有事要与你谈。"我看看他，他也看看我，将指间香烟上一截长长的烟灰弹落，说："你与学生打过赌？"我不明白，但点点头。吴干事又说："你教到第几课了？"我说："课在上，但课文没教。"吴干事又说："为什么？"我想一想，终于说："没有用。"吴干事看看老陈，说："你说吧。"老陈马上说："你说吧。"吴干事说："很清楚。你说吧。"老陈不看我，说："总场的意思，是叫你再锻炼一下。分场的意思呢，是叫你自己找一个生产队，如果你不愿意回你原来的生产队。我想呢，你不必很急，将课交待一下，休息休息，考虑考虑。我的意思是你去三队吧。"我一下明白事情很简单,但仍假装想一想,说:"哪个队都一样,活计都是那些活计。不用考虑,课文没有教,不用交待什么。我现在就走,只是这次学生的作文我想带走,不麻烦吧?"老陈和吴干事望望我。我将课本还给老陈。吴干事犹豫了一下,递过一支烟,我笑一笑,说:"不会。"吴干事将烟别在自己耳朵上,说:"那,我回去了。"老陈将桌上的本子认真地挪来挪去,只是不说话。

我走出办公室,阳光暴烈起来。望一望初三班的教舍,门内黑黑的,想,先回队上去吧,便顶了太阳离开学校。

第二天极早的时候,我回来收拾了行李,将竹笆留在床上,趁了大雾,揹行李沿山路去三队。太阳依旧是白白的一圈。走着走着,我忽然停下,从包里取出那本字典,翻开,一笔一笔地写上"送给王福 来娣",看一看,又并排写上我的名字,再慢慢地走,不觉轻松起来。

会　餐

音河往东流去。一入秋,水小了,河滩上的柳树棵子和一绺一绺的灌木秃立着,准备过冬。

太阳在西边儿地线上还残着半张红脸,凉气就漫开。牛马们于是不肯再走半步,硬橛橛地立等着卸套,任凭扶犁杖的人往死里打。队长叹一口气,说:"回了吧。"牲口知人语,立时刻踏起四蹄来,套还没卸完,就挣着要走。人们把晚上炕头凶老婆的话向牲口们骂,牛马们可就又不懂了,撒开蹄子一直往屯子里跑去。只在书上认识牛的人绝想不到牛跑也如飞,脖子前的那片肉一掀一掀的,赛过马鬃潇洒。

人们把黑袄的下摆揪紧,胸口却敞着,拐着腿,抱着鞭,慢慢往屯子里走,十几张犁就遗在地头。太阳已经完全沉下去,凉气激人。东边儿地线上早升起大圆月亮,微微有些黄。队长回头望了,说:"嗬,赛屁股!"大家笑起来,纷纷问:"明天十五咋吃啊?"队长撒开袄襟儿,手在空中往下一抓,说:"今年这个八月十五,旗里规定要好好办会餐,还要派人到各队

138

视察,要评比。可他妈钱呢?我算计了,夏天来的几个知青,旗里拨了安家费,队上总算还有点儿现金。多打酒,吃了,冬天队上若有钱,好歹补上。这话是咱们说,可不能传到旗里去。"大家都说:"那是,那是。"一个人说,有钱不如给队里置点子挽具什么的,于是大家都骂他憨,说明天就不许他喝酒。那人哈哈一笑,说倒好,留个醒脑子睡老婆。大家就又笑他,说话间到了屯子里。

狗们在昏暗中箭一样蹿出来,又箭一样蹿回去,汪汪叫着。孩子们跑出来,手里捏一点儿饽饽。大人们也不说什么,凭他们的小脏手抓着后裤裆,往屋里钻进去。

队长路过知青的土房,进了灶间,一掀布帘,到了西屋。男知青们正东倒西歪地在炕上,见了队长,也不大动。队长说:"累了,累了,洋学生咋受过这罪。可既来了,不受咋整?说给你们,明天,八月十五,晚上,队里会餐,凡劳动力都有一号,你们都算。早起呢,把你们这炕的被卧挪开,用你们的炕,用你们的灶。会写字画画儿的明天把队部整置整置,闹得漂漂亮亮的,旗里有人下来视察。晚上有酒,有肉,有豆腐,有土豆子,有面饼,撒开肚子吃。女学生们呢?"就起身过到东屋,东屋立时就尖声尖气叫成一片。

早上四点多,窗外就有了响动。有人搬来柴火,又吱吱嘎嘎挑来水,在灶间支起木架。知青们睡不成,就都起身,挪开被卧出来,见了木架,问是干什么的。师傅们说,做豆腐。知青们新奇了,东一句西一句打听起来。师傅们自然很得意,指指划划地说,并邀知青们浆好了的时候来喝。

天亮了,猪圈叫成一片。两只猪被攒蹄扛了来,放倒在草地上。杀猪师傅用膝骨压在猪身上,猪就乱蹬,用一辈子的力气叫着。师傅火了,左手一拧猪耳朵,猪叫就又高上一个八度,右手执刀从项下往胸腔斜里一攮,伤口抖着,血连着沫出来,并不接,只让它流在地上。女知青们掩了眼,杀猪师傅高兴地把刀晃一晃,叫:"你们往后嫁了老公,可不兴这么乱叫乱动!"女知青拾了土圪塔丢他,他躲,就势立起身。队长来了,见血流在地下,急急地问:"咋不接?"杀猪师傅说:"这早晚儿了也不说肝儿咋个处置,我就不管了。"队长瞪了眼,说:"肝儿照例不都是给你?你把这血糟蹋了,肝儿也不能给你了!"杀猪师傅把刀一扔,说:"这猪我也不杀了,往年是往年,今年把斗私批修的话来告诉我,谁知道?"队长拾了刀,说:"还真应了那话:'死了张屠夫,吃不了混毛猪!'"就去杀另外一口猪。那猪不例外也是死挣,就把队长的手碰破。杀猪师傅见不好,急忙抢过刀自己杀,把血也接了。队长胡乱包了手,吩咐说:"肝儿你拿一副吧,那一副炒了给老人们下酒。"杀猪师傅就在猪脚处割开口,用铁条通上去,再吹进气,用线缚了,使棒把气周身打匀,鼓鼓的在热水里刮毛,又把肉卸开,肠头、肚头弄干净,分盆装了。肉拿进灶间,放在西灶上煮。

　　东灶上熬着豆浆。熟了,豆腐师傅叫来知青,一人尝了一碗,都说鲜。大家一边帮他,一边看那豆腐怎么做。原来队长昨晚早派了工磨了一夜豆子。滤了渣的浆煮了三锅,都点了卤,凝了,大瓢舀起来倒进粗布里,粗布就吊在木架上。

有人来把渣和滤下来的汁水拿去喂猪。水滤得差不多,四人提了粗布放在一扇大门板上系好,上面压了磨盘,豆腐师傅就去洗手。知青问:"好了?"师傅说:"等着吃吧。"几个知青仍围了看,不肯相信可以做出豆腐。

日近中午,太阳还是有些辣,地气蒸上来,师傅们赤了膊,都是一身精白的肉,只是脖脸和手是红黑的,倒像化了妆的人。地里的人下午不再出工,纷纷来看,品评着膘肉,吹乎着酒量,打下赌,就手将几个土豆子丢进灶灰里,走时扒出来,在手上掂着吃。鸡、小猪和狗从早上就转来转去。得吃的是狗和鸡,猪因是队上的,总被打跑。可是顽固的也是猪,去了又来,最后把地上的血连土啃下去。孩子们被家里人吓唬着,只远远地看,不肯散去。有的人捏一块肉在嘴里,并不嚼,慢慢走开,孩子跟了去,到远处,才吐给孩子。

净肉煮出来,分盛在桶里。净肉加了豆腐,在一起煮好,分盛在桶里。豆腐单加一些葱再煮,又分盛在桶里。肉汤煮了土豆子,还是分盛在桶里。几十只桶被人提到队部,出来的人嘴都动着。门口有人把守,拦住闲杂人等。之后是烙饼,再就是汤。酒早已有人买来,摆在桌子中央。

天还没黑,人们已经聚在队部外面。劳力们都很兴奋。平日在地里,天地太大,显不出什么,只能默默地做。今日有酒有肉,无异于赛会,都决心有个样子。各人手里拿着自家的碗筷,互相敲着,老人们就不高兴,说像叫花子。

终于队长第一个进门了,大家稳住气跟在他身后。到了屋里,队长先让了屯里几个极有声望的老者和旗里视察的干部坐一小桌,其他自便。墙上用红纸写了语录,贴了四张,又画了工农兵各持武器。大家都说好,都说历年没有手画的画儿,知识青年来了,到底不一样。

照例是旗里的干部先讲话。庄稼人不识字,所以都仔细听,倒也知道了遥远的大事。干部讲完了,大家鼓掌,老人们笑着邀干部坐回去。于是队长讲。队长先用伤了的手捏一本儿语录,祝福了。大家于是跟着祝福。队长说,秋耕已胜利完成,今天就请旗里来的同志给旗里带去喜报。大家要注意增产节约,要想着世上还有三分之二受苦人过不上我们的日子。这会餐,大家要感谢着,不然怎么会有?虽然——可是——吃吧。

于是提上桶来,啪啪地打瓶盖儿。队长给老人们斟酒,老人们颤着手拦,还是满了。队长先端起碗来,又祝福了,敬了,再敬了老人们,一气喝下,大家叫一声好,都端了碗,只喝一口,急忙伸筷。第一巡菜几乎没有嚼就渐见桶底,于是第二巡又上。到第三巡,方才慢下来,说话多起来,而且声儿大起来。

窗户上爬满了孩子们,不动眼珠儿地盯着看,女人们在后面拽不动,骂骂咧咧地走开,聚在门外唠嗑。

屋里的人们已在开始吃饼。喝酒的人们把饼掖好,开始斗鸡一样地划拳,红了眼。女知青们受不住,邀在一起出来。

汤没有人动,于是提出去,一勺一勺舀在孩子们的小手里,孩子们急急地往嘴里泼,母亲们过来指点着他们喝,叱责着。

老人们先出来了。没了长辈，屋里大乱，开始赌起四大碗。知青们出来一个人，与一个壮汉比。于是各喝四大碗，站起，走出来，大家也一拥出来。

空地上早拴好两匹马。两个赌了酒的人各解一匹。知青先上了，别人一鞭，马便箭一样出去，一下将那知青遗在地下躺着，众人都喝彩。壮汉拽着缰绳，却踏不上镫。马转起来，壮汉就随它转。终于踏着，一翻身上去，用缰绳一抽，马便箭一样出去，众人又都喝彩。

女人和孩子们早已拥入屋里，并不吃，只是兜起衣襟收，桌上地下，竟一点儿不剩，只留下水迹。于是女人们和孩子们又都出来，与男人们一起等壮汉回来。

不多时，马回来了，却不见壮汉在上面。一个女人叫起来，往野地里寻去，孩子跟着，被母亲叱住，让兜了两人的菜，先回家去。

月亮照得一地青白。有人叹了，大家就都仰起头看那月亮。那月亮竟被众人看得摇摇晃晃，模糊起来。

节　日

一

眼看麦子就要熟了,却不知道大人们从哪里有了枪。

小龙第一次看见真枪。以往镇里有的,是火药枪,要将黑黑的火药倒进枪筒。枪药不能受潮。受潮了,就不能发火,因此要炒。铁锅,用炭焙热了,放到凉的地上,把受潮的枪药倒在锅里,稳稳地拌,有湿气冒。不冒了,倒出来,就可以了。文化革命前,小荣的爸爸有一次炒枪药,焙干了,别人喊他,他偏头看,药就炸了。小荣的爸爸从此半边脸黑着,一只眼睛像兔眼,一只耳朵像木耳。

小孩子从此不许看炒枪药。鸡可以,围着锅转来转去。

小孩子不许跟着上山看打猎,怕被没有击中要害的野兽冲着。平镇的大人很爱护小孩子,有个三长两短,哭,难过,就都晚了。能想到的,应该先想到。

小孩子可以看枪毙人。平镇离着县城近,镇前有一大片河滩。县里判了死刑的犯人,用大卡车拉来,推到河滩上,验身,跪倒,低头,等待口令。孩子们把耳朵捂上,还是能听到很响的枪声。犯人卧在地上,血流出来。有时死人还能慢慢地翻身,穿白衣的人走过去,弄弄,死人就不动了。小龙很想知道是怎么弄的,但是有人把岗,不能过去。

有一次快喊口令了,突然一个犯人站起来就跑。开枪的兵打惯了不动的目标,又总是近放,所以犯人跑,枪竟不响。后面围观的人都喔地叫起来。枪响了,没打中。再响,还打不中。七八条枪纷纷打,犯人已经跑远了。河滩上的人都笑癫了,没跑的犯人也笑。喊口令的人带两个兵去追,抓回来,忍着笑,枪毙了。这件事后来被传得各种各样,小龙只记得那个人跌跌撞撞地跑,因为河滩上尽是大的圆石头。

所以小龙不是第一次看见真枪,是第一次很近地看见真枪。趁爸爸不注意,摸一下,凉的。

二

试枪的时候,小龙的爸爸要找个目标。小龙的妈妈说,朝天放吧,看打着人。小龙的爸爸说,枪就是打人的。

小荣的爸爸来找小龙的爸爸,说,奶奶的,这回可使着真家伙了,红革造那帮子还闹腾个屁。

小龙的爸爸在裤子上磨着子弹头,说,听说,他们也有枪了。

小荣的爸爸说,差得远,五支队向着咱们,胡师长,就是挺胖的那个,四二年就是八路,跟上头通着气呢。

小龙的爸爸把子弹头往脸上按了按,说,听说,他们也有和上边通气的人。

小荣的爸爸火了，歪着头，说，你还是红造总的人吗？

小龙的妈妈扶着门框说，拿着枪就别吵了，拿着枪吵什么？

两个大人提着枪往外走，左右手换着把袖子挽起来。小龙跟着往外走。

小龙的妈妈叫，你给我回来！

两个大人吓了一跳，站住，回头看。小龙的妈妈过去扯住小龙，说，杀人你还没瞧够哇！

两个大人笑了，走出去。

红革造是县里最先起的造反组织。只三天，大家省悟过来，于是组织纷立。平镇离县城近，被后起的红造总想到，来发展了组织，又被红革造也来发展了组织。平镇往年的大小纠葛，于是有了争斗的实力。因为都标明忠于毛主席，所以对立激烈，终于，有了枪。

平镇的小孩子不许看炒枪药，不许上山看打猎，现在，不许找对立组织的大人的小孩子玩耍。但是，红革造控制平镇的时候，红革造的大人的小孩子可以到街上看游行，看游街，看用棍子、链子打被游街的红造总的大人。红造总控制平镇的时候，红造总的大人的小孩子可以到街上看游行，看游街，看用棍子、链子打被游街的红革造的大人。

三

小龙于是觉得没有意思，瞧瞧鸡，看看鸟。望望天，希望听见枪响。很久很久，还没有响。

小龙慢慢移到院子的门口，站着。之后，跨出门，站着。之后，靠在门框上，手伸到衣服里，挠挠背，挠挠肚皮，突然一闪，蹿到街上，并没有听到妈妈喊，就放心地沿墙根在没人的街上走。

街上没有什么变化。只是照常的新标语贴在旧标语上，照常的鸡在啄纸边的浆糊。小龙跺着脚跑了几步，鸡静静蹿开，歪着头看小龙。小龙恨鸡没有叫，就站在墙边，不让鸡过来。鸡呢，头一抻一抻地踱到街对面，伸开一只翅膀一条腿，探个懒腰，搂搂羽毛，拉了一摊屎，开始用嘴啄磨胸和背。

小龙用手扮作枪，指着鸡，突然，远远的传来枪响。鸡浑然地沉浸在啄磨中。小龙很兴奋，大喊，小荣，小荣，我爸打真枪呢！

小荣一下就从隔壁的门里蹿出来，小荣的妈妈的喊声追着，你个小王八羔子，你死给你妈瞧吧，你个小兔崽子，你那个疯爹，早晚是挨枪的，你跑吧，你个小王八蛋的……

小龙和小荣拼命地跑，街上有了生气。

四

镇口立着一棵大槐树。夏天，树上垂下许多蚕一样的虫子，树叶叫它们吃得零零碎碎。槐树旁有打铁的棚，里面有垒起的灶。打铁的时候，灶里的炭被风箱鼓得一明一暗。小孩子最爱看锤子打在烧红的铁上时，绽开的火星，直到打铁的师傅把锤立放在地上，谁也不看，说，息一程子。灶上有火,却从来不烧水,自有小孩子飞奔回家提水再奔回来。铁匠喝了谁的水,谁就得意,再打铁时,就觉得有权利凑近看,反而被铁匠呵叱。

小荣跑到棚里,蹲到灶上喘气。小龙也爬到灶上喘气。棚里很久没有打铁了,闻着一大股酸味。

小荣说,我妈和我爹干了一仗,我爹干了我妈一巴掌。

小龙说,你爹和我爹一起打枪去了,你听见我爹开的枪了吗?

小荣说,那是我爹开的!

小龙说,我爹开完了才是你爹开呢!

小荣说,你放屁!

小龙说,你放屁!

忽然背后有人说,你们玩儿哪?

小龙和小荣回头看,是小芹。小龙和小荣不说话了,小芹爸爸是红革造的。

小芹的家就在棚后面。小芹靠在门边,弯起一条腿,用手掸鞋子,又跺了几下。小龙不说枪的事,小荣也不说,两个人望着大路从镇里伸出去。

小芹说,我妈给我做新鞋了。

小龙偏头看看,说,新鞋有什么新鲜的。

小芹说,明天过节了。

小龙一愣,说,过什么节?

小芹说,儿童节啊。

小荣说,学都不上了,就没有儿童节了。上学才过儿童节呢。老师说,过节了,就过节了,每年都是。

小芹说,嗳,张老师的腿到现在都没接上,我妈说接不上,就是瘸子了。

小龙说,张光头? 县里来的老师打的,打张光头的时候你们见着了吗?

小荣说,见着了。

小龙说,我也见着了。比我爹打我还打得结实。

小芹说,过节你们干什么呀?

小荣说,我们? 一愣,向镇外一指,说,我们,我们到大渠玩儿,是不是小龙?

小龙高兴地说,嗯! 过节就得有活动,光穿新鞋算什么。

小龙和小荣从灶上跳下来,互相搂着往回走。

小芹说,带我玩儿吗?

小龙停下来,哼哼着不说话。

小芹说,带我玩儿吧。我不跟我爹我妈说。

小龙说,行。

小芹说,也带小良他们玩儿吧。

小荣说,行。可是得听我们指挥。明天晚上吧,别叫大人知道喽。

五

吃晚饭的时候,小龙的爸爸说,得动真的了,红革造想霸了伏麦的水。我们说了,水是我们的,没商量。

小龙的妈妈说,往年说是说,也吓唬,这有了枪,你今年

149

就别去了吧？

小龙的爸爸不说话，吃了一口菜，嚼得嘎嘣嘎嘣的。

小龙说，妈，明天过节了。

小龙的妈妈说，过什么节？

小龙说，儿童节呀，小芹今天都穿新鞋了。

小龙说了小芹就后悔了。小龙的爸爸妈妈都喔了一声。小龙的妈妈说，可不是嘛，那冬天过年的罩褂你明天穿一天吧。

六

平镇的小孩子们悄悄地出到河滩上，只有鸡和狗知道。小龙说，大人们还是看得见。小芹说，你们昨天不是说到大渠玩儿吗？大家就都猫着腰穿过麦地向大渠跑。

傍晚的大渠，东坡顶还有太阳，红黄红黄的，西坡凉下来了，草都有了精神。沟底有水，哗啦哗啦的。小孩子们嚷着，沟外却听不见，小孩子们于是就尖叫，顺着坡斜着跑。虫子飞起来，燕子蹿过来蹿过去。

月亮在水里渐渐小了，天黑下来。三四颗大星星亮亮的不动，动的是火萤子。

小芹说，我的电筒子丢了。

小荣说，你还有电筒子？

小芹说，你们不是说打夜仗吗？我就把电筒子拿来了。丢了可就坏了，我爹我妈就知道了。

大家都很兴奋，摸来摸去地找。小良找到了，大家围过去。

小龙说,怎么使?

小芹说,这么一推,就亮。这么一拉,就不亮了。

小龙说,我看看。拿过来,一推,一道光柱冲出来。小龙哟了一声,让光柱射向天空,虫子在光柱里变成一道道白。

枪声响了。

七

小孩子们吓了一跳,都蹲下来。子弹啾啾的飞过去,细细的光线亮亮地从东拉过西边。立刻,东边也有亮线拉过西边。好一会儿,停下来了。

小龙说,咱们在沟底,打不着咱们。信不信?

小芹哭了,说,回家吧。

小龙说,再试一回。一推,天上又是来来回回的亮线。

小荣说,像打铁!

小良说,像过年放炮仗!

小孩子们高兴了,站起来,小龙再推。

小龙感到有个东西咚地落在坡上,弹起来,他回头看。他看见阳光炸开,而且,声音很大。

电筒子高高地飞起来,落到水里,还亮着。很小的鱼在浑浑的红光里一下一下啄那块圆玻璃。

炊　烟

·

　　老张得了一个闺女。老张说,挺好,就是大了别长得像我,那可嫁不出去。因此,女儿名美丽,自然姓张。

　　老张的大学同学都说,叫个美丽,没什么不好,就是俗了点。老张你也是读过书的人,怎么不能想个雅点儿的呢?

　　老张说,俗有什么不好? 实惠。这年头儿你还想怎么着? 结结实实的吧。

　　老张的同学说,结实? 那叫矿石好了,叫火成岩,水成岩也行。咱们这行就是学了个结实。

　　老张在大学读的地质。

　　老张疼闺女。

　　老张抽烟。老张的老婆说,你要想要孩子,就把烟忌了,书上说,大人抽烟,会影响胎儿的基因。老张正抽到一半儿,马上扔掉,用脚碾灭,戒了。美丽生出来了,老张买了一包烟。老张的老婆说,你叫美丽从小肺就是黑的吗? 老张凄凄的样子。老张的老婆说,你抽吧,别在美丽旁边儿抽。

美丽是冬天生的。春天了,老张的老婆抱着美丽出来晒太阳。起风了,老张说,还不回去,看吹着。老张的老婆说,不晒太阳,美丽吃的钙根本就吸收不了。老张说,那就屋里窗户边儿上晒嘛。老张的老婆说,紫外线透不过玻璃,人体吸收钙,靠的就是个紫外线,隔着玻璃,还不是白晒。老张说,那就等风停了。

老张瞧着老婆给美丽喂奶。老张的老婆书也念得不少,瞧老张老盯着,说,还没瞧够呀,又不是没瞧过。老张说,谁瞧你,我是怕美丽吃不饱。俩人都笑了,美丽换过一口气,也笑了。

秋天了,美丽大了点儿,手会指东西,指妈妈,指爸爸,还会抓耳朵,抓妈妈的头发,抓爸爸的鼻子。

有一天,老张的老婆抱着美丽,老张在旁边挤眉弄眼,逗得美丽嘎嘎乐,两只小手儿孛着。老张的老婆把美丽凑到老张的脸前,美丽的手就伸进爸爸的嘴里。

说时迟,那时快,老张抬手就是一掌,把母女两个打了个趔趄。老张在地质队,天天握探锤打石头,手上总有百来斤的力气。老张的老婆没有提防,就跌倒了。到底是母亲,着地的关头,一扭身仰着将美丽抓在胸口。

美丽大哭。老张的老婆脑后淌出血来,从来没有骂过人的人,骂人了,老张的老婆骂老张。

老张呆了,浑身哆嗦着,喘不出气来,汗从头上淌进领子里。

老张进了医院,两天一夜,才说出话来——

六〇年,闹饥荒,饿死人,全国都闹,除了云南。那年,我毕业实习,进山找矿。

后来,我迷路了。有指南针,没用。我饿,我饿呀。慌,心慌,一慌就急。本来还会想,这下完了。一直就吃不够,体力差,肝里的糖说耗完就耗完。后来就出汗,后来汗也不出了。什么也不敢想,用脑子最消耗热量了。躺着。胃里冒酸水儿,杀得牙软。

后来,从肚子开始发热,脚心,脖子,指头尖儿,越来越烫。安徒生不是写过个卖火柴的小女孩儿吗?这个丹麦的老东西,他写得对。人饿死前,就是发热,热过了,就是死。

我没死。死了怎么还能跟你结婚?怎么还能有美丽?

我醒的时候,好半天才看得清东西。我瞧见远处有烟。当时,我只有一个念头儿,烧饭才会有烟。爬吧。

就别说怎么才爬到了吧。到了,是个人家。我趴在门口说,救个命吧,给口吃的吧。没人应。对,可能我的声音太小。我进去了。

灶前头靠着个人,瘦得牙龇着,眼睛亮得吓人。我说,给口吃的。那人半天才摇摇头。我说,你就是我爷爷,祖宗,给口吃的吧。那人还是摇头。我说,你是说没有吗?那你这灶上烧的什么?喝口热水也行啊。那人眼泪就流下来了。

我不管了,伸手就把锅盖揭了。水汽散了,我看见了,锅里煮着个小孩儿的手。

峡　谷

　　山被直着劈开，于是当中有七八里谷地。大约是那刀有些弯，结果谷地中央高出如许，愈近峡口，便愈低。

　　森森冷气漫出峡口，收掉一身黏汗。近着峡口，倒一株大树，连根拔起，似谷里出了什么不测之事，把大树唬得跑，一跤仰翻在那里。峡顶一线蓝天，深得令人不敢久看。一只鹰在空中移来移去。

　　峭壁上草木不甚生长，石头生铁般锈着。一块巨石和百十块斗大石头，昏死在峡壁根，一动不动。巨石上伏两只四脚蛇，眼睛眨也不眨，只偶尔吐一下舌芯子，与石头们赛呆。

　　因有人在峡中走，壁上时时落下些许小石，声音左右荡着升上去。那鹰却忽地不见去向。

　　顺路上去，有三五人家在高处。临路立一幢石屋，门开着，却像睡觉的人。门口一幅布旗静静垂着。愈近人家，便有稀松的石板垫路。

　　中午的阳光慢慢挤进峡谷，阴气浮开，地气熏上来，石板有些颤。似乎有了噪音，细听却什么也不响。忍不住干咳一两声，总是自讨没趣。一世界都静着，不要谁来多舌。

走近了，方才辨出布旗上有个藏文字，布色已经晒退，字色也相去不远，随旗沉甸甸地垂着。

忽然峡谷中有一点异响，却不辨来源。往身后寻去，只见来路的峡口有一匹马负一条汉，直腿走来。那马腿移得极密，蹄子踏在土路上，闷闷响成一团。骑手侧着身，并不上下颠。

愈来愈近，一到上坡，马慢下来。骑手轻轻一夹，马上了石板，蹄铁连珠般脆响。马一耸一耸向上走，骑手就一坐一坐随它。蹄声在峡谷中回转，又响又高。那只鹰又出现了，慢慢移来移去。

骑手走过眼前，结结实实一脸黑肉，直鼻紧嘴，细眼高颧，眉睫似漆。皮袍裹在身上，胸微敞，露出油灰布衣。手隐在袖中，并不拽缰。藏靴上一层细土，脚尖直翘着。眼睛遇着了，脸一短，肉横着默默一笑，随即复原，似乎咔嚓一响。马直走上去，屁股锦缎一样闪着。

到了布旗下，骑手俯身移下马，将缰绳缚在门前木桩上。马平了脖子立着，甩一甩尾巴，曲一曲前蹄，倒换一下后腿。骑手望望门，那门不算大，骑手似乎比门宽着许多，可拐着腿，左右一晃，竟进去了。

屋里极暗，不辨大小。慢慢就看出两张粗木桌子，三四把长凳，墙里一条木柜。木柜后面一个肥脸汉子，两眼陷进肉里，渗不出光，双肘支在柜上，似在瞌睡。骑手走近柜台，也不说话,只伸手从胸口掏进去,捉出几张纸币,撒在柜上。肥汉也不瞧那钱,转身进了里屋,少顷拿出一大木碗干肉,一副筷,放在骑手面前的木桌上,又回去舀来一碗酒,顺手把钱划到柜里。

骑手喝一口酒,用袖擦一下嘴。又摸出刀割肉,将肉丢进嘴里,脸上凸起,腮紧紧一缩,又紧紧一缩,就咽了。把帽摘了,放在桌上,一头鬈发沉甸甸慢慢松开。手掌在桌上划一划,就有嚓嚓的声音。手指扇一样散着,一般长短,并不拢。肥汉又端出一碗汤来,放在桌上冒气。

一刻工夫,一碗肉已不见。骑手将嘴啃进酒碗里,一仰头,喉节猛一缩,又缓缓移下来,并不出长气,就喝汤。一时满屋都是喉咙响。

不多时,骑手立起身,把帽捏在手里,脸上蒸出一团热气,向肥汉微微一咧嘴,晃出门外。肥汉梦一样呆着。

阳光又移出峡谷,风又蹿来蹿去。布旗上下扭着动。马鬃飘起来,马打了一串响鼻。

骑手戴上帽子,正一正,解下缰绳,马就踏起四蹄。骑手翻上去,紧一紧皮袍,用腿一夹,峡谷里响起一片脆响,不多时又闷闷响成一团,越来越小,越来越小。

耳朵一直支着,不信蹄声竟没有了,许久才辨出风声和布旗的响动。

溜　　索

不信这声音就是怒江。首领也不多说，用小腿磕一下马。马却更觉迟疑，牛们也慢下来。

一只大鹰旋了半圈，忽然一歪身，扎进山那侧的声音里。马帮像是得到信号，都止住了。汉子们全不说话，纷纷翻下马来，走到牛队的前后，猛发一声喊，连珠脆骂，拳打脚踢。铃铛们又慌慌响起来，马帮如极稠的粥，慢慢流向那个山口。

一个钟头之前就感闻到这隐隐闷雷，初不在意，只当是百里之外天公浇地。雷总不停，才渐渐生疑，懒懒问了一句。首领也只懒懒说是怒江，要过溜索了。

山不高，口极狭，仅容得一个半牛过去。不由捏紧了心，准备一睹气贯滇西的那江，却不料转出山口，依然是闷闷的雷。心下大惑，见前边牛们死也不肯再走，就下马向岸前移去。行到岸边，抽一口气，腿子抖起来，如牛一般，不敢再往前动半步。

万丈绝壁飞快垂下去，马帮原来就在这壁顶上。转了多半日,总觉山低风冷,却不料一直是在万丈之处盘桓。

怒江自西北天际亮亮而来,深远似涓涓细流,隐隐喧声腾上来,着一派森气。俯望那江,蓦地心中一颤,惨叫一声。急转身,却什么也没有,只是再不敢轻易向下探视。叫声漫开,撞了对面的壁,又远远荡回来。

首领稳稳坐在马上,笑一笑。那马平时并不觉雄壮,此时却静立如伟人,晃一晃头,鬃飘起来。首领眼睛细成一道缝,先望望天,满脸冷光一闪,又俯身看峡,腮上绷出筋来。汉子们咦咦喂喂地吼起来,停一刻,又吼着撞那回声。声音旋起来,缓缓落下峡去。

牛铃如击在心上,一步一响,马帮向横在峡上的一根索子颤颤移去。

那索似有千钧之力,扯住两岸石壁,谁也动弹不得,仿佛再有锱铢之力加在上面,不是山倾,就是索崩。

首领缓缓移下马,拐着腿走到索前,举手敲一敲那索,索一动不动。首领瞟一眼汉子们。汉子们早蹲在一边吃烟。只有一个精瘦短小的汉子站起来,向峡下弹出一截纸烟,飘飘悠悠,不见去向。瘦小汉子迈开一双细腿,走到索前,从索头扯出一个竹子折的角框,只一跃,腿已入套。脚一用力,飞身离岸,嗖地一下小过去,却发现他腰上还牵一根绳,一端在索头,另一端如带一缕黑烟,弯弯划过峡顶。

那只大鹰在瘦小汉子身下十余丈处移来移去,翅膀尖上几根羽毛被风吹得抖。

再看时,瘦小汉子已到索子向上弯的地方,悄没声地反着倒手拔索,横在索下的绳也一抖一抖地长出去。

大家正睁眼望,对岸一个黑点早停在壁上。不一刻,一个长音飘过来,绳子抖了几抖。又一个汉子站起来,拍拍屁股,抖一抖裤裆,笑一声:"狗日的!"

三条汉子一个一个小过去。首领哑声说道:"可还歇?"余下的汉子们慢声应道:"不消。"纷纷走到牛队里卸驮子。

牛们早卧在地下,两眼哀哀地慢慢眨。两个汉子拽起一条牛,骂着赶到索头。那牛软下去,淌出两滴泪,大眼失了神,皮肉开始抖起来。汉子们缚了它的四蹄,挂在角框上,又将绳扣住框,发一声喊,猛力一推。牛嘴咧开,叫不出声,皮肉抖得模糊一层,屎尿尽数撒泄,飞起多高,又纷纷扬扬,星散坠下峡去。过了索子一多半,那边的汉子们用力飞快地收绳,牛倒垂着,升到对岸。

这边的牛们都哀哀地叫着,汉子们并不理会,仍一头一头推过去。牛们如商量好的,不例外都是一路屎尿,皮肉疯了一样抖。

之后是运驮子,就玩一般了。这岸的汉子们也一个接一个飞身小过去。

战战兢兢跨上角框,首领吼一声:"往下看不得,命在天上!"猛一送,只觉耳边生风,聋了一般,任什么也听不见,僵着脖颈盯住天,倒像俯身看海。那海慢慢一旋,无波无浪,却深得令人眼呆,又透远得欲呕。自觉慢了一下,急忙伸手在索上向身后拨去。这索由十几股竹皮扭绞而成,磨得赛刀。手划出血来,黏黏的反倒抓得紧索。手一松开,撕得钻心一疼,不及多想,赶紧倒上去抓住。渐渐就有血溅到唇上、鼻子,自然顾不到,命在天上。

猛然耳边有人笑:"莫抓住鸡巴不撒手,看脚底板!"方才觉出已到索头,几个汉子笑着在吃烟,眼纹一直扯到耳边。

慎慎地下来,腿子抖得站不住,脚倒像生下来第一遭知道世界上还有土地,亲亲热热跺几下。小肚子胀得紧,阳物酥酥的,像有尿,却不敢撒,生怕走了气再也立不住了。

眼珠涩涩的,使劲挤一下,端着两手,不敢放下。猛听得空中一声唿哨,尖得直入脑髓,腰背颤一下。回身却见首领早已飞到索头,抽身跃下,拐着腿弹一弹,走到汉子们跟前。有人递过一支烟,嚓地一声点好。烟浓浓地在首领脸前聚了一下,又忽地被风吹散,扬起数点火星。

牛马们还卧在地下,皮肉乱抖,半个钟头立不起来。

首领与两个汉子走到绝壁前,扯下裤腰,弯弯地撒出一道尿,落下不到几尺,就被风吹得散开,顺峡向东南飘走。万丈下的怒江,倒像是一股尿水,细细流着。

那鹰斜移着,忽然一栽身,射到壁上,顷刻又飞起来,翅膀一鼓一鼓地扇动。首领把裤腰塞紧,曲着眼望那鹰,抖一抖裆,说:"蛇?"几个汉子也望那鹰,都说:"是呢,蛇。"

牛们终于又上了驮,铃铛朗朗响着,急急地要离开这里。上得马上,才觉出一身黏汗,风吹得身子抖起来。手掌向上托着,寻思几时才能有水洗一洗血肉。顺风扩一扩腮,出一口长气,又觉出闷雷原来一直响着。俯在马上再看怒江,干干地咽一咽,寻不着那鹰。

洗　澡

中午的太阳极辣,烫得脸缩着。半天的云前仰后合,被风赶着跑,于是草原上一片一片地暗下去,又一片一片地亮起来。

我已脱下衣服,前后上下搔了许久。阳光照在肉上,搔过的地方便一条一条地热。云暗过来,凉风拂起一身鸡皮疙瘩,不敢下水。

这河大约只能算作溪,不宽,不深,绿绿地流过去。牧草早长到小腿深,身上也已经出过两个月的汗,垢都浸得软软的,于是时时把手伸进衣服里,慢慢将它们集合成长条。春风过去两个月,便能在阳光下扒光衬衣裤,细细搜捡着虱子们。

远远有一骑手缓缓而来,人不急,马更不急,于是有歌声沿草冈漫开。凡开阔之地的民族,语言必像音乐。但歌声并无词句,只是哦哦地起伏着旋律,似乎不承认草原比歌声更远。

骑手走近了，很阔的一个脸，挺一挺腰，翻下马来，又牵着马，慢慢走到河边，任马去饮。骑手看看我，说："热得很！"我也说："热得很。"他又问："要洗澡？"我说："要洗澡。"他一边解开红围腰，一边说："好得很！好得很！"

骑手将围腰扔在草上，红红的烫眼睛。他又脱下袍子，一扔，压在围腰上。围腰还是露出一截，跳跳的。

骑手把衣服都脱了，阳光下，如一块脏玉，宽宽的一身肉，屁股有些短，腿弯弯的站在岸边，用力地搔身上。

他又问："洗澡？"我说："洗澡。"他就双手拍着胸，向水里蹚去。水没到小腿的一半。

忽然他大吼一声，身子一倾，扑进水里。水花惊跳起来，出一片响声。不待水花落下去，他早又在水里翻过身来，双手挖水泼自己，嘴里嗬嗬地叫着。

我站起来，也不由用手拍着胸腹，伸脚向水里探去，但立刻觉得小肚子紧起来。终于是要洗，不能管凉，慎慎地往下走。

冷不防身上火烫也似凉得抖一下，原来骑手在用力挖水泼过来。我脚下一个不稳，跌到水里。

水还糊住眼睛，就听得骑手在嗬嗬大叫。待抹掉脸上的水，见骑手埋在水里，只露一张阔脸在笑。

我说："啊！凉得很！"骑手说："凉得很！"

我急忙用手使劲搓胸前，脸上，腿下，又仰倒在水里。水激得胸紧紧的，喘不出大口的气。天上的云稳稳地快跑。

骑手又哦哦地唱起歌，只是节奏随双手的动作在变，一会儿双手又随歌的节奏在搓。他撅起屁股,把头顶浸到水里,又开手指到头发里抓,歌声就从两腿间传出来。抓完头,他又叉开腿,很仔细地洗下面的东西,发现我在看他,很高兴地大声说:"干净得很!"

我也周身仔细地搓,之后站起来。风吹过,浑身抖着,腮僵得硬硬的,缩缩地看一看草原。

忽然发现云前有一块黄,惊得大叫一声,返身扑进水里。骑手看看我,我把手臂伸出去一指。

对岸一个女子骑在马上,宽宽的一张脸,眼睛很细,不动地望着我们。

骑手看到了她,并不惊慌,把手在胸前抹一抹,阔脸放出光来,向那女子用蒙语问,意思大约是:没有见过吗?

那女子仍静静跨在马上,隐隐有一些笑意。骑手弯下腰去掬一些水,举到肩上松开手,身上沿着起伏处亮亮地闪起来。

那女子说话了,用蒙语,意思大约是:这另外一个人是跌倒了吗? 骑手嗬嗬笑了,说:"汉人的东西和我的不一样,他恐怕吓着你!"

我分明感到那女子向我盯住看,不由更向水里缩下去。

那女子又向骑手说了:"你很好。"骑手一下子得意得不行,伸开两条胳膊舞了一下,又叭叭地拍着胸膛,很快地说:"草原大得很,白云美得很,男子应该像最好的马,"他的声音忽然轻柔极了,只有蒙语才能这样又轻又快又柔:"你懂得草原。"

那女子向远处望了一下,胯下的马在原地倒换了一下蹄子。她也极快地说:"草原大得孤独,白云美得忧愁,我不知道是不是碰到了最好的马,也许我还没有走遍草原。"

　　骑手呆住了,慢慢低下头去看河水。那女子声音极高地吆了一下马,马慢慢地摆着屁股离开河边跑去。骑手抬起头来,好像在看天上的河水,忽然猛猛地甩甩头发,走到岸上,很快地把衣服穿起来。又一边慢慢裹着围腰,一边看着远去的黄头巾。骑手一摇一摇地去牵走远了的马,唱起歌来,那大致的意思是:

最好的马在呼伦贝尔
马儿在呼伦贝尔最好
因为呼伦贝尔草原最好

最好的马在呼伦贝尔
马儿在呼伦贝尔最好
因为呼伦贝尔骑手最好

马儿跑遍草原
女人走遍草原
但在呼伦贝尔草原停下来

马儿停在这里
女人留在这里

那女子走得极远了，停下来。骑手一直在望着她，于是飞快地翻上马去，紧紧勒住皮缰，马急急地刨几下蹄子。骑手猛一松缰，那马就箭一样笔直地跑进河里，水扇一样分开。马又一跃到对面岸上，飞一样从草上飘过去。

阳光明晃晃地从云中垂下来，燃着了草冈上一块红的火，一块黄的火。

雪　山

　　太阳一沉，下去了。众山都松了一口气。天依然亮，森林却暗了。路自然开始模糊，心于是提起来，贼贼地寻视着，却不能定下来在哪里宿。

　　急急忙忙，犹犹豫豫，又走了许久，路明明还可分辨，一抬头，天却黑了，再看路，灰不可辨，吃了一惊。

　　于是摸到一株大树下，用脚蹚一蹚，将包放下。把烟与火柴摸出来，各抽出一支，正待点，想一想，先收起来。俯身将草拢来，择干的聚一小团，又去寻大些的枝，集来罩在上面。再将火柴取出，试一试，划下去。硫火一蹿，急忙拢住，火却忽然一缩，屏住气望，终于静静地燃大。手映得透明，极恭敬地献给干草，草却随便地着了，又燃着枝，劈劈啪啪。顾不上高兴，急忙在影中四下望，抢些大枝，架在火上。

　　火光映出丈远，远远又寻些干柴。这才坐下，抽一枝燃柴，举来点烟。火烤得头发一响，烟也着了。烟在腔子里胀胀的，待有些痛，才放它们出来，急急的没有踪影，一尺多远

167

才现出散乱,扭着上去。那火说说笑笑,互相招惹着,令人眼呆。渐渐觉出尴尬,如看别人聚会,却总也找不出理由加入,于是闷闷地自己想。

雪山是应该见到了,见到了,那事才可以开始。而还没有见到,于是集了脑中的画片,一页一页地翻,又无非是白的雪,蓝的天,生不出其他新鲜,还不如眼前的火有趣,于是看火。火中开始有白灰,转着飘上去,又做之字形荡下来。咔嚓一声,燃透的枝塌下来,再慢慢地移动。有风,火便小吼,暗一暗,再亮一亮,又暗一暗。柴又一塌,醒悟了,缓缓压上几枝,有青烟钻出来,却又叭的一声,不知哪里在爆。

依然不能加入火,渐渐悟到,距离的友谊,也令人不舍与向往。心里慢慢宽起来,昏昏的就想睡。侧身将塑料布摊开,躺上去,一滚,把自己包了。

时时中觉出火的集会渐渐散去,勉强看看,小小的一点红,只剩一个醉汉的光景。似梦非梦,又是白的雪,蓝的天,说不清的遥远。有水流进来,刚明白是雾沉下来,就什么也不愿再知觉。

梦中突然见到一块粉红,如音响般,持续而渐强,强到令人惊慌,以为不祥,却又无力闪避,自己迫自己大叫。

却真的听见自己大叫,真的觉到塑料布在脸上,急忙扯开,粉红更亮,天地间却静着,原来非梦,只是混沌中不理知那粉红就是晨光中的山顶。痴痴地望着,脑中渐渐浸出凉与热,不能言语。

山顶是雪。

湖　　底

后半夜,人来叫,都起了。

摸摸索索,正找不着裤子,有人开了灯,晃得不行。浑身刺痒,就横着竖着斜着挠。都挠,咔哧咔哧的,说,你说今儿打得着吗? 打得着,那鱼海了去了。听说有这么长。可不,晾干了还有三斤呢。闹好了,每人能分小二百,吃去吧。

人又来催。门一开,凉得紧,都叫,关上关上! 快点儿快点儿,人家司机不等。这就来,也得叫人穿上裤子呀! 穿什么裤子,光着吧,到那儿也是脱,怎么也是脱。

不但裤子穿上了,什么都得穿上,大板儿皮袄一裹,一个一个地出去,好像羊竖着走。

凉气一下就麻了头皮,捂上帽子,只剩一张脸没有知觉。一吸气,肺头子冰得疼。真他娘冷。真他奶奶冷。玩儿命啊。吃点子鱼,你看这罪受的。

都说着,都上了车。车发动着,呼地一下蹿出去,都摔在网上了,都笑,都骂,都不起来,说,躺着吧。

草原冻得黑黑的,天也黑得冷,没一个星星不哆嗦。就不看星星,省得心里冷。

　　骑马走着挺平的道儿,车却跑得上上下下。都忍着说,颠着暖和。天却总也不亮,都问,快到了吧?别是迷了。

　　车也不说一声儿,一下停住。都滚到前头去了,互相推着起来,都四面望,都说,哪儿哪?怎么瞅不见呀?车大灯亮了,都叫起来,那不是!

　　草原不知怎么就和水接上了。灯柱子里有雾气,瞅不远。都在车上抓渔网,胡乱往下扔。扔了半天,扔完了。都往下跳,一着地,嗬,脚腕没知觉,跺,都跺,响成一片。

　　车转了个向,灯照着网。都择,择成一长条,三十多米,一头拴在车斗右边。刚还黑着,一下就能看见了,都抬头,天麻麻亮。都说,刚才还黑着呢。

　　先拢起一堆火。都伸出手,手心翻手背,攥起来搓,再伸出去,手背翻手心,摸摸脸,鼻头没知觉。都瞅水。

　　说是湖,真大,没边儿。湖面比天亮着几成。怪了,还没结冰。都说,该结了,怎么还没结呢?早呢,白天还暖和呢,就是晚上结了,白天也得化。这才刚立秋。妈的,刚立秋就这么冷。后半夜冷。关外不比关里。北京?北京立秋还下水游泳呢!霜冻差不多了,霜冻也没这疙冷。

　　酒拿出来了,说,都喝。喝热了,下水。火不能烤了,再烤一会儿离不了,谁也不愿下了,别烤了,别烤了。都离开了,酒传着喝。

　　天一截比一截亮。湖纹丝不动。

都甩了大羊皮袄,缩头缩脑地解袄扣子。绒衫不脱,脱裤子。往下一褪,毛都乍起来,卵子缩成一团。都赶紧用手搓屁股,搓大腿,搓腿肚子,咔哧咔哧的。

搓热了,搓麻了,手都搓烫了,指尖还冰凉。都佝着腰,一人提一截网,一长串儿,往水里走。

都嚷,妈的,这水真烫啊!要不鱼冻不死呢,敢情水里暖和。你说人也是,咋不学学鱼呢?嘿,人要学了鱼,赶明儿可就是鱼打人了。把人网上来,开膛,煺毛,抹上盐,晾干了,男人女人堆一块儿,鱼穿着袄,喝着酒,一筷子一筷子吃人,有熏人,有蒸人,有红烧人,有人汤。

都笑着,都哆嗦着,渐渐往深里走。水一圈儿一圈儿顺腿凉上来。最凉是小肚子,一到这儿,都吃喝。

水是真清。水底灰黄灰黄的。脚碰到了,都嚷,嘿,踩着了!懒婆娘似的,天都亮了,还不起!别嚷别嚷,鱼一会儿跑了。

网头开始往回兜,围了一大片。人渐渐又走高了,水一点一点浅下去。水顺着腿往下流,屁股上闪亮闪亮的。都叫,快!快!冻得老子顶不住了!

天已大亮,网两头都拴在车斗后面。司机说,好了没有?都说,好了好了,就看你的了!

半天没动静。司机一推门,跳下来,骂,妈的,冻上了,这下可毁了!都光着屁股问,拿火烤烤吧?

司机不说话,拿出摇把摇。还是不行,就直起腰来擦一下头。都在心里说,嘿,这小子还出汗了。

司机的胳膊停在脑门上，不动，呆呆的。

都奇怪了。心里猛地一下，都回过头去。

一疙瘩红炭，远远的，无声无息，一蹿，大了一点儿。屁股上都有了感觉。那红炭又一蹿，又大了一点，天上渗出血来。都噤声不得，心跳得咚咚的，都互相听得见，都说不出。

还站在水里的都一哆嗦，喉咙里乱动。听见那怪怪的声音，岸上的都向水里跑。

湖水颤动起来，让人眼晕，呆呆地看着水底。灰黄色裂开亿万条缝，向水面升上来。

奶奶的！都是鱼。

成　长

王建国生于一九四九年十月一日。

母亲生他的时候,发生难产。医生说,需要产妇的先生签字,是要孩子,还是要大人。等在产科外面的父亲首先纠正说,时代变了,不要叫先生,要叫同志,或者说,孩子的父亲。护士说,好,可以叫同志,孩子现在还不知道生不生得出来,所以还不知道可不可以称父亲,现在要你签字,是保产妇,还是保胎儿?

父亲说,两个人都要。于是剖腹。从肚脐到阴阜竖着剖开,取出婴儿,缝上刀口,日后母亲肚子上留下一条长长的亮疤。

父亲晚上独自回家,长安街上的游行尚未结束,许多人手上举着火把,蜡烛,呼着口号,并不整齐地通过天安门的前面。长安街上有重炮车碾出的轮子印。

父亲想好了,孩子的名,就叫个建国。

建国长到七岁,上学了。第一天老师点名,叫王建国,站起来两个,还有一个也叫建国,但姓李,没有站起来。学校教导处调整了一下,将名为建国而同姓的学生分到不同的班,于是王建国和李建国还在原来的班。

学校开大会的时候,校长,教导主任点名表扬学生,要很清楚地讲明,某年某班的张建国或李建国或赵建国或孙建国或刘建国或王建国如何如何。

学校里老师常常议论的是一个学生叫蒋建国,有老师建议家长应该给孩子改一下名字,家长很愤怒,说,姓蒋的就不能叫建国了吗? 老师认为姓蒋的家长没有体会出问题的实质。

王建国到四年级的时候,老师出了一道作文题:在红旗下长大。王建国写了四百多字,老师认为很好,在班上读了。

五年级的时候,又有一道作文题叫:在红旗下成长。王建国写了一千多个字,老师认为很好,在班上读了,并且推荐给北京市教育局,收进小学生作文选。

考初中的时候,语文试题发下来,王建国打开卷子一看,在五星红旗下成长。想起老师在考试前教的办法是先做会做的题,再做要想一下才会做的题,最后做难题,于是提笔开始写作文,把附在考卷之外的一张白纸也写了一半。

王建国考上一个很好的中学,当了班长,初二就入了共产主义青年团,做过班上的团支部书记和校团委书记。上到高中一年级的时候,校党委书记已经和王建国谈过话,让他提前写入党申请书。教导处也写过报告,推荐重点培养王建国为高中毕业后保送苏联留学的苗子。

但是一九六六年文化大革命了，那一年所有叫建国的孩子十七岁。

王建国后来上山下乡，又转回北京，谋到建筑公司的一个工作，捆钢筋。一九七六年的四五，王建国也写了一首诗，贴到天安门广场。还是一九七六年，建筑公司调到毛主席纪念堂工地，王建国还是捆钢筋。王建国在顶层捆了四个小时后，尿憋了。建筑工的老规矩是就地解决，上上下下几十米高，是合理的。老工人传下来的说法是，撒了拉了才结实。王建国问了班长，班长说上头讨论过了，可以，可也别像以前那么明显。

王建国找了一处，向下看看天安门广场，五星红旗在远处呼啦啦地飘，毛主席他老人家在更远的天安门城楼的像上看着他，左边人民大会堂，右边中国历史博物馆和中国革命历史博物馆，近处是人民英雄纪念碑，纪念堂比纪念碑高，所以看得见纪念碑真正的顶。

高处有风，王建国解决问题后，抖了一下，两眼泪水。

旧　书

吴庆祥十二岁学徒,学的是古书铺的徒。

古书铺和古董店很像,"半年不卖货,卖货吃半年"。吴庆祥的说法是,卖货吃半年的"货",说的是大买卖。大买卖当然不好做,可卖个石印帖啦,卖个寿山石料啦,总是有的,进进出出,总是个买卖。

进进出出的,各种人都有。文人居多,背着手,揣着手,上上下下地看,看了半天,转了半天,出去了。这类是小文人,手头拮据,可也不能小看,小文人不定什么时候成了大文人。小文人的时候侍候得好,成了大文人,书铺的口碑可就出去喽。

大文人常常留下条子,条子上有要找的书。条子上的书找到了,不一定全找到了,也许先找到一本,就送去,叫人家知道你尽力在找。

送书去的时候,总要捎带些别的书,捎什么,揣摸文人的嗜好。有专门好门面的,就捎些门面书,一般也就买下来了,摆在架子上,朋友来了,指给朋友看。

吴庆祥在书铺熬到能送书到买家去,很不容易。

送书的要懂书。第一得识字,说得出送去的是什么书,吴庆祥有识字的精明,进了铺子三年就可以为来买书的人找书了。吴庆祥那时已经变了嗓,也有了身高,一般人还真看不出他才十五岁。

懂书的第二就很难了,版本一项就是个无底洞,各种有关书的花色学问,简直的是烂棉花套子,不是轻易理得出头绪的。

吴庆祥在店里,侍候着来买书的主儿,眼睛睁着,耳朵开着,凡有关书的事,都先强印在脑子里,手脚还得勤快,书铺不是学堂,不是来听说书的,是来给老板卖书的。

印在脑子里的东西,慢慢才明白。不明白的,也许要很久,也许突然有个什么机会,一下子就明白了。明白得越多,也就越容易明白。

吴庆祥有的时候要去海淀的大学送书。骑上店里的车,路边都是荒草。吴庆祥最怕冬天去海淀送书,逆风,天黑得快,回来的时候心里发毛。吴庆祥后来与几个大文人都很好,当然是因为书的关系。

吴庆祥后来嫖妓。宣武门外的伙计很少有不嫖妓的。离得近,铺子上板以后,很寂寞,当然要往有人气儿的地方去。书铺里的书很多,再多也不是人。

吴庆祥染上了梅毒,找人治了,治好了。治好了,再去嫖妓。

白天侍候着卖书,留心着卖书的学问,送书,天晚了,上板。上完板,朝东溜达,找熟的,老价钱的。

北平一九四九年解放,改回原来的名儿,又叫北京。

一九五〇年头儿上,吴庆祥自杀。

对于吴庆祥的自杀,相熟的伙计谁也搞不明白为什么。按说是新社会了,吴庆祥也不是老板,只是个大伙计,成分不能算坏。有什么怕的呢?

取缔窑子?也不至于,新社会了,到处都是新气象,希望正大,怎么一个大男人就寻了短见?

百思不得其解,百思不得其解。店员们凡提起吴庆祥,还是摇头,百思不得其解。

抻　面

　　铁良是满族人,问他祖上是哪个旗的,他说不知道,管它哪个旗的,还不都是干活儿吃饭。

　　铁良在北京是个小有名气的人,名气是抻得一手好面。铁良有个要好的弟兄,也是个有名气的人,名气是和馅儿。大饭庄,有名的饭庄,凡要蒸包子煮饺子烙馅儿饼,总之凡要用到馅儿的,都是铁良这个弟兄去和。天还没亮就起身,和完一个店的再去和另外一个店的,天亮的时候,一天的活儿干完了。肉,菜,料,和在一起,掺高汤打匀。打匀是个力气活儿,而且还不能上午打好的馅儿下午变稀汤儿了,其中有分寸。

　　铁良呢,专在一家做。面是随时有客要吃就得煮的。

　　铁良原来有几股钱在店里,后来店叫政府公私合了营,铁良有些不太愿意,在公家人面前说了几句。公家人也是以前常来店里吃铁良抻的面的主儿,劝了铁良几句。几年以后,铁良知道害怕了,心里感激着那个公家人。

抻面最讲究的是和面。和面先和个大概齐,之后放在案子上苦块湿布"省"着。后来运动多了,铁良说,这"反省"就是咱们的省面。省好了的面,愿意怎么揉掐捏拉,随您便。

省好了的面,内里没有疙瘩。面粉一掺了水,放不多时就会发酸,所以要下碱。下了碱的面,就可以抻了。

有人用舌头试碱放多了还是少了,舔舔,有一股苦甜香,就是合适了。铁良试碱不用舌头,一半儿的原因是抻面是个露脸的活儿,是公开的,客人看着,当面的。铁良用鼻子,闻闻,碱多了,就再放放,"省"碱。

跑堂的得了客人要的数儿,拉长声儿唱给铁良。客人出到街上,靠在铺面窗口儿看铁良抻面,好像是买了一张看戏的站票。

铁良不含糊,当当一手揪出一拳头面,啪,合在一起,搓成粗条儿,掐着两头儿,上下一悠,就一个人长了。人伸开胳膊的长度等于这个人的身高。铁良两手往当中一合,就是两股,再抻再合,就是四股,再抻再合,八股,十六股,三十二股,六十四股,一百二十八股。之后掐去两头,朝脑后一甩,好像是大闺女的辫子飞落到灶上的锅里,客人就笑了,转身回去店里座位上。

锅边儿的伙计用双长筷子搅两下,大笊篱捞出盛到海碗里,海碗里有牛骨高汤,入好面,撒几片芫荽,葱丝儿,带红根儿的嫩菠菜,满天星辣椒油花儿,红、绿、白,啪哒,放在了客人面前。客人挑起一箸子面,撑开嘴吃,热气蒸得额头有一点儿亮。铁良呢,和街上的熟人聊了有一会儿了。

五十年代初,镇压反革命,押去刑场的时候还许犯人点路边的馆子,吃最后一口人间食。有个老头子被押在车上,路过铁良的店,说是去阴间的路上得吃口抻面。于是押进去,老头子张口要龙须面,铁良也不说话,开始抻。

铁良几下就抻好了,亲自放面下锅,霎时捞起,人在汤里双手捧了碗放在老头儿面前。围观的人都伸头去看,说不出话来。老头儿挑起面迎光看看,手上的铐哗啦啦响,吃了一口,说,是这个意思,就招呼上路了。

铁良后来跟人说,这就是当初借钱给我学手艺的恩人,他就是要我抻头发丝儿面,我也得抻出来。

厕　　所

北京是皇城，皇城的皇城是紫禁城。说来话近，民国时将宣统逐出后，将这个大院子用作博物院，凡国民都可进去参观。于是，紫禁城里就永远有走着的国民和坐着的国民，坐着的是走累了的国民。只要紫禁城里不通汽车，大院子里就永远有走着的国民和走累了坐着的国民，因为紫禁城大，而且不可能改小。

这个道理，老吴是早就想通了。

老吴想不通的是，老吴当时在珍宝馆外的公共厕所外排队，生理上有点儿急，所以忽然想不通早年皇上太监三宫六院御林军上朝的文武大臣，这么多人每天在哪儿上厕所？老吴怀了这个心，专门来了三个礼拜天的故宫，结论是当年没厕所，因为考察下来，现在的公共厕所，都是将当年的小间屋改建或新建的。

老吴于是很替皇家古人担忧。

老吴从学术的立场对吃的问题不操心，但一旦吃了，排泄就是一定的了,这个肯定的问题怎么找不到肯定的解决空间呢?吃在皇家不成问题,排泄在老吴的心里倒是个问题了。

老吴于是去找老申。老申八十了,当年在宫里做过粗使太监,现在孤身一人住在朝阳门内大街。老吴找到老申,请教了,老申细着嗓子说,嘻,用桶,桶底铺上炒焦了的枣儿,屎砸下去,枣儿轻,会转圈儿,屎就沉到底下。焦枣儿又香,拉什么味儿的都能遮住。宫里单有太监管把桶抬出去。

老吴问抬到哪儿去?老申说抬出宫去。老吴又问抬出宫再抬到哪儿去?老申就支支吾吾,说自己不是干抬屎专业的。这几年太监成了国宝,经常上电影,老申答不了老吴的问题,有点挂不住,就转了话题透露给老吴太监也有性生活的秘密。

回家后,老吴一边儿感叹焦枣儿粪桶的实际与气派,一边儿到街上公共厕所解决一时之私。

北京人称公共厕所为官茅房。老吴认为这可能是因为最早的街上厕所是官家修的,所以叫官茅房。但这个"最早"早到什么时候,老吴还没考证出来。明清还是民国?也许元大都的时候就有了?总之发明权不在人民政府,要不怎么不叫人民厕所呢?

公共厕所的八个坑儿蹲了四个,都是熟邻居,正议论宣武区虎坊桥新盖了个官茅房,有个小子没房结婚,连夜把男厕所的坑儿填了当洞房,今儿早上大家伙儿一推门,新娘新郎两口子正度蜜月呢!

正笑着,老吴旁边儿的人问老吴,你有富余的纸吗?

老吴明白旁边儿这位没带擦的纸,就直起腰掏兜儿,一掏,才知道自己也没带,就问另外的人,您带的纸有富余吗?

问来问去,原来四个人都没带纸,就又聊起来,等等看再有人来的结果。

果然又来了个人,大家先不好意思问,等那个解了裤子蹲下了,老吴问您带的纸有多吗我们几位巧了都忘了带纸。那人一惊,说,坏了坏了我以为这官茅房里有人就有纸就进来了。

五个人都不说话,听隔壁女厕所有人聊天,也是没办法。

等了近一个钟头,官茅房里居然再没进来人。大家开始怨政府,说官茅房里应该有纸给大家用嘛。老吴说,自己没带就说自己没带,政府管天管地还管擦屁股纸?政府还给你们焦枣儿呢!其他四个人看着老吴,不明白“焦枣儿”是什么意思,也不明白老吴怎么突然站起来了。

老吴系好裤子,说,我的晾干了。

提　琴

　　老侯是手艺人。老侯原来在乡下学木匠,开始的时候锛檩锛椽子。

　　锛其实是很不容易的活儿。站在原木上,用锛像用镐,一下一下把木头锛出形来,弄不好就锛到自己的脚上。老侯一次也没有锛到自己脚上。

　　老侯对没有锛伤自己很得意,说,师傅瞧我还行,就让我煞大锯。

　　煞大锯其实是很不容易的活儿,先将原木架起来,一个人在上,一个人在下,一上一下地拉一张大锯。大锯有齿的一边是弧形的,锯齿有大拇指大。干别的活儿可以喊号子,煞大锯却只能咬着牙,一声不吭,锯完才算。

　　老侯的腰力就是这两样练出来的。后来老侯学细木工,手下稳,别人都很佩服,其实老侯靠的是腰。

　　老侯学了细木工,有的时候别人会求他干一些很奇怪的活儿。老侯记得有人拿来过一只不太大的架子,料子是黄花梨,缺了一个小枨,老侯琢磨着给配上了。

人家来取活的时候,老侯问,这是个什么? 来人说,不知道。老侯心里说,我才不信不知道呢。

不过老侯到底也不知道那个架子是干什么的,这件事一直是老侯的一块心病。

老侯的家在河北,早年间地方上有许多教堂,教堂办学校,学校上音乐课,用木风琴,弹起来呜呜的很好听。老侯常常要修这木风琴。修好了,神父坐下来弹,老侯就站在旁边听。

有一次神父弹着弹着,忽然说,侯木匠,你会不会修另一种琴? 老侯问,什么琴? 神父说,提琴。老侯不知道,嘴上说试试吧。神父就把提琴拿来让老侯试试,是把意大利琴。

老侯把琴拿回家琢磨了很久。粗看这把琴很复杂,到处都是弧,没有直的地方。看久了,道理却简单,就是一个有窟窿的木盒。明白了道理,老侯就做了许多模具,蒸了鱼膘胶,把提琴重新粘起来。神父看到修好的琴,很惊奇。神父于是介绍老侯到北京去,因为教会的关系,老侯就常修些教堂的精细什物,四城的人都叫老侯洋木匠。

老侯因为修过洋乐器,所以渐渐有人来找老侯修各种乐器,老侯都能对付。北京解放了,老侯就做了乐器厂的师傅,专门修洋乐器。

一天有个干部模样的拿来一把提琴,请老侯修。老侯一眼就认出是神父那把琴,老侯没有吭声。老侯知道,跟教会沾关系,是麻烦。因为是修过的东西,所以做起来很快。干

186

部来取琴的时候,老侯忍不住说,您的这琴是把好琴。干部说,不是我的,是单位上的。老侯说,就是不太爱惜,公家的东西,好好保护着吧。是把好琴。

一九六六年夏天,到处抄家砸东西,老侯忽然想起那把琴。厂里不开工,老侯凭记忆寻到那个单位去。

老侯在这个单位里东瞧瞧,西看看。单位里人来人往,大字报贴得到处都是,到处都是加了硷的面浆糊味儿。老侯后来笑自己,这是干吗呢?人家单位的东西,自己找个什么呢?怎么找得到呢?于是就往外走。

可巧就让老侯瞧见了那把琴。琴面板已经没有了,所以像一把勺子,一个戴红袖箍的人也正拿它当勺盛着浆糊刷大字报。

老侯就站在那里看那个人刷大字报。那人刷完了,换了一个地方接着刷,老侯就一直跟着,好像一个关心国家大事的人。

豆　腐

　　孙福九十多岁去世,去世时略有不满,不过这不满在孙福的曾孙辈看来是老糊涂了,他老人家要吃豆腐渣。

　　做豆腐是先将黄豆,大豆,或黑豆磨成浆。你如果说,老孙,这黄豆和大豆不是一种豆子吗?孙福就先生一下气,然后不生气,嘟囔着说:懂个什么。

　　豆子磨成浆后,盛在锅里掺水煮,之后用布过滤,漏下的汁放在瓦器里等着点卤,布里剩下的就是豆腐渣。

　　豆渣是白的,放久会发黄,而且发酸变臭,刚滤好时,则有一股子熟豆子的腥香味儿。豆渣没有人吃,偶有人尝,说,磨老了,或者,磨嫩了。磨老了,就是磨过头儿了,细豆渣漏过布缝儿,混在豆浆里,这样子做出的豆腐里纤维多,不好吃。磨嫩了,就是豆子磨得粗,该成浆的没成浆,留在豆渣里,点浆成豆腐,豆腐当然就少。

　　磨嫩了就需要查查磨。掀开上磨扇,看看是不是磨沟儿磨浅了,或有残。磨沟儿磨浅了,就要剔沟儿。残了不好办,要把磨扇削下去一层,再剔出沟儿来。

做豆腐最难的是点卤。

人常说,画龙难点睛。孙福说,那有什么难?画坏了,重画就是了,豆腐点坏了,重来不了,糟蹋一锅。

点卤前,豆浆可以喝,做豆腐的师傅常常喝豆浆,却不一定吃豆腐,道理在豆浆养人。浆点好卤,凝起来,颤颤的,就是豆腐脑儿。凝起来的豆腐脑儿包在布里,系好,放重物压,水慢慢被挤出布外,布里就是豆腐了。压久了,布里的是豆腐干儿。

打开布,豆腐还是热的,用刀划成一块一块。当天卖不了的,放在冷水里。

孙福学徒做豆腐时,十几岁,还没碰过女人。孙福学点卤,点不好,师傅说,碰过女人没有?孙福摇摇头,脸很红。师傅说,记下,好豆腐就像女人的奶子。

孙福后来讨了女人,摸过之后,叹一口气,说,豆腐,豆腐。孙福的女人听了奇怪,说你做豆腐做出病啦!

第一次世界大战,中国在最后关头赌博一样地参战。孙福当民工,到欧洲打仗去,挖战壕。不久,被德国兵俘虏了,还是挖战壕。

一天,中国战俘被叫在一起,排成一排,命令会做豆腐的站出来。孙福头皮一阵发麻,以为豆腐是罪过,是死罪,但还是站出去。又命令会木匠的站出来,结果是除了会这两样的都赶回去接着挖战壕。

孙福指挥着几个德国人做豆腐,给一个在青岛住过的军官吃。没有几天，德奥战败，孙福又被法国人俘虏了，也没怎么样，接着给在广州住过的一个军官做豆腐吃。做了一次，法国人不满意。孙福想起南方是用石膏点豆腐，就换石膏做卤，法国人说这才是中国豆腐呀。

孙福的曾孙后来怨祖爷爷，为什么不在外国留下来，要不然现在一家子不都是法国人了？孙福说，幸亏我回来了，要不然你小兔崽子还不是个杂种？孙福想说我是舍不得你那豆腐祖奶奶啊。

孙福当年回来的时候，正是五四运动，孙福不懂，还是做豆腐。后来中学里的共青团听说孙福是经过五四的老人，于是来请孙爷爷讲五四革命传统，孙福讲来讲去，讲的是在法国做豆腐。

孙福长寿，活到改革开放，只是一吃豆腐就摇头点头，说机器做的豆腐不行，孙媳妇说机器还是由日本引进的哪！孙福用没牙的嘴说，奶是只有人手才做得出。没有人听懂老头子在说什么，家里人是很久听不懂老头子有时候在说什么了。

家里人最后一次听懂孙福说的话是，给我弄口豆腐渣。

扫　盲

齐主任不是不识字,而是识过的字差不多忘了。

五十年代头几年,兴过扫盲运动。齐主任那时候年轻,街坊都是招呼齐大嫂,也就二十多岁吧,头上别着个束发的小角梳子,听着课,拿下来给别人看。教认字的干部也年轻,也是二十多岁吧,正正经经提醒说,新社会给你们学文化的机会,你们就认真点儿,一天只识这几个字,也要用心啦。

齐家的媳妇是胡同里的俏人,场面上输不得,结过婚的人,嘴里什么都敢,就把每天的日课操练出来。干部静静听了,在小黑板上写下几个字,说,教毛主席万岁你不用心,这几个字你常常用,认真记下吧。来,跟着我念:剥衣—屄,基衣—鸡,剥阿—巴。

认字的笑话传开了,齐家媳妇回家叫男人收拾了一顿。齐家媳妇倒不记恨教书的干部,私下很敬服,又喜欢他安安静静有本事,打算好好学文化,不料运动一个接着一个就来了,从镇压反革命,一路就到了大跃进,大炼钢铁,打麻雀,药

191

老鼠,公共食堂大锅饭,接着又撵进城的叫花子。齐家媳妇一路赶着要强,慢慢在街道居民委员会负起责任来,成了齐主任。

齐主任每月要收扫街费,领着粮店的人发粮票,发油票,发点心票,发布票。夏天发熏蚊子的药,冬天到各家登记买煤买劈柴,流行肝炎通知各家各户买陈嵩蒿熬汤药喝,一天下来,忙忙叨叨,还有家里的三餐四季衣服。一年一年的,齐家媳妇老了,街坊打架,到居委会,进门就喊,老齐呀,你给评评理儿!

多少年了,没有闲工夫静下来再识字。文件精神社论指示,年年有,月月有,天天有,虱子多了不咬,反正叫识字的人念就是了。街道里识字的人出身成分不好,老老实实地念。老齐觉得最像个干部的时候,就是别人念字给她一个人听。

文化大革命的时候,赶上老齐的更年期,阶级斗争的弦绷得紧紧的。人心真是隔肚皮,以为是好好的人,给押走了,原来是坏人,暗藏的,新生的。社论早就说了,千百万个人头落地。

齐主任什么都照指示办,就是不敢逼街道上的孩子们迁户口上山下乡。齐主任自己也有孩子。

齐主任觉得一九七六年真是像崩漏完了就是更年期:亏空,主席都死了,不适应,人敢到天安门广场去闹事。当然得捕人,结果又平反。

这之后的文件精神社论指示,不大能掌握了。以前瞅着不像好人的好人不像坏人的坏人再也掌握不住了。齐主任不想干主任的时候,才发现,不干主任,干什么呢？孩子们都成家立业了。

齐主任于是很烦。街坊孙老太太来报告,十一号南屋老李家的三儿媳妇勾着个男的,今天厂休,关着门在屋里搞腐化。齐主任腾腾腾就去了派出所。

值班的是个年轻的,年轻就年轻吧,齐主任告诉了。

年轻的说,您这么大岁数儿了,想吃什么吃点儿,该喝什么喝点儿。搞腐化,您听见喘了？您是事主儿吗？不是,这不结了！事主儿都不来告,碍着您什么事儿了？告诉您,现在要讲法制了。再说了,我坐在这儿,是这么多钱,我跟了您去,还是这么多钱,您说,我跟不跟您去？

齐主任,老齐,突然想起了年轻时候扫盲干部请她念的那些个字。老齐知道,好日子久远了,要不然真是可以教教这个小警察认认字,泄泄火。

结　　婚

　　老林，男，福建人，单名"企"。最初，老林介绍自己姓名的时候，大家猜不出"林"后面是个什么字，《新华字典》一万一千七百字里，没有这个"哥"和"医"拼在一起的字，"基"？

　　老林坐下来，拿着笔，先在废纸的边上试试，然后在干净纸上确定位置，有起有收地写了一个"企"字，抬头说，嗯？怎么会是"基"嘛！

　　谁也没有料到这么严肃，都松了一口气，说，哦，企。

　　老林是右派，一九七九年才平反，从劳改农场放出来。因为之前是学文的，于是分配到单位里来做文字工作。

　　单位是区里很有名的单位，简称是，大家都习惯用简称，简称是废品站。全称废品公司收购站，不常发音，仅供参考、书写和印刷。例如，大门口的招牌，上级发下来的文件抬头，一律宋体。

　　到废品站工作，第一件事，是职业教育。严格区分废品和垃圾的不同，确立废品的地位，不要一个国家工作人员，自己看不起自己。废品是丧失其原始使用功能，但其某些部分,一般地说,仍有其可利用的价值,与垃圾有本质的不同。

老林问,既然手册里规定垃圾是完全丧失利用价值,为什么还有捡垃圾的呢?大家的顶,经这五雷一轰,都说,是呀,为什么还有捡垃圾的呢?这些日子,中央不是宣传实践是检验真理的唯一标准吗?检验检验,废品研究所的说法,就不一定对。

老孙不识字,因为是党员,所以主持各种学习。老孙老实巴交的,总是刚过钟点,就宣布散会,哪怕重要社论只差一句就念完了。老孙说,大刘,你参加工作十几年了,你给老林具体说说。

大刘把烟叼在嘴角上,谁都不看,嘶嘶地说,我俞他个废品的妈!我说老林哪,要不你怎么成了右派呢,看把你独立思考的。上大学,学什么?学独立思考?

老林说,不是呀,我的专业是音韵。

大刘是粗人,俞字当头,什么都骂,俞姥姥,俞姥爷,俞舅舅,俞大小姨子,大小舅子。不但俞母系,还俞父系,俞奶奶,俞爷爷,俞爹,俞叔,俞姑,兄弟姐妹,都俞,碰上什么俞什么。比如,废铜烂铁论斤收买,称完了,大刘喘着气,说,我俞它个秤砣的。

老林说,大刘俞得这么普遍,有深刻的道理。俞母系,是母系社会血统的确认与反确认,俞父系,也是同样的道理。君臣父子,讲的是政治和血统中的次序,大刘说我俞你妈,就是向对方严厉确定双方在血缘上的次序,我是你爸爸嘛。假如在实际中双方的次序不是这样,那就是骂。公司废品科里只有一个科长,你说我是科长,就好像是骂人,因为实际上不是嘛。另外,大刘肏人,主要是表达情绪时,发音的需要,比如重音啦,节奏啦,并不表示实际的动作。

大家认为老林分析得对,都说,怪不得大伙儿累了,闷了,就喊大刘,大刘哇,来,肏一段儿听听。

大刘还打人。打老婆,打孩子。孩子大了,打不动了。孩子跟当爹的说,杂志上有文章写了,情绪不好,跟性生活欠和谐有关。大刘不承认,却认为老林头脑古怪,肯定是文章上写的道理。

老林有五十了,还没结婚。谁跟他结呢?一个右派。

大刘为人热肠子,发动大家找合适的人。马上还就找着了,就在废品系统。有个女的,也五十了,也是右派平反,也分配到废品公司,因为划成右派前是党员,所以恢复了党籍,在公司里搞统计工作。最重要的是,愿意和老林谈谈。大刘很高兴,因为是他联系的。大刘还从公司打听来老林划成右派的原因:老林说毛主席他老人家的诗有不合音韵的地方。

老林也很高兴,愿意谈谈。大家都很高兴,瞧着俩老单身下班后约了出去,都愿意这事就成了,又议论女的过了四十五,生育怕是不行了。也好,有个伴儿,有个照应。大刘的话儿:性生活嘛,我肏它个不和谐的妈。

两个人谈了没几天,就申请结婚了。大家帮着操持,买床单子,被里被面子,买枕头买褥子,买暖水瓶买茶缸子。公司发了床票椅子票大衣柜票,大家帮着去店里排队,挑,帮着用运废品的车拉回来。房子是借的,大家帮着打扫,帮着布置。

都弄齐了,老林结婚了。大家吃了喜酒,松了一口气,好像自家说不上媳妇的儿子终于成了家。

　　不到一个星期,老林申请离婚了。老林说,两个人睡觉,鞋子,枕头,摆法各不一样,别扭。独身几十年了,又都不愿意改,何必呢?商量了一下,就算了吧,做个分开住的朋友吧。

　　大刘愣了,之后,盦了一段儿,说,没瞅见过这么认真的,要不怎么他们成了右派呢! 俩废品。

洁　癖

老白个儿不高,也说不上矮。圆乎脸儿,额头倒是方的。耳朵有肉。看人的时候,眼睛不大,也不小,正好。嘴干净得像从来没有吃过饭。

老白是很温和的一个人,和老白接触不用久,就能知道,老白有洁癖。

老白上大学的时候,一间宿舍住八个学生。七个学生都不讲究,手巾不拧干,滴一地水。脸盆像图表,高高低低结着灰圈儿。碗筷永远是打饭的时候才洗。十四只袜子,七种味儿。

老白没法子,跟学校说了,走读。四年,风里来雨里去。毕业的时候,同学给老白的赠言是:出污泥而不染。老白说,我是避着才没染。同学说,是呀,所以才劝你呀。

老白后来当然很难。

单位里有同事习惯脱了鞋把脚缩在椅子上办公,思考的时候,慢慢用手指摩挲脚趾,老白就很紧张,因为文件是要传阅的。

发薪水了,会计科给了一小沓儿人民币,五张十元的,一张五元的,一张一元的。老白说,请给换一下。出纳员说,换?换什么?十块五块一块,就这三种!老白说,您看这钱又软又黏,怎么拿着用啊?出纳员说,爱要不要,不要拉倒。

最难熬是上厕所。只是用过的纸积成山这一项,就叫老白心惊肉跳。味儿呛得人流眼泪,老白很奇怪怎么别人还能蹲着聊天儿,说到高兴处,还能抽着气儿笑。

老白谈过恋爱。两个人到郊外僻静地方儿找着块长石头,老白铺了大手绢儿,俩人坐下了。谈得投机,拉手,拥抱,接吻,女的把舌尖儿顶进来,老白一下子就醒了。

大家都说,老白是有病,洁癖。癖,就是改不了的病。

谁也没想到,无产阶级文化大革命把老白的洁癖治好了。不但老白,单位里好多人的病都好了。都说,光想着可别死了,活过来一瞧,吓,病倒都好了。老白变得心很宽,不再计较干净不干净,彻底的温和了,加上有了点儿岁数,显得挺福态。

形势也瞧着要变了,隔一阵就讲落实知识分子政策。机关党委分管人事的书记宣布要家访,了解知识分子的问题。

书记敲了老白的门,进去,很小的一间,白粉墙,白漆窗框,白桌白柜白椅子,白床白被白枕头,高低不平的地都是白的,工具书用白纸包了,只有墨水儿是蓝的。

书记啊了一声,说,听说你这个家不请人家来,二十多年,我是第一个能进来的吧?哈哈,党还是关心你们知识分子的。

老白笑笑,让书记坐了唯一的椅子,自己坐在床边儿,看着书记,好像不认识。

书记从国内讲到国际,又从国际讲到国内,说得高兴,就把手指头伸到鼻孔儿里去挖。挖出来了,就很慢地在手指上揉,话题已经转到当前的四化建设,需要知识分子。知识分子已经定为工人阶级的一部分了,是领导阶级了嘛,所以要体会国家的难处。

书记忽然停下来。

书记发现老白盯着自己的手,明白了,想借手势抹到椅子上,老白紧紧盯着。想擦到鞋底,白白的地叫人发怵。虚举着一只手,终于,慢慢放回到自己的鼻孔儿里。

书记很严肃地说要走了,站起来,老白赶紧把门拉开。

书记站在门口,问有什么问题没有。老白说,没有。

老白听见书记大声地在走廊里擤鼻涕,用脚擦,就摇摇头,把床单轻轻扯平,擦擦椅子,坐下来看书了。

大　风

　　老吴最喜欢的一条毛主席语录是"世界上怕就怕认真二字,共产党就最讲认真"。

　　老吴想,很对。编了四十年刊物,凡经我手签发的文章,从来没有错漏,靠的就是认真。愈是名家,愈要小心。运动来了,他们也写得很急,急,就容易有失误。人没有不出错的,名家也是人嘛。

　　老吴的麻烦是,他把心里的体会在政治学习会上讲出来了。

　　学习会是每个星期都有的,每个人都要发言的。

　　老孙,几个月前是编辑,听了以后,说,你的意思是毛主席也会出错了?

　　老吴脸筋跳着,说,我一些些那个样子的意思也没有!

　　老齐,几个月前也是编辑,点了数下头,说,深挖下去的话,其实有一层恶毒之处,我们都知道,毛主席是当代最伟大的马克思列宁主义者,是中国革命的伟大领袖,把毛主席等同我们这样的人，大家可以想想，是什么性质的问题！

老齐向来说话慢，老吴很有时间镇静下来。

老齐刚说完，老吴就说，你的意思是，敬爱的毛主席他老人家不是人了？

老齐看着老吴，之后，看看老孙，看看其他人，再看着老吴。

老吴一个眼睛是惊叹号，一个眼睛是不用回答的疑问号。

大家都看着进驻杂志社的中国人民解放军宣传毛泽东思想工作队，简称军宣队的班长大李。

大李卷了一支锥形的烟，叼在嘴上，划着火柴，挤起左眼点好，把桌上的帽子甩到后脑勺，话和烟纠缠着出来。

要叫俺说？好，俺说。俺会种地，会打枪，你们哪个会？要不是个文化大革命，俺不会到这个城里，也不会拉扯着你们学习毛泽东思想。学习毛泽东思想就学习毛泽东思想，哪个叫你们仿老婆子拌嘴？寻思俺看不出来呢！骂人不带屑，杀人不用刀，说你们是臭老九，俺寻思了，不屈枉。简简单单一条儿语录儿，吓唬来吓唬去，乌龟咬王八的球，哪个咬到哪个来？要叫俺说，秃子头上走虱虫，明摆着的三个字，共产党，共产党讲究个认真。你们，都算上，哪个是共产党？

是的没有说是，不是的没有说不是，都看着大李。

之后，回去打点行李，下五七干部学校。

干校除了劳动，学习，开批判会，当然还要吃饭。吃了饭，当然还要拉屎。

干校七百人，每天下来，三个茅房的坑，当然都是满的。满了当然掏出去，好能再拉。

粪不难掏，用长把的勺舀到大桶里，把桶挑出去，倒在场上，晾干就是了。难的是防猪吃和狗吃。

猪和狗，都有背景，不是好惹的。猪是贫下中农的猪，狗呢，也是贫下中农的狗。打狗须看主人，轰猪呢，自然也须看主人。

狗改不了吃屎，批判稿上常用来形容除无产阶级以外的阶级的本性的俗语，却是一件需要认真的事。

老齐被分配去看猪和狗。老齐看稿子很快，会认很潦草的字。

于是，不是屎被猪和狗吃了，就是猪和狗叫老齐打了。批判会上，老齐的罪，最轻的是，不认真。老孙发了言，老吴也发了言，大家都发言了。

老齐连夜写了检讨。以后不断地写检讨，因为狗改不了吃屎。

粪倒在场上，晾一两天，就成了粪干。粪干需要大致捣碎，之后扬到地里去。庄稼一枝花，全靠粪当家。不让老齐看猪和狗了。老齐，老吴和老孙，都去捣粪干。

老孙捣得很认真，居然在干校的大喇叭里被表扬了一句。

老吴和老齐，决心更认真。先用石头把粪干砸裂，再砸，粪干成了小块。再砸，粪干由黑变赭。再砸，由赭变黄，变金黄，变象牙白，呈短纤维状，轻轻的，软软的，有一股子热烘烘的干草香气,像肉松。

　　起风了,突然间就很大。

　　粪都在天上。

　　老吴,老齐,老孙,猪,狗,都望着天上。他们觉得,好久没有抬头看过什么了。

散文编

思乡与蛋白酶

我们都有一个胃，即使不幸成为植物人，也还是有一个胃，否则连植物人也做不成。

玩笑说，中国文化只剩下了个"吃"。如果以为这个"吃"是为了中国人的胃，就错了。这个"吃"，是为了中国人的眼睛、鼻子和嘴巴的，所谓"色、香、味"。

嘴巴这一项里，除了"味觉"，也就是"甜、咸、酸、辣、辛、苦、膻、腥、麻、鲜"，还有一个很重要的"口感"，所谓"滑、脆、黏、软、嫩、凉、烫"。

我当然没有忘掉"臭"，臭豆腐，臭咸鱼，臭冬瓜，臭蚕豆，之所以没有写到"臭"，是我们并非为了逐其"臭"，而是为了品其"鲜"。

说到"鲜"，食遍全世界，我觉得最鲜的还是中国云南的鸡枞菌。用这种菌做汤，其实极危险，因为你会贪鲜，喝到胀死。我怀疑这种菌里含有什么物质，能完全麻痹我们脑里面下视丘中的拒食中枢，所以才会喝到胀死还想喝。

河豚也很鲜美，可是有毒，能置人死命。若到日本，不妨找间餐馆（坐下之前切记估计好付款能力），里面治河豚的厨师一定要是有执照的。我建议你第一次点的时候，点带微毒的，吃的时候极鲜，吃后身体的感觉有些麻麻的。我再建议你此时赶快做诗，可能此前你没有做过诗，而且很多著名诗人都还健在，但是，你现在可以做诗了。

中国的"鲜"字，是"鱼"和"羊"，一种是腥，一种是膻。我猜"鲜"的意义是渔猎时期定下来的，之后的农业文明，再找到怎样鲜的食物，例如鸡枞菌，都晚了，都不够"鲜"了，位置已经被鱼和羊占住了。

鱼中最鲜的，我个人觉得是广东人说的"龙利"。清蒸，蒸好后加一点葱丝姜丝，葱姜丝最好顺丝切，否则料味微重，淋清酱油少许，料理好即食，入口即化，滑、嫩、烫，耳根会嗡的一声，薄泪泅濡，不要即刻用眼睛觅知音，那样容易被人误会为含情脉脉，低头心里感激就是了。

羊肉为畜肉中最鲜。猪肉浊腻，即使是白切肉；牛肉粗重，即使是轻微生烤的牛排。羊肉乃肉中之健朗君子，吐雅言，脏话里带不上羊，可是我们动不动就说蠢猪笨牛；好襟怀，少许盐煮也好，红烧也好，煎、炒、爆、炖、涮，都能淋漓尽致。我最喜欢爆和涮，尤其是涮。

涮时选北京人称的"后脑"，也就是羊脖子上的肉，肥瘦相间，好像有沁色的羊脂玉，用筷子夹入微滚的水中（开水会致肉滞），一顿，再一涮，挂血丝，夹出蘸料，入口即化，嚼是为了肉和料混合，其实不嚼也是可以的。料要芝麻酱（花生酱

208

次之),豆腐乳(红乳烈,白乳温),虾酱(当年产),韭菜花酱(发酵至土绿),辣椒油(滚油略放浇干辣椒,辣椒入滚油的制法只辣不香),花椒水,白醋(熏醋反而焦钝),葱末,芫荽段,以个人口味加减调和,有些人会佐食腌糖蒜。京剧名优马连良先生生前到馆子吃涮羊肉是自己带调料,是些什么?怎样一个调法?不知道,只知道他将羊肉真的只是在水里一涮就好了,省去了一"顿"的动作。

涮羊肉,一般锅底放一些干咸海虾米和干香菇,我觉得清水加姜片即可。料里如果放了咸虾酱,锅底不放干咸海虾米也是可以的,否则重复;香菇如果在炭火上炙一下再入汤料,可去土腥味儿;姜是松懈肌肉纤维的,可以使羊肉更嫩。

蒙古人有一种涮法是将羊肉在白醋里涮一下,"生涮"。我试过,羊肉过醋就白了,另有一种鲜。这种涮法大概是成吉思汗的骑兵征进时的快餐吧,如果是,可称"军涮"。

中国的饮食文化里,不仅有饱的经验,亦有饿的经验。

中国在饥馑上的经验很丰富,"馑"的意思是蔬菜歉收,"饥"另有性欲的含义,此处不提。浙江不可谓不富庶,可是浙江菜里多干咸或发霉的货色,比如萧山的萝卜干、螺丝菜,杭州、莫干山、天目山一带的咸笋干,义乌的大头菜,绍兴的霉干菜,上虞的霉千张。浙江明明靠海,但有名的不是鲜鱼,奇怪却是咸鱼,比如玉环的咸带鱼,宁波的咸蟹,咸鳗鲞,咸乌鱼蛋,龙头考,咸黄泥螺。

宁波又有一种臭冬瓜,吃不惯的人是连闻都不能闻的,味若烂尸,可是爱吃的人觉得非常鲜,还有一种臭苋梗也是如此。绍兴则有臭豆。

鲁迅先生是浙江人,他怀疑浙江人祖上也许不知遭过多大的灾荒,才会传下这些干咸臭食品。我看不是由于饥馑,而是由于战乱迁徙,因为浙江并非闹灾的省份。中国历史上多战乱,乱则人民南逃,长途逃难则食品匮乏,只要能吃,臭了也得吃。要它不坏,最好的办法就是晾干腌制,随身也好携带。到了安居之地,则将一路吃惯了的干咸臭保留下来传下去,大概也有祖宗的警示,好像我们亲历过的"忆苦思甜"。广东的客家人也是历代的北方逃难者,他们的食品中也是有干咸臭的。

中国人在吃上,又可以挖空心思到残酷。

云南有一种"狗肠糯米",先将狗饿上个两三天,然后给它生糯米吃,饿狗囫囵,估计糯米到了狗的"十二指肠"(狗的这一段是否有十二个手指并起来那么长,没有量过),将狗宰杀,只取这一段肠蒸来吃。说法是食物经过胃之后,小肠开始大量分泌蛋白酶来造成食物的分化,以利吸收,此时吃这一段,"补得很"。

还是云南,有一种"烤鹅掌",将鹅吊起来,让鹅掌正好踩在一个平底锅上,之后在锅下生火。锅慢慢烫起来的时候,鹅则不停地轮流将两掌提起放下,直至烫锅将它的掌烤干,之后单取这鹅掌来吃。说法是动物会调动它自己最精华的东西到受侵害的部位,此时吃这一部位,"补得很"。

这样的吃法已经是兵法了。

相较中国人的吃,动物,再凶猛的动物,吃起来也是朴素的,表情平静。它们只是将猎物咬死,然后食其血或肉,然后,就拉倒了。它们不会煎炒烹炸熬炖涮,不会将鱼做成松鼠的样子,美其名曰"松鼠桂鱼"。你能想象狼或豹子挖空心思将人做成各种肴馔才吃吗?例如爆人腰花,炒人里脊,炖人手人腔骨,酱人肘子,卤人耳朵,涮人后脖子肉,腌腊人火腿,干货则有人鞭?

吃,对中国人来说,上升到了意识形态的地步。"吃哪儿补哪儿",吃猪脑补人脑,这个补如果是补智慧,真是让人犹豫。吃猴脑则是医"羊痫风"也就是"癫痫",以前刑场边上总有人端着个碗,等着拿犯人死后的脑浆回去给病人吃,有时病人亲自到刑场上去吃。"吃鞭补肾",如果公鹿的性激素真是由吃它的相应部位就可以变为中国男人的性激素,性这件事也真是太简单了。不过这是意识形态,是催眠,所谓"信"。海参,鱼翅,甲鱼,都是暗示可以补中国男女的性分泌物的食品,同时也就暗示性的能力的增强。我不吃这类东西,只吃木耳,植物胶质蛋白,而且木耳是润肺的,我抽烟,正好。

我在以前的《闲话闲说》里聊到过中国饮食文化的起因:

中国对吃的讲究,古代时是为祭祀,天和在天上的祖宗要闻到飘上来的味儿,才知道俗世搞了些什么名堂,是否有诚意,所以供品要做出香味,味要分得出级别与种类,所谓"味道"。远古的"燎祭",其中就包括送味道上天。《诗经》、《礼记》里这类

211

郑重描写不在少数。

前些年大陆文化热时，用的一句"魂兮归来"，在屈原的《楚辞·招魂》里，是引出无数佳肴名称与做法的开场白，屈子历数人间烹调美味，诱亡魂归来，高雅得不得了的经典，放松来读，是食谱，是菜单。

咱们现在到无论多么现代化管理的餐厅，照例要送上菜单，这是古法，只不过我们这种"神"或"祖宗"要付钞票。

商王汤时候有个厨师伊尹，因为烹调技术高，汤就让他做了宰相，烹而优则仕。那时煮饭的锅，也就是鼎，是国家最高权力的象征，闽南话现在仍称锅为鼎。

极端的例子是烹调技术可以用于做人肉，《左传》、《史记》都有记录，《礼记》则说孔子的学生子路"醢矣"，"醢"读如"海"，就是人肉酱。

转回来说这供馔最后要由人来吃，世俗之人嘴越吃越刁，终于造就一门艺术。

现在呢，则不妨将《招魂》录出：

室家遂宗　食多方些
稻粢穱麦　挈黄粱些
大苦咸酸　辛甘行些

肥牛之腱　臑若芳些

和酸若苦　陈吴羹些

胹鳖炮羔　有柘浆些

鹄酸臇凫　煎鸿鸧些

露鸡臛凫　厉而不爽些

粔籹蜜饵　有帐锽些

瑶浆蜜勺　实羽觞些

挫糟冻饮　酎清亮些

华酌既陈　有琼浆些

归来返故室　敬而无妨些

　　这样的食谱，字不必全认得全懂，但每行都有我们认得
的粮食，家畜野味，酒饮，烹调方法。如此丰盛，魂兮胡不归！

　　这个食谱，涉及了《礼记·内则》将饮食分成的饭、膳、
馐、饮四大部分。先秦将味原则为"春酸、夏苦、秋辛、冬咸"，
这个食谱以"大苦"领首，说明是夏季，更何况后面还有冰镇
的"冻饮"，也就是我们现在说的冷饮。

　　难怪古人要在青铜食器上铸饕餮纹。饕餮是警示不要
贪食，其实正暗示了所盛之物实在太好吃了。

　　说了半天都是在说嘴，该说说胃了。

　　食物在嘴里的时候，真是百般滋味，千般享受，所以我们
总是劝人"慢慢吃"，因为一咽，就什么味道也没有了，连辣椒
也只"辣两头儿"。嘴和肛门之间，是由植物神经管理的，这
当中只有凉和烫的感觉，所谓"热豆腐烧心"。

食物被咽下去后,经过食管,到了胃里。胃是个软磨,将嚼碎的食物再磨细,我们如果不是细嚼慢咽,胃的负担就大。

经过胃磨细的食物到了十二指肠,重要的时刻终于来临。我们千辛万苦得来的口中物,能不能化成我们自己,全看十二指肠分泌出什么样的蛋白酶来分解,分解了的,就吸收,分解不了吸收不了的,就"消化不良"。

消化不良,影响很大,诸如打嗝放屁还是小事,消化不良可以影响到精神不振,情绪恶劣,思路不畅,怨天尤人。自己烦倒还罢了,影响到别人,鸡犬不宁,妻离子散不敢说,起码朋友会疏远你一个时期,"少惹他,他最近有点儿精神病"。

小的时候,长辈总是告诫不要挑食,其中的道理会影响人一辈子。

人还未发育成熟的时候,蛋白酶的构成有很多可能性,随着进入小肠的食物的种类,蛋白酶的种类和结构开始逐渐形成以至固定。这也就是例如小时候没有喝过牛奶,大了以后凡喝牛奶就拉稀泻肚。我是从来都拿牛奶当泻药的。亚洲人,例如中国人,日本人,韩国人到了牛奶多的地方,例如美国,绝大多数都出现喝牛奶即泻肚的问题,这是因为亚洲人小时候牛奶喝得少或根本没有得喝,因此缺乏某种蛋白酶而造成的。

牛奶在美国简直就是凉水,便宜,新鲜,管够。望奶兴叹很久以后,我找到一个办法,将可口可乐掺入牛奶,喝了不泻。美国专门出一种供缺乏分解牛奶的蛋白酶的人喝的牛奶,其中掺了一种酶。这种牛奶不太好找,名称长得像药名,总是记不住,算了,还是喝自己调的牛奶吧。

不过,"起士"或译成"起司"的这种奶制品我倒可以吃。不少中国人不但不能吃,连闻都不能闻,食即呕吐,说它有一种腐败的恶臭。腐败,即是发酵,动物蛋白质和动物脂肪发酵,就是动物的尸体腐败发酵,臭起来真是昏天黑地,我居然甘之如饴,自己都感到不可思议。我是不吃臭豆腐的,一直没过这一关。臭豆腐是植物蛋白和植物脂肪腐败发酵,比较动物蛋白和动物脂肪的腐败发酵,差了一个等级,我居然喜欢最臭的而不喜欢次臭的,是第二个自己的不可思议。

分析起来,我从小就不吃臭豆腐,所以小肠里没有能分解它的蛋白酶。我十几岁时去内蒙古插队,开始吃奶皮子,吃出味道来,所以成年以后吃发酵得更完全的起士,没有问题。

陕西凤翔人出门到外,带一种白土,俗称"观音土",水土不服的时候食之,就舒畅了。这白土是碱性的,可见凤翔人在本乡是胃酸过多的,饮本地的碱性水,正好中和。

所以长辈"不要挑食"的告诫会影响小孩子的将来,道理就在于你要尽可能早地,尽可能多地吃各种食物,使你的蛋白酶的形成尽可能的完整,于是你走遍天下都不怕,什么都吃得,什么都能消化,也就有了幸福人生的一半了。

于是所谓思乡,我观察了,基本是由于吃了异乡食物,不好消化,于是开始闹情绪。

我注意到一些会写东西的人到外洋走了一圈,回到中国之后发表一些文字,常常就提到饮食的不适应。有的说,西餐有什么好吃？真想喝碗粥，就咸菜啊。

这看起来真是朴素，真是本色，读者也很感动。其实呢？真是挑剔。

我就是这样一种挑剔的人。有一次我从亚历桑纳州开车回洛杉矶。我的旅行经验是，路上带一袋四川榨菜，不管吃过什么洋餐，嚼过一根榨菜，味道就回来了，你说我挑剔不挑剔？

话说我沿着十号州际高速公路往西开，早上三明治，中午麦当劳，天近傍晚，路边突然闪出一块广告牌，上写中文"金龙大酒家"，我毫不犹豫就从下一个出口拐下高速公路。

我其实对世界各国的中国餐馆相当谨慎。威尼斯的一家温州人开的小馆，我进去要了个炒鸡蛋，手艺再不好，一个炒蛋总是坏不到哪里去吧？结果端上来的炒鸡蛋炒得比盐还咸。我到厨房间去请教，温州话我是不懂的，但掌勺儿表明"忘了放盐"我还是懂了。其实，是我忘了浙江人是不怕咸的，不过不怕到这个地步倒是头一次领教。

在巴黎则是要了个麻婆豆腐，可是什么婆豆腐都可以是，就不是麻婆豆腐。麻婆豆腐是家常菜呀！炝油，炸盐，煎少许猪肉末加冬菜，再煎一下郫县豆瓣，油红了之后，放豆腐下去，勾兑高汤，盖锅。待豆腐腾的涨起来，起锅，撒生花椒面，青蒜末，葱末，姜末，就上桌了，吃时拌一下，一头汗马上吃出来。

看来问题就出在家常菜上。家常菜原来最难。什么"龙凤呈样"，什么"松鼠桂鱼"，场面菜不常吃，吃也是为吃个场面,吃个气氛,吃个客气,不好吃也不必说,难得吃嘛。家常菜天天吃,好像画牛,场面菜不常吃,类似画鬼,"画鬼容易画牛难"。

好,转回来说美国西部蛮荒之地的这个"金龙大酒家"。我推门进去,站柜的一个妇人迎上来,笑容标准,英语开口,"几位?"我觉得有点不对劲,因为从她肩上望过去,座上都是牛仔的后代们,我对他们毫无成见,只是,"您这里是中国餐馆吗?"

"当然,我们这里请的是真正的波兰师傅。"

到洛杉矶的一路上我都在骂自己的挑剔。波兰师傅怎么了?波兰师傅也是师傅。我又想起来贵州小镇上的小饭馆,进去,师傅迎出来,"你炒还是我炒?"中国人谁不会自己炒两个菜?"我炒。"

所有佐料都在灶台上,拣拣菜,抓抓码,丁当五四,两菜一汤,吃得头上冒汗。师傅蹲在门口抽烟,看街上女人走路,蒜瓣儿一样的屁股扭过来又扭过去。

所以思乡这个东西,就是思饮食,思饮食的过程,思饮食的气氛。为什么会思这些?因为蛋白酶在作怪。

老华侨叶落归根,直奔想了半辈子的餐馆、路边摊,张口要的吃食让亲戚不以为然。终于是做好了,端上来了,颤巍巍伸筷子夹了,入口,"味道不如当年的啦。"其实呢,是老了,味蕾退化了。

老了的标志,就是想吃小时候吃过的东西,因为蛋白酶退化到了最初的程度。另一个就是觉得味道不如从前了,因为味蕾也退化了。七十岁以上的老人对食品的评价，儿孙们不必当真。我老了的话，会三缄吾口，日日喝粥就咸菜，能不下厨就不下厨，因为儿孙们吃我炒的蛋，可能比盐还咸。

与我的蛋白酶相反，我因为十多岁就离开北京，去的又多是语言不通的地方，所以我在文化上没有太多的"蛋白酶"的问题。在内蒙，在云南，没有人问过我"离开北京的根以后，你怎么办？你感觉如何？你会有什么新的计划？"现在倒是常常被问到"离开你的根以后，你怎么办？你感觉如何？你适应吗？"我的根？还不是这里扎一下，那里扎一下，早就是个老盲流了，或者用个更朴素的词，是个老"流氓"了。

你如果尽早地接触到不同的文化，你就不太会大惊小怪。不过我总觉得，文化可能也有它的"蛋白酶"，比如母语，制约着我这个老盲流。

一九九六年二月　加州洛杉矶

爱情与化学

这个题目换成"化学与爱情",也无所谓。不过,我们的秩序文化里,比如官场中接见时的名次序列,认为排在前面的一定高贵,或者比较重要,就好像判死刑之后,最先拉出去枪毙的总应该是首犯吧。鲁迅先生有过一个讲演,题目是《魏晋风度与药及酒的关系》,很少有人认为其中三者的关系是平等的,魏晋风度总是比较重要的吧。因此,把"爱情"放在前面,无非是容易被注意,查一下页数,翻到了,看下去,虽然看完了的感想可能是"煞风景"。

那这个容易引起注意的爱情,是什么呢? 我猜这是一个被视为当然而可能不太了解所以然的问题,不过题目已经暗示了,爱情,与化学有关系。

一定有人猜,是不是老生常谈又要讲性荷尔蒙也就是性激素了? 不少人谈到爱情的性基础时,都说到荷尔蒙。其实呢,性荷尔蒙只负责性成熟,因此会有性早熟的儿童,或者性成熟的智障者,十多年前韩少功的小说《爸爸爸》可以是一个例子。顺便说一下的是,当代中国大陆的小说里,疯子和傻子不免多了一点,连带着电影里也常搞些疯子傻子说说"真话"。中国古典小说中常常出现癫僧,说出预言或题旨,因此"癫"是有传统的。

性成熟的人不一定具爱情的能力。那么爱情的能力从哪里来呢?"感情啊",无数小说,戏剧,电影,电视连续剧都"证明"过,有点"谎言千遍成真理"的味道,而且味道好到让我们喜欢。其实呢,爱情的能力从化学来,也就是从性成熟了的人的脑中的化合物来。

不过,话要一句一句地说。先说脑。

《儿子的情人》的作者劳伦斯说过,"性来自脑中",他的话在生理学的意义上是真理,可惜他的意思并不是指生理学的脑。

我们来看脑。

人脑是由"新哺乳类脑"例如人脑,"古哺乳类脑"例如马的脑和"爬虫类脑"例如鳄鱼的脑组成的,或者说,人脑是在进化中层层叠加形成的。

古哺乳类脑和爬虫类脑都会直接造成我们的本能反应。比如,如果你的古哺乳类脑强,你就天生不怕老鼠,而如果你的爬虫类脑强,你就不怕蛇。我们常常会碰到怕蛇却不怕老鼠,或者怕老鼠而不怕蛇的人。好莱坞的电影里时不时就让无辜的老鼠或蛇纠缠一下落难英雄,这是一关,过了,我们本能上就感觉逃脱一劫,先松口气再说。

我是天生厌蛇的人,有一次去一个以蛇为宠物的新朋友家,着实难过了两个钟头,深为自己有一个弱的爬虫类脑而烦恼。顺便要提醒的是,千万不要拿本能的恐惧来开玩笑,比如用蛇吓女孩子,本能的恐惧会导致精神分裂的,后果会非常非常糟糕。

爬虫类脑位于脑的最基层,负责生命的基本功能,其中的"下视丘",有"进食中枢"和"拒食中枢",负责饿了要吃和防止撑死,也就是负责我们人类的"食"。

下视丘还有一个"性行为中枢",人类的"色"本能即来源于此。

我们来看下视丘中这个负责"色"的中枢。

这个中枢究竟是雄性化的还是雌性化的,在它发育的初期,并没有定型。怀孕的母亲会制造荷尔蒙,她腹中的胎儿,也会根据得自父母双方遗传基因染色体的组合,来决定制造何种荷尔蒙,这两方面的荷尔蒙决定胎儿生殖器的构造与发育。

同时,这些荷尔蒙进入正在发育的胎儿的脑中,影响了脑神经细胞发育和由此而构成的联系网络,决定性行为中枢的结构。脑的其他部分,相应产生"男性化脑"或"女性化脑"的基本结构。

这些"硬件"定型之后,就很难改变了。但是在定型之前,也就是脑还在发育的时候,却是有可能出些"差池"的,当这些"差池"也定型下来的时候,就会出现例如同性恋、双性恋的类型。当代脑科学证实了同性恋原因于脑的构造。我们常说"命"，这就是生物学意义上的命，先天性的。

从历史记载分析，中国汉朝刘姓皇帝的同性恋比率相当高，可惜刘家的脑我们得不到了。

好，假设脑发育定型了。

脑神经生理学家证实，古哺乳类脑中的边缘系统是"情感中枢"。因为这个中枢的存在，哺乳类比爬虫类"有情"，例如我们常说的"舐犊情深"，哪怕它虎豹豺狼，只要是哺乳类，都是这样。爬虫类则是"冷酷无情"，这怪不得它们，它们的脑里没有情感中枢。

人类制造的童话，就是在充分利用情感中枢的功能，小孩子听了童话觉得很"真实"，大人听到了也眼睛湿湿的。童话里的小红帽儿呢？由于情感中枢的本能趋使，结果让大灰狼吃了自己的奶奶，又全靠比情感中枢多了一点聪和明，免于自己被吃。

常说的"亲兄弟明算账"，无非是怕自己落到童话的境界。话说回来，情感中枢对人类很重要，因为它使"亲情"、"友情"乃至"爱情"成为可能，不过说到现在，爱情还只是"硬件"的可能罢了。

在这个边缘系统最前端的脑隔区，是"快感中枢"。经典的性高潮，是生殖器神经末梢将所受的刺激，经由脊髓传到脑隔区，积累到一个程度，脑隔区的神经细胞就开始放电，于是人才会有性高潮体验。不过，脑神经生理学家用微电流刺激脑隔区，或者将剂量精确的乙酰胆碱直接输入到脑隔区，脑隔区的神经细胞也能放电,同样能使人产生性高潮体验。这证明了性高潮是脑的事,可以与我们的生殖器神经末梢无关。

我相信不少人听说原来如此,会觉得真是煞风景,白忙了。当初这个脑神经生理关系发现之后,确实有人担心人类会成为电极的性奴隶,你我不过是些男女电池,现在看来还不至于,不过毒品对脑隔区也会产生同样的影响,倒是我们要注意的。

临床报告说,有些脊髓受伤的男性,阴茎仍然可以勃起乃至射精,却没有性高潮体验;另一种则是生殖器麻木不仁,却能由刺激第二性感区,甚至手臂胸腹而产生性高潮体验。我以前在北京朝阳门内有个忘年交,一个当年宫里的粗使太监告诉过我,"咱们也能有那么回事儿",我知道他没吹牛,因为太监制度只严格在下身,断绝精子的产生与输出,同时也断绝男性激素的产生,但是,上面的脑隔区的"快感中枢"却还在,也算百密一疏吧。

不过,边缘系统中,还有一个"痛苦中枢",难为它恰好与"快感中枢"为邻,于是不管快感中枢还是痛苦中枢放电,常常"城门失火,殃及池鱼",使另一个中枢受到影响。所以俗说的"打是疼,骂是爱",或者文说的性虐狂或受虐狂(俗称"贱"),即来源于两个中枢的邻里关系。

"喜极而泣","乐极生悲","极",就是一个中枢神经细胞放电过量,影响到另一个中枢的神经产生反应。女性常会在性高潮之中或之后哭泣,雄猿猴在愤怒的时候,阴茎会勃起,这是两个中枢共同反应,而不是哲学上说的"物极必反"。我认识的一个小提琴高手,凡拉忧郁的曲子,裤裆里就会硬起来,为此他很困扰,我劝他不妨在节目单里印上痛苦中枢与快感中枢的脑神经生理结构常识。

我初次见马友友演奏大提琴时的面部表情,很被他毫无顾忌的类似性行为时的面部表情分神。演奏家,尤其在演奏浪漫派音乐时,都控制不了他们自己的面部表情。

能直接作用于边缘系统也就是情感中枢的艺术是音乐。音乐由音程、旋律、和声、调性、节奏直接造成"频律"(不是旋律),假如这个频律引起痛苦中枢或快感中枢的强烈共振(不是共鸣)而导致放电,人就被"感动",悲伤,兴奋,沮丧,快活。同时,脑中的很多记忆区被激活,于是我们常常听到或看到这样的倾诉,"它使我想起了什么什么……"每个人的经验记忆有不同,于是这个"频律",也就是"作品",就被赋予多种意义了。名噪一时的"阅读理论",过于将"文本"自我独立,所以对音乐文本的解释一直施展不利,因为音乐是造成频律直接影响中枢神经的反应,理性"来不及"掺入。

有一种使母牛多产奶的方法是放音乐给它听,道理和人的生理反应机制差不多,幸亏牛不会成为音响发烧友,否则养牛也真是会破产的。

景象和视觉艺术则是通过视神经刺激情感中枢,听觉和视觉联合起来同时刺激情感中枢的时候,我们难免会呼天抢地。不过刺激久了也会麻木,仰拍青松,号角嘹亮,落日余晖,琴音抖颤,成了令人厌烦的文艺腔,只好点烟沏茶上厕所。

音乐可以不经由性器而产生中枢神经放电导致快感，因为不经由性器，所以道德判断为"高尚"，所以我们可以一遍一遍地听而无"耳淫"的压力，所以我们说我们得到"净化"。孔子说听韶乐后不知肉味，你看，连"进食中枢"都被抑制了，非常净化，不过孔子说的是实话。

说起来，艺术无非是千方百计产生一种频律，在展示过程中加强这个频律，听者、读者用感官得到这个频律，而使自己的情感中枢放电。我们都知道军队通过桥梁时不可以齐步走，因为所产生的谐振会逐渐增强，以至桥梁垮掉。巴赫的音乐就有军队齐步走过桥梁的潜在危险。审美，美学，其实可以解释得很朴素或直接，再或者说，解释得很煞风景。

常说的"人之异于禽兽几何"，笑话讲成"人是因为会解几何题，才与畜生不一样"。不过分子生物学告诉我们，人与狒狒的 DNA 百分之九十五点四是相同的，与最近的亲戚矮黑猩猩、黑猩猩、大猩猩的 DNA 百分之九十九是相同的，也就是说，"人之异于禽兽不过百分之一"，很具体，很险，很庆幸，是吧？

不过在脑的构成里，人是因为新哺乳类脑中的前额叶区而异于禽兽的。这个前额叶区，主司压抑。前额叶区如果被破坏，人会丧失自制力，变得无计划性，时不时就将爬虫类脑的本能直接表达出来，令前额叶区没有被破坏的人很尴尬，前者则毫不在意。

说到现在，我们可以知道，爬虫类脑，相当于精神分析里所说的"原我"和"原型"或"潜意识"和"集体潜意识";新哺乳类脑里的前额叶区,相当于"超我";"自我"在哪里?不知道。美国国家精神卫生署(不是精神文明署,因为缩写为NIMH)脑进化与行为研究室的主任麦克连说,"躺在精神科沙发上的,除了病人,还有一匹马,一条鳄鱼",这比弗洛伊德的说法具体明确有用得多了。

压抑是文明的产物。不过这么说也不全对,因为比如狼的压抑攻击的机制非常强,它们的遗传基因中如果没有压抑机制的组合,狼这个物种早就自己把自己消灭了。这正说明人之所以为人,是因为能够逐步在前额叶区这个"硬件"里创造"压抑软件"的指令,控制爬虫类脑,从蒙昧,野蛮以至现在,人类将这个"逐步"划分为不同阶段的文明,文明当然还包括人类创造的其他。不同地区、民族的"压抑软件"的程序及其他的不同,是为"文化"。

古希腊文化里,非理性的戴奥尼索斯也就是酒神精神,主司本能放纵,理性的阿波罗也就是太阳神精神,主司抑制,两者形成平衡。中国的孔子说"吾未见有好德如好色者",一针见血,挑明了本能与压抑本能的关系。

不幸文化不能由生物遗传延续,只能通过学习。孔子说"学而优则仕",学什么?学礼和技能,也就是当时的权力者维持当时的社会结构的"软件",学好了,压抑好了,就可以"联机"了,"则仕"。学不好,只有"当机"。一直到现在,全世界教育的本质还是这样,毕业证书是给社会组织看的。受过高等教育的人,脸上或深或浅都是盖着"高等压抑合格"或

"高等伪装成功"的印痕,换取高等的社会待遇。

前面说过的快感中枢与痛苦中枢的邻里关系,还会产生"享受痛苦"的现象。古老文化地区的诗歌,小说,戏剧,电影,常常以悲剧结尾,以苦为美。我去台北随朋友到 KTV,里面的歌几乎首首悲音,闽南语我不懂,看屏幕上打出的字幕,总是离愁别绪,爱而不得,爱之苦痛等等,但这确实是娱乐,消费不低的娱乐。

一般所谓的"深刻"、"悲壮"、"深沉"等等,从脑神经的结构来看,是由痛苦中枢放电而影响到快感中枢,于是由苦感与快感共同完成满足感。如果痛苦不能导致快感,就只有"悲惨"而无"悲壮"。这就像巧克力,又苦又甜,它产生的满足感强过单纯的糖,可是我们并不认为巧克力比糖"深刻"。

所以若说"'深刻''悲壮'里有快感",我相信不少人一定会有被亵渎的感觉。这说明文化软件里的不少指令是生理影响心理,心理影响文化,文化的软件形成之后,通过学习再返回来影响心理,可是却很难再进一步明白这一切源于生理。文化形成之后,是集体的形态,有种"公理"也就是不需证明的样子,于是文化也是暴力,它会镇压质疑者。

"沉雄"、"冷峻"、"壮阔"、"亢激"、"战栗"、"苍凉",你读懂这些词并能陶醉其中时,若还能意识到情感上的优越,那你开始对快感有"深刻"的感觉了,可是,虚伪也会由此产生,矫情的例子比比皆是,历历在目。

中国文化里的"享受痛苦",一直有很高的地位,单纯的快乐总是被警惕的。"苦其心志,饿其体肤,天将降大任于斯",虽然苦痛但心感优越,警惕"玩物丧志",责备"浑身没有二两重"。我们可以看出一个很清晰的压抑的文化软件程序,它甚至可以达到非常精致的平衡,物我两忘,但它也可以将一个活泼的孩子搞得少年老成。

不过前额叶区是我们居然得以有社会组织生活的脑基础。我们可要小心照顾它,过与不足,都伤害到人类本身。人类如果有进步,前额叶区的"压抑软件"的转换要很谨慎,这个谨慎,可以叫做"改良"。

无产阶级文化大革命是一次软件设计,它输入前额叶区的是"千条万绪就是一句话:造反有理"和"革命不是请客吃饭,不是做文章,不是绘画绣花,不能那样雅致,那样文质彬彬"。将新哺乳类脑的情感中枢功能划限于"阶级感情",释放爬虫类脑,"革命是暴动,是一个阶级推翻一个阶级的暴烈的行动","要武嘛"。当时的众多社论,北京清华附中"红卫兵"的"三论造反有理",都是要启动释放爬虫类脑功能的软件程序。

"三论造反有理"同时是一组由刺激痛苦中枢转而达到快感的范文,好莱坞的英雄片模式也是这样,好人一定要先受冤枉,受暴力之难,刺激观众的痛苦中枢,然后好人以暴力克服磨难,由快感中枢完成高潮,影片适时结束。

由于前额叶区的压抑作用,人类还产生了偷窥来疏解心理和生理上的压抑。爬虫类和古哺乳类不偷窥,它们倒是直面"人"生的。艺术提供了公共偷窥,视觉艺术则是最直接的偷窥,偷窥包装过的或不包装的暴力与性。

扯得真是远了,爱情还在等待,不过虽然慢了一点儿,但是前面的啰嗦会使我们免去很多麻烦。

人类的"杜莱特氏症"历史悠久,生动的病历好看过小说。这种症状是因为病人脑中的"基底核"不正常造成的。基底核负责制造"邻苯二酚乙胺",即"多巴胺",多巴胺过多,人就会猛烈抽搐或者性猖狂。多巴胺过少,结果之一为"帕金森氏症",治疗的方法是使用"左多巴",注意量要精确,否则老绅士老淑女会变成色情狂的。

你觉得可以猜到爱情是什么了吧?且慢,爱情不仅仅是多巴胺。

脑神经生理学家发现,人脑中的三种化学物质,多巴胺(dopamine),去甲肾上腺素(norepinephrine)和 phenylethyl-amine(最后这种化学物我做不出准确译名,总之是苯和胺的化合物)。当脑"浸"于这些化学物质时,人就会堕入情网,所谓"一见钟情",所谓"爱是盲目的",所谓"烈火干柴"等等,总之是进入一种迷狂状态。诗歌,故事,小说,戏剧,电影,对此无不讴歌之描写之得意忘形,所谓"永恒的题材"。

今年《收获》第四期上有叶兆言的小说《一九三七年的爱情》,我读的时候常常要猜男主人公丁问渔脑里的基底核的情况,有时想,觉得可以戏仿"字典小说"写成一部"病历小说"。从症状上看,丁问渔的基底核有些问题,多巴胺浓度稍稍高了一点,但他的前额叶区里的文化抑制软件里,有一些他所在地区的文化软件里没有的"骑士精神",所以他还不至于成为真正的性猖狂。"骑士精神"是欧洲文化里"享受痛苦"、性自虐的表现之一，塞万提斯笔下的唐吉河德的悲剧是欧洲文化中时间差的悲剧，桑丘用西班牙的世俗智慧保护了主人，叶兆言笔下的丁问渔的悲剧则不但是时间差而且是文化空间差的悲剧，南京车夫和尚显然不是桑丘，连自身都难保。丁问渔的悲剧有中国百年来一些症结的意味，却难得丁问渔不投机。叶兆言要处理的真是很复杂，可惜丁问渔死得简单了，从悲剧来讲，他死得有点不"必然"。不过我这么讲实在是一种监工式的站着说话不腰疼，何况我还不配监工。

上面提到的脑中的三种化学物质，生物学上的意义是使性成熟的男性女性产生迷狂，目的是交配并产生带有自己遗传基因的新载体，也就是子女后代。男女交合后，双方的三种化学物质并不消失，而是持续两到三年，这时若女方怀孕，迷狂则会表现出"亲子"、"无私的母爱"，俗说"护犊子"、"孩子是自己的好"。我如果说"母性"无所谓伟大不伟大，只是一种化学物质造成的迷狂，一定会得罪天下父母心，但脑生理学认为，这正是人为了维护带有自己基因的新生儿达到初步独立程度的不顾一切，这个初步，包括识别食物，独立行走，基本语言表达，也就是脑的初步成熟。爬虫类和古哺乳类的后代的脑是在卵和胎的时期就必须成熟。它们一降生，已经会识别食物和行走。爬虫类只护卵，小爬虫一破壳，就各自为政；古哺乳类则短期护犊，之后将小兽驱离，就像我们从前在日本艺术科教片《狐狸的故事》里看到的。

人脑中的上述三种化学物质"消失"后，脑生理学家还没有找出我们不能保持它们的原因,你们大概要关心迷狂之爱是不是也要消失了? 当然,虽然很残酷,"老婆(也可以换成老公)是别人的好"。生物遗传学家解释说,遗传基因的这种安排,是为了将"迷狂"的一对分开,因为从偶然率上看,交配者的基因不一定是最佳的,只有另外组合到一定的数量,才会产生最佳的基因组合,这也是所谓的"天地不仁"吧。

基因才是我们的根本命运。当人类社会出现需要继承的权力和财富时,人类开始向基因的"尽可能多组合"的机制挑战,造成婚姻制度,逐渐进化到对偶血缘婚姻,以便精确确认有财富和权力继承权的基因组合成品,并以法律保护之。这就是先秦儒家的"道"的来源,去符合它,就是"德",否则就是"非德",我们现在则表达为"道德"或"不道德"。古代帝王则没有什么道德不道德,干脆造成太监,以确保皇宫内只有一种男性基因在游荡。

我们的历代文化没有指责"食"的,至多是说"朱门酒肉臭,路有冻死骨",这是不公平,而不是"食"本身有何不妥。不过酒有例外,因为酒类似药,可以麻痹主司压抑的前额叶区。酒是殷的亡国原因之一,我们很难想象现在的河南商丘地区,当年满朝醉鬼,《礼记》上形容殷是"荡而不静,胜而无耻",情况严重到周灭殷之后明令禁酒。

麻烦的一直是"色",因为色本来是求生殖的事,但基因所安排的生理化学周期并没有料到人类会有一个因财产而来的理性的婚姻制度,它只考虑"非理性"的基因组合的优化。人类发明的对偶婚姻制度,还不到两万年吧,且不说废止了还不到一百年的中国的妻妾制,这个制度还不可能影响人类基因的构成,既然改变不了,人类就只有往前额叶区输入不断严密化的文化软件来压抑基因的安排,于是矛盾大矣,悲剧喜剧悲喜剧多矣。

说实在的,你我不觉得"与天斗,其乐无穷,与地斗,其乐无穷",终有觉悟到人非世界的中心,也就是提出环保的一天,而"与人斗,其乐无穷""八亿人,不斗行吗"同样荒诞,但是与基因斗,是不是有点悲壮呢?

有分教,海誓山盟,刀光剑影,红杏出墙,猫儿偷腥,醋海波涛,白头偕老,杜十娘怒沉百宝箱,包龙图义铡陈世美,罗密欧与朱丽叶,唐璜与唐吉诃德,乔太守乱点鸳鸯谱,汪大尹火烧红莲寺,卡门善别恋,简爱变复杂,地狱魔鬼贞操带,贞节牌坊守宫砂,十八年寒窑苦守,第三者第六感觉,俱往矣俱往矣又继往开来。

清朝的采蘅子在《虫鸣漫录》里记了一件事,说河南有个大户人家的仆人辞职不干了,别人问起原因,他说是主人家有件差事做不来。原来每天晚上都有一个老妇领他进内室,床上帐子遮蔽,有女人的下体伸出帐外,老妇要他与之交合,事后给不少钱。他因为始终看不到女人的颜面,终于支持不了,才辞职不做了。

事情似乎不堪,却有一个文化人类学所说的"生食"与"熟食"的问题。这个仆人是"熟食"的,不是"关了灯都一样",他不打"生食"的工,钱多也不打。

人被迫创造了文化,结果人又被文化异化,说得难听点,人若不被文化异化,就不是人了。爱情也是如此。古往今来的爱情叙说中,"美丽"、"漂亮"几乎是必提的迷狂主旋律,似乎属于本能的判断,其实,"美丽"等等是半本能半文化的判断。美丽漂亮之类,常常由文化价值判断的变化而变化。"焦大绝不会爱林妹妹",话说得太绝对了,农村包围城市之后,文化大革命之中,焦大爱林妹妹或者林妹妹爱焦大,见得还少吗?

文化是积累的,所以是复杂的,爱情被文化异化,也因此是复杂的。相较之下,初恋,因为前额叶区里压抑软件还不够,于是阳光灿烂;暗恋,是将本能欲望藏在压抑软件背后,也还可以保持"纯度"。追星族是初恋暗恋混在一起,迷狂得不得了,青春就是这样,像小兽一样疯疯癫癫的,祝他们和她们青春快乐。

这两年风靡过的美国小说《廊桥遗梦》,是一本严格按照脑生理常识和文化抑制机制制作的小说。首先是迷狂,女主角的血统定为拉丁,这个血统几乎是西方文化中迷狂的符号(电影改编中女主角用斯特里普,效果弱了);迷狂的环境选在美国中部(直到现在美国中部还是以保守著称,总统选举的初选一直就在小说里的爱荷华州,看看美国最基础的价值观大概会支持哪位竞选者),这里有占主流的婚姻家庭传统价值。小说的构造是压抑机制成功,造成巨大的痛苦。你还记得前面介绍过的脑袋里的那个邻里关系吗?于是结尾造成享受痛苦。不要轻视商业小说,它们努力要完成的正是"典型环境里的典型性格"(俄文以前错将"性格"译成"人物",中文也就跟着错了),再运用科普常识和想象力,成品绝不伪劣假冒,当然会将我国的中年知识分子收拾得服服帖帖。

说起文化的复杂,王安忆最近的小说《长恨歌》里透露出上海的文化软件中有一个指令是"笑贫不笑娼"。姿色是一种资本,投资得好,利润很大的,而贫,毫无疑义是没有资本。其实古来即如此,不过上海开埠早,一般的中国人又多是移民,前额叶区里的旧压抑软件的不少指令容易改变,于是近代商业资本意识更纯粹一些,于是上海也是中国冒险家的乐园。何需下海?当年多少文化人就是拥到海里以文化做投资,张爱玲一句"出名要早"点出投资效益。王琦瑶初恋之后,晓得权力是男人的这个文化指令,于是性投资于李主任,不久即红颜薄命,之后的四十多年,难能保住了李主任留下的金子,可红颜到老还是薄命。

人脑中的边缘系统提示我们,如果爱情消失了,我们还会有亲情和友情,只要有足够的智慧,不愁"白头偕老"。

生物学家的非洲动物观察报告说,群居的黑猩猩中,有时候会有一只雄黑猩猩叱退群雄,带着一只自己迷恋上的雌黑猩猩,隐没到丛林深处讨生活。

一九九六年十月　上海青浦

艺术与催眠

不知道动物是不是,反正人类是很容易被催眠的。我猜动物不被催眠,它们必须清醒准确,否则生存就有问题了。腿上睡了一只猫,你抚摸它,它"幸福"地闭上眼,一会儿就打起呼噜来,好像被主人催眠了。可是一旦有什么风吹草动,它立刻就反应,从你的腿上一跃而下,显出猫科的英雄本色,假虎假豹一番,而主人这时却在心里埋怨自己的宠物"真是养不熟的"。狗也是这样,不过狗的名声比猫好,就是它"忠","养得熟",养得再熟,如果它对风吹草动毫无反应,人也会怨它。我写过一篇小说,说有一天人成了动物的宠物,结果比人是主人有意思得多。

前两三年,台湾兴过一阵"前世"热。起因是一个美国人,魏斯(Brian L. Weiss),耶鲁大学的医学博士,迈阿密西奈山医学中心精神科主任,他写了一本书(Many Lives, Many Masters),声称通过他的催眠,被催眠者可以真的看到他或她的前世是什么人。台湾一个出版社将魏斯的这本书翻译成中文,名《前世今生——生命轮回的前世疗法》,造成轰动,两年就卖了超过四十万本,而《前世今生》的原文版在美国六年才卖到四十万本。

我在台北打开电视的时候,正好让我看到台北的"前世今生催眠秀"。"秀"是 show,节目的意思,被催眠的人中,不少是各类明星。现场很热烈。

严格说来,这是那种既不容易证为真,也不容易证为伪的问题。世界范围里历来有过不少轰动一时的"前世"案例,比如一九五六年风靡美国的畅销书《寻觅布莱德伊·莫非》(The Search for Bridey Merphy),至今还可以在旧书店碰到这本书,说是催眠师伯恩施坦因将露丝·席梦思深度催眠,结果这位家庭妇女用爱尔兰口音的英语讲出她的前世:一七九八年十二月二十日生于爱尔兰的寇克镇,名字叫布莱德伊·莫非。席梦思讲的前世都很有细节,而且前世的死期也很具体,享年六十六岁。

当时连载此书部分内容的"丹佛邮报"在轰动的情况下,派记者巴克尔去爱尔兰寻证"布莱德伊·莫非",结果是有符合的有不符合的,比如席梦思提到的两个杂货商的名字和一种两便士的硬币就是符合的,而她提到她前世的丈夫执教的皇后大学,当时是学院。

事情愈发轰动,质疑者也不少,"丹佛邮报"的对手"芝加哥美国人报"就是怀疑者,于是也发起调查。不过"芝加哥美国人报"采取的是去找"露丝·席梦思",调查的结果是露丝就住在芝加哥,有个从爱尔兰移民来的婶子,爱叨唠爱尔兰的种种事情;露丝家的对面也住着一个爱尔兰女人,婚前正是姓莫非,结论不免是露丝在深度催眠下讲出的前世,是她日常所听的再综合。《寻觅布莱德伊·莫非》立刻自畅销榜上掉落。

十几年后,六十年代末英国又出了一个轰动的"前世"案例,说是南威尔士有个催眠师布洛克山姆(A. Bloxham)给一个叫简·依万丝的家庭主妇进行深度催眠并录了音,结果简回忆出自己的七个前世,从古罗马时代的家庭主妇一直到现在的美国爱荷华的修女,非常惊人,于是英国 BBC 广播电视节目的制作人埃佛森(J. Iverson)制作了布洛克山姆的催眠录音带节目。

埃佛森在节目中记录了他对简所说过的一切的调查。简所说的七个前世的时代的历史学者都认为简的叙述具有可观的知识,可是简说自己的历史知识程度只到小学。简曾叙说她的前世之一,一一九〇年是一个曾在约克某教堂的地窖里躲避杀害的犹太妇女,根据描述,埃佛森认为那个教堂应该是圣玛丽亚教堂,可是约克一带的中世纪教堂都没有地窖,除了约克大教堂,但简否认是约克大教堂。

一九七五年春天,圣玛丽亚教堂整修为博物馆时,在圣坛下发现了一个房间,曾经是个地窖!精彩吧?

不过,威尔森(I. Wilson)在《脱离时间的心智》(Mind out of Time)这本书里对上述提出质疑。他举了一个例子,说有一位 C 小姐被催眠后,回忆自己前世曾是理查二世时代女伯爵毛德(Maud)的好朋友,查证之下,C 小姐对当时的细节描述相当准确,不过 C 小姐声明她从来没读过相关的书。可惜

C小姐后来泄露了一个名字"E. 霍特",追查之下,原来有个爱米丽·霍特(Emily Holt)写过一本《毛德女伯爵》,C小姐的描述与书的内容一模一样。

我认为C小姐不是要说谎,她只是将遗忘了的阅读在催眠状态下又回忆出来了。所以当我听到"台北催眠秀"里的明星们在催眠中叙说的"前世"差不多都是某外国公主、贵妇,我猜她们日常最动心的读物大概是"白马王子",也是西方古代"纯情片"的票房支持者。

被催眠后,人的回忆力增强。美国有个马尔库斯(F. L. Marcuse)博士写过一本《催眠:事实与虚构》(Hypnosis:Facts & Fictions),书里提到一个例子,说有个囚犯因为遗产的事需要找到他的母亲,但是他从小就离开家乡了,结果怎么也想不起来家乡在哪里,而且连在哪个州都忘了。监狱里的医生于是将他催眠,让他回到小时候的状态,但还是想不起来。不过这个囚犯却想起来小时候搭过火车,医生就叫他回想站上播音器报站的声音,于是在催眠的诱导下,小站站名的发音浮现脑海,可惜叫这个名字的站全美有六个。不料囚犯又想起来家乡小镇上一个家族的姓,结果站名和姓,让他最终找到了母亲。

催眠能帮助成年人回忆出他们幼儿园时期的老师和小朋友的名字,当然,你也猜到了,催眠也可以诱导受害者或目击者回忆出不少现场细节,帮助警方破案。

一九九四年初美国加州有个案子,是一个叫荷莉的女子因为厌食症求医,医生伊莎贝拉告诉荷莉,百分之八十的厌食症是因为患者小时候受过性侵犯。结果荷莉后来想起自己五到八岁时被父亲葛利骚扰、强暴过十多次。伊莎贝拉在罗斯医生的协助下，用催眠药催眠荷莉，荷莉于是在催眠状态下回忆起被父亲强暴的更多细节。

催眠后的第二天，荷莉开始当面指控父亲，隔天，荷莉的母亲要求离婚。事情闹开了，葛利工作的酒厂解雇了葛利。

觉得莫名其妙的葛利，一状告到法院，控告伊莎贝拉和罗斯催眠他的女儿，将乱伦的想法输入她脑中。法院举行了听证会，哈佛大学的厌食症专家说儿童期遭到的性骚扰与厌食症的发展没有关系，宾西法尼亚州大学的心理系教授则认为催眠不具确定真相的功能，但是病人会变得敏感。结果是法庭判两位医生"无恶意，但确有疏忽"，赔偿葛利先生五十万美元。

因为美国这类官司每年大概有三百件，所以有一群蒙受过不白之冤的人成立了一个基金会，专门协助控告"胡乱植入记忆"的医生。

因此催眠虽然会增强人的记忆力，但是人也会在被暗示的催眠状态下产生虚构和扭曲，出现极为尴尬的结果。法国是搞催眠研究比较早的国家，因此法国法院不许催眠资料作为证据，美国大多数法院也规定如此。

前面提到的马尔库斯的那本书里，还有一个有意思的案例是讲有个男子常常会冒出一段自己也不明白的话来，听来像一种古代语言，譬如我们突然听到"制书律不分首从拟监斩候"的感觉。细查之下，有本书里真有那样一段话，这个男子在图书馆里偶然看到过一眼。

有一种催眠学英语的方法，据说效率非常之高。我没有去试过，我怕被误植了一些莫名其妙的东西在脑里，改就难了。有一个美国人当面向我指出过"洛杉矶时报"的一些拼写错误。我只不过是个写书的，又不必"打入主流社会"（天，"融入"已经能叫人假笑得脸都麻了，"打入"会是一副什么嘴脸呢），日常在舌头上滚来滚去的就是那么多词儿，应付个警察，打个问讯足够了，碰到不懂的，知之为知之，不知为不知，谁还能宰了你？

扯远了，回来说催眠。俄国的催眠学家瑞伊阔夫（V. Raikov）在六十年代（那时还是苏联）以一百六十六个容易进入深度催眠的小有艺术基础的人为实验对象，分别暗示他们是某某艺术大师。结果这些人在有了新的"身份"之后，不再对自己原本的名字有反应，甚至对镜子里的自己都不认识了。瑞伊阔夫让他们在催眠状态下画画儿，拉琴，下棋，结果下棋者的棋术令前世界国际象棋王塔尔（M. Tal）印象深刻；画画儿者的画很有拉斐尔的样子；拉提琴者的演奏像极了克莱斯勒。瑞伊阔夫据此在莫斯科举办过"催眠画展"。

而且，现代"心理神经免疫学"开始注意到一个人的心理状态怎样影响其神经系统和免疫系统。其实古希腊就有祭司暗示病人"会在梦中见到神，神会有指示"的疗病法，中国的《黄帝内经》则实在得多，不涉及神。

米瑞思（A. Meares）提到过一个催眠案例，说有个人患有严重的皮炎，长时间治疗都不能改变，他一天到晚看着自己的皮炎，非常沮丧。后来米瑞思为他施行催眠疗法，暗示他你的那些东西开始消失了，消失得越来越多，当你看到它们消失的时候,你的胳膊就垂下来了。经过两次催眠疗法,这个人的皮炎开始有改善,病好了。

鲁迅嘲笑过中医药方里的药引子,讽刺说蟋蟀也要原配的。中国草医也有不少偏方,比如我父亲得了肝炎,有个偏方说要找一片南瓜叶,上面要有七颗家雀儿,也就是麻雀的屎,吃了就好了。天,到哪里能找到?夏天收留个小雄蛐蛐儿,再留个"童养媳",秋天一定是原配,可是一张叶子上正好落了七颗麻雀屎,这麻雀岂不都成了 NBA 里的乔丹?另有一个治肝炎的药引子是生吞一只活的癞蛤蟆,我父亲想了很久,说他吞不下去。不过,如果你去找那样一张南瓜叶,因其难找,找的心情必是"诚"的,催眠的结果必能调动你的生理机能;如果你真的吞下一只活蛤蟆,自我催眠的效果也真就到了极限,"包治百病",何止区区一个肝的发炎。

我当年做知青的时候,乡下缺医少药。有个上海来的知青天天牙痛,听说山上有个寨子里有个巫医会治牙痛,择日我们一伙人就上去了,走了几个钟头,大汗淋漓,到了。巫医倒也有个巫医的样子,说取牛屎来,糊上,在太阳底下晒,把牙里的虫拔出来就好了。景象当然不堪,可天天牙痛更不堪,于是脸上糊了牛屎,在太阳底下暴晒。牛屎其实不脏的,因为牛的消化吸收能力太强了,又是反刍细嚼慢咽,否则怎么会吃进去的是草,挤出来的是奶?又怎么会出大力替人受罪犁田拉车?牛屎在蒙古是宝,烧饭要靠它,火力旺,烧完了只有一点灰,烧得很充分,又很干净。

好,终于是时候到了,巫医将干了的牛屎揭下来,上海来的少年人一脸的汗，但牙不痛了。巫医指着牛屎说，你看，虫出来了。我们探过头去看，果然有小虫子。屎里怎么会没有虫？没有还能叫屎吗？

不要揭穿这一切。你说这一切都是假的，虫齿牙不是真有虫，天天牙痛是因为牙周炎。好，你说得对，科学，可你有办法在这样一个缺医少药的穷山沟儿里减轻他的痛苦吗？没有，就别去摧毁催眠。只要山沟儿里一天没有医，没有药，催眠就是最有效的，巫医就万岁万万岁。回到城里，有医有药了，也轮不到你讲科学，牙医讲得比你更具权威性。

神、鬼、怪，不可证明它们是否实在。中世纪的神学要证明上帝的实在，是帮倒忙，毁上帝，不过倒由这个实证引发了文艺复兴的科学精神。宗教是人类的精神活动，非关实证。不少著名的科学家周末会去做礼拜，不少神职人员也在科技刊物上发表科学论文，宗教的归宗教，科学的归科学。科学造成的"信"与宗教的"信"，不是同一个"信"。

权威带有催眠的功能。老中医搭过脉后，心中有数，常常给那些没有什么病的人开些例如甘草之类无关痛痒的药，认真嘱咐回去如何煎，先煎什么后煎什么，分几次煎，何时服用，"吃了就好了"。吃了真就好了。西医也会同理认真开些"安慰剂"，也是吃了真就好了。如果我来照行其事，吃了白吃，因为我不具医生资格，天可怜见，我连赤脚医生都没做过。小学生信老师而不信家长，常常是家长比老师马脚露得多，权威先塌掉了。

发明"图像凝视法"的西蒙顿治疗癌症病人时，除了正规下药理疗,同时要病人想象有数百万道光芒正在杀向癌细胞。报告上说,正规疗法配合此法,癌症病人存活月数增加一倍,少数病人的肿瘤有缓解。我们不是也经过什么"鸡血疗法"、"甩手疗法"、"喝水疗法"吗? 我母亲有一次开刀,正赶上"针刺麻醉"盛行,被说服了,上了手术台,一刀下去,"麻什么麻,疼啊! 可是有外宾参观,咱们一个党员,怎么好说实话呢?"关云长刮骨疗毒还要拉个人下棋转移痛点注意力呢。

催眠可以用来减少主观的痛感。牙科和生孩子都有心理预期的"痛",医生采取催眠抑制主观的"痛"以后,真正的痛觉也会迟钝。我记得汤沐黎画过一幅歌颂针刺麻醉的油画,里面好像有个正在念毛主席语录的护士,这应该是中国绘画史上对具体催眠手段的正式纪录,挺有历史意义的。

无产阶级文化大革命是一次成功的催眠秀,我们现在再来看当时的照片,纪录片,宣言,大字报,检讨书等等,从表情到语言表达,都有催眠与自我催眠的典型特征。八次检阅红卫兵,催眠场面之大,催眠效果之佳之不可思议,可以成为世界催眠史上集体催眠的典范之一。我和两个朋友当年在北京看过一本关于催眠的书,免不了少年气盛,议论除了导师舵手领袖统帅,完全够格再加个催眠师。

后来做知青的时候,遇到出大力的苦活儿累活儿,所谓"大会战",照例是要集体念语录催眠的,像"一不怕苦,二不怕死",还有"下定决心,不怕牺牲"等等。说实在的,苦和死,怕与不怕都一样,活儿总是要干的,逃不掉。我认为人类进步的一大动力就是怕苦,于是想方设法搞一点减轻劳苦的花招儿,轮的发明,杠杆的利用,看来看去无一不是怕苦的成果。我利用电脑写东西,理由就是可以免去抄稿之苦。

凡流行的事物,都有催眠的成分在。女人们常常不能认识自己的条件而乱穿戴,是时装宣传的成功同时也是自我催眠的成功。

催眠是人类的一大能力,它是由暗示造成的精神活动,由此而产生的能量惊人。艺术呢,本质上与催眠有相通的地方。

我在几年前出的《闲话闲说》聊到过艺术与催眠,不妨抄一下自己:

依我之见,艺术起源于母系时代的巫,原理在那时候大致确立。文字发明于父系时代,用来记录母系创作的遗传,或者用来篡改这种遗传。

为什么巫使艺术发生呢?因为巫是专职沟通人神的,其心要诚。表达这个诚的状态,要有手段,于是艺术来了,诵,歌,舞,韵的组合排列,色彩,图形。

巫是专门干这个的,可比我们现在的专业艺术家。什么事情一到专业地步,花样就来了。

巫要富灵感。例如大瘟疫,久旱不雨,敌人来犯,巫又是一族的领袖,千百只眼睛等着他,心灵脑力的激荡不安,久思不获,突然得之,现在的诗人当有同感,所谓创作的焦虑或真诚,若遇节令,大丰收,产子等等,也都要真诚地祷谢。这么多的项目需求,真是要专业才应付得过来。

所以艺术在巫的时代,初始应该是一种工具,但成为工具之后,巫靠它来将自己催眠进入状态,继续产生艺术,再将其他人催眠,大家共同进入一种催眠的状态。这种状态,应该是远古的真诚。

宗教亦是如此。那时的艺术,是整体的,是当时最高的人文状态。

艺术最初靠什么?靠想象。巫的时代靠巫想象,其他的人相信他的想象。现在无非是每个艺术家都是巫,希望别的人,包括别的巫也认可自己的想象罢了。

艺术起源于体力劳动的说法,不无道理,但专业与非专业是有很大的区别的,与各人的先天素质也是有区别的。灵感契机人人都会有一些,但将它们完成为艺术形态并且传下去,不断完善修改,应该是巫这种专业人士来做的。

应该说,直到今天艺术还是处在巫的形态里。

你们不妨去观察你们搞艺术的朋友,再听听他们或真或假的"创作谈",都是巫风的遗绪。当然也有拿酒遮脸借酒撒疯的世故,因为"艺术"也可以成为一种借口。

……

当初巫对艺术的理性要求应该是实用,创作时则是非理性。

话是引得有些颠三倒四，事情也未必真就是这样，但意思还算明白。

艺术首先是自我催眠，由此而产生的作品再催眠阅读者。你不妨重新拿起手边的一本小说来，开始阅读，并监视自己的阅读。如果你很难监视自己的阅读，你大概就觉到什么是催眠了。

如果你看到哪个评论者说"我被感动得哭了"，那你就要警惕这之后的评论文字是不是还在说梦里的话。

有些文字你觉得很难读下去，这表明作者制造的暗示系统不适合你已有的暗示系统。

先锋或称前卫艺术，就是要打破已有的阅读催眠系统。此前大家所熟悉的"间离"，比如一出戏，大家正看得很感动，结果跑出来个煞风景的角色，说三道四，让观众从催眠状态中醒过来。台湾的"表演工作坊"有出舞台剧叫《暗恋桃花源》，用戏中的两个戏不断互相间离，让观众出戏入戏得很过瘾。可惜《暗恋桃花源》后来拍成电影时，忘了电影也是一个催眠系统，结果一出间离的好戏被电影像棉被包起来打不破，糟蹋了。先锋艺术虽然打破了之前的催眠系统，必然又形成新的催眠系统，比如大家熟悉的"意识流"，于是就有新先锋来打破旧先锋形成的催眠系统，可是好像还没有谁来间离"意识流"。

不过，以"新"汰"旧"很难形成积累。一味淘汰的结果会是仅剩下一个"新"，太无趣。积累是并存，各取催眠系统，好像逛街，这就有趣了。

音乐是很强的催眠，而且是最古老的催眠手段。孔子将

"礼"和"乐"并重，我们到现在还能在许多仪式活动中体会得到。孔子又说过听了"韶乐"之后，竟"三月不知肉味"，这是典型的催眠现象，关闭了一些意识频道。

法国的普鲁斯特写过一部《追忆似水年华》，用味道引起回忆往事的过程，正是以"暗示"进入自我催眠的绝妙叙述。

电影是最具催眠威力的艺术，它组合了人类辛辛苦苦积累的一切艺术手段，把它们展现在一间黑屋子里，电影院生来就是在模仿催眠师的治疗室。灯一亮，电影散场了，注意你周围人的脸，常常带着典型的催眠后的麻与乏。也有兴奋的，马上就有人在街上唱出电影主题歌，模仿出大段的对白，催眠造成的记忆真是惊人。当然，也有人回去裹在被子里暗恋不已。

电视好一些，摆在明处，周围的环境足以扰乱你进入深度催眠。但是人的自我催眠的能力实在太强了，哪儿都不看，专往屏幕上看，小孩子还要站得很近地看，遭父母呵斥。

自我催眠还会使人产生多重人格。作家在创作多角色的小说时，会出现这种情况，而评论家则喜好判断那些角色的人格是否完整，或者到底哪个角色的人格是作者的人格，或者作者的人格到底是什么样的。敏感的读者常常也做这类的判断。我猜现在常搞的作家当场签名售书的时候，赶去的读者一定带有一部分鉴别"假劣伪冒"的心情。我前些年也让书商弄过两三次这类活动，结果是读者很失望，看来我实属"假劣伪冒"。

有个要领奖的朋友问我"领奖时如何避免虚伪与虚荣"？这个难题可比昆德拉的"媚俗"，你怎么做都是"媚俗"，连不做都是"媚俗"。我说，观察，观察观众，观察颁奖人，观察司仪，观察环境，也观察你自己。这实际是一个造成两重人格的方法，将冷静的一重留给"自己"，假如颁奖现场发生火灾，你会是最先发现的。

成熟的演员是最熟练的多重人格创造者，当然有些人也会走火入魔到扮演的那一重人格里，失去监视的人格，搞得回不过神儿来，不思饮食，所谓陷入深度自我催眠。催眠案例中，有的被催眠者并非是失去全部的"自我意识"，他们常常有一个意识频道是清醒的，看着自己干着急。老托尔斯泰曾经说他原本并没有安排安娜自杀，可是安娜"自己"最后自杀了，他拿她没有办法。

我实在想说，审美也许简单到只是一种催眠暗示系统。

美国的精神卫生署在八十年代研究过"多重人格"者，发现他们的脑波随人格的转换而不一样。巫婆神汉常常做"灵魂附体"的事，说起来是在做多重人格的转换，你在证明那是真的时候，先要检查一下你自己是否被催眠和自我催眠。赵树理在《小二黑结婚》里写小芹的娘是个巫婆，降神的同时还在担心锅里的"米烂了"，七十年代我在鄂西的乡下见到的一个神汉就敬业多了，灵魂屡不附体之后，他悄悄嚼了一些麻叶。他大概是累了，那时候天天学大寨，没有农闲，降灵又是非法的。

也许你们应该意识到：我写的这些文字是不是也有催眠的意味呢？

一九九六年十二月　上海青浦

248

魂与魄与鬼及孔子

读中国小说，很久很久读不到一种有趣的东西了，就是鬼。这大概是要求文学取现实主义的结果吧。

可鬼也是现实。我的意思是，我们心里有鬼。这是心理现实，加上主义，当然可以，没有什么不可以。

不少人可能记得六十年代初有过一个"不怕鬼"的运动，可能不是运动，但我当时年纪小，觉得是大人又在搞运动，而且出了一本书，叫《不怕鬼的故事》。这本书我看过，看过之后很失望，无趣，还是去听鬼故事，怕鬼其实是很有趣的。后来长大了，不是不怕鬼，而是不信鬼了，我这个人就变得有些无趣了。

怕鬼的人内心总有稚嫩之处，其实这正是有救赎可能之处。中国的鬼故事，教化的功能很强并且确实能够教化，道理也在这里。不过教化是双刃剑，既可以安天下，醇风俗，又可以"天翻地覆慨而慷"，中国无产阶级文化大革命能够发动，有一个原因是不少人真的听信"资产阶级上台，千百万颗人头落地"，怕千百万当中有一颗是自己的。结果呢，结果是不落地的头现在有十二亿颗了。

中国文学中，魏晋开始的志怪小说，到唐的传奇，都有笔记的随记随奇，一派天真。鬼故事而天真，很不容易，后来的清代蒲松龄的《聊斋志异》，虽然也写鬼怪，却少了天真。

我曾因此在《闲话闲说》里感叹到莫言：

莫言也是山东人，说和写鬼怪，当代中国一绝，在他的家乡高密，鬼怪就是当地世俗构成，像我这类四九年后城里长大的，只知道"阶级敌人"，哪里就写过他了？我听莫言讲鬼怪，格调情怀是唐以前的，语言却是现在的，心里喜欢，明白他是大才。

八六年夏天我和莫言在辽宁大连，他讲起有一次回家乡山东高密，晚上近到村子，村前有个芦苇荡，于是卷起裤腿涉水过去。不料人一搅动，水中立起无数小红孩儿，连说吵死了吵死了，莫言只好退回岸上，水里复归平静。但这水总是要过的，否则如何回家？家又就近在眼前，于是再涉到水里，小红孩儿们则又从水中立起，连说吵死了吵死了。反复了几次之后，莫言只好在岸上蹲了一夜，天亮才涉水回家。

这是我自小以来听到的最好的一个鬼故事，因此高兴了很久，好像将童年的恐怖洗净，重为天真。

中国文学中最著名的鬼怪故事集应该是《聊斋志异》,不过也因此让不少人只读《聊斋志异》,甚至只读《聊斋志异》精选,其他的就不读或很少读了,比如同是清代的纪晓岚的《阅微草堂笔记》。

《阅微草堂笔记》与《聊斋志异》不同。《聊斋志异》标明全是听来的,传说蒲松龄自备茶水,请人讲,他记录下来,整理之后,加"异史氏曰"。我们常常不记得"异史氏"曰了些什么,但是记住了故事。这也不妨是个小警示,小说中的议论,读者一般都会略过。读者如逛街的人,他们看的是货色,吆喝不大听的。

《阅微草堂笔记》则是记录所见所闻,你若问这是真的吗?纪晓岚会说,我也嘀咕呢,可我就是听人这么说的,见到的就是这样。所以纪晓岚常常标明讲述者,目击的地点与时间。鲁迅先生常常看《阅微草堂笔记》,我小时候不理解,随着年龄的增长,渐渐懂了。《阅微草堂笔记》的细节是非文学性的,老老实实也结结实实。汪曾祺先生的小说、散文、杂文都有这个特征,所以汪先生的文字几乎是当代中国文字中仅有的没有文艺腔的文字。

明清笔记中多是这样。这就是一笔财富了。我们来看看是怎么样的一笔财富。

《阅微草堂笔记》记载了这样一个故事,说是乾隆年间,户部员外郎长泰公家里有个仆人,仆人有个老婆二十多岁,有一天突然中风,晚上就死了。第二天要入殓的时候,尸体突然活动,而且坐了起来,问"这是什么地方"?

死而复活，大家当然高兴，但是看活过来的她的言行做态，却像个男人，看到自己的丈夫也不认识，而且不会自己梳头。据她自己说，她本是个男子，前几天死后，魂去了阴间，阎王却说他阳寿未尽，但须转为女身，于是借了个女尸还魂。

大家不免问他以前的姓名籍贯，她却不肯泄露，说事已至此，何必再辱及前世。

最初的时候，她不肯和丈夫同床，后来实在没有理由，勉强行房，每每垂泪至天明。有人听到过她说自己读书二十年，做官三十年，现在竟要受奴仆的羞辱。她的丈夫也听她讲梦话说积累了那么多财富，都给儿女们享受了，钱多又有什么用？

长泰公讨厌怪力乱神，所以严禁家人将此事外传。过了三年多，仆人的死而复活的老婆郁郁成疾，终于死了，但大家一直不知道她是谁来附身。

用白话文复述这个故事最大的困难在于"她"与"他"的分别，不过我们可以用"他"来指说魂，用"她"来指说魄。魂是精气神，魄是软皮囊，所以"魂飞魄散"，一个可以飞，一个有得散。

清朝的刘炽昌在《客窗闲话》里记载了一个故事，说有个翩翩少年公子，随上任做县官的父亲去四川。不料过险路时马惊了，少年人坠落崖底，魂却一路飘到山东历城县的一个村子，落到这个村子一个刚死的男人的尸体里，大叫一声："摔死我啦！"

他醒来后看到周围都是不认识的人，一个老太婆摸着他说:"我儿,你说什么摔死我了?"公子说:"你是什么人敢叫我是你儿子?"周围的人说:"这是你娘你都不认得了?"并且指着个丑女人说"这是你老婆",又指着个小孩说"这是你儿子"。

公子说:"别瞎说了!我随我父亲去四川上任,在蜀道上落马掉到崖底。我还没有娶妻,哪里来的老婆?更别说儿子了!而且我母亲是皇上敕封的孺人,怎么会是这个老太婆?"

周围的人说:"你别说昏话了,拿镜子自己照照吧!"公子一照,看到自己居然是个四十多岁的麻子,就摔了镜子哭起来:"我不要活了!"大家听了是好气又好笑。

公子饿了,丑老婆拿糠饼来给他吃,公子觉得难以下咽,于是掉眼泪。丑老婆说:"我和婆婆吃树皮吃野菜,舍了脸皮才向人讨了块糠饼子给你吃,你还要怎么着呢?"公子将她骂出门外,看屋内又破又脏,想到自己一向华屋美食,恨不得死了才好。晚上老婆领着小孩进来睡觉,公子又把他们骂出去。婆婆只好叫母子两个同她睡。

第二天,一个老头来劝公子,说:"我和你是老哥们儿了,你现在变成这样,我看乡里不能容你这种不孝不义之人,你可怎么办呢?"公子哭着说:"你听我的声音,是你朋友的声音吗?"老头:"声音是不一样了,可人还是一样啊。我知道你是借尸还魂,可你现在既然是这个人,就要做这个人该做的事,就好像做官,从高官降为低官,难道你还要做高官的事吗?"

公子明白是这么回事,就请教以后该如何办。老头说:

"将他的母亲作你的母亲待,将他的儿子当你的儿子养,自食其力,了此身躯。"公子说自己过去只会读书,怎么养家糊口?老头就想出一个办法,说麻子原来不识字,死而复生居然会吟诗做文,宣扬出去,来看的人会很多,办法就有了。

公子按着去做,果然来看怪事的人很多。公子趁机引经据典,很有学问的样子,结果就有人到他这里来读书。公子能开馆教书,收入不错,足以养家,只是他借住在庙里,不再回家,家里人既得温饱,也就随他。

后来公子考了秀才,正好有个人要到四川去,他就写一封信托人带去给父亲。公子的父亲见了信,觉得奇怪,但还是寄了旅费让公子来见一见。

公子到了四川家里,父母见他完全是另一个人,不愿意认他,两个哥哥也说他是冒牌的。公子细述以前家里的一应细节,父亲倒动了心,可是母亲和两个哥哥执意要赶他走。父亲想,这样的话即使留下来,家里也是摆不平,只好偷偷给了他两千两银子,要他回山东去。

从世俗现实来说,看来我们中国人看肉身重,待灵魂轻。再进一步则是"只重衣冠不重人",连肉身都不重要了,灵魂更无价值。上面两个灵魂附错体的故事,让我们的司空见惯尖锐了一下。说起来,公子还是幸运的,到底附了个男身,不但可以骂老婆,还考了个秀才有了功名,而那个不肯说出前身的男魂,因为附了女身,糟糕透顶,可见不管有没有灵魂,只要是女身,在一个男性社会里就严重到"辱及前世",还要"每每垂泪到天明"。纪晓岚的这则笔记,女性或女权主义者可以拿去用,不过不妨看了下面一则笔记再说。

清代大学者俞樾在《右台仙馆笔记》里录了个故事,说中牟县有兄弟俩同时病死,后来弟弟又活了,却是哥哥的魂附体。弟弟的老婆高兴得不得了,要带丈夫回房间。丈夫认为不可以,要去哥哥的房间,嫂子却挡住房门不让他进。附了哥哥的魂的弟弟只好搬到另外的地方住,先调养好病体再说。

十多天后,弟弟觉得病好了,就兴冲冲地回家去。不料老婆和嫂子都避开了,这个附了哥哥魂的人只好出家做了和尚。

上举三则笔记都太沉重了些,这里有个笑里藏"道"的。也是清朝人的梁恭辰在《池上草堂笔记》里有一则笔记,说李二的老婆死了,托梦给李二,讲自己转世投了牛胎,托生为母牛,如果李二还顾念夫妻情分,就把她买回家。李二于是按指点去买了这头母牛回来,养在家中后院。但是这头母牛却常常跑回去,在大庭广众之中与邻居的公牛交配,李二也只好眼睁睁地瞧着。

民间如此,官方怎么样呢?史中记载,大定十三年,尚书省奏,宛平县人张孝善有个儿子叫张合得,大定十二年三月里的一天得病死亡,不料晚上又活过来。活了的张合得说自己是良乡人王建的儿子王喜儿。勘查后,良乡确有个王建,儿子王喜儿三年前就死了。官府于是让王建与张合得对质,发现张合得对王家的事知道得颇详细,看来是王喜儿借尸还魂,于是准备判张合得为王建的儿子。但事情超乎常理,于是层层上报到金世宗，由最高统治者定夺。

金世宗完颜雍的决定是：张合得判给王建，那么以后就会有人借这个判例作伪，用借尸还魂来搅乱人伦，因此将张合得判给张孝善才妥善。

这让我不禁想起孔子的"不语怪力乱神"。我小时候凭这一句话认为孔子真是一个有科学精神的人，大了以后，才懂得孔子因为社会的稳定才实用性地"不语怪力乱神"。《论语》里的孔子是有怪力乱神的事迹的，但孔子不语怪力乱神的实用态度最为肯定。"敬鬼神而远之"，话说得老老实实；"未知生，焉知死"，虽然可商榷，但话说得很噎人。

《孔子家语》里记载子贡问孔子"死了的人，有知觉还是没有"？孔子的学生里除了颜回，其他人常常刁难他们的老师，有时候甚至咄咄逼人，我们现在如果认为孔子的学生问起话来必然恭恭敬敬，实在是不理解春秋时代社会的混乱。孔子的几次称赞颜回，都透着对其他的学生的无奈而小有感慨。大概除了颜回，孔子的学生们与社会的联系相当紧密，随便就可以拎出个流行问题难为一下老师。这可比一九七六年后考入大学的老三届，手上有一大把早有了自己的答案的问题，问得老师心惊肉跳。

子贡的这一问，显然是社会中怪力乱神多得不得了，而孔子又不语怪力乱神，于是子贡换了个角度来敲打老师。

孔子显然明白子贡的心计，就说："我要是说有呢，恐怕孝子贤孙们都去送死而妨害了生存；我要是说没有呢，恐怕长辈死了不孝子孙连埋都不肯埋了。你这个子贡想知道死人有没有知觉,这事不是现在最急的,你要真的想知道,你自己死了不就知道了吗?"

子贡怎么反应,没有记载,恐怕其他的学生幸灾乐祸地正向子贡起哄呢吧,都不是省油的灯啊。

好像还是《孔子家语》,还是这个子贡,有一次将一个鲁国人从外国赎回鲁国,因此被鲁国人争相传颂夸奖,子贡一下子成了道德标兵。孔子听到了,吩咐学生说,子贡来了你们挡住他,我从此不要见这个人。子贡听说了就慌了,跑来见孔子。

大概是学生们挡不住子贡,所以孔子见到子贡时还在生气,说:"子贡你觉得你有钱是不是?"子贡是个商业人才,手头上很有点钱,孔子的周游列国,经济上子贡贡献不菲,"鲁国明明有法律,规定鲁国人在外国若是做了奴隶,得到消息之后,国家出钱去把他赎回来。你子贡有钱,那没钱的鲁国人遇到老乡在外国做了奴隶怎么办?你的做法,不是成了别人的道德负担了吗?"

孔子的脑筋很清晰。哪个学生我忘记了,问孔子"为什么古人规定父母去世儿子要守三年的丧"?孔子说:"你应该庆幸有这么个规定才是。父母死了,你不守丧,别人戳脊梁,那你做人不是很难了吗?你悲痛过度,守丧超过了三年,那你怎么求生计养家糊口?有了三年的规定,不是很方便吗?"

孔子死后,学生中只有子贡守丧超过了三年,守了六年。以子贡这样的商业人才,现在的人不难明白六年是多大的损失。好像是曾参跑来怪子贡不按老师生前的要求做,大有你子贡又犯从前赎人那种性质的错误了。子贡说,老师生前讲过超出与不足都是失度(度就是中庸),我觉得我对老师感情上的度,是六年。

屡次被孔子骂的子贡,是孔子的最好的学生。颜回是不是呢? 我有点怀疑,尽管《论语》上明明白白记载着孔子的夸奖。

不过扯远了,我是说,我喜欢孔子的入世,入得很清晰,有智慧,含幽默,实实在在不标榜。道家则总有点标榜的味道,从古到今,不断地有人用道家来标榜自己,因为实在是太方便了。我曾在《棋王》里写到过一个光头老者,满口道禅,捧起人来玄虚得不得了,其实是为遮自己的面子。我在生活中碰到不少这种人,还常常要来拍你的肩膀。汪曾祺先生曾写过篇文章警惕我不要陷在道家里,拳拳之心,大概是被光头老者蒙蔽了。

不过后世的儒家,实用到主义,当然会非常压制人的本能意识,尤其是一心只读圣贤书的人。这必然会引起反弹,明清的读书人于是偏要来谈怪力乱神,清代的袁枚,就将自己的一本笔记作品直接名为《子不语》。我们也因此知道其实说什么不要紧,而是为什么要这么说。

还有篇幅,不妨再看看明清笔记中还有什么有趣的东西。

梁恭辰在《池上草堂笔记》里记了个故事,说衡水县有个妇人与某甲私通而杀了亲夫,死者的侄子告到县衙门里去。某甲贿赂验尸的仵作,当然结果是尸体无伤痕,于是某甲反告死者的侄子诬陷。这个侄子不服，上诉到巡按，巡按就派另一个县的县令邓公去衡水县复审。邓公到了衡水县，查不出证据，搞不出名堂。

晚上邓公思来想去，不觉已到三更时分，蜡烛光忽然暗了下来。阴风过后，出现一个鬼魂，跪在桌案前，啜泣不止，似乎在说什么。

邓公当然心里惊惧，仔细看这个鬼魂，非常像白天查过的那具尸体，鬼魂的右耳洞里垂下一条白练。

邓公忽然省悟，就大声说："我会为你申冤的。"鬼魂磕头拜谢后就消失了，烛光于是重放光明。

次日一早，邓公就找来衡水县县令和仵作再去验尸。衡水县令笑话邓公说："都说邓公是个书呆子，看来真是这样。这个人做了十年官，家里竟没有积蓄，可知他的才干如何，像这种明明白白的案子，哪里是他这样的人可以办的！"

话虽这样说，可是也不得不去再验一回尸体。到了停尸房，邓公命人查验尸体的右耳。仵作一听，大惊失色。结果呢，从尸体的右耳中掏出有半斤重的棉絮。

邓公对衡水县县令说："这就是奸夫淫妇的作案手段。"妇人和某甲终于认罪。

这个故事，中国人很熟悉，包公案，狄公案，三言二拍中都有过，只不过作案的手段有的是耳朵里钉钉子，有的是鼻子里钉钉子，还有的是头顶囟门钉钉子，几乎世界各国都有这样的作案手段，我要是个验尸官，免不了会先在这些经典位置找钉子。

破案的路径差不多都是托梦,鬼魂显形,《哈姆雷特》也是这样,只不过凶手是往耳朵里倒毒药,简直是比较犯罪学的典型材料。你要是对这则笔记失望的话,不妨来看看纪晓岚的一则。

《阅微草堂笔记》里有一则笔记说总督唐执玉复审一件大案,已经定案了。这一夜唐执玉正在独坐,就听到外面有哭泣声,而且声音愈来愈近。唐执玉就叫婢女去看看怎么回事。婢女出去后惊叫,接着是身体倒地的声音。

唐执玉打开窗一看,只见一个鬼跪在台阶下面,浑身是血。唐执玉大叫:"哪里来的鬼东西!"鬼磕头说:"杀我的人其实是谁谁谁,但是县官误判成另一个人,此冤一定要申啊。"唐执玉听说是这样,心下明白,就说"我知道了",鬼也就消失了。

次日,唐执玉登堂再审该案,传讯相关人士,发现大家说的死者生前穿的衣服鞋袜,与昨天自己见到的鬼穿的相同,于是主意笃定,改判凶手为鬼说的谁谁谁。原审的县令不服,唐执玉就是这样定案了。

唐执玉手下的一个幕僚想不通,觉得这里一定有个什么道理,于是私下请教唐执玉,唐执玉呢,也就说了昨晚所见所闻。幕僚听了,也没有说什么。

隔了一夜,幕僚又来见唐执玉,问:"你见到的鬼是从哪里进来的呢?"唐执玉说:"见到时他就已经跪在台阶下了。"幕僚又问:"那你见到他从哪里消失的呢?"唐执玉说:"翻墙走的。"幕僚说:"鬼应该是一下子就消失的,好像不应该翻墙离开吧。"

唐执玉和幕僚到鬼翻墙头的地方去看,墙瓦没有裂痕,但是因为那天鬼来之前下过雨,结果两个人看到屋顶上有泥脚印,直连到墙头外。

幕僚说:"恐怕是囚犯买通轻功者装鬼吧?"

唐执玉恍然,结果仍按原审县令的判决定下来,只是讳言其事,也不追究装鬼的人。

两百多年前的那个死囚可算是个心理学家,文化学者,洞悉人文,差一点就成功了。幕僚是个老实的怀疑论者,唐执玉则知错即改,通情达理,不过唐执玉的讳言其事,也可解作他到底是读圣贤书出身,语怪力乱神到底有违形象。

一九九七年五月　上海青浦

还是鬼与魂与魄，这回加上神

　　人类学者认为"自我意识"的发生，是很晚近的。知道这一点，可以很好地避免"以今人度古人"的混乱发生。

　　"自我意识"对于今人，也就是当下的我们，已经是常识，而且常识到我们现在看神话，根本是以"自我意识"去理解神话，体会神话，结果常常闹笑话。无产阶级文化大革命中的文字材料，可以整理出一大本用现代语词写成的《中国当代神话笑话选》。

　　中国文化中，"自我意识"是什么时候发生的呢？这个大诘问中的"中国"，是有概念问题的。传说时代，有"中国"这个概念吗？我姑且用我们混乱的约定俗成来讲这个中国。

　　研究意识发展史的西方学者认为，"自我意识"的出现，起码在埃及金字塔之后。公元前十一世纪的荷马史诗《伊利亚特》，描述的是神话时期，那个时期，神话就是历史。之后的《奥德赛》，则开始有了"自我意识"，这个脉络是清晰的。

　　相当于《伊利亚特》的神话样式，中国却是公元后十六世纪的明代有一本《封神榜》,讲中国在公元前十一世纪的传说。作者陆西星是个有"自我意识"的人,来写三千年前的神话时代,除去他使用的他的当代语词,在神话学上,陆西星做得相当准确。

而相当于《奥德赛》,则是中国西周时的《诗经》。《诗经》里的"颂",是记录神话传说,"风"、"雅"则全是"自我意识"的作品,大部分还相当私人性,而且全无神怪。很难想象那时会产生如此具有"自我意识"的作品。

更进一步的是之后的屈原的《天问》,问上问下问东问西,差一步就是质疑神怪了。我们若设身处地于屈原,是能觉得一种悍气和痛快的,当然其中不免有些"以今人度古人"。

不过孔子是文字记录中最早最明确的"自我意识"者。孔子"敬鬼神而远之","未能事人,焉能事鬼",想想他处在一个什么时代!到了汉代的董仲舒,反而"天人合一",为汉武帝的专制张目。在此之前,只是顺天命而已,没有人视自己为神的代表。《尚书》中的周天子亦只是顺天命,有一份谦逊。谦逊是一种自我意识,用来形容周代初年,也许合适也许不合适。

与董仲舒同时的司马迁,则是自我意识很强的人,所以他的《史记》现代的中国人读来还是同情和感叹。司马迁简直就是和董仲舒对着干,笔下的刘姓皇帝,全都没有龙种的样子。我怀疑司马迁写陈胜吴广揭竿而起时做手脚的细节,把写好字的布条塞到鱼肚子里,半夜学狐狸叫,像是说,你们刘家,比这也好不到哪里去,何来的天人合一?

意识史学者叶奈思(J. Jaynes)定义过"自我意识",即"以其思想与情感而成为一个独特个体"。孔子和司马迁都有事迹证明他们是有很强的自我意识的人,但这并不等于说,当时的所有的人都是如此,而且随着时间的推移,自我意识会在社会中越来越强。相反的,自我意识在历史和现实中,载沉载浮,忽强忽弱,若即若离,如真似假,混杂在载体之中。

这个载体,是由人类的神、鬼、魂所体现的潜意识。在人类行为的沼泽中,这些潜意识,频频冒泡儿,经久不息。它混杂了集体潜意识和集体潜意识中的个人经验。

这个潜意识,常常表现为神、鬼、魂、魄。

中国人认为"魂"是类似精神的东西,人受到惊吓,有时候会"魂飞"。"魄"呢,则是物质性的魂,所以我们常常会说"魂飞魄散"。魂飞魄散之后呢,留下的是尸。假如魂飞了而魄不散,这个尸就是僵尸。

中国民间传说和明清笔记小说中关于僵尸的故事是很多的。清代袁枚的《子不语》里有则"飞僵",说有个僵尸会飞来飞去吃小孩子,村里人发现了这个僵尸藏匿的洞,于是请道士来捉。道士让一个人下到洞里,不停地摇铃铛,这样僵尸就不敢回洞了。道士和另外的人则在外面与僵尸斗来斗去,天亮的时候,僵尸倒在地上,大家用火将僵尸烧掉。

"僵尸野合"说的是有个壮士看到一具僵尸从墓中出来,到一家墙外,墙里有个穿红衣的妇人抛出一条白布带子,僵尸就拉着布带子爬墙过去了。壮士跑回墓中将棺材盖子藏起来，不久僵尸回来了，找不到棺材盖子，很是窘迫，于是又回到那家墙外，又跳又叫，可是红衣妇人拒绝僵尸进去。鸡叫的时候，僵尸倒在地上，壮士约了别人到这家去看，发现这家停放有一具棺材，一个女僵尸倒在棺材外面。大家知道这是僵尸野合，于是将两具僵尸合在一起烧掉了。

如此看来，僵尸是有食、色欲望的，同时有暴力。洋僵尸也是如此，美国半夜过后，电视里常放这类电影，喜欢僵尸题材的人可大饱眼福，同时饱受惊吓。

我们不难看出，"魄"，可定义为爬虫类脑和古哺乳类脑；"僵尸"，是仍具有爬虫类脑和古哺乳类脑功能的人类尸体，它应该是远古人类对凶猛动物的原始恐惧记忆，成为我们的潜意识。

于是，我们也可以定义"魂"，它应该就是人类的新哺乳类脑，有复杂的社会意识，如果有自我意识，也是在这里。

中国人认为"鬼"是有魂无魄，所以鬼故事最能引起我们的兴趣，牵动我们的感情，既能产生对死亡的恐惧，同时又是轮回中的一段载体。

还是袁枚，还是《子不语》，有个"回煞抢魂"的故事。说是淮安县有个姓李的人与妻子非常恩爱，却在三十多岁时死了。入殓的时候，他的妻子不忍将棺材钉上，从早到晚只是哭。

按习俗人死后九到十八天，煞神会带亡魂回家，因此有迎煞的仪式，亲人都要回避。可是这次煞神来的时候，妻子不肯回避,她让子女到别处去,自己留在灵堂。二更的时候,煞神押着丈夫的魂进来,放开叉绳,自顾自大吃大喝起来。丈夫的魂走近床前揭开帐子,躲在里面的妻子就抱着他哭,可是觉得丈夫像一团冰冷的云,于是用被子将魂裹起来。煞神一见就急了,过来抢夺,妻子大叫,子女也都跑来了,鬼只好溜掉了。妻子将包裹着的魂放到棺材里,丈夫的尸体开始有气,到天亮的时候,丈夫苏醒过来。这一对夫妇后来又过了二十年。

也是清代的李庆辰在《醉茶志怪》里录了个故事,说是有个姓朱的人有天夜里经过一条小巷,看到一个男人在一户人家的后窗往里看,就上前责备说:"偷看人家,像个什么样子?"那个人却不理他,还是看。

姓朱的大怒,就去拉这个人。这个人忽然回过脸来,只见他面如朽木,发如蓬草,眼有凶光,说:"关你什么事!"接着用手扭住姓朱的背,姓朱的觉得这个人的手凉如冰雪,抓得自己很痛,可是刹那间这个人又不见了。

姓朱的吓得狂奔而逃。第二天有人告诉他,鬼偷看的那家人娶再嫁的媳妇。大家都说姓朱的看到的是新娘的前夫。

明清笔记小说中最多的是反映被压抑的性的潜意识欲望,这类鬼故事最受人欢迎,中国人差不多人人都有不少这类的故事。这类鬼故事在功能上类似黄色笑话,只不过有关性的鬼故事倾向于满足人类对于性与死亡的焦虑。

再者,就是男性在鬼故事里满足于总是美丽的女鬼自动投怀送抱。这在男性制造的礼法社会中活生生地总是难于遇到,遇到,则是艳遇,哪怕是鬼。

那么男人在男鬼身上希望什么呢? 清代大学问家俞樾在《右台仙馆笔记》里记了个男鬼求嗣的故事。

咸宁地方有个姓樊的男子,好酒好赌,四十多岁就死了。他的魂到一位叔祖家里捣乱,叔祖说:"我与你无冤无仇,你为什么找我的麻烦?"鬼说:"我死后没有子嗣啊。"

叔祖就不明白了,说:"你自己浪荡,不讨妻继子嗣,怎么怪到我头上来了呢? 而且我和你的血脉并不很近,怎么来找我呢?"

鬼说:"我没有田产,谁肯来做我的子嗣? 你现在总管我们樊氏,总要你开口,才有个办法,而且算数。"

叔祖说:"你生前不考虑子嗣,为什么死后倒惦记这件事呢?"鬼就说:"我死后,祖宗都骂我,如果你不替我立子嗣,我无颜面对祖宗啊。"

叔祖于是在族会上提议选一个近支血脉的人做鬼的子嗣,安排了以后,鬼就离去了。

鬼故事差不多就是在表达我们在文化中不得释放的潜意识。自我意识属于显意识,因此它也会压抑潜意识。如果说自我意识强的人就不语怪力乱神,只是子不语罢了,孔子还要祭神如神在呢。

一九九七年七月　洛杉矶

足球与世界大战

炎热的夏天就要来了。这话有毛病。夏天当然是炎热的,所以"夏天就要来了"足矣,不必啰嗦炎热。

不过人是感情动物,常常顾不上语法逻辑,变得语无伦次。记得我小时候有个邻居,骂起她的儿子,真是恨铁不成钢,出口就是"王八羔子","小杂种"。她这个儿子是我的同学,有一次忍不住问他:"你要是王八羔子,你爸你妈就是王八了?"结果是我被"王八羔子"追得满街跑。"必也正名乎"是要付出代价的。

今年,一九九八年,又到了四年一次的世界杯足球赛,照例会有二十多亿人进入疯狂,这个夏天会非常非常炎热。所以,炎热的夏天就要来了。

世界杯足球赛煽动起来的攻击性热情,几乎是四年一次的世界大战,奥林匹克运动会无疑是逊了一筹。一九三〇年之所以要办这么个世界杯足球赛,就是因为觉得奥林匹克运动会中的足球赛,实在不足以满足足球运动的疯狂。

我们不妨随便看看我们在过去将近七十年里的疯狂。

一九二八年，国际足球总会主席雷米在阿姆斯特丹开会的时候，建议办四年一次的国际足球大赛，提案通过。

法国工匠做出一个重一公斤半，也就是我们的三斤重的镀金奖杯，样子是胜利女神直立展翅，命名为 RIMET 世界杯，也就是"雷米"世界杯。

一九三〇年，首届世界杯国际足球赛开始，乌拉圭捧走了金杯。之后，意大利保持了奖杯八年，巴西保持了八年。所谓八年，就是连续夺得两届冠军。

一九七〇年，巴西再次夺得冠军。依照规则，巴西永久拥有这个三斤重的金杯。一九七四年开始，世界杯改称FIFA世界杯，FIFA是国际足球总会的缩写。这个奖杯，是由意大利米兰的工匠制造。

这个杯，属于 FIFA 的永久财产，意大利和当年的西德虽然各得了三届冠军，却不能永久拥有，只能保存复制品。

这样一来，巴西岂不是占了便宜？没有。巴西永久拥有的那个"雷米"奖杯，被人偷走了，大家也就摆平了。

一九六六年全世界最轰动的大事不是中国的无产阶级文化大革命，而是那个世界杯"雷米"失窃。后来英格兰的一只狗在一个菜园子里找到它，狗的主人柯伯特于是得到一大笔奖金。柯伯特决定奖励狗吃一个星期的鱼子酱，一个狗食公司马上跟进，免费供给一年的狗食。我的经验是，狗吃过高级食品后，普通食品就很难下咽了。

不过"雷米"金杯在一九八三年再次失窃，一般认为它已被熔毁。巴西足总永久拥有的那一座,是复制品。

也是和食品有关,一九七四年足球世界杯前,扎伊尔队到埃及踢热身赛,带去调理好的猴儿肉,结果埃及厨子与他们大吵,大骂他们残忍。经过协调,决定由扎伊尔队自己煮,而且只能在自己的房间里吃。

美国有三大球,棒球,篮球,美式橄榄球,但是没有足球。美国人觉得长时间不进球的运动有点莫名其妙,起码没有效率,因此美国从小学到大学,都没有足球课。一个美国孩子,从小学就熟悉三大球的玩法,想想我们对乒乓球的熟悉程度吧。三大球的术语,尽人皆知。赛林格的著名小说的题目被中译成《麦田守望者》,其实它是棒球里外野捕手的意思,也就是我们常看到的那些跑到最远处接球的人。

一九五〇年,美国队在世界杯足球赛中以一比〇击败英格兰队。可能吗?要知道足球这个游戏是英国人发明的,美国人发明的篮球,因此英国报纸将记者发回去的比数改成英格兰以十比一胜美国队,次日见报,举世哗然。不过,美国人也认为赢得侥幸的,美国队盖耶特金飞身接应队友巴尔的长射,顺势将球顶入,场上的另一个队友柯夫认为"盖耶特金肯定不知道球是怎么进的"。

一九七四年荷兰邮政局局长认为荷兰队铁定赢,于是开机印了荷兰队成为冠军的邮票,结果是只能悄悄销毁。当然这件事还是传出来了,否则我也不会写在这里。

一九八六年世界杯足球赛时,意大利一个修道院特准修士们熬夜看电视转播。按规定,修道院晚上十点半必须就寝。如此一来,修士们就可以在十六世纪的小房间里畅饮啤酒,大呼小叫。不过,上帝永远是看现场的。

并非足球强国的人才对足球疯狂。孟加拉一位三十岁的妇女是喀麦隆球迷,一九九〇年八强大战时喀麦隆输给英格兰,她竟自杀了,遗书上写道:"喀麦隆离开了世界杯,就是我该离开世界的时候了。"

孟加拉如同我国,从未踢出过亚洲分区,不过一九九四年为了看转播,孟加拉的大学生发动游行,要求当局推迟期末考试。

足球甚至有关人格。苏格兰一家医院的厨子坎普对苏格兰在一九七八年世界杯赛中的表现甚为不满,登报声明从此不做苏格兰人,要做英格兰人。为此,坎普请了老师补习正统英语,改掉自己的苏格兰腔。

一九七八年,阿根廷主办世界杯赛,游击队刺杀了主事的退休将军,不过游击队马上宣布停火,支持筹办世界杯。

巴西球王贝利说过:"在巴西,只要赢了世界杯,政府怎么胡来都行,人民一点不在乎。"

赚人发疯的钱,是一笔大买卖。一九九四年,二十亿人通过电视转播看世界杯比赛,电视公司得到的广告收益是上百亿美元。

哪个国家主办世界杯足球赛,哪个国家就赚钱。一九六二年,智利大地震,但坚持不让出世界杯的主办权。一九七八年,阿根廷通货膨胀严重,因为主办世界杯而解除了危机。

可惜,今年的世界杯主办国与亚洲无缘,否则亚洲的金融危机也许会转化,而不会像专家们预言的那样需要三年。

不过,据美国一家研究机构做的调查,一届世界杯下来,全世界会损失四千亿美元。一九八二年,当时的西德对当年在西班牙举办的世界杯赛作了研究,发现德国工人旷工在家看电视转播,损失了六亿工时,等于政府损失了四十多亿美元。

足球近似规则化的暴力,攻击性非常强,当然比拳击还差了一截。

一九三〇年首届世界杯足球赛,阿根廷队对墨西哥队时,阿根廷吃了五次十二码罚球;对智利时又大打出手,裁判只好召警察入场;决赛时对乌拉圭,大批阿根廷球迷持械入场,我估计阿根廷队若输了的话,大批棍棒是打本国队员的。

一九三四年意大利队与西班牙踢成平局,大批队员受伤。隔日再战时,两队只好换上新的队员。

一九五四年巴西对匈牙利,踢球加踢人,从场上一路混战到休息室。

贝利在一九六二年一开赛就被弄伤,一九六六年被恶整之后宣布不再涉足世界杯足球赛。

球迷暴动还用我说吗?

除了暴力,巫术也不缺席。一九八二年秘鲁对喀麦隆,秘鲁的巫师沙马尼哥说他感应到喀麦隆的巫师对秘鲁队施法术,于是召集了十二名巫师,各持大刀、棍棒和桦木条,在首都利马郊外集合。沙马尼哥念咒,其他巫师则挥舞法器,之后沙马尼哥宣布已经制伏了喀麦隆巫师召来的恶灵。秘鲁队与喀麦隆队比赛的结果是,零比零,两队后来都没能打入复赛。

喀麦隆的巫师检讨之后,在一九九○年再度作法,他们要足球队员穿特定颜色的衣服,请球迷将老鼠和鸡放进球场。做这些事情时都要小心,一九八九年十一月,一名津巴布韦的选手遵巫师嘱,赛前公然在球场撒尿,结果被罚终身禁赛。

阿根廷的一位家庭主妇说:"比赛开始前,我绕着椅子按顺时针方向转两圈,再按逆时针转两圈,阿根廷就会赢。"

阿根廷的总统梅南也一样。他一九九○年说:"我总是在这儿(总统府)看转播,每次都穿同样的衣服,打同一条领带。"他认为这样会给阿根廷队带来运气。我觉得看球赛还戴领带实在是严肃了,不过总统先生可能认为足球是严肃的事情。

意大利前总统帕廷尼常请意大利国家队到总统府吃饭。一九八二年的那次世界杯赛前,已经八十五岁的他,还特别嘱咐意大利国家队的主力队员罗西说:"记住射门!还有,躲开铲球!"铲球躲不躲得开,专业球员不一定能处理好,但专业球员如果记不得射门,也别别踢了。意大利队夺了冠军回来,罗西将自己的球衣赠给老总统,报答他的赤子之心。

邓小平则是每天深夜准时收看转播,而且还要录下反复看重要段落,是专业球迷。顺便说一下的是,我看报道说中国国家足球队到韩国比赛,回国后教练的感言是原来韩国队每天吃牛肉,所以体力强。体力是由高质量的饮食保证的,这是常识,国家队不会连常识都不知道吧？所以我怀疑报道有误。记得初中时参加游泳训练,教练说"家里供不起每天二两牛肉的,以后就不要来了",我以后就没有再去了,只到玉渊潭去游浑水。

世界杯足球赛期间,性似乎是关闭的,所以才有"足球寡妇"的说法。一九九四年世界杯期间,一对瑞典夫妇去朋友家看现场转播,之后,太太没兴趣,先睡了。到瑞典射入一球的时候,先生摇醒太太,太太不想听,于是夫妇吵将起来,结果是太太大怒,抄起剪刀就是一下,然后忿忿睡去。客厅里主人还在电视机前狂喜,谁都不知道有一个人倒在血泊中死去。

爱尔兰是个穷地方,但是到了世界杯期间,砸锅卖铁也要飞到主办国去看球赛,或者在酒吧里看转播一醉方休。球赛终于全部赛完,足球寡妇们递给足球先生的是离婚书。

泰国卫生部副部长一九九四年说:"泰国妇女希望世界杯永远不结束。"因为时差的关系,泰国男球迷看现场转播是在夜里,声色场所当然是不去了。

我觉得足球赛中最惨的是裁判。

裁判足球赛,很多判断是主观的,哲学上称"自由心证",俗话说就是"随你怎么吹了"。

一九七四年世界杯赛,扎伊尔对南斯拉夫,扎伊尔队的二号踢了裁判的屁股,裁判转回头来却将扎伊尔队的十三号罚出场。这是二十亿人都眼睁睁地看到的自由心证。

在攻击性这样强烈的运动中做裁判,裁判员挣的是性命钱。一九八九年哥伦比亚的一位巡边员,刚下计程车,就被几个人持乌兹冲锋枪扫射身亡。

阿尔及利亚的一位裁判掏红牌罚一个队员出场时,反而是自己被当场殴打致死。

裁判也需检点自己,不要火上浇油。第一届世界杯时,离赛时结束还有六分钟,巴西裁判就吹哨鸣金止战。忙什么呢?

一九六二年智利对意大利,被裁判罚出场的队员竟能赖在场上十分钟不出去。智利的球员放了一拳在对手脸上,裁判视若无睹。这位裁判大概是早已雇好保镖了。

最危险的是一九七八年,阿根廷队必须踢进四球,而且要赢三个球以上才能出线,于是买通秘鲁队和裁判。结果这一场对阿根廷队大放水,两个越位进球,裁判硬是“有看没有见”,巴西队赢得好端端的竟落了个出局。

有人说,国际争端,不如以足球赛的方式解决。我以前也不知好歹地附议过,可是细想想,原来危险很大。足球不能解决国际争端,它只能煽起不可遏制的攻击冲动,只能使国际争端中仅有的理性丧失。让足球只是一种游戏就好了,就好像让文学只是文学就好了,不要给它加码。任何事都是这样,按常识去做,常常在于智慧和决心吧。

一九九六年十一月,中国足协国家队管理部主任在全国足球工作会议上说:“与其窝窝囊囊地输,不如悲悲壮壮地死。”

一九七四年世界杯赛前,扎伊尔总统对即将出发的扎伊尔球队说:"不赢球,就是死。"结果胆战心惊的扎伊尔队连一场都没有赢过。总统先生何苦来?

中国如果想赢得世界杯冠军,还是要老老实实从常识做起,第一就是饮食要改变,老老实实吃牛肉,猪肉再香,也不能吃了。老老实实吃奶皮子,乳酪,"起司",难吃也要吃,这样才能满场飞。

我喜欢看英国人、德国人的足球,他们跑起来像弹弓射出去的弹丸,脚下不花巧,老老实实地传,老老实实地飞奔,这才是体育运动。

写到这里,突然想到好像还没有看过有关足球的小说。想了想,想不太通,算了,不想了,还是准备看转播吧。

一九九八年三月　美国洛杉矶

跟着感觉走?

大概十年前了吧,流行过一首歌叫《跟着感觉走》。不过,好像跟着感觉走了一阵子,又不跟着了,可能还是跟着钱走来得实在吧。这倒让我想起历来的读书人,好像只谈感觉的问题,而不太谈吃饭的问题。谈,例如古人,也只是说"穷困潦倒",穷困到什么地步? 不知道。怎样一种潦倒? 也不清楚。正史读到"荒年"、"大饥",则知道一般百姓到了"人相食"的地步,这很明确,真是个活不下去的地步。

鲁迅写过一个孔乙己,底层读书人,怎样一种潦倒,算是让我们读来活生生的如同见到。还有《浮生六记》的夫妇俩,也很具体,当然历代不少笔记中也有小片段,遗憾在只是片段。

我在贵阳的时候,见到过一本很有趣的书,讲若上京赶考,则自贵阳出发时雇驴走多少钱,雇马走多少钱。第一天走到什么地方要停下来住店,多少钱,一路上的吃喝用度,都有所需银两细目。直到北京卢沟桥,当晚可住什么店,多少钱,第二天何时起身入城,在京城里可住哪些店或会馆在哪里,各多少钱,清清楚楚,体贴爽利。最有意思的是,说过娘子关时可住的一个店中有一位张寡妇,仅此一句,别无啰嗦。

我手上有一本四十年前陈存仁先生在香港写的《银元时代的生活》,常常闲来无事前后翻翻。陈存仁先生原是上海的一个医生,后来到香港还是行医,行医之余,写一些银元时代的生活的连载短文,慢慢集成一本书。书中对清末到抗战爆发这一段生活,记载甚详,包括一屉小笼包多少钱,什么地方的一席宴多少钱,什么菜。他编过一部有名的药典,抄写工多少钱,印刷多少钱。他因行医的关系,与民国元老吴稚晖有交往,也被章太炎收为关门弟子。这些交往,陈先生写来细节饱满,人情流动,天生无文艺腔。有个事情如果不是陈先生全过程的叙述,我们会以为怎么可能发生?原来民国初建时的一大摊革命事务里,有一项是立法废除中医中药,陈先生张罗着到南京请愿,才将中医中药保留下来。

我也是不长进,过于庸俗吧,很感兴趣这些细节。三十年前我去乡下插队,首先碰到的就是一日三餐的问题。初时还算有知青专款拨下去,可度得一时,后来问题就大了,不由得想到念书时灌到脑子里的古代诗人的三餐。

李白千古风流,可是他的基本生活是怎样的,看诗是知不道的。他二十五岁开始漫游,除了一年多在长安供奉翰林,一日三餐不成问题,其余,直到去世的三十五年中,都在漫游,每天具体的三顿饭,不必三顿,哪怕一天一顿好了,都是怎么解决的?诗中他常喝酒,酒虽然会醉人,但还是有营

278

养的。有酒,起码就有一些下酒菜,可以抵挡一天没有问题。而且,古代的酒类是果酒,类似现在的"绍兴加饭"或"女儿红",或者米酒,类似日本的 SAKE,即清酒,可以喝得多而慢醉,只要不吐,就可以吸收成为热量。

李白他们的古代,一般人,尤其文人,是不喝我们现在这种白酒,也称为"臭酒"的。"臭酒"是两次以上蒸馏,消耗粮食的量很大,多是河工,也就是黄河防洪的服徭役者喝,或苦力喝,再有就是土匪,一是抵寒,二是消乏,三是壮胆。我们现在社会上流行喝臭酒,是清末至民初军阀时期兴起来的,说实在,酒品很低,虽然广告做得铺天盖地。

李白若喝臭酒,什么诗也做不出来,只有昏醉。张旭的酒后狂草,也是低度果酒的成果。武松喝的那过不了岗的三碗,是米酒类,稍烈一点,但危险一来,要能做汗出了,才好打虎。

洋人的情况差不多。所谓酒神精神,是饮果酒,也就是葡萄酒后的精神。伏特加算最烈的了,离二锅头还差着一截,我去俄国、丹麦、瑞典,见他们常喝。寒带人多数人有忧郁症,这与阳光少有关,尤其长达半年的白夜,真是会令人忧郁至极,酒可以麻醉忧郁。到他们的地区,看他们的画,读他们的诗,小说,听他们的音乐,都是符合的,不符合的,反而是异国色彩。

我的一些朋友,有忧郁症的,模仿起寒带艺术来真的是像,说模仿不对,是投契。没有忧郁症的,就是模仿了,东西总是有点做作。前些年美术圈兴过一阵"怀斯"风,几年下来,我们看在眼里,心下明白谁是投契,谁是投机。怀斯,是有忧郁症的,忧郁得很老实,并老老实实地画自己的忧郁。美国有不少患忧郁症的人,极端的会自杀。医生有时不给他们开药,只是说,到热带去度个假吧。忧郁症是因为起神经传导作用的去甲肾上腺素降低,吃些三环类的药就好了,只不过药效过后容易再犯,变成对药物产生依赖,于是容易更忧郁,所以还是度假的好。从报道上看,写《哥德巴赫猜想》的诗人徐迟的自杀,应该是患有严重的忧郁症。

病症影响情绪,这是每个人都有体会的,不要说癌症了,就是一个伤风鼻子不通,也会使一些人痛感生活之无趣。欧洲艺术史上有所谓浪漫主义时期,察检下来,与彼时的肺结核病有关。

结核病的症状是午后低烧,苍白的脸颊上有低烧的红晕,眼球因为低烧而眼压增大,角膜也就绷紧发亮,情绪既低沉忧郁又亢奋,频咳。在没有电灯的时代,烛光使这样一副病容闪烁出异样的色彩,自有迷人处。萧三是这样的艺术家的代表人物。那时肺结核可说是一种时髦病,得了是又幸又不幸。

我国在上个世纪末这个世纪初,鸳鸯蝴蝶派的小说里,肺结核的男女主角一个又一个,这股风气由欧洲传来,林琴南译的《茶花女》,风靡读书人,于是读书人做小说下笔也就肺结核起来。当时的读书人,觉得肺结核有时代感,健健康康的,成什么样子? 其实中国小说早有一个肺结核的人物,就是《红楼梦》中的林黛玉。那时还没有肺结核这个词,结核病统称"痨病",但曹雪芹写林黛玉的症状很细,包括情绪症状,所以我们可以确定,林黛玉是结核美人。

现在具有现代感的病是什么,前些年是癌症,由日本传来,弄得华语地区的电视连续剧,一集一集的总会拍到医院病房去,鲜花和闪电中,最后的隐情。其实最现代的是艾滋病,但是小说家编剧人好像还没拿捏好,嫌它有乱交的麻烦,再说吧。

治疗肺结核病后来变得很简单,现在这种病几乎不再发生了。很巧,这时浪漫主义也结束了。

我这么讲可能很不厚道,可是当时作家好像也不厚道,无病不成书。如果以病症为常识,来判断艺术的流派或个人的风格,其实是可以解魅和有更踏实的理解的。

电影《莫扎特传》对莫扎特的葬礼有一个暗示,就是丧葬工人泼洒了几锹石灰到尸袋上。莫扎特的音乐清朗澄明,不像病人所为,但说他被缠于债务,贫病交加,什么病呢?莫扎特难道是用音乐超拔自己的困境,包括病?贝多芬则是先天性梅毒,导致盛年耳聋,而且梅毒引发狂躁与沮丧,当时还没有发明盘尼西林这种特效药,梅毒无疑就成了贝多芬不可抗拒的命运,例如他几次的恋爱都不可能结果为婚姻。我们知道了这一层,对他晚年的作品,例如弦乐四重奏,无疑听得出来剧痛与暂时缓解的交替,惊心动魄。我们知道,贝多芬拒绝用药,是他执著那些交替可以转换成音乐状态吗?舒曼不幸也是先天性梅毒,最后导致精神分裂,我们听他的晚期的作品,例如钢琴五重奏,明显的失误,无与伦比的魅力,同时在一起。

鲁迅患有肺结核,这也是他的死因。我们讲过了肺结核引起的情绪症状,"一个也不宽恕"的绝决,《野草》中的绝望,就多了一层原因。他晚年的文章几乎都很短,应该与体力有关。

这并非说艺术由疾病造成,而是文思的情绪,经由疾病这个扩大器,使我们听到看到的有了很难望其项背的魅力。当然,也有人装疯卖傻,哄抬自己,一谈到价钱,疯还是疯,但是一点也不傻。只可怜不明就里者,学得很累,钱呢,花得很冤枉。跟着感觉走,不知道会走成什么样。

所以我们不妨来谈谈感觉或者情感。

你们肯定猜到我又要来谈常识了。不错,不谈常识谈什么? 世界上最复杂的事是将复杂解为简单。当然,最简单的事也就是将明明简单的事搞得很复杂,我们可以从民生的角度原谅长篇大论的一点是,字多稿酬也就多了。

法国有个聪明人福科,好像是他讲的,"知识也是一种权力。"对中国人来说,我们不需旁征博引,只要略想想科举时代的读书,就明白了。"书中自有黄金屋,书中自有颜如玉",书中还可以有一人之下万人之上,总之,可有的多了。但问题还有另一面,常识也是一种知识,只是这种知识最能解构权力。五四时代讲的科学,现在看来都是常识,却能持续瓦解旧专制。过了半个世纪,有一句话,"实践是检验真理的唯一标准",还是一句有关常识的话,因为之前,实在是一点常识都没有了。

不过常识这个东西也有它的陷阱。常识是我们常说的智商的基础,智商这个词我们知道是由 IQ 翻译而来。我们还有一个由日文汉字形词而来的"知识",当年曾用过"智识"。我觉得还是"智识"好,因为"智"和"识"是同类的,"知",如果是"格物致知"的那个知还好,否则只是"知道"。

八十年代初兴过一阵智力竞赛,类似"秦始皇是哪一年统一中国的"这种题铺天盖地,有些单位举办这种竞赛,甚至影响到职工福利的分配。但这是"知道竞赛",我不知道的,你告诉我,我就知道了,很简单的事。智力是什么? 是对关系的判断。你告诉我秦始皇是怎么一回事,中国当时是怎样一种情况,问"秦始皇会怎样做"? 这才是智力所在。中国有个说法是"小时了了,大未必佳"。小时了了是五岁识得一千字,大未必佳是上大学了还不会洗脚。我在台湾听到诺贝尔化学奖得主李远哲先生讲,如果在家里没有做过家务,例如洗碗,成绩再好,我也不收他做化学博士研究生。

IQ 是 Intelligence Quotient 的缩写,它在西方行之有年,传到中国,也用来测之有年。不过,这个 IQ 是大有问题的。

IQ 是指,智力年龄÷实足年龄×100 之后的那个值。这个值若是 120 以上,算"聪明",不足 80 的,是"愚蠢",而且永远就是这样的,变不了。小时了了,大未必佳。小时了了是 IQ 绝对 120 以上,但是,大未必佳,也许会低于 80 很多。我们几乎人人都有这种身边的例子,小时的玩伴一直到大学毕业的同学,聪明,老师宠爱,亲友赞不绝口,五年过去了,十年过去了,当初被讥为"傻蛋"、"呆瓜"、"蠢猪"的孩子,留级生,常补课的,三脚踢不出个屁的,反而有出息得多。最有意思的是高材生们还在咀嚼当年的豪言壮语,智力低下到竟还没有明白那些目标既非豪也不壮,只是一点学生腔罢了。最令我惊异的是,我在美国遇到不少从中国来攻读学位的,也是如此。"美国"这个词,也是一种魅,好像它等同 IQ。因为中国人出国还非易事,这种魅还不易除,不过这些年来开始渐渐明朗了。

我有一次在聚会时说:"所谓好学生是一个问题只知道标准答案的人。"你如果明白一个问题有两种以上的答案,好,你苦了,考试一定难及格。事后才知道,这个意思结结实实得罪了一些人,这是我活该,因为我也把"好学生"表达为一种答案的形式了,可见我的 IQ 确实不到 80,也就是愚蠢。这个岁数还这样,改也难了。

IQ 的问题,在其计算公式的产生地也越来越遭到质疑,所以近十年来,EQ 的重要性很快地超过 IQ 的重要性。

EQ 是 Emotional Intelligence 的意思,译为情商,不过时髦的人直称 EQ,似乎用汉语说"情商",有 IQ 不足的嫌疑。

你会说,这已经是老生常谈了嘛,尤其丹纽·荀曼(Deniel Goleman)一九九三年写了那本畅销书《情感智力》(Emotional Intelligence)之后,EQ 已经成了常识。没错,我就在说这个常识。

也许你还记得我写过一篇《爱情与化学》,那篇文字里介绍过爬虫类脑是我们人类脑里的最原始部位,它主管着我们最基本的生命本能。这之后发展出古哺乳类脑,其中有个

"情感中枢"。

情感中枢中最古老的部分是嗅叶,负责接收和分析气味。气味对古老动物的重要,可说是攸关性命。食物可食否,是否为性对象,捕捉与被捕捉的辨别,都靠与气味的记忆的比对结果。

嗅叶只有两层细胞,第一层负责接收气味并加以分类,第二层负责传递反射讯息,通知神经,指挥身体采取何种反应。

当嗅叶进化发展成情感中枢时,脑才开始有情绪功能。而在进化过程中,逐渐形成的情感中枢逐步修正学习与记忆这两大功能,古哺乳类动物才有了更复杂的反应的可能。当然,气味是反应的基础,以至情感中枢里有了一个嗅脑部分。

一亿年前,到了新哺乳类动物的脑,也就是灵长类动物和之后人类的脑,开始增添了几层新细胞,智能开始出现了。

我这样的描述,是要警惕的,因为进化的情形并非是说有就有了。我们解剖看到脑的组成,之后描述了大的区别,至于进化过程的实证,生物学家还在寻找。

人类的脑,最终进化出了对感觉可以加以思考,也可以对概念、符号产生感觉的功能。脑神经的互联更为复杂,有更多的反应,情绪也就精致起来,可以对感觉有感觉。新哺乳类脑的情感中枢在脑神经的结构中是个非常非常重要的角色,对脑部的其他功能有非常非常大的影响,到了可以左右我们的思考能力的地步。

不过,我们要回到情感中枢的嗅脑那一部分,因为里面有两个部分极为重要，一个命名为海马回，一个命名为杏仁核，都是因为它们的形状，而非其功能。

我们知道，杏仁核的功能，是纽约大学神经科学中心的约瑟夫·勒杜克斯（Joseph leDoux）发现的。没有这个发现，EQ 的重要性不会超过 IQ。

勒杜克斯发现，当负责思考的大脑皮层对刺激还没有形成决定的时候，杏仁核已经指挥了我们的行为。我们有很多悔之莫及的行为，就是因为杏仁核的反应先于大脑皮层的思考，不免失之草率。

在这个发现之前，医学界认为感觉器官先将感觉信息传到丘脑，转为脑的语言，再传到大脑皮层的感觉处理区，整理成感觉，形成认知和意义，再传到情感中枢，决定如何反应，再通知其他脑区和全身。通常的情况确实如此，这意味着，杏仁核是依靠来自大脑皮层的指令来决定情绪反应。

勒杜克斯的革命性发现是，除了我们已经知道的丘脑到大脑皮层的神经元，他找到了我们以前没有发现的丘脑直达杏仁核的一小绺神经元。这样，杏仁核抢先于大脑皮层的处理过程，激发出情绪反应与相应的行为反应方式，先斩了再说。

勒杜克斯用实验证明了杏仁核处理过我们从未意识到的印象和记忆。他以极快的速度在试验者眼前闪过图形，试验者根本没有察觉，可是之后，他们会偏好其中的一些很奇特的图形，也就是说，我们在最初的几分之一秒，已经记得内容并决定了喜欢与否，情绪可以独立于理智之外。

至于海马回，则是一个情境记忆库，用来进行信息的比对，例如，关着的狼与荒野中的狼，意义不一样。海马回管的是客观事实，杏仁核则负责情绪意义，同时也是掌管恐惧感的中枢。如果只留下海马回而切掉杏仁核，我们在荒野中遇到一只狼不会感到恐惧，只是明白它没有被关着而已。又如果有人用一把枪顶在你脑袋上，你会思考出这是一件危险的事，但就是无法感到恐惧，做不出恐惧的反应和表情，同时也不能辨认别人的恐惧表情，于是枪响了。这是不是很危险？

杏仁核主管情绪记忆与意义。切除了杏仁核，我们也就没有所谓的情绪了，会对人失去兴趣，甚至会不认识自己的母亲，所谓"绝情"，也没有恐惧与愤怒，所谓"绝义"，甚至不会情绪性地流泪。虽然对话能力并不会失去，但生命可以说已经失去意义。

杏仁核掌管的恐惧，在动物进化中地位特殊，分量吃重，因为它决定了动物在生死存亡之际的反应，战还是逃。

杏仁核储存情绪记忆，当新的刺激出现，它就将之比对过去的记忆，新的刺激里只要有一项要素与过去相仿佛便算符合，它就开始按照记忆了的情绪经验启动行为。例如我们讨厌过一个人，以后只要这个人出现，我们不必思考就讨厌他或她。勒杜克斯称此为"认识前的情绪"。

这样，虽然杏仁核的反应是为保护我们的生存，但在一个变化迅速的环境里，我们不免会受到误导。因为一，很可能旧的情绪记忆相对新的刺激已经过时；二，杏仁核的反应虽然快，但失之草率。

我们的童年时期,是杏仁核开始大量储存情绪记忆的时期,这也就是一个人的童年经验会影响一个人一生的原因。一个成人,在事件发生时,最先出现的情绪常常就是他的杏仁核里童年就储存下来的情绪模式。你可以明白,父母常在小孩子面前吵架甚至动手,小孩子虽然小到还抱着奶瓶,但他已经"看"在杏仁核里了,他只是还不能思考这个记忆。这也就是最危险的。虐待,娇宠,虚伪,等等等等,小孩子将来有得好受了。前些年在美国爱荷华大学发生中国留学生卢刚杀人事件,是一个典型的 EQ 出了问题的例子,因为卢刚的 IQ 没有问题。童年,少年处在无产阶级文化大革命时期的人,他们的杏仁核,就是国家的情绪命运,跟着感觉走?

如果你还记得我在《爱情与化学》里介绍过的前额叶,你就知道事情还有补救。前额叶主司压抑,它的理性作用可以调节杏仁核的"冲动"。前额叶会在刺激的瞬间对各种可能进行评估,选出最佳决策,再策动行为。

这就是最基本的 EQ。

我们的社会,强调了知识,强调了知识经济,这似乎是没有问题的。但是没有 EQ,"人"将不"人","社会"将不"社会"。"劳动创造了人类",这个"劳动"如果讲的是工具使用,促使 IQ 不断发展,是有问题的。我看这个"劳动"应该解为劳动组织,这个组织,就是不断成熟的社会关系,它的成熟,是由人类的前额叶与杏仁核的互相平衡造成。我们的前额叶里都是一些什么软件?我们有怎样的行为被孩子的杏仁核记忆为情绪?

孔子在两千多年前就提出"仁",我们意识到那是个 EQ 的里程碑吗?孔子的教材里当然有彼时的 IQ 成果,但他的弟子们在《论语》里,记载的都是老师的 EQ 啊,那里面有迫切的情绪焦虑。两千年后的子孙没有了自己环境中的 EQ 问题吗?一个富足但是 EQ 低下的社会,是个可怕的社会吧? EQ 是不是较 IQ 来得重要而且迫切呢?

你如果说我既然用一种知识的形式讲出以上,所以是一种 IQ,所以 IQ 比 EQ 重要而且迫切,我当然只好闭嘴,去讲 EQ 对艺术的重要了,不过,那是下一个题目了。

一九九八年五月　墨西哥城

艺术与情商

一九八五年，评家说这一年是中国文学转型的一年，这一年，当时还是西德的一个叫 Patrick Suskind，中文译音为苏斯金（台湾译音为徐四金，正好与我的一个朋友重名）的人出版了他的一本小说 Das Parfun，意思是香水。

《香水》轰动西德，一下卖出了四十万本，旋即再轰动世界，被译成二十七种文字。苏斯金在一九八四年写过一个单人剧剧本《低音大提琴》，一直到现在还是德国常演出的剧。

出了《香水》之后，一九八七年，苏斯金有个短篇《鸽子》，九一年则有短篇《夏先生的故事》。《夏先生的故事》配插图，现在给小说做插图真是罕见，插图者是我最喜欢的漫画家桑佩（Jean – Jacques Sempe），我不太买小说，但这一本买了，算收藏。

《香水》实在是一本很绝的小说，绝在写的是嗅觉。小说开始的一段，我个人认为可删，（是不是狂妄了？）将第二段作为开始：

我们要讲的这个时代,城里到处弥漫着咱们当代人无法想象的臭味儿。道儿上是堆肥臭;后院是尿骚臭;楼梯间是烂木头味儿、老鼠屎味儿;厨房是烂菜帮子味儿;屋儿里憋着一股子陈年老灰味儿;卧房里是黏床单子味儿,潮被子味儿,尿壶的呛人味儿;烟囱是硫磺的臭鸡蛋味儿;皮革场是碱腥味儿;屠宰场是血腥味儿;人身上一股子汗酸味儿,衣服老不洗是股子酸臭味儿,嘴里喷烂牙味儿,胃里涌出来葱头的热臭味儿;上点儿年纪以后,就是一股子乳酪的哈啦味儿,酸奶和烂疮味儿。

河边儿臭,教堂臭,桥根儿臭,皇宫也臭。乡下人和教士一样儿臭,学徒和师傅的婆娘臭成一个样儿;贵族从头臭到脚;皇帝也臭,臭得像野畜生,皇后臭得像头老山羊,无冬无夏。十八世纪,还控制不了诸多细菌的祸害,人类拿它们没法子,凡是活物儿,别管老还是小,没有不臭的。

巴黎是法国最大的城圈子,所以最臭。这首善之区有个地方,打铁街和铁器街之间的无名尸坟场更是臭得出格儿。八百年了,主官医院和间壁的教区,成打的大车运来死人,堆到沟里,一层摞一层,天天如此,积了有八百年。一直到后来,法国大革命前,有几个死人堆塌了,漾出来的咸臭味儿让塞纳河边儿的人不是嚷嚷就算了,而是暴动。闹到后来,关了坟场,再起出几百万的烂骨头,运到蒙马特地下坟场,原来的地方儿,搞成个菜市儿卖吃的。

我特别用北京方言译了这一段,觉得这样才有味儿。苏斯金用味道画了一张巴黎的地图。苏斯金当年为写《香水》,一个人骑辆摩托车到法国南方香水产地转游,戴着墨镜什么也看不清,顶着头盔什么也听不见,所以,嗅觉就成了他仅有的感觉了。

说实在的,当今的北京,上海,不是也可以用味道辨认的吗?清朝咸丰年间,日本的一些崇拜中国文化的学者组了个团到北京旅游观光,以偿景仰。不料到了北京,大清国的帝都,路边有屎,苍蝇撞头,脏水出门就泼到街上,垃圾沿墙越堆越高,这些日本汉学者受的打击实在是大,有的人回去后不再弄汉学,有的则是自杀,真正做到眼不见为净。

我去印度,也是这样。印度有个特别处是烧各种香的味道。巴基斯坦则是本国航空公司的飞机上也是国味儿,羊膻气。美国加利福尼亚州南部,因为紫外线过于强烈,花不香,人好像住在电影里。

日本是冷香型,竹林中有一种苦凉的草香气,尤其雨后。

美国的香型是热香型,进干花店,一股子又甜又热的味道像热毛巾裹头,熏得眼珠子都突出来。我还是喜欢冷香型,例如茉莉花,梅花,当然最好还是兰花香,所谓王者香。桂花闻久了会觉得甜,有点儿热。夜来香闻久了是臭的。闽南的功夫茶,第一道倾在一个细高的杯子里,之后倒掉,将杯子放到鼻子底下闻,雅香入脑。天津的小站米,蒸或煮后,香味细甜。

说到臭,以前插队第一次坐马车到村里,路上眼睁睁地看到马放了一个屁,却闻不到味儿,于是等马再放屁,还是没有味儿,真是惊奇,原来还有不臭的屁。

最可怕是黄鼠狼的屁,臭得极其尖锐锋利。有的人的狐臭可以达到"无可比拟"的水平。唐朝时长安的胡人非常多,陈寅恪先生考证"狐臭"原来是"胡臭",即胡人的体臭,可是唐诗里好像没有哪一首感叹到,大概是没人有勇气将臭入诗。安禄山会做胡旋舞,臭味儿当然四散,玄宗皇帝和杨贵妃似乎闻不到,看得高兴地笑起来。

我写过一篇小说《洁癖》,讲一个人有洁癖,这在北京当然是很难过的,"最难熬是上厕所。只是用过的纸积成山这一项,就叫老白心惊肉跳。味儿呛得他流眼泪,老白很奇怪怎么别人还能蹲着聊天儿,说到高兴处,还能抽着气儿笑"。

动物是不食自己的粪便的,只有互食。粪便的味道阻止了排泄者回收自己的排泄物。"回收没有价值"等于"回收物没有价值",于是开骂,"狗改不了吃(人)屎","人类的狗屎堆","屁话","不须放屁,且看天地翻覆"。这最后一句是毛泽东的诗作,无产阶级文化大革命中曾被中央乐团编成交响合唱,"不须放屁"之后,有长号的拖音摹仿,其实远不如现场施放准备好的气味来得够情绪。不过,你也可以就此明白为什么唐朝诗人不将当时普遍的体臭入诗了。

当艺术还与原始宗教不可分的时候,气味是原始宗教中负责激起情绪的重要手段,流传下来的手段大概只有燃香一项了。"燃香沐浴",燃香,是制造规定的味道,沐浴则有祛除自己体味儿的作用;"斋戒",也就是禁食,则是降低排泄物的产生。外清里清,虔诚的情感状态来了。

我不妨引一下上一期关于嗅觉的部分:

> 情感中枢中最古老的部分是嗅叶,负责接收和分析气味。气味对古老动物的重要,可说是攸关性命。食物可食否,是否为性对象,捕捉与被捕捉的辨别,都靠与气味的记忆的比对结果。

> 嗅叶只有两层细胞,第一层负责接收气味并加以分类,第二层负责传递反射讯息,通知神经,指挥身体采取何种反应。

> 当嗅叶进化发展成情感中枢时,脑才开始有情绪功能。而在进化过程中,逐渐形成的情感中枢逐步修正学习与记忆这两大功能,古哺乳类动物才有了更复杂的反应的可能。当然,气味是反应的基础,以至情感中枢里有了一个嗅脑部分。

怪的是,艺术逐渐从宗教中分离后,愈分离得厉害,愈不带气味。歌,没有气味;诗,没有气味;音乐,也没有;画,有一点,但是"墨香"、"纸香"或"油画颜料的亚麻油味"。

电影被称为"综合艺术",而且它与时代科技发展紧密相随,但是电影就是没有味道。电影中最尴尬的镜头就是情人们在花丛中激情不已,观众闻到的只是电影院里各种奇怪的味儿。电影是只有"脏"没有"臭"的艺术。

我还记得参加过的一次电影拍摄。有个镜头是需要男女相吻，但女演员嫌男演员总是吻得时间过长，有被吃豆腐的感觉。我建议她吃一点韭菜或蒜一类的东西。果然，再拍时男演员只吻了一下就立刻离开她的嘴。不过放映效果是情人男吻了一下情人女，之后就目光炯炯地深情地望着情人女。我至今不知道的是女演员到底吃了点儿什么，因为拍摄现场找到蒜之类的东西的可能性太小了，我总不能怀疑她吃了屎吧？上个时代的美国性感男星克拉克·盖博，我想你多多少少总看过那部根据小说《飘》改编的电影《乱世佳人》吧？好，你想起来了。盖博是有名的口臭，与他有吻戏的女演员都有点胆战心惊，据说有导演喊"停"之后女演员昏倒的情况。

美国电影协会今年票选出美国的一百部名片，《乱世佳人》排名第四。如果你认为《公民凯恩》不应该排第一，《乱世佳人》就可以排到第三；如果你认为《卡萨布兰卡》和《教父》（第一集）不够排第二和第三，那《乱世佳人》就是第一了。评选的结果一出来，美国的录相带店又铺天盖地地贴出《乱世佳人》的那张著名的接吻海报，我经过的时候看到，想，导演为什么还不喊"停"？幸亏电影没有味儿。

艺术没有味儿，于是艺术只好利用视觉和听觉引发情感。

我们需要再回忆点常识。上一期讲到"情感中枢的嗅脑那一部分，里面还有两个部分极为重要，一个命名为海马回，一个命名为杏仁核，都是因为它们的形状，而非其功能。

"……当负责思考的大脑皮层对刺激还没有形成决定的时候，杏仁核已经指挥了我们的行为。我们有很多悔之莫及的行为，就是因为杏仁核的反应先于大脑皮层的思考，不免失之草率。

"……这样，杏仁核抢先于大脑皮层的处理过程，激发出情绪反应与相应的行为反应方式，先斩了再说。

"……至于海马回，则是一个情境记忆库，用来进行信息的对比，例如，关着的狼与荒野中的狼，意义不一样。海马回管的是客观事实，杏仁核则负责情绪意义，同时也是掌管恐惧感的中枢。如果只留下海马回而切掉杏仁核，我们在荒野中遇到一只狼不会感到恐惧，只是明白它没有被关着而已。又如果有人用一把枪顶在你脑袋上，你会思考出这是一件危险的事，但就是无法感到恐惧，做不出恐惧的反应和表情，同时也不能辨认别人的恐惧表情，于是枪响了。这是不是很危险？

"杏仁核主管情绪记忆与意义。切除了杏仁核，我们也就没有所谓的情绪了，会对人失去兴趣，甚至会不认识自己的母亲，所谓'绝情'，也没有恐惧与愤怒，所谓'绝义'，甚至不会情绪性地流泪。虽然对话能力并不会失去，但生命可以说已经失去意义。

"……杏仁核储存情绪记忆，当新的刺激出现，它就将之比对过去的记忆，新的刺激里只要有一项要素与过去相仿佛便算符合，它就开始按照记忆了的情绪经验启动行为。例如我们讨厌过一个人,以后只要这个人出现,我们不必思考就讨厌他或她。勒杜克斯称此为'认识前的情绪'。

"……我们的童年时期,是杏仁核开始大量储存情绪记忆的时期,这也就是一个人的童年经验会影响一个人一生的原因。一个成人,在事件发生时,最先出现的情绪常常就是他的杏仁核里童年就储存下来的情绪模式。"

造型艺术里的"真",所谓"写实",就是要引起与海马回里的情境记忆的比对,再引起杏仁核里的情绪记忆的比对,之后引发情绪。这是一瞬间的事。

我们可以由此讨论一下八十年代后期举办的一些人体画的展出。据学院派的意见,人体画是艺术,不是色情。但同样是艺术,静物画展不会引起人潮涌动的效果吧?所以,前提是裸体是引起同类异性性冲动的形象记忆,引发的情绪就是色情。不少国家的法律只规定生殖器部位的裸露程度来判定色情与艺术的分界线。

使裸体成为艺术,是在于大脑部分的判断,而这是需要训练的,而训练,不是人人都可以得到的。即使是美术学院这样的训练单位,模特也是不许当众除衣的,而是先在屏幕后除衣,摆好姿势,再除去屏幕。除衣是情境记忆,它会引发色情的情绪。

裸体模特隐避除衣,是本世纪初从欧洲引进的。当学生有过一定的训练之后,模特的进入程序就不严格了,最后达到可以走动,和学生聊天。美术学院的学生一定还记得第一次人体课开始时的死寂气氛吧?还记得多少年后仍在讲述的笑话吧？怎么会当了教授之后就误会凡人百姓都受过训练呢？

凡人百姓的训练是生活中的见惯不怪。我姥姥家的冀中，女人结婚后日常天热可不着上衣，观者见惯不怪，常常是新调来的县上的干部吓了一跳。所以不妨视冀中人为裸体艺术家，将县上新干部视为参观裸体艺术展的观众。一般来说，愈是乡下，裸体艺术家愈多，愈是城里，训练反而愈少。

知青初去云南，口中常传递的是女人在河里当众洗澡，绘声绘色，添油加醋，情绪涌动。几年之后，知青们如十年的老狗，视之茫茫。

这就是同样的形象反复之后，海马回都懒得比对了，也就引不起杏仁核的情绪比对了，也就没情绪了。我怀疑如果给畜生穿上衣服，一万年之后，它们也会有关于色情与艺术的争论。

人体艺术，真实可贵在你还爱人体。通过画笔见到的人体，会滋生出包括性欲但比性欲更微妙的情感。这不是升华，是丰富，说升华是暴殄天物。

音乐，我在《爱情与化学》里说过了，此不赘。

文学有点麻烦。麻烦在字是符号。识得符号是训练的结果，我们中国人应该记得小学识字之苦。训练意味着大脑在工作，所以人类的大脑里有一个专门的语言区。嗅叶，海马回，杏仁核都不会因符号而直接反应，它们的反应是语言区在接受训练时主动造成与它们的联系，联系久了，就条件反射了。例如先训练"红灯要停住"，之后见到红灯，就引起大脑的警觉,指挥停住。红灯这一图像符号经过反复训练,可以储存到海马回里归为危险情境,但当我们想事情的时候,还是会视而不见闯红灯。我小的时候常看到公共汽车司机座旁有个警告"行车时请勿与司机交谈",就是这个道理。

上个月,我的车被人从后面撞了两次。一次是后面的驾驶人在打手机,一次是后面的驾驶人在骂她的孩子。我现在从后视镜里不但要看后面车的情况,还要看驾驶人的情况,我觉得他们的海马回随时会有问题。

所以当我们阅读的时候,所谓引起了兴趣,就是大脑判断符号时引起了我们训练过的反应,引起了情感。文学当中的写实,就是在模拟一个符号联结系统,这个联结系统可以刺激我们最原始的本能,由这些本能再构成一个虚拟情境,引发情绪。所谓"典型",相对于海马回和杏仁核,就是它们储存过的记忆;相对于情感中枢,就是它储存过的关系整合,如此而已。"典型人物"大约属于海马回,"典型性格"大约属于情感中枢。

而先锋文学,是破坏一个既成的符号联结系统,所以它引起的上述的一系列反应就都有些乱,这个乱,也可称之为"新"。对于这个新,有的人引起的情感反应是例如"恶心",有的人引起的情感反应是"真过瘾",这些都潜藏着一系列的生理本能反应和情感中枢的既成系统整合的比对的反应。巧妙的先锋,是只偏离既成系统一点合适的距离,偏离得太多了,反应就会是"看不懂"。《麦田守望者》是一个偏离合适的例子,所以振振有词的反感者最多;《尤利西斯》是一个偏离得较远的例子,所以得到敬而远之的待遇。不过两本书摆在书架上,海马回是同等对待它们的。

电影,则是直接刺激听觉和视觉,只要海马回和杏仁核有足够的记忆储存,情感中枢有足够的记忆,不需训练,就直接进入了。引起的情绪反应,我们只能说幸亏电影不刺激嗅觉,还算安全。

实在说来,现代人的海马回里,杏仁核里,由电影得来的记忆储存得越来越多,所以才会有"那件事比电影还离奇"的感叹。

我建议研究美学的人修一下有关脑的知识,研究社会学和批评的人也修一下有关脑的知识,于事甚有补益。我不建议艺术创作的人修这方面的知识,因为无甚补益,只会疑神疑鬼,真实状态反而会被破坏了。写侦探小说的除外。

修艺术例如绘画学分的美国学生,你若问他你学到了什么,他会很严肃地说 thinking,也就是思想。这是不是太暴殄天物呢?因为学别的也可以学到思想呀,为什么偏要从艺术里学思想?读《诗经》而明白"后妃之德",吾深恶之,因为它就是 thinking 之一种。

IQ 弄好了,可以导致思想,但仅有智商会将思想导致于思想化,化到索然无味,心地狭小,于是将思想视为权力,门面,资本。如此无趣的人我们看到不少了。

EQ 也可以搞到不可收拾,但我还是看重情商。情商是调动、平衡我们所有与生俱来的一切,也许它们作为单项都不够优秀,但调和的结果应该是一加一大于二的状态。

身外之物,也许可以看淡,但身内之物不必看淡。佛家的禁欲,多是禁身内之物对身外之物的欲,办法是否定身内之物这个前提。少数人可以生前做到,多数人只能死后做到。这么难的事,实在是太难为一般人了。但一般人调和身内之物之间的平衡,则是自觉经验多一些就大体可以做到,不难的。平衡了,对外的索求,不是不要,而是有个度。有度的人多了,社会所需就大体有个数了,生产竞争的盲目性就缓解多了。盲目都是对于自身不了解。

这像不像痴人说梦?我觉得像,因为我们对自身的了解几乎还没有开始,无从开始情商的累积。我们大讲特讲智商的匮乏,将仅有的情商也作智商看待,麻烦事儿还在后头呢。

不过说到情商这一节,也就可以回答《爱情与化学》那一节的疑问了。假如爱情的早期性冲动在情感中枢中留下记忆,此记忆建立了情感中枢里的一个相应的既成系统,当化学作用消失了之后,这个系统还会主动运行的话(主动运行的意思是不受盲目的支配),原配的爱情就还有。否则,就是另外的爱情了。记住,爱情是双方的,任何一方都有可能败坏对方的记忆,而因为基因的程序设计,双方都面临基因利益的诱惑。

我们可以想想原配爱情是多高的情商结果,只有人才会向基因挑战,干这么累的活儿。

一九九八年七月　洛杉矶

闲话闲说

——中国世俗与中国小说

这个话题,恐怕很难讲清。

一个人能历得多少世俗?又能读得多少小说?况且每一篇小说又有不同的读法。好在人人如此,倒也可以放心来讲。

放心来讲,却又是从何讲起?

世俗里的"世",实在是大;世俗之大里的"俗",又是花样百出。我喜欢这花样百出,姑且来讲一讲看。

一

不妨从我讲起。

我是公元第一千九百四十九年、中华民国第三十八年四月生人。中华人民共和国同年十月成立,所以我呢算是民国出生,共和国长大。

按某种"话语"讲,我是"旧中国"过来的人,好在只有半年,所以没有什么历史问题,无非是尿炕和啼哭吧。

现在兴讲"话语"这个词,我体会"话语"就是"一套话"的意思,也就是一个系统的"说法"。

"历史问题"曾经是可以送去杀、关、管的致命话语,而且深入世俗,老百姓都知道历史问题是什么问题。

我出生前,父母在包围北平的共产党大军里,为我取名叫个"阿城",虽说俗气,却有父母纪念毛泽东"农村包围城市"革命战略成功的意思在里面。十几年后去乡下插队,当地一个拆字的人说你这个"城"字是反意,想想也真是宿命。

回头来说我出生前,共产党从北平西面的山上虎视这座文化名城,虽然后来将北平改回旧称为北京,想的却是"新中国"。

因此一九四九年在这个城市出生的许多孩子或者叫"平生",或者叫"京生",自然叫"建国"的也不少。一九五六年,我七岁上小学一年级,学校里重名的太多,只好将各班的"京生""平生""建国"们调来换去。

二

大而言之,古代中国虽有"封建"与"郡县"两制之分,但两千多年是"郡县"的延续,不同是有的,新,却不便恭维。

虽然本无新旧,一旦王朝改姓,却都是称做"创立新朝",那些典礼手续和文告,从口气上体会,也算另一种"创立新中国"吧。

次大而言之,一八九八年的戊戌变法,若将"郡县"改为

"君主立宪",也就真是一个新中国,因为这制度到底还没有过,可惜未成。

这之前四年的甲午战争,搞了三十年洋务的直隶总督北洋大臣李鸿章得知日本军舰刚刚换了新锅炉,节速比北洋水师军舰的高,在清廷主和以保实力。被动开战,则我旧中国人民不免眼睁睁看到了清廷海军的覆灭,留学英国回来的海军军事人才的折损。

这刺激比五十四年前与英国的鸦片战争要大,日本二十四年前才开始明治维新,全面学习西方。

"戊戌"之后清廷一九〇〇年相应变法,废除科举,开设学堂,派遣留学生,改定官制,准备推行三权分立的宪政,倒也按部就班。

此前一八七二年,已经容闳上议,清廷向美国派出第一批小童公费留学生,其中有我们熟知的一八八一年学成回国的铁路工程师詹天佑。

容闳自己则是一八四七年私费留学美国,入了美国籍,再回上海做买办。曾国藩委派他去美国买机器,他则建议清廷办合资公司。

你们看一个半世纪之后,一些拿了绿卡的中国留学生,还是在做同样的事情,这是有"古典"可寻的。

三

其实清廷有一项改革,与世俗之人有切肤的关系,即男人剪辫子。

也是按部就班,先海军,因为舰上机器极多,辫子绞进机器里很是危险,次新军,再次社会。

男人脑后留长辫,是满人的祖法。清廷改革中的剪辫,我认为本来是会震动世俗的,凡夫君子摸摸脑后,个个会觉得天下真要变了。

冲击视觉的形体变化是很强烈的,你们只要注意一下此地无处不在的广告当不难体会。

不过还没有剪到社会这一步,一九一一年,剪了辫子的新军在武昌造成辛亥革命,次年中华民国建立,清帝逊位。以当时四万万的人口来说,可算得是少流血的翻新革命。

秦始皇征战六国,杀人无算,建立一统的郡县制,虽然传递了两千年,却算不得善始。两千多年后,清帝逊位,可算得善终吧。

凡以汉族名分立的王朝,覆灭之后,总有大批遗民要恢复旧河山,比如元初、清初。

民初有个要复清的辫帅张勋,乃汉军旗,是既得满人利益的汉人。另一个例子是溥仪身边的汉人师傅郑孝胥。

日本人在关外立满洲国,关内的满人并不蜂拥而去。满族本身的复辟欲望,比较下来,算得澹泊,这原因没有见到什么人说过,我倒有些心得,不过是另外的话题了。

欧洲有个君主立宪小国,他们的虚位皇帝是位科学家,因为总要应付典礼实在无聊麻烦,向议会请废过几次,公民们却不答应。保鲜的活古董,又不碍事,留着是个乐子。另一个例子,你们看英国皇室的日常麻烦让几家英国报纸赚了多少钱!

设若君皇尚在虚位,最少皇家生日世俗间可以用来做休息的借口。海峡两岸的死结,君皇老儿亦有面子做调停,说两家兄弟和了吧,皇太后找两家兄弟媳妇儿凑桌麻将,不计输赢,过几天也许双方的口气真就软了,可当今简直就找不出这么个场面人儿。

不过这话是用来做小说的,当不得真。

四

若说清逊之后就是新中国,却叫鲁迅先生看出是由一个皇帝变成许多皇帝,写在杂文和小说里面。

冯玉祥将逊位的溥仪驱逐出紫禁城,中国的近代史几乎就是一部争做皇帝史,又是杀人无数。

你们对中国的近当代史都熟,知道孙中山先生说过"革命尚未成功,同志仍需努力"。什么"革命"没有成功?当然是指革命的结果新中国。相同的"志"是什么?当然还是新中国。

中国共产党的新中国"新"一些。马克思主义和列宁主义,都是当时中国要学习的西方文化里的现代派,新而且鲜。

恩格斯"甲午战争"时才逝去,列宁则一直活到一九二五年,而且一九一七年的俄国革命,震动世界,建立一种从来没有见过的国家制度,不管后果如何,总是"新"吧?

中国从近代开始,"新"的意思等于"好"。

也就因此,我们看毛泽东从"新民主主义"到"无产阶级文化大革命"其间的历次经济和政治运动,不断扫除一切的旧,是要建立一个新中国。

这些旧,包括戊戌变法甚至辛亥革命,算算到一九四九年还不够五十年,从超现实的观念上来说,却已经旧了。

五

我家离北京宣武门外的琉璃厂近,小时候常去逛,为的是白看画。六十年代初,荣宝斋挂一副郭沫若写的对联,上联是"人民公社好",下联是"吃饭不要钱",记不清有没有横批,总之是新得很超现实。不要说当时,就是现在,哪个国家可以吃饭不要钱?

六四年齐白石先生的画突然少了,几乎没有。听知道的人说,有个文化人买了齐白石画的一把扇子,回去研究,一面是农田里牧童骑牛,另一面题诗,最后的一句"劫后不值半文钱",被认为是齐白石攻击土地改革的铁证,报到上面内部定案,于是不宜再挂齐白石的画。

到了一九六六年"横扫一切牛鬼蛇神",其实已经没有什么可横扫的了,还是要横扫,竟持续了十年。

六

以一个超现实的新中国为号召,当然凡有志和有热情的中国人皆会趋之,理所当然,厚非者大多是事后诸葛亮,人人可做的。

这个超现实,也是一种现代的意思,中国的头脑们从晚清开始的一门心思，就是为迅速变中国为一个现代国家着急。凡是标明"现代"的一切观念，都像车票，要搭"现代"这趟车，不买票是不能上的。

看七十年代以前的中国，你就能由直观觉出现实与观念有多大差距，你会问，现代在哪里？超出了多少现实？走马观花，下车伊始就可以，不必调查研究，大家都不是笨人。

但是，看一九六六年的中国，你可能会在"艺术"上产生现代的错觉。

六六年六七年的"红海洋"、"语录"歌、"忠"字舞，无一不是观念艺术。想想《毛主席语录再版前言》可以谱上曲唱，不靠观念，休想做得出来。你现在请中国最前卫的作曲家为现在随便哪天的《人民日报》社论谱个曲，不服气的尽管试试。李劫夫是中国当代最前卫的观念作曲家。

"红海洋"也比后来的"地景艺术"早了十年，毛主席像章可算做非商业社会的"普普艺术"吧。

六六年秋天我在北京前门外大街看到一面墙壁红底上写红字，二十年后，八六年不靠观念是搞不出来的，当时却很轻易，当然靠的毛泽东的观念，靠的是"解放全人类"的观念。

凡属观念，一线之差，易为荒谬。比如"解放世界上三分之二的受苦人"的观念认为"世界上有三分之二的人生活在水深火热之中"。

这样一种超现实国家的观念与努力，近十多年来，很多中国人不断在批判。当然不少人的批判，还不是"批判"这个词的原义，很像困狠了的一个哈欠，累久了的一个懒腰。

我呢,倒很看重这个哈欠或懒腰。

七

扫除的"旧"里,有一样叫"世俗"。一个很明显的事实是,一九四九年以后,中国的世俗生活被很快地破坏了。

五十年代有部很有名的电影叫《董存瑞》,讲的是第三次内战时人民解放军攻克热河时炸掉堡垒桥的董存瑞的成长故事。电影里有个情节是农民牛玉合在家乡分了地,出来参加解放军,问他打败蒋介石以后的"理想",说是回家种地,一亩地,两头牛,老婆孩子热炕头儿,大家就取笑他。董存瑞的呢? 是建设新中国。

这两样都很感动人,董存瑞当然不知道他手托炸药包象征性地炸掉了"一亩地,两头牛,老婆孩子热炕头儿"。互助组,合作社,初级社,高级社,人民公社,一级比一级高级,超现实,现代,直到毛泽东的"五七"指示,自为的世俗生活早就消失了。

农民的自留地,总是处在随时留它不住的境界,几只鸡,几只鸭,都长着资本主义尾巴,保留一点物质上的旧习惯旧要求和可怜的世俗符号,也真是难。

一九六六年的无产阶级文化大革命提出的破"四旧",我问过几个朋友,近三十年了,都记不清是四样什么旧,我倒记得,是"旧习惯、旧风俗、旧思想、旧文化"。这四样没有一样不与世俗生活有关。

"新"的建立起来了没有呢? 有目共睹,十年后中国的

"经济达到了崩溃的边缘"。

北京我家附近有一个饭馆,六六年文化大革命的时候贴过一张告示,大意是从今后只卖革命食品,也就是棒子面儿窝头,买了以后自己去端,吃完以后自己洗碗筷,革命群众须遵守革命规定。八六年的时候,同是这家饭馆,墙上贴了一条告示:"本店不打骂顾客。"

我的经历告诉我,扫除自为的世俗空间而建立现代国家,清汤寡水,不是鱼的日子。

八

我七八岁的时候,由于家中父亲的政治变故,于是失去了一些资格,六六年不要说参加红卫兵,连参加"红外围"的资格都没有。

在书上的古代,这是可以"隐"的,当然隐是"仕"过的人的资格,例如陶渊明,他在田园诗里的一股恬澹高兴劲儿,很多是因为相对做过官的经验而来。老百姓就无所谓隐。

殊不知新中国不可以隐,很实际,你隐到哪里?说彭德怀元帅隐到北京西郊挂甲屯,其实是从新中国的高层机构"隐"到新中国的低层机构去了。

若说我是边缘人吧,也不对,没有边缘。我倒希望"阶级斗争"起来,有对立,总会产生边缘,但阶级敌人每天认错,次次服输,于是就制造一种新的游戏规则,你不属于百分之九十五,就属于百分之五。真是一种很奇怪的"数目字管理"。

我在云南的时候,上面派下工作组,跑到深山里来划分阶级成分。深山里的老百姓是刀耕火种,结绳记事,收了谷米,盛在麻袋里顶在头上另寻新地方去了,工作组真是追得辛苦。

更辛苦的是,不拥有土地所有权的老百姓,怎么来划分他们为"地主""富农""上中农""中农""下中农""贫农""雇农"这些阶级呢?所以工作组只好指派"成分",建立了低层机构,回去交差,留下糊里糊涂的"地主""贫农"们继续刀耕火种。

九

还是在云南,有一天在山上干活儿,忽然见到山下傣族寨子里跑出一个女子,后面全寨子的人在追,于是停下锄头看,借机休息一下。

傣族是很温和的,几乎看不到他们的大人打孩子或互相吵架,于是收工后路过寨子时进去看一下。问了,回答道:今天一个运动,明天一个运动,现在又批林彪孔老二,一定是出了"琵琶鬼",所以今天来捉"琵琶鬼",看看会不会好一点。

这"琵琶鬼"类似我们说的"蛊",捉"琵琶鬼"是傣族的巫俗,若发生了大瘟疫,一族的人死到恐慌起来,就开始捉"琵琶鬼"烧掉,据说可以止瘟疫。

我在乡下干活儿,抽烟是苦久了歇一歇的正当理由,不抽烟的妇女也可在男人抽烟时歇歇。站在那儿抽烟,新中国最底层机构的行政首长,也就是队长,亦是拿抽烟的人没有办法,顶多恨恨的。

中国地界广大，却是乡下每个村、城里每条街必有疯傻的人，病了傻了的人，不必开会，不必学习文件，不必"狠斗私字一闪念"，高层机构低层机构的一切要求，都可以不必理会，自为得很。

设若世俗的自为境地只剩下抽烟和疯傻，还好意思叫什么世俗？

十

我上初中的时候，学校组织去北京阜成门内的鲁迅博物馆参观，讲解员说鲁迅先生的木箱打开来可以当书柜，合起来马上就能带了书走，另有一只网篮，也是为了装随时可带的细软。

我寻思这"硬骨头"鲁迅为什么老要走呢？看了生平展览，大体明白周树人的后半生就是"走"，保全可以思想的肉体，北京，厦门，广州，上海，租界，中国还真有地方可避，也幸亏民国的北伐后只是建立了高层机构，让鲁迅这个文化伟人钻了空子。

不过这也可能与周树人属蛇有关。蛇是很机敏的，它的眼睛只能感受明暗而无视力，却能靠腹部觉出危险临近而躲开，所谓"打草惊蛇"，就是行路时主动将危险传递给蛇，通知它离开。蛇若攻击，快而且稳而且准而且狠，"绝不饶恕"。

我从七八岁就处于进退不得，其中的尴尬，想起来也真是有意思。长大一些之后，就一直捉摸为什么退不了，为什么无处退，念自己幼小无知，当然捉摸不清。

其实很简单，就是没有了一个可以自为的世俗空间。

十一

于是就来说这个世俗。

以平常心论，所谓中国文化，我想基本是世俗文化吧。这是一种很早就成熟了的实用文化，并且实用出了性格，其性格之强顽，强顽到几大文明古国，只剩下了个中国。

老庄孔孟中的哲学，都是老人做的哲学，我们后人讲究少年老成，与此有关。只是比较起来，老庄孔孟的时代年轻，所以哲学显得有元气。

耶稣基督应该是还不到三十岁时殉难，所以基督教富青年精神，若基督五十岁殉难，基督教恐怕不会是现在这个样子。

我们若是大略了解一些商周甲骨文的内容，可能会有一些想法。那里面基本是在问非常实际的问题，比如牛跑啦，什么意思？回不回得来？女人怀孕了，会难产吗？问得极其虔诚，积了那么多牛骨头乌龟壳，就是不谈玄虚。早于商周甲骨文的古埃及文明的象形文字，则有涉及哲学的部分。

甲骨文记录的算是中国"世俗"观的早期吧？当然那时还没有"中国"这个概念。至于哲学形成文字，则是在后来周代的春秋战国时期。

我到意大利去看庞贝遗址，其中有个图书馆，里面的内容当然已经搬到拿波里去了。公元七十九年八月，维苏威火山爆发，热的火山灰埋了当时有八百年历史的庞贝城，当然也将庞贝城图书馆里的泥板书烧结在一起。

三百年前发掘庞贝以后，不少人对这些泥板古书感兴趣，苦于拆不开，我的一位意大利朋友的祖上终于找到一个拆解的办法。

我于是问这个朋友，书里写些什么呢？朋友说，全部是哲学。吓了我一跳。

十二

道家呢，源兵家而来，一部《道德经》，的确讲到哲学，但大部分是讲治理世俗，"治大国若烹小鲜"，煎小鱼儿常翻动就会烂不成形，社会理想则是"甘其食，美其服，安其居，乐其俗"，衣、食、住都要好，"行"，因为"老死不相往来"，所以不提，但要有"世俗"可享乐。

"无为而无不为"我看是道家的精髓，"无为"是讲在规律面前，只能无为，热铁别摸；可知道了规律，就能无不为，你可以用铲子，用夹子，总之你可以动热铁了，"无不为"。后来的读书人专讲"无为"，是为了解决自己的困境，只是越讲越酸。

《棋王》里捡烂纸的老头儿也是在讲无不为，后来那个老者满嘴道禅，有点儿世俗经验的人都知道那是虚捧年轻人，其实就是为遮自己的面子，我自己遇到超过一个加强营的这种人，常常还要来拍我的肩膀摸我的头，中国人常用的世俗招法，话大得不得了，"中华之道"。我倒担心缺根弦儿的读者，当时的口号正是"振兴中华"，赢球儿就游行，失球儿就闹事,可说到底体育是什么呢？是娱乐。

爱因斯坦说民族主义就像天花，总要出的。我看民族主义虽然像天花，但总出就不像天花了。

汪曾祺先生曾写文章劝我不要一头扎进道家出不来，拳拳之意，我其实是世俗之人，而且过了上当中邪的年纪了。

道家的"道"，是不以人的意志为转移的自然秩序，所谓"天地不仁"。去符合这个秩序，是为"德"，违犯这个秩序的，就是"非德"。

十三

儒家呢，一本《论语》，孔子以"仁"讲"礼"，想解决的是权力品质的问题。说实在"礼"是制度决定一切的意思，但"礼"要体现"仁"。《孟子》是苦口婆心，但是倾向好人政府。

孔、孟其实是很不一样的，不必摆在一起，摆在一起，被误会的是孔子。将孔子与历代儒家摆在一起，被误会的总是孔子。

我个人是喜欢孔子的，起码喜欢他是个体力极好的人，我们现在开汽车，等于是在高速公路上坐沙发，超过两个小时都有点累，孔子当年是乘牛车握轼木周游列国，我是不敢和他握手的，一定会被捏痛。

平心而论，孔子不是哲学家，而是思想家。传说孔子见老子，说老子是云端的青龙，这意思应该是老子到底讲了形而上，也就是哲学。

孔子是非常清晰实际的思想家，有活力，肯担当，并不迂腐,迂腐的是后来人。

后世将孔子立为圣人而不是英雄,有道理,因为圣人就是俗人的典范,样板,可学。

英雄是不可学的,是世俗的心中"魔",《水浒》就是在讲这个。说"天下大乱,群雄并起",其实常常是"群雄并起,天下大乱"。历代尊孔,就是怕天下乱,治世用儒,也是这个道理。

儒家的实用性,由此可见。

孔子说过"未知生,焉知死",有点形而上的意思了,其实是要落实生,所以"未能事人,焉能事鬼",这态度真是好,不像老子有心术。现在老百姓说"死都不怕,还怕活吗",时代到底不一样,逼得越来越韧。

有时间的话,我们不妨从非儒家的角度来聊聊孔子这个人。

儒家的"道",由远古的血缘秩序而来,本是朴素的优生规定,所以中国人分辨血缘秩序的称谓非常详细,"五服"之外才可通婚,乱伦是大罪过,"伦"就是道。

之后将血缘秩序对应到政治秩序上去,所以"父子"对"君臣",父子既不能乱,君臣也就不许乱了。去符合这种"道",是为"德",破坏这种"秩序"的,就是"非德"。

常说的"大逆不道","逆"就是逆秩序而行,当然也就"不道",同乱伦一样,都是首罪。

"道貌岸然",也就是说你在秩序位置上的样子,像河岸一样不可移动错位。科长不可摆出局长的样子来。

所以儒家的"道",大约可以用"礼"来俗说。我们现在讲待人要有礼貌,本义是对方处在秩序中的什么位置,自己就要做出相应的样貌来,所谓礼上的貌。上级对下级的面无表情,下级对上级的逢迎,你看着不舒服,其实是礼貌。

最先是尊礼的孔子觉得要改变点儿什么,于是提出了"仁"。

十四

道德是一种规定,道变了,相应的德也就跟着变。

像美国这样一种比较纯粹的资本主义秩序,钱就是道,你昨天是穷人,在道中的位置靠后,今天中了"六合彩",你的位置马上移到前边去。

我认识的一位中国女作家,在道中的位置也就是级别,有权坐火车"软卧",对花得起钱也坐"软卧"的农民,非常厌恶,这也就是由"道"而来的对别人的"非德"感。中国人不太容暴发户,暴发户只有在美国才能活得体面自在。

"五四"新文化亦是因为要立新的道德,所以必须破除旧道德,"五千年的吃人礼教"。文化大革命"破四旧立四新",标榜的立新道德,内里是什么另外再论,起码在话语上继承"五四"革命传统的,我体会是中国共产党。

最看得见摸得着的"道德"是交通法规,按规定开车,"道貌岸然",千万不可"大逆不道"。英国对交通的左右行驶规定与美国不同,"道不同不相与谋",不必到英国去质问。

十五

有意思的是,诸子百家里的公孙龙子,名家,最接近古希腊的形式逻辑,他的著作汉时还有十四篇,宋就只有六篇了,讲思辨的文字剩不到两千字。

虽然《道德经》也只有五千言,但公孙龙子是搞辩论的,只剩两千字就很可惜。

一般来讲,不用的东西,容易丢。与庄周辩论的另一个名家惠施,要不是《庄子》提到,连影子都找不见。

这与秦始皇焚书有关,可秦皇不烧世俗实用的书,例如医药书,种树的书,秦始皇烧思想。

能统一天下的人,不太会是傻瓜,修个长城,治下的百姓才会安全受苦。世俗不能保持,你搜刮谁呢?

可长城修到民不聊生,也就成了亡国工程。

十六

常有人将道家与道教、儒家与儒教混说,"家"是哲学派别。

留传下来的儒道哲学既然有很强的实用成分,那么"教"呢?

鲁迅在《而已集·小杂感》里写过一组互不相干的小杂感,其中的一段杂感是:"人往往憎和尚,憎尼姑,憎回教徒,憎耶教徒,而不憎道士。懂得此理者,懂得中国大半。"

这一组互不相干的小杂感里,最后一段经常被人引用,就是："一见短袖子,立刻想到白臂膊,立刻想到全裸体,立刻想到生殖器,立刻想到性交,立刻想到杂交,立刻想到私生子。中国人的想象惟在这一层能够如此跃进。"这好懂,而且我也是具有"如此跃进"想象力的人,不必短袖子。现在全裸的图片太多,反倒是扼杀想象力的。

可是"不憎道士"的一段,我却很久不能懂。终于是二十岁里的一天在乡下豁朗朗想通,现在还记得那天的痛快劲儿,而且晚上正好有人请吃酒。

什么意思? 说穿了,道教是全心全意为人民,也就是全心全意为世俗生活服务的。

十七

道教管理了中国世俗生活中的一切,生、老、病、死、婚、丧、嫁、娶,也因此历来世俗间暴动,总是以道教为号召,从陈胜吴广,黄巾赤眉,汉末张角一路到清末的义和拳,都是。不过陈胜那时用的还是道教的来源之一巫签。

隋末以后,世俗间暴动也常用弥勒佛为号召,释迦牟尼虽是佛教首领,但弥勒下世,意义等同道教,宋代兴起一直到清的白莲教,成分就有弥勒教。

太平天国讲天父,还要讲分田分地这种实惠,才会一路打到南京,而洪家班真的模仿耶教,却让曾国藩抓到弱点,湘军焉能不胜太平军?

道教由阴阳家、神仙家来,神仙家讲究长生不老,不死,迷恋生命到了极端。

"一人得道,鸡犬升天",都成仙了,仍要携带世俗,就好像我们看中国人搬进新楼,阳台上满是旧居的实用破烂。

道教的另一个重要资源是巫签,翻一翻五千多卷的《道藏》,符咒无数,简直就是"十万个怎么办",不必问为什么,照办,解决问题就好。

巫教道教原来是没有偶像神的,有形象的是祥兽,羽人。张光直先生说"食人卣"上祥兽嘴里的那个人是巫师,祥兽送巫师上天沟通,我相信这样的解释,而怀疑李泽厚先生在《美的历程》里的"狞厉的美"。

彝器供之高堂,奴隶既无资格看见,怎么会被"狞厉"吓到? 奴隶应该是不准进电影院看"恐怖"片的人。"食人"卣,"狞厉"美,是启蒙以后的意识形态的判断。

回到话题来,佛教传入后,道教觉到了威胁。

佛教一下带那么多有头有脸的神来竞争,道教也就开始造偶像神,积极扩充本土革命队伍,例如门神的神荼郁垒终于转为秦叔宝和尉迟敬德。

《封神演义》虽是小说,却道着了名堂。名堂就是,道教的神,是由世俗间的优秀分子组成,这个队伍越来越壮大,世俗的疾苦与希望,无不有世俗所熟悉的人来照顾,大有熟人好办事的意思,天上竟一派世俗烟火气。

十八

这些年来兴起的气功热、特异功能热、易经热,都是巫道回复,世俗的实际需要。不解决世俗实际的"信仰"失落,传统信仰当然复归。

我觉得更有意思的是近年来毛泽东逐渐成为道教意义上的"神",世俗间以他的像来驱邪避难。而在此之前,他的命相,开国时辰,死亡大限与唐山大地震天示征兆,则在世俗间流传。最有意思是他在陕北与胡宗南周旋时在葭县请和尚算命的传说,当时的那个庙现在香火鼎盛。

人类学家不妨记录一下我们亲见的一个活人怎样变为一个道教神的过程,人证物证都还在,修起论文,很是方便。

十九

再来看儒教。

举例来说,儒家演变到儒教的忠、信,是对现实中的人忠和信。

孝,是对长辈现实生活的承担。

仁,是尊重现实当中的一切人。

贞,好像是要求妻子忠于死去的丈夫,其实是男人对现实中的肉欲生活的持久独占的哀求,因为是宋以后才塞进儒教系统的,是礼下庶人的新理性,与世俗精神有冲突,所以经常成为嘲笑的对象。

礼、义、廉、耻、忠、信、恕、仁、孝、悌、贞、节……一路数下来,从观念到行为,无不是为维持世俗社会的安定团结。

讲到这种关头,你们大概也明白常提的"儒道互补",从世俗的意义说来,不是儒家道家互补,而是儒教管理世俗的秩序,道教负责这秩序之间的生活质量。

这样一种实际操作系统,中国世俗社会焉能不"超稳定"?

二十

而且,这样一个世俗操作系统,还有自身净化的功能。

所谓世俗的自身净化,就是用现实当中的现实来解决现实的问题。比如一个人死了,活着的亲人痛哭不止,中国人的劝慰是:人死如灯灭,死了的就是死了,你哭坏了身体,以后怎么过?哭的人想通了,也就是净化之后,真的不哭了。

悲,欢,离,合,悲和离是净化,以使人更看重欢与合。

可以说,中国的世俗实用精神,强顽到中国从传统到现实都不会沉浸于宗教,长得烦人的历史中,几乎没有为教义而起的战争。

中国人不会为宗教教义上的一句话厮杀,却会为"肏你妈"大打出手,因为这与世俗生活的秩序,血缘的秩序有关,"你叫我怎么做人"?在世俗中做个人,这就是中国世俗的"人的尊严",这种尊严毫不抽象。

中国古代的骂阵,就是吃准了这一点,令对方主帅心里气恼,面子上挂不住,出去应战,凶吉未卜。我在乡下看农民或参加知青打架,亦是用此古法。

二十一

再者,我们不妨找两个例子来看看中国世俗的实用性如何接纳外来物的。

中国人的祖宗牌位，是一块长方形的木片，就是"且"字，甲骨文里有这个字，是象形的阴茎，中国人什么都讲究个实在。我前面已经讲过中国人对祖先亲缘的重视。

母系社会的祖是"日"，写法是一个圆圈当中一点，象形的女阴，也是太阳。中国不少地区到现在还用"日"来表示性行为。甲骨文里有这个字，因为当中的一点，有人说是中华民族很早就对太阳黑子有认识，我看是瞎起劲。

比起父系社会的"且"，"日"来得开阔多了。

后来父系社会夺了这个"日"，将自己定为"阳"，女子反而是"阴"，父者千虑，必有一失，搞不好，这个"日"很容易被误会为肛门的象形。

中国古早的阴阳学说，我总怀疑最初是一种夺权理论，现在不多谈。

男人自从夺了权，苦不堪言，而且为"阳刚"所累。世俗间颓丧的多是男子，女子少有颓丧。

女子在世俗中特别韧，为什么？因为女子有母性。因为要养育，母性极其韧，韧到有侠气，这种侠气亦是妩媚，世俗间第一等的妩媚。我亦是偶有颓丧，就到热闹处去张望女子。

明末到中国来的传教士，主张信教的中国老百姓可以祭祖先，于是和梵蒂冈的教皇屡生矛盾。结果是，凡教皇同意中国教民祭祖的时候，上帝的中国子民就多，不同意，就少。

耶稣会教士利玛窦明末来中国，那时将"耶稣"译成"爷苏"，爷爷死而苏醒，既有祖宗，又有祖宗复活的奇迹，真是译到中国人的心眼儿里去了。

天主教中的天堂，实在吸引不了中国人，在中国人看来，进天堂的意思就是永远回不到现世了。反而基督的能治麻风绝症，复活，等同特异功能，对中国人吸引力很大。

原罪，中国人根本就怀疑，拒绝承认，因为原罪隐含着对祖宗的不敬。

二十二

另一个例子是印度佛教。

印度佛教西汉末刚传入的时候，借助道术方技，到南北朝才有了声势，唐达于鼎盛，鼎盛也可以形容为儒、道、释三家并立。其实这时的佛教已是中国佛教的意义了。

例如印度佛教轮回的终极目的是要脱离现实世界，中国世俗则把它改造为回到一个将来的好的现实世界，也就是说，现在不好，积德，皈依，再被生出来，会好。这次输了，再开局，也许会赢，为什么要离开赌场？

释迦牟尼的原意是离开赌场。

观音初传到中国的时候，还是个长胡子的男人，后来变成女子，再后来居然有了"送子观音"。

这也怪不得中国人情急时是阿弥陀佛太上老君一起喊的。

佛祖也会呵呵大笑的，因为笑并不坏慈悲。

说到中国佛教的寺庙，二十四史里的《南齐书》记载过佛寺做典当营生,最早的中国当铺就是佛寺。

唐代的佛寺,常常搞拍卖会,北宋时有一本《禅苑清规》,详细记载了拍卖衣服的过程,拍卖之前,到处贴广告,知会世俗。

元代的时候,佛寺还搞过类似现在彩票的"签筹",抽到有奖。

佛寺的放贷、收租,是我们熟知的。鲁迅的小说《我的师父》,汪曾祺的小说《受戒》,都写到江南的出家人几乎与世俗之人无甚差别。

我曾见到过一本北洋政府时期北京广济寺主持和尚写的回忆录,看下来,这主持确是个经理与公关人才。主持和尚不念经是合理的,他要念经,一寺的和尚吃什么?

印度佛教东来中国的时候,佛教在印度已经处于灭亡的阶段,其中很大的原因是印度佛教的出世,中国文化中的世俗性格进入佛教,原旨虽然变形,但是流传下来了。

大英博物馆藏的敦煌卷子里,记着一条女供养人的祈祷,求佛保佑自己的丈夫拉出屎来,因为他大便干燥,痛苦万分。

二十三

至于禅宗,更是改造到极端。

中国禅宗认为世界实在得不得了,根本无法用抽象来表达,所以禅宗否定语言,"不立文字"。"说出的即不是禅",已经劈头一棍子打死了,你还有什么废话可说!

你们可以反问既然不立文字，为什么倒留下了成千上万言的传灯公案？

我的看法是因为世界太具体，所以只能针对每个人的不同，甚至每个人不同时期的实在状态，给予不同点拨。如果能用公案点拨千万人，中国禅宗的"万物皆佛"也就是妄言诳语，自己打自己的嘴巴了。

所谓公案，平实来看，就是记录历代不同个人状态的个案，而留下的一本流水账，实际是"私案"。现代人被那个"公"字绕住了，翻翻可以，揪住一案，合自己的具体状态，还好说，不合的话，至死不悟。

"说出来的即不是禅"是有来头的，老子说，"道，可道，非常道"，可以说出来的那个道，不是道，已经在否定"说"了。庄子说，"得鱼忘筌"，捕到鱼后，丢掉打鱼的篓子，也是在否定"说"，不过客气一点。有一个相同意思的"得意忘形"，我们现在用来已不全是原意了。

据胡适之先生的考证，禅宗南宗的不立文字与顿悟，是为争取不识字的世俗信徒。如此，则是禅宗极其实用的一面。

二十四

既然是实用的世俗文化系统，当然就有能力融合外来文化，变化自身，自身变化。

有意思的是，这种不断变化，到头来却令人觉得是保持不变的。我想造成误会的是中国从秦始皇"书同文"以后的方块象形字几乎没有变。汉代的木简，我们今天读来没有困难，难免让人恍惚。

你们都知道宋朝的李清照，她的丈夫赵明诚好骨董，李清照写《金石录后序》讲到战乱时如何保留收藏，说是插图多的书先丢，没有款识的古器先丢，原则是留下文字最为重要。读书人认为文字留下了，根也就保住了。

不识字的中国老百姓也晓得"敬惜字纸"，以前有字的纸是要集中在一起烧掉的，类似一种仪式，字，是有神性的。记得听张光直先生说中国文字的发生是为通人神，是纵向的，西方文字是为传播，是横向的。

我想中国诗发生成熟得那样早，而且诗的地位最高，与中国字的通神作用有关吧。这样地对待文字，文字焉敢随便变化？

我们可以注意一下词，词的变化和新词很多。大体说来，翻译佛经产生了很多新词，像"佛"、"菩萨"、"罗汉"、"金刚"、"波罗蜜"等等。

第二次是元杂剧，为了记录游牧民族带来的叠音，像"呼啦啦"、"滑溜溜"等等。有个朋友问我"乌七麻黑"怎么写，我说"乌七麻"大概是以前北方游牧民族带来的形容"黑"的词的音写，或者"七麻"是，加在"乌黑"当中，也许都是语音助词，总之多么多么"黑"就是了，将"乌"和"黑"写对，其他随便。

第三次仍然是为了适应外来文明，也就是近代。科学中化学名词最明显，生生造出许多化学元素的表音表义字，等于词。明末徐光启、李之藻那辈人翻译欧洲传来的数学天文知识,中国字词将将够,对付过去了。清末以后,捉襟见肘,说了几十年的"社会主义"、"共产主义"、"资本主义"、"反动"、"主任"、"主席"、"主观"、"传统"等等等等,都是外来语,直接从日本搬来的词形。鲁迅讲"拿来主义",他们那个时代,正是拼命拿来的时代。

二十五

我们看现在读书人的文章,外来的关键词不胜枚举,像什么"一元论"、"人道"、"人权"、"人格"、"人生观"、"反映"、"原理"、"原则"、"典型"、"肯定"、"特别"、"直觉"、"自由"、"立场"、"民族"、"自然"、"作用"、"判断"、"局限"、"系统"、"表现"、"批评"、"制约"、"宗教"、"抽象"、"政策"、"美学"、"客观"、"思想"、"背景"、"相对"、"流行"、"条件"、"现代"、"现实"、"理性"、"假设"、"进化"、"教育"、"提供"、"极端"、"意志"、"意识"、"经验"、"解决"、"概念"、"认为"、"说明"、"论文"、"调节"、"紧张",大概有五百多个。

我知道我再举下去,你们大概要疯了,而以上还只是从日文引进中文的几个例子,而且不包括直接译自西方的词,比如译自英文 Engine 的"引擎",lndex 的"引得","引得"后来被取自日文的"索引"代替了。

如果我们将引进的所有汉字形日文词剔除干净,一个现代的中国读书人几乎就不能写文章或说话了。

你们若有兴趣,不妨找上海辞书社编的《汉语外来词词典》来看看，一九八四年初版，收词相当谨慎。我的一本是一九八五年在湖南古丈县城的书店里买到，一边看一边笑。

二十六

从世俗本身来讲，也是一直在变化的，不妨多看野史、笔记。

不过正史也可读出端倪，中国历代的皇家，大概有一半不是汉人。孟子就说周文王是"西夷之人"。秦更被称为"戎狄"。常说的唐，皇家的"李"姓，是李家人还没当皇帝时被恩赐的。这李家人生"虬髯"，也就是卷毛连鬓胡子，不是蒙古人种，唐太宗死前嘱咐"丧葬当从汉制"，生怕把他当胡人埋了。

陈寅恪先生的《唐代政治史述论稿》上篇《统治阶级之氏族及其升降》里的考证非常详细，你们有兴趣不妨读读，陈先生认为种族与文化是李唐一代史事的关键，实在是精明之论。

我去陕西看章怀太子墓，里面的壁画，画的多是胡人，这位高干子弟交的尽是外国朋友，更不要说皇家重用的军事大员安禄山是突厥人，史思明是波斯人。安禄山当时镇守的河北，通行胡语，因此有人去过了河北回来忧心忡忡，认为安禄山必反。

唐朝人段成式的《酉阳杂俎》，你们若有兴趣，拿来当闲书读，一天一小段，唐的世俗典故，物品来源，写得健朗。

也是唐朝人的崔令钦的《教坊记》，现在有残卷，里面记的当时唐长安、洛阳的世俗生活,常有世俗幽默,又记下当年的曲名,音乐大部分是外来的,本来的则专称"清乐"。

二十七

我想唐代多诗,语句比后世的诗通俗,是因为新的音乐进来。

唐诗应该是唱的,所谓"装腔",类似填词,诗配腔,马上就能唱,流布开来。

唐传奇里有一篇讲到王之涣与另外两个大诗人在酒楼喝酒,听到旁边有一帮伎女唱歌,于是打赌看唱谁的诗多。

我们觉得高雅的唐诗,其实很像现在世俗间的流行歌曲、卡拉OK。

白居易到长安,长安的名士顾况调侃他说"长安米贵,白居不易",意思是这里米不便宜,留下来难哪,这其实是说流行歌曲的填词手竞争激烈。

白居易讲究自己的诗通俗易懂,传说他做了诗要去念给不识字的妇女小孩听,这简直就把通俗做了检验一切的标准了。

做诗,自己做朋友看就是了,为什么会引起生存竞争?看来唐朝的诗多商业行为的成分,不过商品质量非常高,伪劣品站不住脚。

唐代有两千多诗人的五万多首诗留下来,恐怕靠的是世俗的传唱。

唐的风采在灿烂张狂的世俗景观,这似乎可以解释唐为什么不产生哲学家,少思想家。

二十八

大而言之,周,秦,南北朝,隋唐,五代,元,清,皇家不是汉人。辛亥革命的"驱逐鞑虏,恢复中华"若说的是恢复到明,明的朱家却是回族,这族谱保存在美国。

汉族种性的纯粹,是很可怀疑的,经历了几千年的混杂,你我都很难说自己是纯粹的汉人。在座有不少华裔血统的人生连鬓胡须,这就是胡人的遗传,蒙古人种的是山羊胡子,上唇与下巴的胡须与鬓并不相连。

中国历代的战乱,中原人不断南迁。广东人说粤语是唐音,我看闽南语亦是古音,以这两个地区的语音读唐诗,都在韵上。

北方人读唐诗,声音其实不得精神,所以后来专有金代官家的"平水韵"来适应。毛泽东的诗词大部分用的就是明清以来做近体诗的平水韵。

所谓的北方话,应该是鲜卑语的变化,例如入声消失了。你想北方游牧民族骑在马背上狂奔,入声音互相怎么会听得到? 听不到岂不分道扬镳,背道而驰? 入声音是会亡族灭种的。

内地说的普通话,台湾说的国语,都是北方游牧民族的话。杭州在浙江,杭州话却是北方话。北宋南迁,首都汴梁也就是现在的开封,转成了南宋的临安也就是现在的杭州,想来杭州话会是宋时的河南话?

殷人大概说的是最古的汉话,因为殷人是我们明确知道的最古的中原民族,不过炎帝治下的中原民族说的话,也可算是汉话,也许我们要考一考苗瑶的语言?不过这些是语言历史学者的领域。

二十九

我去福建,到漳浦,县城外七十多里吧,有个"赵家城"在山里头,原来是南宋宗室赵若和模仿北宋的汴梁建了个迷你石头城,为避祸赵姓改姓黄。过了一百年,元朝覆亡,黄姓又改回姓赵。汴京有两湖,"赵家城"则有两个小池塘模仿着。城里有"完璧楼",取"完璧归赵"的意思。

我去的时候城里城外均非人民公社莫属,因为石头城保存得还好,令我恍惚以为宋朝就有了人民公社。

中国南方的客家人保存族谱很认真,这是人类学的一大财富。中国人对汉族的历史认真在二十几史,少有人下死工夫搞客家人的族谱,他们的语言,族谱,传说,应该是中原民族的年轮,历代"汉人""客"来"客"去的世俗史。

我去纽约哥伦比亚大学的东亚图书馆,中国的原版地方志多得不得了,回北京后说给一个以前在琉璃厂旧书铺的老伙计听。我这个忘年交说,辛亥革命后,清朝的地方志算是封建余孽,都拉到琉璃厂街两边儿堆着,好像现在北京秋后冬储菜的码法儿。日本人先来买,用文明棍儿量高,一文明棍儿一个大铜子儿拿走,日本人个儿矮棍儿也短,可日本人懂。后来西洋人来买,西洋人可是个儿高棍儿也长,还是一文明棍儿一个铜子儿拿走。不教他们拿走,也是送去造纸,堆这儿怎么走道儿呀?

中国的文化大革命是从秦始皇开始的传统,之前的周灭商,周却是认真学习商的文明制度。我们看陕西出土的甲骨上的字形,刻得娟秀,一副好学生的派头。孔子是殷人的后裔,说"吾从周",听起来像殷奸的媚语,其实周礼学殷礼,全盘"殷"化,殷亡,殷人后裔孔子坦然从周,倒是有道理的。

秦始皇以后,历代常常是民族主义加文化小革命,一直到辛亥革命的"驱逐鞑虏,恢复中华",都是。元朝最初是采取种族灭绝政策,汉人的反弹是"八月十五杀鞑子"。

之后一九六六年的文化大革命,新鲜在有"无产阶级"四个字,好像不关种族了,其实毁起人来更是理直气壮的超种族。论到破坏古迹,则太平天国超过无产阶级文化大革命。

三十

现在常听到说中国文化只剩下一个吃,但中国世俗里如此讲究吃,无疑是看重俗世的生活质量吧?

我八五年第一次去香港,当下就喜欢,就是喜欢里面世俗的自为与热闹强旺。说到吃,世间上等的烹调,哪国的都有,而且还要变化得更好,中国的几大菜系就更不用说了。

粤人不吃剩菜,令我这个北方长成的人大惊失色,北方谁舍得扔剩菜?从前北京有一种苦力常吃的饭食叫"折箩",就是将所有的剩菜剩饭汇在一起煮食。我老家的川菜,麻辣的一大功能就是遮坏,而且讲究回锅菜,剩菜回一次锅,味道就深入一层。

中国对吃的讲究,古代时是为祭祀,天和在天上的祖宗要闻到飘上来的味儿,才知道俗世搞了些什么名堂,是否有诚意,所以供品要做出香味,味要分得出级别与种类,所谓"味道"。远古的"燎祭",其中就包括送味道上天。《诗经》、《礼记》里这类郑重描写不在少数。

前些年文化热时,用的一句"魂兮归来",在屈原的《楚辞·招魂》里,是引出无数佳肴名称与做法的开场白,屈子历数人间烹调美味,诱亡魂归来,高雅得不得了的经典,放松来读,是食谱。

咱们现在到无论多么现代化管理的餐厅,照例要送上菜单,这是古法,只不过我们这种"神"或"祖宗"要付钞票。

商王汤时候有个厨师伊尹,因为烹调技术高,汤就让他做了宰相,烹而优则仕。那时煮饭的锅,也就是鼎,是国家最高权力的象征,闽南话现在仍称锅为鼎。

极端的例子是烹调技术可以用于做人肉,《左传》、《史记》都有记录,《礼记》则说孔子的学生子路"醢矣","醢"读如"海",就是人肉酱。

转回来说这供馔最后要由人来吃,世俗之人嘴越吃越刁,终于造就一门艺术。

香港的饭馆里大红大绿大金大银,语声喧哗,北人皆以为俗气,其实你读唐诗,正是这种世俗的热闹,铺张而有元气。

香港人好鲜衣美食,不避中西,亦不贪言中华文化,正是唐代式的健朗。

三十一

内地人总讲香港是文化沙漠,我看不是,什么都有,端看你要什么。比如你可以订世界上任何地方的任何书,很快就来了,端看你订不订,这怎么是沙漠?

香港又有大量四九年居留下来的内地人,保持着自己带去的生活方式,于是在内地已经消失的世俗精致文化,香港都有,而且是活的。

任何时候,任何地方,沙漠都在心里。

你们若是喜欢看香港电影,不知道了不了解香港是没有电影学院的。依我看香港的电影实在令人惊奇。以香港的人口计算,香港好演员的比例惊人。你们看张曼玉,五花八门都演得,我看她演阮玲玉,里弄人言前一个转身,之绝望之鄙夷之苍凉,柏林电影奖好像只有她这个最佳女演员是给对了。

香港演员的好,都是从世俗带过来的。这就像以前中国电影演员的好,比如阮玲玉、石挥、赵丹、上官云珠、李纬的好,也是从世俗带过来的。现在呢,《阿飞正传》这种电影,也只有香港才拍得出来。

三十二

中国读书人对世俗的迷恋把玩,是有传统的,而且不断地将所谓"雅"带向俗世,将所谓"俗"弄成"雅",俗到极时便是雅,雅至极处亦为俗,颇有点"前'后现代'"的意思。不过现在有不少雅士的玩儿俗,一派"雅"腔,倒是所谓的媚俗了。

你们若有兴趣,不妨读明末清初的张岱,此公是个典型的迷恋世俗的读书人,荤素不避,他的《陶庵梦忆》有一篇"方物",以各地吃食名目成为一篇散文,也只有好性情的人才写得来。

当代的文学家汪曾祺常常将俗物写得很精彩,比如咸菜、萝卜、马铃薯。古家具专家王世襄亦是将鹰、狗、鸽子、蛐蛐儿写得好。肯写这些,写好这些,靠的是好性情。

中国前十年文化热里有个民俗热,从其中一派惊叹声中,我们倒可以知道雅士们与世俗隔绝太久了。

有意思的是,不少雅士去关怀俗世匠人,说你这是艺术呀,弄得匠人们手艺大乱。

野麦子没人管,长得风风火火,养成家麦子,问题来了,锄草,施肥,灭虫,防灾,还常常颗粒无收。对野麦子说你是伟大的家麦子,又无能力当家麦子来养它,却只在客厅里摆一束野麦子示雅,个人玩儿玩儿还不打紧,"兼济天下",恐怕也有"时日曷丧"的问题。

我希望的态度是只观察或欣赏,不影响。

三十三

若以世俗中的卑陋丑恶来质问,我也真是无话可说。

说起来自己这几十年,恶的经验比善的经验要多多了,自己亦是爬滚混摸,靠闪避得逞至今。所谓"俗不可耐",觉到了看到了也是无可奈何得满胸满腹，再想想却又常常笑起来。

揭露声讨世俗人情中的坏，从《诗经》就开始，直到今天，继续下去是无疑的。

中国世俗中的所谓卑鄙丑恶，除了生命本能在道德意义上的盲目以外，我想还与几百年来"礼下庶人"造成的结果有关，不妨略说一说。

本来《礼记》中记载古代规定"刑不上大夫，礼不下庶人"，讲的是礼的适用范围不包括俗世，因此俗世得以有宽松变通的余地，常保生机。

孔子懂这个意思，所以他以仁讲礼是针对权力阶层的。

战国时代是养士，士要自己推荐自己，尚无礼下庶人的迹象。

西汉开始荐举，荐举是由官员据世俗舆论，也就是"清议"来推荐新的官员，这当中还有许多重要因素，但世俗舆论中的道德评判标准，无疑是荐举的标准之一。汉代实现"名教"，"清议"说明"名教"扩散到俗世间，开始礼下庶人。汉承秦制，大一统的意识形态是否促进了礼下庶人呢？

魏晋南北朝的臧否人物和那时的名士行为，正是对汉代延续下来的名教的反动。

从记载上看，隋唐好一些。

礼下庶人，大概是宋开始严重起来的吧，朱熹讲到有个老太太说我虽不识字，却可以堂堂正正做人。这豪气正说明"堂堂正正"管住老太太了，其实庶人不必有礼的"堂堂正正",俗世间本来是有自己的风光的。

明代是礼下庶人最厉害的时候,因此贞节牌坊大量出现,苦贞、苦节,荼害世俗。晚明读书人的颓风,或李贽式的特立独行,亦是对礼下庶人的反动。

清在礼下庶人这一点上是照抄明。王利器先生辑录过一部《元明清三代禁毁小说戏曲史料》,分为"中央法令"、"地方法令"、"社会舆论"三部分,仅这样的分法,就见得出礼下庶人的理路。略读之下,已经头皮发紧了。

民国初年的反"吃人的礼教",是宋以后礼下庶人的反弹,只不过当时的读书人一竿子打到孔子。孔子是"从周"的,周是"礼不下庶人"的。我说过了,被误会的总是孔子。

三十四

"刑不上大夫"是维护权力阶层的道德尊严,这一层的道德由不下庶人的礼来规定执行。孔子入太庙每事问,非常谨慎,看来他对礼并非全盘掌握,可见礼的专业化程度,就像现在一个画家进到录音棚,虽然也是搞艺术的,仍要"每事问"。孔子大概懂刑,所以后来做过鲁国的司寇,但看他的运用刑,却是防患于未然,有兵家的"不战而屈人之兵"的意思。

先秦以前世俗间本来是只靠刑来治理,所谓犯了什么刑条,依例该怎么罚。"民可使由之不可使知之"。孔子反对当时晋的赵简子将刑条铸在鼎上公之于众,看来刑的制定和彝器,规定是不让"民"看到而知之。

大而言之,我体会"礼不下庶人"的意思是道德有区隔。

刑条之外,庶人不受权力阶层的礼的限制,于是有不小的自为空间。礼下庶人的结果,就是道德区隔消失,权力的道德规范延入俗世,再加上刑一直下庶人,日子难过了。

解决的方法似乎应该是刑既上大夫也下庶人,所谓法律面前人人平等,礼呢,则依权力层次递减,也就是越到下层越宽松,生机越多。

你们看我在这里也开起药方来,真是惭愧。

三十五

中国的读书人总免不了要开药方,各不相同。

一九六六年的夏天,北京正处在无产阶级文化大革命最有戏剧性场面的那段时期,毛泽东接见红卫兵,抄家,揪斗走资派,著名的街道改换名称。一天中午,我经过西单十字路口,在长安大戏院的旁边有一群人围着,中国永远是有人围着,我也是喜欢围上去搞个明白的俗人,于是围了上去。

原来是张大字报,写的是革命倡议,倡议革命男女群众夏天在游泳池游泳的时候,要穿长衣长裤,是不是要穿袜子记不清了,我记得是不需要戴帽子。

围着的人都不说话,好像在看一张讣告。我自己大致想象了一下,这不是要大家当落汤鸡吗?

游泳穿长衣的革命倡议,还没有出几百年来礼下庶人的恶劣意识,倒是围着的人的不说话,有意思。

像我当时那样一个十几岁的少年,你不提穿长衣游泳,我倒还没有想到原来是露着的,这样一提,真是有鲁迅说的

"短袖子"的激发力。我猜当时围着的成年人的不说话，大概都在发挥想象力，顾不上说什么了。我想现在还有许多北京人记得西单的那张大字报吧？

丹麦的安徒生写过一篇《皇帝的新衣》，我们不妨来篇《礼下庶人的湿衣》。

我在美国，看选举中竞选者若有桃色新闻，立刻败掉，一般公民则无所谓，也就是"礼不下庶人"的意思。因此美国有元气的另一个特点是学英雄而少学圣贤。我体会西方所谓的知识分子，有英雄的意思，但要求英雄还要有理性，实在太难了，所以虽然教育普及读书人多，可称知识分子的还是少。

三十六

"五四"的时候有一个说法，叫"改造国民性"。

也许有办法改造国民性，比如改变教科书内容曾改变了清末民初的读书人，所以民初有人提倡"教育救国"，是个稳妥可行的办法，只是中国至今文盲仍然很多。

但通过读书改造了自己的"国民性"的大部分读书人，又书生气太重，胸怀新"礼"性，眼里揉不进砂子，少耐性，好革命，好指导革命。

我在云南的时候，每天扛着个砍刀看热带雨林，明白眼前的这高高低低是亿万年自然形成的，香花毒草，哪一样也不能少，迁一草木而动全林，更不要说革命性的砍伐了。我在内蒙亦看草原，原始森林和草原被破坏后不能恢复，道理都就在这里。

我后来躺在草房里也想通了"取其精华，去其糟粕"是一厢情愿，而且它们连"皮之不存，毛将焉附"的关系都不是，皮、毛到底还是可以分开的。

　　糟粕、精华是一体，世俗社会亦是如此，"取"和"去"是我们由语言而转化的分别智。

　　鲁迅要改变国民性，也就是要改变中国世俗性格的一部分。他最后的绝望和孤独，就在于以为靠读书人的思想，可以改造得了，其实，非常非常难做到，悲剧也在这里。

　　所谓悲剧，就是毁掉英雄的宿命，鲁迅懂得的。但终其一生，鲁迅有喜剧，就在于他批判揭露"礼下庶人"的残酷与虚伪，几百年来的统治权力对这种批判总是扑杀的。我在这里讲到鲁迅，可能有被理解为不恭的地方，其实，对我个人来说，鲁迅永远是先生。

　　我想来想去，怀疑"改造国民性"这个命题有问题，这个命题是"改造自然"的意识形态的翻版，对于当下世界性的环境保护意识，我们不妨多读一点弦外之音。而且所谓改造国民性，含礼下庶人的意思，很容易就被利用了。

　　中国文化的命运大概在于世俗吧，其中的非宿命处也许就是脱数百年来的礼下庶人，此是我这个晚辈俗人向"五四"并由此上溯到宋元明清诸英雄的洒祭之处。

三十七

　　世俗既无悲观，亦无乐观，它其实是无观的自在。

　　喜它恼它都是因为我们有个"观"。以为它要完了，它又元气回复，以为它万般景象，它又恹恹的，令人忧喜参半，哭笑不得。

世俗总是超出"观"，令"观"观之有物，于是"观"也才得以为观。

我讲来讲去，无非也是一种"观"罢了。

三十八

大致观过了世俗，再来试观中国小说。

"五四"以前的小说一路开列上去不免啰嗦，但总而观之，世俗情态溢于言表。

近现代各种中国文学史，语气中总不将中国古典小说拔得很高，大概是学者们暗中或多或少有一部西方小说史在心中比较。

小说的价值高涨，是"五四"开始的。这之前，小说在中国没有地位，是"闲书"，名正言顺的世俗之物。

做《汉书》的班固早就说"小说家者流，盖出于稗官。街谈巷语，道听途说者之所造也"，而且引孔子的话"是以君子弗为也"，意思是小人才写小说。

我读《史记》，是当它小说。史是什么？某年月日，谁杀谁。孔子做《春秋》，只是改"杀"为"弑"，弑是臣杀君，于礼不合，一字之易，是为"春秋笔法"，但还是史的传统，据实，虽然藏着判断，但不可以有关于行为的想象。

太史公司马迁家传史官，他当然有写史的训练，明白写史的规定，可你们看他却是写来活灵活现，他怎么会看到陈胜年轻时望到大雁飞过而长叹？鸿门宴一场，千古喋谈，太史公被汉武帝割了卵子，心里恨着刘汉诸皇，于是有倾向性的细节出现笔下了。

他也讲到写这书是"发愤"，"发愤"可不是史官应为，却是做小说的动机之一种。

《史记》之前的《战国策》，也可作小说来读，但无疑司马迁是中国小说第一人。同是汉朝的班固，他的功绩是在《汉书》的《艺文志》里列了"小说"。

三十九

到了魏晋的志怪志人，以至唐的传奇，没有太史公不着痕迹的布局功力，却有笔记的随记随奇，一派天真。

后来的《聊斋志异》，虽然也写狐怪，却没有了天真，但故事的收集方法，蒲松龄则是请教世俗。

莫言也是山东人，说和写鬼怪，当代中国一绝，在他的家乡高密，鬼怪就是当地世俗构成，像我这类四九年后城里长大的，只知道"阶级敌人"，哪里就写过他了？我听莫言讲鬼怪，格调情怀是唐以前的，语言却是现在的，心里喜欢，明白他是大才。

八六年夏天我和莫言在辽宁大连，他讲起有一次回家乡山东高密，晚上近到村子，村前有个芦苇荡，于是卷起裤腿涉水过去。不料人一搅动，水中立起无数小红孩儿，连说吵死了吵死了，莫言只好退回岸上，水里复归平静。但这水总是要过的，否则如何回家？家又就近在眼前，于是再蹚到水里，小红孩儿们则又从水中立起,连说吵死了吵死了。反复了几次之后,莫言只好在岸上蹲了一夜,天亮才涉水回家。

这是我自小以来听到的最好的一个鬼故事,因此高兴了很久,好像将童年的恐怖洗净,重为天真。

四十

唐朝还有和尚的"俗讲",就是用白话讲佛的本生故事,一边唱,用来吸引信徒。我们现在看敦煌卷子里的那些俗讲抄本,见得出真正世俗形式的小说初型。

宋元时候,"说话"非常发达,鲁迅说宋传奇没有创造,因有说话人在。

不过《太平广记》里记载隋朝就有"说话"人了,唐的话本,在敦煌卷子里有些残本,例如有个残篇《伍子胥》,读来非常像现在北方的曲艺比如京韵大鼓的唱词,节奏变化应该是随音乐的,因为有很强的呼吸感。

周密的《武林旧事》记载南宋的杭州一地就有说话人百名,不少还是妇女,而且组织行会叫"书会"。说话人所据的底本就是"话本"。

我们看前些年出土的汉说书俑,形态生动得不得了,应该是汉时就有说书人了,可惜没有文字留下来,但你们不觉得《史记》里的"记""传"就可以直接成为说的书,尤其是《刺客列传》?

宋元话本,鲁迅认为是中国小说史的一大变迁。我想,除了说话人,宋元时民间有条件大量使用纸,也是原因。那么多说话人,总不能只有一册"话本"传来传去吧?

汉《乐府》可唱,唐诗可唱,我觉得宋诗不可唱。宋诗入理,理唱起来多可怕,好比文化大革命的语录歌,当然语录歌是观念,强迫的。宋词是唱的。

中国人自古就讲究说故事,以前跟皇帝讲话,不会说故事,脑袋就要搬家。

春秋战国产生那么多寓言,多半是国王逼出来的。

王蒙讲了个《稀粥的故事》,有人说是影射,闹得王蒙非说不是,要打官司。其实用故事影射,是传统,影射得好,可传世。

记得二十年前在乡下的时候,有个知青早上拿着短裤到队长那里请假,队长问他你请什么假?他说请例假吧。队长说女人才有例假,你请什么例假!他说女人流血,男人遗精,精、血是同等重要的东西,我为什么不能请遗精的例假?队长当然不理会这位山沟里的修辞家。

我曾经碰到件事,一位女知青恨我不合作,告到支书前面,说我偷看她上厕所。支书问我,我说看了,因为好奇她长了尾巴。支书问她你长了尾巴没有?她说没有。

乡下的厕所也真是疏陋,对这样的诬告,你没有办法证明你没看,只能说个不合事实的结果,由此反证你没看。幸亏这位支书有古典明君之风,否则我只靠"说故事"是混不到今天讲什么世俗与小说的。

四十一

元时读书人不能科举做官,只好写杂剧,应该说这是中国世俗艺术史上的另一个"拍案惊奇"。

元的文人大规模进入世俗艺术创作,景观有如唐的诗人写诗。

元杂剧读来令人神往的是其中的世俗情态与世俗口语。

"杂剧"这个词晚唐以来一直有,只是到元杂剧才成为真正的戏剧,此前杂剧是包括杂耍的。台湾"表演工作坊"来美国演出过的《那一夜我们说相声》,体例非常像记载中的宋杂剧。

金杂剧后来又称"院本",是走江湖的人照本宣科,不过这些江湖之人将唱曲,也就是诸宫调加进去,慢慢成为短戏,为元杂剧做了准备。从金董解元的诸宫调《西厢记》到元王实甫的杂剧《西厢记》,我们可以看出这个脉络。

中国古来的戏剧的性格,如同小说,也是世俗的,所以量非常之大。道光年间的皮簧戏因为进了北京成为京剧,戏目俗说是"唐三千宋八百",不过统计下来,继承和新作的总数有五千多种,真是吓死人,我们现在还在演,世俗间熟悉的,也有百多出。

元杂剧可考的作者有两百多人,百年间留下可考的戏剧六百多种。明有三百年,杂剧作者一百多人,剧作三百多种,少于元代,大概是世俗小说开始进入兴盛,精力分散的原因。由元入明的罗贯中除了写杂剧,亦写了《三国演义》,等于是明代世俗小说的开端。

四十二

皮簧初起时,因为来路乡野,演唱起来草莽木直,剧目基本来自世俗小说中演义传奇武侠一类，只是搞不懂为什么没有"言情"戏，倒是河北"蹦蹦戏"也就是现在称呼的"评剧"原来多有调情的戏。百五十年间，多位京剧大师搜寻学问，终于成就了一个痴迷世俗的大剧种。例如梅兰芳成为红角儿后，齐如山先生点拨他学昆腔戏的舞蹈，才有京剧中纯舞蹈的祝寿戏"天女散花"。

此前燕赵一带是河北梆子的天下，因为被京剧逐出"中心话语"，不服这口气，年年要与京剧打擂台比试高低，输赢由最后各自台前的俗众多寡为凭。

我姥姥家是冀中，秋凉灌冬麦，夜色中可听到农民唱梆子，血脉涌动，声遏霜露，女子唱起来亦是苍凉激越，古称燕赵之地多慷慨悲歌之士，果然是这样。

戏剧演出的世俗场面，你们都熟悉，皮簧梆子的锣鼓铙钹梆笛，古早由军乐来，开场时震天价响，为的是镇压世俗观众的喧哗，很教鲁迅在杂文中讽刺了一下。

以前角儿在台上唱，跟包的端个茶壶在幕前侍候，角儿唱起来真是地老天荒，间歇时，会回身去喝上一口，俗众亦不为意。以前意大利歌剧的场面，也是这样，而且好的唱段，演员会应俗众的叫好再重复一次，偶有唱不上去的时候，鞠躬致歉居然也能过去。开场时亦是嘈杂，市井之徒甚至会约了架到戏园子去打，所以歌剧序曲最初有镇压喧哗的作用，我们现在则将听歌剧做成一种教养，去时服装讲究，哪里还敢打架？

你们听罗西尼的歌剧序曲的 CD 唱片，音量要事先调好，否则喇叭会承受不起，因为那时的序曲不是为我们在家里听的。话扯得远了，还是回到小说来。

四十三

明代是中国古典小说的黄金时代，我们现在读的大部头古典小说，多是明代产生的，《水浒传》、《西游记》、《金瓶梅词话》、《封神演义》、"三言"、"二拍"、拟话本等等，无一不是描写世俗的小说，而且明明白白是要世俗之人来读的。

《三国演义》、《东周列国志》、《杨家将》等等，则是将历史演义给世俗来看，成为小说而与史实关系不大。

我小的时候玩一种游戏，拍洋画儿。洋画儿就是香烟盒里夹的小画片，大人买烟抽，就把画片给小孩子，不知多少盒烟里会夹一张有记号的画片，碰到了即是中奖。香烟，明朝输入中国，画片，则是清朝输入的机器印刷，都是外来的，所以画片叫"洋"画儿。

可是这洋画儿背后，画的是《水浒》一百单八将。玩的时候将画片摆在地上，各人抡圆了胳膊用手扇，以翻过来的人物定输赢，因为梁山泊好汉排过座次。一个拍洋画儿的小孩子不读《水浒》，就不知道输赢。

明代的这些小说，特点是元气足，你们再看明代笔记中那时的世俗，亦是有元气。明代小说个个儿像富贵人家出来的孩子，没有穷酸气。

我小的时候每读《水浒》，精神倍增，凭添草莽气，至今不衰。俗说"少不读水浒"，看来同感的俗人很多，以致要形成诫。

明代小说还有个特点，就是开头结尾的规劝，这可说是我前面提的礼下庶人在世俗读物中的影响。

可是小说一展开，其中的世俗性格，其中的细节过程，让你完全忘了作者还有个规劝在前面，就像小时候不得不向老师认错，出了教室的门该打还打，该追还追。认错是为出那个门，规劝是为转正题，话头罢了。

《金瓶梅词话》就是个典型。《肉蒲团》也是，它还有一个名字《觉后禅》，简直就是虚晃一招。"三言""二拍"则篇篇有劝，篇篇是劝后才生动起来。

四十四

《金瓶梅词话》是明代世俗小说中最自觉的一部。按说它由《水浒》里武松的故事中导引出来，会发展英雄杀美的路子，其实那是个话引子。

我以前与朋友夜谈，后来朋友在画中题记"色不可无情，情亦不可无色。或曰美人不淫是泥美人，英雄不邪乃死英雄。痛语"，这类似金圣叹的意思。兰陵笑笑生大概是不喜欢武松的不邪，笔头一转，直入邪男淫女的世俗庭院。

《金瓶梅词话》历代被禁，是因为其中的性行为描写，可我们若仔细看，就知道如果将小说里所有的性行为段落摘掉，小说竟毫发无伤。

你们只要找来人民文学出版社一九八五年版的《金瓶梅词话》洁本看看，自有体会。后来香港的一份杂志将洁本删的一万九千一百六十一个字排印成册，你们也可找来看，因为看了才能体会出所删段落的文笔逊于未删的文笔，而且动作重复。

《金瓶梅词话》全书一百回，五十二回无性行为描写，又有将近三十回的程度等同明代其他小说的惯常描写，因此我怀疑大部分性行为的段落是另外的人所加，大概是书商考虑到销路，捉人代笔，插在书中，很像现在的电视插播广告。

"潘金莲大闹葡萄架"应该是兰陵笑笑生的，写的环境有作用，人物有情绪变化过程，是发展合理的邪性事儿，所以是小说笔法。

说《金瓶梅词话》是最自觉的世俗小说，就在于它将英雄传奇的话头撇开后，不以奇异勾人，不打诳语，只写人情世态，三姑六婆，争风吃醋，奸是小奸，坏亦不大，平和时期的世俗，正是这样。它的性行为段落，竞争不过类似《肉蒲团》这类的小说。

《肉蒲团》出不来洁本，在于它骨头和肉长在一起了，剔分不开，这亦是它的成功之处。

我倒觉得志怪传奇到了明末清初，被性文字接过去了，你们看《灯草和尚》、《浪史》等等小说，真的是奇是怪。本来性幻想就是想象力，小说的想象性质则如火上泼油，色情得刁钻古怪，缺乏想象力的初读者读来不免目瞪口呆。

不过说起来这"色情"是只有人才有的，不同类的动物不会见到另类动物交合而发情，人却会这样，因为人有想象力。人是因为"色情"而与动物有分别。

《金瓶梅词话》应该是中国现代小说的开山之作。如果不是满人入关后的清教意识与文字制度,由晚明小说直接一路发展下来,本世纪初的文学革命大概会是另外的提法。

历史当然不能假设,我只是这么一说。

四十五

晚明有个冯梦龙,独自编写了《喻世明言》、《警世通言》、《醒世恒言》俗称"三言"的话本小说,又有话本讲史六种,是整理世俗小说的一个大工程。他还做有笔记小品五种,传奇十九种,散曲、诗集、曲谱等等等等差不多总有五十多种吧。

他辑的江南民歌集《山歌》,据实以录,等同史笔,三百年后"五四"时的北京大学受西方民俗学、人类学影响开始收集民歌,尚有所不录,这冯梦龙可说是个超时代的人。

晚明还有个怪才徐文长,就是写过《四声猿》的那个徐渭,记载中说他长得"修伟肥白",大个子,肥而且白,现在在街上不难见到这样形貌的人,难得的是"修","修"不妨解为风度。他还写过个剧本《歌代啸》,你们若有兴趣不妨找来看看,不难读的,多是口语俗语,妙趣横生,荒诞透顶,大诚恳埋得很深,令人惊讶。我现在每看荒诞戏,常常想到《歌代啸》,奇怪。

晚明的金圣叹,批过六部"才子书",选的却是雅至《离骚》、《庄子》,俗到《西厢》、《水浒》,这种批评意识,也只有晚明才出得来。

晚明实在是个要研究的时期，郡县专制之下，却思想活跃多锋芒，又自觉于资料辑录，当时西方最高的科学文明已借了耶稣会士传入中国，若不是明亡，天晓得要出什么局面。你们看我忍不住又来假设历史，不过"假设"和"色情"一样，亦是只有人才有的。

我无非是具体想到晚明不妨是个意识的接启点，因为它开始有敏锐合理的思想发生，对传统及外来采改良渐近。

四十六

到了清代，当然就是《红楼梦》。

倡导"五四"新文学的胡适之先生做过曹家的考证，但我看李辰冬先生在《科学方法与文学研究》里记述胡先生说《红楼梦》这部小说没有价值。胡先生认为没有价值的小说还有《三国演义》、《西游记》等等。

我在前面说到中国小说地位的高涨，是"五四"开始的，那时的新文学被认为是可以改造国民性，可以引起革命，是有价值的。鲁迅就是中断了学医改做文学，由《狂人日记》开始，到了《酒楼上》就失望怀疑了，终于完全转入杂文，匕首投枪。

胡先生对《红楼梦》的看法，我想正是所谓"时代精神"，反世俗的时代精神。

《红楼梦》，说平实了，就是世俗小说。

小的时候，我家住的大杂院里的妇女们无事时会聚到一起听《红楼梦》，我家阿姨叫做周玉洁的，识字，她念，大家插嘴,所以常常停下来,我还记得有人说林姑娘就是命苦,可是这样的人也是娶不得,老是话里藏针,一年三百六十五天可怎么过?我长大后却发现读书人都欣赏林黛玉。

不少朋友对我说过《红楼梦》太琐碎,姑嫂婆媳男男女女,读不下去,言下之意是,既然文学史将它提得那么伟大,我们为何读不出?我惯常的说法是读不下去就不要读,红烧肉炖粉条子,你忌油腻就不必强吃。

评论中常常赞美《红楼梦》的诗词高雅,我看是有点瞎起劲。曹雪芹的功力,在于将小说中诗词的水平吻合小说中角色的水平。

以红学家考证的曹雪芹的生平来看,他在小说中借题发挥几首大开大合的诗或词,不应该是难事,但他感叹的是俗世的变换,大观园中的人物有何等见识,曹雪芹就替他们写何等境界的诗或词,这才是真正成熟的小说家的观照。小说中讲"批阅十载",一定包括为角色调整诗词,以至有替薛蟠写的"鸡巴"诗。

曹雪芹替宝玉、黛玉和薛蟠写诗,比只写高雅诗要难多了!而且曹雪芹还要为胡庸医开出虎狼药方,你总不能说曹先生开的药方是可以起死回生的吧?

四十七

我既说《红楼梦》是世俗小说,但《红楼梦》另有因素使它成为中国古典小说的顶峰,这因素竟然也是诗,但不是小说中角色的诗,而是曹雪芹将中国诗的意识引入小说。

七十年代初去世的加州大学伯克利校区的陈世骧先生对中国诗的研究评价，你们都知道，不必我来啰嗦。陈世骧先生对张爱玲说过，中国文学的好处在诗，不在小说。

我来发挥的是，《红楼梦》是世俗小说，它的好处在诗的意识。

除了当代，诗在中国的地位一直最高，次之文章。小说地位低，这也是原因。要想在中国的这样一种情况下将小说做好，运用诗的意识是一种路子。

《红楼梦》开篇提到厌烦才子佳人小人拨乱的套路，潜台词就是"那不是诗"。

诗是什么？"空山不见人，但闻人语响。返景入深林，复照青苔上"，无一句不实，但联缀这些"实"也就是"象"以后，却产生一种再也实写不出来的"意"。

曹雪芹即是把握住世俗关系的"象"之上有个"意"，使《红楼梦》区别于它以前的世俗小说。这以后差不多一直到"五四"新文学之前，再也没有出现过这样的小说。

这一点是我二十岁以后的一个心得，自己只是在写小说时注意不要让这个心得自觉起来，好比打嗝胃酸涌上来。我的"遍地风流"系列短篇因为是少作，所以"诗"腔外露，做作得不得了。我是不会直接做诗的人，所以很想知道曹雪芹是怎么想的。

四十八

既提到诗，不妨多扯几句。

依我之见,艺术起源于母系时代的巫,原理在那时大致确立。文字发明于父系时代,用来记录母系创作的遗传,或者用来篡改这种遗传。

为什么巫使艺术发生呢? 因为巫是专职沟通人神的,其心要诚。表达这个诚的状态,要有手段,于是艺术来了,诵,歌,舞,韵的组合排列,色彩,图形。

巫是专门干这个的,可比我们现在的专业艺术家。什么事情一到专业地步,花样就来了。

巫要富灵感。例如大瘟疫,久旱不雨,敌人来犯,巫又是一族的领袖,千百只眼睛等着他,心灵脑力的激荡不安,久思不获,突然得之,现在的诗人们当有同感,所谓创作的焦虑或真诚。若遇节令,大收获,产子等等,也都要真诚地祷谢。这么多的项目需求,真是要专业才应付得过来。

所以艺术在巫的时代,初始应该是一种工具,但成为工具后,巫靠它来将自己催眠进入状态,继续产生艺术,再将其他人催眠,大家共同进入一种催眠的状态。这种状态,应该是远古的真诚。

宗教亦是如此。那时的艺术,是整体的,是当时最高的人文状态。

艺术最初靠什么? 靠想象。巫的时代靠巫师想象,其他人相信他的想象。现在无非是每个艺术家都是巫,希望别的人,包括别的巫也认可自己的想象罢了。

艺术起源于劳动的说法,不无道理,但专业与非专业是有很大的区别的,与各个人先天的素质也是有区别的。灵感契机人人都会有一些,但将它们完成为艺术形态并且传下去,不断完善修改,应该是巫这种专业人士来做的。

四十九

所以现在对艺术的各种说法,都有来源:

什么"艺术是最伟大的"啦,

什么"灵感""状态"啦,

什么"艺术家不能等同常人"啦,

什么"创作是无中生有"啦,

什么"艺术的社会责任感"啦,

什么"艺术与宗教相通"啦,

什么"艺术就是想象"啦,

等等等等,这些要求,指证,描述,都是巫可以承担起来的。

应该说,直到今天艺术还处在巫的形态里。

你们不妨去观察你们的艺术家朋友,再听听他们或真或假的"创作谈",都是巫风的遗绪。当然也有拿酒遮脸借酒撒疯的世故,因为"艺术"也可以成为一种借口。

诗很早就由诵和歌演变而成,诗在中国的地位那么高,有它在中国发生太早的缘因。

中国艺术的高雅精神传之在诗。中国诗一直有舒情、韵律、意象的特点。"意象"里,"意"是催眠的结果,由"象"来完成。

将艺术独立出来,所谓纯艺术,纯小说,是人类在后来的逐步自觉，是理性。

当初巫对艺术的理性要求应该是实用，创作时则是非理性。

我对艺术理性总是觉得吉凶未卜，像我讲小说要入诗的意识，才可能将中国小说既不脱俗又脱俗，就是一种理性，所以亦是吉凶未卜，姑且听我这么一说吧。

五十

另外，以我看来，曹雪芹对所有的角色都有世俗的同情，相同之情，例如宝钗，贾政等等乃至讨厌的老妈子。

写"现实主义"小说，强调所谓观察生活，这个提法我看是隔靴搔痒。

你对周遭无有同情，何以观察？有眼无珠罢了。

我主张"同情的自由"，自由是种能力，我们其实受很多束缚，例如"道德"，"时髦"，缺乏广泛的相同之情的能力，因此离自由还早。即使对诸如"道德"、"时髦"，也要有同情才完全。

刘再复早几年提过两重性格，其实人只有一重性格，类似痴呆，两重，无趣，要多重乃至不可分重，才有意思了。

写书的人愈是多重自身，对"实相"、"幻相"才愈有多种同情，相同之情，一身而有多身的相同之情。

这就要说到"想象力"，但想象力实在是做艺术的基本能力，就像男子跑百米总要近十秒才有资格进入决赛，十一秒免谈。

若认为自称现实主义的人写小说必然在说现实,是这样认为的人缺乏想象力。

五十一

世俗世俗,就是活生生的多重实在,岂是好坏兴亡所能剔分的? 我前面说《红楼梦》开篇提到厌烦才子佳人小人拨乱的套路,只不过曹雪芹人重言轻了,才子佳人小人拨乱自是一重世俗趣味,犯不上这么对着干,不知曹公在天之灵以为然否?

这样一派明显的中国古典小说的世俗景观,近当代中国文学史和文学评论多不明写,或者是这样写会显得不革命没学问? 那可能就是故意不挑明。

这样的结果,当然使人们羞于以世俗经验与情感来读小说,也就是胡适之先生说的"没有价值"。

周作人先生在《北平的好坏》里谈到中国戏,说"中国超阶级的升官发财多妻的腐败思想随处皆是,而在小说戏文里最为浓厚显著",我倒觉得中国小说戏文的不自在处,因为有礼下庶人的束缚。

"没有价值",这是时代精神,反世俗的时代精神。其实胡适之、朱自清、郑振铎诸先生后来在西方理论的影响下都做过白话小说史或俗文学史,只是有些虎头蛇尾。

相反,民初一代的革命文人,他们在世俗生活中的自为活跃,读读回忆录就令人惊奇。

五十二

《红楼梦》将诗的意识带入世俗小说,成为中国世俗小说的一响晨钟,虽是晨钟,上午来得也实在慢。

《红楼梦》气长且绵,多少后人临此帖,只有气短、滥和酸。

《红楼梦》造成了古典世俗小说的高峰,却不是暮鼓,清代世俗小说依世俗的需要,层出不穷。到了清末,混杂着继续下来的优秀古典世俗小说,中国近现代的世俗小说开始兴起,鼎盛。

清末有一册《老残游记》不妨看重,刘锷信笔写来,有一种很特殊的诚恳在里面。

我们做小说,都有小说"腔"在,《老残游记》没有小说腔。读它的疑惑也就在此,你用尽古典小说批评,它可能不是小说,可它不是小说是什么呢?

《老残游记》的样貌正是后现代批评的一个范本,行话称"文本",俗说叫"作品",可后现代批评怎么消解它的那份世俗诚恳呢?

不过后现代批评也形成了"腔",于是有诸多投"腔"而来的后现代小说,《老残游记》无此嫌疑,是一块新鲜肉,以后若有时间不妨来聊聊它。

五十三

晚清一直到一九四九年前的小说,"鸳鸯蝴蝶派"可以说是这一时期的一大流派。

像我这样的人，几乎不了解"鸳鸯蝴蝶派"。我是个一九四九年以后在中国内地长大的人，知道中国近现代的文学上有过"鸳鸯蝴蝶派"，是因为看鲁迅的杂文里提到，语稍讥讽，想来是几个无聊文人在大时代里做无聊事吧。

又见过文学史里略提到"鸳鸯蝴蝶派"，比如郑振铎诸先生，都斥它为"逆流"。我因为好奇这逆流，倒特别去寻看。一九六四年以前，北京的旧书店里还常常可以翻检到"鸳鸯蝴蝶派"的东西。

"鸳鸯蝴蝶派"据文学史说兴起于一九〇八年左右。为什么这时会世俗小说成为主流，我猜与一九〇五年清廷正式废除科举制度有关联。

此前元代的不准汉人科举做官，造成汉族读书人转而去写戏曲，结果元杂剧元曲奇盛。清末废科举，难免读过书的人转而写写小说。

另一个原因我想是西方的机器印刷术传进来，有点像宋时世俗间有条件大量使用纸。

五十多年间"鸳鸯蝴蝶派"大约有五百多个作者，我一提你们就知道的有周瘦鹃，包天笑，张恨水等等。当时几乎所有的刊物或报纸的副刊，例如《小说月报》、《申报》的"自由谈"等等，都是"鸳鸯蝴蝶派"的天下。"五四"之前，包括像戴望舒、叶圣陶、老舍、刘半农、施蛰存这些后来成为新文学作家的大家，都在"鸳鸯蝴蝶派"的领地写过东西。

一九七六年到一九八六的十年间，亦是写小说的人无数,亦是读过书的人业余无事可做,于是写写小说吧,倒不一定与热爱文学有关。精力总要有地方释放。

你们只要想想有数百家文学刊物,其他报刊还备有文学专栏,光是每个月填满这些空儿,就要发出多少文字量!更不要说还有数倍于此的退稿。粗估估,这十年的小说文字量相当于十年文化大革命写交代检查和揭发声讨的文字量。

八四年后,世俗间自为的余地渐渐出现,私人做生意就好像官家恢复科举,有能力的人当然要去试一试。写小说的人少了,正是自为的世俗空间开始出现,从世俗的角度看就是中国开始移向正常。

反而前面提到的那十年那么多人要搞那么多"纯"小说,很是不祥。我自己的看法是纯小说,先锋小说,处于三五知音小众文化生态比较正常。

五十四

"鸳鸯蝴蝶派"的门类又非常多:言情,这不必说;社会,也不必说;武侠,例如向恺然也就是"平江不肖生"的《江湖奇侠传》,也叫《火烧红莲寺》;李寿民也就是"还珠楼主"的《蜀山剑侠传》;狭邪色情,像张春帆的《九尾龟》、《摩登淫女》,王小逸的《夜来香》;滑稽,像徐卓呆的《何必当初》;历史演义,像蔡东藩的十一部如《前汉通俗演义》到《民国通俗演义》;宫闱,像许啸天的《清宫十三朝演义》,秦瘦鸥译自英文,德龄女士的《御香缥缈录》;侦探,像程小青的《霍桑探案》等等等等。又文言白话翻译杂陈,长篇短篇插图纷披,足以满足世俗需要,这股"逆流",实在也是浩浩荡荡了些。

这些门类里,又多有掺混,像张恨水的《啼笑因缘》,就有言情、社会、武侠。

我小的时候大约六十年代初,住家附近的西单剧场,就上演过改编为曲剧的《啼笑姻缘》。当时正是"大跃进"之后的天灾人祸,为了转移焦点,于是放松世俗空间,《啼笑姻缘》得以冒头,嚷动四城,可惜我家那时穷得可以,终于看不成。

这样说起来,你们大概会说"这哪里只是什么鸳鸯蝴蝶"?我也是这样认为,所谓"鸳鸯蝴蝶派",不要被鸳鸯与蝴蝶迷了眼睛,应该大而言之为世俗小说。

你们若有兴趣,不妨看看魏绍昌先生编辑的《鸳鸯蝴蝶派研究资料》,当时的名家都有选篇。不要不好意思,张爱玲也是看鸳鸯蝴蝶派的小说的。

我这几年给意大利的《共和报》和一份杂志写东西,有一次分别写了两篇关于中国电影的文字,其中主要的意思就是一九四九年以前的电影,无一不是世俗电影,中国电影的性格,就是世俗,而且产生了一种世俗精神。

中国电影的发生,是在中国近当代世俗小说成了气象后,因此中国电影亦可说是"鸳鸯蝴蝶派"的影像版。这是题外话,提它是因为它有题内意。

清末至民国的世俗小说,在"五四"前进入鼎盛。二十年代,新文学开始了。

五十五

这就说到"五四"。

我一九八六年去美国漪色佳的康奈尔大学,因那里有个很美的湖,所以这音译名实在是恰当。另一个译得好的是意大利的翡冷翠,也就是我们现在说的佛罗伦斯。我去这个名城,看到宫邸教堂用绿纹大理石,原来这种颜色的大理石是这个城市的专用,再听它的意大利语发音,就是翡冷翠,真是佩服徐志摩。

当年胡适之先生在漪色佳的湖边坐卧,提出"文学革命",而文学革命的其中之一项是"白话文运动"。

立在这湖边,不禁想起自己心中长久的一个疑问:中国古典世俗小说基本上是白话,例如《红楼梦》,就是大白话,为什么还要在文学革命里提倡白话文?

我的十年学校教育,都是白话文,小学五年级在课堂上看《水浒》入迷,书被老师没收,还要家长去谈话。《水浒》若是文言,我怎么看得懂而入迷?

原来这白话文,是为了革命宣传,例如标语,就要用民众都懂的大白话。胡适之先生后来说"共产党里白话文做得好的,还是毛泽东"就讲到点子上了。

初期的新文学白话文学语言,多是半文半白或翻译体或学生腔。例如郭沫若的文字,一直是学生腔。

我想对于白话文一直有个误会,就是以为将白话用文字记录下来就成白话文了。其实成文是一件很不容易的事。白话文白话文,白话要成为"文"才是白话文。

"五四"时期做白话文的三四流者的颠倒处在于小看了文,大看了白话文艺腔。

举例来说，电影《孩子王》的一大失误就是对话采用原小说中的对话，殊不知小说是将白话改造成文，电影对白应该将文还原为白话，也就是口语才像人说话。北京人见面说"吃了吗您？"写为"您吃饭了？"是入文的结果。你们再去读老舍的小说，其实是将北京的白话处理过入文的。

我看电影《孩子王》，如坐针毡，后来想想算它是制作中无意得之的风格，倒也统一。推而广之，"五四"时期的白话文亦可视为一种时代的风格。

再大而视之，当今有不少作家拿捏住口语中的节奏，贯串成文，文也就有另外的姿式了，北京的刘索拉写《你别无选择》、《蓝天绿海》得此先机。

转回原来的意思，单从白话的角度来说，我看新文学不如同时的世俗文学，直要到张爱玲才起死回生。先前的鲁迅则是个特例。

说鲁迅是个特例，在于鲁迅的白话小说可不是一般人能读懂的。这个懂有两种意思，一是能否懂文字后面的意思，白话白话，直白的话，"打倒某某某"，就是字表面的意思。

二是能否再用白话复述一遍小说而味道还在。鲁迅的小说是不能再复述的。也许因为如此，鲁迅后来特别提倡比白话文更进一步的"大众语"。

鲁迅应该是明白世俗小说与新文学小说的分别的，他的母亲要看小说，于是他买了张恨水的小说给母亲看，而不是自己或同一营垒里的小说。

"鸳鸯蝴蝶派"的初期名作，徐枕亚的《玉梨魂》是四六骈体,因为受欢迎,所以三十年代顾羽将它"翻"成白话。

新文学的初期名作,鲁迅的《狂人日记》,篇首为文言笔记体,日记是白话。我总觉得这里面有一些共同点,就是转型适应,适应转型。

五十六

"五四"时代还形成了一种翻译文体,也是转了很久的型,影响白话小说的文体至巨。

初期的翻译文句颇像外语专科学校学生的课堂作业,努力而不通脱,连鲁迅都主张"硬译",我是从来都没有将他硬译的果戈里的《死魂灵》读过三分之一,还常俗说为"死灵魂"。

我是主张与其硬译,不如原文硬上,先例是唐的翻译佛经,凡无对应的,就音译,比如"佛"。音译很大程度上等于原文硬上。前面说过的日本词,我们直接拿来用,就是原文硬上,不过因为是汉字形,不太突兀罢了。

翻译文体还有另外的问题,就是翻译者的汉文字功力,容易让人误会为西方本典。赛林格的《麦田守望者》,当初美国的家长们反对成为学生必读物,看中译文是体会不出他们何以会反对的。《麦田守望者》用王朔的语言翻译也许接近一些,"守望者"就是一个很规矩的英汉字典词。

中译文里译《麦田守望者》的粗口为"他妈的",其中的"的"多余,即使"他妈"亦应轻读。汉语讲话,脏词常常是口头语,主要的功能是以弱读来加强随之的重音,形成节奏,使语言有精神。

节奏是最直接的感染与说服。你们不妨将"他妈"弱读，说"谁他妈信哪!"听起来是有感染力的"谁信哪!"，加上"的"，节奏就乱了。

翻译文体对现代中文的影响之大，令我们几乎不自觉了。中文是有节奏的，当然任何语言都有节奏，只是节奏不同，很难对应。口语里"的、地、得"不常用，用起来也是轻音，写在小说里则字面平均，语法正确了，节奏常常就消失了。

中国的戏里打单皮的若错了节奏，台上的武生甚至会跌死，文字其实也有如此的险境。

翻译家里好的有傅雷翻巴尔扎克，汝龙翻契诃夫，李健吾翻福楼拜等等。《圣经》亦是翻得好，有朴素的神性，有节奏。

好翻译体我接受，翻译腔受不了。

没有翻译腔的我看是张爱玲，她英文好，有些小说甚至是先写成英文，可是读她的中文，节奏在，魅力当然就在了。钱钟书先生写《围城》，也是好例子，外文底子深藏不露，又会戏仿别的文体，学的人若体会不当，徒乱了自己。

你们的英语都比我好，我趁早打住。只是顺便说一下，中国古典文学中，只在诗里有意识流。话题扯远了，返回去讲"五四"。

五十七

对于"五四"的讲述，真是汗牛充栋，不过大体说来，都是一种讲法。

我八五年在香港的书店站着快速翻完美国周策纵先生的《五四运动史》，算是第一次知道关于"五四"的另一种讲法。我自小买不起书，总是到书店去站着看书，所以养成个驼背水蛇腰，是个腐朽文人的样子。

八七年又在美国读到《曹汝霖一生之回忆》，算是听到当年火烧赵家楼时躲在夹壁间的人的说法。

总有人问我你读过多少书，我惯常回答没读过多少书。你只要想想几套关于中国历史的大部头儿巨著，看来看去是一种观点，我怎么好意思说我读过几套中国历史呢？

一九八八年，《上海文论》有陈思和先生与王晓明先生主持的"重写文学史"批评活动，开始了另外的讲法，可惜不久又不许做了。之后上海的王晓明先生有篇《一份杂志和一个"社团"——论"五四"文学传统》登在香港出版的《今天》九一年第三、四期合刊上，你们不妨找来看看。

他重读当时的权威杂志《新青年》和文学研究会，道出新文学的醉翁之意不在酒。

有意思的是喝过新文学之酒而成醉翁的许多人，只喝一种酒，而且酒后脾气很大，说别的酒都是坏酒，新文学酒店亦只许一家，所谓宗派主义。

我觉得有意思的是，世俗小说从来不为自己立传，鸳鸯蝴蝶派作家范烟桥二十年代写的《中国小说史》大概是唯一的例外，他在六十年代应要求将内容补写到一九四九年，书名换作《民国旧派小说史略》。

新文学则为自己写史,向世俗小说挑战,用现在的话来说,是夺取解释权,建立权威话语吧?

这样说也不对,因为世俗小说并不建立解释权让人来夺取,也不挑战应战,不过由此可见世俗小说倒真是自为的。

五十八

毛泽东后来将"新文学"推进到"工农兵文艺","文艺为工农兵服务"。

工农兵何许人? 就是世俗之人。为世俗之人的文艺是什么文艺? 当然就是世俗文艺。

所以从小说来看,延安小说乃至延安文艺工作者掌权后的小说,大感觉上是恢复了小说的世俗样貌。

从赵树理到浩然,即是这一条来路。平心而论,赵树理和浩然,都是会写的,你们不妨看看赵树理初期的《李有才板话》、《孟祥英》、《小二黑结婚》、《罗汉钱》,真的是乡俗到家,念起来亦活灵活现,是上好的世俗小说。只有一篇《地板》,为了揭露地主的剥削本质,讲乱了,读来让人体会到地主真是辛苦不容易。

当年古元的仿年画的木刻,李劫夫的抗日歌曲如《王二小放牛郎》,等等等等,都是上好的革命世俗文艺,反倒是大城市来的文化人像丁玲、艾青,有一点学不来的尴尬。

五十九

一九四九年后,整个文艺样貌,是乡村世俗文艺的逐步演变,《白毛女》从民间传说到梆子调民歌剧到电影到芭蕾舞就是个活生生的例子。

从小说来看,《新儿女英雄传》、《高玉宝》、《平原游击队》、《铁道游击队》、《敌后武工队》、《烈火金刚》、《红岩》、《苦菜花》、《迎春花》、《林海雪原》、《欧阳海之歌》、《金光大道》等等,都是世俗小说中英雄传奇通俗演义的翻版。才子佳人的翻版则是《青春之歌》、《三家巷》、《苦斗》等等,真也是一个轰轰烈烈的局面。

"文革"后则有得首届"茅盾文学奖"的长篇《芙蓉镇》做继承,只不过作者才力不如前辈,自己啰嗦了一本书的二分之一,世俗其实是不耐烦你来教训人的。

研究当代中国小说,"革命"世俗小说是一个非常明显的线索。

值得一提的是,四十年来的电影,是紧跟在工农兵文艺,也就是"革命"世俗文艺后面的。谢晋是"革命"世俗电影语言最成熟的导演,就像四九年以前世俗之人看电影必带手绢,不流泪不是好电影一样,谢晋的电影也会让革命的世俗之人泪不自禁。

这样的世俗小说,可以总合"五四"以来的"平民文学"、"普罗文学"、"大众文学"、"为人生的文学"、"写实文学"、"社会文学"、"革命文学"等等一系列的革命文学观,兼收并蓄,兵马齐集,大体志同道合,近代恐怕还没有哪个语种的文学可以有如此的场面规格吧?

可惜要去其糟粕,比如"神怪"类就不许有,近年借拉丁美洲的"魔幻现实主义",开始还魂,只是新魂比旧鬼差些想象力。

又比如"言情"类不许写,近年自为的世俗开始抬头,言情言色俱备,有久别胜新婚的憨狂,但到底是久别,有些触摸不到位,让古人叫声惭愧。

"社会黑幕"类则由报告文学总揽,震动世俗。

六十

不过既要讲工农兵,则开始讲历史上"劳动人民的创造","创造"说完之后,你可以闭上眼睛等那个"当然","当然"之后一定是耳熟能详的"糟粕",一定有的,错了管换。虽然对曹雪芹这样的人比较客气,加上"由于历史的局限",可没有这"局限"的魅力,何来《红楼梦》?

话说过头儿了就忘掉我们的时代将来也会是古代,我们也会成古人。

毛泽东对革命文艺有个说法是"革命现实主义与革命浪漫主义相结合",是多元论,这未尝不是文艺之一种。说它限制了文艺创作,无非是说的人自己限制了自己。

但这个说法,却是有来历的,它是继承"五四"新文学的"写实主义"与彼时兴盛的浪漫主义,只是"五四"的浪漫主义因为自西方的十八世纪末十九世纪初的浪漫主义而来,多个人主义因素,毛泽东的浪漫主义则是集团理想,与新中国理想相谐,这一转倒正与清末以来的政治初衷相合,对绝大多数的中国人来说,基本上不觉得突兀。

六十一

说起来,我是读"五四"新文学这一路长大的,只不过是被推到一个边缘的角度读,边缘的原因我在讲世俗的时候说过了,有些景观也许倒看得更细致些。

"五四"的文学革命,有一个与当时的提倡相反的潜意识,意思就是虽然口号提倡文字要俗白,写起来却是将小说诗化。

我说过,中国历来的世俗小说,是非诗化的,《红楼梦》是将世俗小说入诗的意识的第一部小说。《金瓶梅词话》里的"词",以及"话本"小说的"开场诗",并非是将诗意入小说。

在我看来,如果讲"五四"的文学革命对文学的意义,就在于开始诗化小说,鲁迅是个很好的例子,我这么一提,你们不妨再从《狂人日记》到《孤独者》回忆一下,也许有些体会。鲁迅早期写过《摩罗诗力说》,已见心机。

所以我看鲁迅小说的新兴魅力,不全在它的所谓"解剖刀"。

西方的文学,应该是早将小说诗化了,这与中国的小说与诗分离的传统不同。但西方的早,早到什么时候,怎样个早法,我不知道,要请教专门研究的人。我只是觉得薄迦丘的《十日谈》还是世俗小说,到塞万提斯的《唐吉诃德》则有变化,好像《红楼梦》的变化意义。当代的一些西方小说,则开始走出诗化。

"五四"引进西方的文学概念,尤其是西方浪漫主义的文学概念,中国的世俗小说当然是"毫无价值"了。

这也许是新文学延续至今总在贬斥同时期的世俗文学的一个潜在心理因素吧?但新文学对中国文学的改变,影响了直到今天的中国小说,已经是存在。

比如现在中国读书人争论一篇小说是否"纯",潜意识里"诗化"与否起着作用,当然"诗化"在变换,而"纯"有什么价值,就更见仁见智了。

六十二

由此看来,世俗小说被两方面看不起,一是政治正确,"新文学"大致是这个方面,等同于道德文章。我们看郑振铎等先生写的文学史,对当时世俗小说的指斥多是不关心国家大事,我以前每读到这些话的时候,都感觉像小学老师对我的操行评语:不关心政治。

另一个方面是"纯文学",等同于诗。

中国有句话叫"姥姥不疼,舅舅不爱",意思是你这个人没有什么混头儿了。

这是一个母系社会遗留下来的意思,"姥姥"是母系社会的大家长,最高权威,"舅舅"则是母系社会里地位最高的男人。这两种人对你没有好看法,你还有什么地位,还有什么好混的?

"五四"的文学革命,公开或隐蔽,也就到了所谓建立新文学权威话语这个地步。当年文学研究会的沈雁冰编《小说月报》,常批判"礼拜六派",后来书业公会开会,同业抗议,商务印书馆只好将沈雁冰调去国文部，继任的是郑振铎。继续批判。

六十三

中国几十年来的封闭，当然使我这样的人寡闻，自然也就孤陋。

记得是八四年底，忽然有一天翻上海的《收获》杂志，见到《倾城之恋》，读后纳闷了好几天，心想上海真是藏龙卧虎之地，这"张爱玲"不知是躲在哪个里弄工厂的高手，偶然投的一篇就如此惊人。心下惭愧自己当年刚发了一篇小说，这张爱玲不知如何冷笑呢。

于是到处打听这张爱玲，却没有人知道，看过的人又都说《倾城之恋》没有什么嘛，我知道话不投机，只好继续纳闷下去。幸亏不久又见到柯灵先生对张爱玲的介绍，才明白过来。

《围城》也是从海外推进来，看后令人点头，再也想不到钱钟书先生是写过小说的，他笔下的世俗情态，轻轻一点即着骨肉。我在美国或欧洲，到处碰到《围城》里的晚辈，苦笑里倒还亲切。

以张爱玲、钱钟书的例子看，近代白话文到他们手里才是弓马娴熟了，我本来应该找齐这条线，没有条件，只好尽自己的能力到处剔牙缝。

还有一个例子是沈从文先生，我在八十年代以前，不知道他是小说家，不但几本文学史不提，旧书摊上亦未见过他的书。后来风从海外刮来，借到一本，躲在家里看完，只有一个感觉：相见恨晚。

我读史，有个最基本的愿望，就是希望知道前人做过什么了。如果实际上有，而"史"不讲，谈何"历"呢？

我开始写小说的时候，正是无产阶级文化大革命，恰是个没有出版的时期，所以难于形成"读者"观念，至今受其所"误"，读者总是团雾。

但写的时候，还是有读者的，一是自己，二是一个比我高明的人，实际上就是自己的鉴赏力，谨慎删削，恐怕他看穿。

我之敢发表小说，实在因为当时环境的孤陋，没见过虎的中年之牛亦是不怕虎的，倒还不是什么"找到自己"。

六十四

八十年代开始有世俗之眼的作品，是汪曾祺先生的《受戒》。

我因为七九年才从乡下山沟里回到北京，忙于生计，无暇它顾，所以对七六年后的"伤痕文学"不熟悉。有一天在朋友处翻检旧杂志，我从小就好像总在翻旧书页，忽然翻到八〇年一本杂志上的《受戒》，看后感觉如玉，心想这姓汪的好像是个坐飞船出去又回来的早年兄弟，不然怎么会只有世俗之眼而没有"工农兵"气？

《受戒》没有得到什么评论，是正常的，它是个"怪物"。

当时响彻大街小巷的邓丽君，反对的不少，听的却愈来愈多。

邓丽君是什么？就是久违了的世俗之音嘛，久旱逢霖，这霖原本就有，只是久违了，忽自海外飘至，路边的野花可以采。

海外飘至的另一个例子是琼瑶，琼瑶是什么？就是久违了的"鸳鸯蝴蝶派"之一种。三毛亦是。之后飘来的越来越多，头等的是武侠。

六十五

《受戒》之后是陕西贾平凹由《商州初录》开始的"商州系列"散文。平凹出身陕南乡村，东西写出来却没有农民气，可见出身并不会带来什么，另外的例子是莫言。

平凹的作品一直到《太白》、《浮躁》，都是世俗小说。《太白》里拾回了世俗称为野狐禅的东西，《浮躁》是世俗开始有了自为空间之后的生动，不知平凹为什么倒惘然了。

平凹的文化功底在乡村世俗，他的近作《废都》，显然是要进入城市世俗，不料却上了城市也是农村这个当。

一九四九年以后，城市逐渐农村化，以上海最为明显。

我去看上海，好像在看恐龙的骨骼，这些年不断有新楼出现，令人有怪异感，好像化石骨骼里长出鲜骨刺，将来骨刺密集，也许就是上海以后的样子。

《废都》里有庄之蝶的菜肉采买单，没有往昔城里小康人家的精致讲究，却像野战部队伙食班的军需。明清以来，类似省府里庄之蝶这样的大文人，是不吃牛羊猪肉的，最低的讲究，是内脏的精致烹调。

因此我想这《废都》，并非是评家评为的"颓废之都"，平凹的意思应该是残废之都。粗陋何来颓废？沮丧罢了。

中文里的颓废，是先要有物质、文化的底子的，在这底子上沉溺,养成敏感乃至大废不起,精致到欲语无言,赏心悦目把玩终日却涕泪忽至,《红楼梦》的颓废就是由此发展起来的,最后是"落了个白茫茫大地真干净",可见原来并非是白茫茫大地。

你们不妨再去读《红楼梦》的物质细节与情感细节,也可以去读张爱玲小说中的这些细节,或者读朱天文的《世纪末的华丽》,当会明白我说的意思。

我读《废都》,觉到的都是饥渴,例如性的饥渴。为何会饥渴?因为不足。这倒要借《肉蒲团》说一说,《肉蒲团》是写性丰盛之后的颓废,而且限制在纯物质的意义上,小说主角未央生并非想物质精神兼得,这一点倒是晚明人的聪明处,也是我们后人常常要误会的地方。所以我们今天摹写无论《金瓶梅词话》还是《肉蒲团》,要反用"饱汉子不知饿汉子饥"为"饥汉子不知饱汉子饱"来提醒自己。

汉语里是东汉时就开始出现"颓废"这个词了,我怀疑与当时佛学初入中土有关。汉语里"颓废"与"颓丧"、"颓唐"、"颓靡"、"颓放",意义都不同,我们要仔细辨别。

顺便提一下的是,《废都》里常写到"啸",这啸是失传了又没有失传。啸不是我们现在看到的对着墙根儿遛嗓子,啸与声带无关,是口哨。我们看南京西善桥太岗寺南朝墓出土的"竹林七贤"的砖画,这画的印刷品到处可见,其中阮籍嘟着嘴,右手靠近嘴边做调拨,就是在啸。记载上说阮籍的歌啸"于琴声相谐",歌啸就是以口哨吹旋律。北宋儒将岳飞填词的"满江红",其中的"仰天长啸",就是抬头对天吹口哨,我这样一说，你们可能会觉得岳武穆不严肃，像个阿飞。后来常说的翦径强盗"啸聚山林"，其中的啸也是口哨，类似现在看体育比赛时观众的口哨，而不是喊，只不过这类啸没有旋律。

六十六

天津的冯骥才自《神鞭》以后，另有一番世俗样貌，我得其貌在"侃"。天津人的骨子里有股"纯侃"精神，没有四川人摆"龙门阵"的妖狂，也没有北京人的老子天下第一。北京是卖烤白薯的都会言说政治局人事变迁，天津是调侃自己，应对神速，幽默妩媚，像蚌生的珠而不必圆形，质好多变。

侃功甚难，难在五谷杂粮都要会种会收，常常比只经营大田要聪要明。天津一地的聪明圆转，因为在北京这个"天子"脚边，埋没太久了。

天津比之上海，百多年来亦是有租界历史的，世俗间却并不媚洋，原因我不知道，要由天津人来说。

我之所以提到天津，亦是有我长期的一个心结。近年所提的暴力语言，在文学上普通话算一个。普通话是最死板的一种语言，作为通行各地的官方文件，使用普通话无可非议，用到文学上，则像鲁迅说的"湿背心"，穿上还不如不穿上，可是规定要穿。

若详查北京作家的文字，除了文艺腔的不算，多是北京方言，而不是普通话。但北京话太接近普通话，俗语而在首善之区，所以得以滑脱普通话的规定限制，其他省的方言就没有占到便宜。

以生动来讲,方言永远优于普通话,但普通话处于权力地位,对以方言为第一语言的作家来说,普通话有暴力感。内地的电影,亦是规定用普通话,现在的领袖传记片,毛泽东说湖南话,同是湖南人的刘少奇却讲普通话,令人一愣,觉得刘少奇没有权力。

由于北京的政治地位,又由于北京方言混淆于普通话,所以北京方言已经成了次暴力语言,北京人也多有令人讨厌的大北京主义,这在内地的世俗生活中很容易感到。我从乡下回到北京,对这一点特别触目惊心。冯骥才小说的世俗语言,因为是天津方言,所以生动出另外的样貌,又因为属北方方言,虽是天子脚边作乱,天子倒麻痹了,其他省的作家,就沾不多少这种便宜。

六十七

后来有"寻根文学",我常常被归到这一类或者忽然又被拨开,描得我一副踉踉跄跄的样子。

小说很怕有"腔","寻根文学"讨厌在有股"寻根"腔。

真要寻根,应该是学术的本分,小说的基本要素是想象力,哪里耐烦寻根的束缚?

以前说"文以载道",这个"道"是由"文章"来载的,小说不载。小说若载道,何至于在古代叫人目为闲书?古典小说里至多有个"劝",劝过了,该讲什么讲什么。

梁启超将"小说"当"文"来用,此例一开,"道"就一路载下来,小说一直被压得半蹲着,蹲久了居然也就习惯了。

"寻根文学"的命名,我想是批评者的分类习惯。跟随的,大部分是生意眼。

但是"寻根文学"有一点非常值得注意,就是其中开始要求不同的文化构成。"伤痕文学"与"工农兵文学"的文化构成是一致的,伤是自己身上的伤,好了还是原来那个身,再伤仍旧是原来那个身上的伤,如此循环往复。"寻根"则是开始有改变自身的欲望。

文化构成对文学家是一个非常重要的事。

六十八

不过"寻根文学"却撞开了一扇门,就是世俗之门。

这扇门本来是《受戒》悄悄打开的,可是魔术般地任谁也不认为那是门。直要到一场运动,也就是"寻根文学",才从催眠躺椅上坐起来,慌慌张张跑出去。

自此一发不可收拾。世俗之气蔓延开了,八九年前评家定义的"新写实文学",看来看去就是渐成气候的世俗小说景观。

像河南刘震云的小说,散写官场,却大异于清末的《官场现形记》,沙漏一般的小世小俗娓娓道来,机关妙递,只是早期《塔铺》里的草莽元气失了,有点少年老成。

湖南何立伟是最早在小说中有诗的自觉的。山西李锐、北京刘恒则是北方世俗的悲情诗人。

南京叶兆言早在《悬挂的绿苹果》时就弓马娴熟。江苏范小青等一派人马,隐显出传统中小说一直是江南人做得有滋有味,直至上海的须兰,都是笔下世俗渐渐滋润,浓妆淡抹开始相宜。又直要到北京王朔,火爆得沾邪气。

王朔有一点与众不同,不同在他居然挑战。我前面说过,世俗小说从来没有挑战姿态,不写文学史为自己立言,向世俗文学挑战的一直是新文学,而且追到家门口,从旁看来,有一股"阶级斗争"腔。

有朋友说给我,王朔曾放狂话:将来写的,搞好了是《飘》,一不留神就是《红楼梦》。我看这是实话,《飘》是什么?就是美国家喻户晓的世俗小说。《红楼梦》我前面说过了,不知道王朔有无诗才,有的话,不妨等着看。

王朔有一篇《动物凶猛》,我看是中国文学中第一篇纯粹的青春小说。青春小说和电影是一个很强的类,我曾巴望过"第五代导演"开始拍"青春片",因为他们有机会看到世界各国的影片,等了许久,只有一部《我的同学们》算是张望了一下。看来"第五代"真的是缺青春,八十年代初有过一个口号叫"讨回青春",青春怎么能讨回呢?过去了就是过去了。一把年纪时讨回青春,开始撒娇,不成妖精了?

上海王安忆的《小鲍庄》,带寻根腔,那个时期不沾寻根腔也难。到《小城之恋》,是有了平实之眼的由青春涌动到花开花落,《米尼》则是流动张致的"恶之华"。

王安忆后来的《逐鹿中街》是世俗的洋葱头,一层层剥,剥到后来,什么都有,什么都没有,正在恨处妙处。王安忆的天资实在好,而且她是一个少有的由初创到成熟有迹可寻的作家。

南京苏童在《妻妾成群》之前,是诗大于文,以《狂奔》结尾的那条白色孝带为我最欣赏的意象。这正是在我看来"先锋小说"多数在走的道路，努力摆脱欧洲十八世纪末的浪漫余韵，接近二十世纪爱略特以后的距离意识。

当然这样粗描道不尽微意，比如若以不能大于浪漫的状态写浪漫，是浪漫不起来的，又比如醋是要正经粮食来做，不可让坏了的酒酸成醋。总之若市上随手可买到世界各类"精华糟粕"只做闲书读，则许多论辩自然就羞于"为赋新词强说愁"了。

苏童以后的小说，像《妇女生活》、《红粉》、《米》等等，则转向世俗，有了以前的底子，质地绵密通透，光感适宜，再走下去难免成精入化境。

六十九

我读小说，最怵"腔"，古人说"文章争一起"，这"一起"若是个"腔"，不争也罢。

你们要是问我的东西有没有"腔"，有的，我对"腔"又这么敏感，真是难做小说了。一个写家的"风格"，仿家一拥而仿，将之化解为"腔"，拉倒。

我好读闲书和闲读书，可现在有不少"闲书腔"和"闲读腔"，搞得人闲也不是，不闲也不是，只好空坐抽烟。

又比如小说变得不太像小说，是当今不少作家的一种自觉，只是很快就出来了"不像小说"腔。

木心先生有妙语：先是有文艺，后来有了文艺腔，后来文艺没有了，只剩下腔，再后来腔也没有了文艺是早就没有了。

七十

抱歉的是,对台湾香港的小说我不熟悉,因此我在这里讲中国小说的资格是很可怀疑的。

在美国一本中文小说总要卖到十美金以上,有一次我在一家中文书店看到李昂的《迷园》,二十几美金,李昂我认识的,并且帮助过我,于是拿她的书在手上读。背后的老板娘不久即对别人说,大陆来的人最讨厌,买嘛买不起,都是站着看,而且特别爱看"那种"的。这老板娘真算得明眼人,而且说得一点儿不差。店里只有三个人,我只好放下《迷园》,真是服气这世俗的透辟。这老板娘一身上下剪裁合适,气色灵动,只是眼线描得稍重了。

不过我手上倒有几本朋友送的书,像朱天文、朱天心、张大春等等的小说,看过朱天文七九年的《淡江记》并一直到后来的《世纪末的华丽》,大惊,没有话说,只好想我七九年在云南读些什么鬼东西。

我自与外界接触,常常要比较年月日,总免不了触目惊心,以至现在有些麻木了。依我的感觉,大体上台湾香港的文学自觉,在时间上早于内地不只五年。你们若问我这是怎么个比较法,又不是科学技术体育比赛,我不知道,不过倒想问问内地近年怎么会评出来一级作家二级作家,而且还印在名片上到处递人,连古人都不如了。

我向来烦"中学生作文选",记得高一时老师问全班若写一座楼当如何下笔,两三个人之后叫起我来,我说从楼顶写吧。不料老师闻言大怒，说其他同学都从一楼开始写，先打好基础，是正确的写法，你从楼顶开始，岂不是空中楼阁！

我那时还不懂得领异标新，只是觉得无可无不可。后来在香港看一座楼从顶建起，很高兴地瞧了一个钟头。

平心而论，七九年时内地的大部分小说，还是中学生作文选的范文，我因为对这类范文的味道熟到不必用力闻，所以敢出此言。而且当时从域外重新传进来的例如"意识流"等等，也都迅速中学生文艺腔化，倒使我不敢小看这支文学队伍的改造能力。

另外，若七九年的起点就很高，何至于之后评家认为中国文学在观念上一年数翻，而现在是数年一翻呢？

电影亦是如此，八三年侯孝贤拍了《风柜来的人》，十年后内地才有宁瀛的《找乐》的对世俗状态的把握。

七十一

既然说到世俗，则我这样指名道姓，与中国世俗惯例终究不合，那么讲我自己吧。

我的小说从八四年发表后，有些反响，但都于我的感觉不契腻，就在于我发表过的小说回返了一些"世俗"样貌，因为没有"工农兵"气，大家觉得新，于是觉得好，我在一开始的时候说过了，中国从近代开始，"新"的意思等于"好"，其实可能是"旧"味儿重闻，久违了才误会了。

从世俗小说的样貌来说，比如《棋王》里有"英雄传奇"、"现实演义"，"言情"因为较隐晦，评家们对世俗不熟悉，所以至今还没解读出来，大概总要二三十年吧。不少人的评论里都提到《棋王》里的"吃"，几乎叫他们看出"世俗"平实本义，只是被自己用惯的大话引开了。

语言样貌无非是"话本"变奏，细节过程与转接暗取《老残游记》和《儒林外史》，意象取《史记》和张岱的一些笔记吧，因为我很着迷太史公与张岱之间的一些意象相通点。

王德威先生有过一篇《用〈棋王〉测量〈水沟〉的深度》，《水沟》是台湾黄凡先生的小说，写得好。王德威先生亦是好评家，他评我的小说只是一种传统的延续，没有小说自身的深度，我认为这看法是恳切的。

你们只要想想我写了小说十年后才得见张爱玲、沈从文、汪曾祺、钱钟书等等就不难体会了。

七十二

我的许多朋友常说，以无产阶级文化大革命的酷烈，大作家大作品当会出现在上山下乡这一代。

我想这是一种误解，因为无产阶级文化大革命的文化本质是狭窄与无知，反对它的人很容易被它的本质限制，而在意识上变得与它一样高矮肥瘦。

文学的变化，并不相对于政治的变化，"五四"新文学的倡导者，来不及有这种自觉，所以我这个晚辈对他们的尊重，在于他们的不自觉处。

近年来有一本《曼哈顿的中国女人》很引起轰动，我的朋友们看后都不以为然。我读了之后，倒认为是一部值得留的材料。这书里有一种歪打正着的真实，作者将四九年以后中国文化构成的皮毛混杂写出来了，由新文学引进的一点欧洲浪漫遗绪，一点俄国文艺，一点苏联文艺，一点工农兵文艺，近年的一点半商业文化和世俗虚荣，等等等等。狭窄得奇奇怪怪支离破碎却又都派上了用场，道出了五十年代就写东西的一代和当年上山下乡一代的文化样貌，而我的这些同代人常常出口就是个"大"字，"大"自哪里来？

《曼哈顿的中国女人》可算是难得的野史，补写了新中国文化构成的真实，算得老实，不妨放在工具书类里，随时翻查。经历过的真实，回避算不得好汉。

上山下乡这一代容易笼罩在"秀才落难"这种类似一棵草的阴影里。"苦难"这种东西不一定是个宝，常常会把人卡进狭缝儿里去。

七十三

又不妨说，近年评家说先锋小说颠覆了权威话语，可是颠覆那么枯瘦的话语的结果，搞不好也是枯瘦，就好比颠覆中学生范文会怎么样呢？而且，"颠覆"这个词，我的感觉是还在无产阶级文化大革命"造反有理"的阴影下。

我总觉得人生需要艺术，世俗亦是如此，只是人生最好少模仿艺术。不过人有想象力，会移情，所以将艺术移情于人生总是免不了的。

我现在说到"五四"，当然明白它已经是我们自身的一部分了，已经成为当今思维的丰富材料之一，可是讲起来，不免简单,也是我自己的一种狭隘,不妨给你们拿去做个例子吧。

七十四

近几年来,中国小说样貌基本转入世俗化,不少人为之痛心疾首,感觉不出这正是小说生态可能恢复正常的开始。

说到世俗,尤其是说到中国世俗,说到小说,尤其是说到中国小说,我的感觉是,谈到它们,就像一个四岁的孩子,一手牵着爹一手牵着娘在街上走,真个是爹也高来娘也高。

我现在与你们谈,是我看爹和看娘,至于你们要爹怎么样,要娘怎么样,我不知道。

爹娘的心思,他们的世界,小孩子有的时候会觉出来,但大部分时间里,小孩子是在自言自语。我呢,无非是在自言自语吧。

我常常觉得所谓历史,是一种设身处地,感同身受。

我的身就是这样一种身,感当然是我的主观,与现实也许相差十万八千里。

你们也看得出来我在这里讲世俗与小说,用的是归纳法,不顺我的讲法的材料,就不去说。

我当然也常讲雅的,三五知己而已,亦是用归纳,兴之所至罢了。

归纳与统计是不同方法。统计重客观,对材料一视同仁,比较严格;归纳重主观,依主观对材料有取舍,或由于材料的限制而产生主观。

你们若去读"鸳鸯蝴蝶派",或去翻检书摊,有所鄙弃,又或痛感世风日下，我亦不怪，因为我在这里到底只是归纳。

七十五

科学上说人所谓的"客观"，是以人的感觉形式而存在。譬如地球磁场，我们是由看到磁针的方向而知道它的存在；回旋加速器里的微观，射电天文望远镜里的遥远，也要转成我们的感觉形式，即是将它们转成看得到的相，我们才开始知道有这些"客观"存在。不明飞行物，UFO，也是被描述为我们的感觉形式。

不转成人的感觉形式的一切，对于人来说，是不"存在"的。

所谓文学"想象"，无非是现有的感觉形式的不同的关系组合。

我从小儿总听到一句话，叫做"真理愈辩愈明"，其实既然是真理，何需辩？在那里就是了。况且真理面对的，常常也是真理。

当然还是爱因斯坦说得诚恳：真理是可能的。我们引进西方的"赛先生"上百年，这个意思被中国人自己推开的门压扁在外面的墙上了。

这样一来，也就不必辩论我讲的是不是真理，无非你们再讲你们的"可能"就是了。我自己就常常用三五种可能来看世界，包括看我自己。

谢谢诸位的好意与耐心。

创作要目

1979 年　协助父亲钟惦棐先生撰写《电影美学》。

1984 年　《棋王》发表于《上海文学》第 7 期,获第三届
全国优秀中篇小说奖、《中篇小说选刊》优秀
作品奖。

1985 年　《遍地风流》系列短篇《峡谷》、《溜索》、《洗
澡》发表于《上海文学》第 4 期,《遍地风流》
其他篇什陆续在各文学刊物发表。
在 4 月 22 日的《文汇报》上发表随感《话不在
多》,在 7 月 6 日《文艺报》上发表理论文章
《文化制约着人类》,这两篇文章成为文化寻
根讨论的代表性作品。
《孩子王》发表于《人民文学》。
《树王》发表于《中国作家》。

1987 年	小说《孩子王》改编为同名电影，由陈凯歌执导，于 1988 年获第八届中国电影金鸡奖导演特别奖、最佳摄影奖、最佳美术奖；同年获第 41 届戛纳国际电影节教育贡献奖；获比利时 1988 年电影探索评奖活动探索影片奖。同一年，小说《棋王》由导演滕文骥改编为同名电影。
	作家出版社将小说集《棋王》列入"文学新星丛书第一辑"出版，收入《棋王》、《树王》、《孩子王》三个中篇，《会餐》、《树桩》、《周转》、《卧铺》、《傻子》和《迷路》六个短篇。
1992 年	获意大利 NONINO 国际成就奖。
1994 年	在意大利方面安排下，访问威尼斯两个月，撰写《威尼斯日记》一书，首先在台湾出版。
1995 年	《威尼斯日记》获台湾"最佳图书奖"。
1997 年	在《收获》杂志上开设"常识与通识"栏目，至 1998 年，每期发表一篇随笔，共写有十二篇随笔。
1998 年	作家出版社陆续推出阿城的四本书，包括：将

1987 年 9 月至 1993 年 11 月间多次就中国小说话题进行讲谈的集成《闲话闲说——中国世俗与中国小说》，1994 年在威尼斯访问的《威尼斯日记》，1987 年出版的小说集《棋王》的新版本，主要收入阿城下乡时写的短篇小说集《遍地风流》，分"遍地风流"、"彼时正年轻"、"杂色"、"其他"四部分。

1999 年　《常识与通识》结集由作家出版社出版。

贺绍俊

图书在版编目（CIP）数据

阿城选集／阿城著.

－北京：北京燕山出版社，2006.5（2013.5 重印）

ISBN 978-7-5402-1779-2

Ⅰ．阿… Ⅱ．阿… Ⅲ．①短篇小说-作品集-中国-当代

②散文-作品集-中国-当代 Ⅳ．I247.7

中国版本图书馆 CIP 数据核字（2006）第 022053 号

阿城精选集

作　者	阿　城
编 选 者	贺绍俊
责任编辑	张红梅　张　芸
封面设计	小　贾
出版发行	北京燕山出版社
	北京市宣武区陶然亭路 53 号　　邮编 100054
经　销	新华书店
印　刷	北京中科印刷有限公司
开　本	787×1092　1/32
印　张	13
字　数	298 千字
版次印次	2011 年 3 月第 4 版　2013 年 5 月第 7 次印刷
定　价	25.00 元